SUPERNATURAL FICTION WRITERS

CONTEMPORARY FANTASY AND HORROR

Richard Bleiler, Editor

VOLUME II

Guy Gavriel Kay
to
Roger Zelazny

CHARLES SCRIBNER'S SONS®

Supernatural Fiction Writers, Second Edition
Richard Bleiler, Editor

© 2003 by Charles Scribner's Sons. Charles Scribner's Sons is an imprint of The Gale Group, Inc., a division of Thomson Learning, Inc.

Charles Scribner's Sons™ and Thomson Learning™ are trademarks used herein under license.

For more information, contact
Charles Scribner's Sons
An imprint of The Gale Group
300 Park Avenue South, 9th Floor
New York, NY 10010
Or you can visit our Internet site at
http:\\www.gale.com

ALL RIGHTS RESERVED
No part of this work covered by the copyright hereon may be reproduced or used in any form or by any means—graphic, electronic, or mechanical, including photocopying, recording, taping, Web distribution, or information storage retrieval systems—without the written permission of the publisher.

For permission to use material from this product, submit your request via Web at http://www.gale-edit.com/permissions, or you may download our Permissions Request form and submit your request by fax or mail to:

Permissions Department
The Gale Group, Inc.
27500 Drake Rd.
Farmington Hills, MI 48331-3535
Permissions Hotline:
248 699-8006 or 800 877-4253, ext. 8006
Fax: 248 699-8074 or 800 762-4058

Acknowledgment is gratefully made to those publishers and individuals who have permitted the use of the following material in copyright. Every effort has been made to trace copyright, but if omissions have been made, please contact the publisher.

Cover Photographs:
Clive Barker: Photograph courtesy of AP/Wide World Photos. Reproduced by permission. Ray Bradbury: Photograph, 1991, courtesy of Archive Photos, Inc. Reproduced by permission. Marian Zimmer Bradley: Photograph by Jerry Bauer. Reproduced by permission. Terry Brooks: Photograph © Jerry Bauer. Reproduced by permission. Stephen King: Photograph courtesy of AP/Wide World Photos. Reproduced by permission. Anne McCaffrey: Photograph by Edmund Ross. Reproduced by permission of Anne McCaffrey. Michael Moorcock: Photograph by Jerry Bauer. Reproduced by permission.
J. K. Rowling: Photograph courtesy of AP/Wide World Photos. Reproduced by permission. Peter Straub: Photograph by Frank Capri. Archive Photos, Inc. Copyright © Frank Capri/SAGA. All rights reserved. Reproduced by permission.

Jack Vance: Excerpts from "The Moon Moth," in *Galaxy*. Galaxy Publishing Corporation, 1961. Copyright © 1961 by Galaxy Publishing Corporation. Reproduced by permission of the author.

LIBRARY OF CONGRESS CATALOGING-IN-PUBLICATION DATA

Supernatural fiction writers : fantasy and horror / Richard Bleiler editor.--2nd ed.
   p. cm.
Includes bibliographical references and index.
ISBN 0-684-31250-6 (set : hardcover : alk. paper) --ISBN 0-684-31251-4 (v. 1) -- ISBN 0-684-31252-2 (v. 2)
   1. Fantasy fiction--History and criticism. 2. Horror tales--History and criticism. 3. Supernatural in literature. 4. Authors--Biography. I. Bleiler, Everett Franklin, 1920-
PN3435 .S96 2003
809.3'8738--dc21   2002011128

Printed in the United States of America
10 9 8 7 6 5 4 3

Guy Gavriel Kay
1954–

CHRISTINE MAINS

GUY GAVRIEL KAY is one of the few Canadian fantasists to enjoy an international critical reputation; his books have been translated into several languages. His first published work was a trilogy in the high fantasy tradition, decidedly influenced by the work of J. R. R. Tolkien, but he has since written what he calls historical fantasy, re-imagining key moments in the history of Western culture, and in the process producing a body of work that argues for the power of art to help shape a world free of gender bias and religious intolerance. Although he is not always successful in achieving his goal, Kay attempts to transcend the binary oppositions of good and evil, the overly simplistic division of characters into heroes and villains, that is a feature of all too many works of fantasy.

Guy Gavriel Kay was born on 7 November 1954, in Weyburn, Saskatchewan. He attended the University of Manitoba, receiving a B.A. in philosophy in 1975, and then studied law at the University of Toronto. He was admitted to the bar in 1981; although he has never practiced law, he has written several scripts for the CBC program *The Scales of Justice*.

THE FIONAVAR TAPESTRY

In 1974, Kay was invited by Christopher Tolkien to help prepare J. R. R. Tolkien's unfinished work *The Silmarillion* for publication. Perhaps as a natural consequence of that project, which he worked on during 1974 and 1975, his first published work is a Tolkienesque high fantasy: The Fionavar Tapestry, a trilogy comprised of *The Summer Tree* (1984), *The Wandering Fire* (1986), and *The Darkest Road* (1986). Aside from those elements drawn by so many fantasists from Tolkien, including a white-bearded wizard, shining and long-lived elves, and surly dwarves, the story told in the trilogy weaves together strands of several different mythologies: the Matter of Britain, Norse and Celtic myths, even a hint of Native American influence in the Plains-dwelling Dalrei. This seemingly incongruous mixture is explained within the narrative by the fact that Fionavar is the primary world of which all other worlds, including Earth, are only reflections, a concept similar to Roger Zelazny's world of Amber.

The story begins in Canada, as five University of Toronto students—law students Kevin Laine and Dave Martyniuk, Kevin's friend Paul Schafer, medical student Kimberly Ford, and their friend Jennifer Lowell—attend a lecture given by reclusive academic Lorenzo Marcus. Marcus is the Earth-guise of mage Loren Silvercloak, in Toronto with his companion Matt Sören, the exiled king of the dwarves, supposedly to seek guests to attend the High King's anniversary celebrations in Fionavar. Promised that they will be able to attend two weeks of celebrations and return to Toronto as though no time had passed, the five travel to Fionavar, where they are soon swept up in an epic battle between the forces of light and the evil armies led by the dark god Rakoth Maugrim the Unraveller.

One by one, the five seemingly ordinary students take on archetypal or mythic identities. Dave, separated from the rest during the crossing between worlds, is adopted by the Dalrei and finds himself easily slipping into the part of the Warrior. Kim takes over the role of Seer from the aging Ysanne, and Paul, suicidal because of guilt over his girlfriend's recent death, takes the High King's place as a sacrifice on the Summer Tree, dying to be reborn as Pwyll Twice-born. In the second volume, Jennifer, raped and impregnated by Maugrim, learns that she is the reincarnation of Guinevere, while Kevin becomes the goddess's lover, whose sacrifice heralds the end of winter and the return of spring. Their inexperience in their new roles and the resulting distance between them and others is a refreshing change from the matter-of-fact acceptance of power in some other works of fantasy; in Kay's worlds, someone always pays the price for power, and sometimes that price is high.

Kay's tale, like Tolkien's own, is one story broken into three volumes. Unlike other Tolkien-inspired trilogies, it does not fall victim to the dreaded middle-book syndrome, in part because of the introduction of the Arthurian subplot at the beginning of *The Wandering Fire* (1986). Kay's use of the tragedy of the Matter of Britain is emotionally compelling, as Arthur's slaying of the Mayday babies has condemned him to relive, over and over in countless worlds, not only his fate as a Warrior doomed never to witness the outcome of the final battle, but also his betrayal by his wife and companion.

Events move to a final confrontation between good and evil in the third volume, and good does eventually triumph, albeit at a great cost. Unlike some other writers concerned with the struggle between good and evil, Kay is willing to sacrifice even the most beloved of central characters in order to bring emotional depth and true consequences to his story. Like Kevin Laine's self-sacrifice in the second volume, the death in ritual combat of Prince Diarmuid before the climactic battle in *The Darkest Road* (1986) is unexpected and moving. The final volume also emphasizes the theme that fate depends as much on random chance as on free will: Jennifer's determination to let Darien, the child born of her rape by Maugrim, choose his own destiny, even if his choice is to join his father, plays a significant role in the outcome of the final battle.

HISTORICAL FANTASY

Having proven to his satisfaction that high fantasy after Tolkien could be done with depth and significance, Kay made a decision to refocus his writing style. All of the novels published since have been historical fantasies, in which Kay reshapes key moments of the history of Western culture, telescoping centuries into years, renaming central figures, and admitting magic into history when it seems appropriate to his chosen theme. Kay sees fantasy as one way of re-signifying the events and characters of history: the rivalries of the Renaissance city-states in *Tigana* (1990); the Courts of Love in *A Song for Arbonne* (1992); the Christian reconquest of Moorish Spain in *The Lions of Al-Rassan* (1995); and Byzantium during the reign of Justinian and Theodora in *Sailing to Sarantium* (1998) and *Lord of Emperors* (2000), the two books of the duology The Sarantine Mosaic. Kay chooses to write historical fantasy, with an emphasis on the second word in the phrase, rather than historical fiction, in part because fantasy frees him to re-imagine historical figures and events to suit the themes he wishes to explore; the writer of historical fiction is bound to follow the facts, while the writer of historical fantasy is not.

TIGANA

His first novel written after The Fionavar Tapestry contains more magic than he has used since, in the spells worked by wizards and sorcerers; such a use is perhaps acceptable historically because of the setting, evocative of the Renaissance which did boast its own magicians and alchemists. *Tigana* (1990), which explores the difficulty of maintaining a national identity in the face of oppression, was nominated for the 1991 Mythopoeic Fantasy Award and the 1991 World Fantasy Award, and won the 1991 Aurora Award.

Named after one of nine provinces making up the fictional peninsula of The Palm, *Tigana* is inspired by the political situation of Renaissance Italy. Until fairly recently, Italy was not a unified nation but rather a collection of small city-states, fighting amongst each other, which left them vulnerable to repeated invasion from both France and the Hapsburg Empire. These invading forces are paralleled in the novel by Ygrath, ruled by the wizard-king Brandin, and the Empire of Barbadior, represented by the sorcerer Alberico. Both conquerors have plans for the provinces of The Palm; Brandin wishes to conquer territory so that his beloved son Stevan will have a realm of his own to rule over, while Alberico sees his acquisitions in the peninsula as providing a base and resources with which to eventually return to Barbadior to take the imperial throne.

Brandin, with three provinces having already surrendered to him, sends his son against the army of the province of Tigana. Stevan is killed in battle, and Brandin, in his grief, slaughters the Tiganese warriors and then turns his attention to subjugating the province itself. He utterly destroys the culture of Tigana, burning books and shattering statuary and buildings; in a final act of revenge designed to erase even the lingering memory of the people responsible for his son's death, he works a spell that ensures that no one can hear the name of Tigana save for those who were born there before the destruction. In order to outlive even the last of the children born in that time, Brandin artificially prolongs his own life, effectively disinheriting his younger son, and remains in the Palm in order to exercise complete control over the half of the peninsula not dominated by Alberico. Brandin's actions serve to demoralize those old enough to have fought against him, but the next generation, the children too young to fight but old enough to remember their history, grow into young adults determined to restore the power of their home province and to eliminate the domination of both conquerors in order to unite the peninsula—much as did the nineteenth-century nationalists who eventually succeeded in uniting the city-states of Italy into a single nation.

One of Kay's strengths as a writer of fantasy is his ability to avoid the all-too-common polarization that results when the forces of evil have no motivation other than the fact that they are evil and opposed to the heroes. Even in the more conventional fantasy of The Fionavar Tapestry, the wolf-lord Galadan is provided with motivation for his actions and given a second chance at redemption. With the exception of *A Song for Arbonne*, in which the principal representatives of Gorhaut are at times almost caricatures of villains, Kay always blurs the boundaries between good and evil. In *Tigana*, it would seem only natural for the reader to hate Brandin of Ygrath, but Kay undermines that response by his sympathetic portrayal of the love that grows between Brandin and one of his courtesans, the Tiganese Dianora who has insinuated herself into his harem in order to kill him but finds herself in love with him instead. But a simple reversal of the opposition of good and evil is insufficient for Kay's purposes, and he further complicates the issue at the end, when Alessan and his band are successful and both Brandin and Alberico are defeated. The reader's sympathy for the tragically ended love of Brandin and Dianora is subverted with a reminder of the depths to which Brandin was willing to sink in order to exact his revenge.

A SONG FOR ARBONNE

Kay's next work, *A Song for Arbonne* (1992), contains almost no magic at all, although faint traces of the fantastic linger in the use of the two moons, which, as in *Tigana*, figure in the worship of the god and goddess—a spiritual parallel to the underlying contrast of the matriarchal culture of Arbonne and the patriarchal culture of its northern neighbor, Gorhaut. The way in which each culture views the moon-goddess reveals something of their natures; in Arbonne, the goddess is the god's sister and equal, while in Gorhaut, she is his obedient daughter, not worthy of worship. This political and spiritual division into two, Arbonne and Gorhaut, leads to a simpler narrative structure than is usual in Kay's work, and serves at times to reinforce rather than to subvert the good/evil dichotomy conventional in the fantasy tradition.

Arbonne's historical counterpart is Provence, an area in what is now the south of France, and in medieval times the birthplace of the ideals of Courtly Love, which constrained the brute strength of warriors to the service of women and the arts of music and poetry. Because of its devotion to music and its willingness to place women in positions of power, although only rarely, Arbonne is scorned by its northern neighbor, the kingdom of Gorhaut, ruled by the corrupt young king Ademar. Blaise is the son of Ademar's principal advisor. Troubled by the king's behavior and by a scandalous treaty, Blaise leaves Gorhaut to become a mercenary soldier. Eventually he finds himself in Arbonne, where the men are, he mistakenly believes, too in- terested in poetry and music to be good fighters. Used to a society in which women are guarded jealously as property, and are beaten for disobeying their lords and husbands, Blaise is at first inclined to mock its Dukes for bowing to the orders of Signe, who has ruled Arbonne since the death of her husband. His attitude changes as his life becomes entangled with those of the strong and free women of Arbonne: the Countess Signe, the minstrel Lisseut, Beatritz the High Priestess, and especially Ariane de Carenzu, queen of the Court of Love.

Seeing in Blaise a weapon against the hatred and envy of Gorhaut, the leaders of Arbonne convince him to declare himself the rightful king of Gorhaut; when Ademar's forces invade Arbonne, raping, killing, and destroying the fertile land through which they ride, Blaise aligns himself with the forces of Arbonne and eventually wins the battle, ensuring peace between the two nations as well as some improvement in conditions for the women of Gorhaut. His arranged marriage to Ariane's niece, a girl whom he has not met previously, symbolizes the new union of the ancient foes, but also reminds the reader that the world of Arbonne, like its historical counterpart, may treat women better than its neighbors do, but still does not grant women freedom equal to that of men.

Women's response to their treatment creates much of the narrative tension. In fleeing the brutality of the Gorhaut court, Blaise's pregnant sister-in-law provides an excuse for war. The bitter rivalry between Arbonne's two most powerful dukes, Urté de Miraval and Bertran de Talair, caused by the latter's adulterous love for the former's wife—who died giving birth to Bertran's child—has serious political ramifications. Aelis de Miraval's adultery springs from her desire to escape a forced marriage; the fact that women are expected to surrender to marriages arranged by male protectors, even in enlightened Arbonne, complicates the conflict between the matriarchy and the patriarchy.

THE LIONS OF AL-RASSAN

Where *A Song for Arbonne* touches on gender inequality, *The Lions of Al-Rassan* (1995) explores religious intolerance. Kay's setting here is an alternate version of Moorish Spain, during the Christian reconquest. During the early

Middle Ages, Islamic forces had taken control of nearly all of the Iberian peninsula, resulting in a multicultural civilization that was wealthy, educated, and tolerant of the differences between Arabs, Jews, and Christians. The less tolerant Christian kingdoms in the north of Spain, rivals to each other but united in their hatred of the infidels to the south, fought to retake control of the Muslim cities, until only the city of Granada was left to fight the Christian armies with the aid of equally intolerant Muslims from across the Mediterranean. In the novel, Granada is represented by the city of Cartada, ruled by an Asharite king with the advice of his Kindath counsellor and the military aid of Jaddite mercenaries.

The different religious traditions are represented by the central characters: Jehane, a beautiful Kindath physician, her eventual lover, the Asharite commander and poet Ammar ibn Khairan, and their companion, the Jaddite Captain Rodrigo Belmonte, modeled on the historical and legendary figure of Rodrigo Diaz, El Cid. Jehane also loves Belmonte, although he is faithful to his wife Miranda, the mother of his twin sons, and her decision in favor of Ammar is not made out of a lack of sympathy for Rodrigo. The two men, acknowledged leaders of armies at war with each other, nevertheless admire and even care for each other, despite their differing religious backgrounds and cultural histories. Kay presents both men as equally competent, equally worthy of love, equally trapped by loyalties which can only end in opposition. The fact that neither man can be limited to the role of either hero or villain, and that most of the characters are portrayed as complex and sympathetic, means that it is impossible for the reader to choose sides in the conflict. What is evil in Al-Rassan is not any particular person or even any one religion; it is intolerance and the lengths to which intolerance drives otherwise rational human beings that is evil and to be fought whenever possible.

Kay's transferral of the good/evil dichotomy from the individual human onto the intolerance of human institutions is most strongly conveyed during the ritual single combat that precedes the final battle in the holy war between Asharite and Jaddite forces. As leaders of their respective armies, Ammar and Rodrigo are forced to confront each other in a battle to the death. Kay narrates this scene in such a way as to leave the reader uncertain of the identities of the victor and the victim of the duel; it is not until midway through the epilogue that he reveals which of his heroes has lost his life to religious intolerance.

THE SARANTINE MOSAIC

While *The Lions of Al-Rassan* contains no elements of magic at all, Kay's next project does reintroduce magic in the form of pagan gods and the artifacts produced by one of the secondary characters, an alchemist. The two books of The Sarantine Mosaic, *Sailing to Sarantium* (1998) and *Lord of Emperors* (2000), are the chronological next step in Kay's regression through Western history, and there are links here between the narrative world of this story and that of Rodrigo and Ammar. Here the origin of the Asharite religion is revealed, and the inhabitants of the Empire practice a form of the worship of Jad earlier than that found in Al-Rassan. The references to the ruins of the Rhodian Empire and its even earlier predecessor, the Trakesian Empire, obviously Rome and Greece respectively, may provide some clues to Kay's next project.

Sarantium is Kay's version of Byzantium at the height of its power after the collapse of the Western Roman Empire, during the reign of Justinian. Justinian and his Empress Theodora dedicated the Eastern Empire to two projects: one, to rebuild the former Empire by regaining the lost territories to the West and conquering new territory in northern Africa, and two, to glorify the capital city as a cultural as well as political center. To that end, Justinian, like Kay's Emperor Valerius, became a patron of art and architecture, and faced similar opposition regarding the use of religious images; incorporating that controversy into his fantasy, Kay once again touches on the issue of religious intolerance, and one theme explored in this duology concerns the political and clerical response to the power of the artist.

Crispin, a mosaicist working on a small church in what is left of the Rhodian Empire, accepts on behalf of his mentor a summons to attend Valerius' court in Sarantium in order to put his skills to work in building a magnificent new temple which will be Valerius' legacy to history. The fastest and safest way to reach Sarantium is by ship, but it is late in the season so Crispin must make his way through the pagan wilderness, made even more dangerous by the message entrusted to him by the besieged queen of the Antae. And his safety is not assured even after he has reached the city; he quickly finds himself caught up in the intrigues surrounding the royal court, as political and religious rivals plot against the emperor and his dancer-turned-empress. In a surprising turn of events, unexpected both in terms of the conventions of the fantasy genre and the historical facts, these rivals are ultimately successful, as the emperor is assassinated and his empress forced to flee the city. Crispin, his work on the stunningly beautiful but religiously controversial mosaic destroyed, returns to his home and his less prestigious but less dangerous mosaic in Antae.

Aside from the struggle between political and religious factions, another conflict develops surrounding the issue of who controls the legacy that both politicians and artists leave for posterity. Neither Crispin nor Valerius are completely free to portray themselves to the future in the way that they would wish. The artist's work is controlled by his patron, and Crispin must bow to Valerius's wishes in designing his masterpiece. And the image of those who shape history is ultimately controlled by those who survive them—what is known of Justinian and Theodora comes from Procopius's *The Secret History*, which is not flattering, to say the least. Kay narrativizes this biased historical record in the writings of the Emperor's secretary and historian, Petrennius, a bitter and twisted man who takes the side of Valerius's enemies and works to bring about his downfall. Crispin mourns Valerius as a man who attempted to reconcile opposing forces, to bring together those of different religions and different heritages; the failure of both men, and the destruction of Valerius' political and cultural legacy, presages the barbaric and intolerant Dark Ages that will follow, as in the real world.

CONCLUSION

Guy Gavriel Kay is a master of the subgenre of historical fantasy, able to capture not so much the facts of history as the moments of philosophical significance. Through the depiction of complex and sympathetic characters who are as much at the mercy of historical events as are flesh-and-blood human beings, and through his unwillingness to follow the easy and accepted convention of clearly aligning good against evil, Kay argues persuasively in his fiction for a worldview that embraces tolerance for everyone except those who practice and preach intolerance.

Selected Bibliography
WORKS OF GUY GAVRIEL KAY

NOVELS

The Summer Tree. Toronto: McClelland & Stewart, 1984; New York: Arbor House, 1984; London: Allen and Unwin, 1985. (The first book in The Fionavar Tapestry.)

GUY GAVRIEL KAY

The Wandering Fire. Toronto: Collins, 1986; New York: Arbor House, 1986; London: Allen and Unwin, 1986. (The second book in The Fionavar Tapestry.)

The Darkest Road. Toronto: Collins, 1986; New York: Arbor House, 1986; London: Unwin Hyman 1987. (The third book in The Fionavar Tapestry.)

Tigana. Toronto: Viking Canada, 1990; New York: Roc, 1990; London: Viking, 1990.

A Song for Arbonne. Toronto: Viking Canada, 1992; London: HarperCollins, 1992; New York: Crown, 1993.

The Fionavar Tapestry. Toronto: HarperPerennial, 1995. (Omnibus edition containing *The Summer Tree*, *The Wandering Fire*, and *The Darkest Road*.)

The Lions of Al-Rassan. Toronto: Viking Canada, 1995; New York: HarperPrism, 1995; London: HarperCollins, 1995.

Sailing to Sarantium. Toronto: Viking Canada, 1998; London: Simon & Schuster, 1998; New York: HarperCollins, 2000.

Lord of Emperors. Toronto: Viking Canada, 2000; London: Earthlight, 2000; New York: HarperCollins, 2000.

CRITICAL AND BIOGRAPHICAL STUDIES

Allard, James. "'The Unacknowledged Legislators of the World': Songs and Poetry in Guy Gavriel Kay's *A Song for Arbonne*." In *Perspectives on the Canadian Fantastic: Proceedings of the 1997 Academic Conference on Canadian Science Fiction and Fantasy*. Edited by Allan Weiss. Toronto: ACCSFF, 1998.

Cobb, Chris and Mary Anne Mohanraj. "From Tapestry to Mosaic: The Fantasy Novels of Guy Gavriel Kay." *Strange Horizons*. November 13, 2000. On-line magazine; article available at http://www.strangehorizons.com/2000/20001113/kay.shtml.

———. "'We must learn to bend, or we break': The Art of Living in Guy Gavriel Kay's *Sarantine Mosaic*." *Strange Horizons*. November 13, 2000. On-line magazine; article available at http://www.strangehorizons.com/2000/20001113/kay.shtml.

"Guy Gavriel Kay: Lord of Fantasy." *Locus: The Newspaper of the Science Fiction Field*. May 2000. 6-7, 63-64.

Ketterer, David. *Canadian Science Fiction and Fantasy*. Bloomington and Indianapolis: Indiana UP, 1992.

Mains, Christine. "Good vs. Evil is Not Black and White: Ritual Single Combat in the Works of Guy Gavriel Kay." In *Worlds of Wonder: Essays on Canadian Science Fiction and Fantasy Literature*. Edited by Cam La Bossière. Ottawa, ON: U of Ottawa P, forthcoming 2003.

Randall, Neil. "Shifting Focalization and the Strategy of Delay: The Narrative Weaving of *The Fionavar Tapestry*." *Canadian Literature*, 129, (1991).

Siourbas, Helen. "More than just Survival: The Successful Quest for Voice in Guy Gavriel Kay's *Tigana* and Randy Bradshaw's *The Song Spinner*." In *Worlds of Wonder: Essays on Canadian Science Fiction and Fantasy Literature*. Edited by Cam La Bossière. Ottawa, ON: U of Ottawa P, forthcoming 2003.

Webb, Janeen. "Myth and the New High Fantasy: Guy Gavriel Kay's *Tigana*." *The Ringbearer: Journal of the Mythopoeic Literature Society of Australia*, 8, no. 2 (1991). pp. 161-177.

———. "Post-Romantic Romance: Guy Gavriel Kay's *Tigana* and *A Song for Arbonne*." *The New York Review of Science Fiction*, 77: 17 (January 1995).

INTERVIEW

van Belkom, Edo. "Guy Gavriel Kay." In *Northern Dreamers: Interviews with Famous Science Fiction, Fantasy, and Horror Writers*. Kingston, Ontario: Quarry, 1998.

INTERNET RESOURCE

Brightweavings: The Worlds of Guy Gavriel Kay: The Authorized Website. http://www.brightweavings.com/ (A website of interest to researchers on Kay's works, including not-yet-published articles, book chapters, and conference presentations, as well as some comments by the author).

Jack Ketchum
1946–

FIONA KELLEGHAN

JACK KETCHUM ONCE told an interviewer that his favorite horror writer was Herman Melville, for *Moby-Dick*. This apparently wry reply opens one possible way to read Ketchum, who usually establishes his psychological horror fiction in settings as far from civilization as is the open sea; who specializes in portraying obsessive characters absorbed in a terrifying hunt; who shows life as a process of evading or grappling with danger and violence; and who presents the mysterious complexities of the human mind trying, and often failing, to cope with a malign cosmos. Ketchum does not write "just" horror. Like Melville, he deals with the human condition, and he focuses on characters who are predators, victims, and survivors. His villains cruise in homicidal flight paths through their personal whirlwinds of disruption and blood, endangering society as their mental disorders move beyond the borders of reason.

***

Jack Ketchum (pseudonym of Dallas William Mayr Jr.) was born on 10 November 1946, in Newark and raised in Livingston, New Jersey. He is the only child of Dallas William Mayr (1908–1997) and Evelyn Fahner Mayr (1915–1987), also born in New Jersey, of German immigrant stock. Referencing his home town, Ketchum sold a number of early short stories under the pseudonym "Jerzy Livingston."

Ketchum was a precocious reader from an early age. Both parents worked for the war effort during World War II; his mother was an accountant and office manager while his father served in the artillery, firing cannon across the Rhine River in Europe. After the war, the Mayrs moved from Newark to then-rural Livingston on the G.I. Bill. Dallas Mayr Sr. opened a confectionary store called The Sugar Bowl, a luncheonette with groceries as well as magazines, paperbacks, newspapers, and comics, and there Ketchum worked his first job. The young Ketchum would organize the newspapers—gruesome news stories still provide material for his fiction—and arrange the magazines and comics displays. Here he discovered the horror and fantasy fiction magazine *Weird Tales*. Ketchum helped at the family store through his teen years, as a short-order cook in the mornings and as a soda jerk at night. Serving the customers taught him to observe human strengths and foibles, which contributed to his powers of characterization.

Ketchum earned a B.A. degree in English from Emerson College in Boston, afterwards teaching high school in Brookline, Massachusetts, for two years. He entered the world of theater for a while, first writing reviews for a New York organ entitled *Our Town*. In his twenties he criss-crossed the United States, eventually moving to New Hampshire where he "did [his] Thoreau thing way out in the middle of nowhere," as he said in an interview with the horror web site Buried.com in 2002. The experience sent him back to New York in 1970 to engage in an off-off-Broadway theater company that produced a few of Ketchum's one-act plays (two of which he directed) and to act and sing in summer stock repertory. More importantly, perhaps, he returned from New Hampshire with a sense of the solitude and vulnerability of living in the wilds of New England, a setting that occurs repeatedly in his fiction.

Ketchum found the thrills of life as a starving artist wearing thin. He had worked as a garbage collector, lumber salesperson, copywriter, and editor of the paleontological magazine *Fossils*, among other adventures, but he wanted to get serious about writing. He launched a job in the mid-1970s as a literary agent for Scott Meredith, Inc., where he learned contracts, contacts, editing, and marketing. The highlight of his tenure there was agenting for the controversial author Henry Miller (1891–1980) from late 1974 until 1976. His work with this writer, whom Ketchum respects deeply, is recounted in his 1998 memoir "Henry Miller and the Push."

Under the name of Jerzy Livingston, which he used for sales to men's magazines, Ketchum sold his first story, "The Hang-Up," to *Swank* in 1976. The following years saw an exponential increase in his publications of articles, reviews, and fiction. For his novels, he decided upon a pseudonym based on the Texan outlaw Thomas "Black Jack" Ketchum (1863–1901). Ketchum notes that "Jack Ketch" is also, felicitously, British slang for a hangman.

***

In 1981, Ketchum published *Off Season*, which sent a shockwave through the field of horror fiction. It is grounded in the probably apocryphal story of Alexander "Sawney" Bean, the fifteenth-century leader of an incestuous cannibal clan on the coast of Scotland. Set in the ominously named Dead River, Maine, the novel is told from several points of view, a technique Ketchum frequently uses. The hero is weary George Peters, sheriff of this quiet town, though most of the action concerns six friends who visit a rented house for a vacation from New York: Carla, her sister Marjie, Laura, and their boyfriends Nick, Jim, and Dan.

The novel opens at a run with a wild chase scene on September 12, 1981; during the night of September 14, Carla's idyllic retreat is literally shattered by a band of cannibals who migrate along the Maine coast. What follows is a horrifying carnage derby as the man-eaters capture and gruesomely murder five of the six friends. (The survivor is the one the reader least expects to survive.) Meanwhile, the police launch their own manhunt as news of atrocities come in, and Peters, a depressed alcoholic, rallies enough strength at the end to reveal a saddening but noble heroism.

A recurrent image in the novel is that of the scavenging Atlantic crabs of the coast, about whom Peters muses that, like anything else, the crab had found its evil little niche. This idea supports the tale's central notion of a conflict of cultures. Ketchum describes the cannibals almost without moral judgment. The conflict is unresolvable except by predation, dominance, and survival. The cannibals have fierce courage and a family to maintain, but they are doomed when they confront a posse of cops with superior weapons and who are ready to die for each other.

Off Season gathered instant cult fandom and high praise throughout the world of horror readers and scholars. The writer Edward Lee dubbed

Ketchum "the godfather of the splatterpunks," meaning those horror writers who said, more or less, "You want to read horror? Then face exactly what it is we are really talking about—soul-stirring tragic losses, the taint of mortality, the glisten of viscera, poison, putrefaction, and everywhere the eyes of mad creatures inhabiting a world of cruelty and pain." Even the reviewer for the liberal New York weekly, the *Village Voice*, was sickened enough by the novel to title the review, simply, "YECCH!" and to publicly scold its publisher, Ballantine Books, for releasing violent pornography. The novel sold out its initial 400,000-copy print run entirely by word of mouth. The best-selling author Stephen King, meanwhile, offered the blurb: "Ketchum has become a kind of hero to those of us who write terror and suspense. He is, quite simply, one of the best in the business." Plenty of fans agreed. *Off Season: The Unexpurgated Version* was published as a hardcover in 1999 with an introduction by noted novelist-scholar Douglas E. Winter.

Ketchum's next novel, *Hide and Seek* (1984), took liberties with that Halloween favorite, the haunted house story. When four teenagers decide to play a midnight game of hide-and-seek in a derelict house, they discover that the original tenants, now homicidal lunatics, never left the premises. As in many Ketchum novels, the villains are hyperreal—they are supernaturally powerful, vengeful, and murderous. Yet the friends themselves can be dangerous to each other if they ignore the necessity for cooperation. As the narrator says, "I know we are all lonely. Locked off from one another in some fundamental secrecy. But some of us declare war and some of us don't" (p. 95). Three years later, in *Cover* (1987), Ketchum explored a different kind of loneliness in the twisted rage of a Vietnam veteran who finds six weekend campers trespassing on his territory.

The next two books, *She Wakes* and *The Girl Next Door* (both 1989), earned much deserved attention. *She Wakes* is set in Greece, a rugged and primal land Ketchum journeyed through and observed with such a keen eye that the noises, smells, and voices of the people, tavernas, sea, and mountains seem to float live from the page. It is his only truly supernatural novel, and its title refers to the mythological Goddess with Three Aspects—Selene, goddess of the moon; Artemis the Huntress; and Hecate, goddess of darkness and death and bloody sacrifice. Now she walks the earth in the guise of a Greek woman called Lelia Narkisos, thief, liar, and rouser of strife who takes lovers as she will and brutally disposes of them. Six men and women, four of them visitors to Crete, pair off in romantic attachments that will eventually become like the bonds of soldiers in battle, for with Jordan Chase, a psychic who is acutely attuned to the ancient magics that still haunt Greece, they ally themselves in a desperate attempt to prevent Lelia/Hecate from raising an army of the dead and bringing chaos to the world.

The Girl Next Door is generally considered Ketchum's most horrifying novel. Based on the case of sixteen-year-old Sylvia Likens, who was tortured and eventually murdered by her caretaker, Gertrude Baniszewski, in 1965, the novel is narrated by David as a pained reflection of what happened next door in the summer of 1958. When two sisters come to live with their Aunt Ruth, David and the other neighborhood boys spend more time at the house, fascinated and then participating as the sexual abuse and torture begin. David undergoes his own inner torture as he careens among the commands of an adult who is turning hideously insane, the appeal of power over a young girl, and his conscience which cries that he must get out and get help.

The year 1991 saw the publication of *Offspring*, the sequel to *Off Season*, in some ways more horrifying than the original because it portrays parents and children as both victims and cannibals. *Road Kill* (1994) begins one of a number of works concerned with the psychology of serial killers and multiple murders. Carole, sick of abuse by her cruel husband, and her lover, Lee, murder him in the woods. Unfortunately, their act is witnessed by Wayne, who has always longed to kill, and who views them as liberating new friends. When they express horror at his suggestion that they team up, Wayne takes them prisoner in his car and begins a homicidal spree. The conclusion, characteristic of Ketchum's work, leaves few survivors and a hovering air of bleak tragedy.

In *Red* (1995), Avery Ludlow has few pleasures left in life, among them fishing and his faithful dog, Red. The dog is shot by delinquent teen Dan McCormack while his brother and friend look on laughing, and Ludlow determines to get justice. However, the McCormack family is rich, corrupt, and indifferent to the grief of an old man. Ludlow turns to revenge, and the results are indeed bloody red.

Stranglehold (1995) consist of two portraits: one of the making of a sadistic child abuser and one of the disintegration of a family. Arthur Danse (whose name suggests "danse macabre") was himself abused as a child. Now he has a lovely wife, Lydia, and a likeable boy, Robert. However, Lydia gradually recognizes signs that Robert is being raped, and she fights the frustrating world of the legal system to protect her son from her possessive husband. *Stranglehold* epitomizes Ketchum's talent for portraying the psychology of victims of violence and fear. In Ketchum's view, the victim makes the story. Sometimes his victims become survivors—Lydia Danse is a survivor, though she pays a terrible price to save her boy. As Ketchum has told interviewers, he likes and admires women and tries, through his fiction, to avenge the hardships and cruelties so many suffer in real life.

By 1998, Ketchum had published dozens of short stories, and he collected twelve (plus the memoir about Henry Miller) into *The Exit at Toledo Blade Boulevard*. The collection offers grotesquery, laughs, and a great deal of pain, from "The Rifle," in which a mother discovers that her ten-year-old boy shows every sign of growing up to be a serial killer, to the black-comedy, true-crime-based "The Great San Diego Sleazy Bimbo Massacre." Both this book and *Ladies' Night* (1998) were issued as signed, limited editions, the latter because it was considered too violent for mass-market publication. The short novel *Ladies' Night* begins with a faintly science-fictional premise: a tanker with the logo LADIES, INC., overturns on a busy Manhattan street, spilling thousands of gallons of an unidentified, cherry-lollipop-scented liquid. Soon, the women of Manhattan begin to act strangely, at first becoming sexual predators, then turning their anger against men into tooth-and-nail murder. The war between the sexes becomes pure gore as the cherry liquid is paralleled in the final chapters with puddles and runnels of blood.

Ketchum published several chapbooks, memoirs, and novellas before the appearance of his finest novel, *The Lost* (2001), a Bram Stoker Award nominee in 2002. The novel begins in 1965 when three teenagers—the manipulative bully Ray Pye, based on serial killer Charles Howard Schmid, and his fearful friends Tim and Jennifer—decide to camp out in the woods of New Jersey. Ray, who has little in the way of conscience but plenty of anger and weaponry, shoots two girls they see at a nearby campfire. One dies, the other enters a coma. Upon her death four years later, the original policeman investigating the case, Charlie Schilling, is determined to capture the boy whom he knows committed the crimes. The rest of the novel is part police procedural, part killing spree, and wholly gripping.

The title refers to the young people of the 1960s who fell between the cracks, who went neither to war nor to college and who found little else remaining to them except drug abuse and, often, loveless sex. Nearly everyone in the novel, including Ray, says at some point, "What a world!" or "What is the world coming to?" Yet most of the people in the novel are kind and just trying to survive, and Ketchum shows that a few people can poison the world for everyone else. The novel is about both lostness and loss.

There are no winners, and even the survivors are diminished. Ketchum is attracted to writing about real people and the extremes that they find themselves in, either defending themselves from evil or succumbing to evil. He considers the book a call to awareness, strength, and gentleness.

***

The phrase most frequently used in reviews of Ketchum's works is "not for the faint of heart." His matter-of-fact tone is, perhaps, the most terrifying aspect of his fictional violence. Instead of the chapter titles commonly used, Ketchum often divides his books chronologically, each section labeled by date and hour. This police-procedural quality anchors in necessary reality the grotesque, nearly mythic quality of the violence and gore he describes. Although he writes about taboo subjects in every work, his prose is naturalistic. His materials are drawn from newpapers and personal experiences, from what real people do to each other in the real world. His characters may survive, but not intact.

Ketchum's fiction is bleak. He is not drawn to writing the sort of fiction in which humans encounter ersatz monsters such as vampires; he writes from anger at true-life injustices and cruelties. His heroes are those who work for justice, whether teenagers or retired policemen; they cooperate and help each other. His villains are child abusers, wife beaters, and usually drunks; alcoholism serves as a symbol of inability for self-restraint. Ketchum uses the small-town, backwoods setting in order to force his characters into isolation, but even in the crowded Manhattan of *Ladies' Night*, the men fleeing the vengeance goddesses all around them feel terribly alone. His settings convey both the ecstasy of nature and a primitive, potent darkness. The New England his novels return to is a blend of the Maine, New Hampshire, and Vermont that Ketchum lived in during the late 1960s. Like John Steinbeck's California or Jonathan Lethem's Brooklyn, Ketchum's rural New England is mythic. The night with its noises and silences, the forests trembling with concealed life, the cold damp and the warm chablis sunlight, the transition, on a single road, from farm to sea, are all heavy with hidden knowledge.

Ketchum's prose can be sublime, even numinous. In *She Wakes*, he describes the profound, throat-catching experience of clairvoyance felt by the character Jordan Chase:

> He recognized the feelings too—the tuning-fork intensity, the sense of having access for a moment to some impossible vantage point where you could see worlds turning, growing green or barren, imploding or exploding, mountains formed and seas going dry. It was wonderful and terrifying. And it was meant to be watched with humility if it was meant to be watched at all.
>
> Even the elation of it, even the joy, was painful. It could drive you crazy if you let it.
>
> (pp. 14–15)

Likewise, Ketchum's gift for tangible, exquisite sensation balances the pain that his characters suffer. In *Off Season*, when Carla investigates the house she has rented, she discovers a treasure trove:

> The comics looked good. She gathered them up and the smell of them, the old musty paper, pleased her. It was a smell she was very fond of. It stirred adolescent memories of a dime store in upstate New York, circa '64. Mown hay in the summertime. Malteds. Good things.
>
> (p. 20)

Ketchum's short story "The Box" won a 1994 Stoker Award for superior achievement in short fiction; another, "Gone," won the same award in 2001; and "The Haunt" was nominated in 2002. His short stories are gems, but he works best at novel length, where he can build entire worlds, both inside his characters' minds and around them. Another great regionalist, William Faulkner, wrote about the blacks in his 1929 novel *The Sound and the Fury*: "They endured." These two words can serve as an epitaph for all the characters, good and evil, in Ketchum's fiction. They struggle, they strive, they die, or they survive, but they endure.

Selected Bibliography

WORKS OF JACK KETCHUM

Off Season. New York: Ballantine, 1981. Revised as *Offspring: The Unexpurgated Version*. Woodstock, Ga.: Overlook Connection Press, 1999.

Hide and Seek. New York: Ballantine, 1984. Reprint, Springfield, Penn.: Gauntlet Press, 2000.

Cover. New York: Warner, 1987. Reprint, Springfield, Penn.: Gauntlet Press, 2000.

The Girl Next Door. New York: Warner, 1989. Reprint: Woodstock, Ga.: Overlook Connection Press, 1997. (The "corrected definitive" edition.)

She Wakes. New York: Berkley Books, 1989. Revised, Abingdon, Md.: Cemetery Dance Publications, 2002.

Offspring. New York: Berkley Books, 1991.

Road Kill. London: Headline, 1994. Published in the United States as *Joyride*. New York: Berkley Books, 1995.

Only Child. London: Headline, 1995. Published in the United States as *Stranglehold*. New York: Berkley Books, 1995.

Red. London: Headline, 1995; Woodstock, Ga.: Overlook Connection Press, 2002.

The Exit at Toledo Blade Boulevard. Auburn, Wash.: Obsidian Books, 1998.

Ladies' Night. Seattle, Wash.: Silver Salamander Press, 1998. Reprint, Springfield, Penn.: Gauntlet Press, 2002.

Broken on the Wheel of Sex: The Jerzy Livingston Years. Brewerton, N.Y.: Sideshow Press, 1999.

Right to Life. Abingdon, Md.: CD Publications, 1999.

The Lost. Abingdon, Md.: CD Publications and New York: Leisure Books, 2001.

Peaceable Kingdom. Burton, Mich.: Subterranean Press, 2002.

CRITICAL AND BIOGRAPHICAL STUDIES

Bryant, Edward. "*The Girl Next Door*, Jack Ketchum." *Locus*, April 1997, pp. 26, 47.

———. "*The Exit at Toledo Blade Boulevard*, Jack Ketchum." *Locus*, July 1998, pp. 29–30.

———. "*Right to Life*, Jack Ketchum." *Locus*, April 1999, p. 3.

Gwinn, Beth, and Stanley Wiater, eds. *Dark Dreamers: Facing the Masters of Fear*. Baltimore: Cemetery Dance Publications, 2001.

Kennedy, Ann. "A Conversation with Jack Ketchum." *Silver Web*, 14:57–59 (1997).

Piccirilli, Tom. "Words with Jack Ketchum & Edward Lee." *Epitaph*, 1:34–38 (1996).

Wiater, Stanley. "Jack Ketchum." *Mystery Scene*, September-October 1995, pp. 18–19, 77.

———. "A Conversation with Jack Ketchum." *Cemetery Dance* 7:57–60 (Spring 1996).

JACK KETCHUM

INTERNET RESOURCE

"Exclusive Interview with Jack Ketchum." *Buried.com*, February 27, 2002, available at http://www.buried.com/interviews/jack_ketchum.shtml

Stephen King

1947–

RICHARD BLEILER

STEPHEN KING HAS been the subject of scores of Ph.D. dissertations and more than a dozen books, has won significant literary awards, and has appeared in magazines as respected as the *New Yorker*, but his critical reputation is at best uneasy. Significant numbers of critics hold that his very popularity means that he cannot possibly be a good writer. Whether or not King is such a thing depends on how the term is defined, but there is no question that King has never met the editor he needs and has nevertheless flourished. His least efforts become best-sellers; his name on the cover of another book or a magazine guarantees increased sales; virtually all of his works have been filmed; and he receives the accolades and attention that are routinely paid to movie stars and professional athletes. In 1999, when he was critically injured, it made national headlines.

Aggravating the debate is that King frequently uses the works of others as models and inspiration for his novels. The early *'Salem's Lot* (1975) is a classical vampire novel, obviously indebted to such works as Bram Stoker's *Dracula* (1897) and Richard Matheson's *I Am Legend* (1954); *Firestarter* (1980) is almost certainly inspired by John Farris's *The Fury* (1976); *Pet Sematary* (1983) is a retelling of W. W. Jacobs's "The Monkey's Paw;" and *The Tommyknockers* (1987) is clearly inspired by the British motion picture *Quatermass and the Pit* (1967). Other derivations are readily located, but locating them tends to serve no particular purpose apart from showing that King has read and absorbed much supernatural and weird fiction. The question that should be asked is not the source of King's inspiration; it is how well he develops and executes his work.

Though he can be uneven and tends to be best at short stories and novellas, King's moral center has remained reasonably consistent. His is a universe in which good almost always triumphs, albeit sometimes at great cost. This essential optimism—King has stated that he is "convinced that there exist absolute values of good and evil warring for supremacy in this universe [and that] people can master their own destiny and confront and overcome tremendous odds" (*Playboy* interview)—occasionally leads to fiction whose conclusions fail to satisfy, as in *It* (1986), *Rose Madder* (1995), and *Desperation* (1996). When King questions or overturns these values, it leads to such powerful works as *Cujo* (1982), *Dolores Claiborne* (1993), and *The Storm of the Century* (1999). The first is generally King's most disliked novel; he shows that a sympathetic character possessed of heroic courage and determination still can fail. The narrator

525

of *Dolores Claiborne* has literally gotten away with murder, and *The Storm of the Century* recapitulates the theme of *Cujo* and details the decline and collapse of relationships: evil emerges triumphant.

Furthermore, King is generally perceived as a horror writer, but his fantastic horrors are so familiar that they are almost reassuring. Stories of vampires, werewolves, haunted locations, psychically generated monsters, malign imaginary beings, alien possession, revenants, and even characters from (nonexistent) motion pictures tend not to terrify readers inhabiting a world of random violence, the AIDS virus, "ethnic cleansing," and rapid genocide. On the other hand, when King exploits these and additional fears of a contemporary culture—rabies, car crashes, irrational imprisonment, and the government run amok—the results tend to be among his better material. Where he excels are in his depiction of personal relationships, in his portrayal of the lives of blue-collar workers, and in his recognition that the location of his works is as important to the story as the characters. This last is a significant factor in King's work—indeed, critics have linked the contents of his stories to specific locations—and it would not be inaccurate to describe him as a regionalist writer working in the same tradition as such Maine writers as Sarah Orne Jewett and Carolyn Chute.

King himself seems to be at least partially aware of his strengths and weaknesses. He has repeatedly and forthrightly admitted that he is not the finest of prose stylists and has as recently as 2000 stated that he is but a popular novelist who nevertheless cares "passionately about the art and craft of telling stories on paper" (*On Writing*, 2000). Prior to *On Writing*, King's most autobiographical and self-revelatory work was *Danse Macabre* (1981), which combines analyses of contemporary horror archetypes with personal reflections. *Danse Macabre* also offers what remains King's best summation of his creative philosophy: "I recognize terror as the finest emotion . . . and so I will try to terrify the reader. But if I cannot terrify him/her, I will try to horrify; and if I find I cannot horrify, I'll go for the gross-out. I'm not proud."

***

Stephen Edwin King was born on September 21, 1947, in Portland, Maine. His father, Donald, deserted the family when King was about two, leaving behind a few possessions, including an Avon collection of supernatural fiction and a volume of stories by H. P. Lovecraft, about which King has said, "That book, courtesy of my departed father, was my first taste of a world that went deeper than the B-pictures which played at the movies on Saturday afternoon or the boys' fiction of Carl Carmer and Roy Rockwell" (*Danse Macabre*, p. 102). Left with having to raise two children, King's mother, Nellie Ruth Pillsbury King, moved frequently, living in places as disparate as De Pere, Wisconsin, and Stratford, Connecticut, before settling in Durham, Maine. King remained in Maine, matriculating at the University of Maine at Orono in 1970, with a B.S. in English teaching. He married Tabitha Spruce in 1971; they have three children.

Although King had been writing since the 1950s, and wrote through high school and college, his career as a professional effectively began in 1967, when *Startling Mystery Stories* published "The Glass Floor" and paid $35.

During the early 1970s King taught high school and supplemented his income by selling stories to men's magazines and working in a laundry. He had written five unpublished novels—four of which were later published under the pseudonym Richard Bachman—and in 1973 the Kings were so financially desperate that the telephone was removed from their house trailer in Hermon. King conceived a novel based on the ideas of adolescent cruelty and telekinesis but did not like the characters, did not know how to develop it, and threw it away. Tabitha King pulled the manuscript from the wastebasket, assisted with the psychology of characters, and King's misgivings proved wrong. *Carrie* (1974) sold for $2,500; the paperback rights sold for $400,000, enabling King to become a full-time writer. Since then, all of King's mass-market works have been bestsellers.

***

The plot of *Carrie* centers on the coming of age of Carrie White, a tormented and abused high school student. She menstruates in the school's shower and believes she is bleeding to death, for her fanatically religious mother has neglected to inform her of the facts of life. When her classmates pelt her with tampons, Carrie White's dormant telekinetic powers emerge. They emerge lethally at the high school prom: after her classmates viciously douse her with pig's blood, she destroys them and the town. She herself perishes from wounds inflicted by her mother, but the novel concludes on an open and ambiguous note. Carrie White is reviled, and the motives of her classmates are forever questioned, but a concluding letter describes a newborn baby with telekinetic powers. Will this baby grow up to be another Carrie White, or will its loving parents prevent this?

Simple though the novel is, it contains numerous subtexts. The character of Carrie White was based on a composite of several of King's high school classmates, two young women broken by their classmates, and he wrote it intending to show that

> high school is a place of almost bottomless conservatism and bigotry, a place where the adolescents who attend are no more allowed to rise "above their station" than a Hindu would be allowed to rise above his or her caste ....[and that Carrie is] Woman, feeling her powers for the first time and, like Samson, pulling down the temple on everyone in sight at the end of the book.
> (*Danse Macabre*, pp. 169–170)

Carrie also offers adumbrations of King's development as a writer; although it may be classed as science fiction—Carrie White's powers are explained as "genetic recessive"—explanations can be ignored, as King concentrates on the results of the gift, not its cause. In all of his work, King appears less interested in causes than in results, and explanations remain minimal. In "The Mist" (1980) no explanation is offered for the deadly creatures that appear from an eerie mist and trap Maine townspeople in a supermarket. Everything may have been caused by a secretive government organization, the Arrowhead Project, or perhaps it is simply an instance of God—or a god—appearing on Earth.

King's next three novels, *'Salem's Lot* (1975), *The Shining* (1977), and *The Stand* (1978), are concerned with material (embodied) evil and its effects. In King's words, *'Salem's Lot* is "a peculiar combination of *Peyton Place* and *Dracula*" (*On Writing*, p. 85), though the novel's chief subtext does not concern people so much as it does the death of small-town America at the hands (or fangs) of outsiders: *'Salem's Lot* describes a small Maine town overrun by classical (bloodsucking) vampires. The town itself is convincingly described, and King populates it with more than a hundred believable types to show that, small though it is, *'Salem's Lot* is complex and far from idyllic. There are ironies of faith: the Catholic Father Callahgan loses his faith and, despite his expensive crucifix, is humbled by a vampire, whereas two men having faith are able to repel a vampiric attack with crosses made of tongue depressors and adhesive tape.

There is also a well-handled sex-death linkage that makes death from the vampire's bite erotically stimulating, and in all, the most serious fault in *'Salem's Lot* and its short sequel, "One for the Road" (*Maine*, March-April 1977), is conceptual: at the rate that men and women are bitten and become vampires, the United States should long since have become a nation of the undead. Although he hinted at writing a novel-length sequel to *'Salem's Lot*, King has not yet done so, returning to classical vampires only in "Night Flier" (1988), an unexceptional story in which the most memorable image concerns the vampire's bloody urine.

A peripheral element of 'Salem's Lot was a haunted house, but it did little except lend atmosphere. The Shining, on the other hand, is "set in the apotheosis of the Bad Place: not a haunted house but a haunted hotel, with a different 'real' horror movie playing in almost every one of its guest rooms and suites" (Danse Macabre, p. 254). As "Before the Play" (Whispers, August 1982), King's separately published five-part prologue establishes, the Overlook Hotel is a sentient Bad Place with a history of misery and death.

The title of The Shining refers to the psychic powers possessed by five-year-old Danny Torrance. Danny, however, is much less interesting than his father, Jack, a former teacher and recovering alcoholic who is also a talented writer. Jack Torrance is powerfully drawn; as King has admitted, Jack Torrance is autobiographical. Had Carrie not succeeded, King believes he would have become Jack Torrance, a bitter and frustrated man.

The Shining is essentially the story of Jack Torrance's collapse. While serving as winter caretaker in the snowbound Overlook Hotel, Torrance is seduced by Evil and led to try to murder his son and wife when they will not yield. Only the timely arrival of Dick Hallorann, the Overlook's black chef, summoned from Florida because he too has the "shining," saves Wendy and Danny from meeting the fate of the previous caretaker's family. Jack and the Overlook perish when its boilers burst, though Evil endures.

The Stand is a watershed in King's career, simultaneously demonstrating all of his strengths and weaknesses. The first part of the novel describes the accidental escape of a "superflu" from a military installation. The flu, nicknamed "Captain Trips," is 99.4 percent fatal, mutating until the infected can no longer produce antibodies. The world is soon depopulated when the American military, recognizing that the flu has made the United States vulnerable, spreads the virus. Those few who survive Captain Trips are offered a choice via dreams: join the evil Randall Flagg in Las Vegas or the good, 108-year-old Abagail Freemantle in Boulder. Most of the survivors, with the general exception of scientists, reactionary conservatives, militarists, and criminals, move to Boulder and the "Free Zone."

The Stand begins as science fiction in the tradition of M. P. Shiel's The Purple Cloud (1901) or J. D. Beresford's Goslings (1913), and fantasy enters late, with the shared dreams and with the presence of Flagg, who is also called "The Walkin Dude" or "The Dark Man." Flagg is a creature born of modern anxieties, hatreds, and fears—Charles Starkweather was a classmate; he has a flier given to him by Lee Harvey Oswald—and his powers are formidable. He can change into and control crows, weasels, and wolves. He can create magical keys to open electrically sealed cells. His gaze hypnotizes and maddens; he can send his consciousness flying as an eye; he can levitate and create lightning. Recognizing that Flagg is a memorable creation, King has reused him in such works as The Eyes of the Dragon (1984) and the Dark Tower series, where Flagg is identified as Maerlyn (Merlin), whose name indicates his origins, though these vitiate his introduction in The Stand.

The latter half of The Stand, in which the government of the Free Zone is established and its representatives confront Flagg, is overlong and anticlimactic. The 1978 version of the novel has what amount to two endings, neither of which is satisfying. In the first, the long-expected confrontation between good and evil never occurs; instead, the Free Zone's representatives are about to be tortured when an atomic bomb destroys all (save Flagg). In the second ending, Stu Redman—a Free Zone representative who was left behind with a broken leg—is nursed back to health by Tom Cullen, a well-meaning retarded man; and their slow journey back to Boulder is very much a letdown. The 1990 version of the novel adds yet more details, including Flagg's reincarnation and the members of the Free Zone discovering that a baby will survive, thus ensuring the continuation of humanity.

There are problems with *The Stand*, many of which center around the character of Flagg. As King introduces him, Flagg is too powerful to be defeated by the Free Zone's representatives. King thus undermines him, diminishing his powers and weakening him by temper tantrums and emotional outbursts. By steadily reducing Flagg and showing him done in by his own treachery, King shows that the effective life of evil is brief, but this comes at a cost to the novel's suspense. Furthermore, King candidly admits that Mother Abagail and Hallorann of *The Shining* are "cardboard caricatures of superblack heroes, viewed through rose-tinted glasses of white-liberal guilt" (*Playboy*), and the appearance of the spear-clutching simple-minded blacks in Flagg's reincarnation in the 1990 version does not help matters.

King's next two novels—*The Dead Zone* (1979) and *Firestarter* (1980)—share *Carrie*'s theme of the acquisition and disposition of paranormal powers. These, and *Cujo*, which followed, are also works of some depth and can be considered as novels of ideas.

The Dead Zone begins with young Johnny Smith being hit on the head with a hockey puck; part of his brain is injured, and he acquires a mild precognitive ability. As an adult, he is critically injured in a car accident, and when he awakens from a four-year coma, his psychic abilities are much greater. Smith need only touch someone or something belonging to a person to perceive his or her fate, but his brain injury—the dead zone—prevents him from seeing everything necessary. After discovering the identity of a serial killer—it brings him neither glory nor peace—he shakes the hand of aspiring politician Greg Stillson and discovers that the seemingly bluff and friendly man conceals a tigerish temper; if not stopped, he will become president and cause a nuclear war. The reader, who has followed Stillson's career, knows that Smith is correct—Stillson's rise is due to blackmail and intimidation—and Smith's problem is clear. His powers are taken seriously only in retrospect, and his health is failing, the dead zone having turned malignant.

The Dead Zone is permeated with images of cold and motifs of loss that resonate long after the book has concluded. Furthermore, it is a thoughtful book, in that King asks and attempts to answer a number of questions. Some of these are so old they have become clichés: if one could prevent World War II by entering a time machine and assassinating a still innocent Adolf Hitler, should one? The question, and the ethical quandaries it creates, nevertheless remain valid, as do King's additional questions about our purpose in life and God's will.

The titular firestarter is young Charlene ("Charlie") McGee, who can start fires by paranormal means. She acquired her ability because her parents, as college students, partook of Lot Six, an experimental drug that also gave her father, Andy, the ability to "push" people into obeying his orders. The Shop, the government agency that has administered the drug, has watched closely as the McGees "fire-trained" young Charlie. Mistakenly believing that the McGees are fleeing, the Shop captures Charlie, killing her mother. Although Andy McGee is able to free Charlie briefly, the Shop captures and imprisons both. Andy's powers are temporarily exhausted, and Charlie is tricked into starting fires by John Rainbird, a monstrously disfigured Native American assassin. Eventually Andy McGee pushes himself into recovering his powers and tries to escape with Charlie. He does not succeed, and Charlie alone escapes, destroying the Shop and its installations, going forth to tell her story.

Like *The Dead Zone*, *Firestarter* has greater depth than its simple storyline would indicate. The Shop itself is the villain: "Cap" Hollister, who heads its operations, is unpleasant, but he is ultimately pathetic and less vicious than his bureaucracy and its petty and sadistic enforcers. Rainbird is a larger-than-life figure, intelligent, amoral, fascinated with death, and capable of killing without the slightest regret. Finally, the novel is almost a paean to "common people," those who are not tainted by associations with governmental bureaucracies. It is these people who aid the McGees with rides, food, rooms, and money.

Cujo (1981), too, is a study of personalities, marriages, and our society's unhealthy values. False ideals of youth and beauty have led Donna Trenton to take a lover, so that she can pretend she is not getting old. Shoddy production values cause her car to stall while she and her four-year-old son, Tad, are trapped in the car and attacked by Cujo, an enormous rabid St. Bernard dog. Greed—albeit tempered with a sense of responsibility—have caused Donna's husband. Vic, to leave town in a desperate attempt at keeping a vital business account: a much-promoted cereal, sold with the slogan "Nope, nothing wrong here," is in fact quite wrong, for its red dye is indigestible and makes the feces of its eaters appear bloody. Cujo's owners, the Cambers, are fighting for possession of their son; Charity Camber is afraid the boy will become as limited and uncultured as her husband. Indeed, as King emphasizes, Cujo has no free will and is merely an unfortunate dog doing what he must. Humans have brought their fates upon themselves.

King originally intended to publish *Cujo* under his Richard Bachman pseudonym, which is apparently the reason he wrote himself into the novel as Stephen Kemp, Donna Trenton's erstwhile lover. Kemp is a poet and playwright who has published one book. He also works as a restorer of old furniture, an apt metaphor for King's writing, since King himself admits that he is not the most original of writers. In Kemp, King acknowledges his role and makes a self-deprecating joke about himself, his craft, and his position in life.

King's next best-seller was *Christine* (1983), a mildly experimental narrative in which the first and third sections are told by Dennis Guilder, a high school senior, and the middle is told by an omniscient observer. *Christine* has as its themes maturation and coming of age: Guilder and his friend Arnie Cunningham are maturing, and Christine, a 1958 Plymouth Fury, has just reached 21. Maturation involves the loss of innocence, and by the end of the novel few of the characters are innocent and fewer remain alive, for Christine was born evil and is possessed. She destroys the students who have hurt or threatened her or Cunningham.

In late 1983, with *Christine* still on *Publishers Weekly*'s paperback bestseller list, King published two more books, *Cycle of the Werewolf* and *Pet Sematary*. The former was a limited edition, since reprinted as a mass-market paperback; it describes the actions of people in a small town who are menaced by a werewolf over the course of a year. It is enjoyable, though routine.

Pet Sematary attracted considerable attention because King claimed it scared even him. Modeled on what is probably the finest horror story of all time—W. W. Jacobs's "The Monkey's Paw"—*Pet Sematary* tells what happens when Maine doctor Louis Creed discovers that the land behind the children's pet cemetery (its sign is childishly misspelled "*Pet Sematary*") is a haunted Micmac area that will revive the buried dead. King keeps Jacobs's theme, demonstrating that attempting to change fate merely makes life worse, though *Pet Sematary*'s ultimate theme is that one can mean well, yet do terrible things in the name of love. Nevertheless, *Pet Sematary* has few of the terrors of Jacobs's story. King reveals what is knocking at the door, and after the first shock the story becomes predictable, involving "gross-outs" rather than terror.

Following the collaborative *The Talisman* (1984), King's next novel was *It* (1986), which marks the start of an unfortunate and continuing trend in his career. Though his books still contained occasional excellent scenes, many became thematically repetitive, generally showing the effect of an outsider (a monster or a supernatural being) on a small Maine town. Furthermore, his work began to share and reuse a personal mythology, in which a group of people (a *ka-tet*) are bound together by fate to accomplish something. His rationale for this is unknown, but it lacks the resonance of the private mythologies created by such earlier writers as H. P. Lovecraft.

It deals with a monster in the sewers of Derry, Maine. This monster—It—is ultimately rational in origin, having come to Earth in a meteorite, though it possesses a variety of paranormal powers and sometimes catches children while appearing as a clown, Pennywise. In the 1950s a group of seven juvenile outsiders came together and thwarted It, but the survivors must reunite in the 1980s to battle It yet again.

Misery (1987) is one of King's best novels and, like *Cujo*, was originally intended to appear under the Richard Bachman pseudonym. Misery Chastain is the heroine of a series of low-level historical novels by Paul Sheldon, who has come to loathe his creation. Following a car crash, Sheldon finds himself the prisoner of a psychotic nurse, Annie Wilkes, who reads his unpublished manuscript and is horrified that Sheldon has killed her favorite character. Sheldon faces untold misery as he attempts to restore Misery to life in order to please the woman who began as his Constant Reader but becomes his Merciless Editor. Perhaps because of its intended origins, *Misery* is cold and unsympathetic and very convincing in showing a dislike and distrust of fans. Furthermore, as King has noted in *On Writing*, "misery" describes his state of mind when he wrote the novel, for he had become an alcoholic and a drug addict and was killing himself.

Misery was followed by *The Tommyknockers* (1988), which is science fiction, depicting malign aliens taking over a small Maine town. King describes writing it by "working until midnight with my heart running at a hundred and thirty beats a minute and cotton swabs stuck up my nose to stem the coke-induced bleeding" (*On Writing*, p. 96). Following its completion, his wife and family helped him stop drinking and quit his drug use.

The Dark Half (1989) is fantastic, a combination of autobiographical elements and such classical supernatural themes as psychopomps, automatic writing, and the bonds shared by twins. The focus of *The Dark Half* is Thad Beaumont, a respected but unsuccessful writer. When he had writer's block, he created "George Stark" and wrote four violent best-sellers featuring psychopathic Alexis Machine. (The names pay homage to Donald Westlake's Richard Stark novels and a character in Shane Stevens's *Dead City* [1973].) Beaumont's pseudonymous writing is discovered by sleazy law student Frederick Clawson, who attempts to blackmail Beaumont. Beaumont instead goes public with the information and even has a false tombstone created to show that George Stark has been laid to rest. Soon after, however, something emerges from Stark's grave, and killings start before Beaumont finally faces down his alter ego, who does not want to die.

Needful Things (1991) is set in the small Maine town of Castle Rock, used as the setting for *Cujo*, *The Dead Zone*, *The Dark Half*, and several short stories; characters in *Needful Things* also appeared in these other works. In *Needful Things*, Leland Gaunt—who is not human—moves into Castle Rock and opens an antique store called Needful Things. He seems to sell remarkable treasures that satisfy people's innermost desires; in reality, he sells trash, and his prices for his supposed treasures are acts of malicious mischief. Gaunt ultimately causes a battle between the town's Catholics and the Baptists before nondenominational Heaven, operating through Sheriff Alan Pangborn, drives him away. In addition to being thematically repetitive, though with occasional Lovecraftian echoes, the subtext of *Needful Things* involves the destruction of a way of life by outsiders and the wrongful covetousness of cheap and shoddy goods.

Gerald's Game (1992) and *Dolores Claiborne* (1993) are essentially mainstream novels, with a slight element of the fantastic involving psychically shared experiences during a solar eclipse in 1963. Both feature strong women characters. The former describes sexual bondage gone wrong. Jessie Mahout Burlingame resists her husband Gerald's rape fantasy by kicking him so hard that he dies, leaving her handcuffed to a headboard. As the novel progresses, a stray dog enters and dines on Gerald, she recalls the events of 1963, which culminated in her father feeling her breasts and ejaculating on her underwear, she links briefly with Dolores Claiborne, and she sees Death. *Gerald's Game* would be one of King's finest novels were it not for his inability to end it convincingly.

Dolores Claiborne purports to be the oral testimony of sixty-five-year-old Dolores Claiborne, a long-time resident of Maine's Little Tall Island. She is uneducated but cunning, earthy, shrewd, and more intelligent than generally realized, and her testimony is her history, intended to show that she killed her husband, Joe, not her employer, Vera Donovan. Claiborne's marriage yields three children, but Joe is profligate and abusive, and to earn additional money she works for wealthy Donovan, who is equally unhappy. Dolores ends Joe's abuse by hitting him on the head with a pitcher, but she discovers that he has stolen her children's savings and is sexually abusing their daughter. During the eclipse of 1963—during which she sees Jessie Burlingame—she lets Joe believe that she has hidden money, and his greed leads him into an old well. He does not die, however, and nearly escapes before Dolores brains him with a rock.

Insomnia (1994) has been praised for its elaborate thesis, aptly summarized by critic John Grant in *The Encyclopedia of Fantasy* (1997):

> there are four forces that drive the Universe—Life, Death, the Purpose and the Random—and that agents of the purpose are responsible for ending people's lives at the "correct time" while leaving room for the corresponding agent of the Random, who may snatch them away at any moment. But now the Random has imbalanced the relationship between itself and the Purpose, and the Purpose agents draw in an elderly human to help sort things out.

Also essential to the plot is the subject of abortion, which King presents reasonably without bias. On the debit side, the novel is far from being the work of ideas it could be.

Rose Madder (1995) has fewer ideas than *Insomnia* and describes an abused wife—Rose Daniels—being pursued by her husband, Norman, a psychopathic policeman. The fantastic enters in the form of a painting of a woman in a chiton in a classical setting. Rose Daniels enters the painting and discovers that its world is ruled by an alter ego, Rose Madder, who gives her back her courage and, ultimately, imprisons Norman and causes his death at his own hands.

In 1996 King published three novels: the serially issued *The Green Mile*, *Desperation*, and *The Regulators*. The latter purports to be a "Bachman" book, discovered in Richard Bachman's *nachlass*; it is in actuality a mirror of *Desperation*, using many of the same characters and fantastic elements and showing what a Bachman novel could be, even as *Desperation* is written to exemplify a "Stephen King" novel.

The Green Mile is set in a Georgia prison and is the narrative of Paul Edgecombe, who served as the E Block Superintendent, caring for death-row prisoners before they walk the "Green Mile" to their deaths. In 1932 John Coffey, an enormous black man, is brought to E Block, having been found guilty of raping and murdering nine-year-old twins. As the story progresses, Coffey reveals paranormal powers, healing Edgecombe's urinary infection and the warden's cancerous wife, and he is a Good Man, innocent of the charges against him. He nevertheless walks the Green Mile, having conferred the dubious benefit of extended life on Edgecombe, who comes to realize that love can destroy as well as save.

In *Desperation* and *The Regulators*, the force behind the action is *Tak*, a malign deity. In the former, a cross-section of society is imprisoned in the small Nevada mining town of Desperation. Blasting has freed Tak from entombment, who needs bodies to survive. As the desperate humans gradually realize, Tak is being quietly opposed by God, who is also using the prisoners and creating small miracles to assist them in their struggles. Young David Carver experiences a religious epiphany that he is able to share with failed writer John Edward Marinville. The conclusion is bland and religious: humans can make incredible sacrifices, God can be cruel, and God is love.

In *The Regulators*, Tak has possessed an autistic eight-year-old named Seth during a family vacation in Nevada. In Wentworth, Ohio, Tak's powers begin to emerge and cause the area to metamorphose into a quasi-western landscape, and figures from Seth's favorite television shows and motion pictures assume life and shoot the townspeople. Tak's powers are initially limited, and it is up to Seth's aunt Audrey to thwart the monster before he kills her and everybody else. The title of the story derives from a (nonexistent) western motion picture whose images resonate through Seth's mind.

Bag of Bones (1998) is the story of Michael Noonan, a moderately successful novelist whose wife, Jo, has unexpectedly died. As he settles into his lodge on Maine's Dark Score Lake and attempts to comprehend Jo's final actions, he discovers that an impoverished and lovely young widow is being threatened by her wealthy and incredibly vicious father-in-law, and that the town has a guilty secret: decades earlier, a black woman was gang-raped and forced to witness the murder of her child before being murdered. King fails to develop this latter theme, ignoring his politically and socially charged subject to tell a routine supernatural story.

Storm of the Century (1999) is the screenplay of a television miniseries broadcast in February 1999. It describes physical evil—Andre Linoge—entering the small Maine island town of Little Tall. Linoge creates a terrible blizzard, causes havoc, and forces the villagers to make a decision that, no matter how it is resolved, will destroy lives. The screenplay form is congenial to King, and *Storm of the Century* is one of his better works.

The girl of *The Girl Who Loved Tom Gordon* (1999) is nine-year-old Patricia Mcfarland, who becomes lost while hiking in the Maine forest. As she wanders, making a number of wrong decisions that get her further lost, she hallucinates, imagining conversations with friends and with Tom Gordon, ace pitcher of the Red Sox, whose games she hears on her Walkman. Her account is vivid, but King fails to end the novel convincingly.

Published late in 1999, *Hearts in Atlantis* is five novellas that reuse the same characters, all of whom had lives shaped by the Vietnam War; the novellas are also linked by images of hearts (the card game and human hearts) and of loss, particularly Atlantis beneath the waves. The first and longest, "Low Men in Yellow Coats," is set in Connecticut of 1960 and introduces characters whose futures will be described in the other novellas. Young Bobby Garfield, whose mother is money-obsessed and vindictive, befriends elderly Ted Brautigan, who shares books with him and gives him a job: he is to look for for-sale cards that are posted upside down and for low people who wear yellow coats and drive flashy cars. As King's readers will readily recognize, Brautigan is hiding, and ultimately the low men catch him, though not before Bobby has bonded with Brautigan, learned more about his deceased father, and seen his greedy mother humiliated.

In late 1999, King was walking beside the road near his home and was struck by a pickup truck and critically injured. He recovered, albeit with "a gimp leg" (*On Writing*), recounted his experiences in the *New Yorker*, and similarly injured protagonists began to appear in his work. *Dreamcatcher* (2001) features such a character, though the story recounts an alien landing in remote Maine. The aliens are vicious, though the American special forces—led by a Colonel Kurtz—are not significantly better. It is up to civilians to repel the invasion, the battle occurring on a psychic as well as a physical level, the "good" humans being assisted by their psychic retarded friend Duddits. The story fails to convince.

***

Although King has consistently reused characters, his only series is the Dark Tower, currently four volumes, which describes the quest of Roland, the last gunslinger, as he pursues the Man in Black who murdered his father, seduced his mother, and otherwise destroyed his life. Roland's quest occurs in a quasi-post-holocaust world paralleling this world in key points, though Roland's world also permits the existence of magic. In *The Dark Tower: The Gunslinger* (1982), a collection of linked novellas, the terse gunslinger kills the entire population of the town of Tull, befriends a boy named Jake Chambers, and allows Jake to fall to his death in order to pursue the Man in Black. He is vouchsafed a vision and learns that his entire universe is no more than an atom in a weed in a cosmic vacant lot.

The Dark Tower II: The Drawing of the Three (1987) begins with Roland being injured by "lobstrosities," which remove several of his fingers; he spends much of the novel in a high fever. He nevertheless recruits Eddie Dean (a cocaine smuggler) and Odetta Holmes (a crippled woman with multiple-personality disorder, which King refers to as schizophrenia) and administers justice to Jack Mort, the sociopath who injured Odetta.

The Dark Tower III: The Waste Lands (1991) resurrects Jake and introduces the radioactive Waste Lands that Roland's *ka-tet* must cross via Blaine, an insane monorail. Before the ka-tet can ride Blaine, they must fight the remnants of a group of rebels led by the viciously sadistic Tick-Tock Man. The book ends on the monorail, Roland's group engaged in a riddling contest with Blaine, the prize being their lives. The novel itself is a mishmash of ideas and characters taken from, among others, T. S. Eliot, Robert Browning, Harlan Ellison, Robert Louis Stevenson, and J. R. R. Tolkien.

The Dark Tower IV: Wizard and Glass (1997) is largely flashback, showing how Roland loved Susan and lost her to the malevolence of John Farson (an incarnation of Randall Flagg) and Rhea, the Witch of Coos. Susan's death almost destroys Roland, and he mistakenly kills his mother, believing her to be Rhea. The story concludes on an almost parodic note, invoking motifs from *The Wizard of Oz*. Roland and his friends must wear red slippers to enter a castle; the man behind the curtain is the Tick-Tock Man; and the Wizard himself is Maerlyn/Flagg, the evil seducer of Roland's mother. In the opinion of many, this volume constitutes a low point and a misdirection in the series.

***

King wrote six novels as Richard Bachman. The first four—*Rage* (1977), *The Long Walk* (1979), *Roadwork* (1981) and *The Running Man* (1982)—were published as paperback originals.

Fantastic elements are nonexistent, though there are numerous horrific moments. In the first, disturbed student Charles Decker kills several teachers and imprisons his high school class; the class itself exacts its revenge on one of their own. *The Long Walk* lines up 100 teenage boys and has them walk; those who cannot continue are killed, and the last one living gets untold wealth. *Roadwork* is mainstream, depicting working-class protagonist Barton George Dawes, his child, marriage, and career dead, as he attempts to prevent roadwork from destroying his house. *The Running Man* is shaky science fiction, a dystopic view of the future in which Ben Richards attempts to evade hunters and win enough money to provide medication for his sick child.

The fantastic enters *Thinner* (1984), which concerns a gypsy curse laid on overweight lawyer Billy Halleck. He inadvertently kills an elderly gypsy woman with his car, and his well-connected friends see that he is exonerated. The gypsy's father—106-year-old Taduz Lemke—curses those involved in the miscarriage of justice, and Halleck's curse is that, eat though he will, he will lose weight.

Shortly after the publication of *Thinner*, King's pseudonym was revealed. King killed Bachman, ultimately writing an introduction—"Why I Was Bachman"—for an omnibus edition of the first four novels. King's rationale was "I think I did it to turn the heat down a little bit; to do something as someone other than Stephen King. I think that all novelists are inveterate role-players and it was fun to be somebody else for a while—in this case, Richard Bachman" (p. vii). *The Regulators*, discussed previously, was ostensibly an unpublished manuscript discovered in Bachman's papers. It is not known if additional such manuscripts will be found, but, given King's playfulness, it would not be surprising.

***

In collaboration with Peter Straub, King has written two novels: *The Talisman* (1984) and *Black House* (2001). These operate from a premise akin to the Dark Tower series, that there is a magical world adjacent to ours, the Territories. In *The Talisman*, twelve-year-old Jack Hawkins attempts to save his dying actress mother. He learns of the Territories and is befriended by a werewolf, but his quest in this world is hampered by the camp run by the horrible fundamentalist preacher Sunlight Gardner and by his malevolent uncle, who is behind most of the bad things that have occurred to Hawkins and his mother.

Hawkins returns in *Black House*, a young retiree from the Los Angeles police. He has virtually forgotten the Territories and moved to French Landing, Wisconsin, which is plagued by a serial killer. The killer—called the Fisherman because his crimes resemble those of (real) serial killer Albert Fish—involves Hawkins in his crimes, and he joins forces with the town's policeman, Dale Gilbertson, and rediscovers the existence of the Territories. The identity of the Fisherman is revealed early, and much of the story involves Hawkins's gradually locating the man, though the most interesting character is Gilbertson's blind uncle, Henry Leyden, a man with preternaturally acute hearing who hosts a variety of radio programs. Though it can be enjoyable and was praised by a number of reviewers, *Black House* is overly long and not particularly gripping.

***

There have been four mass-market collections of King's short fiction—*Night Shift* (1978), *Skeleton Crew* (1985), *Nightmares and Dreamscapes* (1993), and *Everything's Eventual* (2002)—and, apart from *The Dark Tower: The Gunslinger* and *Hearts in Atlantis*, two collections of linked novellas, *Different Seasons* (1982) and *Four Past Midnight* (1990). There has also been one very limited edition: a mere 1,100 copies of *Six Stories* (1997) were printed, though four of the six stories had been published elsewhere.

The stories in *Night Shift* range from inexplicable shock-horror, as in "The Boogeyman," to gently personal terror, as in "The Last Rung on the Ladder." Several of the stories were cannibalized for later work: "Night Surf" became *The Stand*; "Trucks" served as the basis for *Christine* and the motion picture *Maximum Overdrive* (1986). "Children of the Corn" shows King's strengths at dialogue as it describes a bickering couple discovering that all is not well in an American heartland, for the children have slaughtered the adults; some critics have seen the story as a metaphor for the Vietnam War, though this is unconvincing. "The Lawnmower Man" is a wonderfully gruesome tale in which suburban Everyman Harold Parkette discovers that the man hired to trim his grass swears by Circe, has strangely cleft feet, and runs naked after the lawnmower, eating all that it spews out.

Different Seasons contains four loosely linked novellas, only one of which, "A Winter's Tale: The Breathing Method," transcends the literal. The story is dedicated to Peter Straub, and to some extent King has modeled his work on Straub's *Ghost Story*, using the premise of a club of old men who tell stories to each other. On the less literal level, the men's club becomes a metaphor for the mind, and its numerous rooms are the stories that King has told or plans to tell; King himself is in the story as Stevens, the club's caretaker. "Summer of Corruption: Apt Pupil" and "Fall from Innocence: The Body" are excellent, the former showing what happens when a young boy learns that an elderly neighbor is really a former concentration camp commandant; it has a terrific concluding line. The latter is a coming of age work in which four boys hike to look at the body of a boy their age; there are hints that the death was not natural, and the experience leaves them all changed. It was gracefully filmed as *Stand by Me* (1986), perhaps the best adaptation of a King work to date.

Skeleton Crew includes "The Mist," as well as such works of menace as "The Monkey," which makes an object of terror of a windup toy monkey with cymbals fastened to its hands; every time the monkey claps its cymbals, someone or something close to Hal Shelburn dies violently. The menace in "The Raft" is equally inexplicable: four teenagers are trapped on a raft by an inexplicably deadly being. "The Wedding Gig" is set in 1927, "when jazz was jazz, not noise"; the story manages a convincing irony: the narrator sympathizes with Maureen Scollay, the fat and ugly sister of a minor gangster who becomes a gang leader, but is indifferent to the fate of the black piano player, a decent young man named Billy-Boy Williams. Perhaps the finest story in the collection is "The Reach," published as "Do the Dead Sing?"; it tied for the 1982 World Fantasy Award for Best Short Story. It is the gentle account of ninety-five-year-old Stella Flanders, who has spent her entire life on Goat Island; she begins to see ghosts of loved ones and during a cold spell crosses the Reach, the body of water that separates the island from the mainland.

Two of the stories in *Nightmares and Dreamscapes*—"Dolan's Cadillac" and "My Pretty Pony"—were separately published as limited edition books; the former is a Poe-inspired tale of revenge on a mobster, the latter an account of a young man learning about time. There are pastiches of the works of Raymond Chandler ("Umney's Last Case"), Arthur Conan Doyle ("The Doctor's Case"), as well as works inspired by H. P. Lovecraft ("Crouch End"). "Head Down," an account of Maine's District 2 Little League tournament, is a compulsively readable essay and was first published in the *New Yorker*.

Four Past Midnight is, like *Different Seasons*, a series of loosely linked novellas. The stories in *Everything's Eventual*, whose subtitle—"14 Dark Tales"—indicates the overall tone of the collection, are a blend of literary work and what an introductory note calls "the all-out screamers." "The Man in the Black Suit" is an homage to Nathaniel Hawthorne's "Young Goodman Brown"; it won first prize in the 1996 O. Henry Short Story competition and is one of King's best works. "Riding the Bullet" was originally published electronically—it was one of the first successful e-texts—and is heavily autobiographical, King attempting to relate how anticipating his mother's death made him feel.

***

In 2002, Stephen King announced his retirement from writing, then rapidly retracted and modified his original statement: he would continue to write but no longer seek publication, or he would write enough finish the Dark Tower series, or maybe he would simply slow down a little.

Whatever King's intentions, he will be remembered as one of the world's best-selling writers and as one of the few writers whose name is immediately recognizable. His influence and choice of subject matter effectively created the publishing boom in horror literature of the 1970s and 1980s, and he endured when the market became saturated and people turned elsewhere for reading material. Because of his choice of subject matter, an entire generation of new writers was able to establish themselves.

At the same time, the influence and endurance of the writings is harder to assess. Unlike Dickens (to whom he has occasionally been compared), King did not introduce vivid and enduring characters into mainstream culture; nor did he seek to redress societal abuses and imbalances in his fiction, and King's authorial voice is that of the vernacular storyteller. No one of his novels can be singled out as *best*, as possessing the qualities that will permit it to survive the ultimate passing of its creator. None are stylistically or narratively unique.

King's best work may have been completed, or it may lie ahead, but he has succeeded at writing what interests and amuses him, in a style that has made him accessible to millions and made him the literary equivalent of a brand name, and for that if for nothing else he shall be remembered.

Selected Bibliography

WORKS OF STEPHEN KING

PRIMARY

A comprehensive bibliography of King's writings would fill a book (and it has). The following lists the first editions of the works discussed in the article. Many of King's works have also been published in limited editions issued simultaneously (or almost simultaneously) with the trade editions. No attempt has been made to list such deliberately created rarities.

Carrie. New York: Doubleday, 1974.

'Salem's Lot. New York: Doubleday, 1975.

The Shining. New York: Doubleday, 1977.

The Stand. New York: Doubleday, 1978. Restored edition. New York: Doubleday, 1990.

The Dead Zone. New York: Viking, 1979.

Firestarter. Huntington Woods, Mich.: Phantasia Press, 1980.

Cujo. New York: Viking, 1981.

The Dark Tower: The Gunslinger. West Kingston, R.I.: Donald M. Grant, 1982. (Later editions as *The Gunslinger*.)

Christine. West Kingston, R.I.: Donald M. Grant, 1983.

Cycle of the Werewolf. Westland, Mich.: Land of Enchantment, 1983.

Pet Sematary. New York: Doubleday, 1983.

The Eyes of the Dragon. Bangor, Maine: Philtrum Press, 1984. Revised edition. New York: Viking, 1987.

The Bachman Books: Four Early Novels. New York: New American Library, 1985.

It. New York: Viking, 1986.

The Dark Tower II: The Drawing of the Three. West Kingston, R.I.: Donald M. Grant, 1987.

Misery. New York: Viking, 1987.

The Tommyknockers. New York: Putnam, 1987.

The Dark Half. New York: Viking, 1989.

The Dark Tower III: The Waste Lands. Hampton Falls, N.H.: Donald M. Grant, 1991.

Needful Things. New York: Viking, 1991.

Gerald's Game. New York: Viking, 1992.

Dolores Claiborne. New York: Viking, 1993.

Insomnia. Shingletown, Calif.: Ziesing, 1994.

Rose Madder. New York: Viking, 1995.

The Green Mile New York: Signet, 1996. (Six parts separately published, then cumulated.)

Desperation. New York: Viking, 1996.

The Dark Tower IV: Wizard and Glass. Hampton Falls, N.H.: Donald M. Grant, 1997.

Bag of Bones. New York: Scribners, 1998.

The Girl Who Loved Tom Gordon. New York: Scribners, 1999.

Hearts in Atlantis. New York: Scribners, 1999.

Storm of the Century. New York: Pocket Books, 1999. (Screenplay.)

Dreamcatcher. New York: Scribners, 2001.

SHORT STORIES AND COLLECTIONS

Night Shift. New York: Doubleday, 1978.

Different Seasons. New York: Viking, 1982.

Skeleton Crew. New York: Putnam, 1985.

Dolan's Cadillac. Northridge, Calif.: Lord John Press, 1989.

My Pretty Pony. New York: Library Fellows of the Whitney Museum, 1989.

Four Past Midnight. New York: Viking, 1990.

Nightmares and Dreamscapes. New York: Viking, 1993.

6 Stories. Bangor, Maine: Philtrim, 1997.

Everything's Eventual. New York: Scribners, 2002.

AS RICHARD BACHMAN

Rage. [Richard Bachman, pseud.]. New York: Signet, 1977.

The Long Walk. [Richard Bachman, pseud.]. New York: Signet, 1979.

Roadwork: A Novel of the First Energy Crisis. [Richard Bachman, pseud.]. New York: Signet, 1981.

The Running Man. [Richard Bachman, pseud.]. New York: Signet, 1982.

Thinner. [Richard Bachman, pseud.]. New York: New American Library, 1984.

The Regulators. [Richard Bachman, pseud.]. New York: Dutton, 1996.

WITH PETER STRAUB

The Talisman. New York: Viking/Putnam, 1984.

Black House. New York: Random House, 2001.

NONFICTION/AUTOBIOGRAPHY

Danse Macabre. New York: Everest House, 1981.

On Writing. New York: Scribners, 2002.

King's prefaces to his short story collections contain autobiographical material, as do his introductions to the works of other writers. In addition, King has been widely interviewed. The early interview in *Playboy* (June 1983) remains useful, as do the conversations in *Bare Bones* (below).

SECONDARY

The publication of work on Stephen King has become a cottage industry, with such periodicals as *Cemetery Dance* publishing regular columns on King's writings and doings and hundreds of websites commenting on his fiction. No purpose would be served by listing these, and the following lists major works.

CRITICAL AND BIOGRAPHICAL STUDIES

Beahm, George. *Stephen King Country: The Illustrated Guide to the Sites and Sights that Inspired the Modern Master of Horror.* Philadelphia: Running Press, 1999.

———. *The Stephen King Story.* 2nd revised edition. Kansas City: Andrews and McMeel, 1992.

Collings, Michael. *The Many Facets of Stephen King.* Mercer Island, Wash.: Starmont House, 1985.

———. *Stephen King as Richard Bachman.* Mercer Island, Wash.: Starmont House, 1985.

Collings, Michael and David Engebretson. *The Shorter Works of Stephen King.* Mercer Island, Wash.: 1985.

Docherty, Brian. *American Horror Fiction: From Brockden Brown to Stephen King.* New York: St. Martin's, 1990.

Egan, James. "Sacral Parody in the Fiction of Stephen King." *Journal of Popular Culture,* 23: 125-141 (1989).

———. "'A Single Powerful Spectacle': Stephen King's Gothic Melodrama." *Extrapolation,* 27: 62-75 (1986).

Hoppenstand, Gary and Ray Browne, eds. *The Gothic World of Stephen King.* Bowling Green, Ohio: Bowling Green State University Popular Press, 1987.

Joshi, S. T. *The Modern Weird Tale.* Jefferson, N.C.: McFarland, 2001.

Magistrale, Tony. *Landscape of Fear: Stephen King's American Gothic.* Bowling Green, Ohio: Bowling Green State University Popular Press, 1988.

———. *Stephen King: The Second Decade, Danse Macabre to The Dark Half.* Boston: Twayne, 1992.

Magistrale, Tony and Michael Morrison, eds. *A Dark Night's Dreaming: Contemporary American Horror Fiction*. Charleston, S.C.: University of South Carolina Press, 1996.

Oakes, David A. *Science and Destabilization in the Modern American Gothic: Lovecraft, Matheson, and King*. Westport, Conn.: Greenwood, 2000.

Punter, David. *Gothic Pathologies: The Text, the Body, and the Law*. Houndsmills: Macmillan, 1998.

———. *The Literature of Terror: A History of Gothic Fictions from 1765 to the Present Day. Vol. 2: The Modern Gothic*. 2nd ed. New York: Longman, 1996.

Reino, Joseph. *Stephen King: The First Decade, Carrie to Pet Sematary*. Boston: Twayne, 1988.

Russell, Sharon A. *Stephen King: A Critical Companion*. Westport, Conn.: Greenwood, 1996.

Schweitzer, Darrell, ed. *Discovering Stephen King*. Mercer Island, Wash.: Starmont House, 1985.

Senf, Carol A. "Stephen (Edwin) King" in *American Novelists Since World War II: Third Series*. Edited by James R. Giles. Dictionary of Literary Biography, vol. 143. Detroit, Mich.: Gale, 1994.

Spignesi, Stephen J. *The Lost Works of Stephen King: A Guide to Unpublished Manuscripts, Story Fragments, Alternative Versions, and Oddities*. Secaucus, N.J.: Birch Lane Press / Carol Publishing Group, 1998.

———. *The Shape Underneath the Sheet: The Complete Stephen King Encyclopedia*. Ann Arbor, Mich.: Popular Culture, Ink, 1991.

Underwood, Tim and Chuck Miller, eds. *Bare Bones: Conversations on Terror with Stephen King*. New York: McGraw-Hill, 1988.

———. *Fear Itself: The Horror Fiction of Stephen King*. San Francisco and Columbia, Pa.: Underwood-Miller, 1982.

Westfahl, Gary. "Stephen King" in *St. James Guide to Horror, Ghost and Gothic Writers*, ed. by David Pringle. Detroit: St. James, 1998.

Wiater, Stanley; Christopher Golden; and Hank Wagner. *The Stephen King Universe: A Guide to the Worlds of Stephen King*. Baltimore: Cemetery Dance, 2001.

Winter, Douglas. *Stephen King: The Art of Darkness*. New York: New American Library, 1984.

BIBLIOGRAPHY

Collings, Michael R. *The Annotated Guide to Stephen King: A Primary and Secondary Bibliography of the Works of America's Premier Horror Writer*. Mercer Island, Wash.: Starmont House, 1986. Second edition. *The Work of Stephen King: An Annotated Bibliography and Guide* San Bernardino, Calif.: Borgo, 1996.

Many of the sources cited above also contain bibliographies.

INTERNET RESOURCE

Stephen King's official website is www.stephenking.com

Kathe Koja
1960–

STEFFEN HANTKE

KATHE KOJA WAS born in 1960 in Detroit. She grew up as a child of working-class parents; her father worked as a welder and truck driver for many years, while her mother was a homemaker. She says about herself that she had wanted to write for as long as she can remember, yet considers herself largely self-taught. In 1984 she attended the Clarion workshop at Michigan State University in East Lansing, which encouraged her to start writing professionally and submit her short fiction to magazines. In 1987 she began selling her short fiction, some of which would go into reprint and secure her first awards. Among her first sales in 1988, for example, is "Distances," a story published in the December issue of *Isaac Asimov's Science Fiction Magazine*, which was subsequently reprinted in the *Orbit SF Yearbook 2* in 1989, as well as in *The Year's Best Science Fiction and Fantasy* the same year. Winning the Locus Poll Award in 1989, her two subsequent stories "Skin Deep" and "Points of View" were published in *Asimov's* as well. Together with a few similarly well-received stories, this early success helped her find a publisher for her first novel, *The Cipher* (1991). Also in 1991 she married the artist Rick Lieder, whom she frequently credits for being an inspiration for her work and to whom many of her novels are dedicated. She has one son, and currently lives in Berkley, a suburb of her native city of Detroit.

THE CIPHER

With only a handful of short stories under her belt, Kathe Koja established herself as a novelist with *The Cipher*. It won the Bram Stoker Award for best first novel in 1991, tying for first place with Melanie Tem's *Prodigal* (also published by Dell's Abyss line), and was nominated for the Philip K. Dick Award. Taking place in an unspecified gritty urban setting strongly reminiscent of post-boom Detroit, *The Cipher* confronts its protagonist, Nicholas, with an inexplicable phenomenon immediately recognizable as a conventional element of horror. At the center of the novel is a hole in the floor of a storage room, tucked away inconspicuously inside a decrepit apartment building. Koja's description of the "funhole," as her characters nickname the phenomenon, evokes both terror and fascination: "Pure black and the sense of pulsation, especially when you looked at it too closely, the sense of something not living but alive, not even something but some— process. Rabbithole, some strange motherfucking wonderland, you bet. Get some-

541

body named Alice, tie a string to her...." Unlike the rabbit hole Alice goes down, the "funhole" does not lead anywhere. It is sheer nothingness, the negation of concrete physical objects, which vanish into it without a trace. To satisfy their curiosity and simply to kill time, Nicholas and his friends start experimenting with the hole. When they throw "an asphalt rock, plucked from the parking lot," into the hole, it makes "no sound, no sound at all, can you imagine how spooky that is?" As a number of other objects follow the rock—some retrieved by a string wrapped around them, some irretrievably lost—the results become more and more inconclusive.

Although the hole invites interpretation, it defies all efforts to understand it because it remains situated uncomfortably between proper conceptual categories. (It is "not living but alive, not even something but some—process.") Contrary to both intuition and common sense, your judgment grows hazier "when you [look] at it too closely." In other words, the "funhole," which was Koja's initial suggestion as a title for the novel, is defined more by what it is *not* than by what it *is*. It functions as an extended metaphor that can be turned over and over to yield new visions of lack, deprivation, abandonment, and desolation. In this sense, it represents the epitome of the enigmatic, supernatural presence in all of horror. And yet it is so conceptually condensed, stripped of all mimetic pretense, that it resists all attempts at containing it within genre conventions. Consequently it functions as a conceptual device that invites genre expectations and then cleverly subverts them. *The Cipher* is as much a horror novel as it is a novel about horror as a genre. These self-consciously "literary" qualities of the novel set it aside from much horror fiction published at the same time.

This basic premise has political consequences as well. Koja's insistence upon withholding a definition or explanation for the supernatural phenomenon at the center of the novel provides her with the opportunity to explore the emotional responses of her characters to the supernatural in more depth. This exploration reveals that psychological and social anxieties tend to originate on the inside. There is no threat in *The Cipher* that infiltrates or invades the individual body, psyche, or community from the outside and leads to a dangerous destabilization of boundaries and identities. Bodies, selves, and communities, as Koja herself has stated in an interview, are always already compromised and unstable. Instead of denying our essential fragility, and trying to contain it through discipline or false nostalgia, Koja advocates embracing it and exploring the new modes of being that might be derived from it.

In addition to the book's conceptual minimalism, *The Cipher* is also extremely striking for its austerity in regard to character and plot. In interviews, Koja has described plotting as one of her weaknesses as a writer, which may explain her continued interest in the more condensed form of the short story. In order to turn a vice into a virtue, she often returns to a constellation of three central figures. This permits her to pare down the cast of characters and yet generate intensely focused plots by playing two characters against the remaining one, subtly shifting and re-shifting the balance of power among them. Focused more on the psychology of the individual than on complex social interactions, a novel like *The Cipher* stands in stark contrast to the sprawling Dickensian novels of Stephen King or Peter Straub, which dominated the horror fiction market at the end of the 1980s and the beginning of the 1990s.

What struck most readers of *The Cipher* as unique about the novel, however, was its author's style. Obvious even from the short passage cited above, Koja writes in intense, syntactically fractured prose. Popularized throughout different popular genres by mid-1980s cyberpunk writers like William Gibson, this prose style can be traced back to science fiction writers like Alfred Bester, Theodore Sturgeon, and the British New Wave. It combines a refined pop and cross-cultural erudition with a blunt, even aggressive, sensory immediacy. Koja herself often draws on devices of high modernism like interior monologue. She deftly shifts between linguistic registers, placing clusters of complex expressionistic imagery side by side with naturalistic dialogue, the sublime with the vulgar, the literary with the commonplace. Since some of her novels also use first-person narration, Koja's prose style approximates her characters' subjective experience even further, lending the writing both crystalline clarity and emotional directness.

Since Koja's highly idiosyncratic style has become her trademark over the course of her writing career, reviewers almost invariably comment on it. While someone like Rick Kleffel, for example, phrases his assessment in relatively neutral terms, calling it simply "an entirely original style," Donna Lypchuk complains about "the precious mannerisms that junk up the text" of a later novel, *Strange Angels* (1994). Another reviewer, Gretchen Koot, goes even farther. "Koja often abandons grammar, sentence structure, and, as a result, clarity," Koot writes, concluding that "many of her incomplete sentences are simply unintelligible." Norene Cashen concedes that Koja's prose has the ability to "haunt and comfort, trap and release, frustrate and engross with a bizarre but palpable rhythm," but then notes that, for her taste, these rhythms are "interrupted by too many sentence fragments."

Whereas these reviewers are clearly bothered by Koja's style, others find it intriguing and consider it both integral to the author's artistic project and innovative within the confines of genre fiction. A reviewer of the German edition of *The Cipher*, Thomas Hoehl, describes Koja's prose as "a successful mixture of realism and lyricism," pointing out that the "uncanny drifting off into surrealism" of the novel for both the protagonist and the reader is a direct result of Koja's manipulation of language. Paula Guran appreciates her prose for producing a uniquely synaesthetic reading experience: "You don't just read Kathe Koja, you experience her words with a tactile sense of exploring forbidden territory"—words of praise indeed.

On the whole, her supporters tend to agree that the Koja's skewed lyricism is perfectly attuned to the narrative universe she consistently returns to—a bleak postindustrial cityscape, populated by alienated marginal characters hanging on to their fragile minds and social lives. Like her approach to the central tropes of horror, this setting and style set Koja aside from another kind of horror fiction that occupied the best-seller lists at the time, romantic horror in the vein of Anne Rice. Nothing could be farther from Rice's demon lovers across the centuries than Koja's harsh, unsentimental dissection of post-Reaganomics America.

BAD BRAINS, *SKIN*, AND *STRANGE ANGELS*

Since her 1991 debut, Koja has been producing roughly one novel a year. *Bad Brains* in 1992 was followed by *Skin* a year later, by *Strange Angels* in 1994, and by *Kink* in 1996. *Bad Brains*, the direct follow-up to *The Cipher*, was overshadowed by its predecessor's commercial and critical success, though Koja herself has referred to it in interviews as one of her favorite novels. The story revolves around a young man named Austen, who, after a minor accident, begins to suffer from psychotic episodes. Most of these episodes trigger violent and disturbing hallucinations, which uproot him from his already fragile social environment and send him on a quest to recover a sense of identity. Since Austen was a painter even before his accident, Koja makes the question of insanity part of a larger inquiry into the roots and consequences of artistic creativity. The novel raises questions about the precarious balance between the chaotic and potential antisocial energies of creativity on the one hand, and the procedural disciplines on the other that are necessary to shape and control this energy.

That the protagonist of *Bad Brains* ultimately embraces the new identity with which his hallucinations provide him makes him a predecessor of some of the central figures in Koja's next novel. Much like *The Cipher*, *Skin* garnered enough critical laurels to help define Koja as a writer for a horror audience, receiving a nomination as World Fantasy Award best novel in 1994. *Skin* takes place in a loosely defined avant-garde community, in which two female characters are trying to negotiate the line between art as self-expression and ritualistic self-destruction. With a sharp sense of satire, for which she is seldom credited by reviewers, Koja describes the underground culture of industrial art and body modification, often labeled as "new tribalism," as a network of socially displaced dropouts, self-aggrandizing posers, and inspired autodidacts. In the descriptions of one of the two women creating industrial sculptures out of scrap metal, Koja draws from her father's work as a welder. Meanwhile, the novels' second protagonist performs as a dancer, gradually modifying her body, through a series of surgeries, as an instrument of her art. As one character is trying to draw the other into a more and more radical redefinition of her body and self, Koja returns to the theme of *Bad Brains*, exploring artistic energy, its destructive potential, and the social marginalization it confers upon the artist.

If Koja can be said to have a romantic streak at all, it shows in her concept of the artist as social outsider. Her artists tend to be at the mercy of their own creativity, often unable to channel their talents into socially acceptable roles. They are self-destructive in pursuit of transcendence, which, when it finally arrives, always turns out to be a threat to personal identity. Though this kind of figure may be a staple of romantic and fin de siècle fiction, it is to Koja's great credit that, specifically in the context of the horror genre, she does not employ the threat to her characters' identities to legitimize a return to the status quo. In the figure of the artist, her readers will discover another aspect of the position she takes in regard to the tropes of horror—namely, that while the eruption of chaotic energies into the prosaic world of everyday life does trigger protective and disciplinary ideological mechanisms, these mechanisms belong to the social environment in which the characters function, and Koja herself does not present the lapse into the status quo as inevitable. In the figure of the artist, she shows that a lack of moderation and restraint might be necessary to produce radical forms of otherness, which in turn will broaden the range of available definitions of the self. In this sense her work is closely related to that of such horror writers as Clive Barker and Michael Blumlein, as well as other writers loosely associated with the splatterpunk movement.

Koja's next novel, *Strange Angels*, clarifies this notion of the artist as social outcast by directly contrasting the artist, helpless but inspired in the clutches of his chaotic creativity, with an untalented hack pretending to be an artist. Grant, a mediocre photographer, discovers among the documents kept by his girlfriend, who works in a mental facility, the inspired drawings of Robin, an institutionalized schizophrenic. As Grant gradually gains control over Robin and begins to push him further into his debilitating mental state, Koja expands a hitherto underdeveloped dimension in her work. Though, much like its predecessors, *Strange Angels* is tightly focused on the characters' inner lives, it pays more attention to the specifics of their social environment. Koja examines the theme of marginalization particularly in the light of public health care and its erosion in the late 1980s. As much as *Bad Brains* and *Strange Angels* celebrate the lone figure of the artist, they never fail to critique his or her dreary economic situation. Some readers have objected to Koja's unremitting dreariness, as her characters make do with subsidized housing, eat tasteless food, have joyless sex, and get nickeled and dimed in low-end jobs. Still, seen in the context of Koja's romantic depiction of the artist, this dreariness serves as a reminder that there is nothing glorious about being underpaid, underinsured, and down and out. The two tendencies balance each other throughout her work.

Given the characteristics of Koja's work, it is hardly surprising that *The Cipher* inaugurated Dell's Abyss series in February 1991. Abyss was a conscious attempt to respond to sagging sales figures in the literary horror market by introducing up-and-coming writers, as well as turning away from some of the worn-out clichés that had come to dominate horror fiction at the time. Like Koja, many published by Abyss abandoned the stereotypical American small town for an urban setting. They preferred psychological horror, often with a strong and explicit erotic element, to the supernatural. Body horror often took precedence over more metaphysical themes. And they chose, within the confines of the genre, stylistic experimentation over the formal gentility of the nineteenth-century novel that was typical of so much 1980s commercial horror fiction. The stylistic and thematic similarities shared by most of the writers editor Jeanne Cavelos published under the Abyss imprint illustrate Koja's own position in the horror field. Like Poppy Z. Brite, Melanie Tem, and Lisa Tuttle, she brings a more mainstream conception of the novel to horror fiction, and a more deliberately experimental attitude to her prose.

KINK, SHORT FICTION, YOUNG ADULT FICTION

After roughly forty volumes during a period of seven years, Dell retired the Abyss line with the departure of Cavelos in March of 1998. While Abyss's demise had many writers leaving for small presses, Kathe Koja's next novel, *Kink*, was published by Henry Holt in 1996. Perhaps the choice of a literary mainstream publisher was appropriate because of all of Koja's novels up to this point *Kink* least fits the generic definition of horror. Aside from confirming Koja's declared intention not to be perceived primarily or exclusively as a horror writer, *Kink*'s plot illustrates how consistent she has remained throughout her career. The novel delves into a mènage a troís, an unmarried couple taking in a female friend to live with them. It traces the subtle shifts of power and affection among the three characters and follows them into extreme states of obsession and neurosis. Though there are no traditional horror elements in *Kink*, the novel is permeated with an emotional intensity, a sense of latent violence and claustrophobia, that is strongly reminiscent of horror.

Koja has always been a prolific writer of short fiction. In 1999 she published the collection *Extremities*, which reprints stories that were originally published in such anthologies as Ellen Datlow and Terri Windling's annual *Best New Horror and Fantasy*, as well as containing some new material. Since 1993, she has collaborated on numerous short stories, roughly a dozen of which have been published so far, with renowned science fiction writer Barry Malzberg. Together with him she has also written a novel, which remains unpublished at the present date.

After *Kink*, she took another step in exploring new possibilities as a writer. While her short stories return to the genres of horror and science fiction, her most recent novels have been written for the young adult market. This is hardly surprising because, all along, Koja's preferred characters have been teenagers, or are barely above that age. Her novel *Straydog*, published by Farrar, Straus, and Giroux in 2002, with a cover illustration by her husband, Rick Lieder, reiterates "the theme of the creative outsider," as she herself puts it. So does her next novel for young adults, titled *Buddha Boy*, which is scheduled for publication in the spring of 2002. Rachel, the writer in *Straydog*, is mocked and marginalized; Jinsen, the visual artist in *Buddha Boy*, is hounded and persecuted, while his work itself is physically attacked. Both use their art as a way to endure and to fight back—one peacefully, the other driven by rage. Koja's target is not only the unresponsive social milieu these two teenagers must live in, but, even more importantly, larger forms of violence. For Rachel, this is cruelty to animals; for Jinsen, it is the need to confront and resist systematic bullying. Koja has also finished a novel entitled *The*

Blue Mirror, which she herself describes as "a dark urban fairy tale about a gifted young artist who meets her soul mate among the downtown runaways." The novel has been sold to Farrar, Straus, and Giroux, together with a fourth novel, but no specific publication date has yet been scheduled for either one.

MAINSTREAM WRITER OR GENRE WRITER?

Looking back on Kathe Koja's work over roughly ten years, most of her readers see her as precariously positioned between mainstream fiction and the horror genre. In fact, many of her reviewers have tried to assign her a place in one or the other literary tradition. Donna Lypchuk, for example, has called her "a cross between a post-modern Poe, a beatnik Stephen King and Kafka with a halo of hope." An anonymous reviewer of *Skin* remarks that it "is not a horror novel in the traditional sense, despite the comparisons with Lovecraft and Poe which adorn the cover." Rick Kleffel chimes in, claiming that *Bad Brains* "has more in common with Kafka and Camus than with Stephen King."

Her position between genre and mainstream, as well as her recent transition toward young adult fiction, only highlights the thematic and stylistic consistency of her work more dramatically. The question is not whether Koja varies the degree to which she employs supernatural elements, to which she codes obsession as sexual, or to which her writing has upped the ante on graphic and grotesque violence. What matters is that writing for different audiences has not distracted her from the themes that fascinate her or the prose she writes best. In this sense, all her writing is one ongoing meditation on large philosophical questions—on what it means to be an outsider, on establishing boundaries in the pursuit of our passions, and on the price we pay for intimacy and the surrender of the self to others.

Some might argue—Koja herself among them—that she never qualified as a horror writer in the strict sense to begin with, even when publishers and reviewers placed her in this category. In a strongly segmented publishing market that caters to target audiences rather than simply to readers, her label as a horror writer has always been primarily the result of editorial expediency. Although she has always attracted a devoted readership, and critics have consistently praised her work, remaining unclassifiable has kept her from breaking through to a wider audience. Given the fact that outsiders in Koja's fiction are always perversely empowered by their invisibility, she herself may actually see her position as an opportunity—to continue mapping out a place where she can be a genre of one.

Selected Bibliography

WORKS OF KATHE KOJA

NOVELS

The Cipher. New York: Dell Abyss, 1991.
Bad Brains. New York: Dell Abyss, 1992.
Skin. New York: Dell Abyss, 1993.
Strange Angels. New York: Delacorte, 1994.
Kink. New York: Henry Holt, 1996.

KATHE KOJA

Straydog. New York: Farrar, Straus, and Giroux, 2002.
Buddha Boy. New York: Frances Foster Books, 2003.
The Blue Mirror. Forthcoming.

COLLECTION

Extremities. New York: Four Walls Eight Windows, 1998. (Contains "Arrangement for Invisible Voices," "The Neglected Garden," "Bird Superior," "Illusions in Relief," "Reckoning," "The Company of Storms," "Teratisms," "Angels in Love," "Waking the Prince," "Ballad of the Spanish Civil Guard," "Lady Lazarus," "The Disquieting Muse," "Queen of Angels," "Jubilee," "Pas de Deux," and "Bondage.")

SHORT FICTION

"Happy Birthday, Kim White." *SF International* 1, 1987.

"Distances." *Isaac Asimov's Science Fiction Magazine*, December 1988.

"Skin Deep." *Isaac Asimov's Science Fiction Magazine*, July 1989.

"Points of View." *Isaac Asimov's Science Fiction Magazine*, October 1989.

"The Energies of Love." *Isaac Asimov's Science Fiction Magazine*, December 1989.

"True Colors." *Isaac Asimov's Science Fiction Magazine*, January 1990.

"Illusions in Relief." *Pulphouse* 7, Spring 1990.

"Reckoning." *Magazine of Fantasy & Science Fiction*, July 1990.

"Command Performance." *Amazing Stories*, November 1990.

"Bird Superior." *Isaac Asimov's Science Fiction Magazine*, January 1991.

"The Neglected Garden." *Magazine of Fantasy & Science Fiction*, April 1991.

"Angels in Love." *Magazine of Fantasy & Science Fiction*, July 1991.

"Angels' Moon." In *The Ultimate Werewolf*. Edited by Byron Preiss, David Kellor, Megan Miller, and John Betancourt. New York: Dell, 1991.

"Impermanent Mercies." In *Dark Voices 3*. Edited by David Sutton and Stephen Jones. London: Pan, 1991.

"The Company of Storms." *Magazine of Fantasy & Science Fiction*, June 1992.

"Letting Go." *Pulphouse*, June 1992.

"Persephone." *Isaac Asimov's Science Fiction Magazine*, November 1992.

"By the Mirror of My Youth." In *Universe 2*. Edited by Robert Silverberg and Karen Haber. New York: Bantam Spectra, 1992.

"The Prince of Nox." In *Still Dead*. Edited by John Skipp and Craig Spector. New York: Mark V. Ziesing, 1992.

"Teratisms." In *The Year's Best Fantasy and Horror: Fifth Annual Collection*. Edited by Ellen Datlow and Terri Windling. New York: St. Martin's Press, 1992.

"Metal Fatigue." *Amazing Stories*, February 1993.

"Arrangement for Invisible Voices." In *Dark Voices 5*. Edited by David Sutton and Stephen Jones. London: Pan, 1993.

"Ballad of the Spanish Civil Guard." In *Alternate Warriors*. Edited by Mike Resnick. New York: Tor, 1993.

"The Careful Geometry of Love." With Barry Malzberg. In *Little Deaths*. Edited by

Ellen Datlow. New York: DAW, 1993.

"The Disquieting Muse." With Barry Malzberg. In *Little Deaths*. Edited by Ellen Datlow. New York: DAW, 1993.

"The High Ground." With Barry Malzberg. In *Temporary Walls*. Edited by Greg Ketterer and Robert T. Garcia. Dreamhaven/World Fantasy Convention, 1993.

"I Shall Do Thee Mischief in the Wood." In *Snow White, Blood Red*. Edited by Ellen Datlow and Terri Windling. New York: Morrow, 1993.

"Leavings." In *Borderlands 3*. Edited by Ed Sarrantonio. 1993.

"Rex Tremandae Majestatis." With Barry Malzberg. In *Dinosaur Fantastic*. Edited by Mike Resnick and Martin H. Greenberg. New York: DAW, 1993.

"The Timbrel Sound of Darkness." With Barry Malzberg. In *Christmas Ghosts*. Edited by Mike Resnick and Martin H. Greenberg. New York: DAW, 1993.

"Queen of Angels." With Barry Malzberg. *Omni*, July 1994.

"The Disquieting Muse." In Little Deaths. Edited by Ellen Datlow. New York: Millennium, 1994.

"Literary Lives." With Barry Malzberg. In *Alternate Outlaws*. Edited by Mike Resnick. New York: Tor, 1994.

"Modern Romance." With Barry Malzberg. In *Dark Voices 6*. Edited by David Sutton and Stephen Jones. London: Pan, 1994.

"Three Portraits from Heisenberg." With Barry Malzberg. *Omni*, Fall 1995.

"Buyer's Remorse." With Barry Malzberg. In *How to Save the World*. Edited by Charles Sheffield. New York: Tor, 1995.

"Clubs." *Witness*, 1.9 (1995).

"DMZ." In *Amazing Stories: The Anthology*. Edited by Kim Moran. New York: Tor, 1995.

"Girl's Night Out." With Barry Malzberg. In *Vampire Detectives*. Edited by Martin H. Greenberg. New York: DAW, 1995.

"In the Greenhouse." With Barry Malzberg. Edited by Poppy Z. Brite and Martin H. Greenberg. New York: HarperPrism, 1995.

"Jubilee." With Barry Malzberg. In *Peter Straub's Ghosts*. Edited by Peter Straub. New York: Pocket Star, 1995.

"Mysterious Elisions, Riotous Thrusts." In *Forbidden Acts*. Edited by Nancy A. Collins, Martin H. Greenberg, and Edward Kramer. New York: Avon, 1995.

"Pas de Deux." In *Dark Love*. Edited by Nancy Collins, Martin H. Greenberg, and Edward E. Kramer. New York: Penguin/ROC, 1995.

"The Unchained." With Barry Malzberg. In *Tombs*. Edited by Edward Kramer and Peter Crowther. New York: White Wolf, 1995.

"Waking the Prince." In *Ruby Slippers, Golden Tears*. Edited by Ellen Datlow and Terri Windling. New York: Morrow, 1995.

"The Witches of Delight." With Barry Malzberg. In *Witch Fantastic*. Edited by Mike Resnick and Martin Greenberg. New York: DAW, 1995.

"Lady Lazarus." *Magazine of Fantasy ↪ Science Fiction*, May 1996.

"Homage to Custom." With Barry Malzberg. In *Twists of the Tale*. Edited by Ellen Datlow. New York: Dell, 1996.

"The Inverted Violin." In *Gahan Wilson's The Ultimate Haunted House*. Edited by Gahan Wilson. New York: HarperPrism, 1996.

"Orleans, Rheims, Friction: Fire." With Barry Malzberg. *Magazine of Fantasy & Science Fiction*, August 1997.

"In the Last Chamber." With Barry Malzberg. In *Alternate Tyrants*. Edited by Mike Resnick. New York: Tor, 1997.

untitled, parts 4, 8, 1. Omni Online, April 1998.

"The Doctrine of Color." With Carter Scholz. *Century Magazine* 6, Spring 2000.

"Stray Dog." *Cicada*, September-October 2000.

"At Eventide." In *Graven Images: Fifteen Tales of Magic and Myth*. Edited by Thomas Roche and Nancy Kilpatrick. New York: Ace, 2000.

"Remnants." In *The Green Man: Tales from the Mythic Forest*. Edited by Ellen Datlow and Terri Windling, Viking, 2000.

"Singularities." *Speculative Sex: The Science Fiction Issue*. (Nerve.com online publication.) 2000. Available at http://www.nerve.com/fiction/Koja/singularity/.

"What We Did That Summer." With Barry Malzberg. In *Redshift: Extreme Visions of Speculative Fiction*. Edited by Al Saranntonio. New York: NAL/Penguin Putnam, 2001.

"A Drink at Pandora's." ThePosition.com. (Online publication.) 2002.

"The Oblivion Quartet." *Witness* 2.15 (2002).

"Brandi's Baby." *Cicada*, 2002. Forthcoming.

"Fireflies." *Century*, Fall 2002. Forthcoming.

"Becoming Charise." In *A Wolf at the Door and Other Retold Fairy Tales*. Edited by Ellen Datlow and Terri Windling. New York: S&S Books for Young Readers. Forthcoming.

"Lupe." In *The Swan Sister*. Edited by Ellen Datlow and Terri Windling. Forthcoming.

"Road Trip." World Fantasy Convention 2002 Program Book. Forthcoming.

Dean Koontz
1945–

GREG BEATTY

DEAN KOONTZ'S LIFE resembles the plot of an American success story: a writer lifts himself from a childhood of poverty and abuse through sheer hard work. Koontz has written more than seventy novels, under his own name as well as ten pseudonyms; his books have sold over one hundred and fifty million copies. He has published everything from Gothic romances to science fiction, but it is his suspense novels tinged with the supernatural that have made him a best-seller and won his mature work critical acclaim.

Dean Ray Koontz was born on 9 July 1945, to Ray and Florence Koontz, just one month before the close of World War II. The family lived in Everett, Pennsylvania, until the following year, when they moved instate to Bedford, a town of roughly three thousand, where Dean's father opened a shoe repair shop. Dean lived in Bedford until he graduated from high school.

Koontz evokes Bedford's conservatism, its economically marginal status, and the region's traditional dependence on the coal industry in *Strange Highways* (1995). However, while familiarity with this region—and with small-town life in general—is revealed throughout his work, it was not place that shaped Koontz most powerfully as a writer but people—specifically, his family.

Koontz's father was an abusive alcoholic who experienced severe mood swings. In his later years, Ray Koontz was frequently hospitalized; he was ultimately diagnosed as a borderline schizophrenic. Koontz estimates in several sources, including an interview published in *Sudden Fear,* that his father held forty jobs in thirty-four years, punctuated by periods of unemployment. Ray habitually developed elaborate plans to get rich quick, efforts ranging from inventions to lawsuits. None of them were successful.

The Koontz household was both poor and frightened. Koontz's father terrorized Dean and his mother, sometimes physically abusing them, and vanished for days when drinking. Central to many of Dean Koontz's fictional works are adults whose emotional problems warp their children, from the abusive father who brutalizes animals in Koontz's first published short story, "Kittens" (1965), which appeared in the *The Reflector,* through novels such as *Dark Rivers of the Heart* (1994) and *Intensity* (1995), in which characters fight against the gravitational pull of abusive parents.

Koontz knows this pull very well. As an adult, with his wife, Gerda Ann Cerra, his high school sweetheart whom he married on 15

October 1966, he moved west, first to Nevada in 1975, then to California in 1976, where in 2002 they continued to reside. Koontz has set several of his works in these locales, most notably *The Eyes of Darkness* (1981), in Nevada, and *Whispers* (1980), in California, effectively capturing their inhabitants and geography. In 1977 Dean's father, drinking heavily and nearly destitute, followed Koontz and his wife west and moved in with them, and the couple cared as best they could for Ray Koontz, whose behavior was sometimes violent. Before Ray's death in 1991, he had twice tried to kill Dean.

Koontz's mother, Florence, who died in 1969, had struggled to protect Dean from his father. The figure of the guardian, dedicated to protecting his or her charge from evil, appears in many forms in Koontz's fiction, from the intelligent alien who befriends a human being in *Beastchild* (1970), to the character of Rose in *Sole Survivor* (1997), who struggles to keep genetically engineered children from those who would exploit them.

If his mother's role in the family was that of protector, Dean was the good child who escapes from harm. Koontz read voraciously, especially science fiction and horror, which exposed the reality of his life: the world was not the calm place that mainstream 1950s media representations of America would suggest. Significantly, the character Carl Stanfeuss, in *Twilight Eyes* (1985), reads science fiction to escape from the world that his special sight allows him to see, one in which murderous goblins hide beneath ordinary people's faces.

It is striking how often Koontz's characters wake up to find that they are in another world, or that their entire lives have been cruel hoaxes. Examples occur in *Hell's Gate* (1970), and *Warlock* (1972), among others, and in his first novel, *Star Quest* (1968), a brainwashing drug wears off and the main character finds himself entering a floating library. Writing was Koontz's way to escape to such a library and create such an awakening. By age eight Koontz was writing and illustrating his own stories and selling them to friends and family. Around age eleven, he entered a newspaper contest, writing an essay titled "What It Means to Be an American" which won him twenty-five dollars and a watch.

Koontz attended Shippensburg State College in Pennsylvania, graduating with a degree in English in 1966. While at Shippensburg, he read widely in literature, psychology, and philosophy, and converted to Catholicism for a time. He served on the editorial staff of Shippensburg's literary magazine, *The Reflector*, which published several of his short stories. A teacher submitted one of Koontz's stories and one of his essays to a contest sponsored by *The Atlantic Monthly*. The story won one of five fiction prizes awarded; the essay won an honorable mention. Shippensburg recognized Koontz's achievements in 1989 by awarding him an honorary Ph.D.

After college, Koontz taught for a year in the Appalachian Poverty Program in Saxton, Pennsylvania. Though he shared the liberal idealism sweeping the country and wanted to make a difference, his experience there soured Koontz on change managed through government agencies, an attitude that can be seen in works such as *The Eyes of Darkness*, in which the government experiments on a boy, and *Strangers* (1986), in which the U.S. Army brainwashes citizens who witnessed a UFO.

Koontz moved on to teach at a high school in Mechanicsburg, Pennsylvania, from 1967 to 1969. In 1967 he published his first professional story, "Soft Come the Dragons," in *The Magazine of Fantasy and Science Fiction*. In 1968 he published more stories, and his first novel, *Star Quest*. However, both he and Gerda were frustrated with their jobs, so she proposed a deal: she would support him for five years. He would quit teaching to write full time. He agreed, and moved quickly into a mode of heavy literary production that he maintained throughout his writing career.

Koontz's early work shows promise, but often bears the marks of a young writer working too fast. He also wrote a number of formula works for the money. In part to protect his own name, in part because with some genres, such as Gothic romances, the expectation was for a female author, and in part due to ill-considered advice on marketing, Koontz wrote under a number of pseudonyms. As he has mastered his craft, his artistic ambitions have grown. Koontz has bought the rights to many of these early novels from his publishers. Some he reissued under his own name; others he rewrote. As a result, not only has he dominated the best-seller lists, he has earned a growing critical reputation.

***

Koontz is known as a master of suspense, able to hook readers with the first line of his books and maintain tension until the last page. However, readers may be surprised to realize how infrequently Koontz actually writes supernatural fiction, one of several reasons he resists being labeled a horror writer. Fewer than one of his novels in five is supernatural. If one considers the scientific explanations for such phenomena that are presented in the novels, that number may drop to fewer than one in ten.

However, consistent themes and techniques run throughout Koontz's work, unifying it and creating a sense of his work as primarily in the supernatural vein. His early science fiction novels, for example, tackle religious themes within a naturalistic framework. *Star Quest* describes civil strife, but it is as much about how a just god can allow suffering in the world. *Fear That Man* (1969) in part answers such a question, by describing a god with a material existence, who has been kept captive behind an energy screen. In *A Darkness in My Soul* (1972), God exists, and is accessible, but is insane, perhaps reflecting Koontz's period of atheism. Thematically, Koontz returns again and again to theodicy, asking why people have to suffer. He analyzes the results of overweening ambition and the mind's inability to deal with reality. In each of these situations, morality and emotion are the lodestones that guide his characters through the morass. Koontz finds hope in the heart of good individuals in positive relationships but beyond this he is distrustful; the forms that this intertwined hope and distrust take change with the times, often reflecting shifts in the American sociopolitical landscape.

To address these thematic concerns, Koontz repeatedly introduces into his fictional worlds a rupture in the natural order. Such an event also invariably disrupts the world's moral order. More frequently than he provides an explicit treatment of God, however, Koontz addresses identity and knowledge of the world. As one might expect, given the father that Koontz had, questions of identity become threatening when boundaries are porous, capable of admitting evil, or when they are not settled.

A particularly strong example of this is *Darkfall* (1984), perhaps the most traditionally supernatural of Koontz's work. In this novel a New York City police officer, Jack Dawson, and his children, Penny and Danny, are threatened by Baba Lavelle, a Haitian voodoo *bocor,* or priest of the dark arts. Dawson's moral righteousness makes him largely invincible to Lavelle's voodoo powers, and so an impediment to Lavelle's attempt to exact revenge from the Mafia families who killed his brother. Lavelle opens a passage to hell that allows shape-shifting demons access to the world.

The bulk of the book is an extended chase set in a snowbound Manhattan, in which Dawson and his allies, his partner and new lover Rebecca Chandler, and Carver Hampton, a voodoo *houngon,* or practitioner of white magic, battle a series of demons to protect Dawson's children and save the world. Every crack, seam, or vent in a building becomes an opening for these misshapen forces, which are powered both by their own malignancy and by the city's pool of petty evils, which Lavelle taps. The characterization of good and evil in the novel is at once simplistic—Dawson is righteous, despite his doubts, and his love with Chandler is pure, despite their unmarried state—and refreshing, as Koontz allows his *houngon* humor and human complexities, and gives readers a multiethnic coalition of defenders.

Koontz's stance toward the supernatural in *Darkfall*—his acceptance of demonic forces and his willingness to explain them in terms of magic and morality—can be contrasted with that in another novel from the same period, *Phantoms* (1983). At the opening of this work, almost everyone in the fictional town of Snowfield, California, has been killed or has simply vanished, and only a handful are left to investigate the cause. Primary among them are a doctor, Jenny Paige, and a police officer, Bryce Hammond, who could be variations on *Darkfall's* Chandler and Dawson. All four are ultraresponsible, to the extent that they are haunted by past mistakes that were not their fault.

Once the investigators are in place, the thing responsible for the mass killing begins to torment them. It animates the dead, sings with the voices of those it has eaten, and plays fast and loose with physical barriers. Nothing keeps this thing from killing the town's survivors except its desire to torment them and to have them persuade a scholar, Dr. Timothy Flyte, to come to the town to chronicle these dark events. When he arrives, Flyte argues that a number of mass disappearances through history have been the work of this "Ancient Enemy." This enemy turns out to be a shape-shifting mass of evil with a myriad of powers, but after pleading helplessness for hundreds of pages, the heroes finally use a weapon created by the government to annihilate it. Along the way Koontz proposes both rational and supernatural explanations for his monster, suggesting that it is a biological creature that may have been the basis for various myths, even for the Christian figure of Satan. These explanations fall flat, largely because they do nothing to explain the creature's malignancy, or the sudden success of government science. Koontz, like his characters, functions best when he acknowledges both the credibility of the supernatural and the moral fabric of reality.

Nowhere is this clearer than in Koontz's novel *Twilight Eyes* (1985; revised and rereleased in 1987). As mentioned above, Carl Stanfeuss possesses a form of psychic vision that allows him to see the murderous goblins that hide beneath the flesh of particular humans. These eyes also give him precognitive flashes, intuition into the moral character of the purely human, and less reliable powers such as shared dreams. Carl is on the run, traveling under the alias Slim MacKensie, because he had killed a man, his uncle, that he considered responsible for his family's suffering, including his father's death.

Slim is an evocative figure, at once mythic, metaphorical, and chillingly realistic. His quest to avenge his father and purge the land of goblins is rendered so intensely that one cannot help but sympathize with him. Slim's pained isolation allows him to stand for every abused child who recognizes the evil in his abuser but cannot find a way to be heard—and of the blind distortions fostered by a system that allows such abuse. Koontz's goblin-infested town of Yontsdown is a place of corruption almost on the level of Dashiell Hammett's Poisonville in *Red Harvest*. However, Slim's vision is unreliable and, for more than half the book, unshared. He could be a psychopath with exceptionally vivid delusions. Koontz deepens the novel by setting it in a traveling carnival, where nothing is what it seems and the freakish is mundane. Koontz develops two dozen characters with ease, breathing life into each with well-selected details. Though Koontz explores the theme of the isolated visionary committed to doing good in other books, *The Vision* (1977) and *Cold Fire* (1991) most notably, the dense imagery of *Twilight Eyes* makes it a fine work of supernatural fiction. It would rank higher still if he had not opted for an abrupt, naturalistic explanation that makes neither emotional nor scientific sense, revealing the goblins as an ancient, intentional mutation.

***

If Dean Koontz is not primarily a supernatural writer, what is he? When describing his own work, Koontz uses the term "cross-genre," referring to his tendency to blend elements of mystery, science fiction, horror, and other genres. More specifically, Koontz has called himself "a novelist of the fantastic who writes in a realistic vein" (*Sudden Fear,* p. 26).

This summation sounds contradictory, but illuminates two crucial details about Koontz. First, he is remarkably self-aware with respect to his work. In 1972 he wrote a book titled *Writing Popular Fiction,* in which he detailed his techniques, his beliefs about the role of ideology in fiction, and other issues. Since then, he has rewritten the book, written essays and articles on technique and the fantastic, and allowed himself to be interviewed widely. Advice from some of these interviews is included in *Dark Thoughts: On Writing—Advice and Commentary from Fifty Masters of Fear and Suspense.* Edited by Stanley Wiater, this collection won the 1997 Bram Stoker Award for the best nonfiction horror.

Koontz's self-definition also explains the relationship between the content of his fiction and the experience of reading it. Despite their intensely realistic settings and meticulously researched story lines, his works have the feel of supernatural horror. How does Koontz achieve this effect and what is its significance?

The first step in understanding the tension in Koontz's work is to define the terms "fantastic" and "supernatural." The word "supernatural" refers to something that transgresses the laws of nature. This could be a traditional creature, such as a ghost or a vampire, or an event, such as a premonition that is later validated. Traditional supernatural creatures often follow a set of rules laid down by custom, but one key element of the supernatural is that at some point, reason slips away.

"The fantastic" is more specific. In his study *The Fantastic* (1970), the French literary critic Tzvetan Todorov describes the moment when an event seems to break the natural order. We hesitate, trying to decide if something supernatural has happened or not. The reader, and often the character, is caught at the intersection between two sets of rules, the rational and the supernatural, unsure about what to do next, or even how to resolve the confusion. Koontz tells realistic stories in the language and tone of the supernatural. This puts the realistic content of his fiction in tension with its subtexts.

Koontz does this in literally dozens of ways. The first and most basic technique involves his already noted propensity to address religious themes. In *Dark of the Woods* (1970), a man conquers death, achieving immortality. In *Anti-Man* (1970), Koontz gives us an alien as god, displacing the supernatural with purely naturalistic explanations, but retaining the aura of awe. One of Koontz's early novels, *The Fall of the Dream Machine* (1969), describes a world ruled by a media that has become essentially omniscient. In thrillers such as *Dragonfly* (1975) and *The House of Thunder* (1982), large organizations that operate like deities are critiqued. Koontz communicates the feeling that these power structures can distort reality—and that the way they do so is morally wrong. Sometimes Koontz's characters degrade or pervert religious activities. In *Demon Seed* (1973) a computer that has become, in Koontz's words, "a demi-god," rapes a human woman, inverting the Christian story of the Annunciation.

The title *Demon Seed* illustrates how Koontz uses religious language to refer to otherwise realistic events, imbuing them with the power of their original religious contexts. The superintelligent computer in this novel is not literally demonic, but its actions are as monstrous as any devil's. Koontz's titles often evoke settings of fear, especially variations on darkness, and may pair contradictory words, such as *Cold Fire,* or linked words, such as *Dragon Tears* (1993), that convey something familiar (playing here on the proverbial "crocodile tears") but refer to a transformed physical reality. He builds on this by setting stories in locales where traditional rules do not apply, such as the carnival setting of *Twilight Eyes,* Japan in *The Key to Midnight* (1979; revised and rereleased in 1995), and the frozen world of *Prison of Ice* (1976; revised and reissued as *Icebound* in 1995).

Koontz repeatedly retells the classic story at the intersection of science fiction and horror, of the overreaching scientist who discovers things that man was not meant to know. In several cases, these scientists are involved in attempts to make or remake life, echoing Mary Shelley's Victor Frankenstein and H. G. Wells's Dr. Moreau. Thomas Shaddack in *Midnight* (1989) is a good example; he misuses technology to take over the town of Midnight Cove. In *Watchers* (1987), one of Koontz's finest novels, readers are shown the light and dark possibilities in science. Einstein, a genetically engineered dog, is the ideal of all dogs, raised to the level of human intelligence. He not only protects his humans, he engineers their love affair. His nemesis, the Outsider, is as dark and tortured a creature as has haunted any nightmare. The Outsider is driven by a sense of his own exclusion from the human race, and evokes pity even as he kills.

Koontz further denaturalizes the world by including characters who believe in supernatural powers so strongly that these beliefs shape their world. In *Whispers,* Bruno Frye's mother believes that she was raped by a demon, and that this is the reason she gave birth to identical twins. She was not—the novel is completely naturalistic—but this belief causes her to raise her two boys as one child. This in turn shapes their pathologies, and reinforces, at one point in the novel, the sense that Bruno returns from the dead. Hilary Thomas, who Bruno had been stalking, believed that she had killed him, but "Suddenly, he was not dead anymore" (p. 37). Characters can be so tested by these apparent infractions in natural law that they abandon their faith in reason. In *Invasion* (1975), Don Hanlon is so unsettled by his experiences that he declares that the universe is insane and that humans "are the lunatics in this madhouse" (p. 190).

Bruno Frye's apparent return from the dead is one of many instances in which Koontz takes a traditional image from supernatural horror and re-presents it in a naturalistic framework. Frye is an example of the revenant; Dr. Leben in the 1987 novel *Shadowfires* is another (the German word *Leben* means "to be alive"). Vince Nasco in *Watchers* is a variation on the vampire. A professional assassin, Nasco believes that he absorbs the life force of those he kills. Many Koontz characters exemplify the beast within, or the werewolf, such as the killers Bollinger and Plover in *The Face of Fear* (1977). These characters do not literally change, but are ruled by their bestial desires, as if possessed; more than one critic has noted the parallels between this sort of character and Koontz's father. Koontz also creates many variations on the doppelgänger, supernatural doubles linked by fate. The most striking example occurs in *Mr. Murder* (1993), with Marty Stillwater, a writer, and Alfie, the killer who is his clone. The two are identical, except for the fact that Alfie has no soul (having been raised by a "soulless" organization rather than a loving family). Here too one can see Koontz's father in his fiction, sometimes charming, sometimes terrifying, always with the same face.

The supernatural trope that Koontz most often employs is the ghost: the dead past returns to haunt the living, affecting them without taking a physical form. Nora Devon, the beauty who befriends Einstein, the genetically modified dog, in *Watchers,* sees herself and the world through the eyes of her dead aunt. Ogden Salisbury, the evil scientist in *Night Chills* (1976), was abused as a child. Memories of this pain drive him; Salisbury invents a drug that allows him to control others as he was controlled, creating zombies via biochemistry.

When something strange happens in a science fiction novel, the affected individual has the structure of science to call on, either in the embodiment of scientists or in theories and practices that he or she exercises. In Koontz's work, a disturbing event happens in isolation, as in horror fiction. Sometimes the event causes the isolation, as in *Phantoms* when the biological monstrosity that plagues Snowfield blocks off phone and radio contact with the outside world. In other stories, such as *Invasion*, the isolation is created through location (the characters live in the country), narrative focus, and the characters' psychological makeup. Though it is unclear why, the invading aliens seem to be interested almost exclusively in the Hanlon family. They also act in ways that seem illogical or impossible, as when they kill Don Hanlon's wife, Connie, then return her to life.

Koontz employs two other methods of characterization that contribute to infusing his work with the fantastic. First, intense emotions translate directly to reality. *False Memory* (1999) contains characters who suffer from phobias that manifest suddenly and inexplicably; the fear that the characters experience is so intense that it seems to warp physical reality.

Second, Koontz bases his characters' development on individual morality rather than psychology. This can make his work seem old fashioned, or archaic, like melodrama. Once the moral weight of a character has been established, readers can relax, knowing that good characters, such as house painter Dusty Rhodes in *False Memory* or physician Jenny Paige and her sister Lisa in *Phantoms,* are simply good and will remain so. Since Koontz drew heavily on Freudian psychology early in his career, it is striking to track the shift to an emphasis on free choice and moral action, rather than biology and psychology, employed as the keys to character. The methods mix uneasily in Koontz's early work; Koontz did not find a balance until he read Thomas Harris's serial-killer novel *Red Dragon* (1981). Koontz appreciated the work, but found Harris's almost schematic explanations of the pathology of the Tooth Fairy, the novel's primary killer, lacking. This drove him back to an early literary influence, Charles Dickens. From this point on, Koontz sought a consciously Dickensian method of exploring character, one that emphasized morality.

All of the characterization techniques in play in Koontz's mature thrillers are used in his 1995 best-seller *Intensity*. When *Intensity* opens, psychology student Chyna Shepherd is visiting the family of her best friend, Laura Templeton. An intruder breaks into the house and kills the entire family except Laura, whom the killer kidnaps. Chyna was abused as a child, and this experience allows her to immediately recognize the intruder's intentions as he enters the house. Chyna's presence is not detected by the killer, and she stows away in his motor home, intending to rescue Laura. Once inside the trailer, she finds that it is not what it appears. It is, essentially, a haunted house out of a Gothic novel, only on wheels and invisible to the average eye. The most striking example of its malignancy is the crucified young man in one of the closets. She also finds that Laura has died in the trailer; Chyna has thus been attempting to rescue the dead. Immediately after this discovery, Chyna dedicates herself to killing Laura's killer.

When the killer stops for gas, he kills the station attendants. In the process, he drops a snapshot of Ariel, a beautiful girl he is holding captive. Chyna finds this photo and expands her mission to include saving Ariel. She steals a car and attempts to ambush him. She is captured in turn; he takes her to his home, where he keeps her prisoner. The bulk of the novel describes the war of nerves between the two, and Chyna's attempt to free herself and Ariel. Though the novel is set in a densely detailed and immediately recognizable contemporary California, the characters are as isolated as if they were on the moon.

On the surface, there is little to distinguish *Intensity* from any number of serial-killer novels; Harris's 1988 novel *Silence of the Lambs* has a similar plot. Chyna Shepherd even shares the initials of the latter book's heroine, Clarice Starling. Both are trained in psychology and put themselves in peril by attempting to rescue a captive woman. But Koontz's novel is inherently supernatural.

What makes the novel eerie, however, is its evocation of the familiar. The killer Edgler Vess doesn't just enter a private home, he desecrates a temple (Temple-ton) of domesticity. A police officer, he should have been protecting such temples, not invading them. When Chyna hears Vess, she reacts instantly, and without training; her pain gives her a moral vision as intense as Slim MacKensie's twilight eyes. The girl she sets out to save is Ariel, a name belonging to the bound spirit in Shakespeare's *The Tempest*. Chyna becomes the protective "shepherd" to Ariel that her name suggests. Edgler Vess is also aware of what they are doing; he conjures with his name, telling her that one can make the phrases "God fears me" and "dragon seed" from his name.

Koontz consciously employs genre tropes. Vess believes that he absorbs the essence of those he kills, vampire fashion. The first time Chyna sees him, he is eating a spider in the Templeton's house, like Renfield, the would-be vampire in Bram Stoker's *Dracula*. Though he had been moving quickly before this event, Vess stretches out this moment, and Koontz slows the surrounding narrative, one of many instances in the novel in which emotional intensity has the effect of distorting time and space. Ariel, the abused captive, is described as being "Elsewhere," perhaps Narnia (the imaginary world created by C. S. Lewis); when Chyna escapes from being chained to a chair, she is portrayed as being somehow outside of time.

Finally, both Vess and Chyna are aware of their roles in a heightened and fantastic drama; the artistry of the novel resides in the characters' struggle to determine which script this drama will follow. Will Chyna be the next victim—or will she be the fated obstacle that Vess comes to fear that she is, the obstacle that he has been to those he has killed? Vess sets out to be as false and self-absorbed as his hero Nora Desmond in the movie *Sunset Boulevard;* Chyna consciously rescripts herself from victim to fighter, in part by repeating an incantation that she struggles to validate, "Chyna Shepherd, untouched and alive."

The result of Koontz's choices as a novelist is not simply an intense reading experience, though Koontz certainly provides that. Koontz has often been linked with Stephen King; the two rose to dominance of the best-seller list during roughly the same period; early on, some readers even speculated that it was King, not Koontz, who wrote *Invasion* under the pseudonym Aaron Wolfe. King has sometimes been accused of littering the landscape of the uncanny with the detritus of popular culture, a charge that has also been made against Koontz.

However, novels such as *Intensity* offer another solution to the challenge of making the supernatural believable. By infusing the subtexts of his novels with the supernatural, Koontz makes the entire contemporary American landscape immanent with the fantastic, a place of fear and wonder. He transforms the beliefs of the average reader into objects of power, and makes it possible for the random events and minor crimes of daily life to rise to nearly cosmic importance. As he does so, Koontz communicates a morality of individual responsibility and optimism that seems lifted, like the story of his life, from the pages of the popular literature of the nineteenth century. He is not a literary master on the level of his hero Dickens, and his dedication to genre fiction makes it unlikely that he will ever attain that status. But Dean Koontz is far more than the simple storyteller he modestly claims to be.

DEAN KOONTZ

Selected Bibliography

WORKS OF DEAN KOONTZ

FICTION

Star Quest. New York: Ace, 1968.

The Fall of the Dream Machine. New York: Ace, 1969.

Fear That Man. New York: Ace, 1969.

Anti-Man. New York: Paperback Library, 1970.

Beastchild. New York: Lancer, 1970.

Dark of the Woods. New York: Ace, 1970.

The Dark Symphony. New York: Lancer, 1970.

Hell's Gate. New York: Lancer, 1970.

The Crimson Witch. New York: Curtis, 1971.

A Darkness in My Soul. New York: DAW, 1972.

The Flesh in the Furnace. New York: Bantam, 1972.

Warlock. New York: Lancer, 1972.

Blood Risk. Indianapolis: Bobbs-Merrill, 1973.

Demon Seed. New York: Bantam, 1973.

Hanging On. New York: M. Evans, 1973.

The Haunted Earth. New York: Lancer, 1973.

Surrounded. [Brian Coffey, pseud.]. Indianapolis: Bobbs-Merrill, 1974.

Dragonfly. [K. R. Dwyer, pseud.]. New York: Random House, 1975.

Invasion. New York: Laser, 1975.

The Long Sleep. As John Hill. New York: Popular Library, 1975.

Nightmare Journey. New York: Putnam, 1975.

The Wall of Masks. [Brian Coffey, pseud.]. Indianapolis: Bobbs-Merrill, 1975.

Night Chills. New York: Atheneum, 1976.

Prison of Ice. [David Axton, pseud.]. Philadelphia: Lippincott, 1976. Rev. ed. under Dean R. Koontz published as *Icebound.* New York: Ballantine, 1995.

The Face of Fear. [Brian Coffey, pseud.]. Indianapolis: Bobbs-Merrill, 1977.

The Vision. New York: Putnam, 1977.

The Key to Midnight. New York: Berkeley, 1995.

The Funhouse. [Owen West, pseud.]. New York: Jove, 1980. Novelization of screenplay.

The Voice of the Night. [Brian Coffey, pseud.]. New York: Doubleday, 1980.

Whispers. New York: Putnam, 1980.

The Eyes of Darkness. [Leigh Nichols, pseud.]. New York: Pocket, 1980.

The Mask. As Owen West. New York: Jove, 1980.

The House of Thunder. [Leigh Nichols, pseud.]. New York: Pocket, 1982.

Phantoms. New York: Putnam, 1983.

Darkfall. New York: Berkley, 1984.

Twilight Eyes. Westland, Mich.: Land of Enchantment, 1985.

Strangers. New York: Putnam, 1986.

Shadowfires. [Leigh Nichols, pseud.]. New York: Avon, 1987.

Watchers. New York: Putnam, 1987.

Lightning. New York: Putnam, 1988.

Midnight. New York: Putnam, 1989.

The Bad Place. New York: Putnam, 1990.

Cold Fire. New York: Putnam, 1991.

Hideaway. New York: Putnam, 1992.

Dragon Tears. New York: Putnam, 1993.

Mr. Murder. New York: Putnam, 1993.

Dark Rivers of the Heart. New York: Knopf, 1994.

Strange Highways. New York: Warner, 1995.

Intensity. New York: Knopf, 1996.

Sole Survivor. New York: Ballantine, 1997.

Ticktock. New York: Ballantine, 1997.

Fear Nothing. New York: Bantam, 1998.

False Memory. New York: Bantam, 1999.

Seize the Night. New York: Bantam Doubleday Dell, 1999.

NONFICTION

Writing Popular Fiction. Cincinnati: Writer's Digest, 1973.

How to Write Best-Selling Fiction. Cincinnati: Writer's Digest, 1981.

CRITICAL AND BIOGRAPHICAL STUDIES

Kotker, Joan G. *Dean Koontz: A Critical Companion.* Westport, Conn.: Greenwood, 1996.

Munster, Bill, ed. *Sudden Fear: The Horror and Dark Suspense Fiction of Dean R. Koontz.* Mercer Island, Wash.: Starmont House, 1988.

Ramsland, Katherine. *Dean Koontz: A Writer's Biography.* New York: HarperPrism, 1997.

Wiater, Stanley. *Dark Thoughts: On Writing—Advice and Commentary from Fifty Masters of Fear and Suspense.* Grass Valley, Calif.: Underwood Books, 1997.

William Kotzwinkle

1938–

BUD WEBSTER

WILLIAM KOTZWINKLE WAS born 22 November 1938, in Scranton, Pennsylvania. He enrolled at Rider College in New Jersey at the age of 17, and went on to study at Pennsylvania State University, leaving there in 1957. In 1963 he moved to New York and worked as a short-order cook at Le Figaro Cafe, then became a tabloid-newspaper writer. This last job influenced his comic novel, *The Midnight Examiner* (1989). He also worked as a promotional copywriter for Prentice Hall and was a department store Santa Claus at E. J. Korvette's (which served as background for the 1982 novel, *Christmas at Fontaine's*, and also may have given him significant insight as a writer for children). In 1970, he married writer Elizabeth Gundy and they moved to New Brunswick, Canada. In 1983, they relocated to Maine, where they remain.

As a writer, William Kotzwinkle published his first story, "Marie," in the New Orleans Review in 1969. This was quickly followed by his first book, *The Fireman* (1969). In the ensuing years, he has published more than 40 books and won numerous awards, among them the National Magazine Awards for Fiction (1972 and 1975), the O'Henry Prize (1975), the World Fantasy Award for Best Novel (1977, for *Doctor Rat*), and the North Dakota Children's Choice Award (1983) and the Buckeye Award (1984), both for his 1982 novelization of *E.T.: The Extraterrestrial*. In addition, he was a recipient of the Bread Loaf Writer's Conference Scholarship, offered through Middlebury College in Vermont, and he has been a National Book Critics Circle Award nominee.

THE WRITER AND HIS WORK

It would be easy to dismiss Kotzwinkle as a chameleon, a writer with no voice of his own, and indeed, many critics do just that. However, this badly underestimates an author capable of writing from many viewpoints and with many voices. The same man who wrote the gently whimsical novelization of *E.T.: The Extraterrestrial* also wrote the savage and disturbing *Doctor Rat*, and this should be seen as the significant accomplishment that it is rather than as a limitation.

It would be just as big a mistake to pigeonhole Kotzwinkle simply as a fantasy writer: he writes his stories as they come to him, without regard for labels. *Doctor Rat* (1976) is a dark fantasy;

The Midnight Examiner (1989), a humorous mainstream novel with only mild fantasy elements; the three stories in *The Hot Jazz Trio* (1989) are perhaps best classified as magical realism. Many of his books for children are no more fantastic than any other books written for children.

The truth is that labels simply don't describe Kotzwinkle adequately. He is equally skilled (and, seemingly, equally comfortable) with any and all formats, so that each book, each story, comes as a surprise to the reader, no matter how familiar he or she may be with the writer's past work. In *The Encyclopedia of Science Fiction* (1993), the entry for Kotzwinkle reads in part, "Because he crosses genres with such ease, [he] could fairly be accused of frivolity; but the charge itself seems frivolous when his harsher texts are looked at square."

Kotzwinkle himself rejects any kind of categorization. In an unpublished interview he said, "Labels inhibit the reader's imagination. Is that all Gabriel Marquez is? A magical realist? Absurd. He's a fountain of luminous beauty, a talking lizard, a seductive bird. He's beyond labels, and so, dear friends, am I." Indeed. In that same interview, he discussed the advantages and disadvantages of being *sui generis*, and he indicated that it created more problems than it solved:

> There are no professional benefits to being unclassifiable, only drawbacks. However, had I had the good sense to package myself wisely, I never could have followed the gradients of my own potential. As a kid, I was mesmerized by Steve Brody, who jumped off the Brooklyn Bridge on a bet. I could never get him out of my mind. I tried to imagine everything he went through. Every time I start a book, it's jumping off the Brooklyn Bridge. Like Steve Brody, I have to do it, and once I jump, gravity takes over. I fall through the depths of my own potential, waving my arms in the air as I go. I can't really calculate the impact. If I could, it'd be a sure thing, and if it were a sure thing I wouldn't have jumped in the first place. That's what gave Brody his edge. It wasn't a sure thing. It hadn't been done before. That's what gives me my edge. It hasn't been done before.

Kotzwinkle has been called a "fabulist," a writer of allegorical stories intended to be seen as symbolic. This is all right as far as it goes, but it doesn't go nearly far enough. All writers are allegoricists to one degree or another. In fact, the whole purpose of fiction is to hold a very selective mirror in front of the reader, to present him or her with a model of reality that best illustrates life as the writer wants it to be perceived. The mirror that William Kotzwinkle holds up is a fun-house mirror, one that bends and warps reality and leads the reader gleefully through a landscape that keeps him or her slightly (and sometimes not so slightly) off-balance.

This is as it should be. Too flat a mirror and the reflected reality is of little use to either the reader or the writer: it simply shows what's already there. The fantasist's purpose is to startle the reader with new, unexpected perspectives. This is, perhaps, Kotzwinkle's greatest skill. It's often subtle, occasionally frightening, but always evident.

One example of this skill is his 1987 novel, *The Exile*, in which he frequently shifts the reader's perspective without any warning or foreshadowing whatsoever. The protagonist is Hollywood actor David Caspian who is, like Vonnegut's Billy Pilgrim, unstuck in time. Throughout the book Caspian finds himself changing places with a black marketeer in wartime Berlin, Felix Falkenhayn. Caspian interprets this as encroaching madness, but the reader knows that it isn't, that Falkenhayn is real. One such switch takes place at the home of Caspian's agent, Myron Fish:

> [Caspian] climbed up onto the diving board, and looked out over the wrought-iron fence toward Myron Fish's nearest neighbor—an Arab who was converting an entire hillside into a concrete slab, reason unknown.
>
> He walked to the end of the board and dove off into the bright mirror, cutting through the water

to the bottom, fingers skimming the blue tiles. He glided over them, then turned and swam back upward, toward the rippling, sun-bright surface.

He broke through, and the droplets of water hung lopsidedly in front of him, their descent arrested. Light was reflected from them and he seemed surrounded by a shower of tiny transparent moons. The day had gone; the sun was a spotlight over a pool and the pool was indoors, in a cavernous room filled with people. A party was in progress and it was night in Berlin.

(pp. 89-90)

In his review for the 19 July 1987 *Chicago Tribune*, Douglas Balz said, "Readers will close *The Exile* with a smile, knowing they have witnessed an astonishing feat. They have just seen William Kotzwinkle throw a high wire across an abyss, and then dance across it with effortless ease." This balancing act is one of Kotzwinkle's stocks in trade, and he performs it over and over again in book after book.

Madness is a recurring theme in Kotzwinkle's stories. From David Caspian's fears of onrushing insanity, made worse by his aunt's very real paranoid fantasies about the CIA, to the gleeful psychosis of the 1977 World Fantasy Award winner *Doctor Rat*, to the comic delirium of the titular alien's first experience with alcohol in *E.T.: The Extraterrestrial*, which is shared empathically and publicly by ten-year-old Elliot, the writer explores the myriad facets of madness and shows us both the power and the pain it provides.

Dr. Rat, the main character of the eponymous novel, has, in fact, embraced madness as a way of elevating himself above the other animals used in the laboratory and has assumed in his own mind the mantle of fellow scientist and colleague of the humans who work there. Early in the story, he explains:

My own case is not unusual. I was driven mad in the mazes. The primary symptoms of shivering, whirling, and biting have all passed now, but I've been left with the curiously mad practice of writing songs and poetry. Obviously this is somewhat out of place in a scientific atmosphere and I do my best to suppress the tendency, giving all my attention to writing learned, factual papers. I like to think they're the very latest word in animal behavior.

(p. 4)

While it's possible that there are savants who would dissect these moments of madness to find common threads, and who would then look to the author to try to find these same threads in his own personal experience, it's just as likely that Kotzwinkle simply finds these explorations rich in story possibilities.

The madness in *Doctor Rat*, though, isn't confined to the titular character. Kotzwinkle portrays human experimentation on animals as a horrible and unnecessary insanity committed for foolish reasons. There's no real research going on at the cancer lab that Rat and the other animals call home, only atrocities. When the dogs lead a revolt of the animals that spreads over the entire world, Kotzwinkle almost pornographically details tortures and violence against them in ways that prevent the reader from seeing the human characters as anything but evil. Rat himself is a willing *collaborateur*, and he alone survives the Holocaust.

Like all good funhouses, William Kotzwinkle has more than one warped mirror. He often uses the off-the-wall perspectives of non-human characters, notably in *Doctor Rat*, *E.T.: The Extraterrestrial* and his 1996 novel, *The Bear Went Over the Mountain*. In the latter book, a bear searching for food in the Maine woods comes across a manuscript hidden under a tree by a college professor. The bear reads it, steals it, and makes his way to the publishing world of New York City. Here Kotzwinkle holds up his mirror to show us the shallowness of the literary establishment and its constant, almost desperate need for new and imposing figures to parade in front of the rest of the world. No one seems to notice that Hal Jam is a bear, but it probably wouldn't matter if they did. His celebrity is assured, and that means a hardcover best-seller, a six-figure paperback deal, movie offers, the talk show circuit and all the trimmings. If this also means that the real author of the book, Arthur Branhall, becomes more and more ursine in his frustration, it's a small price to pay.

Interestingly, it apparently wasn't Kotzwinkle's intention to savage the publishing industry or to make social commentary simply for the sake of social commentary; in his own words, "I just described things as they are and they turned into satire." In fact, the book is remarkably good-natured, coming as it does from a writer to whom the literary world hasn't always been kind.

In his novelization of Melissa Mathison's script for the Steven Spielberg blockbuster, *E.T.: The Extraterrestrial*, Kotzwinkle takes what could easily be seen as an overly sentimental and emotionally manipulative story and infuses it with whimsy and wit, and further manages the difficult task of contrasting the isolation and hopes of its characters, human and otherwise: Elliot, an unliked and unlikable boy; Mary, Elliot's mother, divorced and longing for romance; Keys, who hopes to one day find proof of extra-terrestrial life; Harvey, the eternally hungry family dog who wants to be fed; and E.T., who just wants to go home.

Even here, though, Kotzwinkle doesn't limit his "funhousery" to the now-familiar little alien. Any competent writer could have simply elaborated on the script given him and been perfectly safe. Not so Kotzwinkle. He takes his perspective-shifts several steps further, not only using Harvey's viewpoint, but, since E.T. is, after all, first and foremost a botanist, those of vegetables, trees, even houseplants, as well as the odd owl or bat. This takes a special kind of playful mindset, and one that few writers in any field would bother to cultivate. Gerald Jonas, writing in the 29 August 1982 *New York Times Book Review*, said, "[Kotzwinkle's] strong suit here is his imagination and playfulness with language." The author uses his playful imagination to give the characters a depth that film isn't able to delineate, as in this scene which occurs just after E.T.'s ship is forced to leave him behind:

But something in the yard was sending soft signals.

He turned, and saw the vegetable garden.

Its leaves and stems moved in shy patterns of friendliness; sobbing, he crept toward them and embraced an artichoke.

Hiding in the vegetable bed, he took counsel with the plants. Their advice, to go look in the kitchen window, was not welcome.

I'm in all this trouble, he signaled the plant, because of wanting to peek in windows. I can't repeat such folly.

The artichoke insisted, grunting softly, and the extraterrestrial crept off obediently, eyes whizzing around in fearful circles.
(pp. 19-20)

The book quite successfully stands alone and apart from the film. Kotzwinkle takes a frequently maudlin and mawkish script, filled with the director's all-too familiar emotional button-pushing, and turns it into that literary rarity: a novelization that is truly a novel, one that transcends its source almost effortlessly.

William Kotzwinkle's decision to turn to writing, like his writing itself, was more than a little off-beat: "My writing began in an improvisational theater class in college. The lines that came out of me startled me, and at the same time amused the audience of other students. How could I use these lines out of nowhere? The answer, not so obvious at first, was to write them, first in plays, then in short stories, and finally in a novel."

This facility with off-the-cuff ideas is vital to the kind of stories he tells: off-center, off-the-wall, from out of left field. The reader never really knows what kind of story Kotzwinkle has in store for him until he reads it. "In a certain sense," he states, "I am always engaging in improvisation, in order to play my way through scenes in a novel. Playing with another actor would be great fun, because the other actor's wit and intelligence constellates new possibilities in me, which might never surface without that other person."

He has retained a strong interest in plays, for both stage and screen. He adapted his period mystery novel, *Fata Morgana*, for actor Tom Skerrit; he adapted *Jack in the Box*, which was filmed in 1990 as *Book of Love*; he was one of the writers credited with the horror film *Nightmare on Elm Street 4: The Dream Master*; and is currently working with songwriters Jerry Leiber and Mike Stoller (writers of "Hound Dog," "On Broadway," and many other classic R&B hits) on a musical version of his stage adaptation of *Herr Nightingale and the Satin Woman*.

He explains his attraction to the stage like this:

> Screenplays and plays are skeletal. The scenery is left up to someone else. That's quite a burden lifted. I enjoy writing them, and have always felt a natural facility for it. But novels are more enveloping, as they provide a total world, including scenery. The magic of a fully staged production is marvelous, as it was with *Herr Nightingale*, which totally mesmerized the audience. There were my dreams, walking around, and they were wonderful to see, embodied in a talented cast. I suppose there's nothing to compare with it.

Quite a number of his books, including his first, *The Fireman*, were marketed as "children's books," although this largely artificial (if useful) designation bothers him: "Once they became a separate category, it unleashed a river of trash. So much of this writing is condescending, permeated with an austere sense of looking down at the child, or of deliberately writing for the child." No one could accuse Kotzwinkle of condescending to anyone, regardless of age. He takes delight in sharing his stories with his readers, in taking them into all the corners and attics and cellars and showing them the piles of absurdities and wonders they hold.

If he has a literary fault, it's also one of his greatest assets: his passion. Passion drives every page of *Doctor Rat*, for example, sometimes long past the line where he'd made his point. This novel in particular has come under criticism; Robert Stone, in his review for June 1976 *Harper's*, said in part: "It's too contrived, too ingratiating, too soft at the center to carry the weight of its own intentions." Animal experimentation is a subject on which there is much disagreement and very little middle ground. One either accepts it as a necessary evil or rejects it utterly. *Doctor Rat* savagely slams the practice, using dark and gleeful satire to hammer home a point that the author obviously feels strongly about. As a result, the reader is plunged into the horrors of the laboratory from the very first pages, and is carried headlong into even greater horror. Kotzwinkle almost lovingly details vivisections and tests, the mutilations and slow, torturous deaths of those animals unlucky enough to have been "chosen" to serve humanity by dying.

Frequently, the descriptions become so horrible that the reader, no matter which side he takes, is revolted. But this revulsion is as much from the descriptions themselves as from the acts being described:

> In the cage beside them, we actually have three blind rats. In fact, we have twenty-three blind rats, part of a magnificent new experiment . . . that's become the latest rage here at the lab: the fabulous removal of the eggs from a female rat's body and the grafting of them to different parts of a male rat's body—to the tail, to the ear, to the stomach. And for the past twenty-three days, he's been grafting them to their eyeballs! So now it's time we sang that promising young scientist a song.
>
> (pp. 5-6)

In spite of this "flaw of passion," if that is, in fact, an accurate criticism, *Doctor Rat* richly deserved its 1977 World Fantasy Award, winning over books by Ramsey Campbell, Karl Edward Wagner, and John Steinbeck.

INFLUENCES

Trying to guess an author's influences is extremely tricky: critics and reviewers are as likely to insert their own favorite influences, or those that might support their own pet theories, as they are to be accurate.

For example, it's easy for some to see the influences of R. A. Lafferty (author of *Past Master* and *Fouth Mansions*) in Kotzwinkle's work, or Avram Davidson (editor from 1962-64 of *The Magazine of Fantasy and Science Fiction* and author of the Hugo-winning "Or All the Seas With Oysters"), or even Damon Knight (critic, editor of the respected ORBIT series of original anthologies and author of "To Serve Man"). These are good, solid writers, well-grounded in the classics and well-established in the pantheon of speculative fiction. They came up through the pulps and anthologies, or paperback originals, and except for occasional forays into the world of the literary magazines, they remained securely and safely under the umbrella rubric of traditional science fiction. Is it at all outside the realm of probability that Kotzwinkle read them and took their work to heart when creating his own?

Not at all. Many well-regarded fantasists, including Harlan Ellison, Kurt Vonnegut, and Richard Matheson, as well as those mentioned above, began their literary careers writing for pennies a word. In Kotzwinkle's case, however, would that speculation be accurate? In a brief unpublished interview, Kotzwinkle indicated that his influences aren't the standard fantasy writers at all:

> I became acquainted with the real nature of fantasy through Jung's *Memories, Dreams, Reflections*. He demonstrated that we're all boiling with fantasies. What matters is the shape we give them. Graffiti is a fantasy of ego-formation, tinged with aggression. Were a graffiti artist to travel onward in refinement, he might discover fine art. We all have such crude beginnings, and we're all driven by fantasy. When I first read Jorge Borges' *Labyrinths*, I was thunderstruck. *This* was what one could do with fantasy and the erudition of a philosophic and literary tradition. Borges was steeped in Kant, Schopenhauer, and great literature. I steeped myself in the same.

This is a far cry from the commonly-held belief that fantasy writers should arise from the sub-cultural maelstrom of three-cents-a-word magazines, stacks of photocopied rejection letters from harried editors, and regional gatherings of other fantasy and science-fiction writers and their fans, but William Kotzwinkle is a far-from-common writer. Even his experiences as a writer at a tabloid newspaper pushed him towards the fantastic:

> My first assignment was South American Woman Gives Birth to Puppies. When readers wrote in expressing their wonder at this miracle, it was further evidence to me of the fact that we're boiling with fantasy, most of it rising from primitive layers of the mind. There are people walking around America who believe all manner of strange things, real medievalists, and you can also find Cro-Magnons who think their hand prints on a wall represent self, God, and their prey.

William Kotzwinkle began his writing career at a tabloid newspaper, a literary form in which the headline is of the utmost importance: aliens shaking hands with presidents, UFOs appearing in bowling-alley parking lots, bat-boys courting famous actresses, and, yes, South American women giving birth to puppies. In the years since, he has continued to see the world through eyes trained to find the fantastic, the wonderful, in everyday life. With each new book, he gives the reader a wide-angle lens that gathers in light from every corner of existence and focuses in on the beauty, the absurdity, the terror, and the joy that lie just under the surface of the mundane world through which his readers shuffle day after day. His stories are celebrations of the fantastic, celebrations to which we are welcome guests.

WILLIAM KOTZWINKLE
Selected Bibliography

WORKS OF WILLIAM F. KOTZWINKLE

ADULT FICTION: NOVELS

Hermes 3000. New York: Pantheon, 1972.

The Fan Man. New York: Avon, 1974.

Night-Book. New York: Avon, 1974.

Swimmer in the Secret Sea. New York: Avon, 1975.

Doctor Rat. New York: Knopf, 1977.

Fata Morgana. New York: Knopf, 1977.

Herr Nightingale and the Satin Woman. New York: Knopf, 1978.

Jack in the Box. New York: Putnam, 1980.

Christmas at Fontaine's. New York: Putnam, 1982.

E.T.: The Extra-Terrestrial in His Adventure on Earth. New York: Putnam, 1982.

Superman III. New York: Warner, 1983.

Queen of Swords. New York: Putnam, 1984.

E.T.: The Book of the Green Planet. New York: Berkley, 1985.

The Exile. New York: Dutton-Lawrence, 1987.

The Midnight Examiner. New York: Houghton Mifflin, 1989.

The Game of Thirty. New York: Houghton Mifflin, 1994.

The Bear Went Over the Mountain. New York: Doubleday, 1996.

COLLECTIONS

Elephant Bangs Train. New York: Pantheon, 1971.

Jewel of the Moon. New York: Putnam, 1985.

Hearts of Wood and Other Timeless Tales. New York: Godine, 1986.

The Hot Jazz Trio. New York: Houghton Mifflin, 1989.

POETRY

Great World Circus. New York: Putnam, 1983.

Seduction in Berlin. New York: Putnam, 1985.

CHILDREN'S FICTION

The Firemen. New York: Pantheon, 1969.

The Ship That Came Down the Gutter. New York: Pantheon, 1970.

Elephant Boy: A Story of the Stone Age. New York: Farrar, Straus, 1970.

The Day the Gang Got Rich. New York: Viking, 1970.

The Oldest Man (collection). New York: Pantheon, 1971.

The Return of Crazy Horse. New York: Farrar, Straus, 1971.

The Supreme, Superb, Exalted, and Delightful, One and Only Magic Building. New York: Farrar, Straus, 1973.

Up the Alley with Jack and Joe. New York: MacMillan, 1974.

The Leopard's Tooth. New York: Seabury Press, 1976.

The Ants Who Took Away Time. New York: Doubleday, 1978.

Dream of Dark Harbor. New York: Doubleday, 1979.

The Nap Master. New York: Harcourt, 1979.

Trouble in Bugland: A Collection of Inspector Mantis Mysteries (collection). New York: Godine, 1983.

The World is Big and I'm So Small. New York: Crown, 1986.

The Empty Notebook. New York: Godine, 1990.

The Million Dollar Bear. New York: Random House, 1994.

Tales from the Empty Notebook (collection). New York: Marlow, 1996.

Walter the Farting Dog. New York: North Atlantic/Frog, 2001.

OTHER WORKS

William Kotzwinkle has adapted a number of his works for film or stage, including *Jack in the Box* (as *Book of Love*), *The Exile*, *Christmas at Fontaine's*, *Fata Morgana*, *Herr Nightingale and the Satin Woman*, and *Django Rheinhardt Played the Blues.* Not all were produced. He also wrote the text for the Grammy-winning recording of *The E. T. Storybook Album*, specifically for the narrator, Michael Jackson.

CRITICAL STUDIES

Children's Literature Review 6 (1984), pp. 180–185.

Contemporary Literary Criticism 5 (1976), pp. 219–220.

Contemporary Literary Criticism 14 (1980), pp. 309–311.

Contemporary Literary Criticism 35 (1985), pp. 253–259.

Dictionary of Literary Biography, vol. 173: American Novelists since World War II, Fifth Series. Detroit: Gale, 1996.

Collier, Laurie and Joyce Nakamura. *Something About the Author.* Detroit: Gale, 1993.

Pringle, David, ed. *St. James Guide to Fantasy Writers.* Chicago: St. James Press, 1996.

Watson, Noelle, Paul E. Schellinger, et al., eds. *Twentieth-Century Science-Fiction Writers.* Chicago: St. James Press, 3rd ed., 1991.

Lewis, Leon. *Studies in American Literature, Vol. 49: Eccentric Individuality in William Kotzwinkle's The Fan Man, E.T., Doctor Rat, and Other Works of Fiction and Fantasy* Lewiston, Maine: Edwin Mellen Press, 2001.

INTERVIEWS

Flewelling, Lynn. "Interview with William Kotzwinkle." *Bangor Daily News* (Sept. 1994).

Hogan, Ron. "William Kotzwinkle." Beatrice Interviews: http://www.beatrice.com/interviews/kotzwinkle (1996).

Webster, Bud. Unpublished interview with William Kotzwinkle (April 2002.) All quotes by William Kotzwinkle above are from this interview unless otherwise noted.

Nancy Kress
1948–

MAUREEN SPELLER

"ONCE," BEGINS A character in *The Prince of Morning Bells*, "in a time not yet come but not far distant, there was no more magic. All the heroes were dead, and men aspired instead to be accountants, and forgot there had been such things as heroes" (p. 24). This observation characterizes Nancy Kress's approach to writing fantasy as she offers a contemporary perspective on the traditional elements of fantasy. The genre's tropes are examined in detail in each of her three fantasy novels, though the approach varies with each story, providing a subtle but fascinating commentary on the use of fantasy in writing, as well as on the role of women and their relation to power in what had been conventionally seen as a masculine preserve.

Nancy Kress was born in Buffalo, New York, on 20 January 1948, and grew up in East Aurora, New York. After attending the State University of New York at Plattsburgh, where she earned a degree in elementary education, she taught for several years before marrying and starting a family. During this time she began to write, and her first story, "The Earth Dwellers," appeared in *Galaxy* in 1976. Her first novel was published in 1981. For some years, Kress worked variously as an advertising copywriter and as a university instructor while writing fiction part-time. She has been a full-time science-fiction novelist since 1990, with her work typically focusing on genetic engineering.

Nancy Kress made a remarkably assured debut as a novelist with *The Prince of Morning Bells* (1981). Although the novel's cover blurb and, to a lesser extent, its title might have suggested a charming but conventional fantasy, the novel was anything but. Kress's characters were self-consciously participating in a fantastic narrative and throughout the novel provided a commentary on their roles even as they subverted them, sometimes at several different levels simultaneously.

Princess Kirila is well aware, for instance, that she is not a conventional princess in a conventional fairy story. Although the reader is told she spent the first eighteen years of her life doing "the customary princess things," it being implied that this was expected of her, it is also clear that she has received an extensive and liberal education, is able to articulate her restlessness as she reaches adulthood, and also to channel that restlessness into a Quest, while being fully aware that Quests are normally a male occupation.

The purpose of the Quest itself is unusual: to find the Heart of the World. "Wouldn't consider something less ambitious, I suppose? The Holy Grail, overthrowing Evil, something along those lines?" (p. 10) asks her Wizard, while Kirila herself isn't even clear what it is she is asking for, other than that "I'll know what's most important and why—why I should do things" (p. 11). The desire to acquire knowledge will characterize Kirila's dealings with the world, but her knowledge will always be hard-won. Almost from the beginning, the Quest is problematic—the bat given to her by her Wizard as a lucky charm seems intent on pointing out that beauty and knowledge do not belong together (Kirila is of course a beautiful princess) and Kirila's rescuer does not even fit the accepted canon of magical protectors, given that he is a large purple Labrador retriever who talks, and who is, as he points out, not even a young prince, implying that there is no hope of the conventional marriage if he does become disenchanted.

Chessie will nevertheless prove to be a good companion to Kirila; his knowledge of the world gives her quest a goal, the Tents of Omnium, and he is able to offer advice in a guise that is less threatening, though this is no guarantee that Kirila will take any of it. Chessie is determined to fulfill his quest for the Tents of Omnium, but Kirila's desire to find the Heart of the World is such that she is easily distracted from her main goal by the promise of an answer anywhere along the way. Thus she spends a period of time with the Quirks—a scholarly society modeled on the quark (an elementary particle)—who are determined to find the rules of the world, but whose view of the world is already so inflexible that they cannot accept new information unless it fits the existing framework.

She next passes a period of time in the village of Rhuor, where the inhabitants worship a race of white jer-falcons from over the mountains. Their lives are entirely constructed around the infrequent appearances of these creatures, which literally as well as metaphorically represent the only bright spots in their existence—when the birds appear, the world turns to color, while when they disappear, everything turns to gray again. Although Kirila is for a while convinced they know what the Heart of the World is, she eventually realizes that their belief system is so limiting they cannot see beyond its confines and are in fact stifling the thing that shapes their lives.

Though Chessie remains with her faithfully, leading her back to the main Quest after each distraction, when Kirila meets and falls in love with a not overly imaginative prince, obsessed with jousting, and eventually marries him, Chessie continues alone. In seeking to please her new husband and her parents-in-law, Kirila has changed from an adventurous young woman dressed in doublet and breeches who has killed a man in self-defense, to a submissive wife in long, impractical skirts, who runs a house, supervises the laundry, and cooks. And yet, she believes herself to be happy and to have found the Heart of the World.

The story then breaks for twenty-five years, while Kirila and her husband raise a family and rule their pocket kingdom. Only after he dies in a hunting accident does Kirila feel able to renew her Quest, and it is surely no coincidence that Chessie only reappears at this moment, having found the Tents of Omnium but unable to enter them. By now the feminist overtones of the novel have become clear—the various reactions shown by the members of Kirila's family lay out the roles expected of a widowed woman—to remarry or to live quietly in widowhood; to obey the orders of her son, now the king—while underlining that a single older woman has no role at all except to avoid soliciting her children's disapproval by behaving inappropriately. However, Kirila, finally recognizing that her duty is to herself rather than to others, begins to pursue her quest once again.

Kirila is no longer even a typical heroine. Older, less fit than she once was and afflicted by arthritis, her journey is now urgent and focused rather than optimistic and directionless. She tolerates extreme discomfort without noticing it at all, frets over delay, and in the people she meets sees warnings as to what she might become if she doesn't complete her journey. Where once she might have been distracted by Granny Isolda's artistic ability, now she waits only for spring and the chance to continue her journey. Chessie himself has changed, become more a dog and less a person, and more content with his lot.

All Quests have their price, usually the discovery that what is sought has been within one's grasp all along, and this Quest is no exception. Chessie's price is that he is not the prince he thought but a jester and so old he expires almost as soon as he is transformed. Had he remained a dog he would have lived. For Kirila, the price is the knowledge that she was herself the Heart of the World all along, that she made her own world . . . this is reflected in the transformation of the Tents of Omnium into a glorious tapestried city, in a scene reminiscent of Tolkien's "Leaf by Niggle." It is her single-heartedness, her devotion to whatever is at hand, which has carried her along—but as her final guide at the Tents points out, this in itself is a double-edged blessing, which Kirila herself recognizes as the story ends. Having acknowledged her power but also its dangers, she has achieved a balance within herself and become her own woman.

The twin themes of power and responsibility are pursued further in the very different setting of *The Golden Grove* (1984). The eponymous grove is situated on a Mediterranean island, ruled by Arachne and her brother Jaen, and is the site of a mysterious artifact which creates an aura of peace throughout the island, and also influences the island's spiders to produce high quality silk, which is then woven into cloth by Arachne and her women. Home to the descendants of Delernos, a political exile from Thera, who allegedly discovered the island's existence in a manuscript and then searched for it, the island has little to do with the outside world. Its inhabitants rely on Arachne and Jaen to rule them wisely, but Arachne has become so absorbed with the Grove, reflecting the single-heartedness that Kirila was offered but finally rejected, that she has turned her back on her family and her people, and soured her relationship with her brother. When the Grove becomes sickly and its power wanes, Arachne is unable to recognize that it is the very intensity of her fixation with it and her rejection of the rest of Island that has created the problem, upsetting the delicate relationship between grove, island, and people, while her inability to talk to her brother about the problem prompts him to look beyond Island for a solution. In doing so, Jaen brings its existence to the attention of others, thus opening it up to external exploitation and causing the removal of the artifact for investigation elsewhere. It is only when Arachne's obsession with the Grove is finally broken that it can regenerate itself and begin again—by which time Arachne has come to recognize the danger inherent in the Grove, as it begins to exert an influence over her daughter, Amaura, an influence she can no longer feel. As the Grove has always been most fully experienced by Island's children, it's difficult not to see its long-lasting influence over Arachne as her refusal to relinquish her childhood for the responsibilities of adulthood. However, in deciding to send her daughter away from the Grove and from Island, Arachne is also acknowledging the family's need to look beyond its immediate environs in order to survive—only when they do this do they discover the truth about Delernos, a man obsessed by power who has turned his back on his family in order to seek favor at court. Having lived in isolation, the family has lost the wider perspective.

The White Pipes (1985), the last of Kress's fantasies, is also somewhat unconventional. Its protagonist, the first-person narrator, Fia, is a

Storygiver (not a storyteller) who uses potions which allow her to access her deeper consciousness and create actual story-images for viewers to observe, with figures acting out a variety of folktales. She is also a single mother, determined to keep her child, Jorry, the bastard son of a nobleman who currently knows nothing of the child's existence. Fia's entire life since Jorry's birth has been shaped by the need to avoid Brant of Erdulin, fearing that he would take Jorry and educate him as a noble while discarding her, and so she has spent much of her time traveling through obscure kingdoms where her skills are appreciated because they are novel. She is therefore horrified when she arrives in Veliano to perform for the king, only to discover that Brant is one of his advisers. She also quickly realizes that there is someone in the court with the power to manipulate her story images for his or her own gain, and assumes that it is Brant, although his motive is unclear.

In the initial sequences of the novel, Brant seems to behave as we would expect a nobleman to act, colored as our view is by Fia's own belief that he could never have truly cared for her or their child and would not have kept his promise of marriage because of the difference in status between them. Fia's worst fears seem to have been borne out when Brant arranges for the kidnapping of their son and also assaults her, and it is only very gradually, as the threads of the story are unpicked, that Fia comes to appreciate that things are not necessarily as they would appear to be. While she might assume that his brutality is what should be expected of a nobleman, Brant knows that he can only protect Fia by appearing to be brutal, when inwardly he feels very differently towards her.

In many respects, the plot itself is quite ordinary, with its hunt for a magical artifact, the White Pipes, which enable its wielder to control the minds of other people. What sets this novel apart from run-of-the-mill fantasies is its portrayal of various women in the novel, from the queen—who is determined to give the king an heir, but also to seize control of the kingdom—to Brant's wife, Cynda, who has to literally possess her men by taking their belongings to her cottage, a kind of unholy trophy cabinet, and who can exist only so long as she is close to a man who wields power, in this case the king rather than Brant. Fia herself, who has endeavored always to control her own life, stands in contrast to the serving women at the castle, who achieve status through the favor of the castle's men. Kress's portrait of a court that is not necessarily corrupt but in which the king is too unsophisticated to be aware of the intrigues around him is also very well drawn. Seen through the eyes of the outsider Fia, the feeling of oppression and the continual uncertainty over roles, even among the servants, is almost overwhelming, as is the shifting status of the king, who is very much at the heart of his kingdom but of little importance outside it. *The White Pipes* was unusual among fantasy novels of the mid-1980s in trying to address the complexity of male-female relationships rather than attempting to reduce them to simple folk tale formulae. All of Kress's fantasy novels have examined women's relationship with power, using a number of different female viewpoints—from that of the woman in control of her own destiny, who forsakes her duty to others, to that of the woman who has sacrificed everything for her own child—and her women characters have shown a broad range of ages and sympathies.

After *The White Pipes*, Kress turned away from fantasy, and now writes science fiction novels that generally deal with the effects of genetic engineering. She has also written two mainstream biomedical thrillers. However, her science fiction, most notably *Beggars in Spain* (1993) and its two sequels, *Beggars and Choosers* (1994) and *Beggars Ride* (1996), continues to address the themes of power and responsibility first explored in her fantasy novels.

NANCY KRESS

Selected Bibliography

WORKS OF NANCY KRESS

NOVELS AND SHORT STORIES

The Prince of Morning Bells. New York: Pocket Books, 1981.

The Golden Grove. New York: Bluejay, 1984.

Trinity and Other Stories. New York: Bluejay, 1985. (Collection of short stories.)

The White Pipes. New York: Bluejay, 1985.

An Alien Light. New York: Arbor House, 1988.

Brain Rose. New York: William Morrow, 1990.

Beggars in Spain. Eugene, Oreg.: Axolotl, 1991. (Novella.)

The Aliens of Earth. Sauk City, Wis.: Arkham House, 1993. (Collection of short stories.)

Beggars in Spain. New York: Avon, 1993. (Expanded version of the novella listed above.)

Beggars and Choosers. New York: Tor, 1994.

Oaths and Miracles. New York: Forge, 1996.

Beggars Ride. New York: Tor, 1996.

Beakers Dozen. New York: Tor, 1998. (Collection of short stories.)

Maximum Light. New York: Tor, 1998.

Stinger. New York: Forge, 1998.

Yanked. New York: Avon, 1999.

Probability Moon. New York: Tor, 2000.

Probability Sun. New York: Tor, 2001.

NONFICTION

Beginnings, Middles, and Ends. New York: Writer's Digest, 1993.

Dynamic Characters. New York: Writer's Digest, 1998.

CRITICAL AND BIOGRAPHICAL STUDIES

Clute, John. "Nancy Kress." In *The Encyclopedia of Fantasy*, edited by John Clute and John Grant. London: Orbit, 1997.

D'Ammassa, Don. "Nancy Kress." In *St. James Guide to Science Fiction Writers*. Edited by Jay P. Pedersen. Detroit: St. James Press, 1996.

Katherine Kurtz
1944–

KELLY A. O'CONNOR-SALOMON

THE NOVELS OF Katherine Kurtz can be read on several levels. Although they are enjoyable simply for the stories they tell and the characters we get to know, deeper exploration reveals commentary on religion, politics, racism, and gender. The worlds and characters that she creates are varied, complex, and multilayered: the magical Deryni live in a Middle Ages similar to and yet very different from our own; the Knights Templar emerge from our own past; supernatural guardians watch over twentieth-century Britain; an Irish cathedral is protected by gargoyles; even the founding fathers of the United States find new life in her hands. This impressive scope owes much to the variety of life experiences she brings to her writing.

Kurtz was born on 18 October 1944, during a hurricane in Coral Gables, Florida. As the biographical note in several of her books observes, she "has led a somewhat whirlwind existence ever since." Her father, Fredrick, worked as a radar specialist for Bendix Avionics. Her mother, Margaret Carter, was a university honors program administrator, taught English in Venezuela through the Peace Corps, and wrote poetry. Both parents strongly influenced Kurtz as she grew up and she developed both a strong love of reading and an aptitude for science. These two interests merged in her love for what became her favorite literary genre—science fiction. She first encountered science fiction in the fourth grade; however, as she said in a 1980 interview, "[t]echnology and bug-eyed monster stories never appealed to me.... I preferred ESP themes and strong characters" (Elliot, p. 16). Frank Herbert's *Dune* was an early favorite, particularly because of the way Herbert developed his characters and "wove together dialogue and action so that it flowed" (Elliot, p. 19).

After graduating from high school, Kurtz received a four-year science scholarship to the University of Miami, Coral Gables, where she received a B.S. in chemistry in 1966. She started medical school but, after a year, decided to pursue a degree in history instead and received her M.A. from UCLA in 1971. Her first novel, *Deryni Rising*, was published while she was completing this degree.

Kurtz is best known for her Deryni series, which to date totals thirteen novels, a collection of short stories, and two "reference" books. A collection of fan-written fiction edited by Kurtz is due to be published in mid-2002. The story of how Kurtz was discovered is, in fantasy circles, the equivalent of Lana Turner's being discovered in Schwabb's Drug Store—except that Kurtz's story is not apocryphal. While attending her first science fiction convention, Baycon, in Oakland, California, in 1968, she met Stephen Whitfield, who had just published *The Making of Star Trek* with Ballantine. She told him some of her ideas, and he encouraged her to send a proposal for a trilogy to Betty Ballantine. As Kurtz says, "I didn't have enough experience to realize that the odds were almost astronomical against such a thing succeeding. So I wrote my outline and my sample chapters and I sent them off—and two weeks later, got back that magical letter from Ballantine" (Elliot, pp. 20–21). That letter signaled the beginning of Kurtz's success, and *Deryni Rising* was published in 1970.

The Deryni are a magical race that dwell with non-magical humans in a world that many readers will find at least somewhat familiar. The stories focus on the kingdom of Gwynedd and its interactions with surrounding kingdoms. According to Kurtz, these "kingdoms are roughly parallel to our own tenth, eleventh, and twelfth century England, Wales, and Scotland in terms of culture, level of technology, similarity of social structure, and influence of a powerful medieval Church. . . . The major difference, aside from historical personalities and places, is that magic works; for the Deryni are a race of sorcerers" (*Deryni Archives*, p. 1).

However, classifying the Deryni as sorcerers and magicians is not quite correct. As Kurtz explains in her introduction to *Deryni Magic*, "a 'sorcerer' supposedly employs power gained from the assistance or control of evil spirits—which no self-respecting Deryni would espouse—and 'magician,' in our modern world, more often conjures the illusions and legerdemain of stage magic than any real harnessing of extraordinary power and ability" (pp. 1–2). Much of what the Deryni are capable of falls under the category of ESP-type talents. Although they may be born with the potential, Deryni skills must be learned, and some Deryni are stronger and more gifted than others. "At their best, the Deryni might represent the ideal of perfected humankind—the mastery of self and surroundings that all of us might attain, if we could learn to rise above our earthbound limitations and fulfill our highest destinies" (*Deryni Magic*, p. 3).

Some Deryni are capable of acts that even the Deryni themselves cannot explain, and these fall beyond the sphere of the "regular" paranormal. There are some "ritual procedures that, when performed with suitable mental intent and focus, concentrate the operator's own power to produce certain predictable results" (*Deryni Magic*, p. 3). Ward Cubes, which can offer shielding and protection, are examples of this type of magic. However, there are also "supernatural connections . . . which tap into unknown power sources in unknown ways, at unknown cost to the well-beings of one's immortal soul, the certain existence of which is also unknown" (*Deryni Magic*, p. 3). It is in this area that even the most adept Deryni tread with great caution.

Most of the Deryni novels are set up as trilogies that chronicle periods in the history of Gwynedd, but they were not originally published in "historical" order. The trilogy with the chronologically earliest material is The Legends of Camber of Culdi. This series is composed of *Camber of Culdi* (1976), *Saint Camber* (1978), and *Camber the Heretic* (1981). As the first novel opens, a tyrannical Deryni, Imre, sits on the throne of Gwynedd. While it would have been easy to draw black and white distinctions between the Deryni and humans, Kurtz does not do this. As in real life, there are no easy classifications. Many Deryni are appalled by the actions of King Imre and seek a way to overthrow his reign. The rebellion is led by Camber MacRorie, a Deryni nobleman who longs for a humane kingship. An alternative to Imre is found in Cinhil Haldane, an unknown survivor of the human royal house that Imre's family destroyed when they seized power. Although he has been living in a monastery for most of his life, Cinhil is persuaded to accept the throne that is rightfully his. With the restoration of the rightful human line, with their own unique type of non-Deryni magical powers, Camber and his allies believe that Gwynedd's dark days are drawing to a close.

However, after Cinhil is restored to power, the human population of Gwynedd seeks retribution for the evils done to them by Imre and his companions. To a degree this is understandable, but events quickly deteriorate. Deryni are killed, denied basic rights, and declared evil by Gwynedd's religious leaders. Although he worked for the improvement of everyone living in Gwynedd, not just the Deryni, Camber and his family become the focus for much of the hatred; as a result, Camber is forced to fake his own death in order to divert attention from himself and his children. His "death," however, has some interesting side effects, as people begin to attribute miracles to him and clamor for his canonization.

The next trilogy, chronologically, is "The Heirs of Saint Camber," which consists of *The Harrowing of Gwynedd* (1989), *King Javan's Year* (1985), and *The Bastard Prince* (1994). This series follows Camber's children as they attempt to assist the heirs of King Cinhil to live to adulthood and realize the full powers of their kingships. Unfortunately, Cinhil did not father robust children, and Regents have held power long enough to develop a taste for it—and a reluctance to give it up. But Camber's descendants must be constantly on their guard and work in very subtle and discreet ways, for otherwise their own lives would be in danger.

The Chronicles of the Deryni, the next series chronologically speaking, was actually the first to be published. These three novels, *Deryni Rising*, *Deryni Checkmate* (1972), and *High Deryni* (1973), take place about two hundred years after the Camber novels. The Haldanes still rule, and, in some corners, the Deryni are beginning to be reaccepted into society. *Deryni Rising*, which takes place in a very short twenty-four-hour period, is something of a murder mystery, the victim being the latest king, Brion Haldane. Besides discovering the killer, those loyal to the throne also must see to the safety of the heir to the throne, Kelson. Kelson's story continues in the most recent trilogy to be published, the Histories of King Kelson, and in the stand-alone novel *King Kelson's Bride* (2000), in which the young king, after having lost one bride to murder and a second to deception, finally gets a bride he can keep.

The Histories of King Kelson trilogy—*The Bishop's Heir* (1984), *The King's Justice* (1985), and *The Quest for Saint Camber* (1986)—focuses as much on the Deryni trying to rediscover their heritage as it does on Kelson adjusting to his role as king. After two centuries of repression and suppression, many families do not even know that they have Deryni blood. Kelson discovers that his mother is Deryni, but has hidden that part of herself out of shame. Many of the arts that Deryni were famous for in Camber's time, healing, for example, have been all but lost, and this generation must try to piece together bits of information to recreate their culture.

Kurtz apparently does not have a fondness for short stories, having stated, "[m]y ideas are just too big, and I feel constricted by having to squash them down. I don't like to read them, either, because just when a story starts to get good, it's over" (Elliot, p. 20). Nonetheless, she has written several short stories that take place in the Deryni universe, a number of which were published collectively in The *Deryni Archives* (1986). As Kurtz states in the introduction to the collection, most of the stories included "elaborate on incidents or characters that are mentioned in the novels" (p. 8), so perhaps they might be better called "episodes" rather than "short stories."

Five of the stories, "Catalyst," "Healer's Song," "Vocation," "Bethane," and "Legacy," were originally published elsewhere; the other three, "The Priesting of Arilan," "The Knighting of Derry," and "Trial," are original to the book. One benefit of these stories is that they allow the reader of the novels to see characters when they were children, to understand how they came to be in the positions they hold in the novels, or simply to observe them in intimate moments that help flesh out their personalities.

One story that stands out is "The Priesting of Arilan." It focuses on the quest of Denis Arilan, a character in several novels as well, to become a priest. Since Gwynedd's Church, which is modeled on the medieval Catholic Church, sees Deryni as intrinsically evil, they are, as a race, forbidden to seek the priesthood. But Denis is called to that life and feels he must take whatever risks are necessary to realize his vocation.

Denis is not the only Deryni seeking the priesthood; his friend, Jorian de Courcy, actually attempts to be ordained, and as Jorian is being prepared for this final step towards become a priest, Denis wonders if, as they have been told, "God really would strike down any Deryni presuming to seek ordination to the priesthood" ("Priesting of Arilan," p. 101). Jorian is willing to take the risk, but his true identity is discovered and he is executed. In the process of investigating the events surrounding the exposure of his friend, Denis uncovers the fact that it is not God's will at all, but the will of men that has been preventing Deryni from becoming priests. As powerful as they are, all Deryni have one weakness—a drug called *merasha*. Humans are only made sleepy by this drug, but it renders the Deryni powerless. The Church uses this drug in a rather immoral way to ferret out those who would defy the system. But Denis, perhaps with some divine intervention, is able to succeed where no Deryni has for centuries.

Despite some still powerful resistance to Deryni being reaccepted into society, Denis does see some hope for the future. At Jorian's execution, an anonymous voice shouts out support, making Denis believe that opinions are beginning to change. Another indication of a shift in thought is that a few Deryni are being openly welcomed by the King of Gwynedd. One such Deryni, or rather half-Deryni, is Duke Alaric Morgan, and he plays a role in three of the stories: "Bethane," "The Knighting of Derry," and "Trial."

"The Knighting of Derry" is told from the point of view of the human character in the title. Raised hearing about the dangers of the Deryni race, he meets Morgan at a horse fair and finds himself liking Morgan. When they meet again at Derry's knighting, Derry is perceptive enough to realize that much of what Morgan does is not really "magic," but just a way of keeping people off balance:

"Do you do that often?"

"Do what?"

"Simply guess what people are thinking, as any ordinary mortal would do, and then let *them* think you did it with magic?"

As Morgan raised both eyebrows in surprise, Derry sensed he was on to something. Throwing all caution to the winds, he went on.

"You *do* do that, don't you, Your Grace?" he ventured. "I'd heard stories before, but until I saw you today, all in black, deliberately cultivating that faintly sinister air—"

(p. 196)

Morgan, much more used to palace intrigue than the simple honesty he receives from Derry, proposes that the newly dubbed knight enter his service. Derry eagerly accepts, even though working for a Deryni will cause him much difficulty in the future.

Deryni Magic (1990) and the *Codex Derynianus* (1998) are companion texts to the Deryni novels. *Magic* is subtitled "a grimoire," and it is a collection of the various types of magic that readers encounter in the Deryni universe. It also contains several appendices that cover terminology, people, and locations. The *Codex*, which was originally published as a limited edition, has an encyclopedia format and also includes chronologies and maps. A supplement to this text is planned to incorporate information from the more recent novels. *Deryni Tales* (due to be published in mid-2002) is a collection of fan-written short stories that were originally published in *Deryni Archives: The Magazine*, which Kurtz started in 1978 as a "showcase for some of [her] readers' literary efforts" (*Deryni Tales*, p. 6). The one exception to this is "The Green Tower" which was written by Kurtz and is original to this volume. Kurtz's next Deryni project is the much-anticipated Childe Morgan trilogy, which will focus on the character of Duke Alaric Morgan.

To the observant reader, the way the Deryni are treated has resonance in our own history. They have been compared to several minority groups. In a 1989 interview, Kurtz says, "I have a lot to say about the issue of persecution, and of being down on people simply because they're different. I'm commenting on historical factors that enabled really terrible things to happen in our own history, and maybe I can give some insight on how this is possible" ("Evil Days," p. 2). The Deryni are often compared to the Jews, and, in the same interview, Kurtz acknowledges the link:

> In a sense . . . the Deryni fulfill the role in their world, as far as the kind of persecution that they experience because of being so different, that the Jews did in our world. . . . It's always fascinated me, as a human being as well as an historian, how in Nazi Germany they could have been so blind for so long, not to realize what was happening until it was too late to get out. Because the Deryni are doing exactly the same thing—they've been lulled into a false sense of security, saying "Oh, it can't happen here; it can't happen to me. They won't really do what they are threatening to do."
> (p. 2)

Jews were also persecuted in the Middle Ages, the time period for these texts, so an historical parallel can be drawn here as well.

Readers may also see a connection between persecutions inflicted on the Deryni and the mistreatment of women, from the witch-hunts of the Middle Ages to their widespread exclusion from the priesthood even today. The Deryni are suspect because of their magical abilities, powers that are labeled "witchcraft"—and of course it was women who were the primary victims of medieval witch-hunts. Also, to quote Charlotte Spivack, "In a subtler psychological way . . . Deryni also represent the hidden, repressed, feminine side of the human mind, intuitive and mysterious rather than clear and rational" (p. 88). Like women in many religions, the Deryni are forbidden to become priests. Some Deryni, like Denis Arilan, conceal their true heritage and attempt, with mixed results, to realize their calling anyway. This calls to mind stories of women passing for men, such as the legend of Pope Joan, supposedly a woman who made it all the way to the Vatican. "[T]he sacrifice of one's own identity in order to perform a personally or socially useful function is an experience familiar to women through the ages" (Spivack, p. 95). And the distinction drawn between "Deryni" and "human," when the two are visually indistinguishable, calls to mind times in our own history when women were thought of as less than human—or possibly not human at all.

Aside from the Deryni series, Kurtz has published several stand-alone novels: *The Legacy of Lehr* (1986), a young-adult mystery that takes place aboard a spaceship; *Lammas Night* (1988), an occult thriller set during World War II; *Two Crowns for America* (1996), set during the American Revolution and dealing with some of the esoteric traditions that underlie the foundations of the United States; and *St. Patrick's Gargoyle* (2001).

In the novel's Afterword, Kurtz describes *St. Patrick's Gargoyle* as "Katherine at play" (p. 232). While reviews in *Publisher's Weekly* and *Booklist* consider it best for a young adult audience, the novel does have appeal for adult readers and should not be dismissed as simplistic—the book does raise some topical issues. Set in Dublin at Christmastime, the story focuses on Padraig (also known as Paddy), a former avenging angel who, along with his fellow avenging angels, has been reassigned by "The Boss" as a gargoyle. The gargoyles are set to guard various cathedrals and historic structures. As their names come from the buildings they protect, St. Patrick's Cathedral is Paddy's domain. When vandals break into his cathedral, Paddy enlists the assistance of the elderly Francis Templeton to help him retrieve the stolen items.

When Paddy, protector of a Protestant cathedral, and Francis, a Roman Catholic Knight of Malta, first meet, they debate the idea of women priests and allowing priests to marry—pertinent issues both in Ireland and globally:

> "What about the women priests?" Templeton persisted, . . . "I didn't see Our Lord ordain any women."
>
> "Strictly speaking," Paddy said mildly, "I didn't see him ordain *anybody*, man *or* woman. Still, maybe women priests aren't a bad idea. After all, women know about setting tables, and serving a nice meal. They helped with that Last Supper, you know. And they're into vestments. I like vestments."
>
> "Well, they can *sew* the vestments, or *iron* 'em," Templeton muttered. "Just keep 'em off the altar."
>
> "But they're really good at making celebrations," Paddy pointed out. "Especially weddings. . . . So, all in all, women priests ought to have a better handle on stuff like that, right?"
>
> "Well . . ."
>
> "They should let the priests get married, too. How're they supposed to help married people sort out their problems if they don't know what they're talking about? They can't, that's how. Get the women into the act!"
>
> (pp. 17–18)

Topical issues, such as women priests, are another indication of Kurtz's ability to relate her fiction to contemporary concerns.

St. Patrick's Gargoyle is not Kurtz's only foray into the modern world. With Deborah Turner Harris she has cowritten the Adept series. Totaling five books so far—*The Adept* (1991), *The Lodge of the Lynx* (1992), *The Templar Treasure* (1993), *Dagger Magic* (1995), and *Death of an Adept* (1996)—the series revolves around Scottish psychiatrist Sir Adam Sinclair, who is the leader of a Hunting Lodge, "a spiritual force that battles evil" (Kaganoff, p. 54). With the help of his fellow Huntsmen, one of whom is an actual police detective, Adam fights to keep Darkness at bay. In the most recent volume, the characters seek help from John Graham, the hero of *Lammas Night*. Kurtz and Harris have also cowritten two novels about the Knights Templar, *The Temple and the Stone* (1999) and *The Temple and the Crown* (2001). Similar themes can be found in both sets of books. While Kurtz is not sure which series they will add to next, she thinks it will probably be the Adept. The next volume will also serve as a sequel to *Lammas Night*.

In March of 1983, Kurtz married writer and producer Scott MacMillan; they moved to Holybrooke Hall in Ireland in 1986. They have one son, Cameron. Together Kurtz and MacMillan have written two novels—*Knights of the Blood* (1993) and *Knights of the Blood: At Sword's Point* (1994)—about an evil group of vampire Nazis and the time-traveling detective who has to stop them. A third novel is planned.

In addition to the Deryni-related short stories mentioned above, Kurtz has written some non-Deryni stories and edited collections of others. She has edited two anthologies that again revolve around the Knights Templar—*Tales of the Knights Templar* (1995) and *On Crusade: More Tales of the Knights Templar* (1998). A third collection, *Crusade of Fire*, is scheduled for release in late 2002. While the story she included in each of the first two anthologies dealt with characters from her Adept series, her story for the third anthology will focus on Hugues de Payens and the founding of the Templar Order.

Katherine Kurtz's novels, particularly her Deryni series, have become very popular; in addition, *Camber of Culdi* won the Edmund Hamilton Memorial Award in 1977, and

Camber the Heretic received the Balrog Award in 1982. The *Voice of Youth Advocates* listed *Legacy of Lehr* as one of its best science-fiction titles in 1986. As her popularity increases, so will the scholarship of her work. The Deryni short stories in particular lend themselves to use in the classroom, compelling students to talk about issues of race and gender.

Selected Bibliography

WORKS OF KATHERINE KURTZ

DERYNI TRILOGIES

The Chronicles of the Deryni

Deryni Rising. New York: Ballantine, 1970.
Deryni Checkmate. New York: Ballantine, 1972.
High Deryni. New York: Ballantine, 1973.

THE LEGENDS OF CAMBER OF CULDI

Camber of Culdi. New York: Ballantine, 1976.
Saint Camber. New York: Ballantine, 1978.
Camber the Heretic. New York: Ballantine, 1981.

THE HISTORIES OF KING KELSON

The Bishop's Heir. New York: Ballantine, 1984.
The King's Justice. New York: Ballantine, 1985.
The Quest for Saint Camber. New York: Ballantine, 1986.

THE HEIRS OF SAINT CAMBER

The Harrowing of Gwynedd. New York: Ballantine, 1989.
King Javan's Year. New York: Ballantine, 1992.
The Bastard Prince. New York: Ballantine, 1994.

OTHER DERYNI WORKS

The *Deryni Archives*. New York: Ballantine, 1986. (Contains "Catalyst," reprinted from *Moonsinger's Friends*; "Healer's Song," reprinted from *Fantasy Book*; "Vocation," reprinted from *Nine Visions*; "Bethane," reprinted from *Hecate's Cauldron*; "The Priesting of Arilan" and "Legacy," reprinted from *Fantasy Book*; and "The Knighting of Derry" and "Trial.")

Deryni Magic: A Grimoire. New York: Ballantine, 1990.

Codex Derynianus. San Bernadino, Calif.: Borgo, 1998. (With Robert Reginald; a limited edition of 500.)

King Kelson's Bride. New York: Ace, 2000.

NON-DERYNI WORKS

The Legacy of Lehr. New York: Walker, 1986.
Lammas Night. New York: Ballantine, 1983.
Two Crowns for America. New York: Bantam, 1996.
Saint Patrick's Gargoyle. New York: Ace, 2001.

WORKS COWRITTEN WITH DEBORAH TURNER HARRIS

The Adept. New York: Ace, 1991.
The Adept Book Two: The Lodge of the Lynx. New York: Ace, 1992.
The Adept Book Three: The Templar Treasure. New York: Ace, 1993.
Dagger Magic. New York: Ace, 1995.
Death of an Adept. New York: Ace, 1996.
The Temple and the Stone. New York: Warner, 1998.
The Temple and the Crown. New York: Warner, 2001.

WORKS COWRITTEN WITH SCOTT MACMILLAN

Knights of the Blood. New York: New American Library, 1993
Knights of the Blood: At Sword's Point. New York: New American Library, 1994.

WORKS EDITED BY KATHERINE KURTZ

Tales of the Knights Templar. New York: Warner, 1995. (Contains Kurtz's story "Obligations." Introduction and Interludes also written by Kurtz.)

On Crusade: More Tales of the Knights Templar. New York: Warner, 1998. (Contains Kurtz's story "Restitution." Introduction and Interludes also written by Kurtz.)

Crusade of Fire: Mystical Tales of the Knights Templar. New York: Warner, 2002.

Deryni Tales. Edited by Katherine Kurtz. New York: Ace, 2002. (Contains Kurtz's story "The Green Tower." Introductions to the text and to the individual stories written by Kurtz.)

BIBLIOGRAPHIES

Clarke, Boden, Mary A. Burgess, and Mary Wickizer Burgess. *The Work of Katherine Kurtz: An Annotated Bibliography and Guide.* San Bernadino, Calif.: Borgo, 1993. (Bibliographies of Modern Authors, No 7).

CRITICAL AND BIOGRAPHICAL STUDIES

Fry, Carrol L. " 'What God Doth the Wizard Pray To': Neo-Pagan Witchcraft and Fantasy Fiction." *Extrapolation: A Journal of Science Fiction and Fantasy*, 31, no. 4: 333–346 (Winter 1990).

James, Edward. "Katherine Kurtz." *St. James Guide to Fantasy Writers.* Edited by David Pringle. New York: St. James, 1996. Pp. 339–340.

"Katherine (Irene) Kurtz," in *Contemporary Authors Online.* Farmington Hills, Mich.: Gale, 2001. (Available through InfoTrac.)

Spivack, Charlotte. *Merlin's Daughters.* Westport, Conn.: Greenwood, 1987.

Sukraw, Tracy J. "Katherine Kurtz." *Authors and Artists for Young Adults.* Edited by Thomas McMahon. Detroit: Gale, 1997. Pp. 131–139.

KATHERINE KURTZ

INTERVIEWS AND REVIEWS

Elliot, Jeffrey. "Tapestries of Medieval Wonder." *Fantasy Newsletter*, May 1980, pp. 16–21; June 1980, pp. 12–17, 31. (Portions of this interview were reprinted in *Fantasists on Fantasy: A Collection of Critical Reflections by Eighteen Masters of the Art*, ed. by Robert H. Boyer and Kenneth J. Zahorski, New York: Avon, 1984.)

"Evil Days in Gwynedd: An Interview with Katherine Kurtz." *Xignals: Communications from Waldenbooks Otherworlds Club*, February–April 1989, pp. 1–3, 12.

Kaganoff, Penny. "*The Adept*." *Publishers Weekly*, Feb. 8, 1990, p. 54.

INTERNET RESOURCE

Werner, Susan, Melissa Houle, and Carolyn White-Shilts. *Deryni Destination: The Official Deryni/Katherine Kurtz Website*. Home page at http://www.deryni.com. (Included are appearances, current projects, and biographical information.)

Mercedes Lackey
1950–

JUSTIN GUSTAINIS

MERCEDES LACKEY IS one of the most popular and prolific authors in modern fantasy. Although she did not begin writing until the mid-1980s, she published more than forty novels (some coauthored) before the turn of the twenty-first century. Her output in the new millennium has continued unabated, provoking delight among her many fans but mixed reactions from critics.

Born in Chicago, Lackey, the daughter of Edward and Joyce Ritche, was named for the actress Mercedes McCambridge. She majored in biology at Purdue University and graduated in 1972, the same year she married Anthony Lackey (a union that ended in the mid-1980s). Lackey had been an avid reader since childhood, and her abiding interest in the Middle Ages was spurred by the Society for Creative Anachronism, which she joined at Purdue. She lived in South Bend, Indiana, from 1975 to 1981, working as an artist's model and sometime computer programmer.

Lackey moved to Tulsa, Oklahoma, in 1982, having been hired to do computer programming for United Airlines. Feeling culturally isolated in Tulsa, she turned to writing, initially creating "filk"—folk music with fantasy or science fiction themes, often tied to an existing book or series. She also wrote several short stories that appeared in small magazines and fanzines.

In 1985 Lackey met the science fiction and fantasy author C. J. Cherryh, who saw promise in the work of the fledgling writer. Under Cherryh's mentoring, Lackey produced seventeen drafts of her first novel, which was eventually divided into the Arrows trilogy. She has been writing and publishing steadily ever since.

Lackey is married to the artist Larry Dixon, who has illustrated some of her books and coauthored several of them as well. In their limited spare time, the couple rehabilitate injured birds of prey and also serve as volunteer firefighters.

Much of Lackey's fiction can be considered high fantasy—stories in which the author has created an entirely new world separate from the one that we know. Its inhabitants usually include humans and sometimes other, less conventional creatures; its history is not Earth's but may resemble it in some ways; its physics is often altered to include magic; and its cultures are not those of Earth but may be similar to those of our planet's present or past.

Lackey's best-known alternate world is the kingdom of Valdemar, which made its first appearance in the Arrows books. This trilogy, known more formally as The Heralds of Valdemar, consists of *Arrows of the Queen* (1987), *Arrow's Flight* (1987) and *Arrow's Fall* (1988).

Like many of the settings of modern high fantasy, Valdemar bears some resemblance to medieval Europe (minus most of the filth, disease, ignorance, and brutality that characterized the real thing). Valdemar is governed by a system of royalty, travel is done by horse (or horse-drawn conveyance), and combat is conducted with either edged weapons or bows and arrows. Some of the fantasy elements grafted onto this culture include the use of black and white magic, animals that can communicate with humans, demons, and telepathy.

The protagonist of the Heralds of Valdemar trilogy is Talia Sensdaughter, who becomes a Herald (a courier/intelligence agent) to the queen of Valdemar and must endure many tribulations while carrying out her duties for the sovereign.

The next trilogy, Vows and Honor, comprises two novels and a collection of short stories: *The Oathbound* (1988), *Oathbreakers* (1989), and the collection *Oathblood* (1998), which consists of stories written by Lackey over the preceding nine years. This series focuses on Tarma and Kethry, women warriors and blood sisters who fight their way through a series of adventures that involve both mortal and supernatural enemies.

Vows and Honor was followed by a true trilogy called The Books of the Last Herald-Mage, consisting of *Magic's Pawn* (1989), *Magic's Promise* (1990), and *Magic's Price* (1991). This series centers on Vanyel Ashkevron, who, although a weakling as a young man, grows up to become a powerful Herald-Mage—a Herald with magic powers who is charged with safeguarding the land from attack. Ultimately Vanyel saves the kingdom.

The next episode of the Valdemar saga is a single volume, *By the Sword* (1991), also known as "Kerowyn's Tale." Kerowyn, the granddaughter of Kethry (heroine of the Vows and Honor trilogy), is the sole unscathed member of her family following a devastating raid by bandits. With her grandmother's gift of the magic sword Need, Kerowyn succeeds in avenging the attack. She then embarks on a career as a warrior and becomes a heroine in her own right.

The Mage Winds is a trilogy made up of *Winds of Fate* (1991), *Winds of Change* (1993), and *Winds of Fury* (1993). Elspeth, the heroine, is both a Herald and heir to the throne of Valdemar. While on a mission for the queen, she is saved from almost certain death by Darkwind k'Sheyna, whose clan is in serious danger from the malign magic of its enemies. Elspeth lends assistance, and in return Darkwind fights by her side in a desperate battle to save Valdemar from the invading tyrant Ancar.

Although the Mage Wars trilogy is set in the same world as the other Valdemar books, the action occurs about one thousand years earlier than the rest of the saga. Many of the characters who appear in these books—*The Black Gryphon* (1994), *The White Gryphon* (1995), and *The Silver Gryphon* (1996)—are the ancestors of those who play prominent roles in the other Valdemar books. In these tales of Valdemar's forebears, white magic wars against black, and civilization contends against savagery. The forces of light ultimately prevail, but the cost, as always in Lackey's stories, is high in terms of both blood and tears.

With the Mage Storms trilogy, the saga of Valdemar returns to the time period in which the earlier stories are set. As played out in *Storm Warning* (1994), *Storm Rising* (1995), and *Storm Breaking* (1996), Valdemar and its allies are sorely beset by a military threat from the powerful Eastern Empire and also by a series of devastating mage storms—a legacy of the mage wars fought a millennium earlier. The storms disrupt the magic on which the planet depends for its very existence, and only the ghosts of heroes long dead can help a band of brave Valdemarians bring the cataclysm to an end.

The Owls trilogy (also referred to as "Darian's Tale") picks up the story a year later. In *Owlflight* (1997), *Owlsight* (1998), and *Owlknight* (1998), we follow the adventures of Darian Firkin, an orphan living in a small village. Although his initial prospects appear bleak, Darian develops his magical gifts as he grows, forms alliances with several powerful beings and disparate groups, and becomes a hero both to his village and to Valdemar.

With completion of the Owls series, Lackey appears to have drifted away—at least temporarily—from the trilogy format in telling Valdemar stories. *Brightly Burning* (2000), a stand-alone novel, tells the story of Lavan Chitward, who has the ability to start fires psychically. Although at first fearful of his gift, he learns to use it for the benefit of Valdemar. In *Take a Thief* (2001), a stand-alone story that resembles Dickens' *Oliver Twist* in some ways, the young thief Skif is tutored in the arts of knavery by the Fagen-like Bazie. When Bazie is killed, Skiff takes great risks to avenge him, eventually winning respectability as a Herald.

The Valdemar template also forms the basis for the story collection *Sword of Ice and Other Tales of Valdemar* (1997). The eighteen short pieces by other authors are all set within the Valdemar universe, and three of the tales are coauthored by Lackey herself. Lackey has said that she plans to continue writing the popular Valdemar books indefinitely.

***

Lackey's second series, the "Diana Tregarde Investigations," consists of three dark fantasy novels set in the modern world. They feature a female protagonist who is simultaneously a romance writer, white witch, and occult detective (Lackey uses the term "guardian"). In *Burning Water* (1989), Diana Tregarde contends with malign Aztec gods; in *Children of the Night* (1990), she combats psychic vampires; and in *Jinx High* (1991), her opponents belong to a coven of dark sorcerers.

Lackey has declared that the Diana Tregarde series will not be continued. As she once explained in a Web site message to her fans, the books did not sell well. But more important, the occult subject matter attracted the attention of a few deranged individuals. Lackey was subjected to intrusion into her personal life, harassment, and even death threats—reactions she had rarely, if ever, received in response to her high fantasy writings. However, Lackey did venture into similar territory once more with *Sacred Ground* (1994). The protagonist, Jennifer Talldeer, is an Osage Indian shaman and private investigator who specializes in sacred Indian artifacts. The story is similar to the Diana Tregarde adventures, but Lackey has not written a sequel.

The Bardic Voices series is set in a world dominated by a religious hierarchy (not unlike medieval Catholicism) and the equally powerful Musicians Guild. Each wants to control the magic that is the world's main source of power. In between these forces stand the Free Bards, who are opposed to the idea of anyone having a monopoly on magic. In *The Lark and the Wren* (1992), a young woman named Rune rises above her humble circumstances through an act that requires both extreme courage and superb musicianship. By offering to play for the Ghost of Skull Hill, she can gain her fortune—or lose her life. The Ghost reappears in *The Robin and the Kestrel* (1993), a story in which it allies with four young minstrels to oppose the evil plans of a corrupt bishop. *A Cast of Corbies* (1994), coauthored with Josepha Sherman, finds the Musicians Guild adopting rules designed to eliminate the Free Bards. This storyline is continued in *The Eagle and the Nightingale* (1995), in which Free Bard Nightingale allies with a bird-man creature named T'fyrr and convinces the king to preserve the Free Bards. *Four and Twenty Blackbirds* (1997) is a departure for the series, since it is essentially a murder mystery. The story amounts to a police procedural grafted onto the Bardic Voices universe (and thus bears some resemblance to the *Lord Darcy* novels of Randall Garrett and the *Garrett* series by Glen Cook, both of which feature traditional mystery stories set in a fantasy universe).

One group of Lackey's books—which can be subdivided into two distinct subseries—has been called by some the Urban Elves saga. Because all of these novels share the premise that elves have passed from the land of Fairie into our modern world, they fall squarely within the "urban fantasy" genre.

The first subseries is the Bedlam's Bard sequence, consisting of two novels coauthored with Ellen Guon, *A Knight of Ghosts and Shadows* (1990) and *Summoned to Tourney* (1992), and *Beyond World's End* (2001), coauthored with Rosemary Edghill. This series tells the story of Eric Banyon, a Juilliard dropout who ekes out a living playing his flute at Renaissance "Faires." He inadvertently rescues from cursed slumber the elf Korendil, who draws him into a series of struggles within the elf community on Earth, all of which have potentially grave consequences for humans as well. This saga has continued both with and without Lackey's participation: Ellen Guon published *Bedlam Boyz*, a kind of prequel to the first book, in 1993, while Rosemary Edghill coauthored *Spirits White as Lightning* with Lackey in 2001.

The second part of the Urban Elves saga is Lackey's *SERRAted [sic] Edge* series. The title refers to SERRA, the South East Road Racing Association, formed by a group of elves who love fast cars and are also very fond of children. Some of these elves, however, exploit and abuse children. It is the conflict between the two groups (each with its own allies, both human and fey) that drives the action of these novels: *Born to Run* (1992, coauthored with Larry Dixon), *Wheels of Fire* (1992, coauthored with Mark Shepherd), *When the Bough Breaks* (1993, coauthored with Holly Lisle), and *Chrome Circle* (1994, coauthored with Dixon).

Elves also play a central role in a trilogy that Lackey cowrote with Andre Norton. *The Halfblood Chronicles* consists of *Elvenbane* (1991), *Elvenblood* (1994), and *Elvenborn* (2002). The elves of these tales are not the benevolent racing enthusiasts portrayed in the *SERRAted Edge* series but rather creatures who rule their own world and hold humans in virtual slavery—until a young elf-human hybrid with magical power appears, sowing the seeds of rebellion.

In 1995 Lackey began publishing a series of retellings of classic fairy tales. *The Fire Rose* (1995) sets the story of Beauty and the Beast in nineteenth-century San Francisco. *The Firebird* (1996) envisions the Brothers Grimm story taking place in czarist Russia. The ballet Swan Lake is reconfigured as *The Black Swan* (1999), and *The Serpent's Shadow* (2001) revisits the story of Snow White and the Seven Dwarves in 1909 London.

Like many contemporary authors of fantasy and science fiction, Lackey has lent her talents to the growing market created by computer games. "The Bard's Tale," a popular game that has gone through several electronic versions, is set in a universe similar to the kingdom of Valdemar. Not surprisingly, Lackey was asked to supervise the series of novels that grew out of the game. She also coauthored three of them: *Castle of Deception* (1992, with Josepha Sherman), *Fortress of Frost and Fire* (1993, with Ru Emerson), and *Prison of Souls* (1994, with Mark Shepherd). There were five other books in the series, the last of which, *Curse of the Black Heron* by Holly Lisle, was published in 1998.

In an uncharacteristic foray into pure science fiction, Lackey also cowrote, with Ellen Guon, *Freedom Flight* (1994), the first volume of the Wing Commander books, which are based on a popular computer game about an intergalactic war between humans and catlike aliens. Four other volumes followed, written by other authors.

Lackey also penned a science fiction novel with Anne McCaffrey in 1992. *The Ship Who Searched* was the third volume in McCaffrey's The Ship Who Sang series, which concerns a starship piloted by handicapped children who have had their brains hardwired into the ship's control systems.

Lackey's work has continued to extend into new areas of fiction. *The Shadow of the Lion* (2002), coauthored with Eric Flint and Dave Freer, is a fantasy adventure that takes place in sixteenth-century Venice. It is the first of a planned series of books set in this time and place. The fantasy *The Gates of Sleep* (2002) is more like vintage Lackey. Set in early twentieth-century England, the story concerns young Marina Rosewood, a magician in training who is forced to use her untested powers in self-defense against her evil and magically formidable aunt.

***

In interviews, Lackey has described two themes that inform much of her work. One is "there ain't no such thing as a free lunch," the phrasing of which she credits to Robert Heinlein. By this she means that actions have consequences, often both good and bad, and some consequences are not always foreseeable. Further, Lackey shows that no one can achieve anything good without paying a cost—and sometimes the cost is high. The use of magic may slowly destroy the magician; a knight can win a battle but lose his best friend in the fighting; to love one person you sometimes must forsake another, who may react to rejection by becoming your bitter enemy.

The other theme is that there is no single way to truth, or God, or happiness. Lackey's work tends to be unkind to authoritarian institutions—whether commercial, political, or religious. Established churches are often shown to be intolerant and oppressive, and political orthodoxy, in Lackey's worlds, often leads to dictatorship. Some of Lackey's most contemptible villains are parents who abuse or neglect a child because he or she is "different" in appearance or behavior or beliefs. Lackey scorns such conformists who would break a child before breaking the rules.

Lackey's writing has been virtually ignored by critics, apart from perfunctory reviews in the book trade journals. The reasons for this neglect are not clear; certainly Lackey's sales figures and substantial body of work have established her as a major figure in the fantasy genre. One explanation may be that much of Lackey's work falls somewhere between the traditional youth and adult markets. Certainly there are aspects of her books that seem to be aimed at teenagers, who do make up a large part of her fan base. In the typical Mercedes Lackey novel, an abused or downtrodden teenager with a latent magical talent runs away from home, develops the talent by overcoming adversity, has harrowing adventures, and ends up earning the love and respect of a community that he or she has helped to save from evil.

Most of Lackey's writing, however, does not shy away from elements usually considered "adult." Various forms of violence, including torture, are portrayed in fairly frank terms, although Lackey is never gratuitous in this regard. The occasional sex scenes are presented in a forthright manner but without being explicit by contemporary standards. Lackey's books are also tolerant of homosexuality, which she depicts as neither a panacea nor a perversion. Lackey has been nominated three times for the Lambda Award, which acknowledges gay-positive fiction, and she won it in 1991, for *Magic's Price*.

Another explanation for the critics' neglect of Lackey's work may be that there is so very much of it, produced over a fairly short span of years. Critics may generally believe that no one who writes so quickly can also write well. This belief may not hold up when applied to all prolific writers, but in Lackey's case there may be some truth to it. Certainly she has written some first-rate books that are probably destined to become classics of fantasy literature. But many of her works fall short of this mark, and some fall far short. Her plots, while often original, are sometimes formulaic. Her writing is usually fresh but can degenerate into cliché. Some of the characters in her later books bear a very strong resemblance to those in her earlier work. She can be slapdash about details. Even some of Lackey's devoted fans, lamenting that she writes too fast, have expressed the wish that she use her formidable talent to write her stories at a slower pace, and with somewhat greater care.

Mercedes Lackey is nonetheless one of the premier figures in modern fantasy writing, and her legions of fans are always eager for her next book, especially if it takes place in the mythical kingdom of Valdemar.

Selected Bibliography

WORKS OF MERCEDES LACKEY

NOVELS AND SHORT STORIES

Arrows of the Queen. New York: DAW Books, 1987.

Arrow's Flight. New York: DAW Books, 1987.

Arrow's Fall. New York: DAW Books, 1988.

The Oathbound. New York: DAW Books, 1988.

Oathbreakers. New York: DAW Books, 1989.

Reap the Whirlwind. Riverdale, NY: Baen Books, 1989, with C. J. Cherryh.

Magic's Pawn. New York: DAW Books, 1989.

Burning Water. New York: Tor Books, 1989.

Magic's Promise. New York: DAW Books, 1989.

A Knight of Ghosts and Shadows. Riverdale, NY: Baen Books, 1990, with Ellen Guon.

Magic's Price. New York: DAW Books, 1990.

Children of the Night. New York: Tor Books, 1990.

By the Sword. New York: DAW Books, 1991.

The Elvenbane. New York: Tor Books, 1991, with Andre Norton.

Winds of Fate. New York: DAW Books, 1991.

Jinx High. New York: Tor Books, 1991.

Winds of Change. New York: DAW Books, 1992.

The Last Herald Mage. New York: Penguin, 1992.

The Lark and the Wren. Riverdale, NY: Baen Books, 1992.

Born To Run. Riverdale, NY: Baen Books, 1992, with Larry Dixon.

Wheels of Fire. Riverdale, NY: Baen Books, 1992, with Mark Shepherd.

Summoned to Tourney. Riverdale, NY: Baen Books, 1992, with Ellen Guon.

Castle of Deception. Riverdale, NY: Baen Books, 1992, with Josepha Sherman.

When the Bough Breaks. Riverdale, NY: Baen Books, 1993, with Holly Lisle.

If I Pay Thee Not in Gold. Riverdale, NY: Baen Books, 1993, with Piers Anthony.

Rediscovery: A Novel of Darkover. New York: DAW Books, 1993, with Marion Zimmer Bradley.

Fortress of Frost and Fire. Riverdale, NY: Baen Books, 1993, with Ru Emerson.
Winds of Fury. New York: DAW Books, 1993.
The Robin and the Kestrel. Riverdale, NY: Baen Books, 1993.
A Cast of Corbies. Riverdale, NY: Baen Books, 1994, with Josepha Sherman.
The Black Gryphon. New York: DAW Books, 1994, with Larry Dixon.
Chrome Circle. Riverdale, NY: Baen Books, 1994, with Larry Dixon.
Prison of Souls. Riverdale, NY: Baen Books, 1994, with Mark Shepherd.
Storm Warning. New York: DAW Books, 1994.
Sacred Ground. New York: Tor Books, 1994.
Wing Commander: Freedom Flight. Riverdale, NY: Baen Books, 1994, with Ellen Guon.
The White Gryphon. New York: DAW Books, 1995, with Larry Dixon.
The Eagle and the Nightingales. Riverdale, NY: Baen Books, 1995.
The Fire Rose. Riverdale, NY: Baen Books, 1995.
Storm Rising. Riverdale, NY: Baen Books, 1995.
Tiger Burning Bright. New York: Avon Books, 1995, with Andre Norton and Marion Zimmer Bradley.
Elvenblood. New York: Tor Books, 1995, with Andre Norton.
The Ship Who Searched. Riverdale, NY: Baen Books, 1995, with Anne McCaffrey.
Storm Breaking. New York: DAW Books, 1996.
Firebird. New York: Tor Books, 1996.
The Silver Gryphon. New York: DAW Books, 1996, with Larry Dixon.
Four and Twenty Blackbirds. Riverdale, NY: Baen Books, 1997.
Owlflight. New York: DAW Books, 1997, with Larry Dixon.
Sword of Ice and Other Tales of Valdemar. Edited by Mercedes Lackey and John Yezequielian. New York: DAW Books, 1997.
Owlsight. New York: DAW Books, 1998, with Larry Dixon.
Oathblood. New York: DAW Books, 1998.
Fiddler Fair. New York: Baen Books, 1998.
The Chrome Born. Riverdale, NY: Baen Books, 1999, with Larry Dixon.
Werehunter. Riverdale, NY: Baen Books, 1999.
The Black Swan. New York: DAW Books, 1999.
Owlknight. New York: DAW Books, 1999, with Larry Dixon.
The River's Gift. New York: Roc, 1999.
Brightly Burning. New York: DAW Books, 2000.
Beyond World's End. Riverdale, NY: Baen Books, 2001, with Rosemary Edghill.
The Serpent's Shadow. New York: DAW Books, 2001.
Take a Thief: A Novel of Valdemar. New York: DAW Books, 2001.
Spirits White as Lightning. Riverdale, NY: Baen Books, 2001, with Rosemary Edghill.
The Shadow of the Lion. Riverdale, NY: Baen Books, 2002, with Eric Flint and Dave Freer.
Elvenborn. New York: Tor Books, 2002, with Andre Norton.

The Gates of Sleep. New York: DAW Books, 2002.

Exile's Honor. New York: New American Library, 2002.

OTHER WORKS

"A Writer on Writing: The Basic Nuts and Bolts." *Marion Zimmer Bradley's Fantasy Magazine*, 28 (Spring 1991).

"A Writer on Writing: The Pros and Cons of Writers' Circles." *Marion Zimmer Bradley's Fantasy Magazine*, 41 (Summer 1991).

Flights of Fantasy. Edited by Mercedes Lackey and Martin Harry Greenberg. New York: DAW Books, 2000. This volume contains ten original stories about birds of prey, including Lackey's novella *Wide Wings*, which centers on one of the minor characters in *The Black Swan*.

BIBLIOGRAPHIES AND CONCORDANCE

Lee, Teri, Juanita Coulson, and Kerrie Hughes, "The Valdemar Concordance." In *The Valdemar Companion*. Edited by John Helfers and Denise Little. New York: DAW Books, 2001.

CRITICAL AND BIOGRAPHICAL STUDIES

Helfers, John, and Denise Little, eds. *The Valdemar Companion*. New York: DAW Books, 2001.

INTERVIEWS

Taylor, Rebecca. "Interview with Mercedes Lackey." *Voices of Youth Advocates*, 213–217 (October 1992).

Waters, Elizabeth. "Interview with Mercedes Lackey." *Marion Zimmer Bradley's Fantasy Magazine*, 50–52 (Spring 1993).

R. A. Lafferty
1914–2002

CHRIS MORGAN

OF ALL THE contemporary authors generally considered to be part of the fantasy and science fiction genres, Lafferty is without doubt the most original. His originality—and, indeed, his uniqueness, for nobody has been able to imitate him—stem from his themes, approach, and writing style. Lafferty's major themes, particularly in his novels, are inevitably religious, mythological, or both, while his minor themes most often involve the dissemination of peculiar, little-known pieces of knowledge. (He was a man of great erudition, particularly fond of word derivations, folklore, and the more abstruse aspects of mythology and theology, examples of all of which he delighted in explaining to the reader.)

While some of Lafferty's fiction is easily recognizable as fantasy or as science fiction, more falls into neither category or, possessing an allegorical underlay, transcends genres; other portions of his work are strongly autobiographical, or moralistic, or historically based. Yet because of its uniqueness it is better to ignore definitions and categories and to consider all his fiction together.

Lafferty's uncommon approach is one of obliqueness. It is not that he tries to be unclear but that much of his subject matter is too effervescent or too incredible to survive full, detailed scrutiny—only an impression consisting of brief hints and halftruths, analogous to glances from the corner of the eye, can provide the proper setting. The result, however, is one of complexity and, on occasion, a certain degree of confusion for the reader.

Not really divisible from Lafferty's themes and approach is his pixilated, often outrageous, writing style. While quite a few fantasy authors have a readily identifiable style or a strong auctorial presence, Lafferty had both to an unequaled degree. Examples are necessary here:

When you have shot and killed a man you have in some measure clarified your attitude toward him.
("Golden Gate," 1982)

This had been one of the heroic labors required that one of the Argonauts should do. Had Hans failed, they would all have been destroyed by the furies.

This is hero stuff? This?

Yes, yes. Such were the high feats of the primordial heroes and of the early Irish heroes. Do not be fooled by later classical instances. They are derivative.

(*Archipelago*, chapter 1)

The word Surround isn't related to the word Round. It is a short doublet form for Superundate, to be completely covered as with waves. An Island isn't a body of land completely surrounded by water. A Lake is a body of land completely surrounded by water.

(ibid., chapter 6.)

Apparitions are as stone-deaf. They speak their message but they do not hear. You may have noticed this yourself.

("Frog on the Mountain," 1970)

These quotations are typical, although Lafferty always seemed to be trying to avoid the typical in his writing. Most of his work contains much wit, humorous asides, narrative hooks, and apparent overstatements.

Raphael Aloysius Lafferty was born in Neola, Iowa, on 7 November 1914. When he was four his family moved to Tulsa, Oklahoma, where he lived for much of his life. His father was Irish Catholic and worked in the oil-lease business, and Lafferty attended a Roman Catholic school. He had an almost eidetic memory when young, and he always read greatly. His only extended absence from Tulsa was during World War II, when he served in the army for about four and a half years. This included a long posting to the islands of the South Pacific, which had a considerable influence on him and to which references recur throughout his writing. He was an electrical engineer until he retired from that profession in 1970. He did not write at all until he was forty-five (1959); he was fairly prolific, with nineteen novels and about 200 stories published, and much remains unpublished. He had a nonspeculative story published in 1959 and his first speculative story, "Day of the Glacier," in *The Original SF Stories* magazine of January 1960.

Between 1960 and 1968 (when his first novels appeared in print) he had almost fifty stories published. Their originality was recognized very quickly, and they were very well received by critics and readers alike. Nearly all were published as science fiction, principally in the *Galaxy* stable of magazines—*Galaxy, If,* and *Worlds of Tomorrow*—which were all then under the editorship of Frederik Pohl during a period when they were regarded as the best of the science fiction magazines, with *If* winning three consecutive Hugo awards.

Even at the outset of his writing career, Lafferty's stories were strikingly different from everything else appearing in the science fiction magazines. They were refreshingly zany but often concerned with problems pertinent to the 1960s. Certainly they stretched the definition of science fiction, dealing in new ways with some of the older science fiction themes and conventions. They resulted in Lafferty's being regarded as part of a new wave of American fantastic fiction that appeared in the mid-to-late 1960s and included such writers as Samuel R. Delany, Thomas M. Disch, Harlan Ellison, Ursula K. Le Guin, and Roger Zelazny.

An example of Lafferty's high quality from the beginning is his third story to be published, "Through Other Eyes" (1960), in his Institute for Impure Science series. The main characters of the series, Gregory Smirnov, Valery Mok, and Charles Cogsworth, are all there (though not Epiktistes, the sentient computer), and the quality and tone of the story give no indication of its earliness. Typically, it concerns the testing of a new invention—one that enables people to see the world through the eyes of others. The effect is, naturally, shattering, but it is a thinly disguised plea by Lafferty for better human understanding. A well-known later story in the same series is "Thus We Frustrate Charlemagne" (1967). Its time paradox theme is the familiar one of trying to change history, though it contains first-rate historical research and a streak of wild humor, both of which single it out as different. The series includes that complex episodic novel *Arrive at Easterwine: The Autobiography of a Ktistec Machine* (1971), and is continued with stories such as "Great Tom Fool or The Conundrum of the Calais Customhouse Coffers" (1982).

The stories from the 1960's are Lafferty's best work in the sense that they are simpler, more easily understood, and thus more entertaining than his later stories. Several of them have become minor classics, with many reprints to their credit.

"The Six Fingers of Time" (1960) is one such story. It describes how a young man, Charles Vincent, discovers that he possesses the special talent of being able to move faster than the eye can follow. He can enter and leave this speeded-up condition at will. There is the suggestion that this talent is an inherited one, connected with the possession of an extra digit on one's hand (and Vincent has an odd double thumb). Vincent misuses the talent in a puerile manner, playing cruel tricks upon members of the public. A man of similar talent whose face he never sees informs him that he must learn responsibility, and later invites him to join the brotherhood of those who have learned to conquer time—an invitation that Vincent refuses. Yet the moral position of this refusal is not clear, for the shadowy man has the "smell of the Pit" on him. Clearly this is not a God-given gift. Within a year Vincent has worn himself out by this speeded-up living, and he dies of senility.

Lafferty has a liking for writing about groups of prepubescent children. His general standpoint seems to be that they instinctively know things—especially about secret and magical subjects—that adults have forgotten. A delightfully humorous version of this is "Seven-Day Terror" (1962), which is Lafferty's most reprinted story. Clarence, a nine-year-old, makes a device that causes objects to disappear, and his eight-year-old sister manages to take the credit for their reappearance, because she knows they will all reappear after exactly seven days anyway.

A much more serious story is "Among the Hairy Earthmen" (1966), in which a group of alien superchildren spend an afternoon playing on earth. But their afternoon is three centuries of our time, during which they appear repeatedly as various kings and queens of the Middle Ages and Renaissance, using ordinary human beings as cannon fodder in their games. It is an allegory of irresponsibility.

The idea of a group of children with special powers recurs in *The Reefs of Earth* (1968), and an analysis of an educational system that could produce very able children (if enough survived) is found in the bitterly satirical "Primary Education of the Camiroi" (1966).

The frequently reprinted "Slow Tuesday Night" (1965) points to the ephemeral nature of any achievement by postulating a world in which all processes of business and the arts move at a phenomenally rapid pace, so that a lifetime's experience can be had in just one night. An office can be rented and furnished within a minute; a new product can be manufactured and marketed in three minutes; a work of philosophy is written in seven minutes, with a little help from machines ("This was truly one of the greatest works of philosophy to appear during the early and medium hours of the night"); a marriage may last only thirty-five minutes, including honeymoon; a panhandler can become the richest man in the world in just an hour and a half and then be reduced to penury again five minutes later; during the night the entire city is usually rebuilt "pretty completely at least three times."

Lafferty's high regard for American racial minorities, especially Native Americans, Mexicans, and Gypsies, stems from his childhood days when, as an Irish Catholic, he was himself persecuted to some extent and forced to join the racial-minority fringe. His best-known Indian story is "Narrow Valley" (1966), wherein an old Indian spell (aimed at tax avoidance) makes a 160-acre plot of land look like a five-foot ditch. A Gypsy story is "Land of the Great Horses" (1967).

In 1968 Lafferty had his first three novels published. The earliest to appear was *Past Master*, a final nominee for both the Hugo and Nebula awards and still regarded by some as his best novel. Religion and myth are interwoven in a battle between good and evil against a complex background. The human-settled planet of Astrobe is in turmoil despite the near perfection of its wonderful cities, where leisure is the norm and every luxury is available. Millions of people are leaving this society, preferring to live in the dangerous squalor of new slums where they must work hard and have very low life expectancies. To help the situation, Thomas More is brought from the earth of a thousand years earlier, chosen because he may be popular and because of his one honest moment (for which he was executed).

Once on Astrobe, More is manipulated by the governing group, which consists mainly of Programmed Persons—perfect mechanical men, virtually indistinguishable from humans, in whose hands most of the power has been placed. The one fault of the rule of these Programmed Persons, and of Astrobe's utopian ideal, is that it is purely materialistic, suppressing the spiritual side of life. Yet even the Programmed Persons have a spiritual ruler—Ouden, a nothingness, a vortex, which seems to personify evil. On More's side, trying to protect and guide him, are various human mythical archetypes. More runs for world president and wins an overwhelming victory. Very soon, though, he discovers that he is being used to help stamp out everything spiritual upon Astrobe, and he rebels against his lawmakers. He refuses to agree to a clause of this nature and, just as he was a thousand years before, is sentenced to death. A revolution precipitated by the death sentence fails to save More's life but might lead to a new world order.

The Reefs of Earth was the first novel finished by Lafferty (in 1966) but it was published a month or two after *Past Master*. Reminiscent of "Among the Hairy Earthmen," though somewhat less serious, *The Reefs of Earth* is deceptively simple. At one level it concerns a group of six alien children (plus a seventh who is a ghost) determined to kill off all earth's inhabitants and take over the planet. The children are Puca, a race very similar to humans, though sometimes very ugly, like goblins or Neanderthals, and possessing special talents. Generally they are rejected and persecuted by humans, though accepted by Amerindians and blacks. The children fail in their aim (they are, after all, under ten, and there is the suggestion that they may succeed later), and their four parents (they are two families of cousins) all die from a combination of persecution and earth allergy sickness.

At a second level the novel shows up most normal humans (specifically the WASP inhabitants of whichever southern state the novel is set in) as being spiritually deficient and unworthy to live in this world—let alone rule it—while the ethnic minorities are depicted as more intelligent and capable. At another level the whole novel is not to be taken at face value or as an allegory, but is an excuse for a succession of tall tales and doggerel verses. The children delight in telling each other brief ghost and horror stories. This is the *aorach*, a Puca art form. But other characters in the book tell such tales too, and Lafferty inserts many unbelievable snippets into the narration:

> Phoebe Jane piloted them down the river about a mile. She put them in an inlet so hidden that the stars didn't even shine. It was like the inside of a blind shed. "A family lived in this inlet for three generations once, and they never did see the sun," she said. "The parents never saw the faces of their own children. It's so dark in here that you strike a match here and it shines dark instead of light. It's so dark here that you didn't see me go, and I left my voice here to talk with you for two minutes after I'm gone."
>
> (chapter 6)

The other art form of the Puca is the *bagarthach* verse, which can make the person at whom it is aimed do anything, even die. It is doggerel, for which Lafferty has an obvious weakness. All the chapter titles in the novel fit together to make a sixteen-line example of it.

The same verse form, complete with forced rhymes of an outrageousness to rival those of Ogden Nash, is a feature of the author's third 1968 novel, *Space Chantey*. This is another excursion with the archetypes of myth, as a far-future space captain and his crew, returning from war, relive the adventures of Homer's *Odyssey*. The novel is short and patchily episodic. It reaches its greatest heights when the parallels with Odysseus are forgotten and new adventures included. Somehow Atlas is in here, holding the universe together by knowing everything about everything. From Norse myth come some giant trolls (including one who can repair and even improve spaceships with his stone hammer). Most original is a gamblers' world, where the captain, Roadstrum, wins 1,000 planets and then loses 1,024 to a lavatory attendant. As one might expect of mythological archetypes, Roadstrum and his men are occasionally killed, but they never stay dead for long. It is a lightweight work, though one of Lafferty's own favorites.

Myth and religion go hand in hand again in *Fourth Mansions* (1969), another Nebula nominee. The main question in this tremendously complex novel is whether mankind can manage to rise to a new superhuman level (the Fifth Mansion) or whether it must continue its cyclical progression through the previous levels. (The progression is spiritual and mental in nature rather than physical.) As usual in Lafferty's books, the final result is left unclear.

The novel's protagonist is Freddy Foley (there is frequently alliteration in Lafferty's character names), a young journalist who is naive but lucky, an obvious everyman hero type, who comes to fill a Parsifal role and has greatness (a metaphorical Holy Grail) thrust upon him. Circling about him are four power groups who could help or hinder, each characterized by an animal. Already superhuman are the brainweavers, a seven-person mental gestalt (pythons), who want humanity to progress. Opposed to them and trying to control Foley are the revenants, immortal and almost omniscient, changing bodies at will (toads). Then there is a secret Christian brotherhood, the patricks (characterized by the badger), who help Foley and make him their emperor. Last of the four is a young revolutionary, Miguel, who is the self-proclaimed champion of the people (unfledged falcon). Great stress is placed throughout on secret groups who wield enormous power and manipulate large sections of humanity. Despite the complexity there is considerable narrative drive and much violent action, blending to make a very satisfying novel.

The Devil Is Dead (1971) must be considered in tandem with *Archipelago* (1979), the latter being Lafferty's favorite among his novels. Both were finished in 1967, and they are, respectively, volumes two and one in the *Devil Is Dead* trilogy, or, as the author preferred to call it, the Argos Mythos. Each volume contains many references to the other, and there are characters in common. Neither is fantasy in the accepted sense except that the author hints that *Archipelago* may be viewed as a mythological allegory and *The Devil Is Dead* as both a religious and mythological one. *Archipelago* recounts some of the exploits of the Dirty Five, a group of men who meet while serving in the army in the South Pacific in 1943–1945. They are Finnegan, Hans, Casey, Vincent, and Henry, who are also reincarnations of five of the Argonauts (respectively Jason, Orpheus, Peleus, Meleager, and Euphemus). Sometimes their present-day adventures parallel those of the Argonauts, though they seem to spend most of their army service drinking. Later, in civilian life, some of them (together with wives or girlfriends) set up a printing company in New Orleans. Although Lafferty provides details of the earlier lives of all five (sometimes at excessive length), it is the later wanderings of Finnegan upon which he concentrates:

> Was Finnegan a simple schizo in his living several lives? No. He was a complex schizo. His travels ended only with his life, though X. (who claimed to have later congress with him) said they did not end even then. The apocryphal of the Finnegan adventures cannot be separated from the canonical. They raise the question: are there simultaneous worlds and simultaneous people?
>
> (chapter 7)

At the end Finnegan seems to be killed, though this is not clear, and it seems obvious that he will reappear. He does so in *The Devil Is Dead* (a final nominee for the Nebula award), which concentrates on his adventures. The first half of the book consists of a sea voyage from a southern American port to the Greek islands on a small ship owned by the eccentric millionaire Saxon X. Seaworthy. Most, if not all, of the crew and passengers seem to be mythological archetypes. One, named Papadiabolous, is said to be the devil, though Finnegan knows that he is not who he appears to be, because Finnegan has helped to bury a man with the same face on the eve of the voyage.

After a monumental battle between good and evil on the island of Naxos, in which several of the crew are killed, Finnegan becomes a fugitive, hunted around the world by Seaworthy and his associates. An explanation in the last two chapters of how both Papadiabolous and his double were sons of a Pole, Ifreann Chortovitch, who had, literally, been fathered by the devil, is too long and too late. This is a particularly confusing novel at the allegorical level, because personalities and alliances are never made clear. There is even a double of Finnegan, who is either murdered by or merges with him.

Lafferty had four other books published in 1971. *Arrive at Easterwine* has already been mentioned. *The Fall of Rome* is a straightforward nonfiction account of the decades leading up to the entry into Rome by Alaric and his Goths in 410 A.D. (Although it is referred to in some reference works as a novel, it is an undramatized factual account.) *The Flame Is Green* consists of three years of the rollicking, slightly bawdy adventures of Dana Coscuin, a young Irishman from Bantry Bay, in Spain, France, and Poland just before and during the revolutions of 1848. Coscuin becomes involved with various revolutionary groups. Although Coscuin seems to make some miraculous recoveries from severe (or mortal) wounds, these may be attributed to Lafferty's love of the paradoxical overstatement; the novel would not be classifiable as speculative except for the reappearance as a minor character of Ifreann Chortovitch, the son of the devil. Nevertheless, the novel was nominated for a Nebula Award. It was the first in a planned series of four books about Dana Coscuin. Lafferty also published *Strange Doings*, a collection of science fiction stories. The following year, 1972, he had another historical novel published, *Okla Hannali*, the biography of a nineteenth century Choctaw Indian.

Lafferty's next four novels, *Not to Mention Camels* (1976), *Apocalypses* (1977, two novels in one volume), and *Aurelia* (1982), are less satisfactory and did not have the same impact as his earlier works. *Not to Mention Camels* returns to the theme of recurring archetypes. ("'But there *are* no other people!' he cried then. 'There are a dozen or so people. That is all. And they are repeated billions and billions of times.'") They often die but at the instant of death manage to jump to another world, appearing fully adult, though under a different (yet similar) name. Thus Pilger Tisman becomes Pilgrim Dusmano and then Pelian Tuscamondo. He should not be able to recall any of his previous existences, yet he can. A complicating factor is that he is at least partly an artificial creature. He is, perhaps, analogous to the revenants in *Past Master*.

A feature of *Not to Mention Camels* is blood lust, expressed in various unpleasant deaths (such as having one's thoracic organs pulled out by hand and the cavity filled with molten gold) and cannibalism. There are references to *Archipelago*, even though none of the parallel worlds in *Not to Mention Camels* appears to be earth.

Of the two 180-page novels in *Apocalypses*, "Where Have You Been, Sandaliotis?" tells of the greatest confidence trick in the world—the creation of Sandaliotis, a peninsula in the Mediterranean larger than Italy. It is investigated by Constantine Quiche, "the best detective in the world," who discovers it to be an evanescent confection of sea foam and illusion, created to be sold as real estate. It is a memorable work but never convincing.

Also in *Apocalypses* is "The Three Armageddons of Enniscorthy Sweeny." Here Lafferty employs an even more elliptical and indirect approach than normal to suggest that on a parallel earth three stunningly powerful operas (*Armageddons I, II, and III*), performed in 1916, 1939, and 1984, have served to prevent world wars (though it is uncertain whether the final 1984 disaster can be averted, or even whether the world can survive the impact of the third opera).

Aurelia is an extension of "Primary Education of the Camiroi" with added religious symbolism. Aurelia, a fourteen-year-old, is trying to complete her world government project by flying in a spaceship she has built to a backward human-settled planet and governing it for a year. There is no mention here of Camiroi, her advanced planet being known only as "Shining World." Being a poor student, she crashlands on the wrong planet. Its name is never divulged to the reader: probably it is earth; possibly it is counterearth. She never has a chance to govern the planet but is hailed as a kind of messiah; a cult quickly establishes itself around her. Her death is prophesied within three days. Another young offworlder who has just arrived is Cousin Clootie, there to help Aurelia do a proper job. He is her "dark companion." They are light and dark (her name means golden, while his is a Scottish term for the devil), yin and yang, both with cult followings, and they die together by the agency of a spiked yo-yo with yin and yang symbols painted on it. The symbolism is confusing, and a succession of homilies from Aurelia slows down what action there is.

From 1968, when his first novels appeared, Lafferty's short stories began to change. Gradually they became heavier and more intense in their themes and more esoteric in their audience appeal. Rather than appearing in *Galaxy* and *If*, most were first published in Original anthologies, notably Damon Knight's *Orbit* series, which favored experimental stories. For about four years Lafferty's stories were better received than ever, with several award nominations and one Hugo; but since 1973 the pendulum has swung the other way, with his stories being regarded as incomprehensible by increasing numbers of readers.

Examples of some of his most admired efforts include the Nebula nominee "Continued on Next Rock" (1970) and "All Pieces of a River Shore" (1970). Several stories from this period share themes with his novels. For instance, "About a Secret Crocodile" (1970) deals with some of the many secret groups that control aspects of society; it could be part of *Fourth Mansions*. Another highly regarded story, and a Nebula nominee, is "Sky" (1971), about a drug of that name that makes people think they can fly. In 1973 Lafferty won a Hugo Award for his 1972 story "Eurema's Dam," a poignant piece edging into black comedy about Albert, the last of the idiots, who is unable to write properly or to add figures but has to invent tiny machines to do these jobs for him. In adulthood he builds larger and more useful machines that will fill high government office, and they look down on him. His only friend is Charles, a machine that he builds to be as stupid and awkward and inept as himself.

Perhaps it is a testament to Lafferty's originality and unwillingness to compromise the erudite obscurity of much of his later work that he has a good deal of unpublished material of all lengths, including about fourteen novels. Lafferty was a writer who often demanded considerable effort from his readers. Undoubtedly his best work is shorter, and he was unable to sustain his highest standards for more than a few pages. All his novels are episodic; all contain some good passages and many clever lines along with overlong or confused patches.

In 1980 Lafferty had his first stroke, and in 1984, at age 70, he retired from writing. Almost all work published after 1984 was previously unpublished, as opposed to newly written. Furthermore, Lafferty became increasingly ignored by mass market publishers, and the majority of his work appeared as limited editions published by small presses. The best of these small presses could print his work with style, but all lacked the capital to bring complete series into existence, and such works as the final two volumes of Lafferty's Coscuin Chronicles remain unprinted. His most sustained publication from this time is probably the "In a Green Tree" series, which between 1986 and 1990 was published in five slim volumes of two chapters each.

In 1994 a severe stroke completely eliminated Lafferty's writing career and left him inactive; he later developed Parkinson's Disease and Alzheimer's disease. After living with his sister, who died in 1996, he moved to a nursing home in Broken Arrow, Oklahoma, dying on 18 March 2002 at age 87; he left no heirs. His passing received no national notice for several weeks, during which time several other speculative fiction writers died, including Damon Knight, whose passing occasioned far greater publicity. Nevertheless, all who paid tribute to Lafferty paid homage to his incredible originality, likening his works to those of Flann O'Brien and James Joyce, and those paying tribute were as diverse as Gene Wolfe and Neil Gaiman.

There is no question that Lafferty was uneven as a writer and that his short stories tend to be superior to his novels, though the best of his novels are sui generis and remain very good indeed. Furthermore, his earlier works tend to be more exuberant, more wildly original, and more accessible to general audiences, those readers who might have missed Lafferty's very real subtexts but who nevertheless were capable of enjoying the story on its surface level. At the same time, he had a small but persistent and enthusiastic following, and he deserved the World Fantasy Life Achievement Award, given to him in 1990. His great originality has taken fantasy and science fiction into new areas—a tribute that can be paid to only a handful of twentieth-century authors.

As of this writing, virtually all of his major works are out of print, and his stories are being anthologized with increasing rarity. It thus seems unlikely that Lafferty will ever reach the audience the best of his work merits. This is to be genuinely regretted: Lafferty's voice was original, and his love of language, literature, and tall tales—to say nothing of his interests in Native Americans, his concerns about behavior and ethics, and his questioning acceptance of Catholicism—have much to offer. A new generation of readers will be missing one of America's most original writers.

Selected Bibliography

WORKS OF R. A. LAFFERTY

Past Master. New York: Ace, 1968. London: Rapp and Whiting, 1968.

The Reefs of Earth. New York: Berkley, 1968. London: Dobson, 1970.

Space Chantey, New York; Ace, 1968. London: Dobson, 1976.

Fourth Mansions. New York: Ace, 1969. London: Dobson, 1972.

Nine Hundred Grandmothers. New York: Ace, 1970. London: Dobson, 1975. (Short stories.)

Arrive at Easterwine: The Autobiography of a Ktistec Machine. New York: Scribner, 1971. London: Dobson, 1977.

The Devil Is Dead. New York: Avon, 1971. London: Dobson, 1978.

The Flame Is Green. New York: Walker, 1971.

R. A. LAFFERTY

Strange Doings. New York: Scribner, 1971. (Short stories.)

Okla Hannali. Garden City, N.Y.: Doubleday, 1972.

Does Anyone Else Have Something Further to Add? New York: Scribner, 1974. London: Dobson, 1980. (Short stories.)

Funnyfingers & Cabrito. Portland, Oreg.: Pendragon Press, 1976. (Chapbook containing two stories.)

Horns on Their Heads. Portland, Oreg.: Pendragon Press, 1976. (Chapbook.)

Not to Mention Camels. Indianapolis: Bobbs-Merrill, 1976. London: Dobson, 1980.

Apocalypses. Los Angeles: Pinnacle Books, 1977.

Archipelago: The First Book of the Devil Is Dead Trilogy. Lafayette and New Orleans, La.: Manuscript Press, 1979.

Aurelia. Norfolk-Virginia Beach, Va.: Donning, 1982.

Golden Gate and Other Stories. Minneapolis: Corroboree Press, 1982. (Short stories.)

Four Stories. Polk City, Iowa: Chris Drumm, 1983. (Chapbook.)

Laughing Kelly and Other Verses. Polk City, Iowa: Chris Drumm, 1983. (Chapbook.)

Heart of Stone, Dear, and Other Stories. Polk City, Iowa: Chris Drumm, 1983. (Chapbook.)

Ringing Changes. New York: Ace, 1983. (Short stories.)

Snake in His Bosom, and Other Stories. Polk City, Iowa: Chris Drumm, 1983. (Chapbook.)

Through Elegant Eyes: Stories of Austro and the Men Who Know Everything. Minneapolis: Corroboree Press, 1983. (Short stories.)

Annals of Klepsis. New York: Ace, 1983.

The Back Door of History. Weston, Ontario, Canada: United Mythologies, 1988.

Cranky Old Man from Tulsa: Interviews with R. A. Lafferty. Weston, Ontario, Canada: United Mythologies, 1990.

Dotty. Weston, Ontario, Canada: United Mythologies, 1990.

The Early Lafferty. Weston, Ontario, Canada: United Mythologies, 1988.

The Early Lafferty II. Weston, Ontario, Canada: United Mythologies, 1990.

East of Laughter. Bath, England: Morrigan, 1988.

The Elliptical Grave. Weston, Ontario, Canada: United Mythologies, 1989.

Episodes of the Argo. Weston, Ontario, Canada: United Mythologies, 1990.

Grasshoppers and Wild Honey (1920–1942), Chapters 1 &2. Polk City, IOWA: Chris Drumm, 1992.

Half a Sky: The Coscuin Chronicles, 1849–1854. Minneapolis: Corroboree Press, 1984.

How Many Miles to Babylon. Weston, Ontario, Canada: United Mythologies, 1989.

Iron Tears. Cambridge, MA: Edgewood Press, 1992.

Lafferty in Orbit. Cambridge, MA: Broken Mirrors, 1991.

The Man Who Made Models, and Other Stories. Polk City, Iowa: Chris Drumm, 1984.

Mischief Malicious (and Murder Most Strange). Weston, Ontario, Canada: United Mythologies, 1991.

My Heart Leaps Up (1920–1928), Chapters 1 & 2. Polk City, Iowa: Chris Drumm, 1986.

[In a Green Tree, Part I.]

My Heart Leaps Up (1920–1928), Chapters 3 & 4. Polk City, Iowa: Chris Drumm, 1987. [In a Green Tree, Part II.]

My Heart Leaps Up (1920–1928), Chapters 5 & 6. Polk City, Iowa: Chris Drumm, 1987. [In a Green Tree, Part III.]

My Heart Leaps Up (1920–1928), Chapters 7 & 8. Polk City, Iowa: Chris Drumm, 1988. [In a Green Tree, Part IV.]

My Heart Leaps Up (1920–1928), Chapters 9 & 10. Polk City, Iowa: Chris Drumm, 1990. [In a Green Tree, Part V.]

Promonotory Goats. Weston, Ontario, Canada: United Mythologies, 1988.

Ringing Changes. New York: Ace, 1984.

Serpent's Egg: A Fantasy. Bath, England: Morrigan, 1987.

Sinbad: The Thirteenth Voyage. Cambridge, Mass.: Broken Mirrors, 1989.

Slippery, and Other Stories. Polk City, Iowa: Chris Drumm, 1985.

Tales of Chicago. Weston, Ontario, Canada: United Mythologies, 1992.

Tales of Midnight: More Than Melchisedech. Weston, Ontario, Canada: United Mythologies, 1992.

True Believers. Weston, Ontario, Canada: United Mythologies, 1989.

CRITICAL AND BIBLIOGRAPHICAL STUDIES

Bain, Dena C. "R. A. Lafferty: The Function of Archetype in the Western Mystical Tradition." *Extrapolation*, 23 (Summer 1982): 159–174.

Drumm, Chris. *An R. A. Lafferty Checklist*. Polk City, Iowa: Chris Drumm, 1983.

Joe R. Lansdale
1951–

STEFAN DZIEMIANOWICZ

THE TIDE OF books that flooded the horror fiction market in the 1980s came from many sources, including the work of writers whose influences and aspirations sometimes lay outside the genre. Joe R. Lansdale is among those writers for whom supernatural horror and fantasy are just two different dialects in a large vocabulary of literary expression. Over the course of a very active career, he has produced memorable fiction in the western, crime, science fiction, and fantasy markets; edited anthologies; scripted comic books, written books for young readers; and set stories in worlds created by other writers. His versatility ranks him with Richard Matheson, Ed Gorman, Bill Pronzini, Neil Barrett, and other colleagues who regularly cross genre boundaries and whose work resists pigeonholing.

Lansdale's work often blends elements of several types of fiction into a highly original amalgam. Regardless of which genres they borrow from, and in what proportions, Lansdale's stories are uniform in their depictions of an ordinary world subject to unpredictable eruptions of chaos and their vision of the human condition as both bracingly grim and macabrely amusing.

Lansdale's tales also are informed by a strong regional sensibility. He has lived all of his life in Texas and his work reflects the influence of both the southern Gothic and the American tall-tale tradition. Crude gross-out humor and serious reflections on racism, sexism, and other social ills are as much a part of his "voice" as the colloquialisms and slang his characters speak. Owing to their level of uninhibited violence and gore, his stories are sometimes categorized as hard-boiled or "splatterpunk," yet they are just as likely to put readers in mind of the fiction of Mark Twain, Eudora Welty, and Flannery O'Connor as the genre markets in which they are published.

Joe Richard Lansdale was born on 28 October 1951, in Gladewater, once an oil boomtown, in eastern Texas. He was the second son born to Alcee Bee Lansdale, a self-taught mechanic, and Reta Wood Lansdale, who worked in sales. As a child Joe Lansdale absorbed stories and tall tales his family and neighbors told to one another. He also read omnivorously. The fiction of Edgar Rice Burroughs was one of his earliest and strongest influences, and the late-blooming Burroughs would undoubtedly have sympathized with the range of the résumé Lansdale compiled as a fledgling writer: after two years of college, in which he studied (among other subjects) anthropology and archeology, he held a series of jobs that included custodial work, sweet-potato farming, working in rose fields, martial arts instructor, and stints as a bouncer and a bodyguard. He began writing in his preteen years, and placed his first professionally published story, "The Full Count," in the June 1978 issue of *Mike Shayne Mystery Magazine*. By 1981 he was working as a full-time freelance writer. Since the mid-1970s, Lansdale has lived in Nacogdoches, the model for many of the east Texas towns in his fiction. An avid practitioner of martial arts, he has developed his own discipline, Shen Chuan, Martial Science, which he teaches at Lansdale's Self-Defense Systems, a school he maintains in his hometown.

EARLY SHORT FICTION

Lansdale's early short fiction covers a broad terrain that includes suspense, horror, fantasy, science fiction, and even sword and sorcery. It was published in an equally wide variety of markets, ranging from crime digests and biker magazines to the *Twilight Zone*, the professional magazine that in its first decade published many writers associated with the horror boom of the 1980s and 1990s. Some of his earliest sales appeared in theme anthologies for the horror market, and though these stories show his competence at traditional horror storytelling, they bear very little of the personal signature he is recognized for today. "The Princess" (1980) tells of the exhumation and attempted reburial of a living mummy transported from the bogs of Denmark to America. "Waziah" (1980) is a suspenseful tale of two men and a woman trapped by a monster in a remote shack in the Dakotas during a raging snowstorm. "By the Hair of the Head" (1983), written for one of the *Shadows* compilations of dark fantasy, is a traditional tale of a haunting set in a New England lighthouse. In "The White Rabbit" (1981), ghouls in Egypt adopt the shapes of characters from *Alice in Wonderland* and use Carrollian wordplay to beguile an unsuspecting victim. Two notable stories from this period are "Fish Night" (1982) and "Tight Little Stitches in a Dead Man's Back"

(1986). The former, in which two traveling salesmen share a supernatural encounter in the desert, is heavy with dialogue that gives a foretaste of the verbal exchanges Lansdale uses to develop character and plot in his later stories. The latter, written for an anthology of antinuclear fiction, is a postapocalyptic fantasy whose explicit physical horrors have become a trademark in Lansdale's fiction.

At the same time Lansdale placed polished stories in professional markets, he was also publishing a substantial quantity of stories in *The Horror Show*, *Grue*, *Footsteps*, *Time and Space*, *Deathrealm*, *New Blood* and other semiprofessional periodicals. These magazines were bound by fewer restrictions than more-commercial outlets and frequently gave writers a chance to explore offbeat themes or attempt unconventional approaches to their subjects. Lansdale's contributions to these small press venues differ in some regards from his professional sales. The stories are less polished, but they show his quirkier side. They tend to be brief and plotless, developing their single idea in as little space as necessary. Some are written as dramatic monologues spoken by psychotic narrators. Others take a completely deadpan approach to their gruesome horrors. Several are evocative mood pieces that mix the gothic and the lyrical. Tales such as "Bar Talk" (1990), "Saved" (1985), "The Junk Yard" (1989), "The Fat Man" (1987), and "My Dead Dog Bobby" (1987) juxtapose humor with horror and feature grotesques whose sole purpose is to reveal that they are Martian vampires, dangerously deranged pet owners, or turncoats about to feed the unsuspecting reader to a monster lurking in a trash dump. The influence of Robert Bloch, Ray Bradbury, Fredric Brown, Richard Matheson, and other writers from whom Lansdale learned technique is evident in the stories' economy and ghoulish twist endings, and they abound with bizarre horrors clearly inspired by low-budget horror movies and the EC horror comics.

Many of Lansdale's weirdest stories from this interval have no supernatural content. Rather, they begin with an absurd or off-kilter premise and pursue it to the point where the boundary between the realistic and the fantastic begins to blur. The most extreme example is undoubtedly "The Valley of the Swastika" (1982), a tongue-in-cheek homage to Rudyard Kipling's "The Man Who Would Be King" set in the Appalachian Mountains. It tells of an inbred mountain race that worships two motorcyclists because one bears a swastika tattoo that reminds them of the crash-landed Nazi aviator they revered as a god decades before. "Duck Hunt" (1986) starts somewhat more normally with a young boy reluctantly preparing for a duck-hunting trip that will serve as his rite of passage into adulthood. It ends on a surreal note as the boy discovers that the duck is just a totem for what he is really expected to kill. "The Pit" (1987), one of Lansdale's most effective hard-boiled tales, is set entirely within a backwoods arena where two opponents, one white and the other black, are forced to fight to the death by captors whose "minds seemed to click and grind to a different set of internal gears than those on *the outside*" (p. 19). The atmosphere is that of a perverted fundamentalist tent revival meeting, and the fight, fueled by frustrated sexuality and macho attitudes regarding race, plays out like a primal mating ritual. Lansdale provides no back story to explain the pit's existence or customs, leaving his tale open to a number of interpretations. His protagonist provides one: "Sometimes he felt that he had stepped into an alternate universe where the old laws of nature, and what was right and wrong did not apply" (p. 13).

CROSSING GENRES

Lansdale's novels are natural extensions of his short story writing, and several (*The Magic Wagon*, *The Nightrunners*, *The Bottoms*, *The Big Blow*) are expansions of short stories or novellas. With few exceptions, they tend to be episodic and less concerned with plot than with developing their unusual characters or evoking a particular time or place. Lansdale uses their larger scale and looser structure to mix elements from different genres, and pile on odd set pieces and situations whose cumulative weight gives them their sense of skewed reality.

His first published novel, *Act of Love* (1981), is a routine crime thriller about a detective tracking a serial killer dubbed Houston Hacker. The killer's surprise identity, once revealed, represents a betrayal of trust, a theme Lansdale returns to repeatedly in his work as one of the worst expressions of human evil. Most of the novel-length works Lansdale produced between 1981 and 1987 are period westerns inflected with themes and ideas from his work in other markets. There is notable correspondence between Lansdale's westerns and his crime fiction. Both are set in rugged environments where outlaw behavior and murder are regular features of the social climate. The stories reflect a strong sense of good and evil, though this rarely translates to the simplistic pitting of forces of law-and-order against the unlawful. Rather, Lansdale places high value on codes of personal honor and self-sacrifice. His protagonists are not always good men, but much like classic hard-boiled detectives, they are motivated by honorable principles when they bend or work outside the law.

If Lansdale's westerns sometimes play out like crime dramas, they are also laced with images and elements appropriated from horror and fantasy fiction. *Texas Night Riders* (1983; first published under the pseudonym Ray Slater) features an outlaw band whose nighttime raids in black cloaks and hats have a near-supernatural aura. *Blood Dance* (written in the early 1980s but not published until 2000), about a cowboy determined to settle the score with double-crossing desperadoes who killed his partner and left him for dead, includes a Sundance ceremony in which a mystic vision reveals the man's destiny. In *Dead in the West* (1986), Lansdale's most deliberate fusion of the classic western and supernatural gothic, a curse placed by a Native

American medicine man wrongly hanged for a murder causes the dead of Mud Creek to rise as zombies and massacre the living. The novel features one of Lansdale's best-drawn western characters, Jebidiah Mercer, an alcoholic gunslinger turned preacher who is haunted by memories of an incestuous relationship with his sister and who hopes to earn his salvation by eliminating the horror overwhelming the town.

Though the "feel" of his westerns is authentic, Lansdale is acutely aware that modern perceptions of the western frontier have been shaped by the legends of Buffalo Bill, Will Bill Hickok, Calamity Jane, and other outsized personalities, whose exploits lend themselves to exaggeration and folklore. Fascinated by this conflation of history and fiction, as well as the gap that sometimes separates myth from its underlying reality, he has written several fantasies that chart alternate paths that western history might have taken. "Letter from the South, Two Moons West of Nacogdoches" (1986) is presented in the form of a letter written by a modern Native American woman. From details and allusions in her remarks, the reader learns that hers is a world where Native Americans and the Chinese thwarted the manifest destiny of the white man to become the rulers of America. The reader also learns that, though history is different, human nature remains the same and racial and religious prejudices prevail.

"Trains Not Taken" (1987) is almost easily mistaken for a piece of mainstream fiction. At its center is a chance meeting on a train between a disgruntled clerk trapped in an unsatisfying marriage and a bland politician. Lansdale develops these characters with sympathy and pathos—then reveals that they are the folks whom Wild Bill Hickok and Buffalo Bill might have become under different circumstances. "Man with Two Lives" (1982), a nonfantasy, extends this idea with its account of Wild Bill faking his death to escape his notorious reputation and living to a ripe old age under an unremarkable identity.

Lansdale's best-known western, *The Magic Wagon* (1986), is the work that best demonstrates his skill at coaxing fantasy from ordinary materials. Set in the first decade of the twentieth century, when the American frontier has all but closed, it recounts the adventures of a patent medicine show traveling through Texas. The entourage is an unlikely group whose contrasting personalities bring colorful life to their adventures: Billy Bob Daniels, an alcoholic trick shooter who claims to be the son of Wild Bill Hickok; Old Albert, a crusty, old ex-slave wise to the ways of the world; Rot Toe, a wrestling chimpanzee; and narrator Buster Fogg, the orphaned son of a homesteading family. Picaresque and freewheeling, the novel features several scenes where fantasy and realism collide, including Buster's surreal account of the tornado that destroys his home and family (published separately as "The Windstorm Passes"), a sequence in which Billy Bob and an Indian argue over the supposed mummified corpse of Wild Bill, and the finale that ends with a providential bolt of lightning. The effect of these episodes is enhanced by the general carnival atmosphere of the story. The bragging and banter of the medicine show personnel, their outlandish scrapes and escapes, the gullibility of their customers, and the colorful rendering of an older America more open to wondrous possibilities contribute to the novel's feel of a tall tale acted out by characters who loom larger than life.

SURVIVAL

Survival is a key theme in Lansdale's fiction. In some of his more amusing stories, characters face challenges that push them to outrageous extremes to defend their way of life. In other stories, those challenges force a savage battle for self-preservation that prompts the characters to reassess the values by which they define their humanity. Lansdale's sole novel of supernatural horror, *The Nightrunners* (1987), is his best-realized depiction of ordinary people pushed to uncivilized extremes by threats to their well-being. The novel opens with Montgomery and Becky Jones, an educated and progressive couple, retreating to a remote cabin to help Becky convalesce from a brutal rape that would have ended in her murder had it not been interrupted by a good Samaritan. Her main assailant, chillingly amoral teenager Clyde Edson, committed suicide while awaiting arraignment. But his partner in crime, Brian Blackwood, has become a vessel for Clyde's discarnate personality, and under Clyde's instruction he uses Becky's recurring nightmares of the incident like a homing beacon to track her down. In the company of two companions who were also implicated in the rape, Brian pursues Becky and Montgomery to their hideaway, cutting a swath of violence and murder across eastern Texas that ends with a standoff in which Monty and Becky resort to violence almost as vicious as that of their attackers.

The plot calls to mind Sam Peckinpah's revenge film *Straw Dogs* (1971), but Lansdale distinguishes his story through skillful use of supernatural motifs to vivify his depiction of violence as an ineradicable taint of human nature. Violence is a virtual specter that haunts each of the characters on a different level. Mild-mannered Monty is a loving husband who shares his wife's pain with as much understanding as he can. But Becky's rape has made him feel inadequate and revives guilt feelings that have haunted him since childhood when, out of cowardice, he failed to defend his brother against a bully. A sociologist by profession, Monty can understand primitive behavior in theory but is completely at a loss with how to deal with it when confronted with its reality. Though loath to admit it, Monty realizes that violent engagement with Becky's attackers might help restore his compromised manhood.

Becky is haunted by violence in a different way. Ever since the rape, she has suffered nightmares whose content, which includes precognitive visions, suggest that the intimacy of the crime has forged a supernatural link between her and her assailants. The nightmares hinder her recovery and threaten her relationship with her husband. They serve as symbolic representations of the pervasive and inescapable horror of her violation. Like Monty, Becky struggles to resist the belief that the destruction of her assailants is the only way equilibrium can be restored. Lansdale's teenage delinquent does not have the intellectual depth of Monty and Becky, but his haunting is even more frightening because he is channeled by one of Lansdale's most horrifying creations, the God of the Razor:

> The God of the Razor was tall, black—not Negro, but *black*—with shattered starlight eyes and teeth like thirty-two polished, silver stickpins. He had on a top hat that winked of chrome razor blades molded into a bright hatband. His coat... was the skinned flesh of an Aztec warrior and his pants were the same. Raw, bloody fingers stuck out of his pants pockets like stashed after-dinner treats and the Dark Side Clock... which was an enormous pocket watch, dangled from a strand of gut attached to the God's vest pocket—a pocket that was once the fleshy slit that housed an eye. The shoes he wore... were the ragged heads of guillotined Frenchmen from a long-dead revolution. The God's cloven feet fit nicely into these dead mouths and when he walked the heads thudded like medicine balls being slow-bounced along a hardwood floor.
>
> (p. 136)

The God of the Razor has his roots in an earlier Lansdale story, "Beyond the Light" (1981), which proposes a "soul ghoul" that takes possession of unwitting individuals and compels them to commit violent crimes. Lansdale finetunes this idea for *The Nightrunners* with his suggestion that the violent impulses of people such as Clyde and Brian, to which the God of the Razor responds, are latent tendencies that have persisted since primitive times and shaped the course of human history.

If *The Nightrunners* is Lansdale's most dramatic exploration of the savagery that has survived into civilization, then his next novel is his most intentionally zany. *The Drive-In* (1988), which is subtitled "A 'B'-Movie with Blood and Popcorn, Made in Texas," has its roots in the article "Hell through a Windshield"

(1985), an affectionate tribute to the drive-in movie theater and a forerunner of his "Trash Theatre" columns (cowritten with David Webb) on the guilty pleasures of schlock horror films. The article is an exercise in pop sociology that explores the popularity of drive-in theaters as a phenomenon of mass culture, and it ends with a dark fantasy of what might happen to a drive-in audience that found itself trapped in the plot of a dreadful horror B movie. The novel is a full elaboration of that fantasy. Set like much of Lansdale's fiction in the town of Mud Creek, it relates the adventures of a carful of friends who decide to attend the All-Night Horror Show at the local Orbit Drive-In one Friday night. Midway through the show, a strange comet streaks across the sky, and the moviegoers discover that the drive-in is surrounded by a black void that kills anyone who attempts to leave the theater. Over the next few days people carry on as civilly—and uncivilly—as they did before, awaiting rescue. When the food at the concession stands runs out, though, the microcosmic civilization of the drive-in begins to break down. Cannibalism, tribalism, and weird cults that worship the endlessly cycling splatter films on the screen begin to emerge, and life at the drive-in quickly turns into a Darwinian free-for-all.

Lansdale softens this grim scenario with heavy doses of fraternity-house humor from his teen protagonists and situations in the drive-in world where characters act as irascibly and stubbornly as they did in life before. He also lampoons the outrageous stretches of credibility typical of low-budget horror films with a few farfetched creations of his own, notably the Popcorn King, an entity born when a lightning bolt fuses two teenagers—one white and the other black—into a freak endowed with godlike powers. This levity notwithstanding, Lansdale does work serious reflections on human nature into his story. At the point in the novel where life at the drive-in has become its most desperate, the narrator weeps for humanity because "man is not kind at all," and because he has come to the realization that the universe is "a dark empty place" (p. 146). As in *The Nightrunners,* Lansdale looks for an explanation for the flaws in existence that allow the dark side of humanity to show through. In place of the God of the Razor, he blames a "a B-string god," whose world is a low-budget creation that will not permit anything but second-rate actors, shoestring standards, and bottom-lines values (p. 47). Lansdale followed this novel with *The Drive-In 2,* which he subtitled *Not Just One of Them Sequels,* but which, in the best B-movie tradition, reprises characters, set pieces, and the basic plot of its predecessor. Having escaped from the drive-in, the teenage protagonists wander through a primeval landscape that brings out the savage side of human beings and is dominated by Popalong Cassidy, a weird being analogous to the Popcorn King. Popalong, who sports a television set for a head, is the inevitable evolution of a couch-potato misfit who used television as an escape from his miserable life. His embrace of video reality as truth gives him godlike status in the violent world of the drive-in universe.

DEFYING CATEGORIZATION

The year that *The Drive-In* was published, Lansdale also published his best-known short story, "The Night They Missed the Horror Show." It has no fantasy elements and would not merit mention in a discussion of his supernatural fiction did it not make a perfect bookend to his *Drive-In* novels. Indeed, it is possible to read the story as a treatment of those novels' themes in a nonfantasy context. The story features a pair of bored and bigoted teenagers, near carbon copies of the characters in the novels, who decide one Friday night *not* to go to the movies because the film playing, *Night of the Living Dead,* features a black as its hero. The mischief they get into out on the streets, initially as amusing as any in Lansdale's fiction, abruptly turns nasty and leads to an unexpected, inevitably fatal confrontation with a pair of racist rednecks. If there is a message Lansdale is trying to convey here, it may be that real-life horrors, such as racism and criminal indifference toward life, are worse than the fantasized horrors that play out on the screen of a movie theater.

It is hard to find another story in the Lansdale canon that so succinctly expresses its savage worldview, so deftly balances humor and horror, and so casually defies categorization. (Although it won the Bram Stoker Award for best horror novella of 1988, it is much more a piece of regional writing on a horrifying theme.) Not coincidentally, Lansdale has steered increasingly away from traditional fantasy in his writing since its publication. In several stories written in its wake, he has used its basic structure—a chain reaction of events that begin harmlessly but that are accelerated explosively by misunderstanding, misfortune, carelessness, deviousness, and ignorance—as a framework for plots so preposterous that they might as well be fantasy. "Steppin' Out, Summer '68" (1990) features yet another carload of teen delinquents who find more trouble than they bargained for when a quest to turn up a cheap prostitute ends with one of the boys catching fire from volatile moonshine, running in front of a truck that knocks him off a bridge, and falling into the river where he is promptly set upon by an alligator. The Rube Goldberg mechanics with which events progress from bad to worse is macabrely funny and plays out like an urban legend of adolescent recklessness. In "Mr. Weedeater" (1993), an everyman gets a mild taste of the dark side of the Lansdale universe when he attempts to help the title character, a blind man hired to cut the grass in a lot next door to his. Events slowly spiral out of control with the protagonist gradually displaced from his own life by the title character, who seems nothing less than a hypostatized form of the chaos forever threatening to engulf Lansdale's victims.

Lansdale's largest body of fiction in the 1990s is comprised of his novels featuring the unusual detective duo of Hap Collins (white and heterosexual) and Leonard Pine (black and gay). Written in the same antic spirit as the crime novels of Elmore Leonard and Carl Hiaasen, the novels mix Lansdale's usual concerns with the impact of crime and violence on the individual and society with macabre and outrageous plot complications similar to those in his fantasy fiction. His few forays into fantasy since the late 1980s have been notably ambitious. "On the Far Side of the Cadillac Desert with Dead Folks" (1989) is a supernatural western about a bounty hunter and his quarry who team up for a showdown against a horde of zombies. *Batman: Captured by the Engines* (1991) puts a wild pop-culture spin on the shape-shifting theme, pitting the Caped Crusader against Native Americans who can transform into cars and motorcycles. "Bubba Ho-tep" (1999), in which a geriatric Elvis Presley battles a mummy transplanted from Memphis, Egypt, to Memphis, Tennessee, is yet another of Lansdale's riffs on the mythic dimensions of celebrity. Both "The Steam Man of the Prairie and The Dark Rider Get Down" (1999) and *Zeppelins West* (2001) are pastiches of old-fashioned dime novels that work characters and ideas filched from western folklore and the fiction of Jules Verne, H. G. Wells, L. Frank Baum, and Bram Stoker into inventive cross-genre mélanges. A long-time admirer of DC Comics' *Jonah Hex,* a gothic western saga begun in 1972, Lansdale scripted *Jonah Hex: Two-Gun Mojo* (1994), a five-issue comic book series featuring the mysterious bounty hunter whose adventures blend wild west action and supernatural incidents. Lansdale's early fondness for Edgar Rice Burroughs's fiction came full circle when, in 1996, he was asked to finish a Tarzan tale left incomplete at Burroughs's death in 1950. *Tarzan: The Lost Adventure* is a dutiful pastiche of the early Tarzan tales, involving Tarzan in a quest for the fabled city of Ur that is complicated by marvels and monsters of the lost-world type, and punctuated with brutal primitive incidents that resonate with the savage worldview expressed through Lansdale's modern stories.

Even Lansdale's nonsupernatural stories show an occasional streak that suggests he has not eliminated fantasy so much as found new ways to blend it into his story mixes. *Freezer Burn* (1999), a James Cain–type story of sex and betrayal, is set in the world of a traveling freak show whose members are as close to realistic incarnations of the supernatural as one can find in Lansdale's writing. The fantastic and the realistic merge through Lansdale's depiction of the freaks as more human and deserving of sympathy than his scheming, lust-blinded "normals." *The Bottoms*, which won the Mystery Writers of America's Edgar Award for best novel of 2000, is not supernatural, but it offers Lansdale's most eloquent commentary on the purposes that fantasy serves. Redolent with the influence of Harper Lee's *To Kill a Mockingbird*, the novel is set along the banks of the Sabine River in east Texas, during the years of the Great Depression. When the corpses of women who have been sexually violated and mutilated begin turning up in the area, blame falls on the Goat Man, a legendary monster who purportedly lives in the surrounding woods. Throughout the novel Lansdale tantalizes the reader with apparent glimpses of the Goat Man as seen through the eyes of its superstitious adolescent narrator. At the climax, it is revealed not only that the murderer is human, and driven by psychologically explicable motives, but also that the Goat Man is a harmless black simpleton on whom the locals have projected their worst fears. What is more, the Goat Man proves instrumental in saving the narrator and putting a stop to the serial killings. It does not require much interpretation to see this as Lansdale's reminder that fantasy, and fantastic fictions, are tools we use to give to give shape to our worst fears, the better to come to terms with them.

Selected Bibliography

WORKS OF JOE R. LANSDALE

NOVELS AND SHORT STORIES

Act of Love. New York: Zebra, 1981.

Texas Night Riders. New York: Leisure, 1983. [Ray Slater, pseud.]. (Corrected text published by Subterranean Press, 1997.)

Dead in the West. New York: Space & Time, 1986; London: Kinnel, 1990. (Corrected, preferred text published by Crossroads Press, 1995.)

The Magic Wagon. New York: Doubleday, 1986. (Corrected text published by Borderlands Press, 1990.)

The Nightrunners. Arlington Heights, Ill.: Dark Harvest, 1987.

The Drive-In: A "B"-Movie with Blood and Popcorn, Made in Texas. New York: Bantam, 1988; London: Kinnel, 1990.

By Bizarre Hands. Shingletown, Calif.: Marc Ziesing, 1989; London: New English Library, 1992. (Contains "The Pit," "Duck Hunt," "Letter from the South, Two Moons West of Nacogdoches," "Trains Not Taken," "Tight Little Stitches in a Dead Man's Back," "The Night They Missed the Horror Show," "On the Far Side of the Cadillac Desert with Dead Folks," "Hell through a Windshield," "Fish Night" and seven other stories.)

The Drive-In 2: Not Just One of Them Sequels. New York: Bantam, 1989; London: Kinnel, 1990.

Batman: Captured by the Engines. New York: Warner, 1991.

Bestsellers Guaranteed. New York: Ace, 1993. (Expanded edition of *Stories by Mama Lansdale's Youngest Boy*. Eugene, Oreg.: Pulphouse, 1991; contains "The White Rabbit," "The Fat Man," "My Dead Dog Bobby," "By the Hair of the Head," and twelve other stories.)

Writer of the Purple Rage. Baltimore: CD Publications, 1994. (Contains "Mr. Weedeater," "Steppin' Out, Summer '68," "Man with Two Lives," "Bubba Ho-tep," and eleven other stories.)

A Fistful of Stories (and Articles). Baltimore: CD Publications, 1996. (Contains "Bar Talk," "Beyond the Light," and nineteen other stories and articles.)

Tarzan: The Lost Adventure, with Edgar Rice Burroughs. Milwaukie, Oreg.: Dark Horse Comics, 1996.

The Good, the Bad, and the Indifferent. Burton, Mich.: Subterranean Press, 1997. (Contains "Waziah," "Saved," "The Valley of the Swastika," "The Junk Yard," "The Princess," and other stories.)

Freezer Burn. Holyoke, Mass.: Crossroads Press, 1999. (Text is slightly different in the edition published by Mysterious Press, 1999.)

The Long Ones. Orlando, Fla.: Necro Publications, 1999. (Contains "The Steam Man of the Prairie and The Dark Rider Get Down" and three other stories.)

Blood Dance. Burton, Mich.: Subterranean Press, 2000.

The Big Blow. Burton, Mich.: Subterranean Press, 2000.

The Bottoms. Burton, Mich.: Subterranean Press, 2000. (Text is slightly different in the edition published by Mysterious Press, 2000.)

High Cotton: Selected Stories of Joe R. Lansdale. Urbana, Ill.: Golden Gryphon, 2000.

Zeppelins West. Burton, Mich.: Subterranean Press, 2001.

NOVELS FOR YOUNG READERS

Batman: Terror on the High Skies. Boston: Little Brown, 1992; London: Fantail, 1993.

The Boar. Burton, Mich.: Subterranean Press, 1998.

Something Lumber This Way Comes. Burton, Mich.: Subterranean Press, 1999.

GRAPHIC NOVELS/COMICS

Jonah Hex: Two-Gun Mojo. New York: DC Comics, 1994.

Atomic Chili: The Illustrated Joe R. Lansdale. Austin, Tex.: Mojo Press, 1996.

Red Range. Austin, Tex.: Mojo Press, 1999. (With Sam Glanzman.)

ANTHOLOGIES EDITED BY LANSDALE

Razored Saddles. Arlington Heights, Ill.: Dark Harvest, 1989. (With Pat LoBrutto.)

Weird Business. Austin, Tex.: Mojo Press, 1995. (With Richard Klaw.)

OTHER

Anonymous. Interview: Joe R. Lansdale. *The Scream Factory*. Summer 1990, pp. 26–28.

Forshaw, Barry. "The SF-Western-Crime-Horror-Dark Fantasy Man: Joe R. Lansdale Interview." *Interzone*, Aug. 1996, pp. 21–24.

McDonald, T. Liam. "Profiles in Terror: Joe R. Lansdale." *Cemetery Dance,* Spring 1994.

Raisor, Gary L.: "A Conversation with Joe R. Lansdale." *Cemetery Dance,* Winter 1991, pp. 28–30.

Schweitzer, Darrell. "Joe R. Lansdale." David Pringle, ed.: *Horror, Ghost and Gothic Writers.* London: St. James Press, 1998, pp. 346–347.

Schweitzer, Darrell. "A Talk with Joe Lansdale." *Worlds of Fantasy and Horror,* Summer 1996, pp. 51–56.

Wiater, Stanley. "Joe Lansdale." *Dark Dreamers: Conversations with the Masters of Horror.* Lancaster, PA: Underwood-Miller, 1990, pp. 111–118.

Ursula K. Le Guin
1929–

ELIZABETH CUMMINS

URSULA K. LE GUIN is recognized as one of the leading authors of fantasy and science fiction. Her fully realized worlds, tough-minded but gentle characters, invented languages and lyrical prose, and aphorisms about life and art and about home and journey have won her recognition from readers of all ages, critics and scholars from many disciplines. Sometimes she is revered as the sage of our times; sometimes her words are treated as revelations—true now and forever true. But as the chronology of her life and works makes obvious, she is a writer whose well of creativity is regularly filled with new waters. There are identifiable series among her many publications; but the nature of each series changes as her own life experiences, intellectual interests, and artistic experiments broaden and change.

The serial works among Le Guin's fiction are based on place: the created worlds of Orsinia (a fictionalized country in central Europe), Hain (a loose federation of worlds seeded by people from the same planet, which stretches over a trillion miles and whose history spans a million years), the American west coast (the westernmost edge of land, where the continuation of the journey is questioned), and Earthsea (a secondary world, an archipelago where dragons live and magic works and humans find ways to be in the world).

LIFE AND WRITING CAREER

Place and world provide a meaningful approach to the Le Guin biography. Born Ursula Kroeber on 21 October 1929, in Berkeley, California, she has lived in Portland, Oregon since 1959. In more recent years, she has spoken of her identity as a western writer, a sense of place created not only by homes in Berkeley and Portland but also by family ties to the Napa Valley and the Klatsand coastal area of Oregon.

Through her family heritage and her education she has roots in Europe, Colorado, and the American east coast. Her father, Alfred Kroeber (1876–1960), was born in New Jersey of German parents and educated at Columbia University; he is recognized as one of the founders of modern anthropology. Her mother, Theodora Kracaw Brown Kroeber Quinn (1897–1979), grew up in the mining town of Telluride, Colorado, in a family whose ancestors were from Kraków, Poland; she earned both a B.A. and an M.A. at the University of California at Berkeley. Her father's cultural relativism and love of literature, and her parents' propensity for gathering into the Kroeber household Berkeley graduate students, Native Americans, and anthropologists provided an intellectual context that was as critical a part of Le Guin's education as her more formal coursework on the east coast—at Radcliffe College (B.A., 1951) and Columbia University (M.A., 1952 and advanced study).

In 1953 Le Guin married the Georgia native Charles A. Le Guin (b. 1927) in Paris, where they were both Fulbright scholars. Before settling in Portland and raising three children—Elisabeth (1957), Caroline (1959), and Theodore (1964)—the Le Guins lived where Charles Le Guin could complete his Ph.D. in history and begin a teaching career, while Ursula taught courses in French. Her degrees were in the Romance languages, and her love of words, language invention, and translation is evident in her works.

Le Guin's fantasy works are intertwined with her other publications, both chronologically and thematically. They are linked by Le Guin's fascination with world creation and her adroit skill in creating ecosystems and animals, and human races, families, and individuals with unique political systems, histories, architecture, languages, and myths. "Life loves to know itself," she wrote in an early science fiction story, "out to its furthest limits; to embrace complexity is its delight. Our difference is our beauty" ("Winter's King," p. 106). Her works explore similar themes—the ambiguity of truth; the search for balance between individual freedom and community need; the relationship between power and responsibility; the function of authority in storytelling; the problems of perception, coping with change; and the struggle to understand the conjunction of human and nonhuman.

Her earliest publications were in fields in which she continues to publish—nonfiction beginning with a book review (a review of *Jean Lemaire de Belges: Le Temple d'honneur et de vertus*, 1958), poetry ("Folksong from the Montayna Province," 1959), Orsinian fiction (1961), Hainish science fiction ("The Dowry of Angyar," 1964), and Earthsea fantasy ("The Word of Unbinding," 1964). She has branched out into children's picture books and animal stories; since at least the 1980s, she has been involved in other modes for the presentation of her work—performance art, music, film, drama, recordings, photography, and dance. By mid-2002, she had published three nonfiction books—*The Language of the Night: Essays on Fantasy and Science Fiction by Ursula K. Le Guin* (1979), *Dancing at the Edge of the World: Thoughts on Words, Women, Places* (1989), and *Steering the Craft* (1998)—which are important for tracking Le Guin's changing ideas about narrative and genre fiction. In 1993 she published a monograph about the changes in the Earthsea world—*Earthsea Revisioned.* Her twelve books of poetry include fantasy poems and translations, while her nine short story collections are sometimes genre specific, sometimes thematic, and sometimes eclectic. Best known of her seven Hainish novels published between 1966 and 2000 are *The Left Hand of Darkness* (1969) and *The Dispossessed: An Ambiguous Utopia* (1974), while among the three non-Hainish science fiction novels published between 1972 and 1985, *Always Coming Home* (1985) has stirred the strongest debate for its experimental form. The six books of Earthsea (1968–2001) have attracted readers for over three decades, but the seventeen-year hiatus between the first three books and the last three has caused considerable critical evaluation. Among her children's books, the four that constitute the Catwings series (1988–1999) have attracted more attention than her eight picture books.

The richness of Le Guin's stories rewards the reader: grounded in the materiality of Le Guin's invented world, the reader can move freely from story to cosmological questions to political and ethical speculation to narrative theory, and back again. This richness explains why her books garner new readers and inspire rereadings, why

Le Guin is frequently compared with J. R. R. Tolkien, and why her books have won so many awards and accolades. Beginning in 1969 with the *Boston Globe*–Horn Book Award for *A Wizard of Earthsea,* Le Guin's work has been singled out for major awards that include the National Book Award for children's books, a Newbery Honor Book Award, five Nebula Awards (given by the World Science Fiction organization), four Hugo Awards (given by the Science Fiction and Fantasy Writers of America), at least five awards for lifetime achievement, as well as specialized awards from organizations and journals. Further evidence of her major role in contemporary American literature is shown in the numerous books, dissertations, and articles that have been published since 1966, assessing Le Guin's unique place in contemporary literature.

FANTASY GENRE AND EARTHSEA

Le Guin's attitude toward genre definitions in general is that they are useful as long as they are descriptive and not evaluative, inclusive and not exclusive. In his *Strategies of Fantasy,* Brian Attebery suggests that "genres may be approached as 'fuzzy sets,' meaning that they are defined not by boundaries but by a center." Genres have "boundaries that shade off imperceptibly, so that a book on the fringes may be considered as belonging or not" (p. 12). This reference to indeterminate boundaries is compatible with Le Guin's use of the spectrum as an image for distinguishing between fantasy and science fiction.

Since at least 1973 (in the essay "From Elfland to Poughkeepsie," which was later collected in *The Language of the Night*), Le Guin has spoken out against the commercialization of fantasy evident in formulaic novels and their decorative language and against classifications by critics, librarians, professors, reviewers, and bookstores that demean these literatures by using a standard of realistic literature as a moral category. Wryly, Le Guin once offered her publisher a table of contents with a different genre label for each of the eighteen stories in the proposed collection, including such categories as vegetable fantasy, geriatric realism, Gertrudean realism, and revisionary fantasy.

In his essay "About Five Thousand One Hundred and Seventy-Five Words," Samuel Delany (1971) distinguishes fantasy from its relatives by affirming that realistic fiction presents events that "could have happened," science fiction presents events that "have not happened," and fantasy treats events that "could not have happened" (p. 141). In a 1994 interview with Jonathan White, Le Guin stated that fantasy "tells a story that couldn't possibly be true. With fantasy, we simply agree to lift the ban on the imagination and follow the story, no matter how implausible it may be" (p. 103).

For Le Guin, fantasy is the literature of the imagination and of the unconscious, and the exploration of these regions of the human psyche is essential to understanding the nature of being human and moral agency. In an interview with Scott Shuey in 2000, Le Guin spoke of the connection between the power of fantasy to engage the imagination and the world we live in. "The great instrument of moral good is the imagination. . . . You've got to consider bad and good—what is possible and what is not possible—to make an intelligent choice." Fantasy enchants us with a fully realized secondary world in which we experience some of the great difficulties of human experience, such as the coming-of-age process, the fear of death, the recurrence of evil, and the encounter with the stranger or "other." In Le Guin's fantasies, these experiences or stories recur as patterns of images or behavior, such as light and dark, life and death, language and silence, action and restraint, hearth and journey, giving and owning, power and responsibility. "To light a candle is to cast a shadow," one of the Earthsea mages teaches his pupils (in *A Wizard of Earthsea,* p. 44), for in Le Guin's universe, characters must learn that forces that appear to be opposites are complementary. Knowledge of one leads to knowledge of the other; extreme action in one direction brings one around to action in the other.

As Tolkien explained in his touchstone 1939 essay "Of Fairy-Stories" (collected in *The Monsters and the Critics and Other Essays*, edited by Christopher Tolkien, 1983), in order for the fantasy world to enchant the reader, it must be a fully realized world, what he called a "secondary world," with an inner consistency of its own, an appropriate language, and a substantive truth about what it means to be human. In her essay "From Elfland to Poughkeepsie," Le Guin wrote of the work of secondary world creation:

> There is only a construct built in a void, with every joint and seam and nail exposed. To create what Tolkien calls "a secondary universe" is to make a new world. A world where no voice has ever spoken before; where the act of speech is the act of creation. The only voice that speaks there is the creator's voice. And every word counts
>
> (p. 95.)

Such metaphors as Le Guin gives here lead the reader back to the stories themselves, especially the Earthsea books, where "wizardy is artistry."

Earthsea is a fully realized secondary world of island kingdoms and fishing villages, goatherders and wine makers, weavers and dyers, volcanoes and earthquakes, warriors and wizards, witches and harpists, oatcakes and rushwash tea. As an archipelago its existence depends on the balance of earth and sea. This balance, or Equilibrium as it is called, is maintained by the male wizards and sorcerers trained at the School for Wizards on Roke Island. Their power comes from their ability to use the Language of Making, knowing the true names of things. Two other groups use the language—it is the natural language of Earthsea's dragons and it is also used by the village witches, primarily women. Threats to the balance come from wizards and sorcerers with desires for power or immortality, working either on their own or in the service of kings or priests who selfishly seek power without regard for the well-being of the whole. Significant threats require the aid of the leaders of Roke—the archmage and nine masters—and the wisdom of kings, dragons, women, and children.

Writing the Earthsea books over three decades, Le Guin has in effect created two connected Earthsea series. The first series is what became known as the Earthsea trilogy, including *A Wizard of Earthsea* (1968), *The Tombs of Atuan* (1971), and *The Farthest Shore* (1972). After a long hiatus, Le Guin published *Tehanu* (1990); a decade later two more books appeared—*The Tales of Earthsea* (2001) and *The Other Wind* (2001). The first series focuses on the training and deeds of one of Earthsea's greatest archmages—Ged of Gont, culminating in his heroic, singular sacrifice of his powers in order to correct an imbalance created by a powerful mage. The second series focuses on the women, witches, new king, and dragons of Earthsea, culminating in a collaborative story and deed to correct the imbalance created by humans who have broken an ancient contract with dragons.

The first series has three story lines—the life story of Ged, including his coming-of-age experience, the coming-of-age story of Arren, who becomes the first king in eight hundred years of the Inner Lands; and the coming-of-age story of Tenar, priestess-in-training in the kingdom of Karego-At, whose future is unknown. The adult-initiation stories are events of moment for the individual and for the well-being of Earthsea itself. In *A Wizard of Earthsea*, Ged is initiated into the rules of magery, assisted by wise men on both Gont and Roke; in order to take his place as one of Earthsea's greatest mages he must wrestle with and claim as part of himself the dark shadow of ego, pride, arrogance, and despair. Thus Roke's lessons of balancing action and restraint are put into practice.

The next two novels tell double stories—the continued development of Ged as master wizard and new coming-of-age of stories of the young people who are essential to his goal of restoring peace to the Inner Lands. *The Tombs of Atuan* takes Ged to the Kargad kingdom in an attempt to rejoin the Ring of Erreth-Akbe that bears the Rune of Peace. Only the assistance of the young priestess will ensure his success, and she must overcome years of training in which her sense of self has been subsumed by her public identity as the One Priestess. *The Farthest Shore* takes Ged on a quest to heal the break in the Equilibrium made by Cob the Dark Mage, and again he requires the assistance of a young adult. Arren's experience gives him the fortitude to bring Ged back from the land of the dead after Ged has sacrificed his power to defeat Cob; this experience teaches Arren the qualities he will need as he assumes the role of the new king of the Inner Lands.

In the first series, the two male protagonists pass their tests and assume their places in society; Tenar, however, does not assume her mature role. It is as if Le Guin, having created an independent, courageous young woman, could not find a place for her in the hierarchical, patriarchal world she had invented. In interviews since 1990, Le Guin has revealed that, aside from envisioning Tenar as a farmer's wife, she did not know what had become of her. In 1988 Le Guin read a Spanish translation of the trilogy to improve her Spanish, and during this return to Earthsea, she began to see Tenar's story, Tenar's Earthsea. A few years later, the questions left unanswered in *Tehanu* began to seem answerable and to generate new questions, leading to new Earthsea stories beginning in 1997 with the publication of "Dragonfly."

In contrast with the first series, the second series shifts from characters with great powers to those without, from heroic deeds to daily living, from the world of celibate men to the world of women, families, and households. Although some of the same characters reappear against the familiar background of the kingdoms of Havnor and Karego-At, the School of Mages on Roke, and the villages and farms of remote islands, the characters are older and enter into new relationships with one another and with new figures. The characters that bridge the two series are Ged and Tenar, while the most prominent new figure is Tehanu, who apparently was the character that led Le Guin into a fuller exploration of Earthsea's history, the relationship between humans and dragons, and the nature of women's power, which developed into not only finding the origin of the policy of a celibate, male-only society of wizards but also into a broader definition of power itself.

Tehanu appears in the opening chapter of the fourth novel as a six- or seven-year-old child whom Tenar, a widowed farm wife with two adult children, adopts after the child was apparently raped, beaten, and left to die in an open campfire—abuse meted out by a group of adults that included the child's parents. Tehanu's growth into young womanhood and into her double identity as woman and dragon is the key element in the first and last novels of the second series. Ged, having lost his power in *The Farthest Shore*, becomes the husband and father in this new family unit. But between the two novels is *Tales From Earthsea*, five stories that broaden the range of Earthsea's history, beginning with a novella about the dark times, when there was no political unity in Earthsea and the school on Roke was founded, and concluding with a novella set in the time between *Tehanu* and *The Other Wind*.

The central theme of the second series is power and responsibility, but the stories go deeper than acknowledging the human desire for power and the complementary concern as to its responsible use. The second series explores the sources of power in Earthsea in addition to magery, specifically the power of dragons, the "Old Powers" of the Earth, and the power of women's experience.

This expanded but more complicated view of power in Earthsea diminishes the power of the Roke mages; they do not feel as confident about their knowledge of power and their ability to maintain the Equilibrium. In *The Other Wind* when faced with major upheavals—dragons attacking villages in the inner isles, the death of their summoner at the hands of a woman-turned-dragon, their inability to choose a new archmage—the Roke mages turn inward and reenforce the spells that protect Roke. In contrast, the secular individuals and leaders look outward, crossing the seas to encounter dragons, reach friends in trouble, or negotiate with political rivals. Even so, the secular leaders, those men whom society has validated as its leaders, are suspicious or dismissive of the knowledge offered by those on the edges of the patriarchal society—women, witches, children.

The marginal characters, the powerless, provide a model for appropriate decision-making and an opportunity to practice that model. Furthermore, Le Guin's narrative techniques underscore the wisdom of the powerless. The model is that of collaboration; the opportunity to collaborate, however, means acknowledging the power of the powerless, which entails relinquishing the patriarchal model of decision by authority, acquired by those at the top of the hierarchy. *The Other Wind* culminates in a session of collaborative storytelling that leads to choosing how to deal with the changes occurring in Earthsea and threatening the place of humans, the balance between the wildness of dragons and the settled nature of human society.

The act of collaboration is a manifestation of a moral principle that runs throughout Le Guin's work—humans must live their lives recognizing that they are merely a piece of the web of existence. They are not the center of all being in the sense of being more worthy of space, resources, or life than the rest; but they do have a special responsibility for the web because they alone are conscious of it and can thereby make decisions that affect its continued existence. The human maturation process, then, involves not only self-realization but also "other" realization, that is, the ability to connect with the other (individual, animal, stone, plant) while also maintaining the ability to see and respect the differences between self and other. This connection, as Tonia Payne has argued in her 1999 dissertation on Le Guin, affects not only the sense of self and relationship with the ecosystem, but also the act of perception and the shaping of human community.

In the second Earthsea series, Le Guin's narrative techniques demonstrate the power of storytelling and emphasize the collaborative role of the reader. Le Guin alternates focal characters within a single story, undercutting conclusions and refocusing perceptions, not unlike her use of Arren and Ged as focal characters in *The Farthest Shore,* but here in the second series she uses more foci; in *The Other Wind,* for example, Arren, Ged, Tenar, and Alder move in and out of the foreground. In both this novel and the novella "The Finder" (in *Tales from Earthsea*) characters bearing stories initiate narrative obstacles or movement, depending on others' ability to grant authority to the storyteller. The piecing together of multiple stories is crucial for handling the Earthsea crises, so that these stories are also metanarratives about the problematics of authority and the effectiveness of storytelling, similar to what Le Guin was experimenting with in her science fiction—the novel *Always Coming Home* (1985) and the short stories published in the 1990s.

Not only do the new Earthsea stories present the collaborative process of the storytellers themselves, they also show the collaboration of the audience. The reader's collaboration is foregrounded in *Tales from Earthsea*, where the ultimate narrative is that put together by the reader. By collecting together five Earthsea stories from different historical periods and standing in different relationships to the existing Earthsea books, Le Guin calls on the reader to integrate the multiple perspectives. This book of related stories is sometimes called a "composite novel"; Le Guin has also referred to it as a story suite.

Although Le Guin uses a single narrating voice, a historian/storyteller of Earthsea, for all the books, the unity suggested by this consistency is undercut by assertions that stories are incomplete or lost or that with perseverance one might find somewhere in Earthsea someone who could tell yet another version of a particular story. Len Hatfield has argued that the narrating voice in *Tehanu* varies in its distance from the reader and consequently offers the reader the experience of both the immediate story being told and occasional insights into the larger Earthsea story. This double vision characterizes *Tales From Earthsea*; following the five stories is an essay by Le Guin about Earthsea—its history, religion, languages, and people.

The urgency of story collaboration is felt by the reader, not only for solving the immediate threats on Roke and from the dragons, but also for the emotional and psychological health of the central characters (Arren, Tehanu, and Seserakh, the Kargad princess) and for witnessing to these lives. For *The Other Wind* reveals that the dead must be relinquished; the creation of the land of the dead was a violation of the contract between humans and dragons. In that context, then, the story a person tells is the primary evidence of a person's life and consciousness; there is no life after death, only a melding into the ecosystem.

Certainly the second series is distinctly different from the first—written for adults rather than young adolescents and adults, focusing on characters without privilege and power rather than on the traditional hierarchy of male wizards, and putting wisdom in the voices of women rather than in the heroic deeds of mages. However, both Roke and magery remain in Earthsea; what is new is the addition of perspectives from which this world is viewed. Earthsea has been opened up; Le Guin has continued her creation of this secondary world by adding more history and by providing stories of more islands, cultures, people, wizards, and dragons. And when readers look back on Roke or Havnor from these other times, places, and beings, Roke and Havnor look different, smaller; instead of being the center of Earthsea, they are now one of several centers. Le Guin has also noted that "we have lost the gallant young figure with his sword or his mage's staff. That is a clear loss" ("Children, Women, Men, and Dragons" in *Monad: Essays on Science Fiction,* 1990, p. 13). The original trilogy left openings for this revisioning of Earthsea. Like the Earthsea map, which is full of islands not visited in the heroic quests of the first three books, the original stories included unresolved mysteries—a bleak depiction of the land of the dead, the unfinished story of an independent young woman who matched a different kind of power with Ged as archmage, and ferocious dragons in the west who were affected by the actions of Cob the dark mage and who occasionally ventured into human lands.

In a 1996 essay Brian Attebery offered a name for this kind of revisionary writing elsewhere in Le Guin's work—"poaching." In his analysis of Le Guin's short story "The Poacher" (1992), a retelling of the Sleeping Beauty fairy tale in which a young peasant takes up residence in the fairy tale world, Attebery argues that Le Guin has found a way to get inside the fairy tale and yet still be free to change some of the elements. He writes:

> Unlike parody or pastiche, poaching is a way of transforming the tales and redirecting their messages, especially messages about class and gender, without losing their integrity and power. Characters, events, images, storytelling voice, and peasant audience are still in place, but our perception of their relationships have changed. The stories have simply been turned inside out and readdressed, like Poe's Purloined Letter.
>
> (p. 58).

In her essay *Earthsea Revisioned* (1992), Le Guin pointed to the metaphor of double vision to describe the work of *Tehanu*, as author, readers, and characters struggle to bring into focus the patriarchal power and the powers of women and dragons in Earthsea. Not only has she related the work of double vision to her earlier story "Buffalo Gals, Won't You Come Out

Tonight" (in *Buffalo Gals and Other Animal Presences,* 1987), she has identified one of its primary sources—feminist scholarship that she read in the years between the two series (1972–1990), which included *The Norton Anthology of Literature by Women* (1985) and the poet Adrienne Rich's clarion call for "re-vision" (in her 1975 article "When We Dead Awaken: Writing as Re-Vision"), for understanding the strictures on women created by literature and language and for seeing the way to write about how women experience the world.

Insights into this period of Le Guin's reading and maturing can be found in her second nonfiction collection, *Dancing at the Edge of the World: Thoughts on Words, Women, Places.* The essays, speeches, and reviews from 1976 to 1988 show her responses to feminist theory and to her life experiences of passing through middle age (from her forties to her sixties). Poetic and cogent, Le Guin interprets her new learning through images, using the carrier bag as an image of narrative space in which the stories of women and of deeds other than mere conquering can be told, trickster coyote as her muse and transgressive guide for exposing gender as a social construction, borrowing and validating the image of artist-housewife, challenging young women to erupt like a Mount Saint Helens into the mother tongue, representing the uniqueness of women's experience as a crescent of wildness on the edge of the dominant culture.

The critical reception to the Earthsea books has been extensive, primarily in the form of chapters in single-authored books or collections, essays in scholarly journals, and reviews. Children's literature journals and library journals made the earliest responses, beginning in 1969, and continue to consistently pay attention to the Earthsea books. The first critical study was by Eleanor Cameron, a leading writer and critic of children's books, in *Horn Book Magazine* in 1971. Not only did she provide personal information about Le Guin's entry into adolescent literature, she noted the similarity between Carl Jung's and Le Guin's idea of the shadow. Thus began a tradition of interpreting the Earthsea books—both first and second series—against the backdrop of specialized approaches. Jungian, mythic, Taoist, and feminist analyses predominate; but perceptive essays also appeared in the fields of anthropology, linguistics, genre theory, narrative theory, and political science. Particularly refreshing have been essays that examine Le Guin in the larger context of nature writing. An invaluable overview of the Earthsea criticism by Donna R. White appears in her book *Dancing with Dragons: Ursula K. Le Guin and the Critics* (1999).

Response to the first series of books was favorable, evident in the awards and notable book listings they received from librarians and children's literature specialists. Charlotte Spivack (1984) offers a solid Taoist and mythic reading of the trilogy and shows considerable knowledge of the critics who precede her. Coming from medieval studies, T. A. Shippey (1977) suggests that the devaluation of fantasy is partly a result of changed definitions of science, magic, and religion. He argues that Le Guin, with her knowledge of anthropology, undermines the old myths so that the trilogy speaks to the contemporary world. Similarly unique was the approach used by M. Teresa Tavormina (1988) who examined the classical myths in the trilogy. Colin Manlove (1980) introduced a critical approach that, while praising the series for its realistic detail, "unsentimental realism," "metaphoric mode," and style, argued that it was representative of the conservative basis of the fantasy genre. Specifically, Manlove illustrated that the series "portrays the preservation of status quo, looks to the past to sustain the nature and values of the present, and delights in the nature of created things" (p. 287). In light of the second Earthsea series, which subverts the heroic fantasy tradition, Manlove's criticism is worth revisiting.

Le Guin has conducted an energetic dialogue with her readers, beginning with "From Elfland to Poughkeepsie" and "Dreams Must Explain

Themselves" (1973), "Why Are Americans Afraid of Dragons?" (1974), and "The Child and the Shadow" (1975, all of which were collected in *The Language of the Night*, 1979). In these essays, she has spoken primarily about the significance of the genre of fantasy literature and the role of the imagination. She has criticized those aspects of American society that treat the imagination dismissively and those segments of the literary community that either denigrate fantasy literature or produce imitative, commodified fantasy. Her early essays draw on Jungian thought to help explain some of the power of the genre, but she also affirms that her reading of Jung did not come until after she had written her own trilogy; and she points out in later essays how she has drawn away from Jungian thought.

The second series also received positive reviews, but because of the changed view of Earthsea that Le Guin presented, the first book *Tehanu* also elicited several negative reviews and initiated discussions of the relationship between the trilogy and the fourth book. This phase of the critical dialogue began with harsh reviews by John Clute, Robert Collins, and Tatiana Keller to which Le Guin responded with *Earthsea Revisioned*, a lecture presented to the Children's Literature New England institute in 1992, a revision of a 1989 lecture about *Tehanu* ("Children, Women, Men, and Dragons," published *in Monad: Essays on Science Fiction* in 1990).

The first scholarly essay appeared in 1993—Len Hatfield's "From Master to Brother: Shifting the Balance of Authority in Ursula K. Le Guin's *Farthest Shore* and *Tehanu*," which argued that Le Guin had been critical of patriarchy in the first series but in an indirect way. Hatfield asserts that the reader is assisted into this new view of Earthsea through Le Guin's techniques of narrative voice and of authorizing the voices of women, children, and dragons. In 1995 Perry Nodelman objected to Hatfield's analysis and Le Guin's own essay as being attempts to blot out what was really in the original trilogy.

Feminist interpretations of *Tehanu* by Holly Littlefield and Susan McLean both explore the issue of authority in Earthsea. Littlefield contrasts *The Tombs of Atuan* and *Tehanu* in order to show Le Guin's developing feminism between 1971 and 1990. She presents a balanced discussion of Le Guin's critique of patriarchy and her treatment of the issues of gender and power in a number of women in *Tehanu*. McLean also depicts Le Guin's critique of patriarchy and explores the nature of women's power, particularly in the irresolution of the modes of anger and acceptance.

W. A. Senior approaches the four-book Earthsea series from the perspective of cultural anthropology, praising Le Guin's skill in world building and arguing that the ritual of gift giving is the moral and social heart of Earthsea. Warren G. Rochelle's 2001 book on the rhetoric of myth in Le Guin's work includes a chapter on Earthsea in which he points out the changes Le Guin makes in the mythic hero story as Le Guin brings Tenar and the critical acts of living into the foreground.

New scholarship will certainly emerge in response to the two new Earthsea books published in 2001. Early assessments have been made in reviews and essays by long-time readers of Le Guin's work, notably Gary K. Wolfe, Meredith Tax, and Gerald Jonas.

THE BEGINNING PLACE

The Beginning Place (1980) is a novel that is close to the type of fantasy that Jorge Luis Borges, the source of the novel's epigraph, has written. Through realism and fantasy Le Guin tells the story of Hugh and Irena and their difficult journey from adolescence to adulthood. On the verge of adulthood, two individuals—strangers in the normal world—find their way into a fantasy land where they are tested. The novel's epigraph, "What river is this through which the Ganges flows?" refers to two rivers of equal merit—the literal and the metaphorical. In her 1988 introduction to a new edition of *The Book of Fantasy* edited by Borges in 1939, Le Guin notes that Borges's magical realism is a more accurate way to portray the way the world is now. But Le Guin also warns in the introduction that fantasy itself has two sides, which are not of equal merit:

> So fantasy remains ambiguous; it stands between the false, the foolish, the delusory, the shallows of the mind, and the mind's deep connection with the real. On this threshold sometimes it faces one way, masked and beribboned, frivolous, an escapist; then it turns, and we glimpse as it turns the face of an angel, bright truthful messenger, arisen Urizen.
> (p. 10)

This double vision of fantasy is the basis of Le Guin's novel of alternate worlds, and the story should be compared to "Buffalo Gals, Won't You Come Out Tonight." Hugh and Irena need to escape from the pressures of their everyday lives—from their dull jobs as unskilled laborers and each from the oppressive demands of a parent (Hugh from his mother and Irena from her stepfather). However, each initially uses the fantasy world as escapism, including an infatuation for what appear to be perfect love objects. But as the quest develops, Hugh and Irena must make choices, the lessons and consequences of which they take back with them to the real world. Specifically, they learn that sacrifice is not an acceptable mode of either personal or public behavior; that fear must be faced not suppressed; that adult love is more complex than either infatuation or idealization. In the monster they slay, each sees the worst side of the self, which is male for Hugh and female for Irena, a self that lives on pain, suffering, and blindness to the greater world. They emerge from the fantasy world changed—with an early understanding of the nature of adult love, a commitment to living apart from their encompassing families, and an assumption of the role of moral agency that stems from a strong sense of self-worth.

The novel has been the subject of several essays that compare it not only with some of Le Guin's own work ("The New Atlantis," *Very Far Away from Anywhere Else, Always Coming Home*) but also to other works that depict the gateway between a fantasy world and a realistic world (C. S. Lewis's *The Chronicles of Narnia*, Lewis Carroll's *Through the Looking Glass*, Shakespeare's *As You Like It*). Among these, Charlotte Spivack's reading is valuable for its integration of the realistic and symbolic worlds, mythic elements, and discussion of Le Guin's possible sources. Carol Franko focuses on the patriarchal nature of both worlds and Le Guin's "developing feminist ethos" that enables her to reshape narratives as she continued to do in her 1980s fiction.

CHILDREN'S BOOKS

Le Guin's books for children portray the pleasures of the imagination, meeting challenges, and learning to live with animals and respecting their world. She has sustained one story in particular through a series of four books. The Catwings series (1988–1999), illustrated by S. D. Schindler, is animal fantasy. Although the intertwined lives of the cats and the people are portrayed realistically, the cats can fly, they can talk (to each other), and they are portrayed with the characteristics of real animals. The kittens' adventures begin when their mother sends them away from their city home, under a dumpster, which is going to the dogs. The tales invite and exercise the children's imaginations much as the young kittens develop their flying skills in activities that are risky but also simultaneously work and play. Told from the cats' perspective, the stories offer children a way to explore the animal world, and, obliquely, a way to consider some of their own parallel or future experiences—leaving home, accepting one's difference, coping with adversity and trauma. For there is a darkness in the stories; children are not shielded from the dangers and evil in the world. And the narratives show, without sentimentality, the pleasures and responsibility in coexisting with an animal, which cannot be owned or expected to live as humans do and should not be exploited.

Mike Cadden includes the Catwings books in his critical essay analyzing Le Guin's portrayal of the nature of home, arguing that her characters' sense of well-being and security rises from a combination of journeying, being at home in several locations, and resisting isolation. Sandra Lindow discusses Le Guin's knowledgeable handling of the experience of emotional trauma and recovery.

Le Guin's other children's stories show her trying her hand at several categories. *Leese Webster* (1979) is another animal fantasy, the story of a spider who copies the patterns of old tapestries in her webs; after being thrown out of the palace on the end of a duster, she discovers that her artistic webs look more beautiful and jeweled in their new environment. *Solomon Leviathan's Nine-Hundred and Thirty-First Trip Around the World* (1983) is a kind of beast fable; the giraffe and boa constrictor at the center of the tale are philosophers who set out on a quest to reach the horizon. They are helped on their way physically and philosophically when the whale Solomon Leviathan swallows them; the three companions discover that one of the rewards of the quest is the journey itself and the companionship one finds along the way. *A Ride on the Red Mare's Back* (1992) is a fairy tale about a young girl who heroically saves her brother from trolls by using the objects in her possession not as weapons but as gifts. All together, the books emphasize themes similar to those in Earthsea: the importance of community and of accepting responsibility for one's actions.

ANIMAL STORIES

The 1987 collection *Buffalo Gals and Other Animal Presences* mixes fantasy and science fiction, as well as poems, stories, and commentaries, and creates a context for understanding the significance in Le Guin's work of the nonhuman world. In Le Guin's view, the world of existence has no one center but many centers and modes of difference—animal, rock, plant, and human—which are also connected. Humans, alone the conscious being, have a responsibility, Le Guin writes in the introduction, to respect and protect the "continuity, interdependence, and community of all life, all forms of being on earth" (p. 11). Throughout the collection, she portrays beings in the nonhuman world who regard themselves as "people" and who use language. Metaphorically, she subverts the "myth of Civilization" that denies the value of the nonhuman world. Her pieces wittily expose the shortsightedness of species categorization, ethnocentrism, anthropomorphism, and the dualistic split of female/nature and male/culture. In fact, eye imagery leads the reader to re-vision the world of being—that and Le Guin's virtuoso performance of point of view. She invents or discovers the stories that nonhuman beings tell each other and sometimes tell humans—a basalt rock is a word from the earth; the grieving wife is a wild canine trying to reconcile her experience of a loving husband and the repulsive wereman he became; the laboratory animal is an alien who tries desperately, through elaborate maze dances, to communicate with the human scientist who sees it only as a dispensable animal too dumb to correctly complete the maze; the ant is a writer in acacia seeds who was killed for daring to find pleasure in solitude from the community. Le Guin's point of view takes the reader inside the world of the other, from which we look out at the other, which is now human.

In 1988 the title story of *Buffalo Gals and Other Animal Presences*, "Buffalo Gals, Won't You Come Out Tonight," won both the World Fantasy Best Novella and the Hugo Novelette. It concerns a young girl who is rescued by a community of totem animals after a plane crash in the Oregon desert. Coyote and blue jay replace her damaged eye with one of pine pitch, enabling the girl, Myra, to see things from two perspectives. Myra's vision of the animals who have taken her in shades from seeing animal to seeing human images, a quality wonderfully represented in the illustrated, separately published version of this story. Myra, even with the help of the new eye, can only see what her eyes can make, what she can reassemble with the aid of the senses and the imagination—she learns respect without dissolving differences. So the story is a fable of seeing as an act of making; coyote quips, "Resemblance is in the eye" (p. 31). The combination of her new eye with the old one enables Myra to free herself from conventions to embrace the imagination, and to see anew.

Karla Armbruster has approached the story from an ecofeminist perspective, and her discussion could fruitfully be applied to the entire collection. Armbruster analyzes certain ecofeminist positions that inadvertently support the very ideologies being argued against—duality (female/nature and male/culture) and hierarchy (resulting from a perception of difference that leads to a dominance/submission model of relationships). Armbruster points out that too frequently, ecofeminist essays end up endorsing a female/nature essentialism. Armbruster then demonstrates an ecofeminist reading that avoids this pitfall, revealing Le Guin's short story to be a narrative that critiques duality without upholding an essentialist position, that portrays the connectedness of all beings in the world without denying their difference.

POETRY

Throughout Le Guin's books of poetry are poems whose effect on the reader suggests that they are fantasy poems or, at least, poems that use fantastic elements. For example, a number of poems tell stories about historic, mythic, or imagined figures, sometimes using the first-person voice of the central character and often revising the story's androcentricity—Orpheus and Euridice, Saint George and the dragon, Demeter and Persephone, Eve, Medusa, Shiva, Native American women celebrating menses, Queen Isabella of Spain. Poems in the voice of or about things in nature invoke the nonhuman view of the world or contrast the human way of using the world with nature's way of being in the world—Mount Saint Helens, a glacier, a torus, gulls, the water people. The nature poems often allude to Native American mythology or Taoist imagery; sometimes the poems depict the voices of nature as female—for example, the mouth of the Klamath River or the New Mexican cloud women. Some of the longer or serial poems are imaginative responses to places and things such as the henges (sacred prehistoric sites) in Cornwall, England, a Wynn Bullock photograph, the dance ceremonies at Tillai. It is as if the poems have grown out of and into particular stories and places in which the speaker is so immersed in their presence that she can speak in their voices, with the poems sometimes becoming like incantations in Native American poetry or cryptic, meditative Taoist poems.

Of specific interest are the poems about images or events that are akin to those that appear in her Earthsea books, including the long dance, falcon, rowan tree, dragon, vetch, stones of power, land of the dead, and housekeeping. "The Well of Baln" (collected in *Hard Words,* 1981) is unique in being a narrative set in a secondary world that is sustained throughout the poem. These poems could be fruitfully studied for insights into Le Guin's sources and her exploration of certain images and events.

Patrick D. Murphy has analyzed a number of Le Guin's poems to illustrate the basic three types of fantastic poetry—"high fantasy, low fantasy, and revisionist mythopoeia." Following the French literary critic Tzvetan Todorov's classifications of fantasy literature, Murphy states that high fantasy poems are set totally in a fantasy world, low fantasy poems show the "interpenetration" of consensus reality and the fantastic, while the mythopoeic poems offer new versions of old myths or even new myths. Richard D. Erlich's analysis of the poems eschews genre classification and discusses two thematic categories: anger and Taoism, dancing and the gods.

CRITICAL DIRECTIONS

The richness of Le Guin's fantasy literature has stimulated readings by scholars from many fields; extensive critical work has been done, and further assessment is needed.

A specific challenge to Le Guin studies has been made by Donna R. White. In the introduction to her review of the scholarship on Le Guin, she points out that "criticism of Le Guin has become balkanized" (p. 2). Critics in the fields of children's literature and in science fiction—the two areas that have published most of the criticism—are usually unaware of the work in each other's field; and the growing field of ecofeminism/nature writing adds yet another field segmented off from the others. This situation means that integrated studies of Le Guin's oeuvre have not yet appeared and valuable insights from one field are ignored by another.

For example, Le Guin has been playing with double vision for some time and with the fluctuations of perspective, not only in recent fantasy stories such as "The Poacher" but also in science fiction stories such as "The Shobies' Story" (in *A Fisherman of the Inland Sea: Science Fiction Stories*, 1994), and in earlier works such as "Field of Vision" (published in *The Wind's Twelve Quarters*, 1975). In such metanarratives, she exposes the limits of and cultural damage caused by the single-minded point of view, while at the same time revealing the pleasure of the enlarged and transgressive perspective, of walking around to the backdoor, looking behind the throne, or—as in the second Earthsea series—tuning into voices such as a village witch on Gont, a housewife and dairy owner on Semel, a peasant girl from Way, a Karg princess from Hur-at-Hur, an Earthsea seamaster, a king of the Inner Lands, and a raped, burned child. What knowledge do her characters and readers bring back to consensus reality from such experiences? What are the ramifications of this experimentation in terms of narrative theory, cosmology, ethics?

In light of Le Guin's continuing publications, scholars are challenged to balance a desire to interpret Le Guin from a particular critical approach with a desire to remain faithful to the spirit of Le Guin's fantasy and the open endings of individual and serial works. Like a painter who pushes the boundaries of color, Le Guin takes her protagonists to the edge of an apotheosis where they stop short of becoming victorious or defeated, heroic or villainous, mimetic or symbolic, sentimentalized or polemicized, yet the stories still carry drama, beauty, and tension. Her stories are about change, and they begin and end with imminent changes. The protagonists are different at the end—wise but saddened, facing toward home but poised for the journey. As the Master Patterner remarks in "Dragonfly," "What goes too long unchanged destroys itself. The forest is forever because it dies and dies and so lives" (p. 254).

Like Roke's Patterner, the reader and critic must be able to see the expected patterns, the unexpected, and the disarray; for nothing holds permanently, all relationships fluctuate like Heraclitus's river—light and darkness, language and silence, ritual and abyss, male and female, self and other, life and death, action and inaction, power and responsibility.

Aspects of Le Guin's fantasy such as her humor and style have yet to be the subjects of scholarly work. Although many comment on the poetic, oral quality of Le Guin's style, extensive analyses have yet to be written—the rhythm and cadence of her sentences; the emotional weight that accrues in her dramatic scenes, allowing the closing sentences to be at once wrenching and appropriate; the discerning ease with which the details slip together to create an imaginary world.

Specifically, Le Guin's newest Earthsea books invite scholarly assessment. Among the new novellas and stories, "Dragonfly" has received the most comment from reviewers because it is a chronological and thematic bridge between *Tehanu* and *The Other Wind*; but the long opening story "The Finder" is basic to the understanding of the larger Earthsea and the protagonist's long journey may be seen as analogous to Le Guin's own into the new Earthsea of the second series.

On a larger scale, scholars must begin providing readings that examine the connections between the two Earthsea series, an activity similar to Myra's in "Buffalo Gals, Won't You Come Out Tonight" as she tries to adjust to the new pine-pitch eye that coyote has given her: "If she shut the hurting eye and looked with the other, everything was clear and flat; if she used them both, things were blurry and yellowish, but deep" (p. 28).

Selected Bibliography

WORKS OF URSULA K. LE GUIN

Listed are major U.S. editions; genre categories follow those on Le Guin's official Web site: http://www.ursulakleguin.com.

SCIENCE FICTION NOVELS AND STORIES

STORIES OF THE HAINISH

"The Dowry of Angyar." *Amazing* 38: 46–63 (September 1964). Reprinted as "Semley's Necklace" in *The Wind's Twelve Quarters*.

Rocannon's World. New York: Ace, 1966.

Planet of Exile. New York: Ace, 1966.

City of Illusions. New York: Ace, 1967.

The Left Hand of Darkness. New York: Ace, 1969.

The Dispossessed: An Ambiguous Utopia. New York: Harper and Row, 1974.

"The Word for World Is Forest." *Again, Dangerous Visions: Forty-Six Original Stories.* Edited by Harlan Ellison. Garden City, N.Y.: Doubleday, 1972.

Four Ways to Forgiveness. New York: HarperPrism, 1995.

The Telling. New York: Harcourt, 2000.

The Lathe of Heaven. New York: Scribner's, 1971.

"The New Atlantis." In *The New Atlantis and Other Novellas of Science Fiction.* Edited by Robert Silverberg. New York: Hawthorn, 1975.

"The Eye of the Heron." In *Millennial Women.* Edited by Virginia Kidd. New York: Delacorte, 1978.

Always Coming Home. Illustrations by Margaret Chodos. New York: Harper and Row, 1985. Includes cassette tape, "Music and Poetry of the Kesh." Music by Todd Barton. Words by Le Guin.

NON-SCIENCE FICTION NOVEL

Very Far Away from Anywhere Else. New York: Atheneum, 1976.

URSULA K. LE GUIN

STORIES OF ORSINIA

Orsinian Tales. New York: Harper and Row, 1976.

Malafrena. New York: Berkley, 1979.

FANTASIES

THE STORIES OF EARTHSEA

"The Word of Unbinding." *Fantastic* 13: 67–73 (January 1964). In *The Wind's Twelve Quarters.*

A Wizard of Earthsea. Berkeley: Parnassus, 1968.

The Tombs of Atuan. New York: Atheneum, 1971.

The Farthest Shore. New York: Atheneum, 1972.

Tehanu: The Last Book of Earthsea. New York: Atheneum, 1990.

"Dragonfly." In *Legends: Short Novels by the Masters of Modern Fantasy.* Edited by Robert Silverberg. New York: Tor, 1998. In *Tales from Earthsea.*

Tales from Earthsea. New York: Harcourt, 2001.

The Other Wind. New York: Harcourt, 2001.

The Beginning Place. New York: Harper and Row, 1980. Published in the United Kingdom under the title *Threshold.* (London: Gollanca, 1980.)

STORY COLLECTIONS

The Wind's Twelve Quarters. New York: Harper and Row, 1975.

The Compass Rose. New York: Harper and Row, 1982.

Buffalo Gals and Other Animal Presences. Santa Barbara, Calif.: Capra, 1987. (Single-story edition *Buffalo Gals, Won't You Come out Tonight.* Illustrated by Susan Seddon Boulet. San Francisco: Pomegranate, 1987.)

Searoad: Chronicles of Klatsand. New York: HarperCollins, 1991.

A Fisherman of the Inland Sea. New York: HarperPrism, 1994.

Unlocking the Air and Other Stories. New York: HarperCollins, 1996.

The Birthday of the World and Other Stories. New York: HarperCollins, 2002.

POETRY AND POETRY TRANSLATIONS

"Folksong from the Montayna Province." *Prairie Poet*: 75 (fall 1959).

Wild Angels. Santa Barbara, Calif.: Capra, 1974.

Walking in Cornwall: A Poem for the Solstice. 1976. (Chapbook.)

Tillai and Tylissos. With Theodora Kroeber. Saint Helena, U.K.: Red Bull Press, 1979.

Hard Words and Other Poems. New York: Harper and Row, 1981.

In the Red Zone. Illustrated by Henk Pander. Northridge, Calif.: Lord John, 1983.

Wild Oats and Fireweed: New Poems. New York: HarperPerennial, 1988.

No Boats. N.p.: Ygor and Buntho Make Books Press, 1992. (Chapbook.)

Blue Moon over Thurman Street. With Roger Dorband, photographer. Portland, Ore: New Sage 1993.

Going out with Peacocks and Other Poems. New York: HarperPerennial, 1994.

Lao Tzu: Tao Te Ching: A Book About the Way and the Power of The Way. Boston: Shambhala, 1997. (Translation.)

The Twins, The Dream: Two Voices / Las gemelas, el sueño. Houston, Tex.: Arte Publico Press, 1997. (Poems by Diana Bellessi and Ursula K. Le Guin.)

Sixty Odd: New Poems. Boston: Shambhala, 1999.

NONFICTION: ESSAYS AND CRITICISM

Review of *Jean Lemaire de Belges: Le Temple d'honneur et de vertus* edited by Henri Hornik. *Romanic Review* 49: 210–211 (October 1958).

The Language of the Night: Essays on Fantasy and Science Fiction by Ursula K. Le Guin. Edited by Susan Wood. New York: Putnam's, 1979. (Includes "From Elfland to Poughkeepsie.) (Rev. ed. without Wood. New York: HarperCollins, 1992).

Introduction to *The Book of Fantasy,* edited by Jorge Luis Borges, Silvina Ocampo, and Adolfo Bioy Casares. New York: Viking, 1988.

Dancing at the Edge of the World: Thoughts on Words, Women, Places. New York: Grove, 1989.

Steering the Craft. Portland, Ore: Eighth Mountain, 1998.

"Children, Women, Men, and Dragons." *Monad: Essays on Science Fiction* 1:3–27 (September 1990). Revised as *Earthsea Revisioned.*

Earthsea Revisioned. Cambridge: Children's Literature New England, 1993.

Introduction to *The Diaries of Adam and Eve,* by Mark Twain. New York: Oxford, 1996.

BOOKS FOR CHILDREN

Leese Webster. Illustrated by James Brunsman. New York: Atheneum, 1979.

The Adventure of Cobbler's Rune. Illustrated by Alicia Austin. New Castle, Va.: Cheap Street, 1982.

Solomon Leviathan's Nine-Hundred and Thirty-First Trip Around the World. Illustrated by Alicia Austin. New Castle, Va.: Philomel, 1983.

A Visit from Dr. Katz. Illustrated by Ann Barrow. New York: Atheneum, 1988.

Fire and Stone. Illustrated by L. Marshall. New York: Atheneum, 1989.

Fish Soup. Illustrated by Patrick Wynne. New York: Atheneum, 1992.

A Ride on the Red Mare's Back. Illustrated by Julie Downing. New York: Orchard, 1992.

Tom Mouse. Illustrated by Julie Downing. Roaring Brook, 2002.

THE CATWINGS BOOKS

Catwings. Illustrated by S. D. Schindler. New York: Orchard, 1988.

Catwings Return. Illustrated by S. D. Schindler. New York: Orchard, 1989.

Wonderful Alexander and the Catwings. Illustrated by S. D. Schindler. New York, Orchard, 1994.

Jane on Her Own. Illustrated by S. D. Schindler. New York: Orchard, 1999.

ANTHOLOGIES EDITED

Nebula Award Stories 11. New York: Harper and Row, 1977.

Interfaces. With Virginia Kidd. New York: Ace, 1980.

Edges: Thirteen Tales from the Borderlands of the Imagination. With Virginia Kidd. New York: Pocket Books, 1980.

The Norton Book of Science Fiction: North American Science Fiction, 1960–1990. With Brian Attebery and Karen Fowler. New York: Norton, 1993.

OTHER WORKS

King Dog. Santa Barbara: Capra, 1985. Screenplay in book form.

A Winter Solstice Ritual for the Pacific Northwest. With Vonda N. McIntyre. N.p.: Ygor and Buntho Make Books Press, 1991. Prose chapbook.

Findings. Browerville, Minn.: Ox Head, 1992. Prose chapbook.

The Art of Bunditsu. N.p.: Ygor and Buntho Make Books Press, 1993. Prose chapbook.

AUDIO RECORDINGS

The Ones Who Walk Away from Omelas. Read by Le Guin. New York: Alternate World Recordings, 1976. LP recording 7476.

Gwilan's Harp and Intracom. Read by Le Guin. New York: Caedmon, 1977. LP recording TC1556.

The Left Hand of Darkness. Read by Le Guin. Abridged. New York: Warner Audio, 1985. Cassette tape 2142A-2142B.

Rigel Nine: An Opera. Libretto by Le Guin. Music by David Bedford. London: Charisma, 1985.

Music and Poetry of the Kesh. Read by Le Guin. Music by Todd Barton. Ashland, Ore.: Valley Productions, 1985.

The Word for World Is Forest. Read by Laurence Ballard. Miami, Fla.: Book of the Road, 1986. Cassette tape 033.

Uses of Music in Uttermost Parts. Read by Le Guin. Music by Elinor Armer. Port Washington, N.Y.: Koch International Classics, 1996. Compact disk 3-7331-2Y6x2.

Lao Tzu's Tao Te Ching. Read by Le Guin. Musical accompaniment by Todd Barton. Boston: Shambhala Lion, 1997. Cassette tape Z033.

A Wizard Of Earthsea. Read by Le Guin and Harlan Ellison. San Bruno, Calif.: Audio Literature, 2001. Cassette tape.

BIBLIOGRAPHIES

Bratman, David S. *Ursula K. Le Guin: A Primary Bibliography.* 1995. (P.O. Box 662, Los Altos, CA 94023).

Cogell, Elizabeth Cummins. *Ursula K. Le Guin: A Primary and Secondary Bibliography.* Boston: G. K. Hall, 1983.

CRITICAL STUDIES

Armbruster, Karla. "'Buffalo Gals, Won't You Come Out Tonight': A Call for Boundary-Crossing in Ecofeminist Literary Criticism." In *Ecofeminist Literary Criticism: Theory, Interpretation, Pedagogy.* Edited by Greta Gaard and Patrick D. Murphy. Urbana: University of Illinois Press, 1998. Pp. 97–122.

Attebery, Brian. "Gender, Fantasy, and the Authority of Tradition." *Journal of the Fantastic* 7:51–60 (1996).

———. *Strategies of Fantasy.* Bloomington: Indiana University Press, 1992.

Bittner, James. *Approaches to the Fiction of Ursula K. Le Guin.* Ann Arbor, Mich.: UMI Research Press, 1984.

Cadden, Mike. "Speaking to Both Children and Genre: Le Guin's Ethics of Audience." *Lion and the Unicorn* 24:128–142 (2000).

Cameron, Eleanor. "High Fantasy: A Wizard of Earthsea." *Horn Book* 47:129–138 (April 1971).

Clute, John. "Deconstructing Paradise." *Times Literary Supplement,* December 28, 1990, p. 1409.

Collins, Robert. "A Jarring 'Postscript.'" *SFRA Newsletter* 174:45–47 (January/February 1990).

Cummins, Elizabeth. *Understanding Ursula K. Le Guin.* Columbia: University of South Carolina Press, 1990. Rev. ed. 1993.

De Bolt, Joseph, ed. *Ursula K. Le Guin: Voyage to Inner Lands and Outer Space.* Port Washington, N.Y.: Kennikat Press, 1979.

Delany, Samuel R. "About Five Thousand One Hundred and Seventy-Five Words." *SF: The Other Side of Realism—Essays on Modern Fantasy and Science Fiction.* Edited by Thomas D. Clareson. Bowling Green, Ohio: Bowling Green University Popular Press, 1971. Pp. 130–146.

Erlich, Richard D. "Coyote's Song: The Teaching Stories of Ursula K. Le Guin." Science Fiction Research Assoc. Digital Book. http://www.sfra.org.

Franko, Carol. "Acts of Attention at the Borderlands: Le Guin's *The Beginning Place* Revisited." *Extrapolation* 37:302–315 (winter 1996).

Hall, Hal. Science Fiction and Fantasy Research Database. Science Fiction Research Association Web page http//:www.sfra.org.

Hatfield, Len. "From Master to Brother: Shifting the Balance of Authority in Ursula K. Le Guin's *Farthest Shore* and *Tehanu.*" *Children's Literature* 21:43–65 (1993).

Keller, Tatiana. "Feminist Issues in Earthsea." *New York Review of Science Fiction* 28:14–16 (April 1991).

Lindow, Sandra. "Trauma and Recovery in Ursula K. Le Guin's *Wonderful Alexander*: Animal as Guide Through the Inner Space of the Unconscious." Foundation 70:32–38 (summer 1997).

Littlefield, Holly. "Unlearning Patriarchy: Ursula Le Guin's Feminist Consciousness in *The Tombs of Atuan* and *Tehanu.*" *Extrapolation* 16:244–258 (fall 1995).

Manlove, C. N. "Conservatism in the Fantasy of Le Guin." *Extrapolation* 21:287–297 (fall 1980).

McLean, Susan. "The Power of Women in Ursula K. Le Guin's *Tehanu.*" *Extrapolation* 38:110–118 (summer 1997).

Murphy, Patrick D. "The Left Hand of Fabulation: The Poetry of Ursula K. Le Guin." *The Poetic Fantastic: Studies in an Evolving Genre.* Edited by Patrick D. Murphy and Vernon Hyles. New York: Greenwood, 1989. Pp. 13–36.

Nodelman, Perry. "Reinventing the Past: Gender in Ursula K. Le Guin's *Tehanu* and the

Earthsea 'Trilogy.'" *Children's Literature* 23:179–201 (1995).

Olander, Joseph D., and Martin H. Greenberg, eds. *Ursula K. Le Guin.* New York: Taplinger, 1979.

Payne, Tonia L. "'A Heart that Watches and Receives': Ursula K. Le Guin and the American Nature-Writing Tradition." Diss. The City University of New York, 1999.

Rochelle, Warren G. *Communities of the Heart: The Rhetoric of Myth in the Fiction of Ursula K. Le Guin.* Liverpool, UK: Liverpool University Press, 2001.

Senior, W. A. "Cultural Anthropology and Rituals of Exchange in Ursula K. Le Guin's 'Earthsea.'" *Mosaic* 29:101–113 (December 1996).

Shippey, T.A. "The Magic Art and the Evolution of Words: Ursula Le Guin's Earthsea Trilogy." *Mosaic* 10:147–163 (winter 1977).

Slusser, George Edgar. *The Farthest Shores of Ursula K. Le Guin.* San Bernardino, Calif.: Borgo Press, 1976.

Spivack, Charlotte. *Ursula K. Le Guin.* Boston: Twayne, 1984.

Suvin, Darko, ed. "The Science Fiction of Ursula K. Le Guin." Special issue of *Science-Fiction Studies* 2 (March 1976).

Tavormina, M. Teresa. "A Gate of Horn and Ivory: Dreaming True and False in Earthsea." *Extrapolation* 29:338–348 (winter 1988).

White, Donna R. *Dancing with Dragons: Ursula K. Le Guin and the Critics.* Columbia, S.C.: Camden House, 1999.

Yoke, Carl. "Special Ursula K. Le Guin Issue." *Extrapolation* 21 (fall 1980).

INTERVIEWS

Gevers, Nick. "Driven By a Different Chauffeur: An Interview with Ursula K. Le Guin." SF Site. http://www.sfsite.com/03a/ul123.htm.

Greenland, Colin. "Doing Two Things in Opposite Directions." *Interzone,* March 1991, pp. 58–61.

Heideman, Eric M. "An Interview With Ursula K. Le Guin." *Tales of the Unanticipated: A Magazine of the Minnesota Science Fiction Society,* Fall/Winter/Spring 1997–1998, pp. 32–36.

"Ursula K. Le Guin: Not the Establishment." *Locus,* November 1988, pp. 5, 68.

"Ursula K. Le Guin: Return to Earthsea." *Locus,* September 2001, pp. 4–5, 83–84.

"Ursula K. Le Guin: The Last Book of Earthsea." *Locus,* January 1990, p. 5.

Shuey, Scott. "Otherworldly Lecturer." *Spartan Daily* (San Jose State University), 18 April 2000. http://www.spartandaily.org/2news.

White, Jonathan. "Coming Back from the Silence." *Talking on the Water: Conversations about Nature and Creativity.* San Francisco: Sierra Club, 1994. Pp.98–120.

Tanith Lee
1947–

JESSICA REISMAN

SINCE HER FIRST publications in the early 1970s, Tanith Lee has amassed a distinctive body of work. Lee's stories and novels are richly imagined and textured, her writing intelligent, trenchant, and evocative. She has a large readership and is critically well respected, garnering comparisons to such writers as Angela Carter, Oscar Wilde, A. S. Byatt, and Clark Ashton Smith.

Born in London on September 19, 1947, to Bernard and Hylda (Moore) Lee, both ballroom dancers, Lee married John Kaiine, a writer and artist, in 1992 and lives with him in the south of England. She began to write at the age of nine—a fact which is impressive because she did not learn to read until she was nearly eight. Her mother, however, told her stories, many of them fairy tales and fantastic legends that she made up herself. It was her father, Bernard Lee, who finally taught his daughter to read. Once she had the tools, written language came naturally. Asked when she discovered she wanted to write, Lee has said, "How could I discover I was going to be a writer? I *was* a writer. This was my function, clearly demonstrated" (Haut, p. 192).

Lee attended a number of schools in the course of her education, completed at age seventeen. Thereafter she worked at a variety of jobs, from waitress to library assistant. A year at art college when she was twenty-five only reaffirmed that words, not pictures, were her primary passion—though Lee has done illustrations for her stories, some of which have been included as frontispieces to her books. Her first professional sale was in 1968, a brief vignette that appeared in *The Ninth Pan Book of Horror Stories*. She wrote a number of children's stories that were purchased but never actually published because of the publishing firm's financial difficulties. In 1971, Macmillan published her children's novel *The Dragon Hoard*, then two books in 1972, also for children, the picture book *Animal Castle* and a short-story collection, *Princess Hynchatti & Some Other Surprises*.

Meanwhile, her adult fantasy novel, *The Birthgrave*, could not find a home among British publishers. Lee wrote a query letter to the American publishing house DAW Books, which published *The Birthgrave* in 1975. This was the beginning of a relationship that lasted until 1989 and yielded twenty-eight books. In 1976 she was able to become a full-time writer. For that opportunity, or what she describes as "the escape into professional writing and out of the so-called 'real world' that crushes so many of the good and the talented" (Haut, p. 194), she has expressed lasting gratitude.

A prolific writer, Lee has produced two or more books and multiple short stories nearly every year since. Her writing habits follow the dictate of whatever story she is working on. She professes to sometimes work all night, or all day, powering through 150 pages in a month, then becoming stuck on one page for weeks. She dislikes genre designations, and much of her work does either blur or transcend the bounds of fantasy, horror, and science fiction.

Her work has been nominated for the World and British fantasy awards (the latter also known as the August Derleth Award) and a number of Nebulas. In 1980, *Death's Master* was named as British Fantasy Society Best Novel, in 1983 "The Gorgon" was named World Fantasy Best Short Story, and in 1984 "Elle est Trois (La Mort)" won the same award. Also in 1984 she received the SF Chronicle Achievement Award.

***

What is most often noted of Lee is her exquisite prose—elegant, lush, and ironic by turns—along with her insight into the human and the magical. She has garnered a great deal of critical praise, as well as her share of less glowing criticism. Critics appear to agree, whether they find a particular book praiseworthy or not, that Lee is an extremely talented writer whose gifts have only gained power over the years. She has been described as "goddess empress of the hot read and princess royal of heroic fantasy," (Peter Stampfel, *Voice Literary Supplement*) and "a master of the art of storytelling" (Jane Yolen, *Women as Demons,* back cover copy). Her writing is recognized for its lyrical evocation of other worlds and alternate histories and for the depth and complexity of her characters. "Her prose," Michael Swanwick has said, "practically shimmers on the page."

When Lee's style and subject matter do not work, her stories can become perhaps too challenging, with prose composed of literary and mythic reference, rampant metaphor, and simile. Following the separate descents of several characters to madness through the labyrinthine prose in *The Book of the Mad* (1993) leaves some readers dissatisfied. On occasion her characters, particularly some female characters, such as Vivia in the book of the same name, Rachaela, for most of the Blood Opera sequence, and Arpazia of *White as Snow,* can seem so morbidly passive that they feel cold, and readers find it difficult to sympathize with them and care about their story.

Although Lee's province is that of the imagination, and her tales contain much magic and wonder, her adult work is by no means light or frivolous; most of it is quite dark. There is a sharply ironic wit and insight at work in even her most fantastic tales. The characters in her stories are frankly sexual and her writing highly sensual. Ambiguities, the bizarre, the morbid, and the ecstatic are encountered and embodied by her protagonists, whether they are gods, demons, or humans. Lee's work embraces the arcane, the gruesome, the religious and spiritual, revenge, sexuality in all its permutations, love and passion, madness, and great suffering. Her recurring themes include the nature of good and evil; the different powers that lie in love, lust, and passion; and the transformation of the self. Eastern beliefs of reincarnation particularly inform her work, diffused throughout stories that have no overt connection to Eastern traditions. The cycle of life and lives, the immortality of the soul, and the crucible of mortal toils are clearly preoccupations of Lee's. Multiple transformations of identity and gender, as well as physical and spiritual alterations, are to be found in most of her stories. In the Flat Earth series, the demon Azhrarn sacrifices himself to save humanity and is reborn to a human woman; his daughter is known by several different names and identities in the course of her life as an immortal and a mortal. In "Stained with Crimson" from the *Book of the Damned* (1989), Andre St. Jean begins as a man and ends as a woman, Anna

Sanjeanne. A soul about to be born in "Under the Hand of Chance" experiences life as a boy and then as a girl, knowing longing, suffering, and revelation before it is stillborn and must await another chance.

Lee incorporates the myth, legend, and religions of many cultures and civilizations, from pagan, Egyptian, and Greek to Christianity and Renaissance Italy. She takes from any place or time in history that serves her story, often creating alternate, parallel historical periods.

Common among Lee's characters is an eccentricity or perversity of spirit—sometimes physically expressed—which sets them at odds with the world they inhabit. Whether it is the demon lord Azhrarn, Raldnor or Rem of *The Storm Lord* books, Volpa of *Saint Fire*, the reluctant film goddess of the story "Oh, Shining Star," or one of Lee's several shape-changing lycanthropes—to name a small fraction of a large and varied cast—Lee's characters struggle, transform, wound, and are wounded in their journeys, which are typically journeys of self-discovery and self-fulfillment. Her characters are by and large damaged personalities and souls adrift within their own lives.

The combined settings of Lee's work are an endless map of the imagination. Her cities, hovels, palaces, landscapes, and underworlds are vividly imagined and depicted, whether grimly horrific or fantastically beautiful. Response to her stories set in India (*Tamastara*, 1984, and *Elephantasm*, 1993), for example, often assumes she must have traveled there, given the power with which she describes the land and people. Rather than having traveled to India, however, Lee read books and saw movies. She has said in interviews that when she can't see something clearly enough, she shuts her eyes to see it more clearly and no longer feels as if she's merely writing, but as if she's there. For example, a brief line from *Anackire* (1983) conjures the reawakening of an ancient city: "The lives in the city's arid bones flickered like the wings of moths" (in *The Wars of Vis*, p. 663). From "The Demoness" (1976):

> Two hundred pillars upheld the roof in the king's great hall, pillars carved like trees of green marble. Fountains played and pools lay clear as glass, and white birds fluted in the gardens where round fruits grew in clusters under the yellow sky. This was Krennok-dol. At the great gate of bronze hung a bell the size of a warrior, with a tongue the size of a girl-child ten years old.
>
> (in *Women as Demons,* p. 6)

And from *Faces Under Water* (1998):

> "The canal turned, and they came out into wider water. On either side, the dim, dark houses rose, peeling like dying flowers. Iron balconies hung over their heads like empty cages of enormous birds. A lamp burned, one solitary pink ember."
>
> (p. 14)

Lee works comfortably and intimately within a scale of multiple eras or inside the compass of one period of a character's life—though the scope of that life may include such depths and convolutions of mind, spirit, and alternate dimensions that the objective notion of time is rendered fully subjective. A collection of her short fiction often stretches from past to future, treating myth, religion, and technology, most often in terms of their impact upon and involvement with her characters.

The novellas and novels in two of her series, The Secret Books of Paradys and The Secret Books of Venus, collect wide-ranging tales under the umbrella of their locations, an alternate Paris and an alternate Venice. Divided as the books of the mad, the damned, the beast, and the dead (Paradys), and as water, fire, earth, and air, the elements of alchemy (Venus), both series move around freely in time and dimension. Similarly, the stories in The Tales from the Flat Earth sequence roam though many generations of human life in the footsteps of immortal demons: wickedness, death, madness, destiny, and love. Lee's authorial voice in these tales is like Scheherazade's, taking the reader deep into the epic tale with an intimate and attentive intonation.

***

A selective overview of Lee's novels and short-story collections reveals her recurring themes and preoccupations. Her young adult books generally feature a young protagonist who is a misfit in his or her world. *The Dragon Hoard* (1971) plays on many fairy-tale traditions while telling a funny, highly original tale of its own. *Companions on the Road* (1975), *The Winter Players* (1976), *East of Midnight* (1977), and *Shon the Taken* (1979) all narrate the struggles of youthful characters in difficult, dangerous worlds.

In *Prince on a White Horse* (1982), one of Lee's lightest fantasies, a prince and a white horse find themselves questing to rid the world of the frightful Nulgrave—of whom everyone is afraid, though no one is sure why. The horse talks, largely to insist that horses can't talk, and the prince, in classic Lee fashion, can't remember who he is. This coupling of protagonist with pet-as-familiar recurs regularly in both her adult and young adult work. *Black Unicorn* (1991), *Gold Unicorn* (1994), and *Red Unicorn* (1997) feature Tanaquil and her pet peeve, a furry desert beast. Tanaquil, the daughter of a powerful sorceress, has no magic, only the ability to mend anything. The unicorn in each book acts as, or leads Tanaquil to, a door between worlds. In the first book she travels to a perfect, heavenly world, the second a hellish one, and the third an alternate version of her own world. These are fairly dark, uncompromising books, though leavened with comic relief via the peeve. In the first volume Tanaquil discovers her father, a remote and unfeeling king in the city, and her half-sister, whose loneliness equals Tanaquil's own. In the second book, an empress known as the Conqueror and the Child-Eater turns out to be the same lonely half-sister, with whom she's lost touch. Tanaquil is one of Lee's more spirited and engaging protagonists.

The Claidi Journals, *Law of the Wolf Tower* (1998), *Wolf Star Rise* (2000), and *Queen of the Wolves* (2001) also have an engaging female protagonist in Claidi. Her world, too, is a difficult one, fraught with struggle, magic, intrigue, and secrets. *Voyage of the Basset: Islands in the Sky* (1999) features another strong-willed and appealing protagonist in Hope Glover, a house servant in 1867 London who sails out of the mundane world on the *Basset,* a ship that plies the waters, and skies, of the imagination.

The themes in Lee's young adult work appear with much greater intensity in her adult work. *The Birthgrave* (1977) follows a woman who wakes from a mysterious, deathlike sleep in the center of an active volcano without knowledge of who she is or what she is capable of. Her journey through the ruined cities and decadence of a violent and barbaric world is compellingly told. *Vazkor, Son of Vazkor* (1978) and *Quest for the White Witch* (1978) continue the journey with the original character's son, who inherits her strange powers and his father's hatred of her heritage, that of the Old Race. The land where the Birthgrave trilogy unfolds is ancient and legend-haunted. The quest for identity, love, vengeance, and the coming of wisdom that plays out there represents themes that recur in much of Lee's work.

The Book of the Beast (1988), the second volume of The Secret Books of Paradys, is comprised of nine linked stories. The narratives move backward and forward in time, from the Roman beginnings of Paradys as Par Dis to the later period of the opening story in which a young scholar receives an ancient curse through his tryst with Helise, the strange, sexually hypnotic woman haunting his lodgings. The curse infects Raoulin with a demon beast, bird-headed and scaled. As the beast, ravenous, malevolent, and immune to seemingly all methods of destruction, Raoulin is doomed to prey upon the streets of the city. Subsequent stories weave through time, detailing the origins of the beast, Helise's own story, and the beast's passage through other lives, including that of a Jewish scholar and his daughter who attempt to vanquish the curse through the use of Jewish mysticism.

In *Reigning Cats and Dogs* (1995), set in an alternate Victorian London, a giant demon hound is summoned to the city through chance and the work of a secret society that worships Anubis and wishes to cleanse the city of the filthy and unfit—the prostitutes and beggars, the poor and unfortunate. Saul, a man damaged by his brutal childhood, and Grace, a prostitute with an innate gift of healing, are the two protagonists. Cats and dogs move through the streets of the grim city, embodying the best and worst of our own animal natures as a duel between Bast and Anubis—love and hate, compassion and brute power—unfolds.

Both *Lycanthia* (1981) and *Heart-Beast* (1992) also center around the emergence of a beast. The creature of *Heart-Beast*, so brutal and supernaturally inviolate that it turns whole ships and households into ghost dwellings, is seeded in an act of patricide and catalyzed by a cursed, tomb-pilfered gem. The beasts of *Lycanthia* are more traditional wolves, in a novel both erotic and strongly sexual in its depiction of an ancient strain of feral passion meeting a modern hero and finding, in the end, his passion somewhat wanting:

> If he had achieved that mysterious trinity with these two supernatural beings, a power and a sorcery would indeed have come to them, to all three. . . . That the power did not come to him, some unimaginable force far greater and more malefic than the minor spasm of the hailstorm, had proved to the village that there was, in fact, nothing to fear. . . . One other thing it had established, the thing for which both of them, though not deigning to voice it, condemned and disdained him. Though he had shared so much with them, their moods, their activities, their love, he had not actually loved them. He had not actually been capable of oneness with them, or had not been prepared to be.
>
> (p. 218)

As in *Heart-Beast*, a mysterious gem also works upon the character of Sabella in the novel of the same name. Though set in a nominally science-fictional universe—Sabella lives on Novo Mars—*Sabella;, or, The Blood Stone* (1980) is a horror story. The gem turns Sabella into a vampire, though one who is very much alive. In *Kill the Dead* (1980) the dead are also very much alive, requiring the services of ghost killer Parl Dro, a figure as much reviled as needed.

The Blood of Roses (1990) centers around mysteries of blood, vampirism, destiny, and life after death. Set in a medieval forest, rife with forest lords, witches, and Christian priests whose power is of questionable virtue, it follows the fortunes of a young man marked from childhood by a black mothlike creature that drank from his throat. In *Vivia* (1995), a young woman prays to what she believes is an ancient god in the cave shrine beneath her father's rough castle and finds instead a dark power in the form of a shadowy prince who imbues her, through blood and seduction, with eternal life.

The most prominent of the handful of Lee's contemporary fantasies, the Blood Opera books, *Dark Dance* (1992), *Personal Darkness* (1993) and *Darkness, I* (1994), are about the Scarabae, an ancient clan of vampires, as seen through the eyes of their most recent offspring, Rachaela and her daughters, the homicidal Ruth and the luminous Anna. Blending Gothic horror with Egyptian and biblical mythology, the novels are replete with incest, brutal murder, child brides, and recurring souls, unfolding in refined and moody prose which, by virtue of Lee's ironic touch, avoids melodrama.

The serpent goddess of *The Storm Lord* (1977), *Anackire*, and *The White Serpent* (1988) recurs in various lives, moving through individuals and their passions and moving the wars and history of several civilizations. Lee works off of a central concept of a number of religions here; as expressed in the voice of one of the goddess's priests: "Anackire is the symbol. The externalization of the Power inside us all. The face we put on beauty and strength and love and harmony. As writing is the cipher for a sound we only hear" (*The Wars of Vis*, p. 551).

Works such as *Sung in Shadow* (1983), *White as Snow* (2000), and the stories in the collection *Red as Blood, or Tales from the Sisters Grimmer* (1983), take familiar stories—fairy tales or, in the case of *Sung in Shadow*, Shakespeare's *Romeo and Juliet*—and turn them inside out, shedding illumination through their dark and unexplored facets and finding new ways to know them. In the alternate Renaissance Italy of *Sung in Shadow*, where spells, witchcraft, and the Devil are quite real, the tale of Romeo and Juliet plays out as something of a threesome among Romulan, Iuletta, and Mercurio. *White as Snow* finds the myth of Demeter and Persephone in the bones of "Snow White" and produces a dark tale of war, rape, witchcraft, pagan forest ritual, sacrifice, and rebirth told from the perspective of the wicked stepmother—in this case neither clearly wicked nor a stepmother. The title story of *Red as Blood* presents another reinterpretation of "Snow White" in which the stepmother is actually an innocent and the stepdaughter a vampiric evil.

Among Lee's other story collections are *Cyrion* (1982), a series of stories about a mythic figure who appears here and there in various corners and cities of an *Arabian Nights* landscape, encountering the peculiar and mysterious as a swordsman, a sorcerer, and a kind of supernatural detective; *The Gorgon and Other Beastly Tales* (1985), a collection of anecdotes chronicling a variety of beasts; and *Women as Demons: The Male Perception of Women Through Space and Time* (1989), a set of stories examining the nature of relationships between men and women—with particular emphasis on the women, as femmes fatales, witches, the vengeful, the demonic, and the heroic.

Lee's science fiction should be mentioned with her fantasy and horror because it is, almost uniformly, fiction set in futures and science-fictional worlds so advanced that the technology functions like magic for the characters. Wonders abound, though they no more fix the woes or render the struggles of the characters simple than do the sorcery, demons, and gods of Lee's other work. Quite the opposite, in fact; technology becomes a godlike manifestation of the supernatural that challenges the humanity of the protagonists and with which they must contend in order to find themselves, realize love, or be free. Lee has also written radio plays broadcast by the BBC and two episodes of the BBC science fiction television series *Blake's 7*.

Lee is first and foremost a storyteller. Her fiction, deeply imagined, written in beautiful, acutely rendered prose, manages to be eloquent and lush, lyrical and ironic, lucid and bizarre together. She seems to be guaranteed a lasting place in literature as well as on the bookshelves of contemporary readers of supernatural fiction.

Selected Bibliography

WORKS OF TANITH LEE

FANTASY AND HORROR

The Birthgrave. New York: DAW, 1975; London: Futura, 1977.
The Storm Lord. New York: DAW, 1976; London: Futura, 1977.
Volkhavaar. New York: DAW, 1977; London: Hamlyn, 1981.

TANITH LEE

Night's Master. New York: DAW, 1978; London: Hamlyn, 1981.

Vazkor, Son of Vazkor. New York: DAW, 1978. Published in the U.K. as *Shadowfire*. London: Futura, 1979.

Quest for the White Witch. New York: DAW, 1978; London: Futura, 1979.

Death's Master. New York: DAW, 1979; London: Hamlyn, 1982.

Kill the Dead. New York: DAW, 1980; London: Legend, 1990.

Sabella; or, The Blood Stone. New York: DAW, 1980; London, Unwin, 1987.

Delusion's Master. New York: DAW, 1981; London: Arrow, 1990.

Lycanthia; or, the Children of Wolves. New York: DAW, 1981; London: Legend, 1990.

Cyrion. New York: DAW, 1982.

Red as Blood; or, Tales from the Sisters Grimmer. New York: DAW, 1983.

Sung in Shadow. New York: DAW, 1983; London: Futura, 1985.

Anackire. New York: DAW, 1983; London: Futura, 1985.

The Beautiful Biting Machine. New Castle, U.K.: Cheap Street, 1984. (Limited edition of 127 copies.)

Tamastara; or, The Indian Nights. New York: DAW, 1984.

The Wars of Vis. Garden City, N.Y.: Doubleday, 1984. (Omnibus edition of *The Storm Lord* and *Anackire*.)

Night Visions 1. Niles, Ill.: Dark Harvest, 1984. (Limited edition reissued as *Night Visions: In The Blood*. New York: Berkley Books, 1988.)

The Gorgon and Other Beastly Tales. New York: DAW, 1985.

Delirium's Mistress: A Novel of the Flat Earth. New York: DAW, 1986; London: Arrow, 1987.

Night's Sorceries: A Book of the Flat Earth. New York: DAW, 1987; London: Legend, 1988.

The White Serpent: A Novel of Vis. New York: DAW, 1988.

The Book of the Damned. London: Unwin, 1988. New York: Overlook Press, 1990.

The Book of the Beast. London: Unwin, 1988. New York: Overlook Press, 1991.

Madame Two Swords. West Kingston, U.K.: Donald M. Grant, 1988. (Limited edition of 600 copies.)

Women as Demons: The Male Perception of Women Through Space and Time. London: The Women's Press, 1989.

Forests of the Night. London: Unwin, 1989.

A Heroine of the World. New York: DAW, 1989. London: Headline, 1995.

The Blood of Roses. London: Legend, 1990. (Trade edition preceded by limited edition of 200 in the same year.)

Into Gold. Eugene, Ore.: Pulphouse, 1991.

The Book of the Dead. Woodstock, N.Y.: Overlook Press, 1991.

Dark Dance. London: Macdonald, 1992; New York: Dell, 1992.

Heart-Beast. London: Headline, 1992; New York: Dell, 1993.

Personal Darkness. London: Little, Brown, 1993; New York: Dell, 1994.

Elephantasm. London: Headline, 1993; New York: Dell, 1996.

The Book of the Mad. Woodstock, N.Y.: Overlook Press, 1993.

Nightshades: Thirteen Journeys into Darkness. London: Headline, 1993.

Darkness, I. London: Little, Brown, 1994; New York: St. Martin's Press, 1995.

Vivia. London: Little, Brown, 1995; London: Warner Books, 1997.

Reigning Cats and Dogs. London: Headline, 1995.

When the Lights Go Out. London: Headline Feature, 1996.

Louisa the Poisoner. Berkeley Heights, New Jersey: Wildside Press, 1996.

Faces Under Water. Woodstock, N.Y.: Overlook Press, 1998.

Saint Fire. Woodstock, N.Y.: Overlook Press, 1999.

White as Snow. New York: Tor, 2000.

A Bed of Earth. Woodstock, N.Y.: Overlook Press, 2002.

YOUNG ADULT FANTASY

The Dragon Hoard. London: Macmillan, 1971; New York: Tempo, 1984.

Companions on the Road. London: Macmillan, 1975.

The Winter Players. London: Macmillan, 1976.

East of Midnight. London: Macmillan, 1977; New York: St. Martin's Press, 1978.

The Castle of Dark. London: Macmillan, 1978.

Shon the Taken. London: Macmillan, 1979.

Black Unicorn. New York: Atheneum, 1991; London: Orbit, 1994.

Gold Unicorn. New York: Atheneum, 1994; London: Orbit, 1995.

Red Unicorn. New York: Tor, 1997.

Law of the Wolf Tower. London: Hodder, 1998; New York: Dutton, 2000.

Voyage of the Basset: Islands in the Sky. New York: Random House, 1999.

Wolf Star Rise. London: Hodder, 2000. Published in the United States as *Wolf Star.* New York: Dutton, 2001.

Queen of the Wolves. London: Hodder, 2001. Published in the United States as *Wolf Queen.* New York: Dutton, 2002.

SCIENCE FICTION

Don't Bite the Sun. New York: DAW, 1976.

Drinking Sapphire Wine. New York: DAW, 1977. London: Hamlyn, 1979.

Electric Forest. New York: DAW, 1979; London, Hamlyn, 1983.

Day by Night. New York: DAW, 1980.

The Silver Metal Lover. Garden City, N.Y.: Doubleday, 1981.

Days of Grass. New York: DAW, 1985.

Eva Fairdeath. London: Headline, 1994.

OTHER WORKS

Unsilent Night. Cambridge, Mass.: The NESFA Press, 1981. (Poetry and short fiction published in conjunction with Tanith Lee's appearance as guest of honor at Boskone XVIII.)

Dreams of Dark and Light: The Great Short Fiction Of Tanith Lee. Sauk City, Wis.: Arkham House, 1986. (Retrospective collection.)

The Gods Are Thirsty. Woodstock, N.Y.: The Overlook Press, 1996. (Historical novel.)

TELEVISION AND RADIO

Bitter Gate. BBC Radio, *The Monday Play,* June 20, 1977.

Red Wine. BBC Radio, *Thirty-Minute Theatre,* December 3, 1977.

Death Is King. BBC Radio, *The Monday Play,* September 17, 1979.

"Sarcophagus." *Blake's 7*. March 3, 1980.

The Silver Sky. BBC Radio, *Saturday Night Theatre,* August 9, 1980.

"Sand." *Blake's 7*. November 23, 1981.

BIBLIOGRAPHIES

Ashley, Mike. "The Tanith Lee Bibliography." *Fantasy Macabre,* November 4, 1983, pp. 27–36.

Pattison, Jim, and Paul A. Soanes. *Daughter of the Night: An Annotated Tanith Lee Bibliography*. Toronto: Gaffa Press, 1993.

"Tanith Lee: A Selected Bibliography." *Weird Tales,* Summer 1988, p. 45.

CRITICAL STUDIES

Brown, Charles N., ed. "The Many Faces of Tanith Lee," *Locus,* November 1983, p. 4.

Chauvette, Cathy. "Tanith Lee," *Twentieth-Century Science-Fiction Writers*. 3d edition. Edited by Noelle Watson and Paul E. Schellinger. Chicago and London: St. James Press: 1991. Pp. 473–474.

Clute, John. "Tanith Lee," *The Science Fiction Encyclopedia*. Garden City, N.Y.: Doubleday, 1979. Edited by Peter Nicholls. P. 345.

Clute, John. "Tanith Lee," *The Encyclopedia Of Fantasy*. London: Orbit, 1997; New York: St. Martin's Press, 1997. Edited by John Clute and John Grant. Pp. 568–570.

Cowperthwaite, David, ed. *Tanith Lee: Mistress Of Delirium*. Stockport, U.K.: British Fantasy Society, 1993.

De Lint, Charles, ed. "A Celebration Of Tanith Lee." *Dragonfields,* 4:12–25 (1983).

Gasser, Larry W. "Feminism and Tanith Lee's *The Birthgrave.*" *Harbringer,* Spring 1976, pp. 5–7.

Gordon, Joan. "Tanith Lee," *The New Encyclopedia of SF*. New York: Viking, 1988. Edited by James Gunn. Pp. 268–269.

Hardesty, W. H., 3d. "Birthgrave Trilogy." *Survey of Modern Fantasy Literature*. Vol. 1. Englewood Cliffs, N.J.: Salem Press, 1983. Edited by Frank N. Magill. Pp. 116–121.

———. "Volkhavaar." *Survey of Modern Fantasy Literature*. Vol. 4. New Jersey: Salem Press, 1983. Edited by Frank N. Magill. Pp. 2036–2038.

Haut, Mavis. *The Hidden Library of Tanith Lee: Themes and Subtexts from Dionysos to the Immortal Gene*. Jefferson, N.C., and London: McFarland and Company, 2001.

Hearne, Betsy. *Beauty and the Beast: Visions and Revisions of an Old Tale*. Chicago: University of Chicago Press, 1989.

Heldreth, Lillian M. "Tanith Lee's Werewolves Within: Reversals of Gothic Tradition."

Journals of the Fantastic in the Arts, Spring 1989, pp. 15–24.

Larbalestier, Justine. *Opulent Darkness: The Werewolves of Tanith Lee.* New Lambton, N.S.W.: Nimrod Publications, 1999.

Lefanu, Sarah. "Robots and Romance: The Science Fiction and Fantasy of Tanith Lee." In *Sweet Dreams: Sexuality, Gender And Science Fiction.* Edited by Susannah Radstone. London: Lawrence and Wishart, 1988.

Perdone, Kitty. "Blood Sisters." *Midnight Graffiti,* Fall 1989, pp. 46–50.

Smith, Jeanette C. "The Heroine Within: Psychological Archetypes in Tanith Lee's *A Heroine of the World.*" *Extrapolation,* 39:52–56 (1998).

Strickland, Barbara. "From Fantasy to the French Revolution: Tanith Lee's Adventure." *Austin Chronicle,* May 16, 1997, p. 40.

Tymn, Marshall B., Kenneth J Zahorski, and Robert H. Boyer. *Fantasy Literature: A Core Collection and Reference Guide.* New York: Bowker, 1979.

INTERVIEWS

Brown, Charles N., ed. "Tanith Lee: Love & Death & Publishers." *Locus,* April 1998, pp. 4–5, 76.

Garratt, Peter. "Unstoppable Fate: Tanith Lee Interview." *Interzone* 64, October 1992, pp. 23–25.

Nicholls, Stan. "Letting Go of the Here and Now: Tanith Lee Interview." *Fear,* October 1989. Reprinted as "Tanith Lee Has an Art Deco Radio Box in Her Head." In Nicholls's *Wordsmiths of Wonder: Fifty Interviews with Writers of the Fantastic.* London: Orbit, 1993.

Raley, William G., ed. "Coffee Shop: An Interview with Tanith Lee." *After Hours,* Winter 1995, pp. 42–43.

Fritz Leiber
1910–1992

BRIAN STABLEFORD

FRITZ REUTER LEIBER Jr. was born in Chicago on Christmas Eve, 1910. His parents, Fritz and Virginia (Bronson) Leiber, both actors, were then with Robert Mantell's Shakespearean Repertory Company. Although Fritz Leiber Sr. built a bungalow in Atlantic Highlands, New Jersey, to serve as a family home in the summer of 1912, Leiber spent much of his infancy on tour. The experience left an indelible impression on him. He developed, as might be expected, a keen appreciation of the magic of the theater and the necessity of fantasy as a component of life, but when he looked back on the experience in one of his autobiographical memoirs, "Not Much Disorder and Not So Early Sex," he stressed that he was "born into the backstage world" where he could observe "the mechanics of illusion and illusioning" (in *The Ghost Light*, p. 261). He saw far more rehearsals than performances and was never in doubt as to the effort and cost of fantastic production.

Before attending school Leiber was thoroughly familiar with the leading parts in Shakespeare's major tragedies, and the internalization of these roles was the foundation on which he built his prose style. They also influenced his worldview, which never overestimated the human capacity to withstand disaster. "If I have faith in anything in this world," he wrote in the same memoir, "it's in Fantasy and Mystery, [but] it's by no means a certain faith; it has an element of desperation and lost cause about it" (p. 273).

When the time came for Leiber to go to school he was initially lodged with his maternal grandmother, Flora Bronson, in Pontiac, Illinois, but was sent at the age of seven to live with two of his father's sisters in Chicago. He survived the great influenza epidemic of 1918, but it left a legacy of ill health that afflicted him every winter for many years thereafter. He developed a strong interest in science, but as he passed through the education system the focus of his fascination moved from the hard to the soft end of the scientific spectrum—"a quaintly precise trending from the material to the insubstantial," as he put it in another of his autobiographical essays, "Fafhrd and Me" (in *Second Book of Fritz Leiber*, p. 96). During his years at the University of Chicago he broadened his interests even more. Although his personal philosophy was relatively radical, embracing pacifism and progressive liberalism, he spent some time at a theological seminary in New York after his graduation before returning briefly to graduate study in Chicago. While he was still at the university he tried to follow in his father's footsteps by taking parts in productions by Fritz Sr.'s final touring company, but when the Depression killed the company and Fritz Sr. retreated to Hollywood, he began looking in other directions for artistic expression and financial support.

EARLY CAREER

At the University of Chicago, Leiber became friends with fellow chess player, Franklin MacKnight, who was also a devotee of fantastic fiction. MacKnight introduced him to Harry Otto Fischer (1910–1986), a student at the University of Louisville with similar interests, who also had a serious ambition to write. The subsequent correspondence between Leiber and Fischer became the locus of numerous imaginative experiments, of which by far the most important was the invention of two fantastic alter egos, the Gray Mouser (modeled on the diminutive Fischer) and Fafhrd (modeled on the six feet, five inch Leiber). These characters inhabited a fabulous parallel world syncretically compounded out of various ancient mythologies, called Nehwon, and were based in the city of Lankhmar. Lankhmar began as "the city of the Tuatha De Danann" (Celtic migrants to Ireland), but its Celtic elements were soon merged with Mediterranean influences, and its roots were submerged when it began a remarkable evolution of its own. For some time, however, Leiber and Fischer's adventures in what Leiber called "sword and sorcery" fiction remained a private matter. Leiber's first publications—collected much later in the chapbook *In the Beginning* (1983)—were of a very different kind, produced during his brief flirtation with theological studies for the small-press publication *The Churchman*, where they appeared in 1934–1935.

Harry Fischer married the artist and puppeteer Martha McElroy in 1935, and she began to supply Nehwon with a visual dimension. Leiber married the Welsh poet Jonquil Stephens soon after meeting her in January 1936; she was even smaller than Fischer, and elements of her character almost certainly seeped into the Gray Mouser, although the Mouser always remained assertively masculine. Leiber's hope that he might be able to provide an income by professional writing was soon dashed; the novella about Fafhrd and the Mouser that he was working on at the time, "Adept's Gambit," failed to find a publisher, and a short mystery novel (published posthumously as *The Dealings of Daniel Kesserich*) fared no better. He reverted to following his father's example, although he subsequently dismissed his quest to become a movie actor—including a brief appearance in the Greta Garbo vehicle *Camille* (1937)—as "a pretty stupid year that left me with a deep hatred of Hollywood" (*Ghost Light*, p. 337).

Retreating to Chicago, Leiber went to work for Consolidated Book Publishers editing a set of encyclopedias for sale by mail order, writing fiction in his spare time. His son Justin—who eventually became an academic philosopher, although he also published some science fiction—was born in 1938. The job lasted four years, and the experience helped him to obtain a longer-lasting editorial appointment with *Science Digest* in the late 1940s; in between he worked as an instructor in speech and drama at Occidental College in Los Angeles and—partly in order to avoid being drafted during the war years—as an inspector for Douglas Aircraft. All of these jobs were stopgaps, and Leiber never settled into any of them—unlike Harry Fischer, who became so deeply embroiled in making and designing packaging for the General Box Company in Louisville that his writing ambitions never came to fruition.

Leiber corresponded briefly with H. P. Lovecraft between November 1936 and March 1937 (when Lovecraft died) after Jonquil wrote to the great man on her shy husband's behalf; he also met Henry Kuttner and Robert Bloch while he was living on the West Coast. These acquaintances greatly intensified Leiber's desire to write and also helped him obtain a clearer idea of the manner in which his work would have to be slanted if it were to sell. His first sale, in 1939, was "The Automatic Pistol" to *Weird Tales,* but it did not appear until 1940. He sent his new tales of Fafhrd and the Gray Mouser to the adventurous John W. Campbell Jr., editor of *Unknown,* rather than to the staid *Weird Tales* editor Farnsworth Wright; the first of them, "The Jewels in the Forest" (retitled "Two Sought Adventure"), became Leiber's first professional publication in 1939.

Leiber sold several more stories to *Unknown* and *Weird Tales* in the years that followed but found it hard to make progress. He was strongly antipathetic to the idea of writing formulaic fictions employing conventional stereotypes, although the strong element of parody in a hectic compendium of such devices, "Spider Mansion" (1942), apparently went unnoticed. His strong desire to bring weird fiction up to date by devising hauntings uniquely fitted to contemporary urban environments gave rise to such stories as "Smoke Ghost" (1941) and "The Hound" (1942), the opening sequence of the earlier story providing a manifesto of sorts for this ambition. Although there is certainly no shortage of literary accounts of contemporary hauntings, few writers have tried as hard as Leiber to accommodate ghosts to contemporary environments. It is not merely that Leiber's modern apparitions are carefully tailored to their surroundings, but that they reflect distinctively modern anxieties and maladies.

CONJURE WIFE AND *YOU'RE ALL ALONE*

Although John Campbell, who was an unusually passionate and intrusive editor, thought Leiber's ambitions more suited to the pages of *Weird Tales,* it was he who provided Leiber with the scope to work at more adventurous projects, making room in *Unknown* in 1943 for a remarkable novel of contemporary witchcraft, *Conjure Wife,* and that same year encouraging Leiber to move into the field of science fiction in *Gather, Darkness!,* an equally groundbreaking account of rebels against a future dictatorship who disguise their technological sophistication as satanist magic in order to counter the religious impostures of the oppressors.

Conjure Wife is set on a university campus where the wives secretly and routinely practice witchcraft in order to advance their husbands' careers—as wives have allegedly done throughout history. When the rationalist protagonist finds out about his wife's endeavors he insists that she dispossess herself of her magical apparatus, with drastic consequences—and then, much chastened by his inconvenient re-enlightenment, helps her to regain her stolen soul and her powers. Although the second part of the novel is not quite up to the audacious brilliance of the first, *Conjure Wife* achieves a remarkable level of suspense and remains one of the key works in the development of modern weird fiction, proving that the uncanny could still exist not merely alongside but within the most sophisticated apparatus of twentieth-century life.

Leiber began work on another novel for *Unknown,* but the magazine was killed off as a result of the economic restrictions consequent on American involvement in World War II. The opening chapters were eventually adapted into the novella *You're All Alone* in 1950, but the full-length version published in paperback form as *The Sinful Ones* (1953) was very poorly distributed and marred by the intrusion of a number of pornographic passages intended to boost its reader appeal. This absurd fate is a striking testimony to the continuing difficulty Leiber had in finding appropriate publishing opportunities for his work. Although the U.S. literary marketplace had found room for such writers as James Branch Cabell and Thorne Smith in the 1920s and early 1930s, its upper strata were extremely inhospitable to fantastic fiction, and the efforts of writers associated with H. P. Lovecraft to import a greater sophistication and a new experimentalism into the pages of *Weird Tales* always had to compromise with the demand for formularization that was central to the philosophy of pulp fiction.

You're All Alone is an existential fable whose hero discovers that he is one of the rare individuals blessed with genuine free will and the ability to step outside the scripts written for society by a deterministic destiny—and who then finds his freedom threatened by others of the same kind, whose response to their opportunities is more rapacious than his own. Forty years after 1943, when the story was conceived, opportunities would open up for writers of literary fiction to produce fables of a similar stripe—Thomas Berger's *Being Invisible* (1987) and Nicholson Baker's *The Fermata* (1994) are notable examples—but Leiber had to adapt himself as best he could to a very different environment.

1950s AND 1960s

Leiber tried to continue working for John Campbell as a science fiction writer, producing an intriguing exercise in alternative history in *Destiny Times Three* (1945). But after doing his best to reproduce a space opera plot fed to him by the editor (as Campbell's favored writers were routinely required to do) in "The Lion and the Lamb" (1950) he swiftly moved on to less oppressive employers. Because the science fiction genre retained a conspicuous dominance over its fugitive fantasy companion for the greater part of his career, Leiber produced a good deal of work for the science fiction market, but he did his best to maintain his own esoteric interests. He founded his own small-press magazine *New Purposes* in order to further his philosophy and his writing, beginning with the serialization of a mildly surreal novel called *Captain Scatterday's Quest,* the text of which was eventually cannibalized by the more extensively fantasized novel *The Green Millennium* (1953).

Leiber's best hybrid science fiction/fantasy novel, the Hugo-winning *The Big Time* (1958) is a flamboyantly stylish drama (easily adaptable as a stage play) set in "the Place": a recuperation station for soldiers established outside the cosmos while infinity and eternity are undergoing the continual upheavals of a Change War. The station staff are "Demons"—the story's working title was "The Cream of the Damned"—detached from the routine pressures of time and the orthodox burdens of history. Their situation enables them to recognize the true existential plight of human intelligence, forever subject to the vagaries of the Change Wind and never entirely safe from the utter elimination of Change Death. For the Entertainers who work there, the Place really is the Place; although it is nowhere and nowhen, permanently beleaguered by spiders, snakes, and the ultimately-irresistible winds that will never let anything be for very long, it is the only real haven of psychological safety. Like all true Entertainers, Leiber's protagonist understands that while tomorrow and tomorrow and tomorrow creeps in its petty pace to the last syllable of recorded time out there beyond the limelight, the poor player who struts and frets her hour upon the stage lives in an eternal present, always bathed in the sound and fury of the audience's rapt and orgiastic applause. Like *The Sinful Ones,* however, *The Big Time* could only attain its first book publication as half of a paperback "double." Although it achieved much wider circulation and was backed by a collection of Leiber's own stories, it was still a grotesquely unfitting form for such a brilliant and original work.

Alongside these commercial products Leiber was able to issue work that was dearer to his heart in hardcover volumes published by small presses. The Arkham House collection *Night's Black Agents* (1947) gave him an opportunity to put a few unsold stories—including "Adept's Gambit"—into print, and he was able to collect the other early tales of Fafhrd and the Gray Mouser in the Gnome Press edition of *Two Sought Adventure* (1957). *Gather, Darkness!* was, however, issued as a commercial hardcover by Pellegrini and Cudahy in 1950; *Conjure Wife*—which had been filmed in 1944—was reprinted in an omnibus volume issued by Twayne in 1952; and *The Green Millennium* appeared from Abelard. Leiber's productivity improved dramatically during the early 1950s but was interrupted in the middle of the decade by a bout of alcohol-induced incapacity, which also lost him his job at *Science Digest*.

Leiber's alcoholism caused his career to be continually punctuated by periods of inactivity, usually lasting two or three years. He responded to their apparent inevitability by adding drunkenness to the list of fascinations that he routinely celebrated in his work, alongside chess, the theater, cats, and writing itself. The theater generated some of his most heartfelt tales, including "Four Ghosts in Hamlet" (1965); chess some of his most intensely studied, including "Midnight by the Morphy Watch" (1974); cats some of the most lighthearted, as exemplified by the collection *Gummitch and Friends* (1992); and writing some of his most flamboyant, including the underrated satire *The Silver Eggheads* (1959; expanded 1961). Drink, however, produced some of his most original and effective phantasmagorias, including "The Secret Songs" (1962), "The Inner Circles" (1967; also known as "The Winter Flies"), and "Gonna Roll the Bones" (1967).

FAFHRD AND THE GRAY MOUSER

Like everything else Leiber experienced, drink left an indelible impression on the saga of Fafhrd and the Gray Mouser, which continued to serve him as a medium of exotic spiritual autobiography once he had found a useful new home for such material with Cele Goldsmith, who became the editor of the magazine *Fantastic* in 1959. She was such an admirer of Leiber that early in her tenure she published a special issue of his stories, including a boisterously ironic take on his recent troubles embedded in an extravagant account of "Lean Times in Lankhmar" (1959). Unlike John Campbell, Cele Goldsmith was willing to let Leiber take his sword-and-sorcery series in any direction he desired. The relatively slight comedy "When the Sea-King's Away" (1960) was followed by the zestful adventure story "Scylla's Daughter" (1961), the intense *conte cruel* "The Unholy Grail" (1962), the wildly surreal "The Bazaar of the Bizarre" (1963), and a particularly extravagant compendium of black comedy and hectic melodrama, "The Lords of Quarmall" (1964), based on a key fragment that Harry Fischer had provided may years earlier.

Fantastic became a reprint magazine in 1965, shortly after publishing the novella "Stardock" (1965). But the series was reanimated again when Leiber made a deal with Ace Books editor Donald A. Wollheim to reissue it in a number of paperback books. Because Wollheim wanted to lead off with a novel, the first book to appear, out of chronological sequence, was an expanded version of "Scylla's Daughter," *The Swords of Lankhmar* (1968). Leiber wrote some new and rather trivial connective material for the next two volumes in the series, *Swords Against Wizardry* (1968) and *Swords in the Mist* (1968), but he had to write two new long stories to supplement the "The Unholy Grail"—which features the Mouser before he teamed up with Fafhrd—in order to detail Fafhrd's early history and explain how the two characters first met for *Swords and Deviltry* (1970). The writing of the second of these tales, "Ill Met in Lankhmar" (1970), coincided with the terminal illness and death in 1969 of Leiber's wife, Jonquil (who had been a heroin addict for many years), and this harrowing story became the first of several vessels into which he poured his anguish and grief. The new material he added to the stories from *Two Sought Adventure* in order to make up *Swords Against Death* (1970) served a similar function. The subsequent drinking bout was yet another hiatus in the pattern of Leiber's career, and when he began to come out of it, it must have seemed entirely natural to express his feelings in yet more tales of his unconquerable alter ego and his eternally loyal friend. Six such short tales initially issued in 1973–1975 were combined with the novella "The Frost Monstreme" (1976) and the short novel *Rime Isle* (1977) in the belated final volume of the Ace series, *Swords and Ice Magic* (1977). One further volume was added to the series at a later date, *The Knight and Knave of Swords* (1988).

It is entirely fitting that Leiber's literary career began and ended with Fafhrd and the Gray Mouser, bracketed by the marvelously baroque "Adept's Gambit" and the darkly tinted erotic novel *The Mouser Goes Below*, which was mostly written while Harry Otto Fischer was dying in 1986 and eventually made up the final part of *The Knight and Knave of Swords*. The series embraces every kind of fiction that the sword-and-sorcery subgenre can accommodate, but its sprawl is by no means ungainly, and its painstaking reflection of Leiber's life and personality gives it a remarkable coherency as well as an unparalleled poignancy. Although the great pioneer of pulp sword-and-sorcery fiction Robert E. Howard was a more stylish writer than he is sometimes given credit for, it was Leiber who demonstrated conclusively that it was a subgenre of fantastic fiction more hospitable to artistry than many others. Indeed, Leiber's loosely knit series demonstrated that first-rate sword-and-sorcery fiction demanded a remarkable artistic versatility and virtuosity, of which few writers are capable. The boom in genre fantasy that began in 1976 has encouraged the production of a great deal of bad sword and sorcery, but this only serves to underline the complexity of the challenge and the great achievement of the subgenre's acknowledged master.

As with many other Leiber characters, the weaknesses of Fafhrd and the Gray Mouser are usually more evident than their strengths; in an apologetic introduction to *The Swords of Lankhmar* the author observes that "they drink, they feast, they wench, they brawl, they steal, they gamble, and surely they hire out their swords to powers that are only a shade better, if that, than the villains." But this insistent emphasis on their flawed humanity illuminates by contrast the vividly authentic quality of their own heroism and the nature of heroism in general. Unlike many fantastic heroes, Fafhrd and the Mouser do not live in a world where Good and Evil are polarized and personified, but in a world where even the gods are wayward, quarrelsome, meddlesome and mean. They are frequently victimized by cruel circumstance and by their own black moods, but they are survivors avid to extract all the pleasures life provides as compensation for its pains. They sometimes fail and sometimes succeed, but in either case they offer a highly effective account of the sources of human distress and exaltation. They are the product of fabulous and constructive dreaming—but so are the wellsprings of human distress and exaltation.

ASSESSING LIEBER'S WORK

Leiber's ability to project his experiences and emotions into his work with the fervor of a method actor is the source of its effectiveness. His best stories give the impression that they are being intensely lived as well as deftly and artfully performed. This modus operandi made it difficult for him to produce long works but gave him the precious ability to inject a vivid realism into the most bizarre situations, no matter whether they were developed with playful delight, gentle sentimentality, or fierce intensity. His autobiographical memoirs are remarkable for the calm reflectiveness and frankness of their self-analysis, but the constraints of historical accuracy probably inhibit their revelations—a limitation that his best fiction transcends.

Although Leiber proved that sword-and-sorcery fiction is far more elastic, and capable of far greater sophistication, than any of his contemporary practitioners imagined, one thing it could not accommodate was the quest begun in "Smoke Ghost," *Conjure Wife*, and *You're All Alone*. Alongside his tales of Fafhrd and the Mouser he continued to produce accounts of contemporary hauntings in which the nightmarish quality was entirely modern—and in their later phases, teasingly postmodern. The best of his short tales in this vein include "The Girl with the Hungry Eyes" (1949), "The Black Gondolier" (1964), "Belsen Express" (1975), "The Button Molder" (1979), and "The Ghost Light" (1984). His second attempt to extrapolate that kind of sensitivity at novel length was *Our Lady of Darkness* (1977), which was reissued in an omnibus with *Conjure Wife* as *Dark Ladies* (1999). *Our Lady of Darkness* supplies the manifesto outlined in "Smoke Ghost" with an underlying metaphysical theory, featuring "paramental entities" that are the demonic "souls" of modern cities. Although it lacks the fine focus of his best short stories, it remains a tour de force of modern fantasy fiction, artfully combining intellectual fascination and emotional resonance.

Throughout his career Leiber also continued, as he had in *Gather, Darkness!*, to alloy science-fictional imagery with supernatural motifs. Indeed, the posthumous publication of *The Dealings of Daniel Kesserich* in 1997 confirms that he had begun his own experiments of this kind before allying himself with John Campbell. Although clearly influenced by H. G. Wells, the story is closely akin to William Sloane's fantastic mystery *To Walk the Night* (1937), describing a series of seemingly supernatural incidents that turn out to be the result of time-travel experiments in which scientific purity has been muddied by erotic obsession. The most reckless juxtaposition of this kind can be found in "Ship of Shadows" (1969), in which a starship is infested with the entire conventional apparatus of the supernatural imagination; although the tale's abrupt ending suggests that it was originally intended as the prelude to a much longer work, it won a Hugo after appearing in a special issue of *The Magazine of Fantasy & Science Fiction* celebrating Leiber's work. The exuberant alternative worlds story "Catch that Zeppelin!" (1975) and the hallucinatory fantasy "Black Glass" (1978) exhibit a similar cavalier spirit.

Leiber might have written a good deal more in the late 1980s had his eyesight not deteriorated to the point at which he found it impossible to type; his last few stories had to be written, very laboriously, by hand in an exaggerated script. His last works of all—contributions to a column in *Locus* magazine called "Moons & Stars & Stuff" that he had begun in 1982—were dictated. He was married for a second time to Margo Skinner, his companion of some years, shortly before his death on 5 September 1992.

Although Leiber never fit comfortably into any of the marketplaces into which his fiction was launched, he attained considerable critical success and some commercial success within his fields of operation. Although he obtained no financial benefit from the second and third dramatic versions of *Conjure Wife*—a 1960 TV play and the 1962 movie *Burn, Witch, Burn!*—and scant reward for the immense effort he put into his second Hugo-winning science fiction novel, *The Wanderer* (1964), which arrived too early to catch the 1970s boom in disaster stories, he made enough of a living to sustain himself and his family. He eventually collected eight Hugo awards and four Nebulas, as well as several other awards—an awesome total considering that so much of his work appeared in relatively marginal publications. It is arguable that no other career has demonstrated so clearly the difficulties that writers of fantastic fiction face when they seek to write and publish new and unconventional work, but what Leiber did contrive to publish expanded the limits and ambitions of all the subgenres in which he worked, and entitles him to be recognized as one of the finest American short-story writers of the twentieth century.

Selected Bibliography

WORKS OF FRITZ LEIBER

THE FAFHRD AND GRAY MOUSER SERIES (IN ORDER OF INTERNAL CHRONOLOGY):

Swords and Deviltry. New York: Ace, 1970.

Swords Against Death. New York: Ace, 1970. (Incorporates *Two Sought Adventure.* New York: Gnome Press, 1957.) Vols. 1 and 2 were reprinted, with new supplementary material, as *Ill Met in Lankhmar.* Clarkston, Ga.: White Wolf, 1996.

Swords in the Mist. New York: Ace, 1968. Vols. 1, 2, and 3 were reprinted as *The Three of Swords.* New York: Nelson Doubleday SF Book Club, 1989.

Swords Against Wizardry. New York: Ace, 1968. Vols. 3 and 4 were reprinted, with new supplementary material, as *Lean Times in Lankhmar.* Clarkston, Ga.: White Wolf, 1996.

The Swords of Lankhmar. New York: Ace, 1968.

Swords and Ice Magic. New York: Ace, 1977. (Incorporates *Rime Isle.* Chapel Hill, N.C.: Whispers Press, 1977). Vols. 4, 5, and 6 were reprinted as Swords' *Masters.* New York: Nelson Doubleday SF Book Club, 1990. Vols. 5 and 6 were reprinted, with new supplementary material, as *Return to Lankhmar.* Clarkston, Ga.: White Wolf, 1997.

The Knight and Knave of Swords. New York: Morrow, 1988. Reprinted, with new supplementary material, as *Farewell to Lankhmar.* Clarkston, Ga.: White Wolf, 1998.

OTHER NOVELS AND STORIES

Night's Black Agents. Sauk City, Wis.: Arkham House, 1947. (Stories.)

Conjure Wife. New York: Twayne, 1953. (Previously published in *Witches Three*, Twayne, 1952, with "There Shall Be No Darkness" by James Blish and *The Blue Star* by Fletcher Pratt.)

Destiny Times Three. New York: Galaxy Publishing Corp., 1957.

The Green Millennium. New York: Abelard, 1953.

The Silver Eggheads. New York: Ballantine, 1961.

The Sinful Ones. New York: Universal Giant, 1953. (Bound with *Bulls, Blood and Passion* by David Williams.) Revised, New York: Pocket Books, 1980.

The Big Time. New York: Ace, 1961. (Bound with *The Mind Spider and Other Stories*, also by Leiber).

Shadows with Eyes. New York: Ballantine, 1962. (Supernatural stories.)

A Pail of Air. New York: Ballantine, 1964. (Science fiction stories.)

The Night of the Wolf. New York: Ballantine, 1966. (Science fiction stories.)

The Secret Songs. London: Hart-Davis, 1968. (Stories.)

Night Monsters. New York: Ace, 1969. Expanded, London: Gollancz, 1974. (Stories.)

You're All Alone. New York: Ace, 1972. (Novella and stories.)

The Best of Fritz Leiber. Garden City, N.Y.: Doubleday, 1974; London: Sidgwick and Johnson, 1974.

The Book of Fritz Leiber. New York: DAW, 1974. (Stories.)

The Second Book of Fritz Leiber. New York: DAW, 1975. (Stories and essays.)

FRITZ LEIBER

The Worlds of Fritz Leiber. New York: Ace, 1976. (Stories.)

Our Lady of Darkness. New York: Berkley/Putnam, 1977. Reissued, with *Dark Ladies and Conjure Wife,* in *Dark Ladies.* New York: Tor, 1999.

Bazaar of the Bizarre. West Kingston, R.I.: Grant, 1978. (Fantasy stories.)

Heroes and Horrors. Chapel Hill, N.C.: Whispers Press, 1978. (Fantasy stories.)

Ship of Shadows. London: Gollancz, 1979. (Stories.)

The Ghost Light. New York: Berkley, 1984. (Stories and an essay.)

Kreativity for Kats and Other Feline Fantasies. Newark, New Jersey: Wildside Press, 1990.

The Leiber Chronicles: Fifty Years of Fritz Leiber. Edited by Martin H. Greenberg. Arlington Heights, Illinois: Dark Harvest, 1990.

Gummitch and Friends. West Kingston, R.I.: Grant, 1992.

The Dealings of Daniel Kesserich. New York: Tor, 1997.

AUTOBIOGRAPHICAL WRITINGS

"Fafhrd and Me." *Amra,* October 1963. Expanded version in *The Second Book of Fritz Leiber,* pp. 92–114.

"Not Much Disorder and Not So Early Sex: An Autobiographical Essay." In *The Ghost Light,* pp. 251–365.

CRITICAL AND BIOGRAPHICAL STUDIES

Byfield, Bruce. *Witches of the Mind: A Critical Study of Fritz Leiber.* West Warwick, R.I.: Necronomicon Press, 1991.

Frane, Jeff. *Fritz Leiber.* San Bernardino, Calif.: Borgo Press, 1980.

Staircar, Tom. *Fritz Leiber.* New York: Ungar, 1983.

Thomas Ligotti
1953–

DARRELL SCHWEITZER

THOMAS LIGOTTI WAS born on 9 July 1953, in Detroit, Michigan, the son of Gasper and Dolores Ligotti. Few details of his childhood and early life are available, but he is known to have graduated from Grosse Pointe North High School in 1971 and to have attended Macomb County Community College from 1971 to 1973; he received a B.A. in English from Wayne State University in 1977. He worked for a while for the publishing company Gale, but has since relocated to Florida, where he works as a freelance writer and editor.

The first thing any reader must notice about Thomas Ligotti's prose is its distinct voice. There is no mistaking a page of Ligotti for anyone else, though inevitably one reaches for comparisons: Borges, perhaps, or Lovecraft at his most restrained, or Robert Aickman on a very odd day? In the end, it must be, uniquely, Ligotti.

Indeed, the voice of the narrative is very often the central element. Many Ligotti narrators, like Poe's (think of "The Tell-Tale Heart"), have issues to work out, which tend to resolve themselves contrary to the speaker's stated intention. Who is speaking, why, and to whom can often completely distort the reader's expectations and the story's meaning. Sometimes the problem is that the speaker is mad. Others, far less fortunate, suffer because they see things as they actually are. In the Ligotti universe, sanity may be far worse than madness.

This thesis is stated most clearly in an early story, "The Mystics of Muelenburg" (in *Crypt of Cthulhu*, 1987), later collected in *Grimscribe*:

> If things are not as they seem—and we are forever reminded that this is the case—then it must also be observed that enough of us ignore this truth to keep the world from collapsing. Though never exact, always shifting somewhat, the *proportion* is crucial. For a certain number of minds are fated for realms of delusion, as if in accordance with some hideous timetable, and many will never be returning to us.
>
> (p. 112)

The narrator relates how he once knew a man who claimed that, "overnight, all solid shapes of existence had been replaced by cheap substitutes: trees made of flimsy posterboard, houses build of colored foam, whole landscapes composed of hair-clippings," and so forth, which led him to the "greater truth: that all is unreal."

While Ligotti can be profoundly Lovecraftian in his approach, he ultimately diverges from Lovecraft in his thematic conclusion. Lovecraft regarded himself as a scientific materialist. If things are not as they seem in the Lovecraftian universe, that is because humanity, as puny on the cosmic scale as any insect, has not learned the truth, but the awful truth still exists objectively, quite apart from and indifferent to humanity. For Ligotti the source of horror in his stories is that existence itself is nightmare, that nothing makes sense, and ultimately there is no reality, save for the pathetic consensual illusions human beings sometimes create. Indeed, in "The Mystics of Muelenburg," the teller, having stated his thesis, describes his encounter with a master illusionist and profound mystic, Klaus Klingman, who then tells the story of how he (Klingman) was in the town of Muelenberg when just enough of the population ceased to believe in "normal" things so that reality broke down, night did not follow day, and in a strange twilight the very physical shapes of the world began to dissolve into "senseless nightmare." This twilight led to the utter blackness "restored to the memories of the dead." Then the population managed to "awaken." All memory of the bizarre experience was lost, except that of Klingman, who is able to remember through his mystical powers—that is, as long as one accepts the consensus reality in which Klingman exists. The story becomes a kind of "liar's paradox." The narrator abandons Klingman "laughing like a madman," but later is unable to find any trace of him, which pushes veracity even further away, when the narrator begins to experience a breakdown in reality similar to that of Muelenburg. Of course the whole world actually experiences this, but only the narrator can remember anything. He sets down his tale, unable to offer any proof at all.

We see here, also, the other common Ligotti theme, that of psychic contagion. Again, this comes from Lovecraft, but is turned to other ends. In Lovecraft's "The Shadow Over Innsmouth," for example, the hero, having encountered and apparently escaped from the semi-human, frog-like creatures of Innsmouth, discovers to his horror that he is one of them. Perhaps the encounter awakened the innate influences within him. But the Innsmouth folk are a concrete reality. In Ligotti's fiction, it is unreality that is catching.

In "The Sect of the Idiot," in *Songs of a Dead Dreamer*, the protagonist first dreams of deformed, hooded figures in a room. Later, he goes to that room, finding it empty but for strange furniture. Afterward, people begin to shy away from him, and mutter about his own deformity. One of his hands has become an insectile mandible. He is turning into what he has dreamed.

"Nethescurial," one of Ligotti's most brilliant tales, begins like Lovecraft's "The Call of Cthulhu" (or several of Machen's tales, from which Lovecraft seems to have derived the technique) with a report of what the narrator has read in documents he has assembled. The narrator is writing his conclusions in a letter—addressed to whom, we are never told. He has found a "wonderful" antique manuscript by the unknown, admittedly pseudonymous Bartholomew Gray. Mr. Gray travels to a remote island, Nethescurial, where "the real and the unreal swirl freely and madly about in the same fog." Here an archeologist, Dr. N—, has uncovered fragments of a hideous idol, the object of worship by a demonic cult, who might attempt to reassemble the thing and revive its power. Places where fragments of the idol are hidden may be detected by their brooding unreality and "gruesome features"—that is, they resemble much of the dream-landscape of Ligotti's fiction.

Before long, Mr. Gray has become contaminated by exposure to Nethescurial. He has been all along, or now realizes that he is, a member of the modern-day version of the demonic cult. He begins to assemble the idol. He plans to sacrifice Dr. N— to it. But, overwhelmed by the magnitude of what he is doing, he repents, flees, casts the pieces of the idol into the ocean, and composes the manuscript that the letter-writer has found.

This is only the beginning. "Imagine," the frame-narrator (that is, the letter-writer who has found "Mr. Gray's" manuscript) remarks, "all of creation as a mere mask for foulest evil, an absolute evil whose reality is mitigated only by our blindness to it, and evil at the heart of things" (p. 75). This evil, we learn, is the very substance of which the idol of Nethescurial is composed. The narrator goes on: "Imagine the universe as the dream, the feverish nightmare of a demonic demiurge. O Supreme Nethescurial!" (p. 76).

Contagion follows. In a postscript the narrator remarks how, after a night's sleep and dreaming, the contents of the letter seem naive. He has dreamed of the island of Nethescurial and its hideous idol, to which cultists "beyond all hope or consolation . . . willingly abandon themselves" (p. 79). The narrator awakens, but now senses the substance of Nethescurial (the evil that is the universe) oozing beneath the surface of every material object. Try as he may, there is no escape, as he concludes that "Mr. Gray," for all he scattered the pieces of the idol in the sea, had become contaminated by its touch, which in turn contaminated the manuscript, which now contaminates the frame-narrator's letter, and (presumably) contaminates the copy of *Grimscribe* you are holding in your hands, even as the writer attempts a series of denials: "Nethescurial is not the secret name of creation" and finally, "I am not dying in a nightmare" (p. 84). With subtle, sardonic irony, Ligotti has made superb use of the very remoteness of his narratives-within-narratives. The menace of Nethescurial rises toward the reader, through layer after layer of narrative apparatus, like black ooze slowly filling a multi-story house, until the text itself has become part of the story and its inescapable horror. Where other horror fiction has made much of "forbidden texts" that might drive the reader mad, this story, arguably, attempts to be a forbidden text.

"Nethescurial" is the quintessential Ligotti story, expressing his basic theme most clearly, embodying his characteristic techniques and images. (There is also a scene of people-as-puppets, a recurrent motif in Ligotti's fiction, of life seen as an insane Punch-and-Judy show.) Likewise, *Grimscribe* is the essential Ligotti volume, containing also his now classic "The Last Feast of Harlequin," which is surely the best Cthulhu Mythos story written since Lovecraft.

The more famous, admittedly groundbreaking *Songs of a Dead Dreamer* also contains much excellent material (including the astonishing tour-de-force "Notes on the Writing of Horror: A Story"), but doesn't consistently rise to the same heights. This is understandable for a first volume, containing much early work. (Although it must be admitted that Ligotti's very first story, "The Chemyst," in which a madman narrator lures prostitutes into his apartment, feeds them a special drug, and then dreams them into hideously fanciful shapes, is extremely strong.) *Noctuary* is somewhat weaker, perhaps the product of over-production to meet the publisher's demands. There are worthwhile stories in it, but the alleged "novella" that fills out much of the volume, "The Notebook of the Night," is an interesting, but not entirely successful collection of prose-poems and macabre jottings, rather like Lovecraft's "The Fungi from Yuggoth" in prose. As with the Lovecraft sonnet-cycle, "The Notebook" may cause critics to argue for years over its interpretation, and whether it has any continuity at all.

These three volumes constitute the whole of Ligotti's commercially published collections, except for a subsequent selection of the best from them, with a few new stories added, issued as *The Nightmare Factory* (1996). Since then, his publications have been fewer, and mostly issued by small presses.

This is not to suggest that Ligotti is in any sense a one-note writer or spent force. A particularly interesting later production is *In a Foreign Town, in a Foreign Land,* (1998), which comes with a CD by avant-garde musician David Tibet, and is a multi-media story cycle of nightmare set in "remote" places. This suggests that Ligotti himself is beginning to influence the general culture (indeed, he is now the subject of websites in several languages) but that he is making a quiet shift in focus. His earlier stories have been about the discovery of (or contagion by) nightmare in the immediate world close at hand. Now Ligotti's imagination ranges far away. One thinks of Kafka's *Amerika,* a novel set in an imaginary version of the land the author never visited.

Also "far away" are the two as yet uncollected stories of the "Quine Organization," published in *Weird Tales*, "My Case for Retributive Action" (in #324, Summer 2001) and "Our Temporary Supervisor" (in #325, Fall 2001). These exploit the paranoia and stresses of the workplace. The hapless protagonist is sent to a remote and uncomfortable place to work for a large and sinister corporation. He may well spend the rest of his life as a drone, performing incomprehensible tasks, his mind dulled by company-issued drugs, his supervisors unseen and probably inhuman. In the hands of a lesser writer, this, like much of Ligotti's material, could turn into farce, but he maintains his quietly paranoid tone without faltering. The effect is closer to the David Lynch film *Eraserhead* than to typical post-Lovecraftian Cthulhu Mythos fiction.

It is a mistake to think of Ligotti as a Lovecraftian writer, for all he is deeply influenced by Lovecraft. Unsurprisingly, Ligotti's favorite Lovecraft story is "The Music of Erich Zann," about which he has written a revealing essay ("The Dark Beauty of Unheard Horrors"). He is drawn not to Lovecraft's monsters or to his pseudo-bibliography of *The Necronomicon* et al. but to his attempts to penetrate the nature of reality. Robert M. Price has referred to this as Ligotti's "gnostic quest." Traces of this may be found in Lovecraft, Machen, and other classic writers, but Ligotti is not an inbred writer imitating the classics for the delectation of a small body of hardcore fans. He is one of the best-read of contemporary horror writers, at ease with mainstream or avant-garde literature, either American or European. He knows his Lovecraft but is equally influenced by William Burroughs, Bruno Schultz, and possibly Samuel Beckett and Jorge Luis Borges. He has often remarked in interviews that he thinks it fruitful to incorporate the techniques of other types of writing into horror. Part of Ligotti's significance, then, is that he represents a major infusion of outside influences into the hermetically sealed world of supernatural horror fiction. He is fully aware that there are other possible models beyond Lovecraft, Machen, and M. R. James, as admirable as they may be.

At the same time he is the polar opposite of such popular horror writers as Stephen King, in that he makes no attempt to ground his fictions in easily identifiable characters and emotions. His characters are not at all like the plain folks next door. They are as rarefied as Roderick Usher, and their visions and nightmares are abstract, intellectual, and often refutations of the comforts of consensus reality.

It is likewise a mistake to assume that Ligotti is somehow "not good enough" for professional and mass-market book publishers. So far only *Songs of a Dead Dreamer* has reached mass-market paperback. *The Nightmare Factory* is a trade paperback. Ligotti has published one story in *The Magazine of Fantasy and Science Fiction* ("The Last Feast of Harlequin") but has been backed consistently by *Weird Tales*, which devoted a special issue to him in 1991. Otherwise, but for occasional anthologizations, all his work has appeared in the small and amateur presses.

This aspect of his career deserves special consideration, because Ligotti has never been a careerist writer. Instead he has been reclusive, not at all given to self-aggrandizement. He has concentrated on writing uniquely original material without any concern for its commercial potential.

Of course any number of talentless scribblers can rationalize their rejections with the belief (or delusion) that their work is simply too unusual or extreme for staid, conventional publishers, and that only the semi-professional or amateur presses have enough freedom from prior preconceptions to accommodate them. The extraordinary thing about Ligotti is that in his case, this seems actually to be true. Without such publications as *Nyctaclops, Dagon, Crypt of Cthulhu, Eldritch Tales, Fantasy Macabre, Dark Horizons,* and the like, Ligotti's fiction would never have found an audience. The professional editors really can be faulted for having missed something and for (by and large) having failed to seek Ligotti out once he had been discovered in the little leagues of publishing. While such editors may reply that, with his abstract, esoteric dream stories (and no novels, for Ligotti has said that he doesn't enjoy novels and has no inclination to write one), Ligotti doesn't have the potential to be a bestseller like Stephen King or Clive Barker. He does nonetheless have the potential to become a classic writer, appreciated by connoisseurs for generations, and a profound and lasting (if quiet) influence on the horror fiction of the future.

Selected Bibliography

WORKS OF THOMAS LIGOTTI

STORIES

Songs of a Dead Dreamer. Albuquerque, N.M.: Silver Scarab Press, 1985. Revised and expanded edition. London: Robinson Publishing, 1989. New York: Carroll and Graf, 1990.

Grimscribe: His Lives and Works. London: Robinson Publishing, 1991; New York: Carroll and Graf, 1991.

Noctuary. London: Robinson Publishing, 1994; New York: Carroll and Graf, 1994.

The Agonizing Resurrection of Victor Frankenstein & Other Gothic Tales. Woodinville, Wash.: Silver Salamander Press, 1994.

In a Foreign Land, in a Foreign Town. London: Dutro, 1997.

ESSAY

"The Dark Beauty of Unheard Horrors." *Tekeli-li! Journal of Terror*, 4, Winter/Spring 1992.

CRITICAL ARTICLES

Ashley, Mike. "The Knave of Darkness." *Dagon*, 22/23, September-December 1988, pp. 7–9.

Dziemianowicz, Stefan R. "Nothing Is What It Seems to Be: Thomas Ligotti's Assault on Certainty." *Dagon*, 22/23, September-December 1988, pp. 17–26.

Joshi, S. T. "Thomas Ligotti: The Escape from Life." In *The Modern Weird Tale.* Jefferson, N.C., and London: McFarland Publishers, 2001. Pp. 243–257.

Morris, Christine. "Beyond Dualism, an Appreciation of the Writings of Thomas Ligotti." *Dagon,* 22/23, September-December 1988, pp. 10–12.

Price, Robert M. "The Mystagogue, the Gnostic Quest, the Secret Book." *Dagon*, 22/23, September-December 1988, pp. 13–16.

———. "Ligotti's Gnostic Quest." *Studies in Weird Fiction*, 9, Spring 1991, pp. 29–31.

Schweitzer, Darrell, ed. *The Thomas Ligotti Reader.* Holicong, Pa.: Wildside Press, 2002.

INTERVIEWS

Dziemianowicz, Stefan R., and Michael A. Morrison. "The Language of Dread: An Interview with Thomas Ligotti." *Science Fiction and Fantasy Book Review Annual 1990*. Edited by Robert A. Collins and Robert Latham. Westport, Conn.: Greenwood Press, 1991. Pp. 109–118.

Ford, Carl T. "Notes on the Writing of Horror: An Interview with Thomas Ligotti." *Dagon*, 22/23, September-December 1988, pp. 30–35.

Ramsey, Shawn. "A Graveside Chat: an Interview with Thomas Ligotti." *Deathrealm*, 8, Spring 1989, pp. 21–23.

Schweitzer, Darrell. "*Weird Tales* Talks with Thomas Ligotti." *Weird Tales*, 303, Winter 1991–1992, pp. 51–55.

Bentley Little
1960–

KEITH NEILSON

BENTLEY LITTLE'S MOTHER attended the world premiere of Alfred Hitchcock's *Psycho* six weeks prior to his birth and that, he has somewhat facetiously suggested, is probably the reason for his preoccupation with the bizarre and horrific. Little unapologetically considers himself first, last, and only a horror writer. "I am a horror writer and have always tried to make that clear to people," he stated in a 2001 interview with David B. Silva, editor of *Cemetery Dance* magazine. "I've never hidden behind pathetic euphemisms such as 'dark fantasy' (an irritating phrase that is one of my pet peeves). I write horror, and I am very proud and honored to use that word" (p. 23).

Little has always been attracted not only to the subject matter and style of horror fiction, but also to its possibilities as a vehicle for a serious, comprehensive vision of modern life. "It's the chaotic worldview underlying most horror fiction that appeals to me, the sense that anyone can be maimed or killed or ruined at any time as a result of forces or events beyond their control" (Silva, p. 24). Since his first novel, *The Revelation* (1989), which won the 1990 Horror Writers Association Bram Stoker Award for best first novel, Little has, as of mid-2002, churned out twelve novels and over a hundred short stories, clearly establishing him as one of the premier horror writers of what might be called the post–Stephen King generation.

Not surprisingly, King has been one of the two most important literary influences on Little's writing. "I *am* a King disciple. The man's a huge influence on my work and it probably shows," he told Silva. "What impressed me most about King when I first read 'Salem's Lot was the scale of his work, the large tapestry he wove. He painted a portrait not just of a vampire and his victims but of an entire town, and that just blew me away" (p. 25). The other influence is, oddly enough, Dr. Seuss. Little grew up on books like *The Cat in the Hat* and *Green Eggs and Ham*, "stories where this chaotic figure would come into normal people's lives and wreak havoc. . . . Rereading the book to my son recently, I realized that *Green Eggs and Ham* has been the template for much of my work" (p. 25).

On 21 December 1960, Little was born in Mesa, Arizona, which is close to the family vacation home in Payson, Arizona, but grew up primarily in Fullerton, California (in 2002 he continued to maintain residences in both locations). His parents were Larry Little, a teacher, and Roseanna Dobrinin Little, an artist. While pursuing an education, he worked as a newspaper reporter and photographer, video arcade attendant, window washer, telephone book deliveryman, librarian, typesetter, furniture mover, sales clerk, and ad writer. He received a bachelor's degree in communications from California State University at Fullerton (1984) and an M.A. in English with a concentration in creative writing (1986). His M.A. creative writing project was the first draft of *The Revelation*.

Little initially concentrated on short fiction then moved to writing longer works. In the mid to late 1980s his stories started appearing in small genre magazines and his reputation began to grow. When Little approached Dean Koontz at a book signing, the famous author recognized his name and offered to assist him in finding representation. As a result of this encounter, Little signed with a literary agent and *The Revelation* appeared in the fall of 1990.

Most of Little's fiction originates in a real-life experience or observation. His novels are often genre horror stories in regional settings; the small western towns that permeate his fiction are clearly modeled on Payson. *The Revelation* is perhaps the most straightforwardly conventional of his novels. The conflict is basic—good versus evil in an apparently traditional Christian context. The novel opens with a series of frightening and bizarre things that start happening in and around Randall—a church is desecrated; an eighty-year-old woman gives birth to a bizarrely deformed dead baby, which promptly vanishes; a preacher and his family disappears and the wife is later found partially eaten; other locals are killed in weird, terrible ways; and a number of central characters begin to have wild, prophetic dreams involving mutated fetuses, red lightning, and a final apocalypse.

Most of Randall's inhabitants either ignore the growing menace or are helpless to do anything about it, but a small group coalesces into a "team" to confront the deadly threat—the local sheriff, Jim Weldon; a kindly preacher with psychic powers, Father Andrews; and an intelligent newlywed, Gordon Lewis, whose pregnant wife becomes a focus of the evil. The catalyst for the group is a mysterious preacher, Brother Elias, who arrives in the town ready to do combat with Satan. At first he is dismissed as a suspicious fanatic, but the accuracy of his predictions and intensity of his personality convince the other men that he is the only chance for their—and Randall's and possibility humanity's—survival.

The final third of the novel offers one of the most harrowing and protracted conflicts in modern horror fiction. Armed with a curious set of tools, the men travel to Mongolian Ridge, the source of the evil, and confront an army of zombie fetuses, then full-sized reanimated corpses, then monster-sized dead babies, and finally "Satan" himself. I use quotation marks here because by this time Little has made it clear that his novel is no fundamentalist tract. The malign presence that has Randall in its grip generalizes into a kind of primal evil that transcends time and place, and Elias is no simple preacher—his Christian vestments and doctrines are costumes suited to the time and place of his appearance, typical of many that he has used in centuries of battling the dark forces.

The Revelation has many strengths—power, energy, vividness, originality—but also some typical first-novel weaknesses. It is conceptually the least original of Little's books, and Brother Elias's abilities are rather too convenient with respect to the plot; he functions like a deus ex machina. In *The Revelation*, Little stakes out his chosen territory and recruits his basic cast, but it was in his second novel, *The Mailman* (1991) that he found his best subject, not in ancient evil (although he would return to the subject later), but in the modern, everyday world.

The Mailman takes place in Willis, Arizona, whose residents, lifestyles, preoccupations, routines, assumptions, and expectations mirror those of Randall. And as in *The Revelation*, the menace in *The Mailman* begins with ambiguous hints and grows inexorably until it threatens to consume the entire town. But this menace is no primal evil buried in the dark history of the region, but the local mail carrier. Such an elevation of the mundane to the demonic is a trademark of much of Little's best work.

When the former mail carrier of Willis unexpectedly kills himself, he is immediately replaced by "John Smith." At first the mail is not only delivered punctually, but is surprisingly helpful—people receive letters from long-silent relatives and friends, business deals come through, prize contests are won, and the like. But once this new level of service becomes routine, things darken. Bills and expected correspondence are not delivered; letters are misrouted and their contents are offensive or threatening to their recipients. Soon these misdirected epistles begin to provoke the citizens of Willis to hostile reactions: friends turn against each other; neighbors quarrel; relationships collapse; individuals suffer emotional, sometimes self-destructive, breakdowns; and physical violence, even mob violence, threatens.

The focus of the novel is the Albin family—Doug, a high school teacher, his wife, Tritia, and their young son, Billy. Even before the mail delivery becomes strange, Doug is uneasy and suspicious. When thing start going wrong, he is the first one to take action against the mailman, but his efforts are increasingly frustrated. He is dismissed as a crank, much of the hostility aroused by the mailman is directed at him, and his protests to authorities are dismissed or turned against him; the post office insists that "John Smith" does not even exist. Doug tries to enlist the help of his closest friends, but they fall victim to the mailman's powers. His best friend, Hobie, is accused of murdering and mutilating a young woman; the editor of the local paper goes on a shooting spree; Tritia's best friend kills herself.

The mailman finally attempts to invade the Albin family stronghold. Billy is trapped in a play fort that he and a friend had built in the woods, and Tritia is accosted in her own bathroom. Both narrowly escape—and in doing so unearth the clues that Doug needs to mount an effective offense against the mailman. Since the mailman uses "psychic weapons"—the townspeoples' own dark feelings and secrets—Doug knows he must muster a "psychic defense" and does so in a credible, dramatically effective conclusion.

Too many horror novels fail in the final pages because the menace that has seemed invincible is defeated by a relatively trivial, last-minute action on the part of the hero—King's *It* comes to mind. It is a problem basic to the genre—how to create monsters that are awesomely powerful and then dispatch them in a way that is believable. Perhaps the best tactic is to unobtrusively plant a credible weakness early in the book and later exploit it in a way satisfying to the reader. *The Mailman* amply succeeds in doing this.

One additional virtue of *The Mailman* is its humor. In one of the book's pivotal scenes, Doug follows the mailman into the woods and watches him indulge in a curious ceremony. The mailman goes into a wild, spastic dance while chanting unintelligible words, words that at first sound like a strange language but turn out to be the post office motto, chanted over and over. The scene is grotesque and horrific, but is also an example of a rich, dark humor that runs throughout the book and is a strong element in Little's best writing.

Little's next novel, *Death Instinct* (1992), was the first to be set in an urban environment, Phoenix, and the first—and only—to be thoroughly "realistic." A series of chilling, extremely grotesque, elaborate, even artistic murders have traumatized the community. A young single woman, Cathy Riley, and a detective, Lieutenant Alan Grant, find themselves connected in the investigation, he as the chief investigator and she as a kind of magnet for the killer—who turns out to be a young "idiot savant" whose special talent is murder. Little's vivid imagination shows through in the portrayals of ritualistic homicide, but he has referred to

Death Instinct as his least favorite book—although his negative feelings may have been colored by the difficulties that surrounded the novel's publication.

Little originally called it *Killer Savant,* a vivid, provocative title, but his publisher, Signet, changed it to *Death Instinct,* on the theory that the original title "gave away the mystery"—although readers were expected to ascertain the killer the first time he is introduced. The modest sales of *The Mailman* had made Signet uncomfortable about marketing the new novel as straight horror—as well as printing it under Little's real name. Promised a larger print run and a more effective marketing campaign for the book, Little reluctantly agreed to publish the novel under the pseudonym Phillip Emmons. The promotional promises never panned out and *Death Instinct* fared no better than its predecessor. His editor then insisted that Little finish out his three-book contract with a police procedural, so he wrote *The Summoning* (1993), a Chinese vampire story. It was rejected by Signet as expected and Little moved on to Zebra.

The Summoning was inspired by a conversation that Little had with his Chinese girlfriend, now wife, Wai ("Wendy") Sau Li, who told him that in China the traditional vampire has no of fear crosses and garlic, but cannot stand jade and willow trees. The Asian mythology adds an interesting twist to the vampire story, but that is where the book's originality ends. *The Summoning* seems almost an amalgam of King's *Salem's Lot* and a retread of *The Revelation.* The finale also echoes *The Revelation,* but in a less imaginative fashion, and the actual killing of the monster is accomplished much too easily. It is the weakest of Little's novels.

Ironically, *The Summoning,* which had provoked Little's departure from Signet, also became the agency for his return. The president of Signet read and liked the novel and, learning that Little was a former client, suggested that they attempt to bring him back into the fold. At first Little resisted, but upon learning that his former editor had left the organization, he agreed to renew the relationship; Signet published all of Little's subsequent books through 2002. Signet also formalized the titling of his books, continuing the precedent set by Little's first four novels. Two-word titles beginning with "The" has become a Little trademark.

Little's creative production follows a pattern; variations on traditional horror stories set in a small town in the west vie with urbanized stories in which the otherworldly menace is a contemporary institution gone haywire. In addition to the books already discussed, the former include *Dominion* (1996) and *The Town* (2000); the latter consist of *University* (1995), *The Store* (1997), *The Association* (2001), and *The Ignored* (1997). Only two novels, *The House* (1997) and *The Walking* (2000), do not fit into these categories and deserve niches of their own.

In *Dominion,* a teenage couple, Dion Semele and Penelope Daneam, are drawn into a bizarre ritualistic world centered on ancient Dionysian spirits that have converged in a local winery run by women, the "five mothers" of Penelope. In *The Town,* Little transposes the ghost story to the small western town of McGuane, Arizona, with a clever ethnic twist. Gregory Tomasov moves his family from Southern California to his hometown, where he buys a house that, unbeknown to him, is haunted. Weird and violent things begin to happen and the townspeople start blaming the Tomasovs. What makes *The Town* compelling is that the ghost displays elements of Tomasov's ethnic background, and the fact that the group assembled to combat it is a mixture of Russian refugees and local Native Americans.

Three of Little's "contemporary" novels take on three of the largest modern institutions, the state university, the "big box" Wal-Mart/Costco type store, and the homeowners association. In each of them Little simply pushes existing conditions to their extreme and horrific conclusions.

It is not difficult to see where Little got his ideas for *University*. Growing up in Fullerton and attending the local state university, Little witnessed a streak of violent activities that left the academic community stunned: a student murdered a faculty member in his office; a faculty member murdered a student's husband; two individuals jumped from the humanities building into a cement courtyard; and on 12 July 1976, a janitor, Edward Allaway, believing that his wife was having sex with the janitorial staff, went on a killing spree that took seven lives. *University* builds on such incidents as Little turns his fictional college, UC Brea, into a living organism that gradually consumes all trapped within it. Little begins with the tensions and routines typical of every modern campus—academic competition, social divisions and inequities, fraternity snobbishness, "political correctness," latent racism and sexism, bureaucratic confusion and ineptness, artificial complexity and frustration—and magnifies them into a growing apocalypse. Again, we have the small group that senses the growing danger early on and attempts to do something about it—Jim, the editor of the school paper, Stevens, the perceptive professor, Faith, the bright librarian, and a small cadre of friends. The rousing, characteristic Little conclusion becomes a race between the growing mob violence and bloodshed and the frantic efforts of the besieged group to find and act on the beast's vulnerability of the malevolent force before everything is consumed.

Both *The Store* and *The Association* were stimulated by events occurring in Payson. In the early 1980s a Wal-Mart opened in the town and put most of the local retail establishments out of business; Little's run-ins with his own homeowner's association led him to demonize such organizations. Both books follow the pattern of *The Mailman,* but on a much larger scale—the menace is not a single powerful being, but a large, complex institution capable of overwhelming every aspect of the individual's life. In both cases a new organization moves into a small western town and seems to offer idyllic possibilities to its customers—shoppers in *The Store,* homeowners in *The Association.* And in both books the evil is not only pervasive, but also impossible to locate, let alone fight. Between the individual and the malevolent force is a large, complicated, ambiguous institution staffed by networks of bureaucratic morons—Stephen King meets Franz Kafka.

When "The Store" opens in Juniper, Arizona, technical writer Bill Davis does not share his neighbors' enthusiasms. He is bothered by the elimination of zoning laws to facilitate its conspicuous size, the destruction of animal life in the area surrounding the building, and the fact that his best friend is quickly put out of business when the store opens. These negative feelings become more intense when his two daughters become employees and begin to change radically. The citizens of the town go on bizarre shopping sprees for things they couldn't possibly want or use, and finally the store turns Juniper into the equivalent of one big concentration camp. With one of his most original endings, Little has Davis embark on a join-'em-to-lick-'em strategy that provokes one of Little's most satisfyingly ambiguous conclusions.

In *The Association*, like *The Store,* the hero must contend with a faceless bureaucracy, or rather, a bureaucracy made up of neighbors who turn out to be very different than anticipated, an impersonal and increasingly malevolent system, and, behind it all, a mysterious evil presence that may or may not be human. Barry, a horror writer, and his wife, Maureen, move from California to Bonita Vista, an upscale gated community on the outskirts of another small western town, Corban, Utah. At first they appreciate the neatness and security of the gated community, but soon the regulations escalate from mildly annoying restrictions on house colors and lawn length to serious intrusions on their personal lives backed up with penalties that range from fines to dismemberment to death—and Little keeps the reader informed with periodic updates of the "CC&Rs" inserted between chapters. In typical Little fashion, the book climaxes with a confrontation that brings the entire community out to witness a gladiatorial confrontation between Barry and the head of the homeowners' association, whoever or whatever he or it may be.

The satirical thrust of Little's fiction, as well as his dark humor, peaks in *The Ignored*, which focuses not on a particular institution, but on the increasingly impersonal nature of modern life itself, a world in which ordinary people are simply not seen, let alone taken seriously. Bob Jones has a good job, a nice, unremarkable girlfriend, and a pleasant routine, one that is exactly like that of every other average mediocre American male. He is so average, in fact, that after a while nobody notices him no matter what he does, up to and including showing up at work in a clown suit and murdering his boss. Alone and despondent, Jones is finally noticed by a small group of likewise ignored people who call themselves Terrorists for the Common Man and assert themselves through violent actions. Their terrorist acts are indeed noticed, but the perpetrators, alas, are not. Little carries the conceit even further to the possibility of an alternate society for the Ignored, but this last section of the novel flags. Nevertheless, *The Ignored* is an entertaining, amusing, occasionally scary book that is Little's most thought-provoking novel.

In *The House* (1997) and *The Walking* (2000) Little explores new territories, at least from a technical standpoint. All of his other novels have straightforward linear plots. A single protagonist or small group is introduced at the beginning of the book and followed through to the final resolution. In *The House* we are given five separate plot lines that converge. In *The Walking* the narrative alternates between the present and the past with everything coming together in the last chapter.

The House is another variation on the haunted house story. Five individuals—a young man bumming around the West, an unemployed man in Pennsylvania living on his wife's salary, an aging high-school teacher in Iowa, a businesswoman in California, and a video distributor in New Mexico—have no knowledge of each other and nothing in common except similar terrifying dreams about their birth houses and a mysterious butler and his tantalizing, malevolent daughter. They each return to their old home sites—which merge into a single house where they meet and must confront otherworldly evil and their own personal demons.

The Walking moves back and forth between "now"—the present—and "then," the end of the nineteenth century. The "walkers" of the title are animated corpses, and include the father of the novel's protagonist, private detective Miles Huerdeen. These individuals seem to be walking deliberately to an unknown destination. Provoked by this, by reports of other zombies, by his own weird dreams, by a string of bizarre, unexplained deaths that go back decades, and by a prophetic message from a mysterious old woman, Huerdeen organizes a pilgrimage to track the destination of the walkers. That destination is a submerged city, Wolf Canyon, once a haven for witches, later submerged when the government flooded it for a dam. And waiting in Wolf Canyon for his party is the spirit of Isabella, a malevolent, powerful witch, whose curse is behind the reanimations and other dark forces that Miles and his group must deal with.

Little may continue to explore such new directions in future novels. But at the same time, *The Mailman, The Store, The Association,* and *The Ignored* are reminders that many other out-of-control institutions deserve a Little treatment. When Stephen King read *The Mailman* over a decade ago, he unsolicitedly proclaimed Little "the best in the business. A master of the macabre." Since then Bentley Little has more than fulfilled King's description and will, it is hoped, continue to do so.

BENTLEY LITTLE
Selected Bibliography
WORKS OF BENTLEY LITTLE

NOVELS AND SHORT STORIES

The Revelation. New York: St. Martin's, 1989.

The Mailman. New York: Onyx, 1991.

Death Instinct. [Phillip Emmons, pseud.]. New York: Signet, 1992. Published under Bentley Little as *Evil Deeds.* London: Headline, 1994.

The Summoning. New York: Zebra, 1993.

Night School. London: Headline, 1994. Published in the United States as *University.* New York: Signet, 1995.

Dark Dominion. London: Headline, 1995. Published in the United States as *Dominion,* New York: Signet, 1996.

Houses. London: Headline, 1997. Published in the United States as *The House.* New York: Signet, 1999.

The Store. London: Headline, 1997; New York: Signet, 1998.

Guests. London: Headline, 1997. Published in the United States as *The Town.* New York: Signet, 1999.

The Ignored. New York: Signet, 1997.

The Walking. New York: Signet, 2000.

The Association. New York: 2001.

The Collection. New York: Signet, 2002. Short stories.

The Return. New York: Signet, 2002.

INTERVIEWS AND CRITICAL STUDIES

Deja, Thomas. "Little's Shop of Horrors." Fangoria 191.

Silva, David B. "A Conversation with Bentley Little: Writing to His Own Drum." *Cemetery Dance* 34:23–27 (2001).

George R. R. Martin
1948–

E. C. McMULLEN JR.

MANY WRITERS PURSUE their craft with the hope that, one day, they will write something that catapults them into mainstream success. What is often unforeseen, or at least never fully realized, is where that increased recognition will take them. For George R. R. Martin, the increased recognition began with his short story "Sandkings" (1979), first published in *Omni,* a big-budget, high-circulation science fiction magazine owned by Bob Guccione. The success of "The Sandkings"—it was the title story of his third collection of short fiction (1981), was adapted as a graphic novel, was widely anthologized, and became a television show—led to Martin's involvement in television programs and motion pictures, though he voluntarily left these to continue to write the science fiction and fantasy for which he became famous.

BACKGROUND

George Raymond Richard Martin was born in Bayonne, New Jersey, on 20 September 1948, to a lower-middle-class family. His father, Raymond Collins, was a longshoreman and his mother, Margaret (Brady), was a housewife who also worked for a lingerie manufacturer. He attended Northwestern University in Evanston, Illinois, receiving a B.S. in journalism, summa cum laude, in 1970. In 1971 he received his M.A. from the same school. These were among the final years of the Vietnam War, and Martin identified himself as a conscientious objector, serving with the local VISTA volunteers rather than permitting himself to be drafted. In 1973 his lifelong interest in chess led him to direct chess tournaments for the Continental Chess Association; he left VISTA in 1974 and in 1975 married Gale Burnick; the marriage ultimately ended in 1979. In 1976, he became a journalism instructor at Clarke College in Dubuque, Iowa, becoming its writer in residence by 1978.

NOVELS, STORIES, AND TELEVISION

Martin had written as a child, selling "monster stories" to neighborhood children for spare change and giving dramatic readings as added value. His first professionally published work, "The Hero" (1971), appeared in *Galaxy* magazine when he was twenty-two years old and still a student. His first collection, *A Song for Lya,* was published in 1976; the title story won the 1975 Hugo Award for best novella. In 1977 his first major work, the science fiction novel *The Dying of the Light*, was published, as was also his second collection of short fiction,

Songs of Stars and Shadows. In 1981, he collaborated with Lisa Tuttle on the science fiction *Windhaven* (1981), whose story—Maris, a young woman, achieves her lifelong dream of becoming a flyer on a storm-ridden planet—may have had resonance for the recently divorced Martin; it was Tuttle's first novel.

As stated, the appearance of "The Sandkings" was to change Martin's life. It is superficially science fiction, but the science-fictional elements are minimal, and the story is ultimately pure horror with a moralistic and religious subtext, a parable in which absolute power is shown to corrupt absolutely and just desserts are administered by the abused. The story focuses on the sadistic pet owner Simon Kress, who acquires a new kind of pet—the Sandkings, four sets of antlike alien life forms—after he lets his previous pets die of starvation. The Sandkings live in an elaborate terrarium, build castles, and have ritualistic battles with each other. Kress forces them to escalate their battles, and the Sandkings—hive-minds whose intelligence increases—repay him by fighting and sculpting his increasingly twisted visage into their castles; he is ultimately portrayed as an insane deity. Horror erupts when their terrarium is broken and the Sandkings are able to take up residence in the areas surrounding Kress.

"The Sandkings" won the Hugo, Locus, and Nebula awards, and between 1980 and 1998 it was reprinted no fewer than seventeen times, was adapted for various media, and remains popular as an e-title. It should be mentioned that Martin's "The Way of Cross and Dragon"—another story with a religious subtext, and an equally bleak (if not bleaker) resolution—also won a Hugo in 1980, but it was "The Sandkings" that brought Martin to the attention of Hollywood. Moviemakers were looking for the next big science fiction movie: *Star Wars: The Empire Strikes Back* played to sold-out theaters and *Alien* (1979) showed that there was an audience for both science fiction and horror, so the intensely visual "Sandkings" must have seemed perfect. Nevertheless, it was never filmed successfully; the special effects required to create four distinct and believable colors of alien insects did not then exist.

Fevre Dream (1982) was Martin's first fantasy novel. Its events begin in 1857 and occur around the Mississippi River, where businessman Abner Marsh, owner and proprietor of the failing Fevre River Packets, is offered a partnership by the puzzling Joshua York. The *Fevre Dream* is built, and though it is faster than any other steamship on the river, York refrains from racing the boat and instead stops at odd places and brings aboard even odder people. As rapidly becomes evident, York and his friends are vampires, though theirs is a separate race rather than a supernaturally created being. Even as there are good and bad humans, so too are there good and bad vampires, the worst and most dangerous being Damon Julian, the bloodmaster, whose will is law. Julian takes command of the *Fevre Dream*, defeating Marsh and his people and York, and the final conflict between humans and vampires is the novel's climax.

Though *Fevre Dream* is well written, enjoyable, and lively, its biggest problem is its thematic familiarity. Martin humanizes his vampires—they can breed, albeit slowly, and they have dreams and feelings—but there is little that can be done with the genre that hasn't already been done in one form or another, and the historical data are ultimately more interesting than the vampires. Martin's best work generally does not use preexisting fantastic themes, but he uses werewolves to great success in "The Skin Trade" (1986), whose story—set in a dying Rust Belt city—centers on a werewolf working as a repossession man. He is in love with an attractive private detective whose father was mysteriously murdered, and both become enmeshed in hunting for a monster that skins its victims, who tend to be werewolves.

Martin's second fantasy novel, *The Armageddon Rag* (1983), is dramatically different, a contemporary fantasy having its roots in a love for the music of the 1960s. The novel pays explicit homage to J. R. R. Tolkien and W. B. Yeats and has as its background a defunct rock group, the Nazgûl. Though they were enormously popular, the Nazgûl released but five albums. On September 20, 1971, as they were performing pieces from their unreleased *Music to Wake the Dead*, a shot killed the albino lead singer, Henry Hobbins (a.k.a. Hobbit). The killer was never found, the Nazgûl disbanded, and the idealism of the 1960s came to an end. The above background emerges during the investigations of Sandy Blair, once a journalist with the counterculture magazine *Hedgehog*, now a blocked novelist. When he is asked to investigate the murder of Jamie Lynch, the Nazgûl's manager, Blair leaves his life. His investigations are as much about disillusionment from the lifestyle choices made during the 1960s as they are about the Nazgûl, but he learns that the Nazgûl have a new albino lead singer and are planning to reunite and finish their 1971 tour. Blair begins to have recurrent nightmares involving violence, sadism, animated corpses, and revolutions, and there is little doubt that at the conclusion of the Nazgûl's tour, their music will cause hell to erupt and the world to end.

The Armageddon Rag was nominated for the Locus Award and the World Fantasy Award, but it won no major genre awards, perhaps because its final chapter is remarkably weak. Had Martin concluded the novel a chapter earlier, the volume would have been significantly stronger.

In 1986 Martin became the story editor for the re-launch of television's *The Twilight Zone*. The next year, *Omni* published "The Pear-Shaped Man," which tied for the 1987 Bram Stoker award for best novelette. Like Orson Scott Card's "Fat Farm" and *A Planet Called Treason*, and Martin's earlier "The Monkey Treatment" (1983), "The Pear Shaped Man" is a fictionalization of the author's concerns about his body, in particular being overweight. (Martin had been an overweight child and adolescent, had lost weight as an adult, and had regained everything upon achieving Hollywood success.)

"Monkey Treatment" is arguably the superior tale, a hilariously black-humored description of a new form of diet in which the overweight person literally has a monkey set on his back. Nobody else can see the monkey, and it eats everything before its human host can. Horror emerges when the no-longer-obese protagonist realizes that even as he is shrinking, the monkey is growing, and he has no way to remove his tormenter.

In "The Pear Shaped Man," Jessie—a successful artist—finds herself increasingly haunted by the unwanted attentions of the nameless and creepy pear-shaped man, who seems to have no existence apart from a daily diet of Cheez Doodles and Coca-Cola. Fantasy—and horror—enter at the conclusion, when identities are switched and a situation is reestablished. It is possible that the story owes something to Mildred Clingerman's "The Wild Wood" (1957, *Magazine of Fantasy & Science Fiction*), whose plot bears a number of similarities to "The Pear Shaped Man."

In 1986, Martin edited the first of the Wild Card series, a mosaic novel in which different authors share a setting and characters and—generally—depict heroes or superheroes interacting with humanity and frequently saving the world. Martin's friend Howard Waldrop was present in the initial *Wild Cards* (1986) with "Thirty Minutes over Broadway," and his description of Martin's scheme in *Night of the Cooters* (1990) shows how carefully the series was planned: its rules were established and communicated in a private newsletter, *Cut and Shuffles,* and writers were given a variety of points for, among other things, the way in which their characters interacted with the characters created by others. Though individual volumes are uneven, Martin successfully attracted such talent as Roger Zelazny and Sherri S. Tepper, and the series remains popular and continues to be published.

In 1987, Martin became executive story consultant for the television series *Beauty and* the Beast and saw the publication of *Portraits of His Children*, a collection of short stories that, depending on one's mindset, can be classed either as science fiction or as fantasy. Some of the stories are obviously based on events in Martin's life: his love of chess is used in "Unsound Variations," in which a group of middle-age failures must play a climactic chess game against the man who has devoted many lifetimes to ruining them. "The Lonely Songs of Laren Dorr" is a poignant love story, almost a fairy tale, made more poignant by its revelation that love can be used as a weapon. "With Morning Comes Mistfall" is equally poignant and combines a statement about the need for mystery and romance with a strong environmental message.

In 1988, Martin was promoted to producer, then co-supervising producer of "Beauty and the Beast" before the show was permanently canceled in 1990. During the next few years, an increasingly unhappy Martin pursued potential movie and television deals, wrote scripts, adapted other people's work, and watched his own works adapted by others. He ultimately moved to Santa Fe, New Mexico.

A SONG OF ICE AND FIRE

With the epic *A Game of Thrones* (1996) Martin began the series that he calls "A Song of Ice and Fire," in part because the fictional world of the novel is akin to Brian Aldiss's planet Helliconia and has series that last for years. *A Game of Thrones* makes use of Martin's interests in chess and has obvious debts to Tolkien's *Lord of the Rings*, but unlike Tolkien's work, it has strong female characters and blends fantasy, horror, and mystery. The story itself is enormous and richly textured, though at its center are the Starks of Winterfell, a ruling family whose fortunes are followed through several members, including young Bran, whose decision at the beginning to adopt a dire wolf echoes through the book. The fortunes of the Starks change when Lord Eddard Stark receives an appointment to serve the new king, and much of the story is devoted to dynastic squabbles and the working out of political battles. It was continued by *A Clash of Kings* (1999) and *A Storm of Swords* (2000), and when it is finally completed, "A Song of Ice and Fire" will be a notable fantasy series indeed.

As of this writing, Martin is a protean figure. He is one of the few writers adept at any length of narrative, and he is also one of the few who excels at science fiction as well as fantasy and horror. His genre reputation is enormous, and he is establishing a solid and growing critical reputation among mainstream readers as well. He is a writer who richly merits his following; he is a writer to watch.

Selected Bibliography

WORKS OF GEORGE R. R. MARTIN

NOVELS AND SHORT STORIES.

A Song for Lya and Other Stories. New York: Avon, 1976.
Songs of Stars and Shadows. New York: Pocket Books, 1977.
Dying of the Light. New York: Simon and Schuster, 1977.
Windhaven. With Lisa Tuttle. New York: Timescape, 1981.
The Sandkings. New York: Timescape, 1981.

Fevre Dream. New York: Poseidon Press, 1982.

The Armageddon Rag. New York: Poseidon Press, 1983.

Songs the Dead Men Sing. Niles, Ill.: Dark Harvest, 1983.

Nightflyers. New York: Bluejay, 1985.

Tuf Voyaging. New York: Baen, 1986.

Portraits of His Children. Arlington Heights, Ill.: Dark Harvest, 1987.

The Pear-Shaped Man. Eugene, Ore.: Pulphouse, 1991. (Separate printing of short story.)

A Game of Thrones. New York: Bantam Books, 1996. (A Song of Ice and Fire, no. 1.)

A Clash of Kings. New York: Bantam Books, 1999. (A Song of Ice and Fire, no. 2.)

A Storm of Swords. New York: Bantam Books, 2000. (A Song of Ice and Fire, no. 3.)

A Dance with Dragons. New York: Bantam Books. Forthcoming.

The Winds of Winter. New York: Bantam Books. Forthcoming.

AS EDITOR

New Voices in Science Fiction: Stories by Campbell Award Nominees. New York: Macmillan, 1977.

The Science Fiction Weight-Loss Book. Coedited with Isaac Asimov and Martin H. Greenberg. New York: Crown, 1983.

Night Visions 3. With Paul Mikol. Niles, Ill.: Dark Harvest, 1986.

Wild Cards. New York: Bantam, 1986. (Series, with various subtitles and editors.)

CRITICAL STUDIES

Don D'Ammassa. "George R. R. Martin." *St. James Guide to Horror, Ghost, and Gothic Writers.* Edited by David Pringle. Detroit: St. James, 1998. Pp. 388–390.

Richard Matheson
1926–

KEITH NEILSON

IN A CAREER that started in the middle of the twentieth century and is still going strong at the beginning of the twenty-first, Richard Matheson is probably the most successful "hyphenated" writer in modern literature. Novelist-short story writer-screenwriter-television writer, Matheson has never thought of himself as a fiction writer who occasionally pens film scripts (à la Stephen King), nor a screenwriter who turns out the periodic novel (à la William Goldman), but has embraced all his creative projects with equal enthusiasm, denying, in fact, that there are any really important distinctions between them. As Matheson stated in an interview in *The Spook* Internet magazine:

> People ask me what's the difference between writing scripts and novels. To me there's no difference, just that the page looks different. When I write a novel, I'm watching a movie in my head and I'm describing what I'm seeing. And when I write a script, I'm seeing a movie in my head and I'm writing it in script form. But there's no difference otherwise. I write very visually. I think visually in my work.
> (Etchison, "A Conversation with Richard Matheson," *The Spook*, December 2001/January 2002)

Matheson's versatility is also reflected in his wide choice of genres—he has penned outstanding works in the fields of suspense, horror, science fiction, mystery, the Western, nonfiction, even philosophical speculation. Matheson himself has little respect for genre boundaries. "I hate genres.... They're like cubbyholes that the writer gets crammed into. You write a love story and set it on Mars, it's science fiction. You write a love story and set it out west, it's a western. You write a love story, add a murder to it, it's a murder mystery" (Etchison).

Matheson was born on February 20, 1926, in Allendale, New Jersey, and gradually migrated westward—after high school in Brooklyn and military service in World War II (fictionalized in *The Beardless Warriors*, 1960), he attended the University of Missouri (1946–1949), from which he received a Bachelor of Journalism degree, and then finally ended up in Hollywood—where he could conveniently pursue both his major writing interests, fiction and film.

Matheson attracted critical attention with his first published short story, "Born of Man and Woman," which appeared in *The Magazine of Fantasy and Science Fiction* in February of 1950. Because it appeared in a major science fiction periodical and dealt with a postnuclear apocalyptic America, Matheson was initially dubbed a science fiction writer.

If Matheson can be called a science fiction writer, it is in the same sense that his most immediate predecessor and influence, Ray Bradbury, can be so labeled. Like Bradbury, Matheson often sets his characters in the contemporary or near future world surrounded by the paraphernalia of modern technology. But, like Bradbury, it is not social and technological change per se that threaten his characters, but the doubts that these things cast on the nature of reality itself, and the challenge his characters face is not generally to adjust to a new and different world, but rather to confront demons released by that world, demons both external and internal.

A number of his stories and novels have the trappings of science fiction because the genre provides several metaphors well suited to Matheson's preoccupations. Space travel, for example, isolates the individual in the middle of nowhere headed toward unknown, unpredictable destinations, left entirely on his own resources. The threat of nuclear or other apocalypse powerfully presents the notion of an awesome external threat imposed on ordinary people. The prospect of alien invasion, internal as well as external, can put questions of personal identity and objective reality into focus. And earthly existence itself can be made problematic through the possibility of alternate universes that may impinge upon our own, opening holes through which hapless individuals may wander or be seized.

A flood of stories and novels followed on Matheson's initial success, culminating in the outstanding novels of his early career, *I Am Legend* (1954) and *The Shrinking Man* (1956). *The Shrinking Man* also became Matheson's entrée into screenwriting. When a producer approached him about film rights to the novel, Matheson insisted that he write the initial screenplay as a part of the deal. They agreed, he wrote a successful adaptation, and the movie was made as *The Incredible Shrinking Man* (1957). Matheson's dual career then went into high gear.

Between the early fifties and late sixties, Matheson was quite productive. As a fiction writer he continued to turn out short stories, mostly science fiction, fantasy, and horror, with the occasional Western or suspense tale thrown in. Most of them were initially published in genre magazines and later gathered in four paperbacks, *Shock!* (1962), *Shock II* (1965), *Shock III* (1967), and *Shock IV* (1970). In longer fiction he followed up *The Shrinking Man* with the psychic-suspense novel, *A Stir of Echoes* (1958); a haunted house story, *Hell House* (1971); and two romantic fantasies, *Bid Time Return* (also released as *Somewhere in Time*) (1975) and *What Dreams May Come* (1978).

Matheson is best remembered in television for the fourteen episodes he wrote for Rod Serling's *The Twilight Zone*, along with his adaptation of his short story "Duel," which became Steven Spielberg's directorial debut. Other television scripts included several ABC "Movies of the Week" and an adaptation of Ray Bradbury's *The Martian Chronicles* (1980). Feature-length film credits include a series of very loose, darkly comic adaptations for Roger Corman of Edgar Allan Poe classics—"The House of Usher," "The Pit and the Pendulum," "The Raven," "Tales of Terror," and "The Comedy of Terrors"—an adaptation, with Charles Beaumont, of Fritz Leiber's *Conjour Wife* (filmed as *Burn, Witch, Burn*); *Twilight Zone: The Movie*; and scripts from his own novels, *The Young Warriors* (1968), *The Legend of Hell House* (1973), and *Somewhere In Time* (1980).

But since the appearance of *Bid Time Return* in 1978, Matheson's publications have been sporadic. Much of the fiction published between 1978 and the present has been reissues of his earliest works, primarily the Westerns, and initial publications of works completed many years previously, but not printed for one reason or another.

For example, Matheson's first novel, the "mainstream" epic *Hunger and Thirst*, didn't see print until 2000. Although written more than fifty years ago, it was shelved by the author when his agent at the time told him the book was too long and cumbersome (at 750-plus pages) to be commercially viable. When it was finally published, it was put out by a small specialty press. Similarly, the femme fatale ghost story, *Earthbound* (1994), and the neo-noir thriller *Passion Play* (2000), were stories recycled from much earlier periods. This was the case as well for several other works published in the second half of Matheson's career, so the critic must be careful when chronicling Matheson's "development" to distinguish genuinely new material from recycled past efforts.

In the introduction to his *Collected Stories* (1989), Matheson identifies himself as "Mr. Paranoia" and indulges in a fascinating literary and psychological autopsy of his short fiction, one that can easily be extended to his longer fiction and film and television writing. According to Matheson, his archetypal subject is the isolated male, besieged by social, psychological, technological, and otherworldly menace, who fights to understand and survive his plight or even, sometimes, to maintain a hold on his disintegrating identity. He has no allies, or, if he is one of a group, the others share his fate. His weapons are vague and unreliable. Danger lurks as much within as without. As he struggles, the battlefield itself may change or disintegrate around him. If he wins, the victory may seem tenuous and temporary, but if he loses, he may be utterly destroyed.

All of that sounds very bleak, almost Absurdist, more Beckett than science fiction. But there is also from the beginning an optimistic, even Romantic strain in much if not all of Matheson's fiction. This Romantic element becomes more central in the later works, blurring finally into the metaphysical speculation of his most recent efforts.

Although a few of Matheson's early stories and one novel, *Hell House*, focus on a family or group, most of his stories, novels, and scripts feature the same type of protagonist, an intelligent, sensitive middle-class male, sometimes single, sometimes married, but always essentially isolated. Usually, at the beginning of the story he is contented, living an ordered, predictable life in comfortable surroundings. Then something happens to disrupt his status quo—the "thing from the sugar bowl," as the writer George Clayton Johnson termed it. This "thing" may be an overt external menace; an encounter, chance or otherwise, with a destructive person or being; an unleashed personal demon; or even the disintegration of reality itself. Matheson's protagonist seldom deliberately provokes the crisis. Sometimes he is inadvertently responsible for triggering it; more often he is just thrust into a situation without preparation or warning, like, to cite an extreme example, Mr. Ketchum in "The Children of Noah" (1957), who is stopped for a traffic violation in a small New England town and ends up in an oven.

The most bizarre and frightening aspect of the crisis is usually its distorted familiarity. That is, everyday objects, situations, and perceptions are suddenly given new, terrifying qualities. In "Mad House" (1953), Neal, an angry, frustrated writer, is attacked and killed by his own household artifacts. In the short story "Crickets" (1960) that common insect turns out to be sending coded messages from the dead, who are secretly plotting to return. Don Marshall in "The Edge" (1958) goes out for lunch one day and accidentally wanders into a parallel universe. The protagonist in "Disappearing Act" (1953) is even more unfortunate: the world disappears around him as the story ends in midsentence.

The kinds of situations treated in Matheson's short fiction are elaborated more extensively and intensely in his two major early novels, *I Am Legend* and *The Shrinking Man*.

Robert Neville, the hero of *I Am Legend*, lives in a world populated by mindless vampires, the victims of a virulent disease triggered by nuclear war and a series of severe dust storms. "I got the idea" Matheson confided in a *Twilight Zone* interview, "when I was seventeen years old . . . and saw *Dracula*. I figured that if one vampire was scary, then a whole world full of vampires should really be scary" ("TZ Interview I," *Twilight Zone Magazine*, September 1981, p. 46). Neville is the lone surviving "human" and lives barricaded in an apartment at night. During the day, taking advantage of the vampire's traditional vulnerability to sun, he ventures out and stakes as many of them as he can. Thus, he himself has turned into a kind of inverted vampire, who kills by day and must retreat to his "casket" apartment before nightfall or be overwhelmed by hoards of vampires.

Neville's mission becomes complicated by his meeting with Ruth, a young woman who has also apparently survived vampirism. He is wary, but doesn't test her and, sure enough, it turns out that she is not a surviving human, but a new species of vampire, one not subject to vampiric weaknesses, and their meeting was not accidental, but preplanned. But she, too, compromises her mission by falling in love with him and, despite the fact that he had killed her husband, warns him against her colleagues. Neville, however, gives in to his fate rather than flee. He concludes that he is an anomaly in a world that has no place for him. For better or worse, the "new" vampires are now the Earth's dominant creatures and he is as irrelevant as the mindless creatures he was exterminating.

In *The Shrinking Man*, Scott Carey's world is in constant flux, not because it is changing, but because he is as the result of a freak nuclear accident that shrinks him one-sixth of an inch a day. Every day is a little different, but these differences become progressively catastrophic. The dangers and poignancy of Carcy's plight are intensified by Matheson's device of juxtaposing past and present in alternating chapters. In chapter 1 we learn how a nuclear cloud triggered his bizarre malady; in chapter two we watch him, shrunk to four-sevenths of an inch, battle a spider in his cellar. Thus we witness the hero's progressive loss of humanity, alternated with episodes from his courageous last stand—which, ironically, turns into a new beginning.

Like Scot Carey, Tom Wallace, hero of *A Stir of Echoes*, is transformed by an unexpected event, though his change is less traumatic. Indeed, his transformation should have given him power and glory, instead of trauma. When Wallace is hypnotized by his brother-in-law at a party, his latent psychic powers are set free. He begins to see into the future and read the minds and feelings of his family and friends, and even sees a female ghost in his living room at night.

A Stir of Echoes was not Matheson's first use of the "wild talent" as an inciting incident. In "One for the Books" (1955), Fred, a teacher, starts absorbing like a great psychic sponge all of the knowledge found in the classrooms in which he teaches—but unfortunately all of this information is finally drained from him by a bright light and the whole thing turns out to be a plot by aliens to suck out all human knowledge. David, the "Holiday Man" (1957), has an unusual if painful occupation: he predicts fatalities for a big city newspaper. *A Stir of Echoes* is, however, the first novel to feature these kinds of talents.

A Stir of Echoes is also pivotal in the Matheson canon as the first novel in which the male-female relationship is at the center. While the idyllic marriages of Robert Neville and Scott Carey were ruined by their bizarre encounters, neither book pivots on this development. Tom Wallace's marriage, however, is the measure by which everything else in the book is considered. His pregnant wife Anne, already upset by the death of her mother, which Tom had predicted, cannot accept his terrifying abilities. And with the deterioration of the marriage comes the collapse of Tom's mental and emotional stability. Pushed to the edge of insanity, Tom is rescued by a lucid psychiatric explanation of his condition and another round of hypnosis. He takes control of his situation, stabilizes the marriage, identifies the ghost (a previous tenant murdered by a neighbor), and suffers a lucky head wound that returns him to normality.

Although *A Stir of Echoes* is not in a class with its two predecessors—the plot is too contrived, the resolution too easy, and the canvas much smaller—it is crucial in Matheson's development as the novel in which he first put romantic love and psychic experience, the primary subjects of his later fiction, at the center. It is also the first novel to conclude with an unambiguously upbeat ending. The purity of Matheson's paranoia had begun to dissipate.

This emphasis on psychic phenomenon is further pursued in Matheson's next and in some ways oddest novel, *Hell House*, a book that did not appear until 1971, a dozen years after *A Stir of Echoes*. During the sixties Matheson published no novels and only a smattering of short stories—a form he stopped exploring altogether after 1970, except for a single collaboration with his son Richard Christian Matheson. Most of his writing was done for the screen, big and small. This was the period during which he concentrated on *The Twilight Zone* and the Poe adaptations along with several other screen adaptations.

Thus, given his lack of fiction writing activity, it is not surprising that *Hell House* would reflect shifts in interest and emphasis. What is curious is that the novel really stands alone, fitting comfortably neither with the science fantasies of the fifties nor the romantic fantasies of the mid seventies.

Hell House seems to resemble a traditional haunted house story, most notably Shirley Jackson's *The Haunting of Hill House* (although Matheson denies any influence), but with an original science-fictional slant. Three experts in the paranormal—Lionell Barrett, a scientific investigator who uses a machine to neutralize the electromagnetic forces responsible for paranormal activities, Florence Tanner, a spiritualist who relies on love to deal with the otherworldly, and Benjamin Franklin Fisher, a psychic who survived an earlier encounter and wants a second chance—agree to spend time in the Belasco Mansion, a notorious haunted house.

Matheson does an excellent job of conveying the requisite haunted house setting. A pervasive atmosphere of sexual perversion and moral chaos surrounds the occupants as they attempt to deal with a steady onslaught of every sort of psychological and physical horror. In combining traditional haunted mansion motifs with much science-fictional rationalization, he succeeds in mounting a story that is both viscerally scary and intellectually provocative—if a bit farfetched.

But because *Hell House* lacks the usual Matheson hero—or rather keeps him (Fischer) in the background until almost the end of the novel—the reader never really connects with the author's cold, odd, distant characters. *Hell House* is one of Matheson's most cerebral and vivid books, but his least emotional and involving. This is especially surprising, because emotional involvement and sympathetic identification with the characters were to become Matheson's major objectives in his next two novels, *Bid Time Return* (1975) and *What Dreams May Come* (1978).

These two novels also underscore an important shift from science fiction to other genres that coincided with his cessation of short fiction in 1970—by that time science-fictional metaphors no longer fit Matheson's preoccupations. Even the recycled writings of the post-1970 period are suspense thrillers or ghost stories.

While romantic love had been an important element in many of Matheson's previous efforts, *Bid Time Return* and *What Dreams May Come* were his first pure romances. A love story is at the center of both and the overriding question the two novels pose is whether or not the intensity of the hero's passion, love, and devotion can overcome the obstacles that stand between him and his beloved—those obstacles being "time" in the first and "death" in the second. These two books also underscore the importance of the male-female relationship in Matheson's work. Although he almost never makes a woman the central figure in his works, the feminine presence, for better or worse, is almost obsessively central to them—as helpmate, lover, wife, or femme fatale.

The most overt image of feminine destructiveness is probably seen in "Witch War" (1951), in which the telepathic powers of seven giggling teenage girls combine to violently destroy military targets. A more intimate and disturbing example of female voraciousness occurs in "Lover When You're Near Me" (1952), in which the telepathic powers of a "Gnee," a hideous but devoted female alien, gradually overwhelm the consciousness of Lidell, the colonist from Earth. The more realistic story "Day of Reckoning" (1960) features a wife so possessive of her late husband that she turns her son into a homicidal maniac. In "First Anniversary" (1960), Norman's inability to smell his wife Adeline turns out to be the result of her failure to completely control his mind as she, an alien, must do to keep him. Similarly, in "The Likeness of Julie" (1962), it turns out that the male protagonist, a teenager named Eddy, has been manipulated into violence by his supposed female victim, Julie.

In a more traditional manner, Matheson uses the femme fatale as the menace in several ghost stories, including "Wet Straw" (1953), "Slaughter House" (1953), and *Earthbound* (originally published by *Playboy* in a butchered version in 1982, then revised and republished in 1994). In "Wet Straw", John, a recent widower, is plagued by the smell of "wet straw" and other reminders of his dead wife. They grow stronger until she finally returns from the grave to exact revenge for her murder. In "Slaughter House" the femme fatale is the ghost of a young woman named Clarissa, who had murdered her family in 1901.

In *Earthbound* David Cooper and his wife return to the site of their honeymoon to try and rescue their twenty-one-year marriage. But this idyllic vacation turns bad when David encounters Marianna, a sexually charged ghost, and their increasingly graphic encounter not only further threatens the marriage, but drains David of all stability and vitality. But when the succubus attacks his wife directly, David fights back physically and spiritually and, at the risk of life and soul, succeeds in sending Marianna to wherever such ghost are sent. *Earthbound* is a pale reflection of Matheson's earlier horror stories. Marianna never seems like more than a very horny female and the ending is so over-the-top that that it evokes amusement rather than terror. Perhaps Matheson was hearing echoes of Oliver Onion's classic novella "The Beckoning Fair One," and, in updating the concept, lost all of the scariness.

Passion Play, published in 2000 but written fifty years earlier, covers much of the same territory, but in the manner of a 1950s noir novel. A typically ordinary Matheson hero, Ray Thompson, a happily married if frustrated artist, is thrust into chaos by Clarice, a dark sexy temptress. He is seduced and lured into a fight which leads to a false murder charge, a disintegrating marriage, and eventually to a near escape from becoming a murder victim himself. Matheson confessed some bafflement as to why this was not published when written, but in fact the novel is not very good. Thompson is simply too passive and unintelligent to be a credible hero. Until near the end of the book, despite the murder charge, he never really seems in much jeopardy. Eventually his own clumsiness and stupidity put him at the killer's mercy, but, as happens too often in Matheson's fiction, he escapes through no real fault of his own.

In Matheson's later works, the hero tends to be a happily married man and the femme fatale's threat to his marital happiness is almost as important as his physical survival. And at the same time, the power of his romantic love is crucial to his survival. These themes come to fruition in his two most romantic and fantastic novels, *Bid Time Return* (filmed and reissued as *Somewhere In Time*) and *What Dreams May Come*.

Bid Time Return is not the first Matheson work in which the human imagination creates an alternate reality for the main character and transports him into it. In "A World of Difference," a 1960 *Twilight Zone* episode, an actor named Gerry Raigan is able to become his television character, Arthur Curtis, and exits from the reality of his unhappy real life into the happy world of his television character. In "A World of His Own," another *Twilight Zone* episode broadcast the same year, television writer Gregory West peoples his world with creatures of his own imagination, zapping anyone into oblivion who does not live up to his expectations—including Rod Serling.

In *Bid Time Return*, however, Richard Collier's metamorphosis is much more complicated. Given a fatal prognosis due to a brain tumor, thirty-six-year-old screenwriter Richard Collier severs all ties and sets out to lose himself. When his aimless drive brings him to the Coronado Hotel near San Diego, he sees a picture of a turn-of-the-century actress, Elise McKenna, and knows that she is his true love. Obsessed by love, intrigued by mysterious hints in her life, and influenced by a book on the relativity of time, he vows to travel from 1971 to 1896 by sheer willpower—and he does so. They meet, are instantly overwhelmed, and have an intense, ultimately doomed love affair. The romantic power of the book is enhanced by the scrupulously realistic handling of period detail. Contemporary California is juxtaposed against the California of 1896. Matheson captures the feeling, mood, texture, and style of both eras, made more vivid by the comparison. The reader identifies with the hero because of his sensitivity, his intense emotions (made more obvious by his thin, cynical defenses), his romanticism, and his courage. We share his elation at the love affair, but also share an impending sense of doom. When a trivial detail sends Richard back to his own time to die, we are saddened, but not surprised. Was it real time travel or an hallucinatory episode provoked by a brain tumor? The reader is left up in the air. *Bid Time Return* is Matheson's most sensitive and poignant novel.

What Dreams May Come (note that the title does not end in a question mark) is more of a noble failure. Killed in an automobile accident, Chris Nielsen finds himself in the afterlife. Once he adjusts to it, Chris basks in the joys of Matheson's heaven, a tour of which makes up the middle third of the book. This idyllic life is interrupted when Nielsen learns that his widow, Ann, has committed suicide and will have to spend her afterlife in the dark regions. In a harrowing quest, modeled on the Orpheus-Eurydice myth, Chris journeys through "hells within hells" to find her and decides that hell with Ann is preferable to heaven without. The novel ends on the happy note that they will both be reincarnated and will be together for another earthly go-around.

And *What Dreams May Come* is unusual for another reason: it is the only Matheson novel in which the text is followed by a nine-page bibliography. In the final analysis it is less a novel than a dramatized tract and so falls between stools—it is neither engaging enough as a novel, nor intellectually stimulating enough as a treatise to satisfy the reader. But it certainly demonstrates Matheson's increasing interest in the paranormal—or as he likes to call it—the "supernormal."

Despite a gap of two decades, *The Path: A New Look at Reality* (1993) seems like the genuine sequel to *What Dreams May Come*, and is a continuation and elaboration of the ideas promulgated in that book. If *What Dreams May Come* is a thematic novel, *The Path* is a philosophical tract vaguely cast in the shape of a novel. Matheson calls attention to this with the note "Based on the writings of Harold W. Percival," printed below the book's title, and in a brief forward in which he admits that the "answers" to his lifelong metaphysical search are best articulated in Percival's book *Thinking and Destiny* (1979). As he stated in *The Spook* interview: "I was magically drawn to this book. . . . I'd evolved my own metaphysical belief system based on reading hundreds of books. But this book had it all—what did I waste my time for? All I had to do was read this one" (Etchison). Thus, Matheson offers his skills as a fiction writer in the service of Percival's vision, making the ideas accessible to the uninformed reader and, hopefully, stimulating him to further study.

In *The Path* an unnamed first-person Narrator encounters a mysterious Stranger while taking a casual walk around his neighborhood and begins a philosophical conversation—or, rather, engages in a Socratic dialogue, with the Stranger as teacher and himself as acolyte. The dialogue is continued in a series of "Walks" (the basis for Matheson's chapter headings) spread over a number of days. During these successive Walks, the Stranger moves from comments on the sad, precarious state of the world, to discussions of the division between body and spirit, the nature of the "true self," life after death, the ethereal progress of the "doer" self (Matheson never uses the term "soul"), divine judgment (each is his own judge), "hell," reliving misdeeds without perceptual distortion or rationalization, "heaven," where one lives one's idealized life, the nature and process of reincarnation (true learning and improvement can only come from an earthly life), the stages of life, and, finally, the idea that all physical reality is an "exteriorization of thought." Even in Matheson's "simplified" version, this is philosophically heady stuff and very dense reading, provocative if one is sympathetic to Matheson's mystical inclinations, probably unreadable if one isn't.

Mediums Rare, a nonfiction book published in 2000, can almost be seen as an extended footnote to *The Path*. Written in a casual, anecdotal, fragmentary style, it covers the Spiritualist movement from its beginnings up to the advent of "respectable" scientific parapsychology or Extra Sensory Perception (ESP), as it was dubbed by Professor J. B. Rhine in 1934. Although he touches on King Croesus, St. Teresa of Avila, Emmanuel Swedenborg, and Franz Anton Mesmer, it is really with the mid-nineteenth century Fox Sisters, who gave the movement its head start, that Matheson begins his story. From that point on, Matheson systematically, if sketchily, covers the major spiritualists of the second half of the nineteenth century—devoting special attention to Nettie Colburn, whose predictions to Lincoln were important to the Civil War; D. D. Home, who not only claimed contact with the spirit world, but also reportedly was able to levitate himself and do other astounding magical feats; Eusapia Palladino, who admitted mixing trickery with astonishing psychic demonstrations; and finally Edgar Cayce, who combined spiritual contacts with extraordinary healings of the sick. While it is unlikely that Matheson's brief, anecdotal treatments of these figures would convert the skeptical, they do neatly flesh out his shift from detached, cynical "paranoia" to mystical affirmation.

The other original novels published since *Bid Time Return*—two mysteries, *Now You See It. . . .* (1995) and *Camp Pleasant* (2000), and one thriller, *Seven Steps to Midnight* (1993)—are all interesting if uneven throwbacks to the earlier Matheson.

Seven Steps to Midnight (1993) was the first original novel to appear since *Bid Time Return*. The hero, Chris Barton, a government research worker, returns to his home one evening to find out that he no longer lives there: his identity has been assumed by another, neither friends nor family recognize him, none of his identification cards are valid, and he is forced into flight in an attempt to prove his own existence. And if that wasn't bad enough, he is soon pursued by hostile, sometimes violent "agents." He also begins acquiring mysterious instructions, objects, and allies—including, of course, the requisite beautiful female agent. In other words, reality disintegrates around Barton in a manner reminiscent of the agonies endured by many of Matheson's earlier trapped heroes.

But about halfway through the book the protagonist—and the reader—realizes that it is all some sort of elaborate and very artificial plot. He relaxes, we relax, and the good guys show up to explain everything. These final revelations are totally contrived and improbable. *7 Steps* starts well but dissipates for the last hundred pages. A major disappointment.

Now You See It (1995), originally written for the stage then novelized, veers closer to mystery plays like Anthony Shaffer's *Sleuth* or Ira Levin's *Deathtrap* than to Matheson's prior works. A magic show is both the setting for most of the story and a metaphor for the art of the novel. The book is a series of "illusions" with which the characters attempt to fool each other—and the reader. The Great Delacorte, a paralyzed master magician, watches his son Max Jr. duel with his wife, brother-in-law, and agent for control of the act using magic tricks as weapons.

It is not hard to see that the story was originally conceived for the stage. For all practical purposes it looks and feels like a play. Most of the action takes place on a single set, the "Magic Room" of the family mansion, and the action progresses in a series of tightly written scenes that usually feature a reversal or dramatic exposure of an illusion, which leads to another illusion and another exposé and so on until the end of the book when all is finally explained—providing the reader has been keeping score. It is an very clever series of plot reversals—perhaps too clever. While the particulars of each reversal are adroitly concealed, the reader catches on quickly to the fact that they will be coming and that undercuts the mystery and suspense. The other problem in the book is that Matheson's storytelling method—everything is told through the eyes of the paralyzed master magician—seems very contrived and awkward, probably a result of the transition from stage to page.

Matheson's most recent mystery, *Camp Pleasant*, is easily the best of the three. More Agatha Christie than Dashiell Hammett, *Camp Pleasant* has the form and feeling of a classical detective story set in a Summer Camp. Matt Harper, a recently hired counselor, encounters Ed Nolan, the sadistic camp director, his young, sexy, unhappy wife, and assorted oddballs among the staff and young campers. The pressures build as Nolan becomes increasingly devious and brutal until, just prior to a particularly sadistic and dangerous joke he has planned for the young campers, he is found with a knife in his throat. His wife, who by this time Harper has fallen in love with, is charged with the crime. Can he find the real killer before everybody goes home for the summer? It turns out to be not much of a mystery, but the writing is excellent, the novel well-paced, the characters sharply drawn, if one-dimensional, and the setting rendered in vivid sensory detail. Even the ending has some of that ambiguity and sadness characteristic of the best of Matheson's early fiction.

It could be said that Matheson has made a complete 180-degree shift from a paranoiac vision of man trapped in a progressively unstable even disintegrating reality—external and internal—to one of man as a spiritual creature on the brink of ultimate fulfillment. While his work certainly shows a movement in that direction, that would be an oversimplification. Even in the early dark, ironic stories and novels there is usually a glimmer of optimism; even while writing his recent visionary novel-essays he has also written or rewritten stories that harken back to his earlier paranoiac and cynical attitudes. Matheson has always been a moving target, and is one of the most interesting writers in modern fantasy literature.

SUPERNATURAL FICTION WRITERS

Selected Bibliography

WORKS OF RICHARD MATHESON

NOVELS AND SHORT STORIES

Fury on Sunday. New York: Lion, 1953. (Republished as *The Omega Man: I Am Legend*, New York: Berkley, 1971).

Someone Is Bleeding. New York: Lion, 1953.

I Am Legend. New York: Fawcett, 1954; London, Transworld, 1956.

Born of Man and Woman: Tales of Science Fiction and Fantasy. Philadelphia: Chamberlain, 1954; London: Reinhardt, 1956. (Abridged as *Third from the Sun*, New York: Bantam, 1955; London: Transworld, 1961.)

The Shrinking Man. New York: Fawcett, 1956; London: Muller, 1958.

The Shores of Space. New York: Bantam, 1957; London: Transworld, 1958.

A Stir of Echoes. Philadelphia, Lippincott, 1958; London: Cassell, 1958.

Ride the Nightmare. New York: Ballantine, 1959; London: World, 1961.

The Beardless Warriors. Boston and Toronto: Little, Brown: 1960; London: Heinemann, 1961.

Shock! New York: Dell, 1961; London: Corgi, 1962.

Shock II. New York: Dell, 1964; London, Corgi, 1965.

Shock III. New York: Dell, 1966; London, Corgi, 1967.

Hell House. New York: Viking, 1971; London: Sphere, 1977.

Bid Time Return. New York: Viking, 1975; London: Sphere, 1977.

What Dreams May Come. New York: Putnam, 1978; London: M. Joseph, 1979.

Earthbound. London: Robinson, 1989; New York: Tor, 1994. (Restored, uncut version of book originally published in 1982 as by Logan Swanson, after Matheson objected to heavy editing and removed his name.)

Collected Stories. Los Angeles: Dream/Press, 1989. (Contains all but ten of Matheson's published short stories along with appreciations by Ray Bradbury, Robert Bloch, William F. Nolan, Jack Finney, George Clayton Johnson, Harlan Ellison, Stephen King, Dennis Etchison, and his son, Richard Christian Matheson)

Journal of the Gun Years. New York: Evans, 1991.

The Gunfight. New York: Evans, 1993.

The Path: Metaphysics for the '90s. Santa Barbara, Calif.: Capra, 1993. (Republished as *The Path: A New Look at Reality*, New York: Tor, 1999.)

Seven Steps to Midnight. New York: Forge, 1993.

Shadow on the Sun. New York: Evans, 1994.

The Memoirs of Wild Bill Hickock. New York: Jove, 1995.

Now You See It—. New York: Doherty, 1995.

Passion Play. Baltimore: Cemetery Dance, 2000.

Hunger and Thirst. Springfield, Pa.: Gauntlet, 2000.

RICHARD MATHESON

Camp Pleasant. Baltimore: Cemetery Dance, 2001.

Abu and the Seven Marvels. Illustrated by William Stout. Springfield, Pa.: Gauntlet, 2002. (Children's book.)

NONFICTION

Robert Bloch: Appreciations of the Master. New York: Tor, 1995. (Edited by Matheson together with Ricia Mainhardt.)

Mediums Rare. Baltimore: Cemetery Dance, 2000.

TELEPLAYS (PUBLISHED)

Richard Matheson's The Twilight Zone Scripts. Vol. 1. Edited by Stanley Wiater. Springfield, Pa.: Gauntlet, 2001.

Richard Matheson's The Twilight Zone Scripts. Vol. 2. Edited by Stanley Wiater: Springfield, Pa: Gauntlet, 2002.

SELECTED TELEPLAYS (UNPUBLISHED)

"The Enemy Within." *Star Trek.* NBC, 1966.

"Duel." *ABC Movie of the Week.* ABC, January 11, 1972.

"The Night Strangler." ABC, 1973.

"Dying Room Only." *ABC Movie of the Week.* ABC, January 16, 1974. (From his short story.)

"Scream of the Wolf." *ABC Movie of the Week.* ABC, January 16, 1974.

"Dracula." CBS, February 8, 1974.

"The Stranger Within." ABC, 1974. (From his short story.)

"The Martian Chronicles." NBC, 1980.

SELECTED SCREENPLAYS (UNPUBLISHED)

The Incredible Shrinking Man. Universal, 1957.

The House of Usher. American International, 1960.

The Pit and the Pendulum. American International, 1960.

Tales of Terror. American International, 1961.

Burn, Witch, Burn. American International, 1963. (With Charles Beaumont.)

The Raven. American International, 1963.

The Comedy of Terrors. American International, 1964.

The Last Man on Earth. American International, 1964. (As by his pseudonym "Logan Swanson"; from his novel *I Am Legend.*)

The Young Warriors. Universal, 1967. (From his novel *The Beardless Warriors.*)

The Devil's Bride. 20th Century Fox, 1968. (Also released as *The Devil Rides Out.*)

De Sade. American International, 1969. (Story and screenplay.) *The Legend of Hell House.* 20th Century Fox, 1973.

Somewhere In Time. Universal, 1980. (From *Bid Time Return.*)

Twilight Zone—The Movie. Warner, 1983.

Jaws 3D. Universal, 1983. (With Carl Gottlieb.)

CRITICAL AND BIOGRAPHICAL STUDIES

King, Stephen. *Danse Macabre*. New York: Everest House, 1981. Pp. 317–330.

Oakes, David A. *Science and Destabilization in the Modern American Gothic: Lovecraft, Matheson, and King*. Westport, Conn.: Greenwood, 2000. Pp. 63–89.

Rathbun, Mark, and Graeme Flanagan. *Richard Matheson—He Is Legend: An Illustrated Bio-Bibliography*. Chico, Calif.: Rathbun, 1984.

INTERVIEWS

Etchison, Dennis. "A Conversation with Richard Matheson." *The Spook*, December 2001 and January 2002. (An Internet magazine, available at http://www.thespook.com.)

"TZ Interview: Richard Matheson," *Twilight Zone Magazine*, September 1981, pp. 43–50.

"TZ Interview: Richard Matheson (Part Two)," *Twilight Zone Magazine,* October 1981, pp. 14–21.

William Mayne

1928–

JOHN CLUTE

THERE IS A WORD used in Britain to describe a relationship between the land and that which the land holds in its grasp. This word, earthfast, is applied primarily to rocks—standing stones perhaps, planted into the soil three thousand years ago—which the land holds tight and immovable until spring, or dry weather, occasions a relaxing of the grip; when the bondage of that which has been earthfasted loosens. The term has a twofold implication: it points backwards to the bondage of the rock, or the carved stone, or the bones of some entity; and it points to the present moment, when something moves. It is a term that focuses our adherence to the land and allows us to remember that we, who are earthfasts of the planet, are at loose. The title of William Mayne's single most famous fantasy novel is *Earthfasts* (1966), and if one single word can sum up the complex undertakings of his fiction, it is that word.

BACKGROUND

William Mayne seems to ask us to think of him as a person who is almost as anonymous as a rock. He seems to ask us to think of him as nothing but what he writes. He divulges little about his life, though some facts are known. He was born in Hull, on the northeast coast of England, on March 16, 1928. He was a middle-class boy, being the son of a doctor; between 1937 and 1942 he was a pupil at Canterbury Cathedral Choir School, in the far south of the country.

He worked briefly for the British Broadcasting Corporation and worked briefly as a teacher. He wrote from an early age, publishing his first novel, *Follow the Footprints,* in 1953, when he was twenty-five years old. He has published approximately two books a year since that date. He also composes, one of his credits being the incidental music to *Holly from the Bongs* (1966), a nativity play by Alan Garner. He has traveled—he taught for the 1976–1977 academic year at Deakin University in Australia. He lives in the Yorkshire Dales, not far from his hometown. Most of his tales are set within a few dozen miles of his home, but others are set elsewhere, in Wales, London, Cornwall, Greece, the United States, New Zealand, and mythical kingdoms in Eastern Europe. He has remained active for half a century.

MAYNE'S READING OF THE WORLD

From almost the very beginning of his career, critics and readers in general have noticed that

Mayne's books are as much about their settings as they are about the characters who—at times only flickeringly—unfasten themselves sufficiently from landscape to be noted as folk. These characters sometimes seem to come into storyable focus only for the course of the tale; the final moments of many Mayne tales submerge back into the land the stories they tell, and the characters earthfasted into sight to bear the brief burden of the tale similarly return to the ground. Very few of his novels feature protagonists far removed from their home regions; very few of his protagonists leave home at the end of things. A close reading of William Mayne is a close reading of the earth, "the great garden of the world" invaded by the eponymous mole of *The Mouldy* (1983), a short tale about the fragile kingdoms of the natural world, and the inner earths to which the mole returns, once married, once content.

Very little that is supernatural surfaces in the first ten or so years of his career. Of the thirty or so novels published before *Earthfasts* in 1966, most are set entirely in this world, though even as early as *A Swarm in May* (1955), the intensity of his descriptions of the given world, and the deepness of the embedding of his protagonists in their surroundings, together convey a sense of a world supersaturated, as it were, with being. It is a world written and rewritten upon itself, in the way that a palimpsest is inscribed and reinscribed through time. Even the popular Cathedral School sequence, which *A Swarm in May* initiates, plays demandingly with its given venue, and with time's reinscriptions, through a storyline—a boy discovers ancient beehives held fast deep within Canterbury Cathedral—which embeds overwhelmingly the sense that, in Mayne's work, time moves not like an arrow but a loom, weaving together layer upon layer of place.

In the end, in this as in all his greater books, the effect is of sensations too densely woven together to decipher, of codes too overwritten to unpack. The style in which this effect is conveyed is not easy; Mayne, who has never written a book ostensibly for adults, has had to bear for half a century the perception that his work is simply too dense and too demanding for even the young adult market to bear. In *The Member for the Marsh* (1956), much admired by adults for its language and speed, a boy is frightened by a "marsh-dragon" at a place where his dog has been lost; the dragon becomes a pumping engine; the pumping engine exudates an Iron Age settlement. All three phenomena are real within their terms, and separate; all three are woven into one thing. This terrain is difficult.

Most of the books of the next decade share a quest structure of the sort common to much fantasy. Mayne's quests, typical of British as opposed to American fantasy, tend to be centripetal, leading inward to the geographical heart of the place where the story begins (American fantasy quests tend to lead from the beginning place to somewhere else). The treasure to be found in a Mayne quest novel is the genius loci (the genius or central spirit of place) of the land it hides within. It is a unicorn, whether or not "real," in *The Grass Rope* (1957). It is the real street, which underlies the streets of today, in *Underground Alley* (1958), just as the abandoned railway line in *Sand* (1964) underlies the town it once fed. It is the gradual unveiling of the true source of water in a drought-stricken village in Wiltshire in *The Rolling Season* (1960), and it is the eponymous magic ball in *The Glass Ball* (1961), which leads two boys from the monastery on high through their Greek island home village down to the sea below, knitting together for them the luminous lives they lead.

EARTHFASTS SERIES

With *Earthfasts,* which is a full fantasy, the corner-of-the-eye immanence of the genius loci comes implacably into focus. It is a crosshatch tale, a tale about the interweaving intersection of multiple worlds, multiple perceived realities. (For a more extended discussion of "crosshatch" see *The Encyclopedia of Fantasy,* 1997, edited by

John Clute and John Grant.) Young David Wix, who is so acutely atuned to things that he seems fey, and his friend Keith Heseltine are walking in the moors near their home in the northeast of England. They hear drumming at the edge of a hill, "like the thudding of invisible cold flames" (p. 5), and a drummer boy from two centuries earlier works his way out of the earth into 1966, an earthfast freed but intensely bewildered at the new day. He thinks only a little while has passed since he entered a cave to search for King Arthur's treasure. He carries a candle, which he has taken from the cave. He soon disappears back into the time abyss that has kept him bonded to the earth, while aboveground, in 1966, more earthfasts tremble along the crosshatches: a group of standing stones turns into a team of giants, who steal all the pigs in the region; a boggart awakens; David is seemingly struck by lightning, disappears, and is deemed dead. The pace of the tale seems slow but is in fact dense with speed. David and Keith are so caught up in what is happening to them that they seem intagliated against each new sentence that describes their fates, their eyes plastered to the front of the story so they can hardly breathe.

It is a technical feat of storytelling of very great sophistication, and it ranges far afield in its descriptions of a disrupted world. Only after he encounters the awoken Sleeper under the Hill and his troops—"They stood as if they were held, like iron filings, and prickly like them too, against a different force from the one that held Keith to the house and the floor of the world" (p. 131)—does Keith begin to understand that the wresting of the candle from within the earth had broken time, for "King Arthur's time was not yet come" (p. 140). The candle is returned, and the drummer boy, who has been again severed from 1750, is sent to a farm where he will not be terrified. Life is unbroken again.

A year or so later, in *Cradlefasts* (1995), the seams of the world split again. A young girl, fatally ill with tuberculosis, claims to be David Wix's sister Clare. His mother, who had died giving birth to his "real" stillborn sister seven years before, had told David her projected name, but no one else. The child shuttles between town and Swang Farm, near the Jingle Stones, which had turned to giants under time's crosshatch glare. She then dies, though her spirit can be seen becoming transfigured into a boggart, a household entity occasionally aroused by the unhealed knot in time. It is never certain if Clare is a real sister unleashed through the knot, or a fake. All is eventually resolved in *Candlefasts* (2000) which—like so many texts written in the early years of the twenty-first century—shifts back and forth among genres, from fantasy to science fiction and back again. The restiveness in the Dales has been caused through the entrapment there for eons of a spiderlike entity from the far future. David, haunted for years by a deep yearning—at times like profound nostalgia, at other times approaching the ecstasy of a genuine "theophany" (p. 119)—is now a young man. He re-creates the "spider's" grail-like time machine out of stones and crystal. The stones surround Swang Farm. The "spider" escapes. The stones settle into focus. The world is all one time at last. At ease, the boggarts of the farm roam "the garden inside, like pets" (p. 218).

OTHER NOVELS AND STORIES

Although there is very little repetition in Mayne's oeuvre—the "fasts" books are rare in comprising a tightly composed trilogy—themes, patterns of association between protagonists and defining land, are often replayed and re-sorted. *The Battlefield* (1967), for instance, recontemplates what might be called the rhythm of chaos occasioned when the literal rock the world is built of is loosened, and more than one time comes into one place. (Rock, in Mayne's world, seems to represent a deep slowness of time; rock when earthfasted lets the past out.) In *Over the Hills and Far Away* (1968; retitled *The Hill Road* in the United States), a different kind of character, a girl this time, encounters a time-slip deep twin, a witch from a millennium ago, who is in danger. They are lost in literal mists of time, until the mist lifts:

And instead of the hot silence of the uplands, and the sharp noise of the horn, and the threatening song of the enemy, there was the gabble of a tractor working at the hay on the hill; and they were no longer in the middle of battle and the chase, but galloping in a field that had just been cut and made into hay.

"Stop," said Dolly, "stop. We aren't here any more."

(p. 142)

With more complexity than any earlier novel other than *Earthfasts*, *A Game of Dark* (1971) casts into the world (which takes the bait) the twisting psyche of a distressed soul, in this case young Donald Jackson, whose ungiving father is fatally ill after an accident. Rent terribly by guilt and distaste and a hope he cannot understand that his father perish, Jackson enters an otherworld where his conflicts, now external, are transformed into attempts to kill a "worm," that is, a kind of dragon. That this worm and his father are palimpsests of one another becomes gradually clear; but this clarity gives no sure repose. Whuttering back and forth from one world to another, Jackson learns, in the final page of the tale, how to love his father, who dies immediately. "There was no more breathing. Donald lay and listened to the quiet, and went to sleep, consolate" (p. 143).

Just as remarkably, the British edition of *The Jersey Shore* (1973) generates, out of an equally painful family romance, an ending whose release is unalloyed. The setting is New Jersey, in a small town dominated by the Atlantic Ocean. The time is circa 1935. As becomes gradually clear—through an array of effects not dissimilar to those used by Peter Straub, for similar reasons, in his *Mr. X* (1999)—the book's protagonist is black, and the long, tortured tale his white grandfather Benj tells him can only be properly understood when that central fact is also understood. (In view of this, and in view of the fact that much of the book makes little sense when this fact is not understood, it seems all the more inexplicable that the final pages of the American edition of this novel were censored in order to disguise its protagonist's blackness, presumably because American readers were deemed unready to accept a black protagonist and a tale to which miscegenation is central.)

In the novel, the family story of old Benj Thatcher, who had long before emigrated from the disease-ridden fen country of England, deeply engrosses his grandson, young Arthur, who actually comes to pre-inhabit the world described. Years later Arthur, now a World War II pilot on leave, visits Benj's old home, which he recognizes in advance, and discovers Benj's deep story. The woman he had most loved there, but never married, was the black descendant of a slave. After her death in 1886 of fen fever, along with his wife and all their children, Benj left for America, where he married Florence, Arthur's grandmother—who had herself been born a slave—because she was so like his true love. Arthur knocks on the door opposite Benj's old farm. A young black woman opens the door. In the last paragraph of the novel, they fall in love "at first sight" (p. 159).

Some less taxing novels followed. A fairy changeling is found near a Cornish village in *A Year and a Day* (1976) and is adopted by a family for the year and a day he will remain among mortal folk. The family and the land they inhabit with loving humbleness intersect and overarch the child Adam's strange, short life; little happens over the months before he "dies," and soon a new child is born. But the changeling Adam is somehow there:

And the boy was baptized and christened Adam, and he yelled right across the church and had to be taken out afterwards, when he too was a holy Christian man, and Sara and Rebecca sat by the side of the road and cried with happiness while the church of people sang, and Adam listened with them.

(p. 96)

Max's Dream (1977) retells an episode from *The Mabinogion* through the memories in old age of a serving woman left by the boy she loved, a cripple asked to participate in a holy dance and a journey that leaves her alone. Alice, the young protagonist of *It* (1977) sticks her hand into the earth and a poltergeist grabs it and twins her, out of something like vengeance because she will soon time-slip back centuries and kill the witch who had been the poltergeist's person; Alice deals briskly with this complicated set of consequences. Of the three tales assembled in *All the King's Men* (1982), "Boy to Island" is of deepest interest, a complexly crosshatched "Time in Faerie" story. Its young protagonist spends seven years in a kind of day on a fairy island attempting to guide a young woman through labyrinths of deceit and the engulfing rocks to safety, only to find at the end that, once freed, and reunited with the ancient man who has waited so many decades for her, she slides at lightning speed through the years of her life and dies into dust.

Ostensibly for younger children, but much loved by adults, the various Hob stories—four short volumes assembled as *The Book of Hob Stories* (1991), plus two novels, *Hob and the Goblins* (1993) and *Hob and the Peddler* (1997)—comprise a virtual grammatology of intersections between a daylight world and a supernatural being who lives within, and without, the mundane. *Hob and the Goblins* tells more darkly of an upswelling of the underworld, which threatens to engulf the human family Hob takes secret care of. Told with a similar intensity of ellipsis and sudden verb, *The Blemyah Stories* (1987) describe the eponymous beings who, themselves made out of wood, carve misericords of wood throughout a medieval year, which culminates for them in the carving of a nativity scene whose Babe touches a naughty (or knotty) Blemyah and he is cured.

Three novels, each of them ostensibly absent of any real supernatural element, demonstrate the hovering pressure of more complete forms of understanding of the world. Each of them (like so much of Mayne's work) reads as a kind of diorama of the land that shines through their windows. *Tiger's Railway* (1987) tells of the eponymous railway superintendent's habit of stealing trains; the tale is set in a socialist-realist Ruritania called the Bessar District, which threatens constantly to become a Wonderland. In *The Farm That Ran Out of Names* (1990), a Welsh farmer named Owen Tudor is told that the city of Birmingham has expropriated his farm, and all others in his home valley, so that a reservoir can be constructed to feed water to the great distant greedy metropolis. But the village pond, being unowned, has not been expropriated, so Owen builds a Noah's Ark there, immune from the law. Fortunately, after a cold winter, the ark is hurled over a cliff into the next valley, where it settles intact on land for sale, which Owen buys, and life continues in the new-found land.

The powerful *Antar and the Eagles* (1989) stands to one side of Mayne's work in general. The eponymous young boy is the only human character of any significance in the tale; its other main characters are indeed an autonomous tribe of eagles. It is unlike almost any other story in Mayne's vast oeuvre, where animals, whether or not they talk, serve almost invariably as liminal beings, conducting messages back and forth between the surface of the world and time and the deeper world, held fast, in rock, ages ago. Antar is abducted from his unnamed town in an unnamed country by the Great Eagle, whom a gun gravely wounds, and taken to the high cliffs where the eagles under Great Eagle's charge make their home. He is taught to act like an eagle, to fly, to converse properly, to eat proper food. His task is to fly to a neighboring kingdom whose king has illegitimate hold over the golden egg from which the next Great Eagle is due to hatch; otherwise the eagles will die. The boy accomplishes his task, almost dies in the underworld as volcanoes chase him like dragons, and is returned home at last, in time to grow up.

It may be that, as the century darkened and as he grew older, Mayne's sense of the world in turn darkened. Even though he was never a comic writer (individual scenes throughout the years can be hilarious, but always within a controlling frame), a tale like *Cuddy* (1994) seems to bear deeper layers of bleakness within a structure that demands a happy ending, though few endings in Mayne are unseamed. This book may be his most unrelenting attempt yet to construct a grammar of the interactions between world and humans, past and present, bondage and freedom, materially real and utterly real. Cuddy is St. Cuthbert, who lived as a mortal 1,300 years before the action of the tale, which takes place in modern Durham, in the North of England. After his death, his body had been removed from the island he longed to rest in, Inner Farne, near Lindisfarne, where he had served as prior. Partly through the conduit to the present opened by a bear named Beowulf, who has become a teddy bear owned by young Ange, Cuddy's longing to return to what he calls Paradise, or Neorxenawang, begins to crosshatch into the lives of Ange and her friends, all of whom turn out to be relatives, all left-handed, and all related to the Saint's People, who had taken care of Cuddy himself.

The ghost Cuddy requires seven symbolic objects, which have become earthfasted into history and the land over the intervening centuries: staff, bell, cup, cloak, ring, wallet, brush. Dizzyingly, Ange and her cohort are tossed back and forth from time to time and into varying bodies, they are ingested, torn, and blown, but they survive. Cuddy himself, growing in stature, gains the signs of his wholeness and confronts the northern god Tyr, who in monstrous forms has been impeding the search. But even Tyr, in the end, is absolved and absorbed, for Mayne has little truck with villains: the world is too saturated with the gloriousness of being itself to make much room for evil to breathe. Characters are sometimes misled through the interstices of time and things, but they do not hold the reins, or attempt to grasp them, as in more conventional tales of the supernatural.

Two experiments in storytelling can be noted in the work of later years. *The Fairy Tales of London Town: Upon Paul's Steeple* (1995) and *The Fairy Tales of London Town: See-Saw Sacradown* (1996) constitute Mayne's first substantial attempt to incorporate urban fantasy into his oeuvre. The tales are amused, celebratory, haunted by the befogging multiverse of the almost infinitely storied city. They are an attempt, mostly successful, to create a late-century mythology of London retentive of its magic, after a bad century for those who love the metropolis. *The Fox Gate and Other Stories* (1996) assembles a set of linked animal fantasies, the first sustained attempt Mayne has made to tell such tales.

The career of William Mayne remains, it seems, in medias res. *The Worm in the Well* (2002), has a complexity that at some points rivals that of *Cuddy*, though the mode of telling is simpler. It is set at the time of the First Crusade. One lord transgresses against a witch and the way of the world and is turned into the grotesque worm of the title. The second lord, Alan, the protagonist, loses his love, Margaret, through a failure to confront the worm properly. She becomes, literally, a kind of tapestry: a crosshatch between the world and something lost inside the world. She weeps stitches, not tears. Bad waters rise, there are floods, much confusion, actions and interactions. Alan follows instructions regarding the worm, promising to marry its daughter, who is Margaret, and it swallows them up and dissolves, opening them all again to the world. The tale is told lightly, but the Celtic modes within it—specifically the metamorphoses that haunt the turnings of the story—are deeply told.

There is something in this tale of the great urgency that sometimes drives writers who are growing old, but who have more and more to say. William Mayne, now well into his seventies, seems gripped, to the benefit of us all, by this fury.

Of William Mayne's more than 100 books, some are written for younger children and are not listed here; at least forty of the remainder are either fantasy or science fiction, or are tales that hover at the edge of the supernatural. These stories are listed below.

WILLIAM MAYNE

Selected Bibliography

WORKS OF WILLIAM MAYNE

NOVELS AND SHORT STORIES

The Member for the Marsh. London: Oxford University Press, 1956. (Supernatural events are here rationalized.)

A Grass Rope. London: Oxford University Press, 1957; New York: Dutton, 1962.

The Rolling Season. London: Oxford University Press, 1960.

The Changeling. London: Oxford University Press, 1961; New York: Dutton, 1963.

The Glass Ball. London: Hamish Hamilton, 1961; New York: Dutton, 1962.

The Twelve Dancers. London: Hamish Hamilton, 1962.

Earthfasts. London: Hamish Hamilton, 1966; New York: Dutton, 1967. (Earthfasts series, no. 1.)

The Battlefield. London: Hamish Hamilton and New York: Dutton, 1967.

Over the Hills and Far Away. London: Hamish Hamilton, 1968. As *The Hill Road,* New York: Dutton, 1969.

A Game of Dark. London: Hamish Hamilton and New York: Dutton, 1971.

Skiffy. London: Hamish Hamilton, 1972. (Skiffy series, no. 1.)

The Jersey Shore. London: Hamish Hamilton and New York: Dutton, 1973. (The ending of the U.S. edition is rewritten in order to disguise the fact that the protagonist is black.)

A Year and a Day. London: Hamish Hamilton and New York: Dutton, 1976.

It. London: Hamish Hamilton, 1977; New York: Greenwillow Books, 1978.

Max's Dream. London: Hamish Hamilton and New York: Greenwillow Books, 1977.

While the Bells Ring. London: Hamish Hamilton, 1979.

All the King's Men. London: Jonathan Cape and New York: Delacorte Press, 1982. (Stories.)

Skiffy and the Twin Planets. London: Hamish Hamilton, 1982. (Skiffy series, no. 2.)

A Small Pudding for Wee Gowry and Other Stories of Underground Creatures. London: Macmillan Children's Books, 1983.

The Mouldy. London: Jonathan Cape and New York: Knopf, 1983. (Story.)

The Blue Book of Hob Stories. London: Walker Books and New York: Philomel, 1984. (Linked stories.)

The Green Book of Hob Stories. London: Walker Books and New York: Philomel, 1984. (Linked stories.)

The Red Book of Hob Stories. London: Walker Books and New York: Philomel, 1984. (Linked stories.)

The Yellow Book of Hob Stories. London: Walker Books and New York: Philomel, 1984. (Linked stories.)

Gideon Ahoy! London and New York: Viking Kestral, 1987; New York: Delacorte Press, 1989.

The Blemyah Stories. London: Walker Books, 1987. (Linked stories.)

Kelpie. London: Jonathan Cape, 1987.

Tiger's Railway. London: Walker Books, 1987. (Essentially realistic, but set in a Ruritanian Eastern European country.)

Antar and the Eagles. London: Walker Books, 1989. New York: Delacorte Press, 1990.

The Men of the House. London: Heinemann, 1990. (Story.)

The Farm That Ran Out of Names. London: Jonathan Cape, 1990.

The Book of Hob Stories. London: Walker Books, 1991. (Omnibus reprinting of the four 1984 Hob collections.)

Hob and the Goblins. London: Dorling Kindersley, 1993; New York: DK Inc., 1994. (Hob novel.)

Cuddy. London: Jonathan Cape, 1994.

Cradlefasts. London: Hodder Children's Books, 1995. (Earthfasts series, no. 2.)

The Fairy Tales of London Town: Upon Paul's Steeple. London: Hodder Children's Books, 1995. (Stories.)

The Fairy Tales of London Town: See-Saw Sacradown. London: Hodder Children's Books, 1996. (Stories.)

The Fox Gate and Other Stories. London: Hodder Children's Books, 1996. (Stories.)

Hob and the Peddler. New York: Dorling Kindersley, 1997. (Hob novel.)

Midnight Fair. London: Hodder Children's Books, 1997.

Lady Muck. London: Heinemann and Boston: Houghton Mifflin, 1997. (Story.)

Candlefasts. London: Hodder Children's Books, 2000. (Earthfasts series, no. 3.)

The Worm in the Well. London: Hodder Children's Books, 2002.

Anne McCaffrey
1926–

DAVID LANGFORD

ANNE McCAFFREY HAS stated firmly that she is a science fiction storyteller and does not permit the label "fantasy" to be attached to her work. Yet paradoxically her most successful fiction has a mythic, even a fairy-tale, quality. Her famed dragons inevitably carry a weight of legendary associations, while characters often echo the archetypes of Cinderella or the Ugly Duckling as they rise to successful swanhood. It is this quality that entices critics to class her storytelling as "science fantasy" and even to discuss her science fiction in fantasy terms—as in, for example, Mike Ashley's entry devoted to her in *The Encyclopedia of Fantasy* (1997). As Brian Aldiss put it in his essay "Science Fiction's Mother Figure" (in *The Pale Shadow of Science*, 1985), using phraseology perhaps more acceptable to McCaffrey herself: "Anne McCaffrey's dragon novels hover between legend, fairy tale, and science fiction. 'Pure' science fiction is chimerical. Its strength lies in its appetite" (p. 38).

Anne Inez McCaffrey was born in Cambridge, Massachusetts, on April 1, 1926, and took her B.A. in Slavonic language and literature at Radcliffe College in Cambridge, Massachusetts, in 1947. Later academic study of meteorology brought her to the City of Dublin University in Ireland, a country that since 1970 has been her permanent residence. She was married to E. Wright Johnson from 1950 until they divorced in 1970; they had three children. Her first fiction sale was the short story "Freedom of the Race," which appeared in *Science Fiction Plus* magazine in 1953.

McCaffrey's first novel, *Restoree* (1967), is a lighthearted confection of romance and space opera whose engaging heroine, Sara, has painful memories of being the Ugly Duckling. Low on self-esteem, with hairy arms and an oversized nose, she is one of many victims harvested from Earth by repulsive aliens who flay, butcher, and (apparently) eat human prey. By various strokes of luck, Sara reaches planet Lothar—whose people have long battled those same aliens—and finds herself technomagically "restored" as a ravishing beauty with perfect, golden skin. After various setbacks of melodramatic action-adventure, she catalyzes the needed purge of corrupt Lotharian politics and finds true love with a man of high birth. It is a likable romp. A large part of McCaffrey's charm has to do with her unashamed, though here intentionally parodic, use of elements from the gothic or romantic novel traditions in a science fiction context.

THE LAUNCHING OF THE DRAGONRIDERS OF PERN

The author's best-known and most successful piece of science fiction myth making soon followed, with the publication of the first stories about the Dragonriders of Pern, both in *Analog* magazine. "Weyr Search" appeared in the October 1967 issue and "Dragonrider" in two parts, December 1967 and January 1968.

It was one of those rare occasions when something new to the science fiction scene wins immediate mass acclaim. *Analog*'s editor, John W. Campbell, gave both stories star billing on the front cover. The readers, by popular vote, honored "Weyr Search" with the 1968 Hugo Award for best novella—the first ever win by a woman in any Hugo fiction category. McCaffrey's fellow authors in the Science Fiction Writers of America organization gave their own accolade to "Dragonrider": the Nebula Award, again as best novella. With such acclaim from both the fans and the professionals, a one-volume edition of the complete story soon followed: *Dragonflight* (1968). The long saga of Pern was launched.

Again the term "science fantasy" hovers ominously. This is a medieval-seeming world of vaguely feudal society, lords and ladies, craft guilds guarding their secrets, knife duels to the death as an accepted form of litigation, magical-seeming powers of the mind, and—above all—the intelligent, telepathic, highly sympathetic dragons. When asked for her preferred description, the author, in an interview with David V. Barrett in 1984, said: "Soft-core science fiction, in other words, the science does not dominate the story. It's the interplay and interactions of the characters with the science of their planet, not necessarily the science itself" (p. 3).

It can be argued that McCaffrey is consciously and rather ingeniously having it both ways, drawing on the power of mythic fantasy tropes while at the same time deconstructing them in science fiction terms. The prologue of "Weyr Search," as incorporated into *Dragonflight*, sets this up explicitly:

> When is a legend legend? Why is a myth a myth? How old and disused must a fact be for it to be relegated to the category "Fairy-tale"? And why do certain facts remain incontrovertible while others lose their validity to assume a shabby, unstable character?
>
> Rukbat, in the Sagittarian system, was a golden G-type star. It had five planets.
>
> (p. ix)

With the science fiction ground rules of the planet Pern stated, the main story opens in more fantastical mode with the dragonriders' ritual Search for a strong woman who can bond with and ride a soon-to-be-hatched golden dragon. Such queen dragons, now terribly rare, are the all-important breeders. The leadership of a Weyr, an enclave of dragons and riders, is determined by the queens' mating flights: the Weyrleader will be the male human partner of the male dragon (bronze or brown) chosen by the Weyrwoman's queen—a curious form of arranged marriage.

This entire social system is heavy with a sense of stagnation, of rituals that, like those of Mervyn Peake's Gormenghast, have long since become detached from common sense. Why is it important for the Pernese to live in fortified Holds, to scour all vegetation from near their dwellings, to pay a tithe to Dragonweyrs, which for centuries have had no obvious function? Only the sharp-witted dragonrider F'lar has pored over badly preserved historical records to deduce that the legendary menace of "Thread" falling from the sky—the whole reason for the Weyrs' existence—is real and will shortly return.

Astrology in general may be nonsense, but on Pern there is significance in heavenly portents. The Red Star, a rogue planet loose in the Rukbat system, has not made a close approach to Pern in four hundred Turns, four local centuries. But when it does, spores of its native life can cross space and fall to devastate Pern's crops and animals, unless they are sterilized by fire or dragon-flame. An oral tradition of ancient teaching ballads warns of the Red Star's conjunction with human-made landmarks, the Finger Rock and Eye Rock:

> The Finger points
> At an Eye blood-red.
> Alert the Weyrs
> To sear the Thread.
>
> (p. 158)

Such gnomic ballad fragments appear as epigraphs to each chapter of *Dragonflight*, hinting at a long historical background and usefully enhancing the atmosphere of legendary doings.

A particularly memorable Cinderella figure in this novel is the small but tempestuous girl Lessa, who at the outset is quite literally a kitchen drudge, permanently filthy and much bullied and knocked about by her "betters." Soon enough a handsome prince—F'lar the ambitious dragonrider, on Search—arrives to recognize this jewel of pure lineage and psychic talent hidden among grimy pots and pans. Lessa is no passive heroine, though, and the desperately needed reorganization of the sole remaining Weyr to face the return of Thread is much complicated by tensions between this willful new Weyrwoman and F'lar. For some time the relationship is stormy owing to an initial sexual encounter that comes inadvertently close to rape.

One of the recurring scenes of the Pern series, in which considerable emotion is always invested, is the psychic bonding or "Impression" of a newborn dragon by a human. It is a kind of exalted sublimation of the children's-fiction trope of a young rider's rapturous love of her (less often, his) first mount, but here reciprocated and lifelong. (McCaffrey is herself a lover of horses and has for many years run a thoroughbred stud farm in her adopted country of Ireland.)

The inevitable downside of this unbreakable bond is that dragons kill themselves rather than live on after the deaths of their riders, while riders who lose their dragons are emotionally crippled. Another side effect is that the passions of mating dragons spill over to their human partners. In the heat of the mating flight of Lessa's golden dragon Ramoth and F'lar's bronze Mnementh, the virgin Weyrwoman is taken unawares, almost unwillingly, by her and the Weyrleader's inflamed desires.

Despite this slightly gothic shadow over the novel's chief romantic pairing, the story moves on briskly and enjoyably. A single under-strength garrison, Benden Weyr, needs to police all Pern against Threadfall—putting great stress on the dragons despite their innate talent of teleporting through the frigid nonspace known as "*between*" to any distant location that dragon or rider can visualize. Thanks to Lessa's willful disobedience when learning this new discipline, she and Ramoth stumble across the extended ability to jump *between* times, leading to a notable coup as F'lar's dragon forces leap back two hours to make an impossible rendezvous with the first, missed fall of Thread.

There are rousing aerial battles to defend Pern's croplands and forest against the searing, destructive effect of Thread, while at ground level the hunt is on for forgotten technologies—such as flamethrower construction—which can mop up spores missed by the dragons. Overall the cause seems hopeless without the other Weyrs, now empty, whose inhabitants mysteriously went missing centuries ago—until Lessa deduces where and when they must have gone.

In a neat updating of the mythic tradition of supernatural help from the deep past (such as King Arthur sleeping through the ages until Britain's time of greatest need, or the oath-compelled assistance of the cursed Dead in J. R. R. Tolkien's *The Lord of the Rings*), Lessa and Ramoth make a hazardous and draining four-hundred-year backward jump. The Weyrs of long ago learn that they are needed in the future and—excepting Benden—set their course through time for the hour of Pern's greatest need. *Dragonflight* proceeds to a satisfactory conclusion with the arrival of copious reinforcements to help save Pern, and the reunion of F'lar with Lessa.

The closing scene leaves the dragonriders, past and present, joyously carrying out their proper function of battling the Threadfalls, which will continue for decades. One prophetic aside suggests the shape of sequels to come:

> F'lar shook his fist defiantly at the winking Red Eye of the Star.
>
> "One day," he shouted, "we will not sit tamely here, awaiting your fall. We will fall on you, where you spin, and sear you on your own ground."
>
> By the Egg, he told himself, if we can travel four hundred Turns backward and across seas and lands in the blink of an eye, what is travel from one world to another but a different kind of step?
>
> (p. 309)

THE SHIP WHO SANG SERIES

In the year after *Dragonflight*, McCaffrey published the collection of linked stories that she frequently describes as the personal favorite among all her books: *The Ship Who Sang* (1969). Far more evidently than the dragon saga, this is straight science fiction whose heroine Helva is the cyborg "brain" of an interstellar spaceship that has adventures and gets into scrapes in a variety of solar systems.

Again, though, there are underlying mythic resonances that lift this book above the general run of space opera. Helva is an ugly duckling, incurably deformed since birth, a condition introduced without compromise in the opening lines: "She was born a thing and as such would be condemned if she failed to pass the encephalograph test required of all new-born babies. There was always the possibility that though the limbs were twisted, the mind was not" (p. 1). Luckily Helva has a fine mind, which wins part of her rise to swan status. She duly becomes an augmented human, a cyborg "shell person" capable of connecting to and running a spacecraft, a manufacturing plant, or even a city, as though replacing her own useless body. Uniquely among all her peers, she surmounts inbuilt physical obstacles to develop a remarkable singing voice that becomes her trademark. Helva is "the ship who sings."

Additionally she carries fairy-tale echoes of the enchanted princess in a tower of iron (that is, her spaceship), desired but inaccessible. McCaffrey imagines the relation between a brain ship and her ambulant "brawn" partner as potentially highly romantic, rather like the medieval tradition of Courtly Love for a lady who—being intractably virtuous and usually married to another man—can be the object of pure, noble passion untainted by any aspect of physical lovemaking. Indeed Helva preserves her "virtue" or personal integrity in an episode of alien cultural exchange where her mind is temporarily transferred to a physical (though nonhuman) body and she is offered the choice of making this escape permanent. Spurning temptation, she chooses to remain a spaceship.

The loss of Helva's first, platonically beloved partner climaxes the initial story, "The Ship Who Sang" (published in *The Magazine of Fantasy and Science Fiction*, 1961), with a heartfelt evocation of grief. As she related in an article in the November 1990 issue of *New York Review of Science Fiction*, for McCaffrey it was very personal: "I knew it was dramatically correct, and effective. I did not realize as I wrote that I was trying to assuage my grief over my father's death. I still am" ("My Favorite Story," p. 9).

Another parallel with Courtly Love concerns the legends of suitors who become besotted with a picture of a Lady they have never met. The twelfth-century Provençal poet Geoffrey Rudel, for example, supposedly fell in love sight unseen with the Countess of Tripoli and journeyed to his death to see her—as recorded in Algernon

Charles Swinburne's poem "The Triumph of Time" (1878):

> There lived a singer in France of old
> By the tideless dolorous midland sea.
> In a land of sand and ruin and gold
> There shone one woman, and none but she.
> And finding life for her love's sake fail,
> Being fain to see her, he bade set sail,
> Touched land, and saw her as life grew cold,
> And praised God, seeing; and so died he.

Just so, a later partner of Helva falls helplessly in love with the beauty of a computer extrapolation of her genetic makeup, an image showing how she might have looked without that accident of birth. The outcome is less tragic than Rudel's story, with this finally successful partner satisfied with a platonic exchange of conversation and the occasional symbolic caress of Helva's control panel, while she regales him with good coffee and exquisite song. It is one of science fiction's strangest happy endings.

THE KILLASHANDRA SERIES

The importance of music in McCaffrey's life shows clearly in the Helva stories, and a related episode of autobiography was the inspirational seed for *The Crystal Singer* (1982, expanded from two of four linked stories in the four *Continuum* science fiction anthologies, edited by Roger Elwood, 1974–1975). In an author's note that appears in several books, she mentions that she "studied voice production for nine years before arriving at the horrifying conclusion that I was a better stage-director of opera than a singer" (*Dragonflight*, Corgi UK paperback edition, 1970, p. 254). Her singing heroine Killashandra reacts with similar horror when told after ten years' arduous study that despite her perfect pitch, an "unpleasant burr" makes her voice "unsuited to the dynamics of opera," and her intended career as a top soloist is out of the question: "Unfair! Unfair! How could she be allowed to come so far, be permitted to herself, only to be dashed down in the penultimate trial? And to be offered, as a sop, choral leadership? How degradingly ignominious!" (p. 3).

Killashandra's flawed voice makes her another ugly duckling, but she soon learns she has the potential to be a swan on the mystery-shrouded planet Ballybran. Here the singers of the Heptite Guild locate and mine precious crystals via the power of song, recalling the mages of Finland's Kalevala legends, whose potent singing can reshape the physical world. Of course Killashandra is a tremendous success on Ballybran, emerging from her symbiotic adaptation to the planetary ecology with greatly enhanced senses (many candidates are deafened or disabled) and a strong affinity for the especially valuable black crystal, which is the central component of instantaneous long-range communication systems.

As on Lothar and Pern, dangerous exertions or exploits on Ballybran are followed by the sensual pleasures of hot baths, good food, and generally joyous and guilt-free sex. There is a touch of formula here, but it is a useful and time-tested formula. Even better than sex, though, is the magical experience of mining and communing with that subjectively anthropomorphized crystal:

> Killashandra set her nerves for the first incision of the infra-sonic cutter and was relieved to endure less of a shock. Relieved, and dismayed. Was the claim admitting her right to it by lack of protest? Or did one day attune her body to the resonance? She had half wished to experience that pleasuring, that nerve-caressing distraction, as if a highly-skilled lover were inside her body.
>
> (p. 218)

Although the career of crystal singer offers not only such ecstasies but also a greatly prolonged life span, there are repeated warnings about the darker aspects of this devil's bargain. These include Ballybran's deadly "mach storms," physical addiction to the planet so that too long an absence can lead to the kind of rapid aging and death suffered by old-timers who dare to leave the legendary valley of Shangri-La, and chronic memory loss. Indeed the original four-story telling ends in tragedy for our heroine in "Killashandra—Coda and Finale" (*Continuum* 4, 1975), an episode omitted from the sunnier novel.

SERIES AND SPIN-OFFS

All three series books so far discussed developed from shorter work and led to sequels or spin-offs. The Dragonrider series is the most extensive and popular. The Crystal Singer series comprises three books, the second and third being rather less-intense space-operatic adventures than the debut: *Killashandra* (1985) and *Crystal Line* (1992). In the case of *The Ship Who Sang*, McCaffrey indicated reluctance to write more about Helva. In an interview with Chris Morgan, she stated:

> Because *The Ship Who Sang* was sort of my escape valve for a lot of tensions that were in my life in that decade, let's say. Those pressures have since been released or become non-existent. You can't somehow return to a scene like that as easily as you think you can, so I have avoided going back to the Helva setting.... Anyway, you can stretch a theme too far. It becomes too fragile and falls apart. So it's better to push yourself away from the table while you're still a bit hungry.
> (*Extro* 3, July-August 1982, p. 22)

So there have been no further books with Helva as heroine, although two short stories form pendants to the original collection: "Honeymoon" in *Get Off the Unicorn* (1977) and "The Ship That Returned" in *Far Horizons* (1999). By way of compromise, McCaffrey has allowed other authors to cowrite independent novels in this "Helva setting," featuring other brain ships and cyborg city-controllers as their lead characters. The results—see "The Ship Who Sang series" section in the bibliography—are competent and modestly entertaining, but lacking in magic.

Some further examples of McCaffrey's many science fiction series should be briefly mentioned. The "Doona" sequence, opening with *Decision at Doona* (1969), is pure and somewhat simplistic science fiction, although its very catlike aliens suggest the old fantasy motif of talking animals. The "Talent" or "Pegasus" sequence deals with the development, misuse, restraint, and eventual commercial harnessing of such psionic powers as telepathy and teleportation in a realistic future setting. *To Ride Pegasus* (1973) is a collection of linked near-future stories, followed after some lapse of time (and a couple of generations of interior chronology) by the novels *Pegasus in Flight* (1990) and *Pegasus in Space* (2000). The latter are feel-good science fiction adventures, laden with romance, warm friendships, and hearty meals; villains appear but tend to be dealt with almost too rapidly to allow dramatic suspense.

A related series set much further in the future began with *The Rowan* (1990), whose seed was the short "Lady in the Tower" (*Magazine of Fantasy and Science Fiction*, 1959). The series retrospectively acquired the overall title "The Tower and the Hive" as it developed into a multigenerational saga of psionics, romance, and interstellar clashes with genocidal alien "Hivers." The first book's eponymous heroine and her even more talented male partner are still going strong with a large supporting cast of children and grandchildren in the fifth volume, *The Tower and the Hive* (1999). By this point the series has become curiously slapdash, and in place of *Dragonflight*'s adroit, tantalizing feeding of background data into narrative, there are information dumps as clumsy as the following:

> Had the Hivers but known they had met their match in Jeff Raven and Angharad Gwyn aka the Rowan as partners [the speaker, Thian, is referring to his own grandparents], they might have quit while they were ahead.

Not while there were Hiver queens needing planets to colonize," Clancy put in.

And that, of course, brought the entire FT&T organization in at the time of the Deneb Penetration with the Rowan as the focus for the Mind Merge that helped Jeff Raven despatch the Hiver Scouts trying to depopulate his home world.

"And why the Mrdinis decided to ask us, through Mother and Dad, to join forces and defeat the Hivers," Thian said, "since we could take out a Hiver Sphere without having to resort to suicide missions." He leaned back again, pleased with his summation of the events leading up to recent developments.

(p. 24)

Still other series include the "Catteni" and "Acorna" books. The former science fiction adventures begin with *Freedom's Landing* (1995), spun off from the rather unpromising short "The Thorns of Barevi" from *The Disappearing Future* (1970), whose heroine incautiously rescues one of the superstrong humanoid Catteni, is "rewarded" against her will with forced sex, and very rapidly comes to like it. *Acorna: The Unicorn Girl* (1997), with Margaret Ball credited as coauthor, is a text version of what had been first planned as a graphic or heavily illustrated novel. The forehead horn of the not-quite-human girl Acorna can—like the classical unicorn's horn—both heal and purify. Her various undemanding space adventures have an air of being aimed at younger readers; critics have suggested that despite the joint author credit (with Elizabeth Ann Scarborough replacing Ball from the third volume on), McCaffrey's contribution to these novels is minimal.

Meanwhile, the great success story of the Dragonrider series goes on, with no coauthors admitted to this heartland of McCaffrey's literary territory. The original *Dragonflight* has generated not only direct sequels but also parallel subseries and a number of prequels set in the distant past.

The main story line continues in *Dragonquest* (1971) and *The White Dragon* (1978). With the immediate danger of Thread held at bay by the "Oldtimer" reinforcements, some of the tension shifts to political and social issues, in particular the difficulties of accommodating the inflexibly arrogant Oldtimer dragonfolk into the more relaxed, even progressive society of modern Pern. Two new developments with a mythic frisson are the realization of a misinterpreted prophecy and a near-literal trip to Hell.

The prophecy: farmers have long been told to "watch for" certain grubs in the fields, and have dutifully been destroying them, not knowing that these unprepossessing creatures were engineered as a slowly evolving biological defense against Thread, which they eat with impunity despite its searing effect on all other organic life. The hellride: a dragon can go anywhere its rider can visualize, and with the aid of sightings through a newly reinvented telescope, F'lar's half-brother F'nor makes a near-disastrous trip *between* to the unspeakable, airless, corrosive environment of the Red Star. The dream of destroying Thread at the source is, after all, impossible—which temporarily defers the need to answer an agonizing question posed to F'lar in *Dragonquest*:

"Son of my father," began F'nor, "if dragonmen clear the Star of Thread, what further purpose is there for them?"

(p. 228)

Other novelties include the small, cute "fire lizards" native to Pern, from which the dragons were laboriously bred, and various fragments of rediscovered technology. Although the dragons themselves remain magical, and McCaffrey's descriptions of the mutual love between humans and their dragons (or fire lizards) strive for a lyrical intensity, there is a sense that the setting has lost its legend-shadowed innocence. Pern is riddled with understanding, by both characters and readers, of the science fiction machinery underlying its pageantry.

Science fiction problem solving brings F'nor's question to the fore once again, as continuing rediscovery of the first colonists' technology—including a functional artificial intelligence—makes it possible in *All the Weyrs of Pern* (1991) to scavenge the still-orbiting colony ships and alter the Red Star's orbit via a colossal antimatter explosion. Incidental use of suction-cup attachments in vacuum provides a further reminder that McCaffrey writes "soft" rather than "hard" science fiction. Most recently, *The Skies of Pern* (2001) proposes a new role for the Weyrs after a coincidental cometary impact devastates the planet. The resulting floods and tsunamis are conscientiously worked out, with credit to scientific advisers, but are generally familiar from all too many other science fiction treatments of the situation. Nevertheless, McCaffrey is able to end this novel with the reassurance: "There will always be dragons in the skies of Pern!" (p. 447).

A less complicated Pernese spin-off is the "Harper Hall" subseries, written for children and running parallel with the main sequence: *Dragonsong* (1976), *Dragonsinger* (1977), and *Dragondrums* (1979). A musically gifted young girl, Menolly, is irrationally forbidden to make tunes in her harsh Sea Hold home, but becomes the envy of half of Pern by Impressing a record nine fire lizards, and wins a place in the Harper Craft Hall by sheer talent—working closely with Masterharper Robinton, who since his introduction in *Dragonflight* has been an endearing and popular series character. With their convincing feel for music making and childhood frustrations, these stories have an unsophisticated charm.

Other adult novels of Pern likewise parallel the main action, such as *The Renegades of Pern* (1989) with its story of strife and revenge among the narrative's outcasts and misfits at the time of *The White Dragon* and *Dragondrums*. (A troubling continuity problem is that villainies of world-shaking importance in *Renegades* pass unnoticed in the world of *The White Dragon*.) Yet others are set in the saga's deep past. *Moreta, Dragonlady of Pern* (1983) relates a legend of earlier dragonriding days that is commemorated in a famous ballad by the era of *Dragonflight*, a tragedy of errors whose plotting is unfortunately clumsy as McCaffrey visibly steers the hapless heroine to her doom.

With *Dragonsdawn* (1988), the saga goes back to its initial science fiction roots as the ill-fated colonization ships arrive—full of characters whose names are familiar from Pernese settlements and landmarks—to meet the dangers of Threadfall, already well known to followers of the series. Genetic engineering produces dragons with startling rapidity. Further "early Pern" titles are *The Chronicles of Pern: First Fall* (1993) and *Red Star Rising* (1996; published in the United States as *Dragonseye*).

Although cynical readers and critics find McCaffrey's lesser work both exploitative in its sentimentality and prone to deliver overly simplistic solutions to her favored characters' problems, she has won herself an immense, adoring audience—chiefly by her major original creation of Pern. Following the early Hugo and Nebula wins, her further genre awards include the Skylark (presented in memory of science fiction pioneer E. E. Smith), the 1979 Eurocon and Gandalf Awards for *The White Dragon*, two 1980 Balrog Awards for *Dragondrums* and for outstanding professional achievement, and the 2000 Karl Edward Wagner Award for life achievement in fantasy. In 1999 she won the American Library Association's Margaret Edwards Award for lifetime achievement in writing books for teenagers.

McCaffrey's worldwide popularity continues, not despite but because she indulges her fondest readers' insatiable taste for more in a similar vein. To quote the *London Times* review by Walter Ellis that appears on many British editions of her books, "Anne McCaffrey, one of the queens of science fiction, knows exactly how to give her public what it wants."

ANNE McCAFFREY

Selected Bibliography

WORKS OF ANNE McCAFFREY

NOVELS AND SHORT STORIES

Restoree. New York: Ballantine, 1967; London: Rapp and Whiting, 1968.

DRAGONRIDERS OF PERN SERIES

"Weyr Search." In *Nebula Award Stories 3.* Edited by Roger Zelazny. Garden City, N.Y.: Doubleday, 1968; London: Gollancz, 1968.

"Dragonrider." In *Nebula Award Stories 4.* Edited by Poul Anderson. Garden City, N.Y.: Doubleday, 1969; London: Gollancz, 1969.

Dragonflight. New York: Ballantine, 1968; London: Rapp and Whiting, 1969.

Dragonquest. New York: Ballantine, 1971; London: Rapp and Whiting-Deutsch, 1973.

A Time When. Cambridge, Mass.: NESFA Press, 1975. (Extract from *The White Dragon.*)

Dragonsong. New York: Atheneum, 1976; London: Sidgwick and Jackson, 1976. (For children.)

Dragonsinger. New York: Atheneum, 1977; London: Sidgwick and Jackson, 1977. (For children.)

The White Dragon. New York: Ballantine, 1978; London: Sidgwick and Jackson, 1979.

Dragondrums. New York: Atheneum, 1979; London: Sidgwick and Jackson, 1979. (For children.)

Moreta, Dragonlady of Pern. New York: Ballantine, 1983; London: Severn House, 1983.

Nerilka's Story. New York: Ballantine, 1986. (With *The Coelura*, London: Bantam, 1987.)

Dragonsdawn. New York: Ballantine, 1988; London: Bantam, 1988.

The Renegades of Pern. New York: Ballantine, 1989; London: Bantam, 1990.

All the Weyrs of Pern. New York: Ballantine, 1991; London: Bantam, 1991.

The Chronicles of Pern: First Fall. New York: Ballantine, 1993; London: Bantam, 1993. (Collection of linked stories.)

The Dolphin's Bell. Gillette, N.J.: Wildside Press, 1993. (Novella.)

The Dolphins of Pern. New York: Ballantine, 1994; London: Bantam, 1994.

Red Star Rising. London: Bantam, 1996. Reissued as *Dragonseye*, New York: Ballantine, 1997.

The MasterHarper of Pern. London: Bantam, 1998; New York: Ballantine, 1998.

The Skies of Pern. London: Bantam, 2001; New York: Ballantine, 2001.

DOONA SERIES

Decision at Doona. New York: Ballantine, 1969; London: Rapp and Whiting, 1970.

Crisis on Doona, with Jody Lynn Nye. New York: Ace, 1992; London: Orbit, 1993.

Treaty Planet, with Jody Lynn Nye. London: Orbit, 1994. Reissued as *Treaty at Doona*, New York: Ace, 1994.

THE SHIP WHO SANG SERIES

The Ship Who Sang. New York: Walker, 1969; London: Rapp and Whiting, 1971.

PartnerShip, with Margaret Ball. Garden City, N.Y.: Science Fiction Book Club, 1992; New York: Baen, 1992; London: Orbit, 1994.

The Ship Who Searched, with Mercedes Lackey. New York: Baen, 1992; London: Orbit, 1994.

The City Who Fought, with S. M. Stirling. New York: Baen, 1993; London: Orbit, 1995.

The Ship Who Won, with Jody Lynn Nye. New York: Baen, 1994; London: Orbit, 1995.

"The Ship That Returned." In *Far Horizons: All New Tales from the Greatest Worlds of Science Fiction*. Edited by Robert Silverberg. New York: Avon Eos, 1999.

"The Thorns of Barevi." In *The Disappearing Future: A Symposium of Speculation*. Edited by George Hay. London: Panther, 1970.

PEGASUS SERIES

To Ride Pegasus. New York: Ballantine, 1973; London: Dent, 1974.

Pegasus in Flight. New York: Ballantine, 1990; London: Bantam, 1991.

Pegasus in Space. New York: Ballantine, 2000; London: Bantam, 2000.

DINOSAUR PLANET SERIES

Dinosaur Planet. London: Futura, 1977; New York: Ballantine, 1978.

Dinosaur Planet Survivors. New York: Ballantine, 1984. Reissued as *The Survivors*, London: Futura, 1984.

Get Off the Unicorn. New York: Ballantine, 1977; London: Corgi, 1979. (Short stories.)

The Worlds of Anne McCaffrey. London: Deutsch, 1981. (Short stories.)

KILLASHANDRA SERIES

The Crystal Singer. New York: Ballantine, 1982; London: Severn House, 1982.

Killashandra. New York: Ballantine, 1985; London: Bantam, 1986.

Crystal Line. New York: Ballantine, 1992; London: Bantam, 1992.

The Coelura. Columbia, Pa.: Underwood-Miller, 1983.

The Girl Who Heard Dragons. New Castle, Va.: Cheap Street, 1985. (Chapbook, for children.)

PLANET PIRATES SERIES

Sassinak, with Elizabeth Moon. New York: Baen, 1990.

The Death of Sleep, with Jody Lynn Nye. New York: Baen, 1990.

Generation Warriors, with Elizabeth Moon. New York: Baen, 1991.

THE TOWER AND THE HIVE SERIES:

The Rowan. New York: Ace, 1990; London: Bantam, 1990.

Damia. New York: Putnam, 1992; London: Bantam, 1992.

Damia's Children. New York: Putnam, 1993; London: Bantam, 1993.

Lyon's Pride. New York: Putnam, 1994; London: Bantam, 1994.

The Tower and the Hive. New York: Putnam, 1999; London: Bantam, 1999.

ANNE MCCAFFREY

PETAYBEE SERIES

Powers That Be, with Elizabeth Ann Scarborough. New York: Ballantine, 1993; London: Bantam, 1993.

Power Lines, with Elizabeth Ann Scarborough. New York: Ballantine, 1994; London: Bantam, 1994.

Power Play, with Elizabeth Ann Scarborough. New York: Ballantine, 1995; London: Bantam, 1995.

The Girl Who Heard Dragons. New York: Tor, 1994; London: Corgi, 1996. (Short stories.)

CATTENI SERIES

Freedom's Landing. New York: Putnam, 1995; London: Bantam, 1995.

Freedom's Choice. New York: Putnam, 1997; London: Bantam, 1997.

Freedom's Challenge. New York: Putnam, 1998; London: Bantam, 1998.

Freedom's Ransom. New York: Putnam, 2002; London: Bantam, 2002.

ACORNA SERIES

Acorna: The Unicorn Girl, with Margaret Ball. New York: HarperPrism, 1997; London: Corgi, 1998.

Acorna's Quest, with Margaret Ball. New York: HarperPrism, 1998; London: Corgi, 1999.

Acorna's People: Further Adventures of the Unicorn Girl, with Elizabeth Ann Scarborough. New York: HarperPrism, 1999; London: Corgi, 2000.

Acorna's World, with Elizabeth Ann Scarborough. New York: Eos/HarperCollins, 2000; London: Corgi, 2001.

Acorna's Search, with Elizabeth Ann Scarborough. New York: Eos/HarperCollins, 2001.

Nimisha's Ship. New York: Ballantine, 1999; London: Bantam, 1999.

NONFICTION

The People of Pern. Norfolk, Va.: Donning, 1988.

The Dragonlover's Guide to Pern, with Jody Lynn Nye. New York: Ballantine, 1989.

"My Favorite Story." *New York Review of Science Fiction* 27:9 (November 1990).

WORKS EDITED BY McCAFFREY

Alchemy and Academe: A Collection of Original Stories Concerning Themselves with Transmutations Mental and Elemental, Alchemical and Academic. New York: Doubleday, 1970.

Cooking Out of This World. New York: Ballantine, 1973. (Recipes by science fiction authors.)

Space Opera, with Elizabeth Ann Scarborough. New York: DAW, 1996. (Twenty stories with musical themes.)

CRITICAL AND BIOGRAPHICAL STUDIES

Aldiss, Brian. "Science Fiction's Mother Figure." In *The Pale Shadow of Science*. Seattle, Wash.: Serconia, 1985. Pp. 37–49.

Arbur, Rosemarie. *Leigh Brackett, Marion Zimmer Bradley, Anne McCaffrey: A Primary and Secondary Bibliography.* Boston: G. K. Hall, 1982.

Ashley, Mike. "Anne McCaffrey." In *The Encyclopedia of Fantasy.* Edited by John Clute and John Grant. London: Orbit, 1997; New York: St. Martin's, 1997. P. 602.

Barrett, David V. "Fire-Lizards Is Cats; Dragons Ain't Horses; Anne McCaffrey." Interview in *Vector* 123:3–7 (1984).

Bradley, Wendy. "The Big Sellers, 4: Anne McCaffrey." In *Interzone* 34:27–32 (March-April 1990).

Brizzi, Mary Turzillo. *Anne McCaffrey: A Reader's Guide.* Mercer Island, Wash.: Starmont, 1986.

Clute, John. "Anne McCaffrey." In *The Encyclopedia of Science Fiction,* 2nd edition. Edited by John Clute and Peter Nicholls. London: Orbit, 1993; New York: St. Martin's, 1993. Pp. 746–747.

Hargreaves, Matthew D. *Anne Inez McCaffrey: Forty Years of Publishing: An International Bibliography.* [Seattle, Wash.]: Matthew D. Hargreaves, 1992.

———. *Anne Inez McCaffrey: Two More Years of Publishing: A Bibliography of Only U.S. and U.K. Editions.* [Seattle, Wash.]: Matthew D. Hargreaves, 1994.

Morgan, Chris. "Science Fiction with Dragons: An Interview with Anne McCaffrey." *Extro Science Fiction* 3:18–22 (July-August 1982).

Stephensen-Payne, Phil, and Chris Drumm. *Anne McCaffrey, Dragonlady and More: A Working Bibliography,* 4th edition. Leeds, England: Galactic Central, 1996.

Robert R. McCammon
1952–

RICHARD BLEILER AND HUNTER GOATLEY

BETWEEN 1978 AND 1992, Robert McCammon published an even dozen novels and one collection of short stories, almost all of which contained overtly fantastic and horrific elements. This number is small indeed when compared to the output of such contemporaries as Charles Grant, Stephen King, and Dean Koontz, but it nonetheless distinguished McCammon as a consistently gifted and able writer, albeit one whose early works showed an occasional inability to create strong characters and who tended occasionally to sentimentality. Nevertheless, because McCammon's technique improved with each book, his later works—in particular *Boy's Life* (1991) and *Gone South* (1992)—are essentially unclassifiable, blending elements from forms and genres as disparate as the bildungsroman, magical realism, southern gothic, historical novel, and social commentary. In 1999, at what would appear to be the peak of his skills, he retired from writing, citing variously depression, exhaustion from overwork, a desire to spend more time with his family, and frustration with publishers, who insisted he limit himself to writing genre horror fiction when he wanted to explore other literary forms. This self-imposed retreat concluded in 2002, when a small press announced that it would be publishing *Speaks the Nightbird*, a historical novel written in the early 1990s, but it remains uncertain whether McCammon will ever resume writing.

Robert Rick McCammon was born in Birmingham, Alabama, on July 11, 1952, the son of Jack (a musician) and Barbara Bundy McCammon. The marriage failed, and McCammon was raised by his grandparents in Birmingham. He received a B.A. degree in journalism from the University of Alabama in 1974 and currently resides in Birmingham, married to Sally Sanders, with whom he has a daughter, Skye. Despite this strong association with the South, its history and traditions played little substantial role in his early work. Nevertheless, paralleling his development as a writer has been an apparent acceptance of his southern heritage, and the last two novels he produced before his self-imposed hiatus—*Boy's Life* and *Gone South*—are both set in the Deep South and make use of its heritage and traditions. Furthermore, McCammon's works often contain references and asides that cannot be fully appreciated unless one is familiar with Birmingham. The vampire leader Count Vulkan of *They Thirst* (1981), for example, was named for the cast-iron statue of Vulcan set on the Red Mountains on the Birmingham-Homewood border.

Following graduation, McCammon wrote advertising copy for Birmingham businesses and newspapers. Failing to get his short stories into print, he wrote *Baal* (1978), an ambitious effort having as its basis the biblical Book of Revelation and the ultimate conflict between limited Good and limitless Evil. In the afterword to the 1988 edition of *Baal*, McCammon stated that "*Baal* is about power, written at a time when I had none," adding that "you always hear this said to young writers, 'write about what you know.' I wanted to write about things I didn't know, so I consciously set *Baal* in locations as far from the South as possible: Boston, the Middle East, and Greenland. I wanted a global scale and a story that would take the reader to the very edge of Armageddon."

Baal begins in New York City, when Mary Kate Raines is raped by a being that leaves burns where it touched her. She gives birth to a child, Jeffrey Harper, which destroys the lives of the Raines. After Mary Kate kills her husband, the boy is sent to an orphanage, where he matures with uncommon rapidity, develops unpleasant powers, and prefers to be called Baal. He flees the orphanage with his followers and, ultimately, emerges in Kuwait. There he meets an elderly theology professor, James Virga, who has left Boston to discover the whereabouts and fate of his young colleague Donald Naughton, who went to Kuwait to study Baal's sect. Virga rapidly realizes that though Baal is human in shape, he is absolutely evil in intent and is determined to dominate and destroy the world. Virga is powerless to stop Baal and would perish but for the appearance of Michael, a laconic stranger with obvious powers of his own. Michael and Virga follow Baal across the wastes of Greenland and do battle with him, an epic confrontation that ends on a deliberately ambiguous note. Baal and Michael have vanished, locked in titanic and inconclusive struggle, and Virga is about to be rescued, but are those rescuing him Baal's disciples?

McCammon's second published novel was actually his third novel. He had followed *Baal* with *The Night Boat* (1980), but the publisher decided that *The Night Boat* might be too similar to a recently released motion picture called *Shock Waves*. McCammon thus wrote *Bethany's Sin* (1980), after which the publisher decided to publish *The Night Boat*. Upon acceptance of the latter, McCammon decided to become a full-time writer.

Bethany's Sin had its genesis in a Birmingham building McCammon used to pass on his way to work, "a rather forbidding-looking Gothic house with a simple sign out front. That sign said: WOMEN'S CLUB. Nothing else." From observation of this club came the novel, whose premise involves a young couple moving to the small Pennsylvania town of Bethany's Sin and gradually discovering it is a place with lethal secrets and mysteries. In this case, these involve the rebirth of Artemis, incarnate in the person of the wealthy archaeologist Dr. Kathryn Drago. She leads a cult of lethal axe-wielding Amazons who at night ride about town killing townspeople as well as passing strangers. Thematically somewhat uninspired, and with debts to Thomas Tryon's *Harvest Home* (1973)—which likewise involves a lethal matriarchal cult in a small town—*Bethany's Sin* is nevertheless interesting for a barely submerged subtext involving a fear of women. This is not to say that *Bethany's Sin* is a misogynistic work. Rather, McCammon as novelist seemed to be grappling with the awareness that women are frequently outsiders and have their own identities, behaviors, and histories, and that sometimes these run contrary to the accepted and believed norm.

The Night Boat (1980) merges McCammon's interests in World War II and its ordnance with a horrific plot. Set on the small Caribbean Island of Coquina and focusing largely on the guilt-ridden David Moore, an expatriate banker whose sailing accident left his wife and child dead, it describes the horrors that emerge from a sunken German U-boat, mysteriously intact after more than thirty-five years of submergence. The supernatural basis of the story involves a voodoo priest cursing the U-boat's crew to perpetual life in their submarine, and they have become flesh-eating zombies. The supernatural story is less interesting than is the account of the ultimate redemption of Moore, and *The Night Boat* is slight, the least interesting of McCammon's early novels.

McCammon followed the relatively disappointing *Night Boat* with *They Thirst* (1981), a cheerful and sprawling exercise in Grand Guignol that sets classical vampires and their followers in contemporary Los Angeles. Much of the story takes place in the literal shadow of a ruined castle overlooking Hollywood: built by horror-film actor Orlon Kronsteen, it has remained empty following the discovery of Kronsteen's tortured and decapitated body. The inhabitants of Los Angeles—in particular police captain Andrew Palatazin, reporter Gayle Clarke, a sociopathic killer known as the Roach, young Tommy Chandler, actor Wes Richer, and his psychic African girlfriend, Solange—go about their daily lives without realizing that Castle Kronsteen is now the home of Count Conrad Vulkan, a 500-year-old vampire, who is employing the vicious albino motorcyclist Kobra to assist him in his raids on humanity. (Kobra is also one of the people responsible for the death of Kronsteen.) *They Thirst* in part becomes a struggle between limited human good and seemingly limitless supernatural evil, with much of the action occurring during a supernaturally generated sandstorm. There are nevertheless numerous imaginative touches that make *They Thirst* more than a thematic repetition of McCammon's earlier work. First, Vulkan is shown to be but a weakling in comparison to his diabolic mentor the Headmaster, and Vulkan's pride and arrogance are ultimately the cause of his undoing. Next, *They Thirst* has a thread of black humor running through it, and it is one of the first novels to ask where an army of the undead would sleep: a significant portion of the early novel involves Palatazin's attempt to discover why corpses have been exhumed and their coffins stolen. Finally, *They Thirst* shows that McCammon was capable of putting new twists into established stories, and the novel's conclusion is not the defeat of Vulkan but the conclusion of the horrors humans visit on one another.

Mystery Walk (1983), McCammon's fourth novel, was the first to be published in hardcover. It is a complex tale involving the maturation of two young men, each possessing supernatural powers. Billy Creekmore inherited his abilities from his Choctaw mother, and he uses his powers to heal and set spirits to rest. Wayne Falconer has essentially the same powers, but he uses his to raise money for his father's fundamentalist Christian campaign. In addition to sharing psychic abilities, each healer shares a recurrent dream involving an eagle made from smoke battling a snake made of fire. The paths of the two intersect several times, and ultimately they become allies, battling a monstrous supernatural figure, the shape changer, that has directed their lives for its own purposes.

Mystery Walk is ambitious and makes good use of Native American folklore as well as showing the biases directed against Native Americans. It is also the first of McCammon's works to make direct use of the American South: Creekmore and Falconer are from Alabama, and the scenes involving Alabama life and folkways are well presented and convincing. An additional autobiographical element is present in the character of Creekmore, who is McCammon's age. Several scenes in *Mystery Walk* were based on McCammon's experiences as a child, including a tent revival patterned after an actual revival that McCammon's grandfather hosted on his farm.

Much of *Usher's Passing* (1984) is set in the South, though in North Carolina rather than Alabama, and like its predecessor, it convincingly blends folklore, local color, and literary history to great effect. The premise of *Usher's Passing* is that Edgar Allan Poe's "The Fall of the House of Usher" was a fictionalization of some unfortunate events in the lives of the Ushers, and the story begins in New York in 1847, when Hudson Usher, Roderick's brother, confronts a drink-sodden Poe and informs him that he resents Poe's using his family in his stories. Roderick leaves, believing Poe will be forgotten, and the Usher family, already wealthy through its armament sales, grows even wealthier. When the story switches to the present, the Usher fortune is measured in billions, and Rix Usher is one of three Usher children returning to the ancestral mansion to see who will inherit their dying father's fortune.

Although Rix's discoveries and his maturation and acceptance of his heritage form the heart of the novel, the surrounding events and numerous subplots are also well described. Usherland, the estate, is dominated by the Lodge, a sentient treasure house whose walls are distressingly mobile and whose intentions are rarely friendly. Images of physical death and decay are pervasive: a monstrous black panther—Greediguts—roams the grounds, as does the child-stealing Pumpkin Man. A mysterious disease limited to the family, Usher's Malady, affects the oldest Usher, immobilizing and destroying his physical body while sharpening his senses to preternatural acuteness.

An intriguing linkage may be made between Rix and McCammon, whose middle name ("Rick") is phonetically similar. Rix's history shares much with McCammon's own life, including jobs writing ad copy and working on the staff of a B. Dalton bookstore. McCammon was raised by his grandparents, and, as with Rix, it was expected that McCammon would be the kind of person his grandparents wanted him to be: that he would go into the family furniture business and would continue to live in the house his grandparents owned, keeping things as they always had been. McCammon decided he had to live his life his own way, as did Rix.

McCammon followed *Usher's Passing* with *Swan Song* (1987), his longest and most horrific novel to date. Like Stephen King's *The Stand* (1978), its literary model, *Swan Song* follows the lives and actions of a diverse group of characters in a post-holocaust world. King used a super-flu to kill most of the world's population, but he left buildings and civic infrastructure intact, and apart from the emergent supernatural elements, most of the problems faced by his characters are logistical: corpses must be removed, electricity must be restarted, and civil order must be maintained. McCammon went several steps further and destroyed his world with a limited nuclear war, and his characters face plagues, devastation, radiation injuries, and sicknesses, declining food and fuel rations, nuclear winters, and of course, each other.

The Swan of *Swan Song* is Susan Wanda (Swan), a girl with psychic abilities. When the bombs strike, she is nine years old and accompanying her mother through Kansas. She meets Josh Hutchins, an enormous African American wrestler living from paycheck to paycheck, and he becomes her protector in the devastated wasteland. As Josh and Swan travel from town to town, meeting occasional survivors, including the viciously insane Alvin Mangrim, other survivors also travel, their paths occasionally crossing: Sister Creep is a disturbed woman from Manhattan; thirteen-year-old Roland Croninger, a survivor of a survivalist redoubt and a budding psychopath, is accompanied by the much-decorated Colonel Macklin, whose honors are empty and whose memories are haunted by the Shadow Soldier, whose presence enabled him to stay alive at the expense of others.

The fantastic elements in *Swan Song* emerge after the bombs strip away civilization and reveal its underlying magic. Sister Creep finds a circlet of glass embedded with jewels; it is psychically sensitive, warns her of danger, and permits her to watch the slow progress of Josh and Swan. This circlet is sought by a red-eyed being who wants to destroy it, for with its destruction all beauty and hope will end. This being—a shape-shifter who calls himself Friend and who is anything but friendly—allies himself with Macklin and Croninger, who have survived to establish a horrific force, the ironically named Army of Excellence, whose purpose is to kill all who have any trace of disease caused by the nuclear war. (Equally ironically, Macklin and Croninger are both thoroughly diseased.)

Swan Song is perhaps McCammon's most controversial novel, though the controversy is not so much over the subject matter as it is in the novel's technique. Certainly the book is overlong and has some weakly drawn characterizations and a weakly portrayed romance. At the same time, it has an enormous number of characters whose actions are always interesting, much convincing detail, and great strokes of imagination. Furthermore, McCammon is able to depict something as mundane as the passing of a horse with great conviction, and the positive far outweighs the negative. *Swan Song* tied with Stephen King's *Misery* for the 1987 Bram Stoker Award for outstanding achievement in horror and dark fantasy and was the first of McCammon's books to be a *New York Times* best-seller.

Stinger (1988) is science fiction, albeit with a dark sensibility, that tells the tale of a small, dying town in Texas called Inferno and how its inhabitants, at war with one another, react to the arrival of an alien named Daufin—and an alien bounty hunter called Stinger, who is chasing Daufin. The book, which reads like a horror movie from the 1950s, is more than 500 pages long, but the action occurs during one twenty-four-hour period. (Many readers were not aware of the time span until they neared the end of the book and read about the sun rising again.) Like its predecessor, *Stinger* sold nearly a million copies and again made McCammon a *New York Times* best-seller.

Stinger was followed by *The Wolf's Hour* (1989), an odd work featuring a werewolf as protagonist whose action occurs primarily during World War II. Though werewolves are traditionally supernatural beings, McCammon provides a rationale for their existence, and change involves concentration, effort, and stress rather than a full moon. Furthermore, McCammon's werewolves are guided by human consciousness rather than bloodlust, and when Michael Gallatin—the protagonist—is first introduced, it is as a wolf, attacking the Germans in North Africa, demoralizing them and stealing their battle plans. He is later recruited by the Allies to discover the meaning of the term Iron Fist, a grueling quest that has him pursued by Nazis through occupied Europe and Nazi Germany. The novel is well researched and frequently horrific, and it succeeds well in conveying McCammon's interest in World War II and his fondness for James Bond novels. Nevertheless, the work suffers from the same problems that beset all historical fiction: the outcome of the past is not in question, so from the very first the reader knows that the quest must have succeeded.

Also in 1989, McCammon published *Blue World,* his only collection of short stories to date. Most of the thirteen stories contain elements of fantasy and horror, and they are some of McCammon's best work. "Yellowjacket Summer" describes a young mother and her two children stopping in a small Georgia town, only to discover that it is ruled by a psychotic boy who can control yellowjackets. "He'll Come Knocking at Your Door" is also set in the South and shows that everything has a price; being unaware of the cost does not save one from having to pay. "Makeup" involves a thief stealing the makeup case that belonged to horror-film star Orlon Kronsteen (of *They Thirst*): he soon discovers that the makeup converts him into genuine monsters. "Doom City," "I Scream Man," and "Something Passed By" are thematically similar, nightmarish descriptions of domestic situations. "Night Calls the Green Falcon" pays homage to pulp magazines and the adventure serials of the 1940s and 1950s and concludes that the contemporary world still has room for masked crime-solving heroes. "Nightcrawlers" features a drained and breaking Vietnam vet whose ability to project hallucinations and desires leads to a foregone yet chilling conclusion. "Makeup" and "Nightcrawlers" are the only works of McCammon's to have been filmed. "Makeup" was adapted for the TV show *Darkroom* in 1981, and "Nightcrawlers" appeared in 1985 as an episode of *The Twilight Zone* directed by William Friedkin. The "Makeup" adaptation starred Billy Crystal and Brian Dennehy and was played more for laughs than horror, while "Nightcrawlers" is generally regarded as one of, if not the, best of the new *Twilight Zone* shows.

Mine (1990) also makes use of historical events, but its use of the past is to reveal contemporary motivations. The novel has as its premise the idea that the 1960s radical group the Weathermen spawned an even more radical group, the Storm Front. The Storm Front was led by Jack Gardiner, who preferred to be called Lord Jack, and just beneath him in the hierarchy was the enormous and thoroughly psychotic Mary Terrell, who enforced Jack's whims and was generally and aptly referred to as Mary Terror. The group's end came in 1972, in a shootout with the police and the FBI, but Mary Terror survived, and since then she has held a string of low-paying jobs, moved frequently, and become obsessed with babies. (She was pregnant during the shootout but lost the child.) Her path intersects with the wealthy Atlanta suburbanite Laura Clayborne, approximately the same age but whose life has moved in relatively conventional circles, though she is haunted by nightmares. Clayborne is heavily pregnant as the story starts and has just discovered that her husband, Doug, is having an affair. She is thus on her own when Mary, disguised as a nurse, steals her baby in order to present it to Lord Jack.

The story of *Mine* is of course the pursuit of Mary Terrell, with Clayborne and the FBI attempting to discover her whereabouts, and Mary attempting to reunite the Storm Front and locate Lord Jack. Clayborne locates the few surviving members of the Storm Front and interviews them, and ultimately the paths of the two women cross, the climax occurring in the old house in California that the Storm Front used to hold its meetings. During the course of the novel, identities become blurred and realigned: Mary has become more maternal, for she has cared for and genuinely loves the baby, and Clayborne has lost her conventionality and, in her quest for her stolen child, has become obsessive and determined. *Mine* won the 1990 Bram Stoker Award for best novel.

With *Boy's Life* (1991), McCammon not only accepted his southern heritage but used it as the basis for the story. The novel begins in 1964, in the small Alabama town of Zephyr, and is narrated by twelve-year-old Cory Mackenson. He states at the beginning that "we had a dark queen who was one hundred and six years old. We had a gunfighter who saved the life of Wyatt Earp at the O.K. Corral. We had a monster in the river, and a secret in the lake. We had a ghost that haunted the road behind the wheel of a black dragster with flames on the hood. We had a Gabriel and a Lucifer, and a rebel that rose from the dead. We had an alien invader, a boy with a perfect arm, and we had a dinosaur loose on Merchants Street. It was a magic place." It is the last sentence that gives some idea of the novel's complexity and depth, for the volume re-creates the essence of an imaginative childhood in the days before widespread television. It is a time when magical events could happen and when the impossible might reasonably occur.

Boy's Life is nevertheless substantially more than Mackenson's sentimental recollections. The story itself begins and climaxes with the events surrounding a brutal murder—the secret in the lake—and during the course of the novel the old South also begins to die, its customs vanishing and the survivors scrambling to stay alive. Mackenson several times witnesses the passing of power: the horrible Blaylock family is defeated in a battle reminiscent of the climactic gunfight in *High Noon*; the bullying Gordo and Gotha Branlin are defeated when the abused learn to fight back; and the worst aspects of the old South—the white racists—are defeated by the best of the new South. Mackenson witnesses the passing of a close friend and—on a more charming note—a triceratops in a seedy carnival (brought back by Professor Challenger of Doyle's *The Lost World* [1912]) realizes it does not need to put up with abuse and escapes to take up residence in a nearby lake and attacks cars and buses if they pass too close to its territory. In addition to acknowledging Doyle, McCammon pays homage to dozens of his favorite writers and media figures, including Ray Bradbury, Richard Matheson, Eudora Welty, Edgar Rice Burroughs, Boris Karloff, Vincent Price, Bela Lugosi, Gene Autry, and Roger Corman. The book won the 1991 Bram Stoker Award and the 1992 World Fantasy Award for best novel.

The last novel published before McCammon's long hiatus was *Gone South* (1992), a book that is the diametric opposite of *Boy's Life*. The prose in *Boy's Life* was rich, dense and evocative; *Gone South* is spare, almost terse, as it recounts the actions of a series of characters. The focus of the story is Dan Lambert, a carpenter who has developed a brain tumor and leukemia from exposure to Agent Orange in Vietnam. While requesting an extension on a loan, he inadvertently shoots the bank's loan officer, and he goes south, a term combining elements of running away, going insane, and being dead. While on the road he meets a disfigured young woman, Arden Halliday, who tells him of the Bright Girl, a beautiful, perpetually young woman who lives in the Louisiana swamps: Arden believes the Bright Girl will heal her. As Lambert is traveling and seeking salvation and redemption, two grotesque bounty hunters trail him: Flint Murtaugh carries his blind, mute, and retarded undeveloped twin, Clint, embedded in his abdomen, and Cecil "Pelvis" Eisley, a fat Elvis Presley impersonator, carries around an asthmatic little bulldog named Mama. An ambiguously happy ending is ultimately reached.

Although it is stylistically somewhat pallid in comparison to *Boy's Life*, *Gone South* is nevertheless a success as a novel. It is tempting to identify Lambert with McCammon and to see Lambert's quest as a fictional expression of McCammon's need to find something in which to believe and somebody to love, as well as an expression of a wish to live his days in privacy while at the same time permitting his artistic side to reach maturity. Had McCammon's career finished with *Gone South*, it would have been an apt conclusion.

After *Gone South*, McCammon took time off to be a full-time father. When he resumed writing, he turned toward historical fiction and began *Speaks the Nightbird*, set in the Carolina Colony in 1699. The novel tells the story of Rachel, a woman accused of witchcraft in the new and struggling town of Fount Royal, and the magistrate's assistant, Matthew, who begins to doubt the validity of the charges. Against the magistrate's wishes, Matthew begins investigating the truths behind the eyewitness accounts of Rachel's unholy dealings with the Devil and discovers that while there is evil in Fount Royal, it is more man-made than unholy. McCammon spent over a year doing research for the book, including a trip to Williamsburg to study documents from the time period.

After finishing *Speaks the Nightbird*, McCammon encountered an editor who wanted to change the book from what it was to what McCammon felt was more along the lines of a Harlequin romance novel. After trying to work things out with the editor, McCammon found that other publishers weren't interested, for the book wasn't what they expected a "McCammon novel" to be. He eventually pulled the book from consideration and started work on *The Village*, a novel set in World War II about a Russian theatrical troupe whose job is to entertain the Russian troops with government-approved plays depicting proper Russian views and who gets caught behind enemy lines in Germany. Writing *The Village* was an arduous task for McCammon, as he found himself "snakebit" after his editorial experience with *Speaks the Nightbird*, and he began to fear the possibility of more rejections. It should be noted that

McCammon's career began with the publication of his first novel. He had not really experienced rejection before in his career, and he found himself getting depressed. He overcame the depression, but it took him three years to finish *The Village*.

Upon completion of *The Village*, McCammon found that the publishing industry had changed radically in his six years away from it. *Speaks the Nightbird* and *The Village* were offered to publishers, but they didn't believe that the American book-buying public would be interested in historical novels from McCammon, especially since one of the novels did not feature American characters. During the year the books were available, McCammon found he enjoyed life without worrying about deadlines and publisher demands, and in 1999 he announced his retirement from publishing and began enjoying life with his family, catching up on all the things he had never had time to do while he was writing.

Fortunately for McCammon's fans, an employee of River City Publishing, a small publisher in Montgomery, Alabama, had heard McCammon read from *Speaks the Nightbird* at a local college in the mid-1990s and approached him about publishing the book. McCammon liked the idea, and *Speaks the Nightbird* is set for publication in September 2002. However, as of this writing, McCammon sees this as simply the publication of a book and not a return to writing and publishing. It is likely that *The Village* will never be published, although, like the endings of all of McCammon's novels, the future remains open, with untold possibilities for what lies ahead.

Selected Bibliography

WORKS OF ROBERT R. McCAMMON

NOVELS AND SHORT STORIES

Baal. New York: Avon, 1978; London: Sphere, 1979.

Bethany's Sin. New York: Avon, 1980; London: Sphere, 1980.

The Night Boat. New York: Avon, 1980; London: Sphere, 1981.

They Thirst. New York: Avon, 1981; London: Sphere, 1981.

Mystery Walk. New York: Holt, Rinehart, and Winston, 1983; London: Heinemann, 1983.

Usher's Passing. New York: Holt, Rinehart, and Winston, 1984; London: Pan Books, 1986.

Swan Song. New York: Pocket Books, 1987; London: Sphere, 1988.

Stinger. New York: Pocket Books, 1988; London: Kinnell, 1988.

The Wolf's Hour. New York: Pocket Books, 1989; London: Grafton, 1989.

Blue World. London: Grafton, April 1989; New York: Pocket Books, 1990. (Stories.)

Mine. New York: Pocket Books, 1990; London: Grafton, 1992.

Boy's Life. New York: Pocket Books, 1992.

Gone South. New York: Pocket Books, 1992. London: Michael Joseph, 1993.

Speaks the Nightbird. Montgomery, Ala.: River City Publishing, 2002.

ROBERT R. MCCAMMON

AS EDITOR

Under the Fang. New York: Pocket Books, 1991.

Night Visions 8. Arlington Heights, Ill.: Dark Harvest, 1991.

CRITICAL AND BIOGRAPHICAL STUDIES

Adler, Matt. "The Perils and Profits of Mixing Genres: The Work of Robert R. McCammon." In *How to Write Horror and Get It Published.* Edited by Marc A. Cerasini. Brooklyn Heights, NY: Romantic Times, 1989. Pp. 122–127.

"The American Fantasy Interview with Robert R. McCammon." *American Fantasy,* Winter 1988. Pp. 26–31, 64.

Dziemianowicz, Stefan. "Robert R. McCammon." In *St. James Guide to Horror, Ghost and Gothic Writers.* Edited by David Pringle. Detroit: St. James, 1998. Pp. 398–399.

Goatley, Hunter. "The Robert R. McCammon Interview." *Lights Out!—The Robert R. McCammon Newsletter,* July 1989. Pp. 8–14.

———. "Exclusive Interview: Robert R. McCammon." *Lights Out!—The Robert R. McCammon Newsletter,* October 1991. Pp. 23–27.

———. "Exclusive Interview with Robert R. McCammon." *Lights Out!—The Robert R. McCammon Page,* http://www.robertrmccammon.com/interviews/97jan.html) January 1997.

Grabowski, William J. "Interview with Robert R. McCammon." *The Horror Show,* Summer 1985. Pp. 9–13.

———. "Interview with Robert R. McCammon." *The Horror Show—Robert R. McCammon Special,* Spring 1987. Pp. 9–11.

Labbe, Rodney. "Interview with Robert R. McCammon." *Footsteps* 8, November 1987. Pp. 80–84.

Lansdale, Joe. "Interview: Robert R. McCammon." *Twilight Zone Magazine,* October 1986. Pp. 24–27.

Raley, William G. "Coffee Shop: An Interview with Rick McCammon." *After Hours,* Winter 1989. Pp. 40–43.

Strissel, Jodi. "Interview with Robert R. McCammon." *Castle Rock,* November 1988. P. 6.

Taylor, J. R. "Personalities: Robert R. McCammon." *I Cover the War,* October 1987. Pp. 6–8, 20, 21.

———. "Personalities: Robert R. McCammon." *I Cover the War,* October 1988. Pp. 10–13.

Wiater, Stanley. "Horror in Print: Robert R. McCammon." *Fangoria* 44, May 1985. Pp. 32–34.

———. "Interview: Robert R. McCammon." *Fantasy Review* 101, May 1987. Pp. 22–24.

———. "A Sting in the Tale." *Fear,* November-December 1988. Pp. 26–28.

———. "Robert R. McCammon." In *Dark Dreamers: Conversations with the Masters of Horror.* Edited by Stanley Wiater. New York: Avon, 1990. Pp. 145–153.

INTERNET RESOURCES

The official Robert R. McCammon website is www.robertrmccammon.com and is maintained by Hunter Goatley.

Ian McEwan
1948–

JACK SLAY, JR.

LATE IN IAN McEwan's *The Comfort of Strangers*, a woman whose boyfriend has been brutally murdered notices the uneven wear of an official's heels—and for an instant, the narrator notes, "ordinariness prevailed" (p. 127). Such respites occur often in McEwan's work; however, what quickly becomes apparent is that they provide nothing more than a thin veneer to cover over the darkness at the heart of everyday life. In the world of Ian McEwan, ordinariness is little more than a momentary lull in the course of life gone terribly wrong.

***

Ian Russell McEwan was born in Aldershot, England, on June 21, 1948, the son of David McEwan, a soldier, and Rose Lilian (Moore) McEwan, a chambermaid. He spent much of his childhood abroad, stationed with his family in military outposts such as Singapore and Libya. On approaching his teens, McEwan returned to England to attend a state-run boarding school, Woolverstone Hall in Suffolk. He continued his education at the University of Sussex in Brighton, studying French and English and receiving his B.A., with honors, in English literature in 1970. McEwan then went on to the University of East Anglia, where he studied creative writing with Malcolm Bradbury and Angus Wilson, earning an M.A. in 1971. At the same time, he began to submit fiction, making his first sell when *New American Review* bought "Homemade" in 1972; three years later, Jonathan Cape published his first collection of stories, and McEwan's life as a professional writer officially began.

In 1982 McEwan married Penny Allen, an alternative healer and astrologer; together they had two sons before divorcing in 1995. McEwan married his second wife, journalist Annalena McAfee, in 1997. Today, he divides his time between London and Oxford.

Since the early 1970s McEwan has penned some of England's most evocative prose, in works that straddle the division between light and dark, between what is hauntingly possible and brutally real.

***

In a review of McEwan's early work, John Leonard remarked that McEwan's "mind is an interesting place to visit, but I wouldn't want to live there. It is dark, and smells of ether. Freud hangs from the rafters on a meat hook. The footlocker is full of human skulls. Scorpions and bats abound. Every sexual transaction is a failure. We are somewhere between Samuel Beckett and the Rolling Stones" ("Books of the Times: In Between the Sheets," *The New York Times*, August 14, 1979, p. 12C).

McEwan's first collection, *First Love Last Rites* (1975)—winner of the Somerset Maugham Award—set the tone and pace for much of the writing that followed. The stories present a series of shocks: "Homemade" portrays a young boy who seduces and rapes his younger sister; "Butterflies" depicts a man, suffering "chinlessness," who sexually abuses and drowns a child; "Disguises" relates the story of a boy's life with a mad aunt, one who forces him to cross-dress before coming to dinner. Interestingly, the supernatural only occasionally rises to the surface—as in, for example, "Solid Geometry" (originally published in *Amazing Stories*), which is about a man who prefers the company of his great-grandfather's diaries to the incessant intrusions of his wife. Their marriage disintegrates into a sorry, loveless state, the couple exchanging petty cruelties and blows. Eventually, following his great-grandfather's step-by-step instructions, the narrator makes his wife disappear into "the plane without a surface," a mysterious nowhere: "Maisie appeared to turn in on herself like a sock. 'Oh God,' she sighed, 'what's happening?' and her voice sounded very far away. Then she was gone . . . and not gone. Her voice was quite tiny. 'What's happening?' and all that remained was the echo of her question above the deep-blue sheets" (p. 40). More often than not, however, the supernatural world only laps at the edges of McEwan's fiction, making brute reality seem all the more horrible in comparison.

The stories in McEwan's second collection, *In Between the Sheets* (1978), though no less gruesome, are certainly more surrealistic (if not wholly supernatural). Again, the reader is subjected to a series of shocks: "Pornography," for instance, depicts the amputation of a man's penis by the women he has two-timed; "Two Fragments: March 199–" portrays London as a postapocalyptic hybrid of Oz and Sodom, a place where bananas are rarities, the tap water is "slow poison," and dogs and cats are roasted for food. The two most interesting stories, though, are "Reflections of a Kept Ape" and "Dead As They Come." "Reflections" is the heartsick rumination of a very intelligent, exceedingly cultured ape who pines for the lost love of his one-time owner and master Sally Klee. "Dead" describes a millionaire who falls in love with a storefront mannequin. A parody of the foibles of human relationships, the story depicts the man courting, becoming jealous, and eventually "strangling" the mannequin. Like the best of supernatural fiction, both stories are presented as wholly real. It is an instance, as I noted in my book on McEwan (*Ian McEwan*, Twayne, 1996), where "the ordinary becomes absurd, the absurd becomes ordinary" (p. 53).

McEwan's first novel, *The Cement Garden* (1978), is a contemporary horror tale, a postmodern spin on Golding's seminal *Lord of the Flies*. It is the story of a family of four children who, at the sudden deaths of their parents, attempt to survive on their own. Encasing their dead mother in a block of cement in the cellar, the children embark on what they see as a grand adventure. What they discover instead, like the wild crew of boys in *Lord of the Flies*, is the savagery and despair that lurks just beneath the shell of civilization. The novel takes on a surrealistic quality as the fifteen-year-old narrator Jack and his siblings wander through a dreamland of torpidity and emptiness.

Eventually, enveloped by the miasma of their mother's rotting corpse, the family deteriorates: Tom, the youngest sibling, regresses into infancy, sucking his thumb, speaking like a baby, even sleeping in his old baby bed; Jack abandons hygiene, growing filthy and becoming obsessed with masturbation; Sue, the younger sister, isolates herself, spending more and more time beside the cement tomb of her mother. Ultimately, Jack and his older sister Julie seek solace in an incestuous union. However, despite the scene's audaciousness, Michael J. Adams points out in *Postmodern Fiction: A Bio-Bibliographic Guide* that the incest "becomes little more than a desperate need to share experience, any experience, with someone" (p. 460). Jack and Julie's union, then, is simply an attempt to counter the horrors that surround them. The novel concludes as authorities, heralded by slamming car doors and the pattern of a revolving blue light on the bedroom wall, prepare to enter the house, presumably to restore the order meant to be.

McEwan's next novel, *The Comfort of Strangers* (1981), was his first to be nominated for the Booker Prize, Britain's most hyped and coveted literary award. It is also his darkest tale, a story of love and perversion, of sex and cruelty. The narrative concerns Mary and Colin, an unmarried couple on vacation in an unnamed European city. The vacation, though, is really more an attempt to revive a faltering relationship than it is a second honeymoon; the two, subsequently, spend much of their time bickering, getting lost in the maze of narrow streets, then bickering some more. Unexpectedly, one lost evening, the two encounter Robert, a forcibly jovial foreigner, the archetypal false host, who invites them into his home. There Mary and Colin meet his frail, limping wife Caroline and slowly become aware that the strangers' marriage is not the typical union. At one point Caroline confesses to Mary, "By 'in love' I mean that you'd do anything for the other person, and . . . you'd let them do anything to you . . . If you are in love with someone, you would even be prepared to let them kill you, if necessary" (p. 62). At this point the novel takes on a feminist slant, as McEwan's imagined world becomes a microcosm of patriarchal society, one in which male fantasies of dominance are allowed to thrive. Mary and Colin learn that what began as sexual curiosity for Robert and Caroline has developed into a disturbing sadomasochistic relationship, with Robert whipping Caroline, beating her with his fists, and whispering "pure hatred" into her ear as they make love; the perversions culminate with Robert breaking Caroline's back.

What Mary and Colin fail to realize is that they are the next stage in the perverted progression of Robert and Caroline's relationship. The novel ends with the drugged Mary watching helplessly as Robert slices Colin's wrists; stupefied, she "dreamed of moans and whimpers, and sudden shouts, of figures locked and turning at her feet, churning through the little pond [of blood], calling out for joy" (p. 123).

Like McEwan's previous work, *The Comfort of Strangers* is a modern-day horror story, with no supernatural element. Instead, it focuses on the dark side of society: here the labyrinth is endless and the Minotaur is an overweight man wielding a razor.

Critical reaction to *The Comfort of Strangers* and to McEwan's earlier fiction was mixed. McEwan was frequently accused of writing simply to shock, of being overly concerned with blood and perversion. Frustrated with the accusations, McEwan—in an interview with Christopher Ricks in *The Listener*—stated that he refused to write about "what is nice and easy and pleasant and somehow affirming." Rather, for him what was important was to write about "what is bad and difficult and unsettling" ("Adolescence and After: An Interview with Ian McEwan," April 1979, p. 526). He went on to say, "I've yet to meet somebody who said: 'Your stories are so revolting I couldn't read them' " (p. 527). Tellingly, in a 2002 *Newsweek* interview, McEwan admits that when he wrote those early works, he "wanted something savage. I always used to deny this, but I guess what I'm really saying is that I was writing to shock. . . . And I dug deep and dredged up all kinds of vile things which fascinated me at the time" (Jeff Giles, "Luminous Novel from Dark Master," March 18, 2002, p. 62). While the shocks, the gore, and the disturbing focus on the wickedness of humanity are indeed readily apparent in McEwan's early work, it is precisely this unflinching gaze that made him one of today's most distinguished horror writers.

***

McEwan's *The Child in Time* (1987), winner of the Whitbread Novel of the Year Award, represents a turning point for him on several levels. It signaled, for one thing, an abandonment of the desire to shock that marks so much of his early canon; it is a gentler, more affirming novel that, nonetheless, continues to explore many of McEwan's favorite themes: the corruption of politics, regression into infancy, the viability of sustained relationships. The novel is also McEwan's most supernatural work.

Set in a near future—a world of miserable weather and conservative extremism, in which a shoving match at the Olympics can escalate into the "sudden threat of global extinction" (p. 34)—the story concerns the disappearance of three-year-old Kate Lewis, beloved daughter of Stephen and Julie. The novel first chronicles Stephen's unraveling, and then traces how he pieces his shattered world back together: he loses Julie temporarily, falls into an alcoholic squalor, sits on a committee charged by the prime minister with writing an extreme, even brutal, tome on child-rearing, and deals with his agent and friend Charles Darke's abandonment of society and subsequent regression into infancy—but all the while Stephen grows emotionally, as he slowly comes to terms with Kate's disappearance. One of the chief ways that Stephen learns to cope with the loss is through "magical thinking," a process that enables his daughter to continue growing within his mind, allowing Stephen to become "the father of an invisible child" (p. 2).

In addition, the novel is about the seemingly magical malleability of time, the way it seems to stretch and warp, to slow and quicken. For example, the crucial event of the book—and one of McEwan's few overtly supernatural scenes—occurs when Stephen quite literally rips through the fabric of time. Walking through the countryside, Stephen experiences a sense of déjà vu and soon becomes convinced that "the day he now inhibited was not the day he had woken into.... He was in another time" (p. 63). A few minutes later he sees a young couple sitting at the window of a tavern and realizes that the woman is his mother—but his mother as a young woman. Later, back in the present, his mother tells him of getting pregnant before marrying his father, of sitting in a tavern and, in the moment Stephen's father broaches the possibility of abortion, looking outside and seeing a face and *knowing* she is seeing the face of her unborn child. It is in that moment, she tells the adult Stephen, that she decides not to abort her baby. The scene is a chilling, satisfying turn of events, a moment that, in many ways, captures the magical feel of the entire novel. *The Child in Time* is a success, a tremendously affecting novel, beautifully written.

The Innocent (1990), the story of the relationship between British telephone technician Leonard Marnham and German Maria Eckdorf in postwar Berlin, is something of an espionage thriller—and a return to verisimilitude. It is set against the backdrop of Operation Gold, the real-life attempt by British and American forces, in 1955–1956, to tunnel under the city and tap into Soviet communications. Absent entirely are any moments of magical realism, or of the preternatural, and the one nod to horror is the much-touted dismemberment scene—an episode that brazenly recalls McEwan's earlier literature of shock. When Maria and Leonard accidentally kill her ex-husband Otto, they realize they must get rid of the body; to do so, they dismember Otto and hide him in a pair of suitcases. The scene is unflinchingly relayed, McEwan taking obvious pleasure in the gory details:

> [Leonard] was through the bone easily enough, but an inch or so further in he began to feel he was not cutting through things so much as pushing them to one side.... There was a glutinous sound that brought him the memory of a jelly dessert eased from its mold. It was moving about in there;

something had collapsed and rolled onto something else. . . . Both [halves of Otto's torso] tipped to the floor and disgorged onto the carpet.
(pp. 225–227)

A macabre comedy of political manners, *The Innocent*, in the end, contains neither the originality nor the intensity of McEwan's other work.

Black Dogs (1992), McEwan's fifth novel, garnered his second nomination for the Booker Prize. The novel is the story of June and Bernard Tremaine and their acrimonious marriage. She is spiritual, a faithful follower of religion and mysticism; he is a rationalist, a firm believer in intellect and political ideology. Their marriage, then, is a contest of beliefs.

Black Dogs revolves around June's mystical encounter with the beasts referred to by the title. Early in their marriage, June and Bernard hike through postwar France; momentarily separated from her husband, June rounds a bend to encounter a pair of huge, black mastiffs. She breathes a prayer and is, amazingly, able to fend off the dogs' attack with a penknife. It is the moment that changes her life; it is "the defining moment, the experience that redirected, the revealed truth by whose light all previous conclusions had to be rethought" (p. 29). The encounter becomes the centerpiece of her life, leading her into the belief in something more, beyond rationalism and into the mystical world of faith.

When June dies, her presence continues to haunt those she has left behind. For example, shortly after June's death, Jeremy, the Tremaine's son-in-law, visits her home and is prevented from being stung by a scorpion by what he imagines to be June's "presence." After the incident, not wholly convinced, Jeremy imagines June berating him: "I warned you, protected you, it was as simple as that, and if you're prepared to go to such lengths to keep your skepticism intact, then you're an ingrate and I should never have put myself out for you" (p. 100). Later, Jeremy feels her spirit in his protection of an abused child; a "haunting," he calls it, in which June "herself was present, watching me" (p. 107). At other times, June's presence seems more tangible, more obvious. Bernard, for example, tells Jeremy, "I couldn't stop thinking that if the world by some impossible chance really was as [June] made it out to be, then she was bound to try and get in touch [after her death] to tell me that I was wrong and she was right. . . . And that she would do it somehow through a girl who looked like her. And one day one of these girls would come to me with a message" (p. 65). Immediately after this confession, they pass a young woman with "June's mouth and something of her cheekbones" (p. 65); moments later, this same woman rescues Bernard when he is attacked by skinheads. Through such scenes, June's spirit permeates the novel, lingering about the figures of her previous life, a presence not quite a ghost, not completely imaginary. *Black Dogs* is a beautifully wrought novel that immerses itself in the ideology of the real and unreal; it is also one of McEwan's most powerful books.

The late 1990s and the early years of a new century saw McEwan publish three more novels, all critically lauded and commercially successful; they are also all three nonsupernatural stories that, nevertheless, maintain the dark, visceral edge of McEwan's vision.

Enduring Love (1997) tells the tale of Joe Rose, a science journalist, and Jed Parry, a seemingly harmless stranger, two men brought together by a bizarre ballooning incident that ends in death. Soon after the accident, Rose discovers that Parry has, inexplicably, developed a disturbing quasi-religious/romantic fixation on him (what McEwan later reveals to be a true psychological disorder known as De Clerambault's Syndrome). Rose can do little more than watch his orderly, rational world slowly crumble. The novel is a suspenseful and honest examination of love, trust, and, ultimately, forgiveness.

Amsterdam (1998), which at long last won for McEwan the Booker Prize, is the story of old friends Vernon Halliday, the editor of a British newspaper, and Clive Linley, a composer of independent means, who find themselves in an ethical entanglement involving national politics. Their joint decision to publish photographs of the foreign secretary in drag eventually leads the story—as only McEwan can loopily lead it—to the Dutch city of the title and the reciprocal murder of the lead characters. The novel is a savage farce about nasty people doing nasty things; it is also McEwan's most wickedly humorous book.

Atonement (2001), McEwan's eighth novel and fourth nomination for the Booker Prize, is, in many ways, his finest achievement—it is joyfully and precisely written, a novel for the ages. A Jane Austenish story of mid-century British genteelism, the novel focuses on thirteen-year-old Briony Tallis, her dreamy view of the world, and the ineffectual family that surrounds her. Midway through the novel she mistakenly accuses Robbie Turner, the chambermaid's son, of raping her cousin; familial chaos and near-tragedy ensue. It is a darkly tinted novel of love and war, of mistakes made and sins atoned for, a distinguished accomplishment in a distinguished canon.

***

Toward the end of *Atonement*, Briony Tallis settles back to watch her offspring perform a play she wrote some sixty-four years earlier; "I'd been expecting a magic trick," she says, "but what I heard had the ring of the supernatural" (p. 346). The same observation could be made of McEwan's work: there is always, no matter the subject, a "ring of the supernatural," an other-worldliness that lurks on the periphery, a shadowy evil that pushes his characters toward the abyss hidden beneath the surface of everyday life. Though the supernatural is only hinted at in the majority of his work, McEwan nonetheless deserves to be classified as a writer of supernatural fiction, for he revels in the dark and sees clearly the extraordinary within the ordinary, the natural within the supernatural.

Selected Bibiliography

WORKS OF IAN McEWAN

NOVELS AND SHORT STORIES

First Love, Last Rites. London: Jonathan Cape, 1975; New York: Random House, 1975. (Short stories.)

In Between the Sheets. London: Jonathan Cape, 1978; New York: Simon & Schuster, 1978. (Short Stories.)

The Cement Garden. London: Jonathan Cape, 1978; New York: Simon & Schuster, 1978. (Novel.)

The Comfort of Strangers. London: Jonathan Cape, 1981; New York: Simon & Schuster, 1981. (Novel.)

The Child in Time. London: Jonathan Cape, 1987; New York: Houghton Mifflin, 1987. (Novel.)

The Innocent. London: Jonathan Cape, 1990; New York: Talese/Doubleday, 1990. (Novel.)

Black Dogs. London: Jonathan Cape, 1992; New York: Talese/Doubleday, 1992. (Novel.)

Enduring Love. London: Jonathan Cape, 1997; New York: Talese/Doubleday, 1998. (Novel.)

Amsterdam. London: Jonathan Cape, 1998; New York: Talese/Doubleday, 1999. (Novel.)

Atonement. London: Jonathan Cape, 2001; New York: Talese/Doubleday, 2002. (Novel.)

CRITICAL AND BIOGRAPHICAL STUDIES

Leonard, John. "Books of the Times: In Between the Sheets." *The New York Times*, August 14, 1979, section, p. 12C.

Malcolm, David. *Understanding Ian McEwan*. Columbia: University of South Carolina Press, 2002.

Slay, Jack, Jr. *Ian McEwan*. New York: Twayne, 1996.

INTERVIEWS

Giles, Jeff. "Luminous Novel from Dark Master." *Newsweek*, March 18, 2002, p. 62.

Ricks, Christopher. "Adolescence and After: An Interview with Ian McEwan." *The Listener*, April 1979, p. 526.

FILMS BASED ON IAN McEWAN'S WORK

The Comfort of Strangers. Screenplay by Harold Pinter. Directed by Paul Schrader. Skouras, 1991.

The Cement Garden. Screenplay by Andrew Birkin. Directed by Andrew Birkin. October, 1992.

The Innocent. Screenplay by Ian McEwan. Directed by John Schlesinger. Miramax, 1993.

First Love, Last Rites. Screenplay by Jessie Peretz and David Ryan. Directed by Jesse Peretz. Trimark, 1998.

Patrick McGrath

1950–

JAY McROY

RAISED IN THE shadow of Broadmoor Hospital, the "criminal lunatic asylum" outside London at which his father was employed as medical superintendent, Patrick McGrath has emerged as one of the most original voices in contemporary Gothic fiction. Composed in a style that is by turns eloquently economical and lyrically labyrinthine, McGrath's fictions present readers with gloomy and, at times, surreal environments populated by a myriad of haunted grotesques that are—in a literary sense—timeless; one gets the impression that his tormented protagonists would feel strangely comfortable within the bleakest corners of Charles Dickens' London and the murkiest patches of Emily Brontë's moors. Yet, McGrath's characters and themes are very much the products of a twentieth century perspective, and as such, they allow him to re-invent and revitalize the Gothic novel with each new offspring of his rich and morbid imagination.

***

Patrick McGrath was born in London in 1950 and spent much of his early years on the grounds of Broadmoor Hospital, where his father worked from 1955 to 1981. His experiences at Broadmoor had a dramatic impact upon his writing, as evidenced by his thorough understanding of human psychology. From his father, McGrath learned that the mentally ill deserve sympathy rather than scorn, a perspective consistently reflected in his writings; likewise, McGrath's early interest in the Gothic tales of Edgar Allan Poe and H. P. Lovecraft shaped his understanding of storytelling as a practice that reveals information about our deepest, darkest selves even as it obscures the very possibility of ever discovering the "truth." A graduate of the University of London, where he received a B.A. in English, McGrath has worked as an orderly in a mental hospital and as a teacher. In addition to having lived in the vicinity of London, he dwelled in assorted undisclosed locations across the North American continent and spent several years on a "remote" island in the north Pacific. Presently, McGrath resides in London and New York City. He is married to Maria Aitken, an actress who appeared in, among other films, John-Paul Davidson's 1995 cinematic adaptation of McGrath's novel, *The Grotesque*.

In each of his works, McGrath skillfully probes the tenuous social and psychological webs we weave to support our notions of what constitutes "reality." From his debut novel, *The Grotesque* (1989), to his most recent tome, *Mar-*

tha Peake: A Novel of the Revolution* (2000), a menacing yet seductive discourse pours forth from the disturbed minds of McGrath's antiheroic narrators. These testimonials lead readers to ask important questions regarding the speakers' motives and, by extension, the reliability of the information they provide. In this sense, then, McGrath's narrators evoke the simultaneously troubled and elegant raconteurs found in the finest tales of Edgar Allan Poe and Vladimir Nabokov. Immersing the reader within the minds of such characters contributes to each text's prevailing tone, whether it is one of satirically self-conscious melodrama or psychological suspense infused with horror and dread. Furthermore, this rhetorical strategy allows McGrath to exploit and, in subtle yet interesting ways, comment critically upon the Gothic as a literary genre. At times, this approach results in "purple prose," but more often than not the prose is the violent purple of a fresh and incomprehensible bruise, an abrasion one knows is painful and yet one cannot help but touch and retouch, even as one winces.

McGrath's earliest novels, *The Grotesque* and *Spider* (1990), are particularly illustrative of how, from the very beginning of his career, the style and content of his works compliment one another in ways that position the Gothic, and storytelling in general, as a grotesque and monstrous art form. Indeed, readers that immerse themselves within the pages of these books resurface with as many questions as answers. Are the narrators of these respective texts merely paranoiacs wracked with delusions, or are their tales of malevolent deceptions and profound betrayals grounded in "truth" (whatever that increasingly fragile term may denote)? And, what does it mean about our own deep and dark desires when even the characters with which we most sympathize are themselves shadowy and ominous at best? This is not to say that the narrators of these, and indeed each of McGrath's subsequent, novels are not appealing. To the contrary, they compel us to identify with their perverse perspectives. In *The Grotesque*, for example, even the most tangential asides of Sir Hugo Coal, the novel's paralyzed narrator, are filled with biting phraseology and bilious observations that are frequently clever and insightful. Often, such passages evoke sly smiles and silent meaningful nods from readers, the political and philosophical implications of Coal's remarks resonating long after the reader has turned the text's final pages. Furthermore, in an ironic mirroring of Coal's quest to trace the lineage of dinosaurs to modern birds via his own archeological discoveries, the narrative that emerges from the mind of the disabled paleontologist is a story undergoing continual reconstruction. Riddled with wild speculation, contradictory hypotheses, missing links, and flat-out errors, the memoir is, like its author, a literary grotesque of the kind one encounters rarely and never forgets.

However, while *The Grotesque*'s narrator's oft-humorous observations and tone allows McGrath to parody Gothic stereotypes like mysterious butlers and nefarious infidelities, *Spider* is by far the more accomplished of McGrath's early novels. Through the clandestine scribblings of the insane Dennis Clegg, readers enters a dingy, damp, and malodorous industrial landscape infused, in the style of David Lynch's postmodern Gothic films *Eraserhead* and *The Elephant Man*, with the oozing, dripping, and hissing of blocked pipes, steaming grates, and fog-enshrouded gasworks. Like his moniker, which also serves as the book's title, Clegg/Spider ensnares us within a schizophrenic miasma of language and shadow that becomes more complex and mysterious as we struggle to assign a stable meaning to the various narrative threads being spun throughout the novel's pages. In an eerily effective wedding of realism and surrealism, *Spider*, the novel, mirrors the precarious psyche of Spider, the character. As such, *Spider*, not unlike the finest speculative fictions of novelists like William S. Burroughs and filmmakers like David Cronenberg, allows us to question all of those institutions and practices (psychiatry, law enforcement, the family, etc.) that *make meaning* and, as a result, transform us, with greater or lesser degrees of success, into alienated machines distanced from our very selves. As Clegg/Spider tells us:

> "I look at my fingers...they seem so far away from me, at first I think I see a crab of some type lying there on the open page, a yellow crab with horny pincers, a creature unrelated to me...I wonder... what they will find of me when they cut me open after death (if I am not dead already)? An anatomical monstrosity, surely: my small intestine is wrapped around the lower part of my spine and ascends in a taut snug spiral, thickening grossly into the colon about halfway up, which twists around my upper spine like a boa constrictor, the rectum passing through my skull and the anus issuing from the top of my head where an opening has been created between the bones joining the top of my skull, which I constantly finger in wondering horror, a sort of mature excretory fontanelle....
>
> (p. 175)

As McGrath's novel unfolds and we learn more and more about Clegg's macabre and traumatic childhood, these hallucinatory and nightmarish images become increasingly common until the readers begin to suspect — albeit through their own perpetual confusion — that the societal patterns and "methods" too often taken for granted may very well have formed the root of Dennis Clegg's "madness."

In *Dr. Haggard's Disease* (1993) and *Asylum* (1996), McGrath continues his interrogation of the often perforated line between sanity and delusion. The tales are relayed through physicians (a surgeon and psychiatrist respectively) that, far from possessing the facility or desire to heal themselves, ultimately inflict more pain then they relieve. Consequently, these narratives imply that the differences between "health" and "sickness," "sanity" and "insanity," and the social worker and the sociopath may not be as distinct as one might like to imagine. Propelled by powerful undercurrents of sexual obsession, the accounts of these men of science are anything but straightforward, once again revealing "truth" as achingly, frustratingly subjective. Consider, for example, the aptly named Dr. Haggard. Not unlike *Spider's* Dennis Clegg, Haggard is a sad, damaged man, a tortured soul preoccupied with his own corporeal disintegration and, as the novel's title suggests, "disease." A metaphor for pre-World War II England and, in a broader sense, the inescapable weaknesses of the human condition, Haggard's broken, "morphia"-addicted physique and love-scarred psyche are structures as suffocating as the crumbling gothic mansion in which he dwells, and as hopelessly dysfunctional as the passionate yet doomed romance that pains him ceaselessly and propels him towards the novel's explosive conclusion.

Asylum is likewise a grim, neo-Gothic narrative with a "catastrophic" tale of passion and excess twisting, like a thick and impossibly tightening knot, at its murky core. Set primarily within and around the iron gates and damp stone of a maximum-security mental hospital, this story of obsession and emotional anguish unfolds, curiously enough, in the form of a case history stemming from the seemingly detached, "medically sound" observations of Dr. Peter Cleave, a consulting psychiatrist. Through Cleave, we learn of the travails of Stella Raphael, who leaves her psychiatrist husband and young child for the brutal charms of Edgar Stark, a psychotic, murderous artist that is part Hannibal Lecter and part Bill Sykes. And yet, as in McGrath's previous novels, nothing is truly as it seems. Beneath a façade of gentility, the "good doctors" are neither free from the stain of corruption nor operating with the best interest of others in mind. In particular, as the plot develops, it soon becomes apparent that Dr. Cleave, armed with a strangely intimate knowledge of the human will to control, may be working to fulfill his own hidden agenda. Like the menacing patriarchs of conventional Gothic texts, the ostensibly objective Cleave casts a vast, ominous shadow throughout virtually all of *Asylum*, making psychoanalysis itself seem a monstrous weapon and assuring that true "Asylum"—in the sense of security and sanctuary—remains an alien concept on the dreary hospital grounds.

Not surprisingly, this mixture of Gothic and postmodern sensibilities inform McGrath's short fiction as well, as evidenced by the contents of his 1988 short story collection *Blood and Water and Other Tales*. From a miniature Sigmund Freud determined to spread his own form of madness, to Southern plantations reminiscent of the kind one might encounter in the direst stretches of Faulkner's Yoknapatawpha County, these brief and, at times, brilliant tales provide further examples of McGrath's powerful, haunting, yet lyrical vision. *Blood and Water and Other Tales* provided many readers with their first glimpse of McGrath's inimitable style and thematic concerns. Within each of these thirteen stories, readers encounter an imagination that introduces them to their own dark fantasies. Through his deft manipulation of language, McGrath *summons* fear rather than telling his readers that they should be afraid; consequently, readers *experience* horror and the macabre rather than having it thrust upon them in violent or gruesome passages composed for the sole purpose of generating a cheap shock or thrill. *Blood and Water and Other Tales* showcases the skills (and occasional missteps) of a literary master steadily coming into his own. The collection revels in the very images of disease (particularly slow, wasting diseases like malaria and pernicious anemia), and in the daring, yet morosely humorous take on Gothic conventions and human psychology that would soon become the predominant feature of the aforementioned longer, progressively more accomplished works.

***

It is in *Martha Peake: A Novel of the Revolution* that McGrath not only elaborates upon his works' many recurring themes, including "reality" as a social construct, but also uses his unique imagination to evoke both the Hogarthian turmoil of London in the mid eighteenth century and the social/political milieu of late colonial America. In Martha Peake, the violent struggle for power, control, and survival are once again prominent motifs. Furthermore, in keeping with his earlier novels, McGrath skillfully deploys the classic Gothic tropes of physical deformity and architectural decay, using them as metaphors for a larger, more profound moral corruption. In the process, however, he accomplishes two feats that position this novel as a milestone in his development as an important and innovative neo-Gothic novelist. First, through the character of Martha Peake, who "escapes" to America and struggles to overcome the unspeakable abuse she suffered at the hands of Harry Peake, her vicious drunkard father, McGrath presents readers with an allegory for understanding the tribulations of an emerging nation that, although tainted by an imperialist history it is destined to repeat, nonetheless struggles to define itself against a suffocating "parent". Secondly, McGrath chronicles the complex cultural moment that gave rise to the Gothic tradition in British literature, as well as the social turbulence that, at least in part, allowed for the development of a comparable aesthetic in the so-called "New World" across the Atlantic.

It is a testimony to his considerable creative talents and propensity for the speculative that, over a relatively short expanse of time, Patrick McGrath has carved a unique space for himself in literary history. As a premier artist of the neo-Gothic, a genre defined by both the depiction of a world of shadow and the exploration of the limits of pain and pastiche, he deserves his place among such accomplished contemporaries as Iain Banks, Joyce Carroll Oates, and Ian McEwan. But, as a chronicler of sorrow, alienation, and the incessant pangs of corporeal and spiritual disfigurement, he has earned the right to dwell among the likes of Mary Shelley, Emily Brontë, Matthew Lewis, and Edgar Allan

Poe, sages whose at once beautiful and "hideous progeny" remain with us to this day, haunting the darkest corners of our imaginations, crying out to be heard and understood anew.

Selected Bibliography

WORKS OF PATRICK McGRATH

NOVELS

The Grotesque. New York: Poseidon Press, 1989.

Spider. New York: Poseidon Press, 1990.

Dr. Haggard's Disease. London; New York: Viking, 1993.

Asylum. London: Viking, 1996; New York: Random House, 1997.

Martha Peake: A Novel of the Revolution. London; New York: Viking, 2000.

COLLECTIONS

Blood and Water and Other Tales. New York: Poseidon Press, 1988.

The Angel and Other Stories. Harmondsworth: Penguin, 1995.

EDITED ANTHOLOGIES

With Brandford Morrow. *The New Gothic: A Collection of Contemporary Gothic Fiction.* New York: Random House, 1991.

AWARDS

Bram Stoker Award, Best Collection Nominee 1988, *Blood and Water and Other Tales.*

British Fantasy Society, Best Novel Nominee 1996. *Asylum.*

SELECTED INTERVIEWS WITH PATRICK McGRATH

"An Elegant Weirdness" by Pete Crowther, *Fear!* November, 1989.

"Interview with Patrick McGrath" by Kevin B. Parent, (iv) *Journal Wired.* Summer/Fall 1990.

"Enter The Strange Realm Of Patrick McGrath" by Sean Abbott. *At Random*, Randon House, Inc. Winter 1997.

"Interview de Patrick McGrath" by Gilles Menegaldo (Ed. Bernard Vincent). *Sources*, November 1988.

CRITICISM ON PATRICK McGRATH

Freixas, Ramón. "Visiones de in extraño." *Quimera* 103 (1991): 66.

Patricia A. McKillip
1948–

JESSICA REISMAN

PATRICIA A. McKILLIP writes resonant fantasies, bringing the quest theme of high fantasy into ardent, intimate perspective. She is recognized as a uniquely gifted writer whose work garners superlatives at every outing. The lyrical turns of her prose draw readers into worlds rendered with exquisite depth, peopled by characters made vivid and alive with subtle strokes of language.

BACKGROUND

Patricia Anne McKillip was born February 29, 1948, in Salem, Oregon, to Wayne T. and Helen (Roth) McKillip. She was one of six children. Between 1958 and 1962 her Air Force officer father took the family to live in Germany and England. With four younger siblings, she spent a lot of time babysitting and at some point began telling stories to while away the time. At age fourteen, while living in England, she sat down one day by a window looking out on a medieval church and, in a spell of boredom, wrote a short tale which later became her first published book, *The House on Parchment Street.* The next summer she spent writing fairy tales and reading them to her siblings. Except for a period when she thought she wanted to be a concert pianist, she wrote all through high school and college, in many forms, from poems and plays to novels. In an interview in *Locus,* she said: "I started writing because I was too young to know better. And I had an imagination, and I had to do something with it. It's still there—it doesn't grow less with age. In fact it seems, the more you use it, the more you have of it" (August 1992, p. 5).

After attending the College of Notre Dame in Belmont, she earned a B.A. degree in English from San Jose State in 1971 and an M.A. there in 1973. That same year her first two novels, *The House on Parchment Street* and *The Throme of the Erril of Sherril,* were published. With some practicality, she realized she couldn't see herself with a full-time job, so she set out to get herself published before she left college. Though her first publications, and a number of those that followed, are young adult, she says that she never set out to become a children's author but simply wrote what pleased her.

The Forgotten Beasts of Eld, published in 1974, won the World Fantasy award for best novel in 1975; it has not been out of print since. The following year she published *The Riddle-Master of Hed,* the first book in what was to become the Riddle of Stars trilogy. The last book of the trilogy, *Harpist in the Wind* (1979), was nominated for both a Hugo and the World Fantasy award. After this McKillip wrote a contemporary novel and several science fiction works, returning to fantasy in *The Changeling Sea*, published in 1988. She has written fantasies steadily since, among them *Winter Rose* (1996), nominated for the Nebula, as well as many short stories. Other awards McKillip has received include the Locus Poll Award in 1980, the Balrog Award in 1985, and the Mythopoeic Award in 1995.

Though she writes of "imaginary people, impossible places," McKillip's work is filled with the real, from which it draws its depth and savor. In *Faces of Fantasy* she says of the imagination, "It is best fed by reality, an odd diet for something nonexistent; there are few details of daily life and its broad range of emotional context that can't be transformed into food for the imagination" (p. xx). Her other interests in life, among them music, cooking, and art, inform McKillip's fantasies richly, from the music in *Song for the Basilisk* (1998) and the culinary art of *The Book of Atrix Wolfe* (1995) to the charcoal sketching Ducon Greve does in *Ombria in Shadow* (2002). She professes to generally having several projects going at once, and to being driven by a desire to finish one book so that she can get to experience the ones beyond it.

STYLE AND SUBSTANCE

Praise for McKillip is abundant and often passionate. Her use of language, prose style, and imagery are almost unanimously agreed to be elegant, haunting, and beautifully evocative. Even those who may find some of her work lacking in other ways accord her prose this regard. Her work has been described variously as exquisite, lush, truly literary, poetic, graceful, atmospheric, memorable, and has been compared with both dreams and drugs in its elation-producing properties. Her language itself, with its nuance and metaphor, creates as much a sense of the fantastic as the fantastic elements—the talking animals, sorceresses, doors into shadow worlds, and shape-shifters—themselves do. McKillip is also praised for the fact that her stories, fantastic as they are, all succeed on the level of basic human concerns and issues. Many readers and critics find her characters to be well articulated, fully dimensional creations who live off the page for them. The deep sense of history and culture in her worlds, her pacing, plot, and command of symbolism are all likewise well regarded.

Some critics and readers, however, find flaw with some of these same elements. The dreamlike quality of her prose makes for an uncertain and overly demanding reading experience for some. The complexity of her symbolism, odd cant of some syntax, and passages in which it might take more than one reading to decipher exactly what has happened, leave some readers feeling mired. Others find her plots weak and the events and character motivations unclear as the story takes second place to the language and imagery. Occasionally the archetypal nature of many of her characters leads some critics to feel they lack dimension. There is an overall sense that McKillip is a bit cerebral for some tastes.

Certain themes and motifs recur in many of McKillip's novels. As mentioned above, the fantastic in her tales is well rooted in an understanding of fundamental human drives. The inner conflict between love and the desire for power, the redemption and strength inherent in compassion, are central to many of McKillip's characters and their stories. Defining choices are common to her characters' arcs through a narrative, particularly the choice between hate and love—whether to let vengeance, anger, and power be their cause, or to give that focus and space to compassion, love, and the pursuit of truth. Sybel and Coren in *The Forgotten Beasts of Eld*, Nyx in *The Sorceress and the Cygnet*, Caladrius in *Song for the Basilisk,* Morgon in the Riddle of Stars books, all must make such choices.

Legends and stories abound within McKillip's tales. Her characters and worlds are often haunted by a particular story, a kind of founding narrative. The characters and cultures she imagines are usually deeply involved in the activity, as Corleu puts it in *The Sorceress and the Cygnet*, of "tell[ing] story" (p. 4) in one way or another. The nature of the stories ranges from the tales told over food preparation in the great kitchen of *The Book of Atrix Wolf* to the riddles of the Riddle of Stars trilogy.

Riddles and riddling are just one of the motifs McKillip employs in her characters' searches for truth. The unraveling of a mystery of self out of the grip of pain, loss, and anger is an oft-recurring thread in her work. Shape-changing is another motif that appears in more than one book, a fantastical metaphor for the loss and rediscovery of the soul's essence. The role of women in the quest is another theme. She has written in an essay about Tolkein's *Lord of the Rings* that as she grew older she could no longer read the books, finding that there was no place for her in them, no real place for the women. Her female characters take their cue from this, exploring their own place in the traditional quest and faceting those quests in whole new ways.

THE NOVELS

McKillip's *The Throme of the Erril of Sherill*, one of her first publications, is a short children's novel in which the Cnite Caerles is sent by his mournful—and rather vindictive—king, Magnus Thrall, "the King of Everywhere" (p. 5), to find the Throme written by the Erril of Sherill long ago in a land that does not exist within the borders of Everywhere. The Erril's Throme is celebrated as being "a dark, haunting, lovely Throme, a wild, special, sweet Throme made of the treasure of words deep in his heart" (p. 5, 1984). The king lives in shadow and misery for want of the Throme and makes his daughter live there too. Caerles finds many other things, such as a violet-eyed dragon-hound, a star-wand, a golden harp, a child-tree, a bottomless river, a dark well, the house of death, and the "flower wold at the world's end" (p. 102). But all the beings he encounters tell him the Throme does not exist. Finally, barefoot, cloaked in leaves, armorless and swordless—much changed by his journey—he sits down and writes his own Throme. Caerle's Throme pleases the king, until Caerles, unable to lie, admits that he wrote it "of the tales and dreams and happenings of his quest" (p. 97). When the king asks where he found the words for it, Caerles replies, "Everywhere" (p. 104). This configuring of the quest as always for something already within—the honest and heartfelt experience of one's own life—continues on through much of McKillip's work.

In *The Forgotten Beasts of Eld* (1974), Sybel's quest for the pennant-winged, moon-eyed Liralen comes up against her quest for vengeance. This choice is presaged in Coren, her lover, who gives up his vengeance for love of her. Sybel, as a wizard's daughter, and Coren, as the seventh son of a seventh son, both know many strange stories and riddles, as does the wise white boar Cyrin, one of Sybel's fabulous and legendary beasts. One riddle, which Cyrin puts to both Coren and Sybel at different times, goes "The giant Grof was hit in the eye by a stone, and that eye turned inward so that it looked into his mind, and he died of what he saw there" (p. 71, 1984). When Coren says that he does not know what the answer to the riddle might be, Cyrin tells him to ask Sybel what name she spoke before his that day. It turns out to be that of the Blammor, a beast that embodies "the fear that men die of" (p. 73). When the Blammor appear to Sybel on the eve of the war she has fashioned for her revenge, she finds she cannot so easily face the Blammor as before.

> Visions ran through her mind . . . of the death faces of men through the ages meeting the core of their nightmares one final time in rooms without windows, between stone walls without passage. A wet air hovered with the darkness, carrying the cloying scent of pooled blood, of wet, rusted iron;

she . . . heard the faint, last cries like a dark wind from some ancient battlefield, of pain, of terror, of despair. And then her thoughts lifted away from her into some plane of terror she had never known, and she struggled blindly, drowning in it.

(pp. 195–196)

It is seeing a vision of the Liralen, broken and lifeless within this vision of what has become of her own heart, that finally saves her. Later, when she is speaking with the boy she raised as a son, he says "But you had a right to be angry," to which Sybel replies, "Yes, but not to hurt those I love, or myself" (p. 205).

The books in the Riddle of Stars trilogy also bring their main character, Morgon, to the brink of such a decision, more than once. The choice between pursuing that which hurt him through hate, or that which hurt him through love, the choice between violent retribution and peace are, for Morgon, integral to a choice between becoming that which he hates—the cruel and powerful man from whom he has wrested much of his power—and becoming his true self, the Star-Bearer. It's a destiny he struggles with terribly, as it seems to mean the loss of all he knows. The books are composed of journeys bound up in both the denial of truth and self and the inevitable quest for that truth, of self and of others. Raederle, Morgon's intended, who dominates the second book in the trilogy, also struggles against her heritage, that of the ancient race of shape-changers who threaten Morgon. The changing of shape around a central self and the finding of that self through such metamorphosing are integral to the books. Raederle must learn to accept the ability with which she was born, while Morgon begins to learn the wonder of his own power in learning to change into a wolf or a tree.

Morgon is the Prince of Hed, ruler of an island known for its peace and stolidity, but he is born with three stars on his forehead and a talent for riddles.

He looked at himself as though he were a figure in some ancient tale: a Prince of Hed reared to harvest barebacked in the sun, to puzzle over the varied diseases of trees and animals, to read the weather from the color of a cloud, or a tension in a breathless afternoon, to the simple, hard-headed, uncurious life of Hed. He saw that same figure in the voluminous robe of a Caithnard student poring late at night over ancient books, his lips shaping, soundlessly, riddle, answer, stricture. . . . He saw a Prince of Hed with three stars on his face leave his land, find a starred harp in Ymris, a sword, a name, and a hint of doom in Herum. And those two figures . . . the Prince of Hed and the Star-Bearer, stood apart from each other; he could find nothing that reconciled them.

(p. 114)

The stars on his forehead lead the shape-changers to kill his parents, and he is drawn into a quest in which he will lose himself utterly, shaking the foundations of riddle mastery to the ground before he finds the truth. Again and again he must choose to follow the fragile threads of the tenets of riddle mastery and of his own heart through rage, power, hurt, and profound loss.

The Sorceress and the Cygnet (1991) begins and ends with tales, tales of origin and tales that come to life around the characters, dragging them into their twists and turns. Corleu is different from his dark Wayfolk kin, born with the cornsilk hair of his gran's story about his grandfather, a brief liaison in a cornfield. Her pursuit of knowledge and power has estranged Nyx from her family of Ro Holding. Most lately it is an odd and gloomy knowledge Nyx has sought, through the killing of small birds and other such activities performed deep in an inhospitable swamp. Ro Holding is storied, its Cygnet said to have defeated or tricked the Gold King, the Blind Lady, the Dancer, and the Warlock, who the Cygnet broke into pieces so that he became the Blood Star, found only in the shadow of a blood fox. These elements of legend set a struggle in motion when they bespell

Corleu's people and the Wayfolk travel into a mist of frozen time, lost in a dream on the Delta.

> There the sun was invisible by day; at evening it hovered, huge and blood-red, above the silvery, delicate forests. The rich, steamy, scented air clung to everything, even time. . . . The bog mists, the great red sun, the lovely green drugged the eye. The final, glowing moments of sunsets, trees like black fire against a backdrop of fire, burned into memory . . .
>
> (p. 15)

Corleu feels compelled to break them free. He is marked for this by his difference and by his desire to learn more and more "story words" and "Keep saying and keep saying them until I get all the way back to the first thing they mean" (p. 21). So he steps into the Gold King's Dark House, which has fallen from the sky as it does in legend, and steps into story. He isn't released until the heart of Ro Holding, and the heart of Nyx, have been made right again. As one of the figures of the ancient tale of the Cygnet tells Corleu, "When the heart casts a shadow instead of dancing light, there story begins" (p. 224).

A number of now familiar threads can be found in *The Book of Atrix Wolfe* (1995), appearing in a wholly different tapestry of story. When Atrix Wolfe, the greatest mage of the age, falls prey to a black fury, he breaks one of the main tenets of his training—that mages do not meddle in war. He performs a spell to create a thing so terrible that "both armies would end their war to flee from it" (p. 11). Then he abandons his own shape and place in the world in remorse for the death and destruction he has wrought—not yet aware of the real extent of that destruction. His making has torn two otherworldly beings from themselves, changing their shapes tragically. Saro and Ilyos, the daughter and consort of the Queen of the Wood, are lost to her. From this place in time, shadows are cast by not one heart but many. The sense of something frozen in time—that place from which story begins—is echoed when Talis, born the night, twenty years before, of Atrix's making, feels an "odd sense of timelessness" (p. 15) in the book he has found hidden in the stones of the mage school. It is the book Atrix wrote after his making, just before he abandoned the world. The words in the book hide dire meanings beneath their facades, confounding, elusive, and misleading, as is Saro's name, like Deth's in the Riddle of Stars books. Saro, having lost language with her shape, works as a kitchen drudge scrubbing pots. Ilyos has become the awful thing Atrix made. In the course of the story, bits of the highly fantastic, straight from fairy tale, are rendered urgently real; as Saro struggles to form words again, what drops from her mouth are "a hard jewel of light," then a "small, dark bird" (p. 230). What Ilyos says when he finally finds his way back to his own shape recognizes a tenet at the heart of much of McKillip's work: "You were nothing to me. If you were something I did not hate, then you were nothing. And then you spoke, and summoned out of me what you had loved" (p. 232).

The story that haunts *Winter Rose* (1996) is one of patricide, madness, and a curse, which has left ghosts in decaying Lynn Hall, deep in the woods. When Corbet Lynn, the descendant of this tale, comes to rebuild his family's estate, roots and ghosts rise up to tangle into the present. Rois, in pursuing the mystery of what really happened all those years ago in Lynn Hall, and what happens to Corbet Lynn as the story unfolds, is faced with the changing shape of her own self-notion. Eventually, when she holds Corbet through a storm of shapes—echoing the Tam Lin story, which *Winter Rose* plays with— she also begins to find the core of her own spirit. In McKillip's version, it is more Janet/Rois's story, as Rois, through freeing Tam Lin/Corbet, "bears herself in a certain way" (*Locus*, July 1996, p. 7).

Like Talis and Corleu, Cyan Dag in *The Tower at Stony Wood* (2000) is called on a quest—pulled into story—to help others find their way from the darkness within which they are trapped. The telling of tales and the peril and hope present in words, along with the unraveling of a mystery, all figure prominently in the shifting worlds of the story, as do the powers of compassion and love. It is because Cyan Dag sees with his heart and acts on compassion that he is able to speak to the hearts of others and recall them to themselves—though he is generally clueless about what he is doing.

Ombria in Shadow (2002) rests on a founding tale, that of Ombria's shadow city, which haunts the whole narrative. Again it is the shadow cast from a heart—from many hearts—that sets the chain of events in motion. The ruling family of Ombria is in tatters, under the control of a heartless, despotic woman named Domina Pearl. She has cast the whole city under a darkness. Faey, a powerful sorceress, takes her shape from old books and paintings in the undercity, the ruins of ancient Ombria beneath the streets of the current city. Her apprentice, Mag, dresses herself in the clothes and personas of ghosts for her trips above, always disguised. At first believing herself to be a "waxling," she learns that she is human but denies the knowledge to herself, finding it easier to be Faey's waxling. Ducon Greve doesn't know who his father was, and thus doesn't really know who he is himself; but the shadows call to him and he sketches them constantly, forming bits and corners of a story whose beginning and end he doesn't know. As the heart's hope, love, is often wrested from the most terrible of shapes in McKillip's stories, so the characters of Ombria come to find that "the shadow world is [their] hope" (p. 286).

McKillip has also written several works of science fiction and a contemporary novel with overtones of magical realism. Her science fiction is sometimes referred to as science fantasy, and she has been quoted as saying that she doesn't always manage to keep the fantasy out of her science fiction. Whatever genre she is writing in, McKillip's gift with language, the depth and humanity of her characters, and the rich detail of her worlds have set her apart as a peerless luminary in the field.

Selected Bibliography

WORKS OF PATRICIA A. McKILLIP

FANTASY

The Forgotten Beasts of Eld. New York: Atheneum, 1974. Reprinted New York: Berkley, 1984.

The Riddle-Master of Hed. New York: Atheneum, 1976.

Heir of Sea and Fire. New York: Atheneum, 1977.

Harpist in the Wind. New York: Atheneum, 1979.

The Sorceress and the Cygnet. New York: Ace, 1991.

The Cygnet and the Firebird. New York: Ace, 1993.

Brian Froud's Faerielands: Something Rich and Strange. New York: Bantam, 1994.

The Book of Atrix Wolfe. New York: Ace, 1995.

Winter Rose. New York: Ace, 1996.

Song for the Basilisk. New York: Ace, 1998.

The Tower at Stony Wood. New York: Ace, 2000.

Ombria in Shadow. New York: Ace, 2002.

PATRICIA A. McKILLIP

YOUNG ADULT FANTASY

The Throme of the Erril of Sherill. New York: Atheneum, 1973. Republished with "The Harrowing of the Dragon of Hoarsbreath," New York: Ace/Tempo, 1984.

The House on Parchment Street. New York: Atheneum, 1973.

The Changeling Sea. New York: Atheneum, 1988.

SCIENCE FICTION

Moon-Flash. New York: Atheneum, 1984. (YA)

The Moon and the Face. New York: Atheneum, 1985. (YA)

Fool's Run. New York: Warner, 1987.

OTHER WORKS

Stepping from the Shadows. New York: Atheneum, 1982. (Contemporary novel about a girl coming of age and to grips with her own overly powerful imagination; with magic realist overtones.)

"Three Ways of Looking at a Trilogy." *New York Review of Science Fiction* (August 2001).

INTERVIEWS

Perret, Patti. *The Faces of Fantasy.* New York: Tor, 1996. (Photographs of fantasy writers with brief interviews).

Wentworth, Charles, L. "McKillip, Patricia A." *Contemporary Authors New Revision Series.* Vol. 18. Detroit: Gale Research Company, 1986.

"Moving Forward." *Locus* (August 1992), pp. 5, 69.

"Springing Surprises." *Locus* (July 1996), pp. 6, 7.

CRITICAL STUDIES AND REVIEWS

"The Book of Atrix Wolfe." *Kirkus Reviews* (May 15, 1995).

Casada, Jackie. "Song for Basilisk." *Library Journal* (September 15, 1998), p. 116.

———. "Ombria in Shadow." *Library Journal* (January 2002), p. 158.

"The Cygnet and the Firebird." *Kirkus Reviews* (July 15, 1993).

Estes, Sally. "The Book of Atrix Wolfe." *Booklist* (August 1995), p. 1933.

Green, Roland. "Something Rich and Strange." *Booklist* (October 1, 1994), p. 245.

———. "Winter Rose." *Booklist* (July 1996), p. 1812.

Lunde, David. "Patricia McKillip." *Voyages, the 25th World Fantasy Convention Book.* Providence, Rhode Island, 1999. (Souvenir book from convention where McKillip was the guest of honor.)

McHargue, Georgess. "The Forgotten Beasts of Eld." *New York Times Book Review* (October 13, 1974), p. 8.

Shea, Glenn. "The Riddle-Master of Hed." *New York Times Book Review* (March 6, 1977), p. 29.

Silvey, Anita, ed. *Children's Books and Their Creators.* Boston: Houghton, 1995.

"Song for the Basilisk." *Kirkus Reviews* (August 1, 1998).

Steinberg, Sybil. "The Sorceress and the Cygnet." *Publisher's Weekly* (March 29, 1991), p. 81.

St. James Guide to Fantasy Writers. Edited by David Pringle. Detroit: St. James Press, 1996.

St. James Guide to Young Adult Writers. 2d ed. Edited by Tom Pendergast and Sara Pendergast. Detroit: St. James Press, 1999.

"The Tower at Stony Wood." *Publisher's Weekly* (April 17, 2000), p. 57.

Michael Moorcock

1939–

RHYS HUGHES

MICHAEL MOORCOCK IS one of the most versatile and prolific authors of this or any other age. While many of his contemporaries seem intent on narrowing down the outside world to fit their own opinions and desires, he prefers to expand himself in an attempt to fill the world, a process of self-amplification which encompasses the realm of the supernatural as much as that of apparent reality. But for Moorcock, the supernatural is rarely treated as an end in itself. More often, it serves a symbolic or ironic function, and its inherent wonders are parallel to the wonders of the ordinary human spirit, which is never simplified. His generosity of perception, imagination and technique ensure that the weird elements in his work are rigorously original, always employed to serve complex ends. Yet he remains an exceptionally readable writer, utterly devoted to the cause of pure and perfect story.

Although he has experimented with a bewildering variety of genres, usually blurring every distinction between them, there are supernatural landscapes and weird mindscapes in all his writings, the main exceptions being the crime spoofs, *The Chinese Agent* and *The Russian Intelligence*, the elegant erotic fantasy, *The Brothel in Rösenstrasse*, the monumental "mainstream" novels, *Mother London* and *Byzantium Endures* (and the other volumes in the "Colonel Pyat" sequence), and a handful of short stories, in particular those grouped under the heading "Some Reminiscences of the Third World War." Even in these works, which are romantic but basically grounded in reality, the unsettling effects associated with the fiction of the supernatural are present, though their trappings, in the shape of obvious sets of intrusions from other planes, are not. Moorcock employs techniques he learned from writing fantasy even when creating "straight" literature. The results are intoxicating and always uncanny and radical, because they retain the suspense and tension of supernatural fiction, but sublimated into the higher principles of the narrative rather than merely realized as props of plot.

In his more directly supernatural stories, there are semi-plausible explanations for the miraculous and hypernormal events, solutions which are hallucinatory, metaphysical or futuristic. Generally, any rationale is redundant. Moorcock's vision is about refusing to simplify the world, declining to develop an addiction to systems, which he regards as wholly inadequate for a sustainable and coherent modern life, while embracing a code of structure and honor into the existence of the individual. This balancing act is difficult and ambitious, and ensures a richness of tale far beyond the limits of any single category. Moorcock is a supernatural writer without doubt, but he is every other kind too. He is feasibly the only pan-author currently working.

LIFE

Michael John Moorcock (who has also written as Bill Barclay, Edward P. Bradbury, James Colvin, and Desmond Reid) was born in Mitcham, Surrey, on 18 December 1939, son of Arthur and June (Taylor) Moorcock. He worked as an editor for *Tarzan Adventures* (London, 1956–1957) and for the Sexton Blake Library (1958–1961), then served as editor for the Liberal Party (1962–1963). In 1964 he succeeded John Carnell as editor and publisher (from 1967) of *New Worlds*, which under Moorcock's aegis became the pre-eminent science fiction magazine of its day, regularly publishing such writers as Brian Aldiss, J. G. Ballard, Barrington Bayley, Thomas M. Disch, Charles Platt, John Sladek, Norman Spinrad, Gene Wolfe, and Roger Zelazny. Moorcock has also been a songwriter and a member of various rock bands, including the Greenhorns, Hawkwind, Blue Oyster Cult, and Deep Fix. In 1962 he married writer Hilary Bailey, with whom he had two daughters (Sophie and Katherine) and one son (Max). In 1978 Moorcock divorced Bailey and married Jill Riches; in 1983 he married for a third time, to Linda Steele. He has won the British Science Fiction Association Award (1966), the Nebula Award (1967), the Derleth Award (1972, 1974, 1975, 1976), the Guardian Fiction Prize (1977), the Campbell Memorial Award (1979), and the World Fantasy Award (1979).

Moorcock's early works were largely influenced by pulp writers from the first half of the Twentieth Century. The texts produced while he was working at *Tarzan Adventures*, gathered in *Sojan the Swordsman*, are enthusiastic tributes to Edgar Rice Burroughs. They are headstrong, primitive, colourful and not a little awkward. The first, eponymous tale is the most accomplished. The others rush between scenes of action and rescue with an acceleration which is undisciplined rather than dreamlike, but considering the extreme youth of their author they are remarkable in several ways, not least for how they demonstrate Moorcock's talent for creating sympathetic characters in very few words. It is an extraordinary skill. Minor players in Moorcock's fictions often have more depth than the central personalities in the novels and stories of other writers. But the "weird" aspects of the Sojan sequence verge on the conventional. The monsters are just the fauna of an alien planet and have no moral significance. They are xenobiological, not representative or educational. The theology of balance, the denizens of Law and Chaos, now so critical to Moorcock's oeuvre, took a decade after Sojan finally hung up his shield to develop properly.

More imitations of Burroughs came with the *Warrior of Mars* trilogy, published initially as by "Edward P. Bradbury" and later retitled and reprinted under Moorcock's name. Again the perils faced by the protagonist, the adventurer and duellist Michael Kane, are virtually determined by the protocols of the science fantasy romp, and include all manner of hostile beast and man, novel to Kane but natural to the planet where he finds himself marooned, but they also begin to encompass deeper kinds of hazards, psychological and philosophical, and in parts there is a supernatural strangeness distinct from the baser strangeness of simple dirk-and-dirigible Burroughsiana. The trilogy improves as it progresses, with the pompously assertive Kane of *City of the Beast* becoming less of a bully and more of a victim in *Lord of the Spiders* and finally a man of authentic honour in *Masters of the Pit*. This last volume, which is thick with psychological and social consequences, is saturated with humour and is the first novel in which Moorcock demonstrated his massive wit and penchant for satire. Kane is forced to live by the code which his literary predecessors in the Burroughs books always proclaimed but never followed. The result is a wry test of hypocrisy.

The novel can also be read as an assault on simplistic systems. Later, Moorcock was to deliver tougher blows against pulp fantasy, most effectively from inside the genre itself, with the uproarious parable, "The Stone Thing," being perhaps the most notable example.

It was Brian Aldiss who claimed that writers in their dotage appear to develop an obsession with forcing all their previously published work into one grand scheme by writing inappropriate linking texts. Moorcock's own cycle of cycles evolved slowly from the beginning, so naturally that there is no shock of dislocation when a character from a very early work makes an appearance in a seemingly unrelated book decades later. Such is the case with Jephraim Tallow, one of Moorcock's oddest characters, not to mention one of his most resilient and evocative. Partly based on the science fiction writer Barrington Bayley, the subtly troubling Tallow makes his introduction in *The Golden Barge*, a novel written while Moorcock was only 16 and still devouring the pulp writings of Burroughs, Robert E. Howard and Abraham Merritt. But his influences this time were Mervyn Peake and apparently Bertolt Brecht, for he had decided to engage in two different and incompatible traditions of literature at the same time, the high and the very low. Despite its occasionally clumsy grammar and uneven pace, *The Golden Barge* preserves an extraordinary ambience of mystery and deliriousness. The story is so archetypal that it feels old and absolutely right, like a genuine folktale rather than the product of a single author. Although it lacks the polish of works which followed in the years to come, its atmosphere is often superior to the fantasy books of Moorcock's maturity. Not until the *Dancers at the End of Time* series and *Gloriana*, the novel of Tallow's return, was Moorcock able to conjure up the magic of this early novel using his vastly improved prose. Tallow carries a burden of prickly and ancient awe about him. He is quite equal in image, behaviour and faith to any inhabitant of Peake's Gormenghast, which Moorcock has consistently rated as the finest fantasy cosmos ever conceived. In best Peakean style, Tallow is a born radical, unhappy with the arranged chaos around him, selfish, muddled but bravely contemptuous of external authority. His mythomaniac journey down a gigantic river, a simple but effective metaphor for life itself, in pursuit of an elusive barge which represents all unobtainable desires, is profoundly supernatural in tone and progression, though most incidents are not unnatural impositions on his already peculiar world. The most notable paranormal scene concerns a brief transdimensional detour which anticipates the essential importance of parallel and alternative universes in Moorcock's subsequent work. But *The Golden Barge* is an anomaly, the manuscript lying forgotten in a box while its author turned his attention to fantasies of a more traditional slant. It was first published two decades after it was written, so that the debut of the original Tallow lagged slightly behind his reappearance in *Gloriana*, a trick wholly in keeping with the optimism, clumsiness and insensitivity of the character.

THE ELRIC CYCLE

Moorcock's change of direction back towards pulp adventures was the benign fault of E. J. Carnell, editor of *Science Fantasy* and *New Worlds*, who commissioned a set of heroic tales. Carnell's young protégé responded with the figure and mythos of Elric, albino prince of Melniboné, a moody and doomladen catalyst for ethereal and diabolical happenings who is almost a supernatural being himself but whose outlook on existence was generated by one of the author's own soured love affairs. Elric was a deliberate attempt to construct a fantasy character with more complex motivations and personality than were generally to be found within the genre. Elric's habitual melancholy, his frequent rages and ontological and cosmological speculations are mirrored by his backdrop, which is rarely joyful, never peaceful, and often metaphysical. The theology of the universe he dwells in has loose affiliations with Zoroastrianism. There are two vast forces seeking to win ultimate control of everything, Chaos and Law, the former with an agenda of perennial change, the latter with an equal but opposed ethic of utter rigidity. There are neutral powers too, and champions of the Balance, who are willing to swap sides to ensure that neither triumphs. One of the most astounding aspects of the Elric sequence as it gradually develops is the growing realisation that Elric's reality is not hermetically sealed from the one in which the reader lives, but merely a variation on it, and that this theology of balance is applicable to our reality too. In Moorcock's schematic of existence, there are many if not an infinity of universes. This universe of universes, impossibly complex and yet eminently plausible and elegant, allowing a consistent theory of all kinds of "strange" phenomena, is termed the Multiverse, a word which Moorcock coined independently and which has since become his own. Nearly all his protagonists have some awareness of it, and many like Elric make frequent and vital use of it.

It remains a curious fact that writers involved in science fiction, speculative fiction or science fantasy who endeavoured to make authentic predictions about the future almost always were betrayed by real events, whereas those with no real interest in prophecy or futurology have often proved to be astonishingly accurate. Moorcock's literary development and exploration of the Multiverse, its consequences, probabilities, meanings and contradictions are useful as a means of entry into what has recently become a very real and momentous theory of everything in the scientific arena. Throughout the 1960s he developed and refined his cosmology. With such a vast stage to parade his creations upon, and an endless number of opportunities for dramatic philosophical speculation, it is remarkable how full of life and ideas and how carefully explored is his own Multiverse, with paradox and logical impossibility resolved, and no sense of thinness or haste in the cultures of the myriad worlds. Elric is a gloomy attractor of hugely adaptable evils, his travels across many dimensions meddled with by hosts of whimsical and cruel demons, devils, monsters and fantastical spirits, not to mention pantheons of gods and wizards.

The Elric cycle has a convoluted bibliography, in particular the early sections, much of it consisting of frequently retitled novellas assembled into frequently retitled books, a complexity which can make it difficult to read the series in any strict chronological order. But Moorcock has always been intrigued by nonlinearity and his albino prince has provided this almost by default as his cycle has evolved beyond its original rubric. The final adventure of Elric–in terms of his life story–is the very dark novel *Stormbringer*, in which every supernatural debt incurred in the previous tales is finally settled. Moorcock's later additions to the cycle have necessitated the slotting in of new exploits between existing books, increasing the pace of Elric's career to a quite unbearable pitch of frenzy. The early stories had the colour and spirit, but lacked the polish and density. The return of the pale prince in *The Fortress of the Pearl* gave his personality more depth at the cost of a weaker plot. *The Revenge of the Rose* was better, but the greatest Elric novel is the most recent, *The Dreamthief's Daughter*, in which the fusion of the supernatural, realistic, visceral, intellectual, moral and aesthetic elements is seamless.

EREKOSË AND HAWKMOON CYCLES

Elric is certainly the most famous of Moorcock's four basic avatars of the "Eternal Champion," his catch-all hero, but is not necessarily the most compelling. Erekosë is more enigmatic than Elric, tormented by a heightened awareness of his role. He is also a screen on which may be projected other paranormal personalities, who then proceed to engage in extra quests, ostensibly on the side of good but sometimes on evil, or both at the same time. Erekosë himself is a thin presence, but his relative stoicism (his vast difficulties are less self-created than those of the albino) make him a more bearable literary focus than Elric, though he is even more of a loner. *The Eternal Champion*, the first novel in which he makes an appearance, is a smooth fable, simply told but powerful, with some of the rare ambience of *The Golden Barge*, despite a thoroughly melodramatic tone. The following Erekosë exploit, *Phoenix in Obsidian*, is less theatrical and closer to conventional science fantasy, taking its restless protagonist to a world which resembles the future of Earth as delineated in two early short stories which Moorcock has since dismissed as trivial but which are enthralling "fimbulwinter" visions, "The Time Dweller" and "Escape from Evening." After this point, the two cycles of Erekosë and Hawkmoon, yet another "Eternal Champion" avatar, originally overlapped, but a third proper Erekosë novel, *The Dragon in the Sword*, redefined the direction of the character, taking him into a predicament which blended high action with trenchant satire and finally gave him some measure of rest while making the Multiverse blueprint even more elaborate than it already was.

More human than Elric and less diffuse than Erekosë, the character of Hawkmoon is the most likable version of Moorcock's quadrigeminal hero. His cycle is a *bildungsroman* of aggressive responsibility. Dorian Hawkmoon, Duke of Köln, begins as a passive tool of the Empire of Grandbretan, develops a conscience and ends as the champion of freedom in a future Europe spoiled by unjust war and dominated by the obsessive nature of the Grandbretan ethic, which is utterly biophobic and sadistically cultish. A hapless traitor to his own cause, Hawkmoon has few or no special powers, but must face supernatural horrors in a world where magic and technology coexist and where both are generally employed to perverted ends. Many of the images of the Hawkmoon books are the most memorable of any of the "Eternal Champion" cycles, though this series was conceived and written with excessive haste. The irony of a far future Britain representing the "Dark Empire" while a German noble leads the fight against oppression is typical of the wry touch that Moorcock was developing prior to his total mastery of satire in the *Dancers at the End of Time* trilogy. Hawkmoon is sociable and mild mannered. He has guilt but almost no cosmic doom bothering his spirit. His companions are similarly genial and impressive and include the brusque and tarnished Count Brass, who is nominally the central figure of a second Hawkmoon cycle, the final novel of which, *The Quest for Tanelorn*, was an early and somewhat ineffectual attempt at finalising the entire Multiverse scheme. Tanelorn is a place of rest from the infinite struggle between Law and Chaos, a neutral city mostly untouched by the manoeuvres of mad gods and sensible demons. The moment at which Hawkmoon literally merges with his other avatars into a compound hero, his humanity and therefore his worth is diluted, but this magniloquent and unimaginable climax does not compromise the wild harmony of the earlier parts of the cycle.

CORUM CYCLE

The most original avatar of the "Eternal Champion" is Corum, also known as the "Prince with the Silver Hand." Corum manages to strike a balance of voice and personality between the grandiose and cold Elric and the more fallible and human Hawkmoon. He is the last member of—the Mabden—an ancient, arrogant, accomplished race, who are oblivious to the growing threat of mankind, who have recently started to swarm over and conquer the planet. In his isolation, Corum is suddenly outdistanced by history. His people are slain and he is subjected to hours of torture which leave him without an eye and hand, but which give him a thirst for revenge and an authentic reason for moody rage which Elric never really had. The mutilation proves to be a brutal blessing in disguise, for the missing parts are replaced by mystical attachments, a jeweled eye which can peer into the realm of the dead and a metal hand which can beckon its inhabitants back into the world of the living. The genius of this system is that whenever Corum defeats and slays an enemy, whether man or monster, he is then able to call upon it as a temporary ally. Moorcock employs this neat conceit to highly inventive effect.

The initial Corum novels, which form a tight trilogy, involve the hero in a quest of steadily mounting cosmic strain in which his ambition is the annihilation of three Chaos gods. *The King of the Swords*, the third in the cycle, contains some of Moorcock's best apocalyptic writing, simultaneously smooth and wide, with many images of rare power, such as Duke Teer's castle made entirely from blood. The climax of this novel was yet another attempt by the author to dismantle the supernatural bureaucracy of the Multiverse, for the Gods of both Chaos and Law are eventually murdered by other Gods who have no allegiance to either side, and thinking beings are now released from the fated violence of cosmic service, a message that is pure existentialism, concerned with choice and responsibility. The symbol of free will, the "Cosmic Balance," is finally allowed to swing according to the actions and thoughts of mortals rather than divinities. It is not necessarily a happy ending, but it is certainly a liberating one. However, it is clear that Chaos and Law were removed from only one dimension, for they remain key influences in other parts of the Multiverse.

After the completion of his gargantuan mission, Corum was allowed a brief rest to regain his will and strength before he was forced to face the frosty reception of another set of demiurges, a pantheon of senile and rotting alien Gods called the Fhoi Myore. The three books of this second trilogy have been criticised as weary, but in fact they are simply on a smaller and more personal scale than the first three, and the actual prose is of a higher standard, better suited to the psychological aspects of Corum's new relationships in a community which adopts him. Learning to love the company of others is a task as difficult for him as killing an immortal, but he somehow manages both. The flavour of this second cycle comes from Cornish myth. It is darker, colder and more affecting than the grandiose atmospheres of its predecessor. Corum's own murder at the climax of the final volume is surprisingly moving, but it also feels right, for he can no longer find a place in the present. He is an echo which has faded to incoherence and his creator has made the courageous decision to give him a crucial but almost flippant death. One wishes that all fantasy writers could love and leave their heroes so wisely.

Corum is the most visually and mythically striking of the four avatars, but it has been pointed out that whichever incarnation is first encountered by the reader generally becomes the personal favourite. All have different strengths and flaws, though they are variations of each other. When they meet, the subsequent reactions are chemical, holistic and sometimes unsatisfying, though opportunities still exist for them to blend perfectly in an adventure worthy of their combined glooms and talents.

DANCERS AT THE END OF TIME

In terms of style, substance and genuine vitality, Moorcock is one of the very few writers who keeps improving with age. What he was unable to achieve successfully in *The Quest for Tanelorn* was later realised in subtler ways with more sophisticated methods. This time the fusion was a broader, deeper and more complex mix of variations on archetypes, scenes and beliefs, and the result was the hilariously brilliant *Dancers at the End of Time* sequence. The original trilogy presents a future world where technology can produce affects akin to magic. The scenario is not hugely dissimilar in scale and scope to that of Roger Zelazny's celebrated *Lord of Light*, but the writing, allusions and consequences are wittier. As an entertainment, the *Dancers* series is almost unsurpassed in fantasy, but it works on many levels, cultural, political, existential. The naive but resourceful hero, Jherek Carnelian, handles all the issues which dismay Elric, Corum and the rest, but he does it with a lightness of touch that manages not to diminish their importance. He embarks on a steep learning curve armed mostly with flair and charm. In books added to the trilogy, the other inhabitants of his world embark on similar curves. The tone of the supernatural is often present in their frantic, farcical and clever adventures, but it is evoked by means of applied nanotechnology, one of the first occasions in fiction in which this innovation is utilised. This is the point at which science and magic, and thus the natural and supernatural, become identical. The animated, sentient jelly dinosaurs of *Constant Fire* are paranormal by any definition. The spaceship engines which melt them into a sticky mess are not. The interactive moment between the two is neither fully magical nor mechanical but an alloy, a new event forged from opposing traditions of fantastical fiction, the unexplained and the speculative. This mix is one of Moorcock's specialities.

THE VON BEK FAMILY CYCLE

The recent very weird trilogy which began with *Blood* and continued with *Fabulous Harbours* and *The War Amongst the Angels* is another example of the author's range and originality. A blend of gothic history, wild space opera, social satire, metafictional game and ironic romance, this sequence ranges across time and space and beyond at a rate dizzying even by Moorcock's standards. Unclassifiable and highly disturbing, the cycle is notable for presenting its extravagances and wonders in a prose style of cool elegance. In the first volume, a brilliant comedy of extracts from the "Corsairs of the Second Ether", an ersatz pulp space adventure consisting of thousands of chapters, is contrasted with the poignancy of the quest of the hero, expert gambler Jack Karaquazian, for his partner, Colinda Dovero, one of the most stimulating female characters in any of Moorcock's books, most of which feature strong female characters. In the second volume, the literary allusions amplify rather than attenuate the novelty of the plot and subplots, which again often attempt the impossible task of redefining the Multiverse and resolving its complexities. A nice touch is the inclusion (and identification with Elric) of Anthony Skene's character, Monsieur Zenith the Albino, the antihero of an almost vanishingly rare series of thriller yarns composed in the 1920s, and who was a crucial influence on the creation of the Prince of Melniboné. More references to all kinds of literary convention are made in the third and final volume, which demonstrates how even the clichés writers are urged to avoid can be employed to sardonic and fresh effect (chapter one is entitled "I Am Born"). The stylised playfulness and elaborate self-irony of the narrative are reminiscent of the experimental comedies of Raymond Queneau and Boris Vian, though the timbre is gentlemanly and even aloof. The passion of Moorcock's early works has moved offstage, but relocation has not diminished its force.

Of all the author's multiple sequences, the books which are closest in atmosphere and dynamic to the ideals of standard supernatural fiction are the Von Bek adventures, which are unreservedly morbid and grotesque in tone. *The War Hound and the World's Pain* is a horror story set during the Thirty Year's War, in which the blasted landscapes of the domains of Chaos have been imposed on Europe by the agency of men and their violent disputes. Shifts of inner mood generate changes in the exterior world in the manner of the Elric stories, but the darkness and despair around von Bek always feel more real. The Origenistic plot concerns the attempts of Satan to make peace with God and the vested interests which plan to ruin this process. *The City in the Autumn Stars* is set during the time of the French Revolution, and features a descendant of the original von Bek and his escape from Paris to Mirenburg, an archetypal city in the heart of a fictionalised Mitteleuropa. From here he travels by balloon into another dimension, an otherworldly land which overlaps with our own. The gradual building of suspense, the relatively leisurely pace of the narrative and erudite historical details ensure this book has far greater solidity and depth than its predecessor. It is Moorcock's finest fantasy novel, with the possible exception of *Gloriana*, but it is certainly his masterpiece of pure supernatural fiction.

GLORIANA

His most substantial single volume fantasy, *Gloriana*, was composed in three weeks in the grip of a merciless headache. A Peakean romance, it harks back in colour to *The Golden Barge* but approaches its material from a more advantageous position. Plots, intrigues and symbols are its main concern, but the ambience of its setting is murky and gothic, a labyrinthine palace riddled with passages down which whispers may carry for miles and bounded by hollow walls through which old Jephraim Tallow might creep on thieving raids. The suspense associated with supernatural fiction is here present in a fundamentally orgastic sense, for the true climax of the story hinges on the sexual fulfilment of the Queen, ruler of a parallel England which contrives to be both Elizabethan and alien. The incessant energy of her libido seems to power not only events in her own dimension but on other planes of existence. The chapter in which the sorcerer John Dee lectures the Queen on his cosmological theories with the aid of obscure maps is remarkable for the way in which it contrasts and combines a yearning for occult knowledge with sexual frustration and yearning for physical satisfaction.

SHORT FICTION

Moorcock is almost exclusively defined as a novelist rather than a short story writer, which is a tribute to the range and inventiveness of his longer work and its overriding importance in his career. But he has produced many superb short tales, some of which are overtly supernatural in taste and intent. "The Greater Conqueror" is a heady romp through the empire of Alexander the Great, in which it is revealed that the king in question is possessed by a demon. "Consuming Passion" features a bitter artist who realises he is able to start fires by willpower alone. "Wolf" plays with lycanthropy as a metaphor for misogyny. "Goodbye, Miranda" is a parable about a flying lover and his girlfriend. "Environment Problem" is a dark and amusing satire on the cliches of the Faustian pact horror story. The best of Moorcock's short fiction has the power and energy of his novels, if nothing like their scale and depth. His later short tales have been of an extremely high literary quality and include masterpieces such as "Hanging the Fool", which derives many of its motifs and images from Tarot cards. The volume *Earl Aubec* includes much of Moorcock's best work at the short story level, with the notorious novella "Behold the Man" as perhaps its most glaring omission.

Many of his Moorcock's books have relatively slight or tangential connections to the genre of true supernatural literature, although they make use of its tropes and agitations. A collaboration with Storm Constantine, *Silverheart*, has a rich gothic voice, though it lacks the higher motives and philosophy of the original von Bek novels. The story concerns an artificial heart programmed to destroy its owner unless he completes a quest in a given amount of time. It occasionally reads like a cross between a reworking of the first Hawkmoon novel and Jack Vance's *The Eyes of the Overworld*. Whether Moorcock has the will and desire to produce more works in a supernatural vein is difficult to predict, partly because he has always been capable of rejecting a genre and then returning to write one of its key works. The most that can be safely stated is that he is a writer of almost unparalleled enthusiasm and stamina with a seemingly infinite supply of surprises.

MICHAEL MOORCOCK

Selected Bibliography

WORKS OF MICHAEL MOORCOCK

An Alien Heat. London: McGibbon and Kee, 1972; New York: Harper & Row, 1973. The Dancers at the End of Time.

Ancient Shadows. London: MacGibbon and Kee; New York: Harper & Row, 1972.

The Bane of the Black Sword. New York: DAW, 1977; London: Panther, 1984. Contains material from *The Singing Citadel* and *The Stealer of Souls*. Short stories. Elric.

The Barbarians of Mars, as by Edward P. Bradbury. London: Compact, 1965. Reprinted under Moorcock's name and retitled *The Masters of the Pit*. New York: Lancer; London: New English Library, 1971. Warriors of Mars.

Behold the Man. London: Allison and Busby, 1968; New York: Avon, 1970.

Behold the Man and Other Stories. London: Phoenix House, 1994. Omnibus reprint of *Behold the Man*, *Breakfast in the Ruins*, and *Constant Fire*.

Blades of Mars, as by Edward P. Bradbury. London: Compact, 1965. Reprinted under Moorcock's name and retitled *The Lord of the Spiders*. New York: Lancer; London: New English Library, 1971. Warriors of Mars.

Blood. New York: W. Morrow, 1994; London: Millennium, 1995.

Breakfast in the Ruins. London: New English Library, 1972; New York: Random House, 1974.

The Brothel in Rösenstrasse. London: New English Library, 1982; New York: Carroll and Graf, 1987.

The Bull and the Spear. London: Allison and Busby, 1973; New York: Berkley, 1974. Corum.

Byzantium Endures. London: Secker & Warburg, 1981; New York: Random House, 1982.

The Champion of Garathorm. London: Mayflower, 1973; New York: Dell, 1976. Ereköse; Dorian Hawkmoon.

The Chronicles of Corum. New York: Berkley,m 1978. Omnibus edition of *The Bull and the Spear*, *The Oak and the Ram*, and *The Sword and the Stallion*.

The Chinese Agent. New York: Macmillan; London: Hutchinson, 1970. Has its basis in *Somewhere in the Night*.

City in the Autumn Stars. London: Grafton, 1986; New York: Ace, 1987.

Count Brass. London: Mayflower, 1973; New York: Dell, 1976. Dorian Hawkmoon.

Dancers at the End of Time. London: Granada, 1983. Omibus edition of *An Alien Heat*, *The Hollow Lands*, *The End of All Songs*. Revised: London: Millennium, 1993.

Dragon in the Sword. New York: Ace, 1986; London: Grafton, 1987. Erek

Dreamthief's Daughter. New York: Simon and Schuster; London: Earthlight, 2001.

Earl Aubec and Other Stories. London: Millennium, 1993. Reprints *The Golden Barge* and short stories.

Elric at the End of Time. London: New English Library, 1984; New York: DAW, 1985. Elric short stories.

Elric of Melnibone. London: Hutchinson, 1972. Retitled without approval and reprinted with unapproved changes as *The Dreaming City* (New York: Lancer, 1972). Revised:

New York: DAW, 1976. Elric.

The End of All Songs. New York: Harper and Row; London: Hart Davies MacGibbon, 1976. The Dancers at the End of Time.

The Eternal Champion. London: Mayflower; New York: Dell, 1970. Revised: New York: Harper & Row, 1978. Ereköse.

Fabulous Harbours. New York: Avon; London: Millennium, 1995.

The Fortress of the Pearl. London: Golllancz; New York: Ace, 1989.

Gloriana or the Unfulfill'd Queen. London: Allison & Busby, 1978; New York: Avon, 1979. Revised: London: Millennium, 1983.

The Golden Barge. Manchester: Savoy, 1979; New York: DAW, 1980.

The History of the Runestaff. London: Granada, 1979. Omnibus edition of *The Jewel in the Skull, The Mad God's Amulet, The Sword of the Dawn,* and *The Runestaff.*

The Hollow Lands. New York: Harper and Row, 1974; London: Hart Davies MacGibbon, 1975. The Dancers at the End of Time.

The Jade Man's Eyes. Brighton: Unicorn Bookshop, 1973. Elric short story.

The Jewel in the Skull. New York: Lancer, 1968; London: Mayflower, 1969. Revised: New York: DAW, 1977. Dorian Hawkman.

King of the Swords. New York: Berkley, 1971; London: Mayflower, 1971. Corum.

Knight of the Swords. New York: Berkley; London: Mayflower, 1971. Corum.

Legends from the End of Time. New York: Harper & Row, 1976. Omnibus edition of *Ancient Shadows, Pale Roses, White Stars.* Dancers at the End of Time.

London Bone. New York: Scribner/Simon & Schuster; London: Scribner, 2001.

The Mad God's Amulet. London: Mayflower, 1969. Revised: DAW, 1977. Dorian Hawkmoon.

Mother London. London: Secker and Warburg, 1988; New York: Harmony, 1989.

The Oak and the Ram. London: Allison and Busby, 1973; New York: Berkley, 1974. Corum

Phoenix in Obsidian. London: Mayflower, 1970. Retitled: *The Silver Warriors.* New York: Dell, 1973. Ereköse.

The Queen of the Swords. London: Mayflower; New York: Berkley, 1971. Corum.

The Quest for Tanelorn. London: Mayflower, 1975; New York: Dell, 1976. Ereköse, Dorian Hawkmoon.

The Revenge of the Rose. London: Grafton; New York: Ace, 1991. Elric.

The Runestaff. London: Mayflower, 1969. Revised: New York: DAW, 1977. Dorian Hawkmoon.

The Russian Intelligence. Manchester, England: Savoy, 1980.

The Sailor on the Seas of Fate. London: Quartet; New York: DAW, 1976. Elric.

The Singing Citadel. London: Mayflower; New York: Berkley, 1970. Elric short stories.

The Sleeping Sorceress. London: New English Library, 1971; Reprinted as *The Vanishing Tower.* New York: DAW, 1977. Elric.

Sojan. Manchester: Savoy, 1977.

Somewhere in the Night. London: Compact, 1966. Basis for The Chinese Agent.

MICHAEL MOORCOCK

The Stealer of Souls. London: Neville Spearman, 1963. New York: Lancer, 1967. Elric short stories.

Stormbringer. London: Herbert Jenkins, 1965. New York: Lancer, 1967. Revised: New York: DAW, 1977. Elric.

Stormbringer. London: Millennium, 1993. Omnibus edition of *Stormbringer, The Vanishing Tower, The Revenge of the Rose.*

The Sword and the Stallion. New York: Berkley; London: Allison and Busby, 1974. Corum 6.

The Sword of the Dawn. New York: Lancer, 1968; London: Mayflower, 1969. Revised: New York: DAW, 1977. Dorian Hawkmoon.

The Swords Trilogy. New York: Berkley, 1977. Omnibus edition of The Knight of Swords, the Queen of the Swords, and The King of the Swords.

The Transformation of Miss Mavis Ming. London: W. H. Allen, 1977. Retitled: *A Messiah at the End of Time.* New York: DAW, 1978. Retitled: *Constant Fire* in *Behold the Man and Other Stories.* London: Phoenix House, 1994.

The War Amongst the Angels. New York: Avon; London: Millennium, 1996.

The War Hound and the World's Pain. New York: Pocket Books, 1981; London: New English Library, 1982.

Warriors of Mars, as by Edward P. Bradbury. London: Compact, 1965; New York: Lancer, 1966. Reprinted under Moorcock's name and retitled *The City of the Beast.* New York: Lancer, 1970; London: New English Library, 1971. Warriors of Mars.

The Weird of the White Wolf. New York: DAW, 1977. Contains material from *The Singing Citadel* and *The Stealer of Souls.* Elric.

Wizardry and Wild Romance: A Study of Epic Fantasy. London: Victor Gollancz, 1987; revised, 1988. Nonfiction: does not discuss Moorcock's own work but offers insights into the works of others.

AS EDITOR

Before Armageddon: An Anthology of Victorian and Edwardian Imaginative Fiction Published before 1914. London: W. H. Allen, 1975.

The Best of New Worlds. London: Compact, 1965.

The Best SF Stories from New Worlds. London: Panther, 1967–1974.

England Invaded: A Collection of Fantasy Fiction. London: W. H. Allen; New York: Ultramarine, 1977.

New Worlds: An Anthology. London: Fontana, 1983.

The Traps of Time. London: Rapp and Whiting, 1968.

SECONDARY

Ashley, Mike. "New Worlds," in *Science Fiction, Fantasy, and Weird Fiction Magazines*, ed. by Marshall B. Tymn and Mike Ashley. Westport, CT: Greenwood, 1985, p. 423–437.

Bilyeu, Richard. *The Tanelorn Archives: A Primary and Secondary Bibliography of the Works of Michael Moorcock 1949–1979.* Manitoba, Canada: Pandora's Books, 1981.

Clute, John. "Michael Moorcock" in *The Encyclopedia of Fantasy*, ed. by John Clute and John Grant. New York: St. Martin's, 1997, p. 656–660.

Clute, John. "Michael Moorcock," in *The Encyclopedia of Science Fiction*, ed. by John Clute, Peter Nicholls, and Brian Stableford. London: Orbit, 1993.

D'Ammassa, Don. "Michael Moorcock," in *St. James Guide to Science Fiction Writers* 4th ed. Detroit, MI: St. James, 1996, p. 666–670.

Langford, David. "Michael Moorcock," in *St. James Guide to Fantasy Writers*, ed. by David Pringle. Detroit, MI: St. James, 1996, p. 412–416.

James Morrow
1947–

BRIAN STABLEFORD

JAMES KENNETH MORROW was born on March 17, 1947, in Philadelphia, the only child of William and Emily Morrow. After graduating from the University of Pennsylvania in 1969 with a B.A. degree in creative writing he attended the Harvard Graduate School of Education, receiving his master's degree in 1971. His career as an English teacher, launched at the Cambridge Pilot School in Massachusetts in 1970, soon broadened out to encompass enthusiastic promotion of visual media—including film and comics—as educa- tional instruments. In 1972 he married Jean Pierce; their two children, Kathleen and Christopher, were born in 1978 and 1988.

From 1977 to 1979, Morrow was a lecturer in instructional media at Tufts University in Medford, Massachusetts, and from 1978 to 1980 a codirector of the Institute for Multimedia Learning in Westford. During the 1980s, when he became a full-time freelance writer, he wrote a great deal of educational nonfiction and children's fiction, much of the latter supporting educational software packages. Morrow and Jean Pierce were divorced in 1996; he subsequently married Kathryn Smith and moved with her and Christopher to State College, Pennsylvania.

In commenting on the essays written on his work in a special issue of the journal *Paradoxa* in 1999, Morrow says of the early phase of his career that

> Coming of age during the idealistic and activist 1960s, I readily embraced the notion that we might improve the doleful expectations of our disadvantaged youth by first improving the dreadful schools in which they were required to congregate. I decided to become a teacher. It quickly developed, however, that I was much too introverted a man to function effectively in the classroom. And so I drifted into the more abstract side of the education world....
>
> Having made a half-dozen 8mm fantasy and horror films as a teenager, I soon discovered natural allies among those educators for whom the "new media"—movies, photography, radio, television—held great potential as learning tools. The leading light behind this rather messianic media-in-the-schools movement was the Canadian communications philosopher Marshall McLuhan, and for about a year his ideas captivated me.... I grew disenchanted ... [but] the more I ponder the challenges of novel-making, the more I realize that my McLuhanist past is not behind me. I continue to be fascinated by the formal, structural, and theoretical considerations that confront the

practitioner in any medium, including the medium of fiction.

(pp. 158–159)

Given this, it is hardly surprising that Morrow's fiction is scrupulously and ingeniously didactic, using all manner of quasi-pyrotechnic rhetorical devices to make its points. Marshall McLuhan was fond of declaring that he was an explorer, not an explainer—a device he often used to defuse criticism from those who, like Morrow, eventually came to suspect that some of his assertions were simply wrong. Morrow is also an explorer first and an explainer second—but he is a very conscientious explorer, who shows a rare determination to find everything that there is to be found in the furthest territories mappable by the imagination.

Morrow's first novel, *The Wine of Violence* (1981), is framed as science fiction, but the tradition to which it belongs is that of the Voltairean *conte philosophique*—a tradition Morrow's work carries forward as positively and as productively as any modern writer could. A scientific expedition gone astray lands on Carlotta, a world long isolated from other outposts of human civilization. After being attacked by "neurovores" (brain-eaters) its members discover the walled city of Quetzalia, surrounded by a mysterious organic moat. Entomologist Francis Lostwax learns from the Quetzalian doctor Tez Yon—with whom he falls in love—that the moat consists of "noctus," which soaks up the aggressive impulses of the Quetzalians and gives harmless expression to them as cathartic dreams experienced and contained within the context of the religious philosophy of Zolmec.

Lostwax finds Quetzalia's pacifist society attractive, but his fellow expeditionary Burne Newman cannot wait to escape from it. Newman, having discovered that the distilled aggression can be restored to its originators by injection, raises an army of volunteers that he eventually leads to a hard-won victory against the neurovores. Lostwax unwisely injects Tez Yon with noctus in the hope that it will enable her to survive in his world when he takes her home—but she also injects herself and is driven by the double dose to become a serial killer. The bitter climax of the black comedy argues that love is—alas—an inadequate antidote to the human propensity for violence, insufficient in itself to heal the wounds that passion and aggression open up. A corollary conclusion is that religion is similarly imperfect as an insulating force, and would be even if its metaphysical claims were given robust material support.

Like all conscientious designers of utopian societies, Morrow operates as a curious investigator rather than as a committed preacher; Quetzalia is a thought experiment, not a prescription that the meek might seek to follow in attempting to collect their promised inheritance. *The Continent of Lies* (1984) carries forward the themes laid down in *The Wine of Violence* but readjusts the balance to bring the engineered dreams to center stage. Here "cephapples" grown on "noostrees"—popularly known as "dreambeans"—are the hottest medium of entertainment, but their potential as a rewarding medium of experience and education is threatened by the advent of a toxic bean, The Lier-in-Wait, which leaves its consumers in a near-catatonic state, helplessly muttering "My only God is Goth."

Quinjin, a cephapple critic, is hired to track down the source of the rogue beans, and the mission becomes personal when his beloved daughter falls victim to one. After an interplanetary journey through some gloriously gaudy scenery, Quinjin eventually confronts the satanic Simon Kusk, whose ambition is to establish a dark religion with himself at its center. Heroically, he destroys the Hamadryad—the "deathtree" that puts forth the malevolent fruit—but his victory is not without its costs.

Quinjin, whose task is to harrow a custom-designed hell, fares somewhat better than Francis Lostwax, who foolishly corrupted a perverse kind of heaven, but Morrow's carefully constructed heterocosms always recognize the ultimate inescapability of those evils that are so deep-rooted in the human psyche as to be part of its nature. *The Continent of Lies* is more recklessly inventive than its predecessor, but the flamboyance of its narrative serves mainly to accentuate the sharpness of the moral problems it seeks to highlight. *This Is the Way the World Ends* (1986) is spare by comparison, refining its method as it narrows its focus to examine and extrapolate contemporary anxieties about the possibility of nuclear war.

George Paxton, a monument mason and a contented family man, is persuaded to buy a scopas (Self-Contained Post-Attack Survival) suit for his beloved daughter but cannot keep up the necessary payments. A strange woman with black blood offers him a "free" suit if he will visit a surreal MAD Hatter's shop (MAD signifying Mutually Assured Destruction) and sign a document admitting that his purchase of the suit is an admission of complicity in the nuclear arms race. An attack is launched while George is trying to get the suit home; he is shot by a desperate neighbor and wakes aboard a submarine bound for Antarctica to find that he and five other people are to be tried for their complicity in the destruction of the world before a tribunal of the "unadmitted"—anticipatory phantoms robbed by the holocaust of their opportunity to be born.

George's five codefendants all represent groups involved in the politics or implementation of nuclear deterrence, and their culpability is never in doubt. But George—as the representative of the common man—seems to stand a chance of acquittal on the grounds that he is as much a victim as the unadmitted are. Morrow's verdict is, however, meticulously calculated. George cherishes his illusions; he wants to be persuaded that peace can be obtained by preparation for war, just as he wants to be persuaded that the scopas suit is more than a scam and that he really can be united, however briefly, with his dead daughter. The judgment of the unadmitted is that George is guilty of an optimism so misguided as to constitute intellectual treason. When he has been gifted his one final illusion—the equivalent of the condemned man's last meal—he sets about engraving a tombstone for the whole human race.

Morrow had only published one short story, "The Assemblage of Kristin" (1984), before *This Is the Way the World Ends*, but he now began to produce brief satires in some profusion, most of their barbs aimed at religion in general and the Old Testament in particular. "Spelling God with the Wrong Blocks" (1987) and "Diary of a Mad Deity" (1988) were swiftly followed by the earliest items in an elastic series of revisionist accounts that eventually lent their collective title to a 1996 short-story collection: the Nebula-winning "Bible Stories for Adults, No. 17: The Deluge" (1988) and "Bible Stories for Adults, No. 31: The Covenant" (1989). This work of reexamination soon expanded to take in the New Testament in the novel *Only Begotten Daughter* (1990), a bitterly sarcastic account of the advent of a new messiah, this time born female.

Forewarned and philosophically forearmed by the sad precedent of Jesus, the virgin father of Julie Katz is not optimistic about her chances of figuring out what it is that a child of God is supposed to do for contemporary humankind, and knows full well that it will be a thankless task in a world that offers precious little scope for her to do anything at all. Julie is led by her confusion to seek enlightenment in the Dantean Hell run by the ingenious Father of Lies—where Jesus now resides, still doing his best to help sinners—but it is not until she returns to the world that things begin to get really difficult for her. Awkwardly placed between the diffuse God of the philosophers and the concrete God of faith manufacturers, she is inexorably and painfully torn apart.

Only Begotten Daughter is a righteously wrathful book calculated to enrage many of its readers. In the year that it was published, Morrow compiled a pilot version of *Bible Stories for Adults,* issued as No. 8 in a short-lived periodical series, *Author's Choice Monthly,* published by the hyperactive small press Pulphouse. Morrow titled the collection *Swatting at the Cosmos,* recalling in the introduction that this was what his first writing teacher had advised him repeatedly not to do. He left no doubt of his intention to carry on doing it, even more ambitiously than he had so far contrived to do. Even his slightest and funniest short stories always deal with big subjects: slavery and wage slavery in "Abe Lincoln in McDonald's" (1989), the limitations of charity in "The Confessions of Ebenezer Scrooge" (1989)—in which the much-haunted miser learns more subtle lessons from the Ghosts of Christmas Subjunctive, Christmas Conditional, Christmas Future Perfect and several other neglected tenses—and the perils of idolatry in "Arms and the Woman" (1991).

The Nebula-winning novella *City of Truth* (1991) is a fabular account of the utopian city of Veritas, where telling the truth is compulsory, and its equally utopian underworld, Satirev, where lying is not merely permitted but definitely de rigueur. The story carefully compares the advantages of the two modes of existence, eventually coming to the conclusion that some lies—especially those supporting and sustaining the placebo effect—are not merely convenient but so life-enhancing that a society would have to be insane to try to do away with them. Morrow had no intention, however, of meekly joining the ranks of those apologists who would include the idea of God among necessary or desirable illusions. This was one lie that, in his view, required very thorough interrogation and analysis before it could be permitted to stand.

Although the God who makes a dutifully humble cameo appearance at the end of *Only Begotten Daughter* is not judged exceedingly harshly, the paternal and bullying God of the Old Testament is given a much harder time in all the hypothetical arenas in which Morrow takes him on. In his next three novels Morrow set out to develop a counterargument to Voltaire's famous assertion that if God did not exist we should have to invent him. The underlying argument of the "Godhead trilogy" is that even if God did exist, we might do well to ignore him—with the corollary that if God really cared about us, perhaps the best thing he could possibly do for us would be to commit suicide. In *Towing Jehovah* (1994), he does exactly that, casting his body upon the waters of the earth.

The hero of *Towing Jehovah,* Anthony Van Horne, is a disgraced ship's captain ridden by the guilt of having perpetrated an eco-catastrophe. He is given a chance to redeem himself when he is selected by the mournful angels to tow God's dead body to its final resting place in the Arctic. The task is awkward because of the vast size of the corpse, and is further complicated by the determination of the Vatican to keep God's death a secret and the equal determination of a group of militant atheists to make the fact known. Although the passage of the corpse is cloaked by a stubborn fog, the business of towing Jehovah soon becomes vexatious; indeed, such is the mechanical difficulty of maneuvering the body that Anthony's ship runs drastically short of supplies; for want of other sustenance his crew members have no alternative but to dine on its meat, with ambiguous nutritional consequences.

In the end, the commission proves a little too much for the unfortunate Anthony; having failed to deliver the unwieldy cadaver soon enough to the natural cryonic chamber prepared by the Vatican, he loses his ship, but he manages to avoid the traditional captain's fate of going down with her. He is left to extrapolate from his newly enriched personal experience (in association with insights contributed by the unorthodox Jesuit Thomas Wickliff Ockham and the orthodox atheist Cassie Fowler) a hypothesis to explain why God's death had become necessary.

In *Blameless in Abaddon* (1996), Jehovah's corpse suffers the indignity of becoming the main attraction in a Florida theme park—a fate that seems even more ignominious following the discovery that life still lurks in its mysterious cellular depths. This stubborn persistence of life allows the Corpus Dei to be subpoenaed to appear before the World Court in the Hague, charged with inflicting a host of evils upon humankind throughout history. This charge is laid by Martin Candle, a justice of the peace practicing in Abaddon Township, Pennsylvania, who has reacted badly to the news that he will die, messily, of prostate cancer. The World Court initially refuses to hear the case, pleading lack of funds, but Martin's challenge is relished by a multimillionaire professor of medieval literature, Gregory Francis Lovett, who appoints himself defense attorney for the Creator.

Blameless in Abaddon is one of many modern replays of the book of Job, which is by far the most literary and by no means the least contentious exemplary tale in the Old Testament; Morrow had earlier written another version as a one-act play, "Bible Stories for Adults, No. 46: The Soap Opera" (1992). Martin's alter ego, Job, makes a guest appearance in the plot, along with many other Old Testament figures, during a journey through the neural tissue of the corpse intended to plumb the depths of the Divine Mind. The adversary whose challenge to Jehovah prompted the testing of Job is also present, as an interested onlooker. Although he is, inevitably, less sophisticated than the urbane Devil of *Only Begotten Daughter,* he makes a far better case for his own indispensability within the divine scheme.

As in the tribunal featured in *This Is the Way the World Ends*—which might be regarded as a trial run—the prosecution in *Blameless in Abaddon* is conducted with great rhetorical fervor and argumentative skill, but here the defense is much more resilient. Morrow is by no means the only contemporary fantasist to be bold enough to tackle the awkward business of theodicy head on, with a fierce desire to get to the bottom of it—Anne Rice's attempt in *Memnoch the Devil* (1995) and Philip Pullman's in *His Dark Materials* (1995–2000) are virtually simultaneous—but Morrow's combination of philosophical sophistication and narrative force is quite unparalleled. Whether the judgment handed down by the court is right or fair, the evidence is certainly set out in full and argued by both sides with all due determination. This time, the troublesome corpse was set to be cremated—but it was not yet finished with its own demonstrations.

In the final part of the trilogy, *The Eternal Footman* (1999), the suicidal Jehovah, tired of human attempts to evade consciousness of his extinction, celebrates the millennium by disintegrating his body and sending his skull into geosynchronous orbit, where it functions as the ultimate memento mori of the Western world. Then, beneath the mocking glare of the Cranium Dei, the West is subjected to the last and nastiest of all the plagues God has seen fit to visit upon it. Kevin Burkhart, whose mother, Nora, makes a living delivering funeral wreaths, is confronted and swiftly possessed by his "fetch"—his own personal Death—Quincy Azrael. Black "fear syrup" bubbles from Kevin's mouth as his excruciation on the existentialist rack begins, and many others are similarly afflicted.

The pathology of this "abulic plague" is credited to a protein nicknamed Nietzsche-A. People who have only seen their fetches are in a prefatory "Nietzsche-positive" phase, in which they may remain for some considerable time; only after fusion with their fetches do sufferers move to full-blown "thanocathexis." Meanwhile, the monument sculptor Gerard Korty, resentful of the Vatican's misuse of a reliquary he built to contain God's remaining bones, commits himself to a crusade against the plague led by the psychoanalyst Adrian Lucido. Lucido employs a drug named hyperion-15 in association with his own custom-designed religion of Somatocism, whose deities mirror quasi-Freudian stages of human development and are named with anagrams of the name "Diagoras," the fifth-century B.C. Sophist who was the first identifiable atheist.

As American society collapses, Nora Burkhart makes her way south in the hope that Lucido—now based in Mexico—might cure Kevin. She is delayed by the crusade launched against the Jews of America by the Anglo-Saxon Christian Brotherhood, whose battlefields she must cross, but eventually hooks up with Anthony Van Horne, who is taking his own stricken child, to Lucido's clinic. Kevin's subsequent relief is, alas, only a stay of execution; hyperion-15 and Somatocism are merely instruments of procrastination. While Lucido's search for a more permanent "antidote" to thanocathexis leads him into the darkest heart of paganism, Korty returns to the quest to create an appropriate object for the veneration of future ages. The symbolism of his attempt becomes intricately entwined with that of a dream odyssey undertaken by Nora, whose fetch guides her through two contrasted visions of post-theistic existence: the city of Deus Absconditus, in which, as in Satirev, institutions are judged by their efficacy rather than their fidelity to truth or principle; and the technologically retreatist village of Holistica.

God does not come out of the Godhead trilogy well, and the candidates for his replacement fare even worse, but such alternatives as Deus Absconditus and Holistica are found wanting too, just as Quetzalia had been in *The Wine of Violence*. Like the World Court in *Blameless in Abaddon*, Morrow can never quite escape the temptation to let God off the hook. In the special issue of *Paradoxa* devoted to his work he observes that "the average Morrow novel modifies its scoffing through appeals to a modified transcendence. . . . Evidently I want to regurgitate my communion wafers and have them too" (p. 154). In the same commentary he concedes, prompted by Bill Sheehan's article "Of Lunacy and Sorrow: Comedy and Tragedy in James Morrow's *City of Truth*," that his entire body of work has a "thematic core" that berates the unfortunate tendency humans have to sacrifice their own humanity upon the altar of some overdemanding ideal.

Paradoxical as it may seem, there are certain ideas that are so serious that they can only be sensibly addressed in fantasy, by means of comedy. That which is conventionally held sacred has to be denuded of all its insulation before it can be examined with a fresh eye. Aggression extrapolated into murder and warfare, and worship extrapolated into oppression and persecution, are the most serious problems that afflict modern individuals and nations. Sober reportage makes them seem overwhelming and irresistible; their limitations can only be grasped by means of satirical transformation and the evaluative inversions of sarcasm. James Morrow is a master of this kind of narrative alchemy, and part of his artistry lies in never forgetting or failing to provide a counterweight to his caustic deluges of black irony by constantly reminding his readers of the redemptive quality of affection.

More often than not, affection in Morrow's work takes the form of parental love, especially of mothers for their sons and fathers for their daughters. He is too conscientious a writer to reward such emotional attachments with arbitrary miracles of salvation, no matter how hard he forces his characters to try for their attainment. But he is wise enough to assert, continually and insistently, that by constituting their own reward, our most intimate relationships always affirm the virtue as well as the necessity of our struggles against adversity. This is the best that modern *contes philosophiques* have to offer, and it is a conclusion well worth the reaching.

JAMES MORROW

Selected Bibliography

WORKS OF JAMES MORROW

NOVELS AND SHORT STORIES

The Wine of Violence. New York: Holt, Rinehart and Winston, 1981; London: Century, 1991.

The Continent of Lies. New York: Holt, Rinehart and Winston, 1984; London: Gollancz, 1985.

This Is the Way the World Ends. New York: Henry Holt, 1986; London: Gollancz, 1987.

Only Begotten Daughter. New York: William Morrow, 1990; London: Century, 1991.

Swatting at the Cosmos. (In *Author's Choice Monthly,* issue 8.) Eugene, Ore.: Pulphouse, 1990.

City of Truth. London: Legend, 1990; New York: St. Martin's Press, 1992.

Towing Jehovah. New York: Harcourt Brace and London: Arrow, 1994.

Blameless in Abaddon. New York: Harcourt Brace, 1996.

Bible Stories for Adults. New York: Harcourt Brace, 1996.

The Eternal Footman. New York: Harcourt Brace, 1999.

NONFICTION

Moviemaking Illustrated: The Comicbook Filmbook. With Murray Suid. Rochelle Park, N.J.: Hayden, 1973.

Media and Kids. With Murray Suid. Rochelle Park, N.J.: Hayden, 1977.

The Grammar of Media Kit. With Jean Morrow. Rochelle Park, N.J.: Hayden, 1978.

The Creativity Catalogue. With Murray Suid. Belmont, Calif.: Pitman, 1982.

CRITICAL AND BIOGRAPHICAL STUDIES

The Divinely Human Comedy of James Morrow. Special issue, *Paradoxa* 5, no. 12 (1999). (Contains eleven articles on Morrow and two by him—one responding to the articles—plus an introduction and a bibliography.)

Kim Newman
1959–

CLAUDE LALUMIÈRE

BORN IN LONDON on July 31, 1959, Kim Newman is the son of Bryan Michael Newman and Julia Newman (née Christen). He attended Bridgwater College from 1975 to 1977 and received a B.A. with honors in English from the University of Sussex in 1980. In addition to his work as a film critic and writer of fantastic fiction, Newman's multifaceted career has included stints with the Sheep Worrying Theatre Group and the Club Whoopee cabaret band, broadcasting for BBC Radio, and a longstanding and ongoing involvement with the British Film Institute. Kim Newman's most famous creation is the alternate history series Anno Dracula. He has also written under the name Jack Yeovil, mostly novels and stories set in the role-playing shared worlds of Games Workshop. He has collaborated most notably with Neil Gaiman, Stephen Jones, Paul J. McAuley, and Eugene Byrne.

His coedited essay anthology *Horror: The 100 Best Books* (1988) tied for the 1990 Bram Stoker Award (nonfiction). His dark and politically savvy reimagining of the pulp vigilante, "The Original Dr Shade" (1990), won the 1991 British Science Fiction Association Award (short fiction). His novel *Anno Dracula* (1992) was shortlisted for the 1993 World Fantasy Award and the 1994 Bram Stoker Award, came in second in the horror novel category of the 1994 *Locus* Reader's Poll, and won the 1995 International Horror Guild Award. "Coppola's Dracula" (1997), shortlisted for the 1998 World Fantasy Award (novella) and the 1998 Bram Stoker Award (long fiction), won the 1998 International Horror Guild Award (short form). His mosaic *Where the Bodies Are Buried* (2000) won the 2001 British Fantasy Award (collection). In total, Newman has earned more than forty nominations for his work as fiction writer, anthologist, and critic.

***

Newman's first book, *Nightmare Movies: Wide Screen Horror since 1968* (1984)—later revised as *Nightmare Movies: A Critical History of the Horror Film, 1968 -1988* (1988)—was the first of several books of film criticism. It was followed by *Ghastly Beyond Belief* (1985), a humor anthology of science fiction and fantasy quotations coedited with Neil Gaiman. His next book, *Horror: The 100 Best Books*, coedited with Stephen Jones, is an anthology of lively essays by noted contemporary horror writers, each describing their favorite horror book. A number of the selections—for example, John Brunner's *The Sheep Look Up* (1972), a prescient science fiction novel of environmental catastrophe and corporatized government—challenge traditional definitions of horror fiction.

"Dreamers" and "Patricia's Profession," Newman's first two professional fiction sales, to UK genre fiction magazine *Interzone* in 1984 and 1985 respectively, are true to the mid-1980s zeitgeist, cyberpunk (both are included in his 1994 collection, *The Original Dr Shade & Other Stories*). His fifth published story, "Famous Monsters" (1988), proved to be a signature piece: a sad and sardonic monologue by an aging Hollywood actor who happens to be one of H. G. Wells's Martians, set in the aftermath of the First and Second War of the Worlds. Its combination of pop-culture references, film arcana, horror imagery, erudite wit, political engagement, and alternate history deviating not from real history but from classic fiction came to define Kim Newman's most celebrated work.

Nevertheless, his first novel, *The Night Mayor* (1989), harks back to the cyberpunk setting of his early stories (in fact, they share characters). *The Night Mayor* is a wry cyberpunk detective story set in a virtual-reality film noir landscape. The novel makes rich and entertaining use of film history and cinematic imagery. The same year, *Drachenfels*, set in Games Workshop's Warhammer world, appeared. It was the first of several novels written under the name Jack Yeovil. *Drachenfels*'s most important contribution to the Kim Newman canon was the introduction of one of his signature characters, the compassionate vampire Geneviève Dieudonné, who would later resurface in different incarnations in several of Newman's fictional worlds.

The early 1990s would see seven more Jack Yeovil novels, six titles for Games Workshop's Warhammer and Dark Future series, and *Orgy of the Blood Parasites* (1994), a splatterpunk novel of science gone wrong. While Jack Yeovil was busy being such a prolific novelist (and occasional short-story writer), a steady stream of short stories, novels, film criticism, and anthologies bore the Kim Newman byline.

His second book of film criticism, *Wild West Movies: Or How the West Was Found, Won, Lost, Lied About, Filmed and Forgotten*, appeared in 1990. Newman's second novel under his own byline was *Bad Dreams* (1990), a minor splatterpunk novel linking the urban underworld of London with the underworld of the undead. His next novel, *Jago* (1991), an epic horror novel of megalomaniacal cultism and psychic powers, shows considerably more ambition and imagination. It combines a wealth of transmogrified pop-culture icons, a fast-paced horrific thriller, an expansive cast of diverse characters, and a pointed commentary on the politics of the voluminous horror best-sellers of the 1980s.

Nineteen ninety-two was an important year for Kim Newman. With Paul J. McAuley, he coedited *In Dreams*, an anthology of new science fiction and horror stories inspired by pop music. His novella "Red Reign" made its debut in *The Mammoth Book of Vampires*, edited by Stephen Jones. The same year, "Red Reign" was retooled by Newman to form the basis of his most renowned novel, the genre-bending masterpiece *Anno Dracula*.

Dark Voices 5: The Pan Book of Horror (1993), edited by David Sutton and Stephen Jones, saw the first appearance of "Where the Bodies Are Buried," the beginning of an important series of stories that would pastiche 1980s horror movies and brutally criticize the reactionary political context that spawned them.

The next book to sport the Kim Newman byline was *The Quorum* (1994), a Faustian drama that brings back several characters from Newman's short stories. The most interesting aspect of the novel is that it explores in greater detail Newman's oft-recurring villain, Derek Leech, a manipulative British media mogul with more than a whiff of the demonic about him. The Faustian motifs, the detective plot, and the Derek Leech story that combine to form *The Quorum*—although each is filled with inventive moments and intriguing ideas—fail to coalesce in as dramatically satisfying a fashion as did the diverse elements that made up *Jago* or *Anno Dracula*.

Newman's first collection of short fiction was released in 1994: *The Original Dr Shade & Other Stories*. Although entertaining, most of its contents pale in comparison to the dark and intense opening story, the award-winning "The Original Dr Shade," in which a fascist pulp vigilante is triumphantly reborn in Thatcher's economically oppressive Great Britain. The other highlight is the collection's one previously unpublished story, "The McCarthy Witch Hunt." In it, Newman takes the word "witch" literally; in an engaging and viciously hilarious condemnation of the sexual politics of American family values, he sics an intolerant and paranoid Senator McCarthy on Samantha Stevens (of TV's *Bewitched*).

Considerably more important is *Famous Monsters* (1995), his second collection. *Famous Monsters* reprints the bulk of Newman's early signature pieces. Most of the stories in this collection highlight the particular qualities that make up Newman's distinctive style, and most of them show Newman at the top of his form, deftly juxtaposing poetic evocation with pop-culture kitsch and genre history with hard-hitting political commentary. The collection's many memorable stories include the poignant title story, combining film history with H. G. Wells's *The War of the Worlds* (1898); "The Big Fish" (1993), a hardboiled homage to *Weird Tales* featuring the vampire Geneviève Dieudonné and juggling the universes of H. P. Lovecraft, Raymond Chandler, and Second World War politics; the moving ode to Orson Welles and alternate-history pastiche of *Citizen Kane* (1941), "The Snow Sculptures of Xanadu" (1991); the first two "Where the Bodies are Buried" stories (1993 and 1994); and "Übermensch!" (1991), a moody alternate history evoking 1930s German expressionist cinema set in the aftermath of the Second World War on a planet earth where the rocket carrying DC Comics' Superman landed not in Kansas but in Germany.

His 1995 novel, *The Bloody Red Baron*, is a sequel to *Anno Dracula*. Set during the First World War, it continues to explore the ramifications of the events that gave birth to the Anno Dracula timeline by venturing further afield in the world and by moving forward in time (*Anno Dracula* was set in Victorian London). Perhaps not as spectacular in its effects as *Anno Dracula*, it is nevertheless an engaging and entertaining novel that goes beyond merely aping its predecessor and establishes its own voice and themes.

In 1996, Newman edited *The BFI Companion to Horror*, which, although it doesn't ignore literary sources, concentrated mainly on cinema (appropriately, as the volume was prepared for the British Film Institute).

Back in the USSA, a collaborative alternate-history mosaic by Eugene Byrne and Kim Newman, appeared in 1997. It postulates a world where the Communist Revolution took place not in Russia but in the United States. It spans nearly nine full decades of twentieth-century history, from 1912 to 1998. Interestingly, the stories were serialized in the U.K. magazine *Interzone*, but the book was only ever published in the United States, the one book of Newman's to be published there exclusively (while the reverse, a British publication with no American equivalent, has happened to Newman on several occasions).

The third Anno Dracula novel, *Judgment of Tears: Anno Dracula 1959*, came out in 1998. Set in Rome, it pastiches Italian crime movies and James Bond—again, not the equal of the first book, but wildly entertaining and different from yet coherent with its predecessors.

In 1999, Newman published two volumes of film criticism: *Millennium Movies: End of the World Cinema* and, in the BFI Film Classics series, *Cat People*. The latter is a slim but authoritative volume on Jacques Tourneur's classic 1943 horror film of the same name.

That same year Newman scored a mainstream hit with the peculiar novel *Life's Lottery*, a book structured like a "choose your own adventure" game. Characters "reappear in new roles in different strands, often to ironic effect when alternate stories are compared. Occasional SF timeslip opportunities let you switch stories or rethink old decisions. Some lives are touched by spidery horror. ... Others encounter magic, madness, cancer, violence or prison. ... you can always turn back, perhaps noticing the scenes not reachable by any official route, and try again. Inventive, frustrating, compulsive" (Langford, online). Appropriately, the novel is narrated by the "possibly demonic, certainly malign" (*Seven Stars*, p. 384) Derek Leech, a character who is frequently shown throughout Newman's oeuvre as taking perverse pleasure in manipulating, controlling, and/or playing with people's lives. *Life's Lottery* was popular in the U.K. but has yet to be published in the United States.

Also in 1999, the novella *Andy Warhol's Dracula* appeared as a limited edition from the British small press PS Publishing. It revisits the world of *Anno Dracula* and is part of the as yet unpublished mosaic *Johnny Alucard*, the fourth and supposedly final Anno Dracula book. Other Anno Dracula stories published so far include "Coppola's Dracula" (*The Mammoth Book of Dracula*, edited by Stephen Jones, 1997), "Castle in the Desert: Anno Dracula 1977" (*Scifi.com*, 2000), and "Dead Travel Fast" (*Unforgivable Stories*, 2000).

The success of *Life's Lottery* prompted Simon & Schuster U.K. not only to reprint the bulk of Newman's backlist fiction in uniform trade editions to match the design of the new book's dust jacket but also to release two new collections. The first was *Seven Stars*, a solid follow-up to *Famous Monsters* that emphasizes the connections between the different worlds of Newman's multiverse. With that in mind, the book includes a previously unpublished piece by Newman: "Who's Who," a brief alphabetical listing of Newman's major characters and of their different incarnations and appearances. The two concluding Where the Bodies Are Buried stories (1995 and 1996) are also featured in *Seven Stars*.

The showcase piece, however, is the title novella, a deliriously inventive and epic tale pastiching Bram Stoker, ranging in time from ancient Egypt to Newman's cyberpunk 2025, and involving several characters from Newman's recurring cast.

Newman's next collection was *Unforgivable Stories*. Less focused than *Seven Stars*, it still contains a number of strong stories, but also a few minor ones. Also in 2000, all four Where the Bodies Are Buried stories were gathered in one book under that title by specialty publisher The Alchemy Press.

Time and Relative, a Doctor Who novella, was published in 2001. In 2002 BFI Publishing released a film criticism anthology edited by Newman, *Science Fiction/Horror: A Sight and Sound Reader*, rounding up articles from *Sight and Sound*, for which Newman is a contributing editor.

According to the website, *The Kim Newman &Eugene Byrne Alternate History Pages*, also in the works and looking for a publisher is an alternate history series by the two collaborators—the first volume is called *The Matter of Britain*—postulating a world in which Nazi Germany successfully invaded Great Britain.

***

Newman's fiction is made up of a rich and eclectic blend of many influences, narrative traditions, and cultural references. His major works fall most prominently under three headings: contemporary horror, alternate fictional history (deviating from classic works of literature, screen, and comics), and pop-culture pastiche. Very little of his work falls exclusively under one of these banners—Newman's ingenious flair for cross-pollination is a major factor in his fiction's appeal—but, nevertheless, three of his longer works can be taken to represent the apex of each tendency: *Jago*, for modern horror; the Anno Dracula series, for alternate fictional history; and *Where the Bodies Are Buried*, for pop-culture pastiche. But all three works contain elements of each genre.

Jago is in many ways Newman's answer to the formulaic horror thrillers of Stephen King and his ilk. Like these, it is a long novel. Like much of King's work, it is set in a village community (although American New England is replaced with British Somerset) that is disturbed by a powerful and terrifying psychic/supernatural phenomenon. Although King often ultimately situates the blame for the supernatural violence on the hidden darkness—child abuse, racism—that lurks behind the peaceful small-town exterior, the social order itself is never seriously challenged or questioned in his fiction. In *Bag of Bones* (1998), for example, the vengeful ghost is a black woman who, in life, was gang-raped and forced to witness the murder of her child. Instead of using this as a springboard to tell a politically engaged story, King calls up a horde of ghosts for a sentimental finale and ignores the social issues he raised earlier in the novel. The community lives on, peaceful and unchanged. The status quo is restored. Readers are reassured that the supernatural threat has been dealt with and are distracted from the fact that its root causes have been narratively sidestepped.

In *Jago*, things are not so cozy. Reverend Anthony Jago is a charismatic and megalomaniacal psychic. Himself the child victim of abuse of the hands of clergy, he goes on to form a cult that, with the help of his psychic powers, threatens to destroy consensus reality and replace it with a world of his own making. Jago is able to unleash people's most repressed fantasies—because of the abuse he suffered in his youth, he is drawn to revenge fantasies—and transform reality accordingly. The ensuing mess is an orgy of violence and disturbing sex that leaves characters profoundly altered, and, although the threat is neutralized by novel's end, nothing is left pat and comfortable. Unspeakable horrors have been laid bare, and life cannot resume its former state unquestioned. In *Jago*, cults and recognized organized religions both systemically abuse the faithful. Newman condemns their self-serving agendas as hypocritical, malign, and destructive. Status quo society and its oppressions do go on, but readers are left feeling queasy by this prospect, and far from reassured that life will continue as it was. Particularly disquieting is the reaction of the authorities and the media in the wake of Anthony Jago's near-apocalypse, which leaves more than three thousand dead. The blame is laid to a mysterious—and nonexistent—drug and to fringe religious groups (*Jago*, p. 663). The forces in mainstream society that nurtured Jago's evil go unpunished and unchecked, and readers are left with the impression that similar horrors could easily happen again. Unlike in King and other popular fictions reinforcing consensus reality, the triumph of the status quo is not a source of relief but a cause for alarm. All this is peppered with Newman's outré wit, which, in this case, enhances the over-the-top tastelessness of the unleashed horrors to great effect. Punches are not pulled, blows are not softened, issues are not sidestepped.

Anno Dracula began a series that has been career-defining for Newman. A genre-bending cornucopia, this book is a police procedural, a serial killer thriller, a Sherlock Holmes pastiche, a conspiracy novel, a vampire tale, and, most of all, an alternate fictional history of ambitious scope.

In the aftermath of an alternate resolution to the events described in Bram Stoker's *Dracula* (1897), a serial killer nicknamed Jack the Ripper is killing vampire prostitutes on the streets of London. The human Charles Beauregard is recruited by the secret power behind British government, the Diogenes Club, headed by Mycroft Holmes, the brother of the famous detective. The continental vampire Geneviève Dieudonné is in London and befriends Beauregard. All this is connected, leading to Queen Victoria's consort, Dracula.

Anno Dracula is densely populated with characters drawn from literature (Wells's Doctor

Moreau, Polidori's Lord Ruthven, Doyle's Mycroft Holmes and Inspector Lestrade), history (Florence Stoker, Jack the Ripper, Queen Victoria), and Newman's own cast of quirky characters; this is also true of its sequels. Book one in the series is a thrilling epic that evokes myriad versions of Victorian London from literature and history that have become part of the popular imagination. Also, *Anno Dracula* is filled with a great diversity of female characters whose strengths and distinctive personalities allow the author to address the inequities of Victorian gender politics. But Charles Beauregard—"a man who tried always to do the right thing even when there were no right things to do" (*Judgment of Tears*, p. 140)—is the novel's, and the series', most effective character, a hero's hero, whose charm and integrity are manifest throughout.

The Bloody Red Baron takes place during the First World War. Dracula has fled England after the events of *Anno Dracula*. Charles Beauregard has replaced Mycroft Holmes as head of the Diogenes Club. Edwin Winthrop—a character who has appeared in several of Newman's fictions—is Beauregard's new protégé and also the main protagonist. Charles Schulz's Snoopy, P. G. Wodehouse's Bertie Wooster, and Monk and Ham from Lester Dent's Doc Savage novels are only a few of the recruits from the annals of fiction and pop culture to participate in this second foray into the Anno Dracula universe. This tale is very different in mood from its predecessor, concentrating on the aristocratic culture of the vampire fighter pilots.

Judgment of Tears: Anno Dracula 1959 skips a few decades and shifts the locale to Rome, Italy. A vampiric James Bond (here called "Hamish Bond"; "Hamish" is the Scottish form of "James," so this is a nod to Sean Connery, the well-loved Scottish actor who portrayed Bond in the earliest installments of the film series) joins the fray, as do Orson Welles and Charles de Gaulle. Both Beauregard and Dracula meet their final fates. Portions of the book evoke early 1960s cinema, such as Italian crime films, James Bond spectaculars, and Hollywood romantic thrillers (Stanley Donen's 1963 *Charade*, for example), but, in the wake of the sympathetic and heroic Beauregard's death, an aura of mournful introspection suffuses even the wildest goings-on.

Recently, Newman has been publishing a number of shorter works further exploring the Anno Dracula universe. These are supposed to be gathered in the upcoming (but unscheduled, as of this writing) *Johnny Alucard*. In the Anno Dracula series, Newman has created not only an alternate history diverging from Bram Stoker's *Dracula* but a universe gathering together more than a century's worth of fictional and historical characters, invoking readers' own mythologizing of these legendary figures. The Anno Dracula universe unfolds like a pageant of pop culture mythology.

Where the Bodies Are Buried collects the four linked stories of the title series. A no-holds barred satire of the slasher-movie franchises of the 1980s, it chronicles the interlinked destinies of Rob Hackwill, a monstrous serial killer who refuses to remain fictional, and his creator, the horror writer/director Allan Keyes. The first story in the cycle also introduces the serial killer's namesake, a crooked right-wing politician whose inclusion sets the stage for Newman's political deconstruction of the slasher craze. The final story in the sequence, "Where the Bodies Are Buried 2020," finds Newman revisiting the cyberpunk mode of some of his early work. It is an intentional irony that his original story spoofing franchise characters should itself have spawned sequels: "Having written a story about franchise characters, it seemed an obvious move to write a sequel," wrote Newman in the afterword to "Where the Bodies Are Buried II: Sequel Hook" for *Famous Monsters* (p. 340).

***

Kim Newman is a pop-culture bricoleur who explicitly fashions his work from the materials of the fictions that have shaped him as a writer and marked the wider culture in which he writes. The media that have most inspired him are prose fiction, film, comics, and television.

Newman's most obvious literary source of inspiration is Bram Stoker, whose *Dracula* led to the Anno Dracula series; and Stoker's mummy novel *The Jewel of Seven Stars* (1907) served as primary inspiration for Newman's 1999 novella "Seven Stars." Many classic writers provide other raw materials—including characters—for Newman's *Anno Dracula*. John Polidori lends Lord Ruthven from *The Vampyre: A Tale* (1819). The Sherlock Holmes mythos of Arthur Conan Doyle permeates the entire novel, and Mycroft Holmes's Diogenes Club— reimagined as a secret society of spies, adventurers, and behind-the-scenes political manipulators—is a recurring organization in Newman's fictional playground. H.G. Wells is another seminal figure in the Newman pantheon. Wells's Doctor Moreau—from *The Island of Doctor Moreau* (1896)—participates in *Anno Dracula*, and *The War of the Worlds* also feeds into Newman's "Famous Monsters." Robert Louis Stevenson's Henry Jekyll—from *Strange Case of Dr. Jekyll and Mr. Hyde* (1888)—appears as well. Newman probes deeper into Stevenson's classic in the story "Further Developments in the Strange Case of Dr Jekyll and Mr Hyde" (1999; collected in *Unforgivable Stories*).

Pulp magazines such as *Weird Tales*, *Black Mask*, *The Shadow*, and *Doc Savage* have colored many of Newman's fictions, most explicitly 'The Original Dr Shade," "The Big Fish," *Judgment of Tears: Anno Dracula 1959*, and *Seven Stars*. The related stories collected in *Seven Stars* combine to form a universe where outrageous pulp adventure is the secret way of the world.

Allan Keyes from *Where the Bodies Are Buried* is at least partially based on Clive Barker (*Seven Stars*, p. 384). The fandom culture that sprang up around Barker also inspired Newman's 1990 story "The Man Who Collected Barker" (collected in *The Original Dr Shade & Other Stories*).

Newman's pop-culture bricoleur approach is somewhat reminiscent of Philip José Farmer's. Farmer achieved similar effects using some of the same source material in texts such as *A Feast Unknown* (1969), *The Other Log of Phileas Fogg* (1973), and *Greatheart Silver* (1982). The fiction of both writers is constantly invaded by the larger-than-life heroes of their youth. Farmer's innovations paved the way for such shenanigans, but Newman injects a more layered political deconstruction into the game.

The multiversal aspect of Newman's oeuvre—the fact that everything is oddly connected and that different versions of the same characters appear in various settings—recalls Michael Moorcock's comparable oeuvre-encompassing project. Geneviève Dieudonné, for example, has appeared in at least three incarnations: in the Warhammer universe, in the Anno Dracula timeline, and in pulp-pastiche adventure stories such as "The Big Fish" and "Seven Stars." "The three can be told apart because their middle names vary," Newman notes in "Who's Who" (*Seven Stars*, p. 382), "but they are at heart the same girl."

Considering Newman's parallel career as a film critic, it is no surprise that the cinema is evoked everywhere in his fiction. To name the most prominent examples: the 1980s slashers in *Where the Bodies Are Buried*; the classic monster movies in "Famous Monsters"; *Citizen Kane* in "The Snow Sculptures of Xanadu"; hardboiled film noir in *The Night Mayor*; various genres from early 1960s cinema in *Judgment of Tears: Anno Dracula 1959*; the German impressionists in "Übermensch!"; George Romero's zombie movies in "Amerikanski Dead at the Moscow Morgue, or "Children of Marx and Coca-Cola" (1999; collected in *Unforgivable Stories*)—in which Newman characteristically makes explicit and perverts the unquestioned political assumptions of the source material: "Though the rising of the dead is supposed to be a global phenomenon, Romero's movies ... are all about America. Romero's films belong now to the era of the superpower face-off, and I thought it would be interesting to see what might be happening in the then-Soviet Union ... and, more importantly, what it might mean" (*Unforgivable Stories*, p. 82).

Comics characters such as Superman, Green Lantern, Swamp Thing, Snoopy, and Tintin appear (somewhat transformed) in *Judgment of Tears: Anno Dracula 1959*, *Jago*, "Une Étrange Aventure de Richard Blaine" (1999; collected in *Unforgivable Stories*), and "Übermensch!" Newman's supernatural investigator Richard Jeperson is partially inspired by the Marvel Comics character Dr. Strange (*Seven Stars*, p. 384).

The baroque modish style of the British television series *The Avengers* is never far from the surface when Newman creates adventure characters. He has a penchant for pairing, in the manner of John Steed and Emma Peel from *The Avengers*, charmingly eccentric male adventurers with ultra-competent women: Charles Beauregard and Geneviève Dieudonné in *Anno Dracula*; Edwin Winthrop and Catriona Kaye in "Angel Down Sussex" (1999, collected in *Seven Stars*); Richard Jeperson and Vanessa in "The End of the Pier Show" (1997) and "You Don't Have to Be Mad..." (1999), both collected in *Seven Stars*.

Newman's fiction testifies to his deep, broad, and perhaps even obsessive erudition. One of his strengths is to expose the unpleasant and overlooked political and psychological underpinnings of the popular narratives that make up the English/American canon. He does so with verve, intelligence, and an unshakable resolve to laugh at the horrors that seek to crush all our spirits and to have dark, delicious fun in the face of oppressive adversity.

Selected Bibliography

WORKS OF KIM NEWMAN

FICTION

The Night Mayor. London: Simon & Schuster, 1989; New York: Carroll & Graf, 1990. (Novel.)

Bad Dreams. London: Simon & Schuster, 1990; New York: Carroll & Graf, 1991. (Novel.)

Jago. London: Simon & Schuster, 1991; New York: Carroll & Graf, 1993. (Novel; quotations from the London: HarperCollins/Grafton, 1992 edition.)

Anno Dracula. London: Simon & Schuster, 1992; New York: Carroll & Graf, 1993. (Novel.)

The Quorum. London: Simon & Schuster, 1994; New York: Carroll & Graf, 1994. (Novel.)

The Original Dr Shade & Other Stories. London: Simon & Schuster/Pocket Books, 1994. (Collection of fifteen stories with afterwords by the author; foreword by Neil Gaiman.)

Famous Monsters. London: Simon & Schuster/Pocket Books, 1994. (Collection of fifteen stories with afterwords by the author; foreword by Paul J. McAuley.)

The Bloody Red Baron. New York: Carroll & Graf, 1995; London: Simon & Schuster,

1996. (Novel; sequel to *Anno Dracula*.)

Judgment of Tears: Anno Dracula 1959. New York: Carroll & Graf, 1998. Published in the U.K. as *Dracula Cha Cha Cha*. London: Simon & Schuster, 2000. (Novel; sequel to *The Bloody Red Baron*.)

Life's Lottery. London: Simon & Schuster, 1999. (Novel.)

Andy Warhol's Dracula. Leeds: PS Publishing, 1999. (Novella in the Anno Dracula series; introduction by F. Paul Wilson.)

Seven Stars. London: Simon & Schuster/Pocket Books, 2000. (Collection of six stories, with a "Who's Who" of the author's cast of recurring characters and a foreword by Stephen Jones.)

Where the Bodies Are Buried. Birmingham: The Alchemy Press, 2000. (Mosaic of "Where the Bodies Are Buried" and its three sequels; introduction by Peter Atkins; illustrated by Randy Broecker.)

Unforgivable Stories. London: Simon & Schuster/Pocket Books, 2000. (Collection of fourteen stories, with afterwords by the author; introduction by Eugene Byrne.)

Time and Relative. Kent: Telos Publishing, 2001. (Doctor Who novella.)

FILM CRITICISM

Nightmare Movies: Wide Screen Horror since 1968. London and New York: Proteus Books, 1984.

Nightmare Movies: A Critical History of the Horror Film, 1968-88. London: Bloomsbury, 1988. (Updated and revised edition of *Nightmare Movies: Wide Screen Horror since 1968*.)

Nightmare Movies: A Critical Guide to Contemporary Horror Films. New York: Crown Harmony, 1989. (U.S. edition of *Nightmare Movies: A Critical History of the Horror Film, 1968-88*.)

Wild West Movies: Or How the West Was Found, Won, Lost, Lied About, Filmed and Forgotten. London: Bloomsbury, 1990.

Millennium Movies: End of the World Cinema. London: Titan Books, 1999.

Cat People. London: BFI Publishing, 1999. (A BFI Film Classics book.)

Apocalypse Movies: End of the World Cinema. New York: Griffin, 2000. (U.S. edition of *Millennium Movies: End of the World Cinema*.)

AS JACK YEOVIL

Drachenfels. Nottingham: Games Workshop Books, 1989. (Warhammer novel.)

Demon Download. Nottingham: Games Workshop Books, 1990. (Dark Future novel.)

Krokodil Tears. Nottingham: Games Workshop Books, 1991. (Dark Future novel.)

Beasts in Velvet. Nottingham: Games Workshop Books, 1991. (Warhammer novel.)

Comeback Tour. Nottingham: Games Workshop Books, 1991. (Dark Future novel.)

Genevieve Undead. London: Boxtree, 1993. (Warhammer novel.)

Route 666. London: Boxtree, 1994. (Dark Future novel.)

Orgy of the Blood Parasites. London: Simon & Shuster/Pocket Books, 1994. (Novel.)

COLLABORATIONS AND ANTHOLOGIES

Gaiman, Neil and Kim Newman, eds. *Ghastly Beyond Belief*, London: Arrow, 1985. (Compilation of humorous quotes.)

Jones, Stephen and Kim Newman, eds. *Horror: The 100 Best Books*. London: Xanadu, 1988; New York: Carroll & Graf, 1988. Revised as: *Horror: 100 Best Books*. London: New English Library, 1992; New York: Carroll & Graf, 1998. (Anthology of critical essays.)

McAuley, Paul J. and Kim Newman, eds. *In Dreams*. London: Gollancz, 1992. (Anthology of short fiction.)

Newman, Kim, ed. *The BFI Companion to Horror*. London: Cassell, 1996. (Anthology of critical essays.)

Byrne, Eugene, and Kim Newman. *Back in the USA*. Shingletown: Mark V. Ziesing Books, 1997. (Fiction.)

Newman, Kim (ed.). *Science Fiction/Horror: A Sight and Sound Reader*. London, BFI Publishing, 2002. (Anthology of critical essays.)

SOURCES

Brown, Charles N., and William G. Cotento. "The Locus Index to Science Fiction." In Locus Online. 3 November 2001 update. http://www.locusmag.com/index/

Byrne, Eugene. *The Kim Newman & Eugene Byrne Alternate History Pages*. http://www.angelfire.com/ak2/newmanbyrne/

Clute, John and John Grant. *The Encyclopedia of Fantasy*. London: Orbit, 1999.

The Lord Ruthven Pages: The Byronic Vampire in Popular Culture. http://gothic.vei.net/lordruthven/ruthven.htm

McHugh, Maura. *Dr. Shade's Laboratory: The Official Kim Newman Web Site*. http://www.johnnyalucard.com/biblio.htm

CRITICISM OF WORKS BY KIM NEWMAN

Lalumière, Claude. "The Alternate Worlds of Science Fiction." In *The National Post*, December 19, 1998, Books 24. (Column including a review of *Judgment of Tears: Anno Dracula 1959*; available online at http://www.total.net/~clcl/tawosf.html)

———. Review of *Seven Stars*. In *January Magazine*, June 6, 2000. http://www.januarymagazine.com/SFF/7stars.html

———. "13 Contemporary Writers of Weird Horror." In *January Magazine*, October 25, 2000. http://www.januarymagazine.com/features/horror2000.html

———. Review of *Unforgivable Stories*. In *January Magazine*, January 23, 2001. http://www.januarymagazine.com/SFF/unforgivestories.html

———. "Three Fantastic Film Classics." In *Locus Online*, June 15, 2001. http://www.locusmag.com/2001/Reviews/Lalumiere06.html (Reviews of three books in the BFI Film Classics series, including *Cat People*.)

Langford, David. Review of *Life's Lottery*. In Amazon.co.uk. http://www.amazon.co.uk

Andre Norton

1912–

CHARLENE BRUSSO

ANDRE NORTON IS a master storyteller. She has written a bit of everything, from gothic mysteries and historical fiction to far-flung science fiction and high fantasy adventures, and is best known for her work in the latter genre: tales featuring compelling characters and vivid, original settings. Her theme of the outsider in search of a place to belong has made her books especially resonant with young adult readers, a fact that unfortunately led to Norton being branded children's writer for most of her career. Her work didn't begin to draw the critical notice it deserved until the 1980s.

Alice Mary Norton was born on February 17, 1912, in Cleveland, Ohio. She was the second daughter of Bertha Stemm and Adalbert Freely Norton, owner of a rug company. Like many authors, she began writing seriously in high school. She attended Case Western Reserve from 1930 to 1931, intending to become a history teacher, but economics forced her to leave during the Great Depression. She accepted a job as assistant librarian in the Cleveland Library System and spent the next eighteen years working in children's sections of various branch libraries. Advancement was limited by her lack of a college degree, despite the fact that her skills made her an important consultant for those above her.

Prompted by her publisher's insistence that male writers outsold women authors, Norton legally changed her name to Andre Norton in 1934, the year her first published novel, *The Prince Commands*, appeared. Norton began writing full-time in 1950. She also worked as a reader for Martin Greenberg at Gnome Press off and on for eight years. Her first published science fiction story, "The People of the Crater," appeared in *Fantasy Book* in 1947 and later became part of *Garan the Eternal*, written under the name "Andrew North." Her first science fiction novel, *Star Man's Son, 2250 A.D.*, was published in 1952.

Norton moved from Ohio to Winter Park, Florida, in 1966 for health reasons, but in 1997 she relocated to Murfeesboro, Tennessee, where she finally realized a long-time dream to establish a retreat for genre writers. The High Hallack Genre Writer's Research and Reference Library opened early in 1999.

Norton has earned many and diverse accolades, from the Boys' Clubs of America Medal to the Gandalf and the Balrog Fantasy Awards. In 1984 she became the first woman to be awarded the title of Grand Master by the Science Fiction Writers of America.

Norton is very much a series writer, frequently placing multiple novels in a particular locale. This tactic allows the author to develop each world more thoroughly, creating rich, multi-layered settings. Norton's Witch World series is her best known, most enduring, work. To date it includes some twenty-four novels and six story collections; seven of the books and three of the collections are collaborations with other authors. The Witch World series can be subdivided into two distinct sequences based on setting: Estcarp/Escore and High Hallack.

The Estcarp/Escore novels form a roughly linear story arc. Home to a race descended from the mysterious Old Ones, Estcarp is ruled by the Council of Es, a matriachate comprised of Witches gifted with the Power. With enemies on nearly every border, the Witches struggle to hold together a land thinned to a shadow of its former glory.

The High Hallack novels, on the other hand, are smaller in scale and less formally organized. High Hallack is a land of rich, rolling Dales and mysterious wastes, far to the west across the sea from Estcarp. Magic is rare and generally feared, associated as it is with the ancient, often dangerous, ruins left by the mysterious Old Ones.

The core books of the Estcarp/Escore series are *Witch World* (1963), *Web of the Witch World* (1964), *Three Against The Witch World* (1965), *Warlock of the Witch World* (1967), *Sorceress of the Witch World* (1968), *Trey of Swords* (collection, 1977), and *'Ware Hawk* (1983). The High Hallack series consists of the novels *Year of the Unicorn* (1963), *Spell of the Witch World* (collection, 1972), *The Crystal Gryphon* (1972), *The Jargoon Pard* (1974), *Zarsthor's Bane* (1978), *Lore of the Witch World* (collection, 1980), *Gryphon in Glory* (1981), *Horn Crown* (1981), and *Moon Called* (1982).

There is some overlap of settings in the short story collections. Later books such as *Storms of Victory* (1991), *Flight of Vengeance* (1992), *On Wings of Magic* (1994), and *The Warding of Witch World* (1996)—said to be the last Witch World novel, though the series franchise spawned *Ciara's Song* in 1988—are collaborations written by others under Norton's guidance. They extend the scale of Norton's original work very little and generally lack the brisk pace and fluidity of her solo writing.

Witch World introduces a grim land where ancient legends have as much influence over the present as more contemporary events. The book's primary character, ex-U.S. Army Colonel Simon Tregarth, is typical of Norton's protagonists: an outsider thrust into an unfamiliar and dangerous new world, forced to draw on his inner strengths to survive and earn a place for himself. As a stranger in a strange land, Simon's pragmatic exploration of the Witch World parallels the reader's own experience of discovery.

Norton's novel method for getting Simon to the Witch World draws on her deep knowledge of history and legend. Pursued by enemies and out of options, Simon escapes via the fabled Siege Perilous, an arch of stone menhirs once used by King Arthur to test the honor of his knights. The Siege Perilous was said to judge a man's worth and deliver him to his just fate, the time and place where his soul truly belonged. In Norton's hands it wrenches Simon from Earth to a bleak and brooding moor, where he encounters a woman in mail pursued by soldiers and a pack of decidedly un-Earthlike canines. Simon helps her escape and she leads him to safety. Only then does he discover she is one of the nameless Witches of Estcarp. Echoing many a superstitious Earth culture, the Witches renounce their names; to give someone your name is to give him or her power over you.

Estcarp lies precariously sandwiched between enemy nations. To the north, past gray Tor Moor and its Fens, lies hostile Alizon. To the south is a range of jagged peaks where the grim Falconers—even more dogmatically patriarchal than Estcarp is matriarchal—dwell. Beyond is Karsten, where those with Estcarp blood have been "three times horned," outlawed, to be hunted to their deaths.

A third threat comes from over the seas to the west, where the sinister and single-minded Kolder have entered the Witch World through a gate from their own dying planet. The Kolder's advanced technology—aircraft, submarines, and powerful weaponry—is beyond the imagination of the Witch World's pseudo-medieval society. Not even the hearty Sulcarmen, Estcarp's sole allies, sea-rovers who know every ocean current and every inch of coastline, can stand up to the Kolder's superior weaponry or their frightening ability to mind-control prisoners.

This introduces some frequent and important themes in Norton's work: the necessity of balance between powers, with a corollary concerning the danger of introducing superior technology into less developed worlds. Additionally, the Kolder's lack of humanity stresses Norton's belief in the necessity of free will, and the horror of losing it. The Kolder-made zombies fight to the death like machines. To the warriors of Estcarp, men so damaged are men without souls.

As Estcarp divides its ever-diminishing forces between uneasy borders, the Witches at Es Castle search for a means to defeat their enemies. Their own numbers are shrinking. All girl children are tested for sensitivity to magic. Any with signs of talent are taken away to be trained. Only virgin women can use the Power, however, so those most likely to bear Witch offspring are least likely to have children.

Simon respects the authority of the Witches, but he refuses to be intimidated by them. As a professional soldier he offers new perspectives in military strategy, and his experience with Earth's technology gives him a unique ability to understand the Kolder. The biggest surprise, however, is his own sensitivity to the Power and his growing ability to use it.

Simon's diverse skills make him a pivotal element in driving the Kolder back, at least for a little while. In the meantime his relationship with the unnamed Witch he met on Tor Moor grows from mutual respect to friendship and finally love. At the close of *Witch World* she shares her name, Jaelithe, with him and seems willing to give up her magic to have him.

The next five novels in the series expand on the events in *Witch World* in chronological fashion. In *Web of the Witch World* Jaelithe and Simon are able to put an end to the Kolder incursion, but Karsten and Alizon grow increasingly dangerous. More importantly for the couple, Jaelithe discovers that wedding and losing her virginity to Simon has not stripped her of her Power after all. Yet the Council of Es refuses to recognize her, insisting that her Power will fade with time.

While Simon at first fears Jealithe has abandoned him, holding her Power and independence more important than their relationship, they find their way back together when they discover that their individual Powers are now linked and developing in synergy with each other. Even after they use their magic to defeat the Kolder, however, the powerbrokers on the Witch's Council continue to shut the couple out, stonewalling to protect their ancient dogma and influence. After all, Jaelithe is a dangerous distraction to other witches who might wonder about what they've sacrificed for their Power.

Long before it was fashionable to mistrust authority, Norton's Simon and Jaelithe show there is frequently good reason to do so. The Council of Es wields its jealously guarded Power as much to tighten their control as to protect Estcarp. By renouncing her name, a new-made Witch gives up any identity as an individual. She must submit to the wishes of her superiors—just as men, and those women without the Power, must obey the orders of any Witch. Such a chain of command is deeply entrenched in Estcarp's culture, and its rigidity in the face of change is the source of its weakness as well as its strength.

Despite problems with the Council, it is telling that Norton's main characters never consider destroying or replacing it. While warning readers to be wary of formal institutions, Norton never advocates their total removal. The Council of Es is fighting to protect Estcarp and in turn itself. Clearly what serves the larger community is not necessarily the best for the individual.

Matters escalate in *Three Against the Witch World*, as related by the warrior Kyllan, one of the triplets Jaelithe bears Simon. By now the couple have founded the House of Tregarth. Interestingly, Jaelithe follows tradition here and takes Simon's surname—a reminder that despite Norton's forward thinking in other areas, she still holds unswervingly to some traditions.

As if foreseeing contemporary family troubles—or merely showing that every age shares the same problems—Norton illustrates the difficulty of raising a family when both parents are employed in high power, high stress positions. Simon and Jaelithe are well-meaning but distant parents, driven by their sense of duty to place Estcarp's problems above personal matters. With both parents frequently away "on business", sons Kyllan and Kemoc, and daughter Kaththea, come to rely on their caretaker Anghart, an exiled Falconer woman as wily as she is wise.

Then Simon is lost at sea and Jaelithe goes off to save him, leaving Anghart and the children alone to face the Council of Es, that is determined to get Kaththea in its clutches. The three Tregarth offspring have inherited their parents' Power. Each has a different ability yet, like their parents, they share a mind-link and can channel their individual Powers together, multiplying them into one very strong force.

Desperate to stop enemy incursions from the south, the Witches at Es focus their Power and reshape the southern mountains to cut off Estcarp from Karsten, a cataclysmic event that will become known as "the Turning." While the Witches are busy, the Tregarth siblings escape eastward into Escore, the original home of the Old Ones, who cast a mental block to keep those who settled Estcarp from remembering their former home. Long ago Escore was nearly torn apart by immense magical battles between good and evil. Those who could fled west and settled in Estcarp, setting the mind block spell for protection.

Once in Escore, the three siblings stumble into one of the ancient pockets of evil left over from the war and accidentally free ancient powers. Kyllan is sent back to Estcarp under the compulsion of a *geas* spell to recruit people to return to Escore and defend the land. The next three books—*Warlock of the Witch World, Sorceress of the Witch World,* and *Trey of Swords*—describe the struggle to restore Escore, and see each of the Tregarth children settled on their eventual lifepaths. Part of this resolution includes each sibling becoming romantically matched with a mate equal to their abilities and interests. This "pairing off" becomes a fairly predictable part of plot resolution for major characters throughout the Witch World series, a part of the balance of elements and powers her stories frequently demand.

'*Ware Hawk* is the last of the Witch World novels written solely by Norton. Set several years after the Turning, a half-breed woman (half witch blood) is under *geas* to return to the ruins of her ancestral home in Karsten and recover an ancient treasure. She hires a down-on-his-luck Falconer, homeless since the Turning, to guide her over the mountains. They are trailed by a Dark One who covets the treasure, and together they must defeat the evil or be used by it against their will. Norton's story-telling is particularly riveting here, with the forces of evil coming closer to victory than in any other book of the series.

The High Hallack portion of the Witch World series is more intimate in scale, focusing more on characters who tend to doubt or minimize their own strengths until forced headlong into dangerous situations. Female characters take the lead role more often here as well. The series begins with *Year of the Unicorn*, Norton's first novel written from the point of view of a female protagonist. Dales society is feudal, with the land divided between keeps, and there is no central authority akin to the Witches in Estcarp. Beset by forces from Alizon, the lords of High Hallack made a bargain with the mysterious shape-changing Were-Riders from the northern Wastes. In exchange for the Riders' protection, the lords promised thirteen brides of noble blood, to be paid in the Year of the Unicorn.

Gillan, an orphan with little to keep her at the Dales Abbey where she grew up, takes the place of one of the brides and finds herself matched with the Were-Rider Herrel. Her choice earns the enmity of those Riders who were not selected by any bride. They hold Herrel to be the least of their number because of his mixed blood and meager magical ability compared to the rest. When the other Riders learn Gillan can see through the illusions they hold to keep the other brides from seeing things as they really are, Gillan herself becomes a threat. Together she and Herrel must defeat their enemies, drawing power from the bond they share, and their own inner strengths.

In *The Jargoon Pard*, Herrel's ambitious half-sister Lady Heroise plots to gather power by having the sorceress Ursilla swap her baby daughter for Herrel and Gillan's son Kethan, whom she can raise to be the heir of Car Do Prawn, and her pawn. Her plans go awry when Kethan is marked as Were, a shape-changer, and exiled. Living by his wits and the senses of his animal half, a pard (leopard), Kethan must learn self-control, both for himself and his beast nature, as well as how to control the shift between forms. Only then can he stand up to the dark forces called up by Heroise and Ursilla and win his freedom.

The Crystal Gryphon and *Gryphon in Glory* are set in a time slightly earlier than *Year of the Unicorn*, when Alizon brings war to the peaceful Dales. The novels are sequential, told in alternating chapters by Kerovan of Ulmsdale and Joisan of Ithkrypt, Kerovan's bride by proxy marriage when both were children. Born with the taint of the Old Ones obvious in his cloven hooves, Kerovan has faced scorn and distrust all his life. Rumors hint that his mother treated with dark forces before his birth, but no one knows the truth: that she hoped to resurrect the spirit of an Old One in her son's body. To her credit, Joisan discounts the rumors she has heard about Kerovan, determined not to judge a man before she has met him.

When their homes are overrun, each sets off to find the other. When they meet, the sight of Kerovan's cloven hooves and strange amber eyes lead Joisan to believe he is an Old One driven out of hiding by the war. Stung by her assumption, Kerovan hides his true identity and assumes the role she creates for him as Lord Amber. Only when they must stand together against Kerovan's siblings, who seek to call up the Old One to possess him, is the truth revealed.

Although Kerovan and Joisan triumph in that fight, he still fears that he could permanently become "a vessel into which something else was poured," losing himself to the ancient soul meant to wear his body. In *Gryphon in Glory* Kerovan journeys into the Waste to learn who and what seeks to possess him; Joisan follows and helps him finally prove to himself that he is strong enough to control his own destiny.

Although written late in the series, *Horn Crown* is chronologically the first of the High Hallack novels. A band of refugees flee through a gate to another world that they call High Hallack, giving up all memory of Hallack, their original home, and the threat that drove them away. The new land contains the remains of structures and temples left by an earlier race. Although his lord, Garn, has forbidden anyone from entering the ruins, the young warrior Elron is drawn to an ancient Moon Shrine.

Garn's daughter Iynne also feels the pull of the old temple, but Elron agrees to keep her visits there secret—until Iynne disappears. Elron is exiled for helping her deceive her father. Determined to salvage some scrap of personal honor, Elron sets off to find Iynne and bring her safely home.

Likewise Gathea, apprentice of the Wise Woman Zabina, is determined to find Iynne. Gathea knows something of the Moon Shrine's magic and claims Iynne has stolen the power Gathea sought to raise there for herself. Despite their mutual hostility, Gathea and Elron team up and set off in search of the girl. Their quest brings them face to face with ancient powers, both good and evil, stirred by Iynne's magical bumbling. In order to succeed, Elron and Gathea must work together to reset the balance of magic that Iynne disturbed.

The remaining works in the Witch World series are relatively minor in scope, though often quite powerful, particularly Norton's short stories. *Zarsthor's Bane* and *Moon Called* both deal with young women, refugees forced to live in the wilderness, who survive thanks to the help of animal companions. Both are drawn into trouble when they try to help someone in distress, and each must draw on her inner resources to survive and return a stronger person.

Spell of the Witch World consists of three novellas set in High Hallack: "Dragon Scale Silver," "Dream Smith," and "Amber out of Quath." Each shows a different aspect of the Power of the Old Ones that still haunts the land to trick the unwary or reward the worthy. The stories of *Lore of the Witch World* offer a bit more variety. Of these, the strongest are "Falcon Blood," in which a Sulcar woman and a Falconer grudgingly join forces to defeat an ancient evil, and the linked stories "The Toads of Grimmerdale" and "Changeling," where a young woman calls down a curse that alters her life as much as it affects the man on whom she cast it.

Much of the Witch World series has been influenced by the "John Eric Stark" adventure stories of pioneer sword-and-sorcery writer Leigh Brackett. While Simon Tregarth is clearly modeled on Stark—both are self-sufficient heroes from other worlds who must stand strong against dark, alien forces—Norton expands Brackett's concept with her creation of the Witch World, a detailed setting that feels "lived in" and evolves with each book, broadening and deepening so that other characters and storylines can take the lead while maintaining a self-consistent whole.

Norton's Witch World has in turn been a powerful inspiration for other authors, including many of the most successful women science fiction and fantasy writers of the 1970s and 1980s. Marion Zimmer Bradley's popular "Darkover" series, with its sternly matriarchal society and characters gifted with a range of mental/magical abilities, shows the most obvious borrowing from Norton's work. To a lesser extent C. J. Cherryh's "Morgaine" series, Jo Clayton's "Diadem" saga, and Anne McCaffrey's "Pern" stories are also related; each shows the unique influence of Norton's worldbuilding as well as her interest in blending technological elements with magic.

Norton has battled depression for much of her life and her determination to win that fight seems echoed by her stories. The typical Norton protagonist is alone, cut off from friends and family, often trapped in what seems to be a hopeless situation. Norton's heroes and heroines strive against all odds not just to survive but to grow and enrich their lives, ideally to remain independent while forging a strong relationship with another of like mind. No matter how grim the plot, nor how dark the journey (internal *and* external) a character must make, every Norton protagonist is at heart an optimist, determined to make the best of a bad situation, to succeed against all odds.

While this kind of focus can make for highly compelling stories, there is also a danger—and Norton's work, for all its strengths, falls prey to it, particularly with the later books in the Witch World series. Plotlines and characters start to feel formulaic. While resolution never comes easily to any Norton protagonist, all too frequently the main character ends by pairing off romantically with another character who has been a partner in the adventure. While each story stands perfectly well on its own, too many read back to back can become cloying.

Despite this flaw, Norton's works are some of the most enduring in imaginative fiction. Her marvelous storytelling ability makes her stories flow so quickly and effortlessly that the reader can easily fail at first pass to notice the richness of the work. Norton's ability to weave historical elements and bits of classic myths and legends results in worlds that make sense and resonate with believability, whether she takes readers voyaging across galactic vistas or into bleak lands peppered with ruins ripe with the magic of an earlier age.

In the early part of the twentieth century, the typical speculative fiction story pitted Good against Evil on a grand scale. What Norton brought to the genre was a more intimate kind of tale, one where people mattered more than the devices they used or the monsters they slew. No matter how grim the situation, Norton's characters triumph by trusting in themselves and learning to trust others. Victory is achieved by drawing on those inner abilities we think of as most human: self-reliance, independence, honor. At their core, Norton's stories resonate with idealism and belief in this basic principle: As long as one is true to oneself, one can never really be defeated.

Selected Bibliography

WORKS OF ANDRE NORTON

Witch World. New York: Ace, 1963; London: Universal-Tandem, 1970.

Web of the Witch World. New York: Ace, 1964; London: Universal-Tandem, 1970.

Three Against The Witch World. New York: Ace, 1965; London: Universal-Tandem, 1970.

Year of the Unicorn. New York: Ace, 1965; London: Universal-Tandem, 1970.

Warlock of the Witch World. New York: Ace, 1967; London: Universal-Tandem, 1970.

Sorceress of the Witch World. New York: Ace, 1968; London: Universal-Tandem, 1970.

The Crystal Gryphon. New York: Atheneum, 1972; London: Gollanz, 1970.

Garan the Eternal. Alhambra, CA: FPCI, 1972. (Collection).

Spell of the Witch World. New York: DAW, 1972. London: G. Prior, 1977. (Collection).

The Jargoon Pard. New York: Atheneum, 1974.

Trey of Swords. New York: Grosset and Dunlap, 1977; London: Star; 1979. (Collection)

Zarsthor's Bane. New York: Ace, 1978.

Lore of the Witch World. New York: DAW, 1980. (Collection).

Gryphon in Glory. New York: Atheneum, 1981.

Horn Crown. New York: DAW, 1981.

Moon Called. New York: Pinnacle, 1982.

'Ware Hawk. New York: Atheneum, 1983.

OTHER WORKS

The Many Worlds of Andre Norton, edited by Roger Elwood, New York: Chilton, 1974. (republished as *The Book of Andre Norton*, New York: DAW, 1975.)

Joyce Carol Oates
1938–

TODD MASON

JOYCE CAROL OATES, the United States' most prolific living writer to gain widespread critical acclaim, has often sought to exploit (in the best sense, and like most writers) her personal demons, as well as describe the seeming inexplicability and suddenness with which violence and tragedy can enter any person's life. These aims have led her to write of fantastic and supernatural occurrences in some of her most vivid fiction. Disturbing themes and incidents are rarely missing in her work, thus even her most realistic fiction often verges on the horrific, or at least achieves a similar effect in naturalistic suspense. She sees the distinction clearly between these two modes, as she noted ironically in her review essay "Raymond Chandler: Genre and 'Art'" (*Where I've Been and Where I'm Going*, 1999): "[Horror and suspense fiction divide] thematically into two overlapping categories: works in which supernatural forces figure, manifested literally as monsters or symbolically as 'compulsions' in presumably normal people, and works in which obsessive sexual predators stalk their victims. The former might be defined as essentially a juvenile mode, the latter is its adult equivalent" (p. 97).

Nonetheless, she has been deservedly twice awarded the Bram Stoker Award by the Horror Writers Association, once in 1994 for Life Achievement, despite the relative infrequency of supernatural horror fiction among her large body of published work, and again in 1996 for her short novel *Zombie*, despite the lack of any supernatural elements in the latter work, which is set in the form of the diary of a sociopath. Beginning in 1980, with the publication of her Flannery O'Connor tribute "The Bingo Master" in the high-profile anthology of new horror fiction *Dark Forces*, edited by Kirby McCauley, she began publishing some of her new work in anthologies and magazines devoted explicitly to fantastic- and crime-fiction. Stories of hers would first appear, over the following decades, in the anthologies *The Architecture of Fear, The Skin of the Soul, 999* and *MetaHorror*, among others, and in such literate "genre" fiction magazines as *Ellery Queen's Mystery Magazine, OMNI, Twilight Zone Magazine, Century, The Magazine of Fantasy and Science Fiction, Alfred Hitchcock's Mystery Magazine* and *The Spook*, while she continued also to publish in the "generalist" magazines such as *The Paris Review, Harper's, The North American Review* and *The New Yorker* (ironically, *The New Yorker* had never published Oates's fiction until she submitted the original short-story form of "Zombie" directly to then-new general editor

Tina Brown, bypassing the fiction editors there). The little magazine *Conjunctions* falls between these categories to some extent, as its editor Bradford Morrow is a leading proponent of the "New Gothic" in his magazine and elsewhere (including an anthology by that title, largely drawn from *Conjunctions* and including an Oates story); Morrow is a contributing editor of *Ontario Review*, the magazine edited and published by Oates's husband, Princeton professor Raymond Smith, with her collaboration.

Much of her genuinely supernatural fiction has been in short story form, and much of that has been collected to date in two volumes, *Haunted: Tales of the Grotesque* (1994) and *The Collector of Hearts: New Tales of the Grotesque* (1998); several stories in the latter had been previously collected in *Demon and Other Tales*, published by the horror-fiction specialist publishers Necronomicon Press in 1996. (At least two earlier collections, though less purely devoted to "the grotesque," should also be noted here: *Night-side: Eighteen Tales* [1977]—its title story alone would warrant attention—and *Heat and Other Stories* [1991], including what may be Oates's first science fiction story, the grimly surreal "Family.") That year also saw publication of her anthology, *American Gothic Tales*, an historical survey that drew together rarely-collected stories by luminaries such as Herman Melville and Edith Wharton, familiar but major tales by Washington Irving and Ambrose Bierce, and stories from a diverse lot of Twentieth Century writers of horror fiction (occasionally or frequently), all influential in their differing ways, including August Derleth, John Cheever, Peter Straub, Lisa Tuttle, Harlan Ellison, Robert Coover, Shirley Jackson, and Kathe Koja and Barry Malzberg. Oates's introduction to the volume notes that supernatural horror not only was crucial to much of the most notable early American fiction, but also was a key component of the famous sermons which preceded the contributions of Irving and Charles Brockden Brown.

In 1988, her selection of *Tales of H. P. Lovecraft* was published, a survey of the short fiction of the extremely influential existential-horror fiction writer, and in 2001, Carroll & Graf published *The Barrens*, the eighth in a series of intense, often slightly fantasticated crime-fiction novels, all published under her pseudonym Rosamond Smith. The number and variety of Oates's contributions to horror fiction and related fields seems likely to grow considerably with time.

EARLY LIFE AND CAREER

Born June 16, 1938 to the former Carolina Bush and Frederic Oates, she spent her early years in the extremely rural Upstate New York town of Lockport and its environs, attending a one-room schoolhouse for her first five grades, the same one her mother had twenty years before. While she would eventually have both a brother (Frederic Oates, Jr., born 1943) and a sister (Lynn Ann Oates, born 1956), the difference in their ages, Joyce's relative lack of similar-age playmates, and her shyness all encouraged her to live as much as possible within her imagination throughout her youth—when she wasn't keeping company with her parents and other adults (often performing the chores expected of a farm child), or exploring the countryside, either alone or with her few close friends. It was in this period that she developed an abiding interest in the natural sciences as well as literature. Her extensive reading, and involvement with organized religion (more in her experience of local Methodist services than of the Catholic ones she would dutifully attend with her family) also helped foster an interest in moral and philosophical questions. Her father, a former amateur boxer, sparked her interest in the "sweet science," by watching televised boxing matches with her and taking her to see the fights in person. Her lifelong interest in the sport would eventually lead to various requests for her analysis from publishers and broadcasters, including at least two books.

As an intellectually-gifted girl who had no fear of displaying her academic talent (and one not fond of such typically feminine toys as dolls, which would play an occasional sinister part in her later fiction), she often felt alienated, or worse, from many of her classmates. After years of bullying, some of the older boys at her school attempted to gang-rape Oates, then 10 and in the fourth grade; unsurprisingly, this inspired, in no small part, a recurring theme in her fiction: that of the many ways men, particularly older men, can become or attempt to become predators upon women and girls, and how the women and girls must cope with this threat and its consequences. This occurs within the larger context of her continuing study of how violence, physical and otherwise, can happen in "hidden" and unexpected ways, and the inability to determine the true character of people from their public face, or even how they might seem to intimate observers: family, friends, and lovers. Questions of the (at least) dual nature of our public and private selves would also frequently recur in her fiction, as would concrete metaphor for this duality in the forms of characters with twin siblings and doppelgangers, literal and figurative.

Like many young writers, she began attempting to tell tales on paper before she was properly literate. As she recalls in Greg Johnson's *Invisible Writer: A Biography of Joyce Carol Oates* (1998), her illustrated narratives produced at age three or four were accompanied by a scrawl along the bottom of the pages that simulated adult handwriting. Lewis Carroll's *Alice's Adventures in Wonderland* and its sequel were the first books she loved, and she attempted to create her own versions of them, with illustrations that were her attempt to ape John Tenniel's. Not long after, her reading had expanded to include many of the classics literate children are likely to encounter, including the stories of Edgar Allan Poe. As Oates states, in her introduction to Poe's "The Black Cat" in the anthology *Masters' Choice, Volume II* (2000), "Poe's genius is the ability to portray deranged states of mind as if they are utterly natural; in fact, identical to our own" (p. 318). This was a lesson not lost on her.

Along with her love of fiction and other literature, she was a fan of such influential comic books of her era as Entertaining Comics' satirical *Mad* and the sardonic, often gruesome horror anthology *Tales from the Crypt*. Her stepgrandfather, she recalls, was a reader of science fiction magazines and perhaps crime-fiction ones as well (she doesn't mention whether she dipped into his collection, but that she remembers it bodes well for her having done so). Thus, Oates was exposed at an early age to supernatural horror fiction, even if largely indirectly and in the context of much other reading.

Even at a very young age, she was a prolific writer, finishing several novels and a number of short stories before graduation from high school. All but one of these stories, which was published in her high-school literary magazine, have been lost, mostly by intention. Oates would discard most of them after completion or after submission as school projects, seeing them as merely practice for better work to come. The one surviving story, "A Long Way Home," was published in *Will o' the Wisp* in 1956 and has not yet been reprinted in any of her collections (though it has been reprinted in *First Words: Earliest Writing from Favorite Contemporary Authors*, edited by Paul Mandelbaum [1993]).

Oates attended Syracuse University as an undergraduate, beginning in 1956, and began contributing to the student literary magazine *Syracuse Review*; it was there she first read more ambitious little magazines, with a national audience, such as *Kenyon Review*. She achieved her first professional publication in 1958 as one of two winners of a *Mademoiselle* fiction contest, and shortly afterward had her first acceptance (of many) at the important little magazine *Epoch*. Her early published stories, often set in an idealized rural upstate New York based on her hometown and its surroundings, were indicative not only of the strong influence of writers such as Flannery O'Connor and William Faulkner, but also of a lifelong tendency to draw inspiration from her own experiences and those of friends and acquaintances. Often, she might fictionalize events in part by giving persons or places similar but masking names; the Erie County of her youth became "Eden County" in a series of short stories collected as *By the North Gate* (1963), for example. Critic and biographer Greg Johnson repeatedly notes her tagging of characters who are at least somewhat representative of their author with names that, like hers, begin with the letter "J."

This tendency to draw from the lives she knew for story materials often helped give her work an immediacy and timeliness that many other writers of her generation, or at least those often referred to as "serious" writers, didn't strive for to the same degree. Ironic distance and indulgence in mild or playful surrealism marked much of her contemporaries' work in the 1960s. While Oates didn't shy away from surrealism and could be seen to display a certain reserve, frequently engaging in one degree or another of satire, in presenting her characters in her work, most of her fiction was seen in some quarters as, if anything, too aggressively naturalistic, downbeat, and grim. Nonetheless, throughout the 1960s, national attention began to accrue to her fiction, as when *Best American Short Stories* editor Martha Foley included Oates's story "A Legacy" in the "Honor Roll" of stories Foley felt worthy of attention, but not quite worthy of inclusion, in the 1961 volume of the annual. Oates had taken her M.A. in English at the University of Wisconsin in 1961, without much enjoyment, notably aside from meeting and soon marrying fellow graduate student Raymond Smith. She thought she might continue with her studies as a Ph.D. candidate elsewhere, but, as Oates remembered in a *New York Times* interview with Walter Clemons, quoted in *Invisible Writer,* "I hadn't known about [the "Honor Roll" citation] until I just picked up [a copy of the annual] and saw it. I thought, maybe I could be a writer" (p. 93). She ceased pursuit of a doctorate, and, by 1964, had published her first collection of short stories (*By the North Gate*), written her first novel (*With Shuddering Fall* [1964]), and had stories included in both the *Best American Short Stories* and *The O. Henry Awards* volumes, the two most widely-read U.S. annuals of contemporary short fiction; her work frequently would be anthologized by these and other "best-of" anthologies over the next four decades. Her third novel, *them* (1969), won her the National Book Award; it dealt with unhappy lives in the racially and economically-charged climate of Detroit, just across the river from the University of Windsor, where by now Oates was on the faculty. Her next novel, *Wonderland* (1971), judged by Greg Johnson her best to date, verged on the fantastic more than her previous longer work in its "feverish intensity" and incorporated strong elements of the realistic grotesque.

A series of dream-inspired narratives, somewhat influenced by the work of erudite fantasist and literary hoaxer Jorge Luis Borges, was published by Oates as if in translation by her from the work of "Fernandes" in a variety of magazines and collected as *The Poisoned Kiss and Other Stories from the Portuguese* (Vanguard 1975). Though neither the first nor last time that Oates would playfully or seriously take on a new identity to publish her work, it may have been the most elaborate; a trilogy of novels to follow would also demonstrate her interest in metafictional technique.

By 1980, her increasing ambition led her to offer the first of these, a complex family-saga with strong fantasy elements, *Bellefleur* (Dutton). It bore an "Author's Note" warning that in this novel "the implausible is granted an authority and honored with a complexity usually reserved for realistic fiction" (frontispiece), an excellent description of much of the best literary fantasy. This book became her first national bestseller in hardcover, and served as a transition notice that she would be dealing with more straightforwardly fantastic and psychologically-alien themes in at least some of her new work.

THE 1980S AND LATER WORK

A Bloodsmoor Romance (1982) and *Mysteries of Winterthurn* (1984) were, in a sense, follow-ups to *Bellefleur*; complex, intentionally nostalgically reminiscent of Victorian-era writing, and, to some extent, plot-driven examples of romance- and mystery-fiction as well as examinations of families and small-town life; *Mysteries* is presented in the form a popular account of the detective work of Xavier Kilgarven. Neither was a commercial success, and perhaps in part because of this, publication of the next novel in the sequence, the gothic *The Crosswicks Horror*, has been delayed indefinitely. By the 1980s, Oates had firmly established a pattern in her writing projects; she would tend to alternate between large novels and shorter, somewhat less-demanding work: short stories, plays, poetry, essays, and even libretti (her short novel *Black Water* [1992] was adapted as an opera).

Having proven herself an adventurous and at the very least a capable writer in each of the forms she turned her hand to, her growing interest in the explicitly supernatural in fiction since the late 1970s may have come in part from growing confidence in her ability to handle fantastic themes, or her ability, as the recipient of most of the awards and credentials an American fiction writer can achieve, to see such work published and as respected as her work in other modes. Perhaps also her desire to take on fresh challenges was a spur. What she may have previously seen as her "minor" projects were often gaining large audiences and acclaim. For example, the short novel *Foxfire: Confessions of a Girl Gang* (1993) was widely hailed (if also damned by some reviewers as an "angry" book, when Oates meant it to be darkly comic), and was the first of her stories to be adapted as a commercial theatrical film (her earlier short story "Where Are You Going, Where Have You Been?" had been filmed for the PBS television series *American Playhouse* as "Smooth Talk"; "In the Realm of Ice" had also been filmed.). Perhaps it's notable that *Foxfire* goes beyond the chilling self-sacrifice the protagonist of "Where Are You Going" accepts to save her family (a choice so bleak that the "Smooth Talk" adaptation changes the ending of the story considerably), to allow its oppressed young women characters the opportunity to strike back, to an extent, at the society which attempts to damage them; perhaps this less-selfless response disturbed the reviewers in question.

Meanwhile, *Zombie* in its longer form surprised even some who'd come to expect remarkable empathy with her characters from Oates. While not her first novel in confessional form from the point of view of a murderer (*Expensive People* [1968] and the Charles Manson-inspired novella "The Triumph of the Spider Monkey" [1976] preceded it), *Zombie* was at least as relentless as anything that had come before it, in its portrayal of the thoughts and aspirations of a young man completely without conscience.

While some of Oates's academic and literary colleagues had bristled at finding variations and caricatures of themselves in some of her earlier fiction, and a few reviewers found the parallels between the events recounted in *Black Water* and the events surrounding the drowning of Mary Jo Kopechne while in the company of Sen. Edward Kennedy too great for satisfying fiction, there was little complaint about her portrait of someone very much like serial-killer Jeffrey Dahmer. As with her earlier work from a murderer's point of view, and in a manner more reminiscent of Robert Bloch's *Psycho* than of the approach taken by Truman Capote with *In Cold Blood*, Oates re-imagined the events that might arise in a situation similar to Dahmer's, rather than attempt to slightly fictionalize his actual crimes. The protagonist, Quentin P— (his surname is never given), preys sexually upon young men and boys, and aspires to create a sort of zombie sex-slave, through a rough sort of lobotomy that will nonetheless, Quentin hopes, leave his victim capable of expressing its admiration for and devotion to its master. The diary is written in an affectless style, complete with illustrations of the tools necessary for lobotomy and diagrams of the steps necessary to kidnap a victim. Notably, unlike in such predecessors as *Psycho* and Thomas Harris's *Red Dragon*, Quentin is in no real danger of apprehension by the authorities by novel's end; Oates's avoidance of pat endings is as much in play here as her Poe-inspired abilities to make the most monstrous of persons understandable in his own frame of reference, leaving the reader almost sympathetic.

Much of Oates's recent work published in horror-fiction and related magazines, or collected in *Haunted* and *The Collector of Hearts*, offers an intensification of her earlier themes and motifs; her best work in supernatural horror may be ahead of her. When explicitly fantastic elements are introduced to the stories, they are often done so obliquely, as in "The Sky Blue Ball" (in *Collector of Hearts*, originally in *Ellery Queen's Mystery Magazine*, 1995). The protagonist, a fourteen-year-old girl, walking in the town where she attends high school, away from her rural hometown (one of the recurring autobiographical elements of Oates's fiction), sees a child's toy rubber ball fly over a high brick wall; the ball is remarkably similar to one she'd had as a child and loved. She tosses it back over the wall, only to have it tossed back to her. Almost against her better judgment, she engages in what she takes to be a game of catch with an unseen child, until the ball is returned in such a way as to cause her to run out into a road, where she narrowly avoids being hit by a truck. Shaken, she tosses the ball back over the wall, gets no response, and when she finds a means to climb over the wall (landing in a way reminiscent of another incident from Oates's childhood), she finds a deserted lot and a faded, worn ball, obviously much older than the one she'd been tossing. The implication that she had been playing with some earlier, displaced version of herself (a sort of doppelganger) is obvious, but only by deft suggestion.

"Haunted," the short story, on the other hand, offers an all-too-fleshy revenant, who may be an insane drifter or a genuine vengeful spirit, but who definitely is implicated in the horrible death of a young woman who flouts convention. The narrator in this ironic allegory accepts her "punishment" for trespass into an abandoned house (and beyond the behavior of a "good girl"); her friend and fellow trespasser is unrepentant, and pays the price. This is the first of many stories to have been anthologized or shortlisted by Ellen Datlow and Terri Windling in their anthology series *The Year's Best Fantasy and Horror*. Oates would later contribute her short story "The Crossing" (1995) to Datlow and Windling's anthology of new, adult fairy tales, *Ruby Slippers, Golden Tears*.

Several more recent stories demonstrate that the power of Oates's work often leads to the continuing placement of her fiction, much as with *Zombie*, in horror or similar contexts even when no supernatural element is present. The August 2001, issue of *The Spook*, a web-based horror fiction magazine, offered Oates's "Testimony," which is the confession, in deposition-transcript form, of a girl who collaborated with an insanely vicious male rapist-murderer, as he degrades and eventually kills a young woman victim. This story is thematically and incidentally linked to another Oates story, "The Girl with the Blackened Eye" (2000), which deals with an adolescent girl forced into a kind of collaboration with another insanely vicious rapist-murderer, this one a middle-aged man, as remembered many years later by the young woman, who barely survived the ordeal; "Girl," first published in the little magazine *Witness*, was reprinted in the 2001 volumes of both the *O. Henry Awards* and *The Best American Mystery Stories*. The similarities between the two stories do not diminish either as riveting, uncomfortable reading.

In issue 34 of the little magazine *Conjunctions*, Oates published "Four Dark Fables," offering in the space of four pages more consolidation of new and old recurring themes in her work. The fairy tale "The Little Sacrifice" is a cruel vignette in which a young girl suffers so that her masters may know the absolute depth of their depravity, and thus accordingly compensate in the rest of their lives; "Prevailing Faith in 'Free Wil'" is a second-person description of the reader and his doppelganger leading parallel lives without conscious knowledge of the other; "The Revelation" is a nightmare vision that may well be reality, glimpsed only fleetingly (these middle two owe the most to Borges); "There Will Come That Evening" reads almost like a recapitulation of part of the earlier short story "The Doll," wherein Oates's recent recurring theme of the terrors that arise while driving at night is on display; doppelgangers of sorts are hinted at, as well.

Her 2002 short novel *Beasts* indicates no desire to slacken the pace of her exploration of the many forms of exploitation men and women can perform upon one another, nor a diminution of her willingness to let bizarre actual crimes inspire her fiction. An academic setting allows this tale to include some sly satire of academic life, including some at her own expense as conductor of classes in writing. As she gains the largest audiences of her career, thanks in part to her participation in Oprah Winfrey's television book-discussion of her family-saga *We Were the Mulvaneys* (1996) and to the strong commercial success of her Marilyn Monroe-inspired novel *Blonde* (2000), it will be interesting to see what the larger audience might make of her (even) more frightening fiction.

Critics who deal regularly with supernatural fiction often laud Oates not only for her impressive skill, but also for her disregard for arbitrary "genre" boundaries and willingness to incorporate many different elements into any given work, not shying away from fantastic motifs in a primarily realistic story, for example. In this, her work resembles that of a number of "maverick" writers who have in their careers "crossed over" to audiences in various literary subcultures simultaneously, including Robert Coover, William Kotzwinkle, and Jonathan Lethem; perhaps the strongest correspondence of the work of Oates to another writer's, in supernatural fiction and related fields, without either apparently being a direct influence on the other, is to that of Kate Wilhelm, who has written a variety of supernatural as well contemporary mimetic fiction and science fiction, but who may be best known for her sometimes fantasticated crime-fiction, such as the novel *Death Qualified: A Mystery of Chaos*. Their careers have other parallels as well, including a long commitment to teaching creative writing, Oates since 1978 at Princeton University, Wilhelm most visibly in her decades with the Clarion Science Fiction and Fantasy Writers' Workshop. More importantly, both in their fiction can present highly charged topics in, at times, a seemingly dispassionate way, with a clear-eyed assessment of human cruelty and a strong, compassionate feminism informing their work; both demonstrate a continuing desire to expand their range and the varieties of their skill.

Among Oates's essay collections, the aforementioned *Where I've Been, and Where I'm Going* may be the most useful to the student of supernatural fiction, with essays on fairy tales and their social utility, serial killers, children as protagonists, metaphor in horror fiction, and many related matters.

SUPERNATURAL FICTION WRITERS

Selected Bibliography

WORKS OF JOYCE CAROL OATES

NOVELS AND SHORT STORIES

By the North Gate. New York: Vanguard, 1963.

With Shuddering Fall. New York: Vanguard, 1964.

Expensive People. New York: Vanguard, 1968.

them. New York: Vanguard, 1969.

Wonderland. New York: Vanguard, 1971.

The Poisoned Kiss, and Other Stories from the Portuguese. New York: Vanguard, 1975.

The Triumph of the Spider Monkey. Santa Barbara, Calif.: Black Sparrow, 1976 (Chapbook of a novella.).

Night-side: Eighteen Tales. New York: Vanguard, 1977.

Bellefleur. New York: Dutton, 1980.

A Bloodsmoor Romance. New York: Dutton, 1982.

Mysteries of Winterthurn: A Novel. New York: Dutton, 1984.

Heat and Other Stories. New York: Dutton, 1991 (Includes "Family").

Black Water. New York: Dutton, 1992.

Foxfire: Confessions of a Girl Gang. New York: Dutton, 1993.

Haunted: Tales of the Grotesque. New York: Dutton, 1993 (Includes "Haunted," "The Doll," "The Bingo Master," "The White Cat," "The Model," "Extenuating Circumstances," "Don't You Trust Me?", "The Guilty Party," "The Premonition," "Phase Change," "Poor Bibi," "Thanksgiving," "Blind," "The Radio Astronomer," "Accursed Inhabitants in the House of Bly," and "Martyrdom.")

Mandelbaum, Paul, ed. *First Words: Earliest Writing from Favorite Contemporary Authors.* Chapel Hill: Algonquin Books of Chapel Hill, 1993. (Includes Oates's oldest surviving short story, "A Long Way Home" [1956].)

Where Are You Going, Where Have You Been? Selected Early Stories. Princeton, N.J.: Ontario Review Press, 1993.

"The Crossing." In *Ruby Slippers, Golden Tears.* Edited by Ellen Datlow and Terri Windling. New York: Morrow, 1995.

Zombie. New York: Dutton, 1995.

Demon and Other Tales. West Warwick, R.I.: Necronomicon Press, 1996 (A limited edition.).

We Were the Mulvaneys. New York: Dutton, 1996.

The Collector of Hearts: New Tales of the Grotesque. New York: Dutton, 1998.(Includes "The Sky Blue Ball," "Death Mother," "The Hand-Puppet," "Schroeder's Stepfather," "The Sepulchre," "The Hands," "||||||||," "Labor Day," "The Collector of Hearts," "Demon," "Elvis Is Dead: Why Are *You* Alive?", "Posthumous," "The Omen," "The Sons of Angus MacElster," The Affliction," "Scars," "An Urban Paradox," "Unprintable," "Intensive," "Valentine," "Death Astride Bicycle," "The Dream-Catcher," "Fever Blisters," "The Crossing," "Shadows of the Evening," "The Temple," "The Journey.")

Blonde. New York: Ecco Press, 2000.

"Four Dark Fables." *Conjunctions* 34 (2000).

"The Girl with the Blackened Eye." *Witness* 14, no. 2 (2000).

The Barrens. New York: Carroll & Graf, 2001 (As Rosamond Smith).

Beasts. New York: Carroll & Graf, 2002.

The Crosswicks Horror (Unpublished).

ESSAYS AND OTHER WRITING

Where I've Been, and Where I'm Going: Essays, Reviews, and Prose. New York: Dutton, 1999.

Introduction to Edgar Allan Poe's "The Black Cat." In *Master's Choice, Volume II*. Edited by Lawrence Block. New York: Berkley, 2000.

BOOKS EDITED BY OATES

American Gothic Tales. New York: Plume, 1996.

Tales of H. P. Lovecraft: Major Works. Hopewell, N.J.: Ecco Press, 1997.

CRITICAL AND BIOGRAPHICAL STUDIES

Bloom, Harold, ed. *Joyce Carol Oates: Modern Critical Views*. New York: Chelsea House, 1987.

Johnson, Greg. *Understanding Joyce Carol Oates*. Columbia: University of South Carolina Press, 1987.

———. *Joyce Carol Oates: A Study of the Short Fiction*. New York: Twayne, 1994.

———. *Invisible Writer: A Biography of Joyce Carol Oates*. New York: Dutton, 1998 (Includes excellent bibliography.).

Showalter, Elaine, ed. *Where Are You Going, Where Have You Been?* New Brunswick, N.J.: Rutgers University Press, 1994.

Tim Powers
1952–

IAN NICHOLS

THE ESSENTIAL ELEMENTS of science fiction and fantasy are so clearly defined that it sometimes seems easy to write, and this is evidenced by the plethora of fantasy, horror, and supernatural thriller novels on the shelves of bookstores across the world. For many of these, even those by highly talented writers, it is as if the demands of the genre take control of the text from the writer, and the result is a book that is enjoyable but indistinguishable from many, many other novels. Writers who can use the elements of fantasy to their own ends, who can, while working within the genres, use those elements in a genuinely original and creative way, are rare. Tim Powers is one of those writers.

THE SOURCE OF POWERS

Tim Powers was born in Buffalo, New York, on February 29, 1952, the son of Richard Powers, an attorney who had been a marine pilot in both World War II and the Korean War, and Noel (Zimmerman) Powers. The oldest of eight children in an Irish Catholic family which traced its origins back to County Wexford, not far from the John Power distillery, he developed a love of literature early, fostered by his highly literate parents. The family moved to California when he was eight, a move enthusiastically endorsed by Tim and the rest of the children. Although his first days at school, after coming from a Catholic grade school in Buffalo into a public grade school in California, were something of a culture shock, he adapted. Now, he would not happily live anywhere else. He does not miss the snow; as he told John Berlyne in 1999, "ever since [moving to California] I've tried to avoid physical contact with snow. I don't mind it in movies and things, but I don't want to be where it actually is."

When he was eleven years old, his mother introduced him to science fiction, via Robert Heinlein's *Red Planet* (1949) and by thirteen, he had already received his first rejection slip, from *The Magazine of Fantasy & Science Fiction*. Rather than being discouraged by this, he was encouraged: "I was very pleased to have a real rejection slip. I thought look at that! Just like Hemingway! I'm one of the boys! I think I've still got that rejection slip. And so from then on I would, once or twice a year, type up a story and put it in the mail and get another rejection slip." (in Berlyne, 1999).

After high school, Powers attended California State University at Fullerton from 1970 to 1976. Part of the reason for this extended stay was that he took twice as many units for his major in

English literature than was needed. This extensive knowledge of the sources of literature in English is apparent in his writing, which is informed by a great breadth of reading. Along with this, he, and other writers, attended the writing classes of Dorethea Kenny on weekends. One of these writers was James P Blaylock. Powers and he were writing "an interminable unplanned novel" which was never published. The atmosphere was one that fostered creativity, and eventually both writers recognized that the apparent spontaneity of the novels they favored was, in fact, the fruit of extensive planning and plotting.

THE BIRTH OF WILLIAM ASHBLESS

The poet William Ashbless is the major character in Powers' *The Anubis Gates* (1983), which has the best print record of all his novels. Ashbless is also mentioned in many of his other novels and has even been mentioned in a Web site on how to gain a Ph.D. Unfortunately, Ashbless doesn't exist. He is the invention of Powers and Blaylock.

While they were both in college, Blaylock and Powers created Ashbless by writing alternate lines of poetry, "pretentious and portentous but totally nonsense." The poems were published in the university paper and read at writers' workshops for as long as the two could keep straight faces. Both Blaylock and Powers have since used Ashbless in novels, and since *The Anubis Gates,* Powers has included at least a reference to Ashbless in every novel.

PLUNGING INTO PUBLICATION

Powers' first published novel was *The Skies Discrowned* (1976) for Laser Books, sold on the strength of four chapters and a summary. If he had been a known writer at this time, it would only have been three chapters, but Laser Books asked him for another, to prove he could do it. He had been made aware of Laser Books through K. W. Jeter, another young writer, and had sent them his novel because there was little competition; they had rigorous requirements regarding length, restrictions on sex and language, and they didn't pay very much.

His second novel, *Epitaph in Rust* (1976), was also published by Laser Books, and his third was to be part of a series planned by Corgi, in England. The series was to be about King Arthur, reappearing throughout history in different guises, His book was accepted, an advance was paid, and then the series was canceled. Powers submitted the finished novel to Lester Del Rey, who asked him to rewrite it at greater length, and it was eventually published in 1979 as *The Drawing of the Dark*. This was the novel that really launched Powers' career.

Powers was dissatisfied with the way *Epitaph in Rust* had been edited and rewritten by Laser Books, and he sought assurances that this would not occur again. They gave the assurances but went out of business soon after. In the interval between *Epitaph in Rust* and *The Drawing of the Dark,* Powers went back to work at a pizza parlor. Later, after his writing career was established, *Epitaph in Rust* was republished from the original manuscript (NESFA Press, 1989).

If *The Drawing of the Dark* was the novel that established Powers, his fourth novel, *The Anubis Gates*, was the work that stamped his mark on the field of fantasy. It has been in continuous publication since its first printing in 1983, by Ace Books, and won the prestigious Philip K. Dick award. There is a certain ironic justice in this, since Powers knew Dick well before his death, and lived across the hall from him in a block of apartments for some time. He was bequeathed Dick's library and created something of a controversy by selling it. However, his sale of Dick's books took place only after none of the universities he contacted showed any interest in the collection and had been endorsed by Dick before his death.

The path to publication of *The Anubis Gates* was not an easy one, despite Powers' previous success and growing reputation. It was rejected by many publishers, including Lester Del Rey, who had accepted *The Drawing of the Dark*. Eventually the book was submitted to Ace for the second time, and Beth Meacham, an editor there, suggested that it be cut by an eighth. It was, it was accepted, and it has become Powers' most popular novel.

The novel is a time-travel story, in which the protagonist, Brendan Doyle, is thrust back into a nineteenth-century England as we never knew it. Through various loops of time, created by Egyptian black magicians who are out to rule the world, we meet creatures both fine and grotesque, ranging from Lord Byron, who has been brainwashed into an attempt on King George's life, through to a beggar-king killer, Horrabin, who performs odd experiments on his victims. The most satisfying thing about the book, apart from Powers' usual thorough research and scintillatingly evocative writing, is that all the loose ends are tied up, ingeniously and believably.

PAST THE PROLOGUE

Powers has taken his fantastic novels to many different places and times: to other planets in the far future, to a post-holocaust Los Angeles, to Vienna in the sixteenth century and Las Vegas in the twentieth century. He has set stories in London and the Caribbean, on the *Queen Mary* and in the Middle East. The characters are as diverse as the settings, from sword-wielding reincarnations of King Arthur to Las Vegas hustlers; from the fictional poet William Ashbless to the real poet Lord Byron.

While Powers has not been, perhaps, as prolific as other writers, the quality of his work has gained him many awards. Along with Philip K Dick Award, *The Anubis Gates* won the *Science Fiction Chronicle* Award and the Apollo Award. *Dinner at Deviant's Palace* (1985) also won the Dick Award, in 1986. Powers has also won the Mythopoeic Fantasy Award for *The Stress of Her Regard* (published 1989) and the World Fantasy Award and *Locus* Award for *Last Call* (published 1992). *Earthquake Weather* (published 1997) was voted the best fantasy novel in the 1998 *Locus* poll. *Declare* (published 2000) won the International Horror Guild Award and another World Fantasy Award, both for best novel.

Part of the reason for the slow production rate of Powers' novel lies in the meticulous research he does for each of them. Even those things other authors seem to take for granted, such as the swordplay in *The Drawing of the Dark* or *The Skies Discrowned*, is drawn from Powers' own experience in fencing. He has fenced since university. For *Last Call*, which is set in Las Vegas, he and his wife, Serena (they were married in 1980), drove there, duplicating the drive that takes place in the novel. The historical novels are researched with equal thoroughness, as are the supernatural elements of the novels. The Lamia, for instance, in *The Stress of Her Regard,* were suggested by research into what had actually happened to the body of Byron when it washed onto the shore after drowning.

TALKING ABOUT THE NOVELS

It cannot be said that Powers' novels genuinely extend the boundaries of fantasy, horror, or science fiction. Their locus is squarely within the genres and uses the motifs and conventions of those genres. While the novels are highly literate, there seems to be no artifice in them, no obvious attempt to make them *literary* novels. They are most certainly not writerly novels; there is no attempt to draw attention to the text as text, nothing that opposes diegesis. However, they do not sit quietly within the category of readerly texts either.

Part of the reason for this is that while the texts do not employ structural disruptions to challenge the reader, the conceptual challenges disrupt genre expectations. Nothing is really as it seems, as if the surface text is merely an illusion, and the real story can only be seen when the illusory story is pierced. Small things take on meaning, such as the water snakes smoked by Merlin in *The Drawing of the Dark*. The puppetry in *On Stranger Tides* (1987) seems to represent the way in which individuals can be controlled, by fate or other people. The constant themes of changing personalities within a body, the Fisher King, earth magic and blood magic, all challenge readers, but not by asking them to decode a complex message, fragmented and obscure. Rather, the challenge is to dig deeper into what seems simple and plain but which is actually rich and highly referential.

Even the most basic tropes of the genres, such as the stock characters, are enriched to make us think. Pirates are not just pirates, and magicians are not just magicians. As Powers' texts progress, his characterizations make clear that there are reasons for their behaviors that go beyond simple concepts of good and evil, heroes and villains. These have, at times, supernatural origins, at times natural ones, at times psychological ones. Powers manages to link these factors together to produce quite rounded characters, capable of surprising readers with their actions, but these actions are nevertheless consistent with their characters.

Sometimes the links to external referents are not made plain but underlie the text as part of its construction. When researching *Last Call*, Powers "noticed that The Flamingo opened on the day after Christmas, closed just about on Good Friday and re-opened on just about Easter. And again I think 'OK! I get it. No problem!' and [Bugsy] Siegel himself was killed on June 20th-which is the day in Babylonian myth that the fertility god Tammuz is killed" (in Berlyne, 1999).These observed relationships with key mythological events are part of the novel, but only emerge in it as part of the generalized myth of the Fisher King which is centralized in the text. However, they inform that very myth, and are central to the death and resurrection for the sake of fertility which the myth symbolizes.

THE BOOKS THEMSELVES

The Drawing of the Dark takes place in the sixteenth century and centers around Brian Duffy, an expatriate Irish mercenary living in Venice. Through what appears to be an accidentally caused vendetta, but which turns out to be a carefully laid plot, Duffy finds it best to leave Venice and take up an appointment as the bouncer at the Zimmerman Inn, in Vienna. The position is offered to him by Aurelianus, the proprietor of the inn, which has been established in an old monastery and brewery, the source of Herzwestern beer. Duffy is familiar with the beer and the monastery, since he lived in Vienna until three years before the story starts, but, again, had to leave the city in a hurry.

Nothing is as it seems. Duffy's first intimation of this is when he drinks at a tavern with Bacchus, prior to Duffy's passage over the mountains toward Vienna. During this passage, mythical and magical beasts appear to guide and guard him. He reaches the inn and reacquaints himself with Epiphany, the woman whose marriage to a rival had forced him to leave Vienna. Aurelianus arrives, and Duffy's real job is revealed to be the guarding of the Fisher King, as Aurelianus is revealed to be Merlin and Duffy is revealed to be a reincarnation of King Arthur, the ancient guardian of the powers of the West. The inn itself is revealed to be the last resting place of Finn MacCool, the great Celtic Hero, and the Herzwestern is brewed directly over, and in contact with, his body.

The western powers need a guardian, since the forces of the East, under Suleiman, are about to besiege Vienna, and they will destroy the Dark; the mystic Herzwestern beer which alone can revive the injured Fisher King. The physical conflict between nations is itself only a mask for the much greater mystic conflict between the souls of the two hemispheres, their champions being Merlin, for the West, and Ibrahim, for the East. The battles that take place are magical, spiritual, and physical, and all of them are described with great verisimilitude.

While the novel appears on the surface to be a carefully researched and brilliantly written fantasy adventure, it is much more than that. The characters, Duffy in particular, live and breathe, and suffer from much human fallibility. Duffy rejects his job, and he doesn't want to know about magic and past lives. He doesn't get the girl in the end, and she sinks further into drunkenness. Her father, a prophetic artist after the fashion of Blake, dies from neglect, and his masterpiece is so spoiled that it cannot be used for prediction. All these things are not so much to show the heroic nature of humans under great stress but to show us the humanity of heroes.

Some themes emerge that are repeated in other novels. Transference of consciousness is one of these. Brian Duffy's body is taken over by the soul of Arthur, and other characters act as the vellum for palimpsests of those from long ago. The image of departure on water, particularly on rivers, is evoked when Duffy departs down the Donau canal. The dominant theme, though, is that of redemption, for Duffy and the West, and that is repeated in *Dinner at Deviant's Palace*.

Even though published after *The Drawing of the Dark*, *Dinner at Deviant's Palace* is conceptually closer to *The Skies Discrowned* and *Epitaph in Rust*. In many ways it is the transitional text, the missing link between the earlier writing of Powers and the more mature, more considered writing. It was, in fact, conceived before *The Drawing of the Dark*. There is less dwelling on nuance and more action. It is not concerned with the supernatural, and it is the last of Powers' novels that could be described as science fiction.

The novel is a reworking of the Orpheus myth, set in a post-holocaust Los Angeles. This Orpheus is Gregorio Rivas, a musician who was, for some time, a redeemer, rescuing people from the Jaybush Cult. His success rested on his hard-won knowledge of the cult; he was a member who managed to find a way around the will-sapping rituals employed.

Rivas, retired and a successful musician, is approached to "redeem" a woman stolen by the cult, a woman he once loved. This is the introduction of the neomythological Orpheus motif. Rivas pursues her into his social equivalent of Hell, Deviant's Palace. Like Orpheus, he loses her at the end, but not because he looks back. Instead it is because she is not what she was, and he is not what he was. Time has passed, and their experiences have changed them both. He leaves, pursued by demons, with another, and worthier, woman.

Dinner at Deviant's Palace introduces two very important tropes that recur throughout Powers' ouvre. Things that appear to be incomprehensible are explained; they have reasons. The source of the Jaybush powers is a vampiric alien being, and everything descends from that, as everything descends from the historic clash of East and West in *The Drawing of the Dark*. It also introduces the idea of patterns, and the disruption of patterns, another motif repeated throughout his works, up to and including *Declare*.

In *On Stranger Tides*, the Caribbean becomes the setting for a dark fantasy of pirates and the search for the Fountain of Youth. It also makes plain one of the major themes of Powers' works, the person as puppet. The protagonist is John Chandagnac, later known as Jack Shandy, who is a puppeteer and inadvertent swordsman. The magic is vodun, or voodoo, outlined as a system approaching the rigor of a science. It is when the importance of the puppetry is realized by the reader that themes within the novel become plain, and these reflect on Powers' other novels, both prior and post. People are controlled by magic, and a powerful *bocor*, a voodoo witch or priest such as Blackbeard, is able to take over their actions. Making this plain, and fighting with his own skills against the magical puppetry of others, Chandagnac uses the body of one of his foes as a puppet to delay the execution of his love until he can rescue her. With this theme established, the puppetry in other novels becomes clear. In *The Drawing of the Dark,* Duffy is the puppet of both Merlin and Arthur. In *Dinner at Deviant's Palace,* the alien controls people through the Jaybush cult, taking over their bodies and literally making them dance to his will. Even in *Declare,* people are puppets of institutions, or of magic.

The continuing complexity of the themes in Powers' work marks him as a writer who enunciates a consistent vision of the world, and a consistent fictional vision. The themes are interdependent and intersupportive. Perhaps the overarching theme is that of people who rebel against control, who break the puppeteer's strings, whether that puppeteer be tradition, magic, other people, or God himself. In the final analysis, Powers' works are celebrations of the humanity that drives people to triumph over fate, however that fate is conceived.

Selected Bibliography

THE WORKS OF TIM POWERS

NOVELS

The Skies Discrowned. Toronto: Laser Books, 1976; New York: Tor Books, 1986.

Epitaph in Rust. Toronto: Laser Books, 1976; Framingham, MA: NESFA Press, 1989.

The Drawing of the Dark: New York: Del Rey, 1979.

The Anubis Gates. New York: Ace Science Fiction, 1983.

Dinner at Deviant's Palace. New York: Ace Books, 1985.

On Stranger Tides. New York: Ace Books, 1987.

The Stress of Her Regard. New York: Ace Books and London: Charnel House, 1989.

Last Call. New York: William Morrow and London: Charnel House, 1992.

Expiration Date. London: HarperCollins, 1995; New York: Tor, 1996.

Earthquake Weather. London: Legend and New York: Tor, 1997.

Declare. Burton, Mich.: Subterranean Press, 2000.

CRITICAL STUDIES AND INTERVIEWS

Berlyne, John. "Interview with Tim Powers." (September 1999). "Works of Tim Powers" Web site. Available from http://www.timpowers.info. (The Web site includes extensive information on Powers and his works.)

Dembo, Arinn. "Impassion'd Clay: On Tim Powers' *The Stress of Her Regard.*" *New York Review of Science Fiction* 37:1–2 (September 1991).

Kelleher, Fiona. "Getting a Life: Haunted Spaces in Two Novels of Tim Powers." *New York Review of Science Fiction,* 10.7:13–17 (March 1988).

Terry Pratchett
1948–

DAVID LANGFORD

TERRY PRATCHETT'S WRITING career had a precocious start with a short fantasy written at the age of thirteen for his school magazine, and professionally published two years later. After twenty more years and some idiosyncratic novels, he hit his stride with the Discworld series of comic fantasies, whose steadily increasing success in Britain has made Pratchett a regular number-one best-seller in both hardback and paperback.

Terry David John Pratchett was born in Beaconsfield, England, on April 28, 1948. He credits his education more to omnivorous reading in the Beaconsfield Public Library than to the local school. After a period in High Wycombe Technical High School, he entered journalism at Buckinghamshire's newspaper, the *Bucks Free Press*, in 1965, subsequently working on the *Western Daily Herald* and the *Bath Chronicle*. Later he became a publicity officer for the Central Electricity Generating Board (now Powergen), issuing assurances about the safety of nuclear power stations.

That first story was "The Hades Business" (*Science Fantasy* magazine, 1963), in which Hell improves its image with a public relations campaign. Pratchett's first novel, the children's fantasy *The Carpet People*, was written when he was seventeen and published some years later in 1971, with cartoon illustrations by the author. Its fantasy quest has the unusual setting of a carpet's weave, where tribes of microscopic inhabitants regard a stray sugar crystal or a lost coin as almost inexhaustible resources of food or metal, respectively, and ascribe the titanic footsteps of humans walking on the carpet to the malice of a Dark Lord called Fray. The story was heavily revised for its 1992 reissue. In a note from the author in the reissue, Pratchett declared: "I wrote that in the days when I thought fantasy was all battles and kings. Now I'm inclined to think that the *real* concerns of fantasy ought to be about not having battles, and doing *without* kings" (p. 7).

THE EVOLUTION OF DISCWORLD AND ITS SUBSERIES

Pratchett's early career continued with two lighthearted science fiction novels, *The Dark Side of the Sun* (1976) and the parodic *Strata* (1981). The latter mocks the contemporary science fiction fashion for vast artificial constructions—for example, Larry Niven's 1970 *Ringworld*—by introducing a manufactured flat world: "It was like a plate full of continents. A coin tossed into the air by an indecisive god" (p. 57).

A Discworld, in fact. The first comic romp to be set on Pratchett's more enduring fantasy Discworld soon followed: *The Colour of Magic* (1983). Here the disc is supported by four vast elephants who, in accordance with certain ancient cosmological myths, stand on a turtle of immense size: Great A'Tuin. Upon the disc, from the perpetual waterfall around the Rim to the gods' home atop the tallest mountain at the Hub, is a medley of generic fantasylands, a fluid setting for parodic capers. This, at any rate, is how it began—but Discworld has evolved steadily and significantly.

The Colour of Magic comprises four episodes in which inept wizard Rincewind escorts the impossibly naive Twoflower (a traveler from Discworld's "Aurient," embodying various Japanese tourist stereotypes) through seriocomic perils. These begin in the great and malodorous metropolis Ankh-Morpork, whose exotic sleaze, Thieves' and Assassins' guilds, and street names all echo Fritz Leiber's fantasy city of Lankhmar—a favorite haunt of the Leiber sword-and-sorcery heroes Fafhrd and the Gray Mouser, whose Discworld equivalents are Bravd and the Weasel. When Twoflower unwisely introduces the notion of fire insurance to Ankh-Morpork's underworld, the city is soon in flames.

The parody content takes on a flavor of H. P. Lovecraft with a visit to the blasphemous fane of ichor god Bel-Shamharoth, complicated by the Conan-like barbarian Hrun of Chimeria and his unstoppably talkative magic sword Kring (whose ambition is to be a ploughshare). Next, Anne McCaffrey's dragonriders are gently spoofed, with the physical implausibility of huge flying dragons handled by making them purely magical, semi-illusory creatures: "I didn't know dragons could be seen through," Rincewind says wonderingly (p. 116). Finally, leaving parody behind but retaining high spirits, Pratchett takes his adventurers to the unpleasant Rim land of Krull, where a primitive space program aims to launch "chelonauts" off the edge to determine the world-turtle A'Tuin's sex. Inevitably, Rincewind and Twoflower replace the chelonauts.

Capers continue, with a high density of incidental gags, in *The Light Fantastic* (1986). Although Rincewind and Twoflower (rescued by outrageous deus ex machina from the long drop off the Rim) remain rather shallow and static characters, the "anthropomorphic personification" Death—always speaking in DOOM-LADEN CAPITALS—begins his development from a mere brutal ender of lives to a functionary who is obscurely on humanity's side against things worse than himself. The wizards' college Unseen University begins to take form, and a magical accident transforms its librarian into the book-loving orangutan destined to be a popular series character. Thickwitted Hrun gives way to the more interesting Cohen the Barbarian, a living legend but now a very old man who still wields a mean sword, has fond if dwindling hopes of ravishing young ladies, and quests for reliable dentures.

Discworld's popularity was growing by word-of-mouth recommendation. Readers expecting more of the same were slightly startled by the next book, *Equal Rites* (1987), in which young heroine Esk inherits wizard-type magic from her father, making her a misfit in a world where wizards are expected to be men. Pratchett turns a wry eye on what he saw as the genre's recurring magical sexism:

> The fantasy world, in fact, is overdue for a visit from the Equal Opportunities people because, in the fantasy world, magic done by women is usually of poor quality, third-rate, negative stuff, while the wizards are usually cerebral, clever, powerful, and wise. . . . Wizards get to do a better class of magic, while witches give you warts.
> ("Why Gandalf Never Married," Pratchett speech, November 15, 1985)

Esk is raised and almost wholly upstaged by redoubtable witch Granny Weatherwax, who has an iron-willed determination to give people what they need rather than what they want, and ultimately causes upheaval at Unseen University. Meanwhile, imaginatively lyrical passages about the joys and hazards of the witchy practice "Borrowing"—riding in animals' minds—would not seem out of place in Ursula K. Le Guin's *A Wizard of Earthsea* (1968). In a characteristically Pratchettian development, young Esk tries Borrowing on the huge Unseen University building itself: "For the first time in her life she knew what it was like to have balconies" (p. 161).

Mort (1987) successfully fuses humorous invention with deeper thoughtfulness and the recognition that comedy can be strengthened by an underpinning of dark matters. Death hires a young apprentice, Mort, who is all too human and makes a mess of the "Duty": by saving a young princess fated to die, he endangers history and reality. High humor and deep complications ensue.

Dividing the many stories of Discworld into linked subseries, the first and weakest stars the perpetually cowardly and panic-stricken Rincewind, a wizard so incapable that his traditional pointy hat is embroidered with the word WIZZARD, and who after *The Colour of Magic* and *The Light Fantastic* has a leading role in a number of titles, including *Sourcery, Eric, Interesting Times*, and *The Last Continent*. *Sourcery* (1988) introduces a superpowerful young wizard or "sourcerer" who catalyzes a general increase in available magic; the power goes to the heads of Discworld's wizards, and there is all-out magical war. *Eric* (1990), a short travelogue of Discworld past and present, including its creation, its versions of the Aztec Empire and Trojan War, and its Hell, was conceived as a series of picture opportunities for the artist Josh Kirby (who painted covers for British editions of all the Discworld novels and many spin-offs until his death in 2001). Later, deflatingly, the text was issued without Kirby's luxuriant paintings.

Interesting Times (1994) visits the tyrannical Agatean Empire—a pastiche of old and new Chinese stereotypes—at a time when Cohen the Barbarian and his nonagenarian Silver Horde (seven strong in total) plan to seize the Agatean throne. Rincewind here develops his cowardice into something approaching a practical philosophy. *The Last Continent* (1998) runs riot with innumerable Australian jokes and references in a setting which is Discworld's all too close equivalent of Australia, ranging from the aboriginal Dreamtime to opera houses, Vegemite, and drag queens. Rincewind even pioneers the Down Under tradition of corks dangling on strings from one's hat brim, after a less-successful preliminary experiment in which they remained attached to their bottles.

In the Witches of Lancre sequence, Granny Weatherwax of *Equal Rites* goes on to assemble a very small coven in her tiny homeland, Lancre, the other members being outrageous old reprobate Nanny Ogg and flustered New Age witch Magrat Garlick. These form the traditional triad of crone, mother, and maiden, while "Lancre Witches" echoes the Lancashire Witches of seventeenth-century English witch-trial fame. Their byplay, personality clashes, misunderstandings, and refusals to understand are a reliable source of comedy.

Wyrd Sisters (1988) involves the trio in complex shenanigans regarding Lancre's royal succession, as commemorated on stage in a usurper's commissioned propaganda play that begins as whitewash and becomes strangely similar to *Macbeth*. *Witches Abroad* (1991) sees them flying by broomstick to foreign parts, finally reaching an exotic land of fairy tales and voodoo to thwart an unscrupulous fairy godmother (who is Granny's bad sister) and save the local Cinderella from the dire fate that awaits her if she goes to the ball. *Lords and Ladies* (1992) echoes Shakespeare again, with an invasion of murderous elves turning Magrat's wedding plans into a midsummer night's nightmare.

With Magrat married, the coven must recruit another maiden. The quest for runaway young witch Agnes in *Maskerade* (1995) takes Granny and Nanny to Ankh-Morpork and its Opera House, where the story of *The Phantom of the*

Opera is dangerously playing itself out and needs to be diverted. It is a recurring Discworld theme that stories have a real momentum, and that the easy downhill path to the expected default ending may not be the "right" one. The novelette *The Sea and Little Fishes* (1998) features the Lancre Witch Trials, an "informal" contest of witchcraft that is dominated by Granny's relentless, single-minded competitiveness—even when she does not take part. *Carpe Jugulum* (1998), the darkest so far of all the Lancre stories, pits indomitable Granny against almost invulnerable, indestructible, garlic-immune vampires at a time of great uncertainty when the coven's makeup is shifting, with Agnes now the maiden, Magrat a new mother, Nanny Ogg the crone, and Granny perhaps out in the cold. Despite ample comedy, both black and white, there are grim passages and a sense of real menace.

The cowled, skeletal figure of Death appears regularly throughout the Discworld stories, usually in brief vignettes of greeting the newly dead or gently explaining their situation. A third sequence beginning with *Mort* revolves around Death, his fated duties, and later his "granddaughter" Susan (child of Mort and Death's adopted daughter). *Reaper Man* (1991) sees Death pensioned off, subject at last to time, and passing his retirement as a farmhand who is particularly good with a scythe—though challenged by the mechanical threat of a newly invented combine harvester. Meanwhile in Ankh-Morpork, unharvested life energies discharge in poltergeist activity and a just-deceased wizard finds himself unwillingly continuing as a zombie—a new recruit for the city's small but active undead-rights campaign ("You Don't Have to Take This Lying Down.").

Death takes another holiday in *Soul Music* (1994), while Ankh-Morpork is swept by a new craze for rock music thanks to the magical guitar acquired by a fey young musician who looks somehow . . . elvish. Susan and the bumbling Unseen University wizards are soon involved in the manic action, densely larded with musical puns and allusions. *Hogfather* (1996) sees the Ankh-Morpork Assassins' Guild accepting a contract on the Hogfather, Discworld's Father Christmas, who is killed or at least gravely stricken by a devious assassin who begins by kidnapping the Tooth Fairy. All this is instigated by the bean-counting Auditors of Reality, already met in *Reaper Man*, who regard human life and free will as unwanted litter in their tidy cosmos. They make another clean-up attempt in *Thief of Time* (2001) with a scheme to re-create the legendary Glass Clock of Bad Schüschein, as recorded in the Discworld children's book *Grim Fairy Tales*, which slices time so thinly as to stop it altogether. Life and movement necessarily halt, and only a few specially privileged beings remain able to function, such as Susan and the Horsemen of the Apocalypse (including the forgotten fifth, who dropped out before the group became famous).

One of the most consistently successful Discworld subseries is the string of noir fantasy police-procedurals about the exploits of the Ankh-Morpork City Watch. When introduced in *Guards! Guards!* (1989), the Night Watch is at its lowest ebb and consists of four people: depressive alcoholic Captain Vimes, portly coward Sergeant Colon, light-fingered Corporal Nobbs, and desperately literal-minded new recruit Carrot—who begins with such gaffes as arresting the president of the respected Thieves' Guild for being a thief.

Darker doings are afoot as the Elucidated Brethren of the Ebon Night, a vaguely Masonic secret society, learns to summon and control a dragon whose flame-power can melt stone and vaporize people. The plan is to topple the city's efficient but unloved tyrant Lord Vetinari and—a fantasy trope that Pratchett regards with particular suspicion—install a True King qualified by heredity to rule (or at least to take orders from the scheming Supreme Grand Master of the Brethren).

Vimes loves Ankh-Morpork and is at last stimulated to effective investigation by the menace of the dragon: "Of all the cities in the world it could have flown into, he thought, it's flown into mine" (p. 94). Loving the city does not mean liking Vetinari or the citizens, one of whose realistically predictable reactions is a mob attack on the messy but harmless pet swamp-dragons bred by aristocratic Lady Sybil Ramkin, an outsized lady who as part of the ambiguously happy ending is destined to become Vimes's wife. Meanwhile it is gently indicated that, although he would never dream of claiming the throne, the true heir of Ankh-Morpork's long-deposed kings is Carrot.

The dynamic between Vimes and Vetinari the Patrician, balancing personal dislike against reluctant admiration for each other's abilities, is adroitly developed through further Watch novels and leads to such ironies as sullenly socialist Vimes being successively rewarded with a knighthood, a dukedom, and the status of ambassador. *Men at Arms* (1993) expands the Watch under a new policy of racial equality, which in Ankh-Morpork means admitting dwarfs, their traditional enemies the trolls, and even an engaging female werewolf. Meanwhile a serial killer with plans to change the city's rulership has acquired a unique weapon that is only a little ahead of its time: it is, essentially, a high-velocity rifle. Ever ready to rethink fantasy clichés—in this case, that of a world locked into medieval technology—Pratchett has seen that Ankh-Morpork's dedication to the profit motive has brought it to the brink of industrial revolution.

This provides background color in *Feet of Clay* (1996), in which investigation of a sequence of devious "impossible crime" poison attacks on the Patrician takes the still-expanding Watch on an investigation of various city industries. In the absence of internal combustion engines, much motive power is provided by the despised golems, mute clay figures powered by magic and under compulsion to work tirelessly at the filthiest jobs. Even these seeming robots, it proves, have feelings and hopes. When one golem is finally given a voice, there are cries of "Blasphemy" and Vimes, always ready to champion if not to like the underdog, replies: "That's what people say when the voiceless speak" (p. 272).

Jingo (1997) features another assassination attempt directed at a dignitary from Ankh-Morpork's chief rival, the Araby-like country of Klatch. The story moves outside Ankh-Morpork to a futile but mercifully brief war with this desert kingdom, where Carrot blossoms as a Lawrence of Arabia figure and successfully arrests an entire battlefield—a rare occasion, in this subseries, of comedy and plausibility colliding with some damage to both sides. *The Fifth Elephant* (1999) takes the very undiplomatic Vimes on a diplomatic mission to Uberwald, a spooky country whose name (German for "over the wood") recalls Transylvania ("across the woods"). Even distant Uberwald is now closely linked to Ankh-Morpork by trade and the latest communications technology of semaphore towers, alias "clacks" or c-mail, and the Patrician is much concerned that its local dwarf, vampire, and werewolf politics are in turmoil. The utterly amoral and very nearly unkillable werewolves are the major difficulty in Uberwald; a pack's long, murderous, cross-country pursuit of Vimes skillfully varies extreme terror with comic relief. In the end, the local police being ineffective, Vimes deals personally with the neo-Nazi werewolf ringleader—the first time in the series that he has actually killed in cold blood:

"You killed him?"

"No. I put him down."

(p. 300)

Most recently, *Night Watch* (2002) turns aside from the march of progress in Ankh-Morpork with a freak magical accident that hurls Vimes and his latest criminal quarry thirty years back in time. The History Monks who try to keep Discworld events on course (and who featured briefly in *Small Gods*, extensively in *Thief of Time*) would like to put things right, but first there is a historical gap for Vimes to fill. An honorable sergeant-at-arms of the Watch has been prematurely killed by the villain also flung back into the past, and Vimes must carry out his part by teaching the young Vimes to be a good policeman, playing a key role in the imminent Ankh-Morpork revolution . . . and then dying in a needless skirmish, to be remembered and honored thirty years later by the few Watchmen who were there. A tough order for this determined survivor, but comedy still creeps in. When the barricaded People's Republic of Treacle Mine Road drafts a manifesto including Free Love, the local "ladies of negotiable affection" rapidly force an amendment to Reasonably Priced Love.

SOME MORE OR LESS STAND-ALONE DISCWORLD NOVELS

Backtracking to discuss—in order of publication—some more or less stand-alone novels, the first of these is *Pyramids* (1989). This explores Discworld's version of ancient Egypt, a static society with an extensive pantheon of animal-headed gods ("Hat, the Vulture-Headed God of Unexpected Guests") and a culture of mummification and expensive pyramid building that had bankrupted the country. Pteppic, heir to the throne, is called back from his expensive foreign education at the Ankh-Morpork Assassins' Guild when his father dies. At home, he must come to terms with the musty stagnation of a desert land that—since Discworld pyramids literally store and discharge temporal energy—has lived far too long on borrowed time. There are also plenty of black jokes about embalming, such as the traditional apprentice gag during the disembowelment stage: "Look . . . your name in lights. Get it?" (p. 62).

In *Moving Pictures* (1990), the alchemists of Ankh-Morpork invent "octo-cellulose," magical film stock that triggers the founding of a motion picture industry at nearby Holy Wood. Since this is fantasy, the movie cameras contain teams of very tiny demons, painting each frame as it clicks past and blowing hard to dry the result. Hollywood jokes and references come thick and fast, but the power of belief and star-worship compelled by movies is a dangerous thing here on Discworld where the fabric of reality is thin, and attracts sinister attention from Outside. Which leads, almost logically, to the memorable image of a giant woman climbing the city's highest tower while clutching a terrified ape—the Librarian—in one hand, and being strafed by wizards from a flying broomstick. Meanwhile the cranky Gaspode the Wonder Dog, who can talk yet never gets the attention paid to his photogenic but very stupid canine companion Laddie, steals the show.

Incidentally, this manic novel marks a change in Unseen University. Previous wizards had regularly been killed off, usually by one another, and replaced, with the Librarian the only fixed point. *Moving Pictures* introduces a set of genially comic wizards whom Pratchett liked enough to keep: Archchancellor Mustrum Ridcully, an alarmingly hearty devotee of huntin', shootin', and fishin', and his supporting cast of bickering college fellows, such as the Chair of Indefinite Studies, Lecturer in Recent Runes, Dean of Pentacles, and Bursar. They reappear in many later books, including the already mentioned *Reaper Man*, *Lords and Ladies*, *Soul Music*, *Interesting Times*, *Hogfather*, and *The Last Continent*. Often they provide a strand of broad comedy that contrasts with a novel's other, less farcical story lines.

Very much darker, *Small Gods* (1992) again takes readers to a previously unvisited desert country: Omnia, a theocracy whose savagely monotheistic church of the great god Om denies the shape of the world. Doctrine insists that Discworld is spherical, though heretics in the final tortures of the "Quisition" may defiantly whisper (echoing Galileo's *Eppur si muove*): "The Turtle moves!" In a familiar paradox, the oppressive atmosphere of an unforgiving, crusading Church Militant stifles the religious impulse. Discworld's gods derive power from worship, and when Om decides to incarnate himself he finds that he is down to one last true believer—the hero Brutha, a slow-thinking novice monk—and so can manifest only as a humble, powerless tortoise. Many harrowing complications and a number of deaths follow before the church can be reformed under Brutha, who makes a New Deal with the reempowered Om: "No smiting. No commandments unless you obey them too" (p. 249). This tough-minded yet still humorous story may be Pratchett's finest novel.

Another attack on the Patrician, but on his reputation rather than his life, is central to *The Truth* (2000), which rings the changes on Ankh-Morpork crime capers by moving Vimes and the familiar Watch characters aside in favor of William de Worde, Discworld's first investigative reporter. Introduced as a professional letter-writer in the spin-off "encyclopedia" *The Discworld Companion* (1994), de Worde is standing in just the right or wrong place when the next phase of industrial revolution arrives: the invention by dwarf craftsmen of movable-type printing. The resulting journal, *The Ankh-Morpork Times* ("The Truth Shall Make Ye Fret"), mixes ghastly small-town journalism, fondly recalled by Pratchett from his own newspaper days, with blundering investigation that annoys the Watch, attracts serious death threats and sabotage attempts, and finally solves the mystery with inside information from the anonymous source "Deep Bone"—Gaspode the Wonder Dog from *Moving Pictures*, now working with one of Ankh-Morpork's most dysfunctional street people as a "thinking-brain dog."

Many subseries strands are woven together in *The Last Hero* (2001), a short novel that, like *Eric*, was designed to be illustrated, this time by Paul Kidby. Cohen the Barbarian and the remnants of his Silver Horde plan to revenge themselves on the gods who have allowed them to grow old, by climbing to the gods' mountain home "Dunmanifestin" and setting off a fifty-pound keg of Agatean Thunder Clay, having the approximate effect of a nuclear weapon. This, the Patrician learns, will incidentally end the world. So something must be done. Assisted by the massed wizards, Leonard of Quirm (the Discworld's Leonardo da Vinci, inventor of a submarine in *Jingo* and of all too many terrible weapons such as the rifle of *Men at Arms*) obligingly devises space technology powered by flaming swamp dragons. The suicide crew that sets off on a very strange course *under* the Disc comprises Leonard, Carrot, and Rincewind, plus an unwitting stowaway whose discovery is reported in the memorable message: "Ankh-Morpork, we have an orangutan" (p. 105). It is a splendidly silly romp, well and copiously illustrated, and ultimately touching.

A slightly different Discworld venture is *The Amazing Maurice and His Educated Rodents* (2001), written for children and starring talking animals who are in no way cute. Like Gaspode, Maurice the cat and his troupe of rats have enhanced intelligence thanks to magically contaminated waste from the Unseen University rubbish dump. They make their living by Maurice's Pied Piper scam: the rats infest a town ("One rat, popping up here and there, squeaking loudly, taking a bath in the fresh cream and widdling in the flour, could be a plague all by himself" [p. 31]), and the team's boy associate gets a fee for piping them away. But to Maurice's frustration the rats are developing ethical scruples about widdling in the flour, while the latest town on their tour conceals horrors generated by an altogether nastier adult racket run by rat-catchers; the story takes on grisly convolutions.

SPIN-OFFS AND COLLABORATIONS

The phenomenal success of Discworld has led to a huge amount of spin-off material in all imaginable media. The nonfiction section of the bibliography is confined to printed material by or cowritten by Pratchett himself. Of particular interest are *The Science of Discworld* (1999) and its sequel, written with Ian Stewart and Jack Cohen. In both, Pratchett contributes a Discworld novella in which Ridcully's wizards study the unthinkable "Roundworld," a world without magic—our own. These fictional chapters alternate with nonfiction commentary by Stewart and Cohen, experienced popularizers of science, who expand on the many emerging discussion points. This is possible because Discworld operates by a skewed logic that jests with or parodies scientific method, rather than ignoring it as in so many other fantasylands.

Outside Discworld there is one collaborative novel of some note, *Good Omens* (1990), written with Neil Gaiman. This reworks the legend of the coming of the Antichrist with particular reference to the movie sequence that began with *The Omen* (1976). A babies-exchanged-at-birth twist results in the fateful child being brought up as, essentially, the irrepressible brat from Richmal Crompton's famous William Brown children's stories—indeed the reluctantly abandoned working title was *William the Antichrist*. (Gaspode the Wonder Dog's perpetual grumbling self-justification also owes something to William.) In the end, all the forces of Heaven and Hell cannot quite refute the dreadful reasonableness of boyish logic.

Non-Discworld comedies for younger readers comprise the Bromeliad trilogy and the open-ended Johnny Maxwell sequence. The former, though centering on a race of four-inch "nomes" who surreptitiously share our world (similar to, but much larger than, the microscopic Carpet People), is actually science fiction about visiting aliens. The latter inflicts various improbable adventures on the ordinary English boy Johnny Maxwell, moving into supernatural territory with the second book, *Johnny and the Dead* (1993). Here development plans for a "disused" cemetery become important to Johnny when he discovers that he can talk to the ghostly inhabitants and hear their objections to the scheme, precipitating him into comic tangles of town politics.

Pratchett is an extremely hardworking author, indeed a confessed workaholic who embarks on new projects within hours of completing old ones. His skillfully deployed comic techniques have evolved to rely mostly on the solid humor of character and situation, decorated with verbal sleights, real-world allusions ("Vetinari" mocks the Medici of Renaissance Italy), puns (a purveyor of inferior sausages in *The Truth* "can't make both ends meat" [p. 13]), old saws with new twists (someone turns the tables on a foe in *Hogfather*: "The worm is on the other boot now" [p. 129]), and his trademark footnotes, which no genre author but Jack Vance has used to such ironic and outrageous effect.

Few awards go to writers of humorous fantasy, but Pratchett won the 1990 British Science Fiction Association Award for *Pyramids*, was named Book Club Associates Fantasy and Science Fiction Author of the Year in 1994, received the state honor the Order of the British Empire for services to literature in 1998, and in 2001 was given a special British Book Award ("Nibbie") for contributions to bookselling. Of the last, he observed: "It's an industry award and an award for causing them to sell skiploads of books does have a certain four-square honesty about it" (*Ansible*, March 2001, p. 164).

Terry Pratchett's deserved popularity continues. Further Discworld novels are in the pipeline.

Selected Bibliography

WORKS OF TERRY PRATCHETT

NOVELS AND SHORT STORIES

The Carpet People. Gerrards Cross, England: Colin Smythe, 1971. Revised edition, London: Doubleday, 1992. (For children.)

TERRY PRATCHETT

The Dark Side of the Sun. Gerrards Cross, England: Colin Smythe, 1976; New York: St. Martin's, 1976.

Strata. Gerrards Cross, England: Colin Smythe, 1981; New York: St. Martin's, 1981.

DISCWORLD SERIES

The Colour of Magic. Gerrards Cross, England: Colin Smythe, 1983; New York: St. Martin's, 1983.

The Light Fantastic. Gerrards Cross, England: Colin Smythe, 1986; New York: Signet, 1988.

Equal Rites. London: Gollancz, 1987; New York: Signet, 1988.

Mort. London: Gollancz, 1987; New York: Signet, 1989.

Sourcery. London: Gollancz, 1988; New York: Signet, 1989.

Wyrd Sisters. London: Gollancz, 1988; New York: Roc, 1990.

Pyramids (The Book of Going Forth). London: Gollancz, 1989; New York: Roc, 1990.

Guards! Guards! London: Gollancz, 1989; Garden City, N.Y.: Science Fiction Book Club, 1991.

Eric, with Josh Kirby (illustrator). London: Gollancz, 1990. Reissued without illustrations, London: Gollancz, 1991; New York: Roc, 1995.

Moving Pictures. London: Gollancz, 1990; New York: Roc, 1992.

Reaper Man. London: Gollancz, 1991; New York: Roc, 1992.

Witches Abroad. London: Gollancz, 1991; New York: Roc, 1993.

Small Gods. London: Gollancz, 1992; New York: HarperCollins, 1994.

Lords and Ladies. London: Gollancz, 1992; New York: HarperPrism, 1995.

Men at Arms. London: Gollancz, 1993; New York: HarperPrism, 1996.

Soul Music. London: Gollancz, 1994; New York: HarperPrism, 1995.

Interesting Times. London: Gollancz, 1994; New York: HarperPrism, 1997.

Maskerade. London: Gollancz, 1995; New York: HarperPrism, 1997.

Feet of Clay. London: Gollancz, 1996; New York: HarperPrism, 1996.

Hogfather. London: Gollancz, 1996; New York: HarperPrism, 1998.

Jingo. London: Gollancz, 1997; New York: HarperPrism, 1998.

The Last Continent. London: Doubleday, 1998; New York: HarperPrism, 1999.

The Sea and Little Fishes. London: HarperCollins, 1998. (Novelette as half of promotional chapbook for the anthology *Legends*, edited by Robert Silverberg.)

Carpe Jugulum. London: Doubleday, 1998; New York: HarperPrism, 1999.

The Fifth Elephant. London: Doubleday, 1999; New York: HarperCollins, 1999.

The Truth. London: Doubleday, 2000; New York: HarperCollins, 2000.

Thief of Time. London: Doubleday, 2001; New York: HarperCollins, 2001.

The Last Hero, with Paul Kidby (illustrator). London: Doubleday, 2001; New York: HarperCollins, 2001. (Novella.)

The Amazing Maurice and His Educated Rodents. London: Doubleday, 2001; New York: HarperCollins, 2001. (For children.)

Night Watch. London: Doubleday, 2002; New York: HarperCollins, 2002.

SUPERNATURAL FICTION WRITERS

BROMELIAD TRILOGY

Truckers. London, Doubleday, 1989; New York: Delacorte, 1990. (For children.)

Diggers. London, Doubleday, 1990; New York: Delacorte, 1990. (For children.)

Wings. London, Doubleday, 1990; New York: Delacorte, 1991. (For children.)

The Bromeliad. Garden City, N.Y.: Science Fiction Book Club, 1998. (Omnibus of above three novels.)

Good Omens: The Nice and Accurate Prophecies of Agnes Nutter, Witch, with Neil Gaiman. London: Gollancz, 1990; New York: Workman, 1990.

JOHNNY MAXWELL SERIES

Only You Can Save Mankind. London: Doubleday, 1992. (For young adults.)

Johnny and the Dead. London: Doubleday, 1993. (For young adults.)

Johnny and the Bomb. London: Doubleday, 1996. (For young adults.)

NONFICTION

The Unadulterated Cat, with Gray Jolliffe (illustrator). London: Gollancz, 1989.

DISCWORLD SERIES SPIN-OFFS

The Streets of Ankh-Morpork: Being a Concise and Possibly Even Accurate Mapp of the Great City of the Discworld, with Stephen Briggs and Stephen Player (illustrator). London: Corgi, 1993. (Map and chapbook.)

The Discworld Companion: The Definitive Guide to Terry Pratchett's Discworld, with Stephen Briggs. London: Gollancz, 1994. Revised and expanded edition, London: Gollancz, 1997.

The Discworld Mapp: Being the Onlie True & Mostlie Accurate Mappe of the Fantastyk & Magical Dyscworlde, with Stephen Briggs and Stephen Player (illustrator). London: Corgi, 1995. (Map and chapbook.)

The Pratchett Portfolio, with Paul Kidby (illustrator). London: Gollancz, 1996. (Art book.)

Unseen University Diary 1998, with Stephen Briggs. London: Gollancz, 1997.

Ankh-Morpork City Watch Diary 1999, with Stephen Briggs. London: Gollancz, 1998.

A Tourist Guide to Lancre: A Discworld Mapp, with Stephen Briggs and Paul Kidby (illustrator). London: Corgi, 1998. (Map and chapbook.)

Assassins' Guild Yearbook and Diary 2000, with Stephen Briggs. London: Gollancz, 1999.

Death's Domain: A Discworld Mapp, with Paul Kidby (illustrator). London: Corgi, 1999. (Map and chapbook.)

Fools' Guild Yearbook and Diary 2000, with Stephen Briggs. London: Gollancz, 1999.

Nanny Ogg's Cookbook, with Stephen Briggs. London: Corgi, 1999.

The Science of Discworld, with Ian Stewart and Jack Cohen. London: Ebury Press, 1999. (Discworld novella alternating with chapters of popular science exposition by Stewart and Cohen.)

Thieves' Guild Yearbook and Diary 2002, with Stephen Briggs. London: Gollancz, 2001.

The Science of Discworld II: The Globe, with Ian Stewart and Jack Cohen. London: Ebury Press, 2002. (Format is the same as that of *The Science of Discworld.*)

Discworld (Reformed) Vampyres' Yearbook and Diary 2003, with Stephen Briggs. London: Gollancz, 2002.

CRITICAL AND BIOGRAPHICAL STUDIES

Butler, Andrew M. *The Pocket Essential Terry Pratchett*. Harpenden, England: Pocket Essentials, 2001.

Butler, Andrew M., Edward James, and Farah Mendlesohn, eds. *Terry Pratchett: Guilty of Literature*. Reading, England: Science Fiction Foundation, 2000.

(Critical essays.)

Langford, David. "Equal Rites." *Foundation*, 40:99–101 (Summer 1987).

———. "Terry Pratchett." In *St. James Guide to Fantasy Writers*. Edited by David Pringle. Detroit: St. James Press, 1996. Pp. 486-488.

———. "Terry Pratchett." In *The Encyclopedia of Fantasy*. Edited by John Clute and John Grant. London: Orbit, 1997; New York: St. Martin's, 1997. Pp. 783–785.

———. "Who's Who: Terry Pratchett" and "Fantasy Worlds: Discworld." In *The Ultimate Encyclopedia of Fantasy*. Edited by David Pringle. London: Carlton, 1998. Pp. 165–166 and 238–240.

———. "Chapter One: Discworld Delights" and "Chapter Six: Discworld Revisited." In *A Cosmic Cornucopia*, with Josh Kirby (artist). London: Paper Tiger, 1999. Pp. 12–27 and 83–103.

Kathryn Ptacek
1952–

RICHARD BLEILER

KATHRYN PTACEK HAS been a professional writer since 1979, during which time she has published nearly twenty novels, several of which have won literary awards. That she is not better known as a writer of fantasy and horror is that the majority her publications have been historical romances, written under such pseudonyms as Kathryn Atwood, Kathleen Maxwell, and Anne Mayfield, and her lengthiest effort to date—a fantasy trilogy set in a China that never was, The Land of Ten Thousand Willows—appeared as paperback originals under the pseudonym of Kathryn Grant and have not been reprinted. Nevertheless, her genre work as a whole—the fantasy trilogy and numerous novels blending suspense and horror—though sometimes uneven, shows her to be a consistently talented and able writer. The two horror anthologies she has edited—*Women of Darkness* (1988) and *Women of Darkness II* (1990)—have been influential in showcasing the works of such influential and capable women writers as Lisa Tuttle, Lucy Taylor, Kit Reed, Poppi Z. Brite, and Tanith Lee.

BACKGROUND

Kathryn Anne Ptacek was born in Omaha, Nebraska, on September 12, 1952, the only child of Les and Rose Ptacek. She matriculated the University of New Mexico, earning a B.A. in journalism with a minor in history in 1974. Among her instructors were the young-adult novelist Lois Duncan and noted mystery novelist Tony Hillerman. Following her graduation, she held a variety of positions, including working as telephone solicitor for the New Mexico Association of Retarded Citizens and as a technical writer for the University of New Mexico's Computing Center, but she became a professional writer following the 1979 sale of her first novel, *Satan's Angel* (1981), a historical romance. Since 1982 she has been married to the professional writer Charles L. Grant, also profiled in these volumes, although they have yet to collaborate. "We had planned on it, but our interests didn't mesh. He wanted to do an American historical; I wanted to do one set elsewhere. Plus, our styles are just incredibly different," states Ptacek (private communication).

NOVELS

Gila! (1981, as by Les Simons), Ptacek's first suspense novel, is quasi–science fiction, an enthusiastic homage to such 1950s environmental horror movies as *Them!* (1954). *Gila!*

describes the advent of giant gila monsters in the American Southwest. The gila monsters are ill-tempered and quite mobile; unless they are stopped, they will reach Albuquerque and cause untold deaths and destruction. Working first to discover the cause of some unexplained deaths, and then to see that the proper weapons are used on the gila monsters, is attractive and plucky herpetologist Dr. Kate Dwyer, assisted by her lover, full-blooded Apache Dr. Chato Del-Klinne. The novel is a cheerful romp, with the gila monsters eating idiotic politicians, offensive journalists, and fanatical environmentalists alike, but its strong environmental concerns—as voiced through Dr. Dwyer, who explains that the desert is a complex ecosystem in its own right—provide it with a serious subtext.

Ptacek's next horror novel, *Shadoweyes* (1984), is also set in the American Southwest and reuses the character of Chato Del-Klinne, but it is an overtly supernatural horror work. Something is destroying the people of Albuquerque, and Del-Klinne and Laura Rainey, an energetic newspaper reporter, know that the killer is not a bear run amok, a knowledge also shared by a variety of corrupt local politicians. The golden-eyed monsters are occasionally referred to as witches, but they are evileyes, the shadoweyes of the title, called into existence in part because of the removal and misuse of a sacred Native American fetish. Nevertheless, as the novel establishes, the genuine monsters are human and of human origin and include those who would defile sacred traditions for ready money as well as entrenched local politicians who will do almost anything to maintain their power. A vicious and casually racist social system is limned with some care, and although Del-Klinne is ultimately successful in repelling the shadoweyes, his efforts have merely removed a supernatural menace known and accepted by very few. He will return to an ungrateful and unkind world that remains largely unaltered.

Blood Autumn (1985) abandons the American southwest to set its events in India and England during the 1850s and Savannah, Georgia, during the 1880s. The story itself hinges on a lamia, the beautiful and deadly August, whose sexually voracious charms no man can resist. The historical descriptions are well researched and presented—Ptacek's acknowledgments thank, among others, the Georgia Historical Society—but although the conclusion is appropriately open-ended, the novel itself fails to engage or convince that its menace is genuine.

With *Kachina* (1986), Ptacek returns to the American southwest, though it is the southwest of 1880. The story itself initially focuses on a couple—young Elizabeth Stephenson, married to the much older and domineering anthropologist William—as they explore the New Mexico territories, with William hoping to study an isolated tribe, the Konichine. Though she has permitted William to boss her in "civilization," in the southwest isolation Elizabeth reveals herself to be intelligent, resourceful, and her husband's equal (if not superior) in many areas, including anthropology, for the Konichine have a history of matriarchal rule and are more willing to talk with her than with William. More: following a series of dreams and discoveries, Elizabeth begins to believe she is a primitive goddess, the Kachina Outcast Woman. She takes a local lover, kills her husband, and even leads Indian raids against white incursions. She is ultimately brought down by Natchez Curry, a bounty hunter sent to stop her by Governor Lew Wallace.

Kachina is occasionally uneven as a narrative, but it is nevertheless a novel of some complexities. The scenes and descriptions of southwestern life are very well presented, and one regrets that Ptacek has not continued to make use of this region, for her descriptions of it are convincing. Also convincing are Elizabeth Stephenson's character, and the events surrounding her are appropriately ambiguous. She may be supernaturally possessed, commanding ghost forces. Or she may be, as Curry avers, "an impressionable white woman who felt sorry for the Indians and who has gone mad," her ghost forces no more than "some other Indians . . .

making those raids" (p. 299). Finally, regardless of whether one interprets the work rationally or as a work of fantasy, the novel's subtext shows the destruction of traditional matriarchal ways by corrosive American "values."

In Silence Sealed (1988) reuses the lamia of *Blood Autumn* but is effectively a prequel, its events occurring a generation earlier in the Greece of 1824. In Missolonghi, Winston Early, a young Englishman on his grand tour, encounters the dying George Gordon, Lord Byron, who tells him, via extended flashbacks, of the events behind the early deaths of John Keats and Percy Bysshe Shelley: they were seduced and destroyed by the Kristonosos sisters, August and Athina. Byron dies of injuries caused by the sisters, and Early returns to England, where he discovers to his horror that Athina Kristonosos has preceded him. Worse yet, his father Richard has married her, and she has been joined by her sister.

Ptacek has stated that *In Silence Sealed* is her favorite novel, and it is an enjoyable blending of her interests in history, literature, romance, and supernatural horror. On the debit side, there are numerous scenes of explicit sexuality, and although it would be unreasonable to expect a contemporary novel utilizing lamias to eschew sexuality, at the same time these scenes slow the action and, by very virtue of their physicality, reduce the element of menace that the supernatural unknown brings with it.

The three novels that comprise the Land of Ten Thousand Willows series—*The Phoenix Bells* (1987), *The Black Jade Road* (1989), and *The Willow Garden* (1989)—are an odd and often amusing mishmash of historical romance and supernatural adventure set in an alternate world, one in which England has established commercial ties with China and in which the magics of all cultures coexist, as do such creatures as benign dragons, malevolent serpentine beings, and the all-pervasive Darkness. Though dates are essentially meaningless in alternate worlds, the stories themselves are dated from 1662 to 1664, and the series follows the life of the young Emperor Ty-Sun, who must find a wife within three years of his father's death or forfeit the throne. Upon leaving his palace confines and lands, he has numerous adventures, gradually loses most of his company, and ultimately ends up in England, where at Hotspur, the site of the English monarchy, he meets and falls in love with Blessing Dunncaster, a beautiful young Puritan witch whose songs have magical potency. Nevertheless, the path to their return to the Land of Ten Thousand Willows and eventual union is not smooth. Blessing initially blames Ty-Sun for the death of her brother, after which she is kidnapped by the pursuing forces of Darkness, and Ty-Sun is forced to enter the astral plane and rescue her. During the course of their journey almost all of their company perishes—though some perish more fully than others—and their path takes them through hell, after which they discover that Ty-Sun's land has been ravaged and remains under constant attack from the Darkness. Ty-Sun must defend the land, though against the Darkness there is no consistent defense, and the series concludes on a surprising note: after Ty-Sun defeats the malign Black Madonna, he and Blessing unite, but their future is in the afterlife, and their departure strips China of its magic.

The character of Chato Del-Klinne reappears as the protagonist of *Ghost Dance* (1990). Although he has been invited to assume academic positions, he is contentedly working in a Las Vegas, Nevada nursery and courting the attractive Anglo woman Sunny, when one of his academic friends is found brutally murdered. Events escalate, and Del-Klinne discovers that the historic Ghost Dance religion—hitherto believed destroyed at the Battle of Wounded Knee in 1890—has resurfaced and is being practiced by a variety of Indians. Del-Klinne becomes involved as a Ghost Dancer and notices an odd correlation between the dances and such environmental phenomena as earthquakes and tornadoes. He learns too that while the Indian

Ghost Dancers of 1890 believed that their magical shirts would protect them from the bullets of the white army, the Ghost Dance practitioners of the 1990s have a more ambitious goal: the radioactive elimination of all whites from the North American continent.

It would not be unreasonable to say that although *Ghost Dance* is quite readable, it is not entirely successful as a novel. One of the more capably drawn characters is assassinated, unnecessarily, early in the volume, and questions concerning the power of belief and the validity of the Ghost Shirts are shunted aside, never directly addressed. Although there is the sense that the world is in peril from the forces awakened by the new religion, there is also never any sense that Del-Klinne will fail in his attempt at ending the menace and re-establishing the status quo.

The Hunted (1993) contains no overt supernaturalism, though the young protagonist, Jessie Morrison, is the reincarnation of a victim of the concentration camps, with her "spells" (fugues) permitting her to re-experience the Nazi horrors. She discovers that the local pediatrician Emerson Thorne is a far from benign figure: at Auschwitz, he was one of the camp doctors who experimented on the prisoners. The novel's subject matter awakens strong feelings in readers: the reviewer for *Publisher's Weekly* excoriated the book for its poor plotting and predictable resolution, though it has also been praised by the scholar Don D'Ammassa as having "minimal horror content, but still notable for its strong characterizations and finely crafted suspense."

SHORT FICTION

Much of Ptacek's short fiction has been anthologized, but there has yet to be published a collection of her short stories, though these are often her most original work, relying on minimal supernaturalism to present internal states. "Each Night, Every Year," "Mi Casa," and "Snow" present adults attempting to deal with elderly and dying parents, while in "The Grotto," dying Ceil Ucello Wallace visits Tuscany and learns of a hidden grotto, sacred to a goddess. "The Visit" and "Skinned Angels" make use of traditional Judeo-Christian angels, though both end on horrific notes. Several of the stories make use of a woman protagonist who has sacrificed something (or everything): in "Snow," Jean has sacrificed her life for her mother, as has Virginia of "Healing Touch," though the self-sacrificing mother of "Little Contrasts" turns the tables on her abusers. In "Hair," and "Driven," women attempt to take control over their lives, though "Three, Four, Shut the Door" inverts the situation and shows to great effect a woman who has lost control and become obsessive-compulsive.

As of this writing Kathryn Ptacek has been concentrating her genre efforts on short fiction and has not written an overtly supernatural novel in nearly a decade; indeed, her fictional output seems to have dramatically diminished, though she prepares a market report for *Hellnotes*, edits the monthly newsletter of the Horror Writers Association, and regularly writes and distributes a market newsletter, *The Gila Queen's Guide to Markets*. Her return to fiction is anticipated with some eagerness.

Selected Bibliography

WORKS OF KATHRYN PTACEK

NOVELS

Gila! As by Les Simons. New York: Signet, 1981.

KATHRYN PTACEK

Shadoweyes. New York: Tor, 1984.

Blood Autumn. New York: Tor, 1985.

Kachina. New York: Tor, 1986.

The Phoenix Bells. As by Kathryn Grant. New York: Berkley, 1987.

In Silence Sealed. New York: Tor, 1988.

The Black Jade Road. As by Kathryn Grant. New York: Berkley, 1989.

The Willow Garden. As by Kathryn Grant. New York: Berkley, 1989.

Ghost Dance. New York: Tor, 1990.

The Hunted. New York: Walker, 1993.

SHORT STORIES

"Driven." In *Dark Love*. Edited by Nancy A. Collins and Edward E. Cramer. New York: Penguin/Roc, 1995.

"Each Night, Each Year." In *Post Mortem: New Tales of Ghostly Horror*. Edited by Paul F. Olson and David B. Silva. New York: St. Martin's Press, 1989.

"The Grotto." In *Grotesques: A Bestiary*. New York: Graven Images/Berkley, 2000.

"Hair." In *Phobias*. Edited by Wendy Webb, Richard Gilliam, Edward E. Kramer, and Martin H. Greenberg. New York: Pocket Books, 1994.

"Healing Touch." In *Eldritch Tales*, 27. 9: 21–29 (Summer 1992).

"The Lake." In *NECon 2000 Commemorative Volume*. Bristol, R.I.: NECon, 2000.

"Little Contrasts." In *White of the Moon*. Edited by Stephen Jones. Nottingham, U.K.: Pumpkin Books, 1999.

"Mi Casa." In *Gothic Ghosts*. Edited by Wendy Webb and Charles Grant. New York: Tor, 1997.

"Skinned Angels." In *Dark Terrors 3*. Edited by Stephen Jones and David Sutton. London: Gollancz, 1997.

"Snow." In *The Definitive Best of The Horror Show*. Edited by David B. Silva. Baltimore: Cemetery Dance, 1992.

"Three Four, Shut the Door." In *More Phobias*. Edited by Wendy Webb, Richard Gilliam, Edward E. Kramer, and Martin H. Greenberg. New York: Pocket Books, 1995.

"The Visit." In *Heaven Sent*. Edited by Peter Crowther and Martin H. Greenberg. New York: DAW, 1995.

AS EDITOR

Women of Darkness. New York: Tor, 1988.

Women of Darkness II. New York: Tor, 1990.

SECONDARY

D'Ammassa, Don. "Kathryn Ptacek." *St. James Guide to Horror, Ghost & Gothic Writers*. Edited by David Pringle. Detroit: St. James, 1998.

Philip Pullman
1946–

ANDREW BUTLER

PHILIP PULLMAN HAS come to prominence in a new golden age of British fantasy or supernatural writers for children and, in terms of sales, is perhaps the closest rival to J. K. Rowling, author of the popular Harry Potter series. On top of winning the Carnegie, Smarties, and Whitbread Awards for children's fiction, Pullman in 2002 won the overall Whitbread Prize, the first time the children's winner has done so. Popular and critical success, due largely to the His Dark Materials trilogy, is balanced by criticism from some Christian groups, which have objected to his theological explorations. However, the trilogy is just one part of a publishing career dating back into the 1970s.

***

Philip Nicholas Pullman was born to Alfred Outram Pullman, an airman, and Audrey Pullman in Norwich, England, on October 19, 1946. With his father and stepfather Pullman spent time in various countries, including Australia, where he read Norman Lindsay's *The Magic Pudding* (1918) and discovered Batman and Superman comics, and Rhodesia (now Zimbabwe). He returned to the United Kingdom and lived in Wales from the age of eleven. At school he fell under the influence of his English teacher, Enid Jones, and read English at Exeter College, Oxford, graduating in 1968. After a series of jobs, he taught in a number of middle schools in Oxfordshire. In 1970 he married a hypnotherapist, Judith Speller. After 1988 he taught, part-time, at Westminster College, Oxford, specializing in Victorian fiction, fairy tales, and folktales. He became a full-time writer in 1996, but still gives occasional lectures and speeches. He has also been a reviewer of children's fiction.

Pullman's first book, *The Haunted Shore* (1972), was written for adults (it has since been suppressed by the author), but his later books and stories have been marketed to younger readers. In interviews he has insisted that he does not just write for children, but for whatever audience he can attract. In a sense this is true of all children's fiction, in that agents, editors, librarians, teachers, and parents all intervene between the author and the child reader. Pullman's works have been targeted by their publishers at younger children aged four to eight, children aged eight to twelve, and Young Adult or Teenage readers, but it is perhaps more profitable to divide most of the books into the categories of

809

the "penny dreadful," the fairy tale, or as part of the His Dark Materials trilogy.

***

The "penny dreadful" is a literary genre that began as an offshoot of the Gothic horror novel in the nineteenth century, and combined complex, melodramatic plots with supernatural elements. Books of this type were designed to shock and thrill and sold many copies at a penny each. Pullman's modern-day equivalents are perhaps more ambiguous in their use of the supernatural, although the first of them, *Count Karlstein* (1982), certainly invokes demons.

The protagonist of this tale, Heinrich Müller, has made a bargain with the Demon Huntsman to become Count Karlstein and gain an estate. In order to maintain his wealth he must make a human sacrifice a decade later. He decides that he will sacrifice his two orphaned nieces, Lucy and Charlotte, but a maid overhears his plan and helps them to safety. The plot is made more complex by the appearance of their former teacher and an escaped impostor and by the revelation of the identity of the true Count Karlstein. The two nieces spend much of their time reading penny dreadfuls, and compare their various experiences to the titles they have read. At the close of the 1991 version of the novel, Charlotte continues reading, whereas Lucy begins writing the narrative of *Count Karlstein*, and in a corner three children listen to another tale being told. Pullman achieves an extratextual dimension by incorporating brief comic strips into the narrative, drawn by Patrice Aggs. This device allows the author to show what the characters look like and contains some of their dialogue; it also allows inanimate objects such as books, a clock, various animal heads, and two phantoms to comment upon the action.

Pullman had developed the illustrated-narrative form in *Spring-Heeled Jack* (1989), with prose and cartoons taking up roughly the same amount of the book; the illustrations for this volume are provided by David Mostyn. In *Spring-Heeled Jack*, Rose, Lily, and Ned are headed for a ship bound for America, having escaped from an orphanage. They are ambushed by Mack the Knife, who wants a locket they are carrying. He kidnaps Ned, and Rose and Lily must rescue him. They are aided in their attempt by an Able-Seaman, Jim, and the eponymous Jack. Jack was a legendary figure whose terrorized England throughout the mid- and late 1800s, much like the more familiar Jack the Ripper. In 1837, the Spring-Heeled Jack of legend attacked a woman named Polly Adams in southwest London and, over the next forty or more years, was credited with attacks on a number of other people as well. In the early penny dreadfuls, the figure became a crime-fighting avenger.

In Pullman's tale Jack becomes a kind of Batman, inspired by the comics the author had read as a child. The comic strips economically show action and dialog, as well as a mouse and a cat's commentary on the narrative. Further intertextuality comes in the form of epigrams to each chapter, which are quotations from sources as diverse as Dumas's *The Three Musketeers* (which Pullman had adapted for the stage) and Hergé's *Adventures of Tintin*. In a moment of self-referentiality, one chapter epigram quotes Pullman's *Spring-Heeled Jack*.

Pullman's use of the penny dreadful narrative finds its most sustained form in the Sally Lockhart books, beginning with *The Ruby in the Smoke* (1985), which was originally written as a school play. Set in the nineteenth century, the book's protagonist is sixteen-year-old Sally, whose father has drowned in the South China Sea, leaving her orphaned and caught up in a conspiracy to obtain a valuable ruby. Even though several people who have helped her are murdered by the henchmen of an evil Chinaman, Ah Ling, she is able to enlist the aid of a young photographer, Frederick Garland, and a lawyer's clerk, Jim Taylor, to establish the truth about the death of her father and the nature of the ruby. In the follow-up novel, *The Shadow in the Plate* (1986), Frederick is employed to photograph a ghost at a séance and Sally, now twenty-two and an investment advisor, is determined to get to the bottom of a scam which has cost one of her clients her life savings. In a third installment in the series, *The Tiger in the Well* (1990), Sally and her daughter by the her late lover (Frederick) are forced to go on the run when Sally is sued for divorce by a man she has never heard of and had never married. She discovers that the plot is an attempt at revenge by an old adversary, who is rumored to have a demon for a servant.

Sally manages to surround herself with (mainly male) helpers in the first two books, but she is still strong, level-headed, intelligent and resourceful, and perhaps a precursor to Lyra from Pullman's His Dark Materials trilogy. Events isolate Sally in the third book, but she finds a multitude of female help, and realizes the precarious position of women in the nineteenth century. At the same time she gets an education in the nature of capitalism, as she meets workers in London's East End who have been employed in ventures in which Sally and her clients had invested. The novel endorses a socialist message, and Sally reaches political maturity in this volume.

The fourth book in the series, *The Tin Princess* (1994), somewhat sidelines Sally and shifts the attention to Jim Taylor and Adelaide, a character last seen in *The Ruby in the Smoke*. Adelaide is to marry Prince Rudolf of Eschtenburg, the heir to the throne of the Ruritanian kingdom of Razkavia. Jim attempts to act as a bodyguard to the heir, and finds himself drawn into a conspiracy for control of the throne. This is the most disappointing of the four books, in part because of the absence of Sally from much of the narrative, and in part because the author retreats from the socialist, potentially republican, ending of the third novel. The novels' generic status is problematic, since many of the overt fantasy and supernatural elements turn out to have a materialist, misperceived basis. The construction of a Victorian London which in some ways pastiches Charles Dickens and, especially, Wilkie Collins, perhaps offers us an alternate history.

***

In parallel with these books, Pullman has also been working on the retelling of fairy tales or folktales, a subject that he has taught at Oxford University. *The Wonderful Story of Aladdin and the Enchanted Lamp* (1993) is a lavishly illustrated but straightforward retelling of one of the *Arabian Nights* tales. *Puss in Boots* (2000) is also illustrated in color, and contains speech balloons so that some of the action is conveyed in comic-book style. On the death of his miller father, Jacques is left only a cat, but the cat, who can speak, aids him in killing an ogre and marrying the king's daughter.

In *The Firework-Maker's Daughter* (1995) Pullman tells a coming-of-age story about a girl in a Chinese context. The heroine wishes to be a maker of fireworks, and rushes off to pass an endurance test with a goddess without taking the necessary offerings. She discovers that the gifts she needs are actually within herself rather than to be found in physical objects. This appears to be an original tale written by Pullman; it draws upon the structure of many tales, but also contains elements of satire about advertising and the nature of belief.

Clockwork, or All Wound Up (1996) is a complex tale which draws attention to its own fictiveness, partly by putting Fritz, a story-teller, at the center of the narrative and commenting on his story-telling abilities, but also by including boxed commentaries in which the implied author criticizes the characters' actions. Fritz tells a tale about the death of Prince Otto, who turns out to have a clockwork heart. The tale is interrupted by the appearance of Dr Kalmenius, one of the characters from the story, who offers to help Karl, an apprentice clock-maker, pass his training by providing a clockwork knight. The narrative loosely alludes to *Pinocchio* and the Tin Woodman in *The Wizard of Oz*, for the power of love is able to transform a clockwork boy into a real one. In this book Pullman shows again that he is brave enough to kill major characters, and explores the inevitability of certain outcomes once events have been set up in a particular way. The metaphor of clockwork here suggests a sense of predestination of events, as, despite the best will of the implied author, characters are punished for their actions or their potential actions. Pullman's notion of evil, also explored in *Tiger* and the His Dark Materials Trilogy, is that it is deeds that are evil rather than people; however this distinction is hard to maintain in *Clockwork* since the authorial asides provide commentary on the killed person's character: "I'd save the wretch if I could, but the story is wound up, and it must all come out. And I'm afraid Karl deserved a bad end. He was lazy and bad-tempered, but worse than that, he had a wicked heart."

In *Mossycoat* (1998), effectively a short story, Pullman turns to a northern English folktale and translates it into modern English. The narrative is a variation on *Cinderella*; here the heroine, Mossycoat, is able to escape an unsuitable marriage thanks to the wiles of her mother, and gains titular clothes in the process. Mossycoat finds work as a cook in a royal castle but attends a ball wearing the mossycoat as a disguise. She anonymously wins the heart of the prince but is, inevitably, identified by her lost slipper. Aside from a few wishes, the tale lacks the magical transformation of the more familiar, traditional version of the story, a narrative to which Pullman returned in the following year, in *I Was a Rat!* (1999).

The rat in question, named Roger, is one of the creatures who had been transformed by the Fairy Godmother into a page boy, so that Cinderella could go to the ball, and who for some reason did not revert to type on the stroke of midnight. Roger is at first adopted by a kindly, childless couple, but his inability to deal with the human world leads him to fall into the hands of the manager of a freak show, to be used as a burglar, and finally to be treated as a monster by the tabloid press. The book is hard to locate in time and space: its subject matter places it in the fairy-tale seventeenth or nineteenth century, but its satire on child psychiatry, social services bureaucracy, and the hypocrisy of newspapers suggests a much more recent date.

***

Pullman draws on much more canonical texts in his magnum opus, the His Dark Materials trilogy. While his inspirational sources are not immediately apparent in the first volume, *Northern Lights* (1995), they are clearly John Milton's *Paradise Lost* and William Blake's *Songs of Innocence and Experience* and *The Marriage of Heaven and Hell*. Lord Asriel is planning to refight the War in Heaven as described by Milton, and to overthrow the Authority who has set himself up as God. Asriel wants to replace the Kingdom of Heaven with the Republic of Heaven. Because this is a different world from our own, it is not clear who won the original war and Pullman, being a Blakean, believes that Milton's Satan is the Messiah. Asriel's morals and actions are therefore ambiguous.

In his preparations for the battle Asriel is investigating the phenomenon of Dust, and has discovered a leakage between universes near the North Pole. His expeditions lead the Master of Jordan College, Oxford, to plot to kill him, but the plot is discovered by Lyra, supposedly Asriel's orphaned niece, but in reality his daughter.

Another element, which Pullman was partly inspired to create by Heinrich von Kleist's writings on puppets, is the daemon. Every human in this universe has one of these creatures, which are part guardian angel, part Jungian archetype, and part imaginary friend. Daemons can shapeshift, taking the form of various animals until their human owner's puberty, when they settle down, Lyra and her daemon, Pantalaimon, head north on a quest to find Asriel and rescue a kidnapped friend. She discovers that there are experiments to separate children from their daemons, killing both in the process. This is being masterminded by Mrs. Coulter, who is revealed to be Lyra's mother.

In the second book, *The Subtle Knife* (1997), the action partly shifts to a universe that seems like our own, where Lyra meets Will, a boy who probably caused someone's death and who is looking for his father. From the narrative of a capable, resourceful female hero, the emphasis shifts to a more traditional, albeit teenaged, male hero. Lyra subjugates her needs to Will's as they travel between universes with the aid of a knife he has acquired. (Early in the first book Lyra had been given a divining device, the Alethiometer, which tells her to trust Will.) In the final volume, *The Amber Spyglass* (2000), Lyra spends much of her time in a coma, guarded by Mrs. Coulter, before she is rescued by Will in time for a final battle and an attempt to assassinate her by the Inquisition.

The first two volumes received critical adulation from adults and children alike, but the third volume has fared less well. Perhaps the extended wait for the appearance of the third volume led readers to feel less satisfied with its much longer narrative, and it is true that the ending disappointed many.

Pullman's work has been criticized from a number of quarters, especially from the religious right. Pullman's critique of religious institutions, in particular the Inquisition, has offended some Christian pressure groups, and his reimagining of the War in Heaven, his Blakean sympathies, his depiction of the death of God (actually an impostor), and his final, atheistic, insistence on the materiality of the universe as opposed to the notion of the afterlife is thought of by some as blasphemous.

On the other hand, some critics, myself included, feel that he has not gone far enough. Having established the finality of death in the first volume, it feels like a sentimental betrayal to be able to visit the dead and say farewell to them after all. The insistence on changing this world rather than aiming for heaven could be read as a rejection of the possibilities of fantasy.

In a number of interviews Pullman has condemned post-Tolkien fantasy for its avoidance of real-life issues. He has faulted C. S. Lewis' Narnia Chronicles for their punishment of sexuality, especially in his treatment of the character of Susan. In contrast he sees, albeit ironically, his own work as "stark realism," although this is perhaps true in the same way that Blake's prophetic volumes interweave political history and what we would see as metaphysics or fantasizing. His Blakean championing of sexuality would be more convincing if he did not separate Lyra and Will after their sexual union, exiling them to separate universes. This plot development is consistent with his treatment of the sexual protagonists in his other works. For instance, he kills off Sally and Adelaide's partners in the Lockhart books, and does something similar in his mainstream novel, *The White Mercedes* (1992).

Other criticisms of Pullman's work focus on his treatment of gender and class issues. For instance, his decision to replace Lyra with Will as central character has upset some readers, and highlights some problems with his female characters. Lyra is portrayed as a new Eve, a betrayer; Mrs. Coulter's actions are almost all evil; and Mary Malone, former nun turned particle physicist, is set up as the serpent-betrayer.

Finally, the sensitivity that Pullman showed to class issues in *Tiger* seems undermined in the way he allocates daemons among the characters of the His Dark Materials trilogy. Servants in these tales are always given dogs for daemons, unlike higher-born characters. Pullman seems to imply that some people are born to be servants and should achieve no higher in position. This seems to suggest a predestination, also elaborated in *Clockwork*, and seems to limit the possibility that a better world could be fought for in the here-and-now.

***

Pullman's inventiveness and ambition is great, and he has produced an impressive body of work to date. It remains to be seen whether he can successfully marry his political message (at the risk of conflating his beliefs with those of Sally and David Goldberg in *Tiger* and those on the final page of *The Amber Spyglass*) with his passion for storytelling. He plans to publish further fairy tales, more novels featuring Sally Lockhart or her friends and relatives, and a companion novel to His Dark Materials Trilogy.

Selected Bibliography

WORKS OF PHILIP PULLMAN

NOVELS AND SHORT STORIES

The Haunted Storm. London: New English Library, 1972.

Galatea: A Novel. London: Gollancz, 1978.

Ancient Civilisations. Illustrated by Gary Long. Exeter: Wheaton, 1981.

Count Karlstein. London: Chatto and Windus, 1982. Rev. ed. Appeared as *Count Karlstein, or the Ride of the Demon Huntsman.* Illustrated by Patrice Aggs. London: Doubleday, 1991.

The Ruby in the Smoke. Oxford: Oxford University Press, 1985. (Sally Lockhart, Book 1.)

"Video nasty," In *Cold Feet*, edited by Jean Richardson. London: Hodder and Stoughton, 1985. (Short story).

The Shadow in the Plate. Oxford: Oxford University Press, 1986. Rev. ed. appeared as *The Shadow in the North.* Harmondsworth: Penguin, 1988. (Sally Lockhart, Book 2.)

How to Be Cool. London: Heinemann, 1987.

Spring-Heeled Jack: A Story of Bravery and Evil. Illustrated by David Mostyn. London: Doubleday, 1989.

The Broken Bridge. London: Macmillan, 1990.

The Tiger in the Well. New York: Knopf, 1990. (Sally Lockhart, Book 3.)

The White Mercedes. London: Macmillan, 1992. Reissued as *The Butterfly Tattoo.* London: Macmillan, 1998.

The Wonderful Story of Aladdin and the Enchanted Lamp. Illustrated by David Wyatt. London: Scholastic, 1993. (Picture book.)

The New Cut Gang: Thunderbolt's Waxwork. Illustrated by Nick Harris. London: Viking, 1994.

"Something to Read," In *Point Horror*, edited by A. Finnis. London: Scholastic, 1994. (Short story.)

The Tin Princess. Harmondsworth: Puffin, 1994. (Sally Lockhart, Book 4.)

The Firework-Maker's Daughter. Illustrated by Nick Harris. London: Doubleday, 1995. U.S. edition illustrated by S. Saelig Gallagher. New York: Arthur A Levine, 1999.

Northern Lights. London: Scholastic, 1995. U.S. edition released as *The Golden Compass*, New York: Knopf, 1996. (His Dark Materials, Book 1)

The New Cut Gang: The Gas-Fitters' Ball. Illustrated by Mark Thomas. London: Viking, 1995.

Clockwork, or All Wound Up. Illustrated by Peter Bailey, London: Doubleday, 1996.

The Subtle Knife. London: Scholastic, 1997. (His Dark Materials, Book 2.)

Mossycoat. Illustrated by Peter Bailey. London: Scholastic, 1998.

I Was a Rat!... or The Scarlet Slippers. Illustrated by Peter Bailey. London: Doubleday U.K., 1999. U.S. edition illustrated by Kevin Hawkes, New York: Knopf, 2000.

The Amber Spyglass. London: Scholastic/David Fickling, 2000. (His Dark Materials, Book 3.)

Puss in Boots. Illustrated by Ian Beck. London: Doubleday, 2000. (Picture book.)

PLAYS AND TELEPLAYS

Sherlock Holmes and the Adventure of the Sumatran Devil. First production: Polka Children's Theatre, Wimbledon, 1984. (Published as *Sherlock Holmes and the Adventure of the Limehouse Horror*, London: Nelson, 1993.)

The Three Musketeers. First production: Polka Children's Theatre, Wimbledon, 1985.

Frankenstein, First production: Polka Children's Theatre, Wimbledon, 1987. Oxford: Oxford University Press, 1991.

How to Be Cool. ITV, broadcast August 1989.

I Was a Rat! BBC1, broadcast December 2001.

OTHER WORKS

Using the Oxford Illustrated Junior Dictionary: A Book of Exercises and Games. Illustrated by Ivan Ripley, Oxford: Oxford University Press, 1995. (New edition illustrated by David Mostyn, Oxford: Oxford University Press, 1999.)

Detective Stories. Illustrated by Nick Hardcastle. London and New York: Kingfisher, 1998. (Edited collection.)

CRITICAL STUDIES AND INTERVIEWS

Achuka Interviews. Philip Pullman. http://www.achuka.co.uk/ppint.htm.

Brown, Tanya. "Philip Pullman: Storming Heaven." *Locus* 45, no 478 (December 2000): 6.

Clute, John. "Phillip (Nicholas) Pullman." *The Encyclopedia of Fantasy.* Edited by John Clute and John Grant. London: Orbit, 1997. P. 791.

Lenz, Millicent. "Philip Pullman." In *Alternative Worlds in Fantasy Fiction.* Edited by Peter Hunt and Millicent Lenz. London and New York: Continuum, 2001. Pp. 122–169.

Roberts, Susan. Interview with Philip Pullman. http://www.fish.co.uk/culture/features/pullman_intereview.html

Anne Rice
1941–

CHRISTOPHER TREAGUS

THOUGH ANNE RICE had already been creating worlds and stories since her childhood, it was not until the tragic death of her young daughter that she would finally pen the creation that would catapult her into fame within both the literary world and that of the gothic subculture, revitalizing a field and a monster that had been dead for at least a generation.

Interview with the Vampire was a turning point for both its creator and its subject. The vampire as a genre had been on its last leg. The stories had become stale and even the monster itself weary and tired, having no more ability to scare or enthrall. Yet just as it was suffering its final death, Anne Rice breathed new life back into the vampire, resurrecting it from its grave as surely as the monster itself had resurrected so many before. All it took was a bit of fresh blood, and a new perspective.

There may have been hints of the seductive, amoral, romantic vampire in all the old tales—after all, much of the modern archetype was based upon John Polidori's "The Vampyre" (1819), whose primary character, Lord Ruthven, was modeled after the poet Lord Byron, a seductive, amoral, and romantic figure in his own right—but no one had explored it as actively or thoroughly as did Rice in 1975 when she wrote *Interview*. The genre would never be the same afterward. Now every other vampire follows her model. Bram Stoker himself has been reduced almost to a mere footnote.

Yet Anne Rice never set out to be the idol of the vampire world. Though she recalls cheerfully times in her youth when she would go see matinee horror films with her sister Alice, and would be scared out of her mind, it was not a genre that she ever set out to redefine. In fact, despite a background that was ideal for the creation of supernatural fiction and fantasy worlds, Anne Rice had never intended to write horror at all, though it would seem to be a destiny she could not deny.

Anne Rice was born in New Orleans on October 4, 1941, and was given the name of Howard Allen Frances O'Brien, an odd moniker designed to honor past family members. It was a most unusual name for a girl, but she was not raised in an ordinary household. Anne's mother, Katherine, had progressive ideas and believed that children should be treated like adults and given the freedom to do and act as they pleased—within reason. If they wanted to run around naked out back, they were allowed. If they didn't feel like going to classes, they were not required to. By the time she began to attend school, Rice acquired the nickname Anne, choosing it for herself in order to fit in better with the other children.

Despite the relative freedom that Anne and her sisters Alice and Tamara enjoyed in their youth, however, they were conversely restricted by the moral code of their Irish Catholic upbringing. The conflict between idealistic freedom and being bound by religious tradition would be a constant theme of Rice's fiction in later years.

Rice was introduced to the worlds of culture and literature at a young age and was raised with a rich story telling tradition. She would listen to tales told her by her mother, father, aunts, uncles, and her older sister Alice. She also played elaborate games with her siblings, (one of whom, Alice Borchart, became a writer herself) in which they would create fantasy worlds and characters. Many children play such games, but what made Rice's world different was that her fantasy characters adapted and grew. They aged, fell in love, and got married. Sometimes they even died. This was the foundation of the kind of detailed universe for which Rice would be so known in later life. Certainly it provided for practice and experience with vast networks of world building and creating dynasties of characters.

But this is not to say that Anne's youth was entirely cheerful. An awkward child, Rice did not fit in well at school. She was always on the outside, looking in. She had few friends, and preferred the company of her imaginary people to that of real children her age. Her mother, an alcoholic who grew more and more ill as time went by, died when Anne was fourteen, an event that marked the end of her childhood. Afterward, Rice began to take over household duties and to help care for her younger sister. It was a dark and lonely time, further coloring the worlds that she would one day create. Without the protective influence of her mother, high school became even more difficult than elementary school. Eventually Anne's father moved the family to Texas and re-married.

Anne fit in even less well in Texas, though she did meet her future husband, the poet Stan Rice at the University there—though at the time, he couldn't have been less interested in her. Anne, however, was confident that one day they would be together.

Eventually Anne left Texas for San Francisco, where she lived for several years before coming in contact with Stan again. After an on again, off again relationship, they were finally married in 1962. Stan was well on his way to becoming an established poet, yet Anne's literary career was still several years from taking off. She had enrolled in political science classes at the University of San Francisco, and though she occasionally wrote short stories, she was not actively pursuing writing. Stan was supposed to be the writer in the family.

By 1965, however, Anne Rice began to emerge from under the shadow of her husband. Among her early works was a short story version of *Interview with the Vampire*. It was also during this period that she first began to explore the eroticism that would become a staple of her later writing with two pornographic stories. "The Sufferings of Charlotte," of which the only copy was loaned out to a friend and eventually stolen, and "Nicholas and Jean," a novella about a love affair between a man and a boy. In May, her first story, "October 4, 1948" was published in the University of San Francisco literary magazine. The following year, in June 1966, the first chapter of "Nicholas and Jean" appeared there as well. It was during this period, as well, that Rice's daughter Michele was born, on September 21, 1968.

By 1969, Rice had been published in several college and small literary magazines, though true success was some time off. Her first long piece, "Katherine and Jean" was a reworking of "Nicholas and Jean" that she turned in for her graduate thesis in 1972. The work could have seen publication, but Rice's burgeoning career was side tracked when her daughter Michele was diagnosed with leukemia.

Dealing with the illness of their daughter was a very difficult time for Stan and Ann Rice. Both their careers and financial stability suffered as they put everything thing they had into saving the child. The pressures also put a strain on their marriage that grew even more difficult as Michele came closer to losing her battle. By the end, Stan thought it would be a far greater mercy to let the child go, than for her to linger; while Anne clung desperately to the little girl as though she could prevent her from leaving. Despite their best efforts, Michele died in August of that year.

The death of their child was followed by a period of despondency and depression for both Anne and Stan, and they would soon both turn to writing to express the sorrow and loss they felt.

Stan's reflections became the book of poetry, *Some Lamb*, which also brought him his greatest success, though it would pale to that of the soon to be rising star of his wife. Having no idea where to start in her own expression, Anne turned to some of the older tales she had never completed, thinking she would make one of them into a novel length work. Eventually she settled upon the short story "Interview with the Vampire."

Over the next six weeks, Anne poured out her emotions into this book; expressing all her concerns, fears, and sadness. Her lost daughter became Claudia, the child trapped forever in eternal youth. Her husband was the original model for Lestat, alternately alluring and cruel, representing her own ambivalent feelings toward Stan's attitude regarding their daughter at the end of her life. Anne Rice herself was cast as the young mother who had lost her own child and becomes Claudia's companion in death.

The story follows the experiences of Louis, who, as a young man of twenty-five, becomes a vampire. Unlike other such creature's in literature and the movies, he is a product of the New World. Traditionally vampires had come from crumbling castles in Eastern Europe, or the more culturally refined societies of places such as France and England. Louis is from a deep South plantation near New Orleans in the late eighteenth century. By being from this continent, he becomes instantly more identifiable to the American public. His concerns are much closer to ours, and we are better able to understand what it is like to be a vampire.

Louis experiences fully the sense of loss and regret that one feels for the dead, as he his mourning for his own death. Lestat, his creator, seems to revel in his death. The two are almost diametrically opposed, yet tied together by their isolation, until Lestat chooses another companion for them, the little girl Claudia. She is an orphan who has lost her mother and, if left to the world, would more than likely die. Together Lestat and Louis save her from that fate—but bring her into an even worse destiny.

Through each of Anne Rice's characters in her first novel, the reader sees and experiences the different viewpoints in vampiric existence. Armand, the self proclaimed oldest living vampire of *Interview* at four hundred years, represents the more traditional, old world archetype. His is crafted after the Byronic image used for Polidori's "Lord Ruthven" more than a century earlier. Beautiful to behold, amoral, and cunning, yet harboring a secret void that can never be filled, no matter how much blood is taken, or whatever companionship is sought. Lestat is the epitome of Rice's take on vampirism. Orphaned by his own creator, he struggles on his own for understanding, breaking all the rules and taboos of mortal and immortal kinds, then glorifies in the discovery of his godlike powers. Louis is the cursed immortal still attached to his human life, never truly able to distance himself for it. Therefore, he sees himself as damned, and evil. As all humans do at one point or another, he questions everything, from the existence of god, to the meaning of life. Yet as the immortal who never gives up his humanity, he is the most predatory and wanton killer of them all. Claudia represents the bitterness and hatred that vampire existence could come to inspire. As a young girl of five, she was made into a vampire, becoming trapped in a shell that will never change or grow, though her mind continues to mature. By her appearance, she is condemned to always be a young girl, despite that she ages 65 years. And she rightly resents it.

Louis, as a truly New World vampire, additionally epitomizes some of the failings of our own society, for there is a common sense that living in such a mixing pot of cultures, we have somehow lost connection to our past. His journey in the second half of *Interview* to find his roots, the heritage of his dark blood, in many ways echoes our own desires to understand from where we came ourselves.

Horror was already gaining in popularity when *Interview* hit the streets, with the success of Stephen King and novels such as *The Exorcist, The Others,* and *Rosemary's Baby.* What Rice tapped into went even further than all these, however. Other writers of the time had provided an overview of true evil as it impacted our world. Anne Rice not only personified it, but made it human. For the first time we could understand its motives, and even feel for it. For many, it would cause an uncomfortable turn to look inward and see the darkness within ourselves that we may share with these monsters. *Interview* came at just the right time. In the late 1970s, when our fascination with evil was on the rise.

In many ways Anne Rice's career is a case study of the importance of timing and resilience. From the time she completed *Interview,* Rice was determined that this book would be published, even if she had to bind it herself and sell copies out of the trunk of her car.

The summer after it was written, Rice attended the Squaw Valley writers conference, where she met Phyllis Seidel, a young literary agent through whom *Interview* found its way to Alfred A. Knopf, which purchased it for a $12,000 advance—which was unheard of for a new, unknown author's first book. In 1976, the paperback rights sold to Ballantine for $700,000, and then the movie rights went to Paramount for $150,000.

Despite this success, however, Rice's subsequent novels strayed from the supernatural elements that had made *Interview* such a hit, and her advances and readership have suffered. Her career has been marked by a series of ups and downs; for every achievement she has made with her vampire fiction, she has had several critical or publishing failures.

Her second novel, *The Feast of All Saints* (1979), was passed up by Knopf despite the phenomenal success of *Interview.* Though it later sold to Simon & Schuster for $150,000, it was far from a success, selling 20,000 copies, well below expectations; paper back rights only brought in $35,000. *The Feast Of All Saints* began a trend of decreasing advances and lack luster critical acclaim. Her next novel, *Cry to Heaven,* was published in 1982. This time it was Simon & Schuster who did not want it, though Knopf did—for $75,000.

Anne Rice was determined to write what she wanted, when she wanted. *The Claiming Of Sleeping Beauty* (1983), was in part an exploration of her own sexual fantasies. Wounded by poor critical reception of some of her later day novels and wishing to be judged by the work alone and not by the expectations of her name, Rice originally published the book as A. N. Roquelaure and sold it to Dutton. It was followed by *Beauty's Punishment* (1984). *Exit To Eden* (1985), another pornographic novel, was published under the name Anne Rampling by Arbor House for an advance of $35,000. Rice then penned the last of her Roquelaure novels, *Beauty's Release* in 1985.

In *The Vampire Lestat* (1985) Rice further blurred the lines between good and evil and matched the success of *Interview With The Vampire.* This time it is Lestat's perspective that reveals the dark truths of vampiric existence, not Louis.

Lestat's induction as a vampire is much more chaotic and confused than Louis's. Just after bestowing what has come to be referred to as "The Dark Gift" Magnus, Lestat's creator, quickly throws himself into the fire, leaving

Lestat on his own as he struggles to come to terms with his new existence. For a time, he creates others to share in his new life, but he finds that their companionship won't fill the void that has grown in his soul. When he meets Armand for the first time, he learns of the ancient vampire Marius, Armand's creator. Lestat sets off to find him in an attempt to learn the heritage of their kind, echoing the similar journey that Louis and Claudia take in the first novel.

The Queen Of The Damned (1988) unites all the disparate vampires from across the world as the oldest, most powerful among them, Akasha, awakens from a deep sleep and begins a plight of mass destruction—killing both her own kind and humans alike—particularly the male members of the species. Her descendants must put aside centuries of hostility to find a way to work together to prevent her plan, yet this is further complicated when Lestat himself comes under Akasha's power.

In writing *Queen*, Rice gave shape to two other eternal creatures; an immortal man late to appear in *The Mummy, Or Ramses, the Damned* (1989) and an incubus spirit which provided the inspiration for Lasher, the creature of *The Witching Hour* (1990), which spawned the Lives of the Mayfair Witches series. An organization that documents paranormal activity called The Talamasca is also introduced in these pages, which has come into prominence throughout the rest of Rice's supernatural fiction, and yet resides on the horizon as a specter that will one day be unveiled in a book of its own.

The Mummy, or Ramses the Damned, born out of a love of 1950's horror genre films, was first designed for a CBS television mini-series. But as production got underway and revisions were made to the script, Rice did not care for the direction the story was going, and eventually withdrew from the project. She then took her original story outline to Ballantine and presented the idea as a Trade Paperback original.

Ramses is a novel that glorifies in the old B-movie tradition, where a previously undisclosed tomb has been uncovered, complete with a curse inscribed upon the door, and a mummy in a gilded sarcophagus—only to soon rise again to take a horrible vengeance on those who have made this discovery. Where Rice's story differs from the usual tale, however, is that her mummy is not a lumbering monster but a beautiful and articulate immortal man. Ramses was once the lover of the famed Cleopatra, and now that he is awake, he wants to revive her as well. When he locates her mummy, he takes his immortality elixir and sprinkles it on her body. What comes back to life is not the girl he once loved, but a mindless monster.

The Witching Hour (1990) is the story of Lasher, a creature of spirit who longs for a physical form. For centuries he has been manipulating generations of the Mayfair family in an attempt to find the right combination of genes to breed a mortal body he can inhabit. The Mayfairs have their own tales, their own dark secrets, plights, and ambitions, and their history is richly detailed and lovingly recounted.

Throughout her career, Anne Rice has been far more successful with her vampire fiction than with any other, though this has not stopped her from the occasional forays into other subjects—particularly erotica. *Belinda* was released in 1986 under the pen name of Anne Rampling, though Rice made no secret of her true identity this time; her own name was also on the cover. This time she tells the story of a forbidden passion. Forty-four year old illustrator of children's books, Jeremy Walker, falls for a sixteen year old girl, and becomes obsessed.

The Servant Of the Bones (1996), tells of the creation of a ghost assassin, and more recently in *Violin* (1997) again deals with ghosts, this time following the exploits of a 19th century aristocrat who follows his violent to 20th century New Orleans. Future plans have her desiring to write what Rice calls an "autobiography" concerning the life of Jesus Christ.

Her vampires, however, are what have made Anne Rice a household name. Since *Queen of the Damned,* she has released two more in the original series, *The Tale of the Body Thief* (1992) and *Memnoch the Devil* (1995), and began a second chronicle, The New Tales of the Vampires, in which she fleshes out the lives and stories of characters from the earlier novels. These include *Pandora* (1998), *The Vampire Armand* (1999), *Vittorio* (2000), and *Blood And Gold* (2002).

The Tale Of The Body Thief again deals with the theme of an immortal being wishing for the experiences of mortal flesh. Lestat, after finding that he can not kill himself, and growing bored with his existence, is offered a chance to "exchange" his vampiric body for one of a mortal man for a short period of time. When he foolishly agrees, he soon finds that the man with whom he has made the bargain has stolen his vampiric body. Lestat must seek him out before he can do too much damage in his name.

In *Memnoch The Devil,* having exhausted and triumphed over all other enemies and rivals, what is there left to give a being such as Lestat any challenge? Perhaps a fallen angel? Or the devil himself? In *Memnoch* Lestat faces a creature that could be just such a challenge.

The New Tales Of The Vampires are essentially the accounting of David Talbot, once a member of the Talamasca, now a vampire himself, as he accumulates the tales and histories of the others of his kind. *Pandora* tells of the origin of the vampire who helped rescue Marius when he was trapped and left for dead by their progenitor Akasha in *Queen of the Damned. The Vampire Armand* who has been both a bane and a source of pleasure to Louis, Lestat, and so many others, also has his own story told, as does *Vittorio,* who was born and created in Florence during the height of the DeMedeci influence. In *Blood And Gold* we follow Lestat's old mentor and Armand's creator, Marius, throughout history, from the classic Roman age, on through to the modern era, as he does his best to protect the secret of the King and Queen, the first vampires who are known simply as They Who Must Be Kept.

Despite unveiling ever more mysteries about her vampires, Rice has been anything but idle in the Lives of The Mayfair Witches series as well. In 1993, she continued the tale began in *The Witching Hour* with its followup, *Lasher,* detailing the plight of the incubus creature who had finally attained a mortal body at the end of the previous novel, and now seeks for a mate.

In 1995's *Taltos,* Rice delves even deeper into the history of this being, revealing the hidden nature of its true identity. And in 2001, she combined her witches and vampires into one novel. *Merrick* focuses on Merrick Mayfair, who comes from another branch of the huge family and has put her necromantic powers to work for the Talamasca. Louis makes his first return since a brief scene in *The Tale of the Body Thief,* requesting that Merrick use her powers to reach the spirit of Claudia—to disastrous results. When Lestat wakes from his slumber, all three are re-united once again, nearly thirty years after their initial creation. This time they are linked inexorably to the Lives of the Mayfair Witches.

What marks Anne Rice's fiction and makes it stand out above the works of others is her attention to detail, and the rich tapestry of characters which she weaves. Every novel is a world to itself, yet each one serve to further expand upon her universe. Familiar characters move comfortably from one story or series to he next as easily as any one of us might travel from one city to another. There can be little doubt that it was due to her unique childhood that Rice became so adept at world creation, drawing from the games with imaginary people she played in her youth and the horror movies she would watch at matinee showings. Every experience of her life has become a part of this fictional world, which is why even her vampires ring so extraordinarily true. For she has managed to capture something of the conflict within us all; the quest for meaning in our lives. It is for this insight that, despite her setbacks and disappointments, Anne Rice has had one of the most successful careers in modern supernatural literature.

ANNE RICE

Selected Bibliography

WORKS OF ANNE RICE

Interview With The Vampire, Alfred A. Knopf, 1977.

The Feast Of All Saints, Simon & Schuster, 1979.

Cry To Heaven, Alfred A. Knopf, 1982.

The Claiming Of Sleeping Beauty, Dutton, 1983. (Published under the name A. N. Roquelaure.)

Beauty's Punishment, Dutton, 1984. (Published under the name A. N. Roquelaure.)

Beauty's Release, Dutton, 1985. (Published under the name A. N. Roquelaure.)

Exit To Eden, William Morrow, 1985. (Published under the name Anne Rampling.)

The Vampire Lestat, Alfred A. Knopf, 1985.

Belinda, William Morrow, 1987. (Published under the names Anne Rampling and Anne Rice.)

The Queen Of The Damned, Alfred A. Knopf, 1988.

The Mummy, Or Ramses The Damned, Alfred A. Knopf, 1989.

The Witching Hour, Alfred A. Knopf, 1990.

The Tale Of The Body Thief, Alfred A. Knopf, 1992.

Lasher, Alfred A. Knopf, 1992.

Taltos, Alfred A. Knopf, 1995.

Memnoch The Devil, Alfred A. Knopf, 1995.

Servant Of The Bones, Alfred A. Knopf, 1996.

Violin, Alfred A. Knopf, 1997.

Pandora, Alfred A. Knopf, 1998.

The Vampire Armand, Alfred A. Knopf, 1999.

Vittorio, The Vampire, Alfred A. Knopf, 2000.

Merrick, Alfred A. Knopf, 2001.

Blood And Gold, Alfred A. Knopf, 2002.

BIBLIOGRAPHY

Books about Anne Rice and her Universe:

Ramsland, Katherine. *Prism of the Night: A Biography of Anne Rice,* New York: Dutton/Penguin Group, 1991.

Ramsland, Katherine. *The Vampire Companion,* New York: Ballantine Books, 1993.

Ramsland, Katherine. *The Witches' Companion,* New York: Ballantine Books, 1994.

Related material:

Borchart, Alice. *Devoted.* New York: Dutton/Penguin Group, 1995. (Introduction by Anne Rice.)

Borchart, Alice. *Beguiled.* New York: Dutton/Penguin Group, 1997. (Introduction by Anne Rice.)

J. K. Rowling
1965–

BRIAN STABLEFORD

JOANNE KATHLEEN ROWLING was born on July 31, 1965, in Chipping Sodbury, near Bristol. Her father, Peter Rowling, was an engineer and manager for Rolls-Royce. Her younger sister Dianne was born two years later. The family lived in the Bristol suburb of Yate until they moved to Winterbourne, and then—when Joanne was nine—to the village of Tuthill, near Chepstow, in the Forest of Dean. Rowling was educated at Wyedean Comprehensive, where she eventually became Head Girl. She studied French and Classics at Exeter University, spending her year abroad in Paris. She went on to take a teaching qualification at Moray House Teacher Training College in Manchester, then moved to London, where she worked as a secretary and as a research assistant for Amnesty International.

In 1991 Rowling went to Oporto in Portugal to teach English as a foreign language; her job required her to work in the afternoons and evenings, and she spent the mornings writing. She had already conceived the idea of the Harry Potter series in the summer of 1990, while traveling on a train from Manchester to London. She married TV journalist Jorge Arantes in 1992, but they were divorced in 1993, when Rowling returned to Britain with her infant daughter, Jessica (named after the most rebellious of the Mitford sisters), and a suitcase full of chapters and notes for the Harry Potter project. Her subsequent adventures, as seen in retrospect, have already taken on a quasi-folkloristic quality that has easily surpassed the legend formulated by Hans Christian Andersen in *The Fairy-Tale of My Life* (1855).

Rowling settled in Edinburgh, where her sister Dianne—who had formerly worked as a nurse—was now studying law. Suffering from depression and caught in a poverty trap because the cost of child care made it uneconomical to work, she formed the habit of taking long walks through the city and then, while Jessica slept, writing chapters of *Harry Potter and the Philosopher's Stone* (later titled *Harry Potter and the Sorcerer's Stone* in the United States) in coffeeshops. She finished the novel in 1995, the year in which her mother, Anne, died of multiple sclerosis at the age of forty-five. She worked as a French teacher until the novel was accepted for publication early in 1997, at which point she was able to obtain a grant from the Scottish Arts Council that enabled her to buy a computer to facilitate the completion of *Harry Potter and the Chamber of Secrets* (1999).

Published in June 1997, *Harry Potter and the Philosopher's Stone* won the Smarties Book Prize Gold Medal and was short-listed for the *Guard-*

ian Fiction Award and the Carnegie Medal. American rights were sold at auction in September 1997 for $105,000. Warner bought the film rights in 1999, and when the third novel, *Harry Potter and the Prisoner of Azkaban*, was published in the same year, the three books took over the top three slots on the U.S. best-seller lists. Soon afterward, Rowling became the highest-earning woman in Britain. She bought Kilchassie House, a nineteenth-century mansion in Perthshire, in the autumn of 2001 to serve as a home for the new family created by her marriage—on Boxing Day of that year—to Dr. Neil Murray.

Harry Potter and the Sorcerer's Stone tells the story of Harry's abrupt realization that there is more to life than living in the cupboard under the stairs at 4 Privet Drive in the Surrey village of Little Whinging, suffering appalling maltreatment at the hands of the Dursleys, on whose doorstep he was abandoned as a babe-in-arms. The Dursleys had been obliged to take him in because Petunia Dursley was the sister of Harry's mother, but the obligation was as fearful as it was dutiful because they knew that there had always been something very odd about Harry's family. The reader, who has been alerted to the nature of this oddness and informed about the circumstances in which he was orphaned by a prelude, shares Harry's enthusiasm in discovering that he is a wizard, entitled to enroll at Britain's school of wizardry, Hogwarts Academy.

Harry's determination to claim his heritage is impeded by the Dursleys' bitter hatred of all things magical, but their increasingly desperate attempts to keep him from responding to his invitation to Hogwarts are hopeless; they are, after all, mere Muggles (nonmagical folk). Harry catches the Hogwarts Express from platform nine and three-quarters at King's Cross Station, and is carried away to a new life. (The train on which Rowling first conceived Harry Potter must have been bound for Euston, but King's Cross was the departure point for a much earlier train on which her parents had first met.)

The basis of all creativity, according to Arthur Koestler's *The Act of Creation*, is the forging of new and startling "bisociations." Harry's career at Hogwarts is, on the one hand, a conventional tale of boarding-school life, involving time-tabled lessons, various teachers (some kind, some stern, all supervised by a benign and near-godlike headmaster), dining halls, dormitories, common rooms, sports fields, the forging of friendships firm enough to last a lifetime, and the making of petty enemies capable of casting a malevolent blight over the minutiae of everyday existence. This process is, however, dexterously bisociated with an education in another and very different way of being, in which everything—including all the items listed in the previous sentence—is magical. Harry himself, although he is an utter novice yet to be introduced to the most elementary magical techniques, is also a ready-made hero with a reputation that has preceded him. When he was still preconscious in his cradle he not only survived a magical assault by the infamous dark wizard Voldemort (whose name is so terrible in its effects that only Harry and the headmaster, Albus Dumbledore, dare pronounce it) but deflected the lethal spell back upon its sender, reducing Voldemort to helplessness.

In the beginning, the only strong evidence of Harry's innate talent is provided by his activities on the sports field, where he becomes a key player for his house team in the wizards' game of Quidditch. Quidditch is played at a hectic pace by teams of flying broomstick riders; it involves several balls and is open to many kinds of dangerously dirty tactics. Significantly, Harry becomes his team's Seeker, charged with locating and seizing the Snitch, the golden ball whose capture brings a Quidditch game to its conclusion. As *Harry Potter and the Sorcerer's Stone* moves toward its climax, though, Harry is forced to exercise himself in more serious matters.

Voldemort did not perish in his abortive assault on the infant Harry, having merely been reduced to a similar but much less prepossessing condition. While Harry has been growing from childhood to adolescence Voldemort has also been "growing up" for a second time—and he, of course, has had the advantage of knowing exactly what this process entails and what his ultimate goal is. Harry grows wiser and more powerful by slow and measured degrees, but Voldemort is already monstrously ingenious as well as utterly malevolent; as the series progresses they are engaged in a kind of obstacle race that becomes more explicit at every step, in which Harry must win every stage as well as the overall contest.

Given this situation, Harry stands in dire need of the friends he makes at Hogwarts. Dumbledore, some of the teachers, and the gargantuan groundskeeper, Hagrid, are already fully committed to his side, but they cannot provide the kinds of support he can only get from his peers. The roles played in Harry's career by his newfound friends Ron Weasley and Hermione Granger are no less vital for the fact that both of them begin their school careers in much the same state of ignorance as he. Hermione, as a "Muggle-born" whose talents have arisen haphazardly, makes up for her own lack of experience with a fearsome appetite for study, while Ron, who comes from an old wizard family, has the invaluable—if not unproblematic—asset of a set of older brothers.

Alas, Voldemort has friends too, despite the purge that followed his defeat; those of his acolytes who escaped prosecution (mostly, it eventually turns out, by making deals with the wizards' court and the Ministry of Magic) hate Harry as fervently as Dumbledore's party approve of him. Most have retained their nasty habits even though their petty treasons have left many of them almost as fearful of the prospect of Voldemort's return as their rivals are.

Harry's principal enemy among his peers is Draco Malfoy, the son of Lucius Malfoy (who, it eventually turns out, remains a steadfast "Death Eater" and a virulently racist enemy not merely of Muggles but of Muggle-born magicians). Draco Malfoy is, however, an overt adversary, whose enmity can be assumed, and is not overly difficult to counteract. Figuring out which of the adults with whom Harry becomes associated might be enemies is a much more problematic business, in which hasty judgments are likely to prove disastrously mistaken. The plots of the first four novels in the series all hinge on confusions of this sort. Characters tacitly assumed to be allies sometimes turn out, when the chips are down, to be deadly enemies—and just as often, it transpires that characters assumed to be adversaries are potentially valuable allies.

Such switches are, of course, part of the ordinary routines of plotting, but in Rowling's stories they take on a deeper significance because they are intricately interwoven with fundamental questions about the politics and morality of magic. In *Harry Potter and the Sorcerer's Stone* the lines between good and evil are drawn in conventional terms, but those terms become increasingly confused and problematic as the series progresses and matures. The basic story format of the first four volumes involves unidentified villains secretly hatching plots that Harry must thwart, first by ingenious detection and then by brave confrontation—but instead of merely repeating this formula, Rowling has subjected it to a sequential process of complication. As Harry becomes increasingly able to penetrate the mysteries surrounding him he becomes increasingly alert to the significance of those mysteries within a much wider context. Even more importantly, as he is forced to make increasingly courageous stands against Voldemort and his allies he becomes increasingly conscious of what he is fighting for. Voldemort, as his own name and the nicknames of his followers suggest, is no mere pulp villain who exists merely to be knocked down repeatedly by a hero; the evil that he embodies becomes more complicated with every volume, increasingly shaded with subtleties even though its stark menace increases by leaps and bounds.

This gradual sophistication of a robust formula gave Rowling the scope to construct plots that became more and more complicated—considerably more, by volume three, than those found in the general run of children's books. As their mysteries grow in complexity the sequels embrace deeper moral ambiguities; characters as morally complex as the enigmatic Severus Snape, who is a perennial obstacle to Harry's efforts even though Dumbledore seems to trust him implicitly, are a great rarity in children's fiction.

Despite such minor indulgences as the hectic broomstick riding in Quidditch, Rowling maintains a careful discretion in her use of magic in *Harry Potter and the Sorcerer's Stone*. Many writers of children's fantasies are carelessly profligate in their use of the casual narrative flourishes that can all too easily be contrived by the arbitrary use of magic. There is, of course, an irreducible element of deus ex machina about the escapes that Harry contrives from his dangerous encounters with the forces that oppose him, but Rowling skillfully maintains their dramatic tension and she never shirks the business of allowing Harry to suffer real injury when he is slow on the uptake—even, sometimes, when he is not. By virtue of this narrative skill and her willingness to allow bad consequences to materialize, Rowling was able to equip the later novels in the series with powerful climaxes whose dramatic tension reaches an extraordinarily fine pitch. Although the unalerted readers of *Harry Potter and the Sorcerer's Stone* must have been securely captivated long before the climax, it was surely the extraordinary suspense of Harry's first confrontation with Voldemort—driven by the desperate necessity of keeping the eponymous stone out of his hands—that boosted their reading experience to a level of excitement that many of them had never previously been able to achieve.

The striking quality of the climax of the first volume created obvious problems for the novel's successors. The escalating pattern of the series plan required that this trick should not merely be repeated but further exaggerated on each subsequent occasion. Very few writers have ever attempted such a thing—almost all writers of children's series content themselves from the beginning with a straightforwardly repetitive pattern in which the units are mere clones strung out in a potentially infinite but essentially flat line—and no one has yet succeeded. *Harry Potter and the Chamber of Secrets* (1999) is, however, just as well-balanced and carefully controlled in its build-up as its predecessor, and even more melodramatic in its final confrontation. It introduces a nice comic figure in Gilderoy Lockhart, the narcissistic author of bestsellers describing his (wholly fictitious) exploits in combating the black arts, but an even more effective introduction is that of Dobby the House-Elf, whose ambiguous role is cleverly conceived and developed. The eventual revelation of the location of the Chamber of Secrets and the monster it contains are handled with remarkable dexterity, neatly weaving comic and melodramatic plot threads together into a thoroughly satisfying knot.

Harry Potter and the Prisoner of Azkaban increases the melodramatic component of the series considerably, while simultaneously contriving a new dimension of moral complication by introducing the wizards' prison, Azkaban. Azkaban, where most of Voldemort's supporters were sent when his campaign was thwarted, is a striking extrapolation of penological theory, being guarded by the hideous, soul-sucking Dementors, whose phobic effect on Harry raises the question of what kinds of means can properly be justified by the end of defeating and confining evil. Dumbledore fears that the Dementors' appointment might eventually prove direly unwise, although the administrators the apparatus of magical government seem blissfully blind to its own follies. By virtue of these additions to Hogwarts' world, the third volume is noticeably darker in tone than its predecessors, although the plot is careful to maintain its elements of comic relief. (The gradual reduction of the series' comedy element has been compensated to some extent by the release of two complementary chapbooks on behalf of the charity Comic Relief: *Quidditch Through the Ages*, by Kennilworthy Whisp, and *Fantastic Beasts and Where to Find Them*, by Newt Scamander (both, 2001). The second item comes with ready-inserted marginal notes in various hands, and they are both profoundly funny.)

The escapee from Azkaban featured in the plot of the third volume is Sirius Black, allegedly one of Voldemort's key supporters, who is widely supposed to be making his way to Hogwarts for the express purpose of annihilating Harry. Although Remus Lupin is a great improvement on Gilderoy Lockhart as a teacher of Defense Against the Dark Arts, Harry seems ill-equipped to deal with this threat—a prospect that is more than enough to put him off his stroke at Quidditch. The eventual climactic confrontation, involving the four pseudonymous makers of the invaluable Marauder's Map and an unjustly condemned hippogriff, tests him once again to the limit. Fortunately, Harry's limit is not something static; as he grows in knowledge and power it extends considerably—sufficiently to allow him to become an underage entrant in an international competition of school champions of wizardry in *Harry Potter and the Goblet of Fire* (2000).

Harry soon figures out that his unsought entry into the championship is part of a plot to kill him, but he is much slower to realize that there is far more to the scheme than mere murder. The reader, forewarned that Voldemort intends to make use of Harry before killing him, must watch the hero make mistake after mistake because he does not realize the complexity of the challenge that faces him. He is surrounded by powerful figures—Dumbledore has summoned the aid of the legendary and much-scarred fighter of dark forces Alastor "Mad-Eye" Moody, and various other representatives of magical government, including Bartimeus Crouch, Ludo Bagman, and the Minister for Magic, Cornelius Fudge, make their presence felt—but it is obvious to the reader that this company includes at least one traitor. Even the comedy relief provided by Rita Skeeter, a reporter for the *Daily Prophet* determined to apply the lowest strategies of yellow journalism to the coverage of Harry's exploits, merely serves to add one more to the plague of troubles afflicting him.

It is a testament to Rowling's skill that even adult readers, who are sure to notice the symbolic quality of the names she gives to characters even if they cannot appreciate all the niceties of her borrowings from Latin and French, are still likely to be taken completely by surprise by her carefully precorroborated plot twists. What they are sure to observe, however—perhaps unlike their younger counterparts—is the gradual accumulation, especially *in Harry Potter and the Goblet of Fire*, of vital materiel to be hoarded for the eventual climax of the series. By the end of this volume the emerging battle lines have become much clearer to everyone except the inglorious Fudge and his fellow mandarins, and the first preparations for a truly titanic final battle are in hand.

The remarkable history of Harry Potter is all the more astonishing because publishers had begun to fear in the early 1990s that the drastic shortening of the periods for which books were routinely displayed in bookshops no longer allowed time for "word-of-mouth" publicity to take effect, and thus militated against the possibility of spontaneous best-sellers arising out of unprompted reader response. The reduction of display time had, however, run in parallel with an increase in the sophistication of technologies by means of which opinions could be disseminated; J. K. Rowling was the author who demonstrated that word-of-mouth publicity could now spread with amazing speed and effect. Although her first book was issued by Bloomsbury, a small publisher of relatively recent provenance—having been turned down by those that had massive publicity machines at their disposal—it generated such enthusiasm among its readers that it not only achieved unprecedented success but did so with amazing rapidity. Even more remarkable was the fact that although *Harry Potter and the Sorcerer's Stone* delighted its initial target audience of eight- to eleven-year-olds, it attracted so many admirers from beyond that age range that Bloomsbury eventually found it politic to issue a special "adult paperback" edition of the series in more staid packaging.

Critics and historians who had been declaring the traditional English public-school story dead and buried for more than thirty years contracted a severe case of egg on the face when the Harry Potter series proved so popular. "The school story proper, that is one which does not look beyond the small enclosed world of school, is dead," Marcus Crouch wrote in 1972 in *The Nesbit Tradition: The Children's Novel 1945-1970*. "It died many years ago of exhaustion and social change.... The possible variations of school, playing-field, bullies, friendship, were arithmetically predictable, and they had been used up" (p. 161). Since 1972 we have, of course, seen a dramatic upsurge in American school stories, spearheaded by films and TV dramas aimed at a teenage audience, but there are immense differences between the cultural situation of American high schools—particularly those in small towns—and schools in Britain. It was not obvious before Harry Potter that the rewards reaped by employing supernatural devices to exaggerate teenage anxieties in high school settings—as pioneered by numerous "Prom Night" schlock-horror movies and perfected by the TV version of *Buffy the Vampire Slayer*—could be transplanted into British school story fiction; attempts by writers like Diana Wynne Jones and Gillian Cross had only achieved a limited success. Rowling succeeded where others had not by grasping the nettle more firmly. The Harry Potter books exploit to the full a fact that many critics and historians of children's fiction had steadfastly refused to notice or grasp: that "the small enclosed world of school" is, of necessity, a microcosm of something much larger, and that such a microcosm is capable of doing far more than merely reflecting and celebrating a preexistent ideological system.

The public school story was always consumed as a species of fantasy, and its decline had far more to do with the terminal decay of its innate ideology than with the evolution of the actual education system; the format remained available for anyone bold enough and clever enough to retain and exploit the most appealing aspects of the fantasy while reconstructing the implicit ideology in such a way that the microcosm of the school implied a very different and much more interesting macrocosm. There is certainly a sense in which Rowling's Hogwarts harks back to a generations-old tradition, but critics are mistaken if they think this makes it an essentially conservative institution. Although Hogwarts is structurally similar to the mythical public schools employed as arenas for teenage dramatics by Talbot Baines Reed and Angela Brazil, the manner in which its structures are manned and managed is exemplary of a society whose divisions and distinctions are different from, and much more modern than, those of pre-war Britain. Indeed, as Hogwarts evolves through the first four volumes of the series, its situation in the wider world comes to reflect something far broader than any kind of insular nationalism; in *Harry Potter and the Goblet of Fire* the macrocosm reflected in Hogwarts' microcosm is an entire world, enriched in several different ways by the metaphysical and metaphorical qualities of the microcosm's magic.

The Harry Potter series, as planned and advertised, will eventually extend to seven volumes, each one covering a year in Harry's secondary school career (thus taking him from his eleventh birthday, which occurs shortly after the beginning of the first book, to the brink of eighteen at the conclusion of the last). Harry is by no means the first hero of children's fiction to grow older—although the majority do remain existentially static—but it is unusual indeed for this kind of character development to happen according to such a fixed and far-reaching pattern. This is because most children's books have a target audience whose age range is fairly narrowly confined, limiting the extent of the maturation that a particular central character may undergo. As Rowling's plan unfolds, the Harry Potter books will have to mature in themselves as their hero grows, changing their implicit target audience as they emerge into the marketplace.

The first four books have evolved considerably in accordance with this resolution; they have grown considerably in both size and complexity, and the balance between humor and melodrama has shifted inexorably toward the latter. The demands made on the reader by the 636-page *Harry Potter and the Goblet of Fire* are much greater than those made by *Harry Potter and the Sorcerer's Stone*; the fourth book's seriously scary climax adds a further element to an escalating series whose projected seventh item will inevitably be called upon to attain a level of dramatic tension and a narrative scope rarely seen in adult supernatural fiction, let alone children's fantasy. What Rowling has demonstrated beyond the slightest shadow of doubt, however, is that even young children are nowadays capable of following complex plots and savoring rousingly melodramatic climaxes, provided that an adequate narrative incentive is provided. It is a considerable compliment to her audience, as well as to her, that she has not yet overestimated the intellectual and imaginative capacity of her fans. If she can carry the project through to a satisfactory conclusion it will be an unparalleled achievement; thus far, she has not faltered.

The real reason why traditional public school stories died out had nothing to do with any exhaustion of arithmetical permutations of plot elements, and everything to do with the failure to make any better connection between their microcosm and the surrounding macrocosm than the observation that the bloody mess of World War I had been hatched from the playing fields of Eton (an observation whose evil significance even its maker failed to realize). Rowling has not made that mistake, and knows full well what the significance is, not merely of what she has already done but of what might be done if the connection can be taken to its furthest and strongest extreme. The remainder of the series will succeed, one hopes, in doing exactly that. Perhaps the British school story, like Lord Voldemort, was always fated to rise again from its pit of ignominy—but it is doubtful that anyone else could have drawn it forth with such a thunderous éclat.

Selected Bibliography

WORKS OF J. K. ROWLING

NOVELS

Harry Potter and the Philosopher's Stone. London: Bloomsbury, 1997. As *Harry Potter and the Sorcerer's Stone*. New York: Scholastic, 1998.

Harry Potter and the Chamber of Secrets. London: Bloomsbury, 1998. New York: Scholastic, 1999.

Harry Potter and the Prisoner of Azkaban. London: Bloomsbury. New York: Scholastic, 1999.

Harry Potter and the Goblet of Fire. London: Bloomsbury. New York: Scholastic, 2000.

OTHER WORKS

Fantastic Beasts and Where to Find Them, by Newt Scamander. London: Bloomsbury and New York: Scholastic, 2001.

Quidditch Through the Ages, by Kennilworthy Whisp. London: Bloomsbury and New York: Scholastic, 2001.

David J. Schow
1955–

DARRELL SCHWEITZER

BORN IN MARBURG, Germany, on July 13, 1955, David J. Schow was adopted by American parents and raised in the United States. He attended the University of Arizona, but dropped out before taking a degree. Schow married Christa Faust in 1995; he lives in Hollywood, California.

Schow inevitably got himself labeled a writer of "splatterpunk" (an ostentatiously "loud" type of horror fiction, contemporary, hip, and characterized by no-holds-barred explicitness) with the publication of a feature article, "Inside the New Horror" by Philip Nutman in the October 1988 issue of *Rod Serling's The Twilight Zone Magazine*. The article opens with a full-page photograph of Schow, along with colleagues John Skipp, Craig Spector, J. K. Potter, and Jeff Conner (the publisher of Scream Press), grimacing at the camera. It goes on to effusively declaim the merits of the new "movement." There is even a sidebar on the reporter, Nutman, as "splatter-critic." The lead story in the issue, prominently billed, is the first installment of Schow's two-part novella, "The Falling Man." The article on splatterpunk was intended to be, as Schow later described it, a preemptive strike, whereby certain new, hot horror writers would label themselves before someone else labeled them. Schow himself is credited with coining the term "splatterpunk."

The creation of a new horror movement had the effect of making the writers involved more visible. They had captured the field's attention, unquestionably, but it is clear that, quite early on, Schow had the foresight to wonder "What next?" He seems to have distanced himself from the movement almost immediately after aligning himself with it. Significantly, no story by Schow is included in the 1990 manifesto-anthology *Splatterpunks: Extreme Horror*, edited by Paul M. Sammon, and as early as an interview in the spring 1990 *Weird Tales*, conducted by Bill Warren, he refers to splatterpunk in the past tense. In a 1996 interview published in *Cemetery Dance*, he described "the Splatterpunk image" as "the image that's one channel on the dial," and goes on to say, "I detest doing the same thing over and over, even within the range of explicit stuff or violent stuff or loud stuff. I am trying to vary my dynamic ranges" (p. 48).

The point is well taken, because Schow's "dynamic range" has always been broad, and more significantly, when splatterpunk melted away like—as any of the splatterpunks might have put it—the doggy-pee-stained snows of yesteryear, it was Schow who was left standing, very much an individual writer of considerable range and talent. The critic S. T. Joshi has suggested that it is more likely that splatterpunk will be remembered because of Schow than the other way around.

Schow's first published work was, rather atypically, science fiction, sold to the magazine *Galileo* in the late 1970s. He seems to have gone through the usual phase of writerly poverty, then supported himself by penning men's action-and-adventure novels (some under the pseudonym Stephen Grave) for a series he has since playfully referred to as the Eviscerator. The experience formed the basis for a satirical fantasy, "Pulpmeister" (in *Seeing Red*, 1990), in which a hack writer meets his own character, then tries to set up the character to write his books, only to discover that this killer-cum-mercenary-cum-hero is not a very good writer ... at least not at first.

By 1987, Schow had won a World Fantasy Award for the short story "Red Light" (collected in *Lost Angels*, 1990), which contains a certain amount of loud and sarcastic, but still deftly precise, prose ("She pulled off her workout shirt and aired a chest that would never need the assistance of the Maidenform Corporation, breasts that would soon have the subscribership of Playboy eating their fingernails" [p. 15]), but is actually a sensitive and haunting story about a photographer who is unable to resist photographing a celebrity model until he has virtually consumed her soul; she ultimately disappears. The protagonist, like a lot of Schow heroes, is a cynic hoping for redemption. He brags about discarding lovers like tissues, but he claims to actually love this particular woman. He has difficulty forming any sort of stable relationship. His narrative voice, sarcasm and all, is an authentic one.

Schow certainly could, when he chose to, write in the splatterpunk mode, with such "classics" of the form (seldom described without laughter) as "Jerry's Kids Meet Wormboy" (In *Black Leather Required* [1994] and Skipp and Spector's *The Book of the Dead* [1989] an anthology of stories extrapolating from the premise of director George Romero's film "Night of the Living Dead' and its sequels), which is exceedingly gross but far more parodic than genuinely frightening. The saving grace of this and such stories as "Blood Rape of the Lust Ghouls" (in *Seeing Red*)—about a film critic who vents his frustration writing hostile reviews of gore flicks, then finds himself magically transported into one—is that Schow does not take them seriously.

More genuinely frightening are such stories as "Night Bloomer" (in *Seeing Red*, 1990), about a nasty corporate worker who dispatches his boss with the seed of a lethal plant, only to find that the seed's hideous growth continues within himself. "Life Partner" (in *Black Leather Required*), about a woman who prefers her lover dead, is on one level a witty satire of sexual conflict. The story, however, creates genuine unease. The novella "The Falling Man" combines several familiar Schow tropes (explicit sexuality, difficult or failing relationships, the vanishing of a loved one) to considerable effect, as does "Pamela's Get" (in *Lost Angels*), in which a dead woman's imaginary companions try to assume reality on their own.

It is impossible to discuss Schow's fiction without mentioning Hollywood. The author is very much the product of Southern California culture, and a lifelong fan of fantastic TV and films. Indeed, the first book he published under his own name was *The Outer Limits: The Official Companion* (1986), which grew out of a series of articles he and Jeffrey Frentzen wrote for *Rod Serling's The Twilight Zone Magazine*. His 1990 story "Monster Movies" (in *Lost Angels*) is simply a paean to classic horror movies. "Gills" (in *Crypt Orchids*, 1998) is a deadpan, funny story about an entity resembling the Creature from the Black Lagoon, living in semiretirement in Hollywood and griping about shoddy remakes of his original exploits. "One for the Horrors" (in *Seeing Red*) is an eerie, touching story about a mysterious theater that shows classic films with never-before-seen footage, and even films that were never made. "Coming Soon to a Theatre Near You" (also in *Seeing Red*) tells of a cinema haunted by a truly preternatural supply of cockroaches—again a loud, outrageous story bordering on knowing, controlled parody.

Schow is primarily known as a short story writer, for all the hack adventure novels and television and film work that he is credited with. By 2002, two novels had appeared under Schow's name. A yet-to-be-issued third novel is described by Schow in the 1996 *Cemetery Dance* interview.

Discussion of the first of the novels attributed to Schow, *The Kill Riff* (1988), is beyond the scope of the present volume. It is a psychological thriller, about a man whose daughter is killed in a riot at a rock-and-roll concert and gradually slides into madness as he stalks and kills members of the band. It is a riveting narrative, fast-paced and filled with convincing details, but ultimately less interesting than Schow's second novel, *The Shaft* (1990), which by contrast is definitely in the supernatural mold.

The Shaft seems to contain some autobiographical elements. Schow mentioned in an interview that he once had a six-month job in Chicago, but he was so unenamored of the Windy City that he maintained an apartment in Tucson, Arizona, during the entire period. Indeed, the depiction of a wintry Chicago is very much that of an uncomfortable Southern Californian removed reluctantly from his environment: cold, dark, filthy, menacing. This is more than exaggeration or hype. It contributes effectively to the novel's atmosphere as one of the characters, a drug dealer, is forced to flee his familiar, sunny home (in this case, Florida, not California) to Chicago after the accidental death of his boss's latest sex toy. In the dark, strange world of Chicago's underclass, he resumes his trade and takes up residence in an outrageously dingy apartment building, the Kenilworth Arms, which is no ordinary slum dwelling, as in one chapter it seems to literally devour one of its tenants.

Into this environment come two other characters, an artist fleeing a failed relationship, and a prostitute. Despite their differences, they become companions in a struggle for survival against menaces both natural (drug dealers and gangsters, the police) and supernatural. In the building's central ventilation shaft dwells a quasi-Lovecraftian monster, the presence of which is never completely rationalized in the course of the novel but may be seen as an outward manifestation of the evil spirit of the Kenilworth Arms. Indeed, the building is one of the great haunted establishments in supernatural fiction, ranking alongside Shirley Jackson's Hill House and Stephen King's Overlook Hotel.

The strengths of the novel are many. Schow uses vulgarity and explicit material not to shock, but to produce a genuinely convincing portrait of the people and events described. Schow's prose is like a series of ugly but evocative photographs, selected and snapped from precisely the right perspective. The characterizations are entirely believable. While it is useless to speculate how many gangsters and drug dealers Schow has actually met, one must credit either his imagination or his reportorial skills for the way that he is able to convince the reader that he knows exactly how these people act and think. At times he can almost make them sympathetic—or perhaps it is more accurate to say that he makes us understand how they justify themselves from their own points of view. The supernatural menaces are effective because they enhance the already menacing sense of place and situation. As if it is not bad enough that someone has to climb down a filthy, fetid airshaft in a Chicago slum apartment in the dead of night in the middle of the winter to retrieve a bundle of cocaine (which might mean the difference between life and death and promise a better future for the characters), there also happens to be a monster down there—and the building itself seems to be alive and malevolent.

The Shaft is a fine example of "urban horror" in the tradition that goes back as far as Charles Dickens's "No. 1 Branch Line, the Signalman"

(1866) but is exemplified by such classic Fritz Leiber stories as "Smoke Ghost" (coincidentally, also set in Chicago), "The Hound," and "You're All Alone." Inexplicably, in 2002 this book had still not been published in the United States, although the original short story, which also failed to sell until it appeared in the Schow issue of *Weird Tales,* was later published in *Black Leather Required.*

In the absence of his promised third novel, Schow in the early years of the new century continued to demonstrate a mastery of the short story. His 2001 collection, *Eye,* contains several first-rate tales, some of them supernatural, some borderline. "Blessed Event" is about fears associated with pregnancy and childbirth. One of the characters, beneath his human guise, is a bizarre, beaked entity that can devour a woman's fetus "the way a gull swallows a fish" (p. 52), then insert its own "meat" instead. For this reason, a man has murdered and disemboweled his girlfriend. He tells his tale to a pair of detectives. It is certain by the end of the story that the bird-headed things exist, but there is no explanation of their nature or reason for existence. They could as readily be extraterrestrials, demons, or projections of human fears.

"Watcher of the Skies" is somewhat difficult to categorize. Indeed, it is an original to the collection because Schow could not sell it separately—too science fictional for the weird/horror magazines, too horrific for the science fiction ones. The story concerns children who befriend something, a creature that very likely is a stranded space alien. But this is the nightmare version of *E.T.* without magic or a happy ending. Eventually adults kill the alien and treat the children as if they had done something shameful. Eventually, as the children grow up, the incident passes away with their childhood and becomes an effective metaphor for the seeming irrationality of adults, to whom children can never explain certain very important things.

Other stories in the book reiterate now familiar Schow themes. In "Calendar Girl" we meet a man who (unsurprisingly) has had a long series of unsuccessful or superficial relationships with women. He now works for a pornography publisher and discovers that a model currently being featured in the publisher's magazines seems to be the very same center-spread girl he has fixated on since adolescence, completely unchanged despite the passage of decades. It turns out that she is indeed the same, an immortal being kept alive by her "lovers," who give her years of their lives in order to keep her young.

"Entr'acte" is about a man who receives a phone call in the middle of the night; the caller instructs him to get away immediately, because the woman in the bed beside him is not human. This happens to be the case, but the man's lover manages to make him forget the discovery (even though he has scars from his encounter with her true, alien self) and things go on as before.

"Holiday" is almost a reverse image of the same story, and is one of the very few weird tales (perhaps the only one) narrated by a tattoo. A crude, drunken boor, very much a caricature of a typical Schow protagonist, has acquired a tattoo during one of his all-night binges. It is exactly what one would expect, a female figure with enormous breasts, hips, and pubic hair, but little else. But this figure is alive, and resents its grotesque appearance. Being unable to come to any sensible terms with its host, it spreads over his entire body and absorbs him, becoming a normal woman with a tattoo of a caricatured man rapidly disappearing from her shoulder.

Some of the other stories are not fantastic, such as "Two Cents Worth," which is an interesting parallel to Ray Bradbury's "The Pedestrian," about a man who is deemed a social deviant because he reads books, and "Quebradora," about an American murderer who flees south and finds a new life and a kind of redemption behind a Mexican wrestler's mask.

A survey of Schow's short fiction, from *Seeing Red* and *Lost Angels* through *Eye* makes clear that Schow is not a supernatural writer of the Lovecraftian or Leiberesque sort, with his focus on the cosmic and on intrusions from beyond the realm of human experience, nor is he, like Thomas Ligotti, primarily preoccupied with questions of the unreality of existence. Even when Schow uses fantastic tropes (either classically supernatural or taken from the imagery of science fiction), his focus is on the immediate, Earth-bound world of interpersonal relationships, more often than not sexual relationships. That the woman in "Entr'acte" is some sort of alien or demonic being is only of interest because of the way she highlights gender tensions, in this case, to borrow the phrase Schow attributes to Gordon van Gelder, editor of *The Magazine of Fantasy and Science Fiction*, the perception of "Woman as Other."

Similarly, "Watcher of the Skies" is more about the relationships between children and adults than it is about visiting aliens. In these concerns and approaches, Schow may be placed firmly in the Southern California school of horror and fantasy writing, that which is typified by Rod Serling's *The Twilight Zone* TV show and the writers centered around him, particularly Richard Matheson, Charles Beaumont, and William F. Nolan. Schow's work contains more explicit sexual content than that of the former writers, as is unsurprising for a product of his generation. He happened to be writing in a time when considerably more explicitness was allowed, but unlike many other, lesser talents, he has generally used this freedom to good effect, rather than for gratuitous shock.

Selected Bibliography

WORKS OF DAVID J. SCHOW

NOVELS

The Kill Riff. New York: Tor, 1988.

The Shaft. London: Macdonald, 1990.

SHORT STORY COLLECTIONS

Lost Angels. (Includes the novella "The Falling Man") New York: New American Library, 1990.

Seeing Red. New York: Tor, 1990.

Black Leather Required. Shingletown, Calif.: Mark V. Ziesing, 1994.

Crypt Orchids. Burton, Mich.: Subterranean, 1998.

Eye. Burton, Mich.: Subterranean, 2001.

OTHER WORKS

Silver Scream. Arlington Heights, Ill.: Dark Harvest, 1988. Anthology edited by Schow.

The Outer Limits: The Official Companion. With Jeffrey Frentzen. New York: Ace, 1986.

Wild Hairs. Northridge, Calif.: Babbage, 2001.

INTERVIEWS

Schweitzer, Darrell. "A Conversation with David Schow." *Cemetery Dance* 24 (Summer 1996), Pp. 48–56.

Warren, Bill. "Weird Tales Talks with David Schow." *Weird Tales* 51, no. 3 (Spring 1990), Pp. 17–25.

CRITICAL STUDIES

Joshi, S. T. "David J. Schow and Splatterpunk." *Studies in Weird Fiction* 13 (Summer 1993), Pp. 21–27.

Nutman, Philip. "Inside the New Horror." *Rod Serling's The Twilight Zone Magazine*, October 1988, Pp. 24–29; 85.

Michael Shea
1946–

BRIAN STABLEFORD

APART FROM THE facts that he was born in Los Angeles in 1946 and attended the University of California there is little biographical information about Michael Shea available as a matter of public record. When invited to elaborate, he observed that "writers often have boring lives" and suggested the following additions: "After post-university years of transcontinental hitchhiking and European travel (more hitchhiking) Shea settled into a life of scrabbling for a living. He has done the usual: construction, carpentry, housepainting, flophouse night-clerking [and] has even descended to teaching (adults). His most precious possessions (and nearly his only ones) are his dear wife, the holographer/artist Linda Cecere Shea, his firstborn Della and second-born Jake" (personal correspondence, March 6, 2002).

Shea's first-published novel, *A Quest for Simbilis* (1974), is set in the far future scenario devised by Jack Vance in *The Dying Earth* (1950), and describes further adventures of one of Vance's characters, Cugel the Clever, whose original appearance was in *The Eyes of the Overworld* (1966). The use of the far future as a venue for fantasy fiction had been pioneered in the 1930s by Clark Ashton Smith in a series of stories set in Zothique. Smith had set earlier stories of much the same type in prehistoric sunken continents such as Hyperborea and Atlantis, but had decided that the exaggeratedly Decadent trappings of such settings were compromised by the reader's knowledge that the future of their neighbors must have been one of progressive evolution to modern civilization. Zothique, by contrast, is the perfect milieu for Decadent fantasy, because the entire solar system containing its world is doomed to perish when the sun dies; everything that happens there is cursed with a magnificent futility. Individual humans may retain the hope that they will live out their lives before oblivion claims everything, but the lack of any guarantee exacerbates their existential angst, and they know that there is no point in building any kind of heritage for the sake of generations to come.

The tales of Zothique are possessed of an inherent black comedy that Smith elected to embellish with fabulously gaudy prose. Vance's adaptation of the scenario differed little in its physical detail, although he was careful not to remain dependent on the obsolete theory by which Lord Kelvin had calculated the likely age of the sun on the assumption that its heat was being generated by gravitational collapse. Stylistically, however, Vance preferred to decorate his black comedies with a more delicate and more explicit wit. Of all the characters he developed for the dying Earth, Cugel is perhaps the most carefully fitted to the tone of the stories: a casual liar, dyed-in-the-wool cheat, and opportunistic thief, who is not quite as clever as he thinks he is. He often comes through his picaresque exploits as much by luck as judgment, and is all the more sympathetic because of it.

Shea's Cugel, still pursuing a feud with Iouconnu the Laughing Magician, whose earlier phases had been mapped by Vance, has suffered a mishap by virtue of mispronouncing a spell that has left him stranded on a barren shore of the Sea of Cutz. There he meets Mumber Sull, the Thane of a fishing village that lies in territory once claimed by the legendary magician Simbilis, whose long absence has created an opportunity for usurpers to move in and take over. Sull persuades Cugel that they might benefit from teaming up to find Simbilis, whose power would be more than adequate to return Cugel to a more hospitable place, as well as ridding his own village of its new governors. Their journey takes them through a series of challenging encounters, including a gruesome escapade in the vaults beneath Cannibal Keep, a hazardous game that wins them the right to use a narrow bridge across a vast chasm, and a failed attempt to do a favor for the obese rulers of the strange city of Waddlawg. Worse misfortune befalls them in the city of Millions Gather, which is a center of trade between the upper world and the demonic underworld, and they are taken as prisoners into the demons' realm—but this is a necessary step, because the underworld is where Simbilis is allegedly to be found, campaigning against the demon hordes from his beleaguered citadel. As things turns out, the great magician is engaged in a rather different and much more ambitious project, which puts the petty concerns of Mumber Sull and Cugel into a broader context.

The bizarre underworld of *A Quest for Simbilis*, whose hyper-Boschian imagery adds an extra order of magnitude to the exotic surfaces pictured by Smith and Vance, became Shea's key contribution to farfuturistic fantasy. His next few stories, set in similar scenarios, abandon the trappings of Vance's dying Earth and substitute Nifft the Lean for Cugel. Initially a kind of literary clone, Nifft soon began to develop a more rounded character of his own, and a legendary status within his own world—which led to the tales of his adventures being collected and collated by one Shag Margold, who serves as an ironic and wryly sceptical commentator. Two of the four adventures assembled in the World Fantasy Award-winning *Nifft the Lean* (1982)—the novellas "Come Then, Mortal, We Will Seek Her Soul" and "The Fishing of the Demon Sea"—involve journeys into netherworlds undertaken by Nifft and his bulkier companion-in-arms, Barnar Hammer-Hand. The former story is an elegant, sarcastic fantasy that carefully recomplicates and mercilessly subverts the basic plot of Orpheus's descent into Hades. The land of the dead featured therein is by no means comfortable, but it pales when set beside the gloriously phantasmagoric demon realm featured in "The Fishing of the Demon Sea."

Whereas the first descent undertaken by Nifft and Barnar was a willing one, the second is undertaken under the sternest compulsion—as it would have to be, given that no sane person would ever enter such an Inferno willingly, despite the awesome treasures it contains. They are dispatched to rescue a fool, and in order to do so they must find and recruit the aid of Gildmirth, a resident magician stranger by far in his capabilities and ambitions than Simbilis. Laying hands on the object of their search and freeing him from captivity is merely a prelude to further hazards; getting such an inconvenient burden back to the surface in one piece doubles the difficulties faced during the the descent, especially as their route brings them into intimate contact with a titanic refugee from a further and even more hellish underworld: a demon's demon, interrupted in his attempt to burst out into the greater universe but not rendered entirely harmless.

By comparison with these two items, the shorter tales of "The Pearls of the Vampire Queen" and "The Goddess in Glass" are modest. The former is a tale of ingenious thievery that would be almost conventional were it not for its breezy ostentation. In the latter, Nifft is a virtual bystander observing a minor crisis in the affairs of an insectile "goddess"—actually an extraterrestrial visitor—whose vast size and exceedingly long reproductive cycle contrive a dramatic reversal of familiar existential comparisons between man and insect. This was a theme that Shea was to develop at considerable length, with ingenious variety and to great effect, in further phantasmagoric fantasies and a sequence of brilliant horror stories.

Shea's third novel, *The Color out of Time* (1984), is a sequel to H. P. Lovecraft's "The Color out of Space," detailing occurrences following the resurgence of the exotic alien entity featured in the earlier story. The valley containing the farm whose well was blighted in Lovecraft's story has been dammed and the diseased terrain submerged beneath a man-made lake. The narrator and his companion are the first tourists camping by the lakeside who notice that anything is wrong; their attempts to alert the authorities and warn their fellow campers are thwarted by the increasingly intrusive entity, but they are aided in their attempt to tackle it head-on by a resident of the area who remembers the initial infestation and has spent her life—with a little help from H. P. Lovecraft—gathering armaments against exactly such a resurgence. In a Lovecraft story there would be no possibility of any resistance capable of winning more than a temporary respite, but Shea was already well-used to pitting his heroes against seemingly impossible odds and bringing them out alive. The three allies contrive a robust and thrilling response to the demonic invader of which no Lovecraftian protagonist would ever have been capable; his other Lovecraftian fantasy, the delectably nasty-minded, "Fat Face" (1988), is far less lenient.

Shea followed *The Color out of Time* with another ambitious farfuturistic fantasy, *In Yana, the Touch of Undying* (1985), which introduces a new anti-hero in Bramt Hex, an uncommitted student of arcana who gives way to a momentary romantic whim and decides to court a rich widow. The decision is unfortunate; he is quickly embroiled in a scheme to sell a local brothel to demons—a move requiring a translocation to the underworld and certain changes in working practices to which the resident whores strongly object. The botched deal does, however, put Hex on the trail of the legendary land of Yana, where the secret of immortality is rumored to be had for the taking, and he sets off to find it. The quest is, inevitably, a very difficult one, involving numerous bizarre phases and many ironic misfortunes, but in the end he does reach his destination, and contrives to make the inevitable descent into the underworld that attainment of his goal requires. Once there, however, he is forced to recognize that the realization of his heart's desire is by no means as simple and straightforward as it once seemed. The imagery of the story is a little restrained by Shea's standards (though not, of course, by anyone else's), but it contains some marvelous set pieces; its relaxed humor and its calculatedly languid flavor combine into a unique piquancy, and it is one of the finest examples of modern Decadent fantasy.

The aquatic monster of *The Color out of Time* has distant kin in Nifft's *Demon Sea*, and on the alien world where human explorers meet the eponymous titan in the science fiction novella "Polyphemus" (1981), one of several stories Shea published in *The Magazine of Fantasy & Science Fiction*. Monsters extrapolated from marine life-forms by vast inflation were, however, sidelined in subsequent work in favor of insects and arachnids. Other alien visitors eatured in Shea's fantasy and science fiction stories include the inquisitive arachnid anthropologist in "The Angel of Death" (1979), whose benevolence is tested to an ironic limit byits encounter with a psychotic serial killer, and the desperate castaway in the uncompromisingly gruesome "The Autopsy" (1980), whose if tiny size does not diminish the threat it poses in its determination to survive. The most distinctive of the set is, however, "The Horror on the #33" (1982), an exceptionally fine existentialist fantasy in which death rears an ugly insectile head in deeply discomfiting circumstances.

"Uncle Tuggs" (1986) is a more conventional conte cruel about a vengeful ghost, remarkable mainly for its moral cynicism. A similarly nonjudgmental cynicism was cleverly extrapolated into a satirical account of the future of mass entertainment in "The Extra" (1987) before reaching a new apogee in the fine novella *I, Said the Fly*, which appeared in *The Sixth Omni Book of Science Fiction* in 1989 before the separate publication of an expanded version. *I, Said the Fly* is yet another tale of alien invasion, this time as part of an exercise in colonization, whose human protagonist takes less inspiration than he might from the media project in which he is involved as he is gradually brought to see things from the insectile invaders' point of view. The brief "Delivery" (1987) is cut from the same cloth.

There was a considerable hiatus in Shea's publications in the early 1990s, although the blurb accompanying "Fat Face" when it was reprinted in the first in the series of *The Year's Best Fantasy* (later *The Year's Best Fantasy and Horror*), edited by Ellen Datlow and Terri Windling, announced that he had two novels forthcoming, entitled *Momma Durtt* and *The Plunderers*. Shea reports that the as-yet-unsold *Momma Durtt* is "a contemporary supernatural thriller (comic horror) about a pollution-poisoned Earth gone murderously mad" and that "*The Plunderers* is a novel that has been first drafted....about alien parasites, quite elaborate, [with a] contemporary setting" (personal correspondence, March 2, 2002). He began publishing short fiction again in 1994, and began publishing novels again shortly thereafter. *The Mines of Behemoth* (1997) and *The A'rak* (2000) continue the adventures of Nifft the Lean, the former explaining how he eventually came to part company with Barnar Hammer-Hand and the latter linking him with a new and rather reluctant partner in Lagademe the Nuncio, who serves within the story as an alternate narrator.

The Mines of Behemoth is set in a region of the far future Earth insulated from demonic activity by the vastly extensive nest of an alien hive whose members are nourished on demon flesh. Although the nest is in the underworld, its neighborhood has been all but purged of demonkind by ruthless predation; only unusually clever and unobtrusive demonic parasites can thrive in close proximity. The humans living on the surface, ever anxious to exploit economic opportunities, have sunk a series of shafts into the nest in order that the gargantuan larvae may be "milked" of their "sap"—which is to say their fluid flesh. This would not normally be the kind of work to which Nifft would stoop, but Barnar's nephew, Costard, has run into trouble while trying to ruin a sap mine, and Barnar is duty-bound to help him out. Nifft becomes more enthusiastic when an entrepreneur named Ha'Awley Bunt offers to pay a huge sum for a quantity of ichor exuded by the Queen, whose collection is a more dangerous enterprise. Then again, the demonic netherworld is strewn with treasures, which are less well guarded in this region than in any other—although that situation is complicated by the presence of another ultra-demonic titan from the lower regions interrupted in his upward drive toward the light. The expedition is a great success—but in Shea's universe, even the greatest success is likely to turn to horridly ironic failure, and the disasters that befall Costard and Bunt affect Nifft and Barnar too.

Like "The Goddess in Glass," the Behemoth Queen and her entourage are probably extraterrestrial in origin, and although it poses many practical problems for its human neighbors, the net effect of the nest's presence is relatively benign. There is no puzzle relating to the origin of the A'rak, which is definitely extraterrestrial, but there is a great deal of ambiguity about the relationship that the giant arachnid forges with its human associates on the island of Hagia. It agrees to serve as their god, to reward them with gold, and to maintain their prosperity by providing unassailable protection for the vaults in which the gold is kept (thus gifting Hagia with the only safe banks in the entire pirate-ridden world). All it asks in return is a few discreet human sacrifices, offered on a regular basis, with which to feed its children—but the number of the A'rak's children have grown as the island's people has thrived, and the witches who inhabit the neighboring islands of the Astrygal chain take the view that its discretion has been merely a preparatory phase. Lagademe the Nuncio is a messenger hired by the witches to make a seemingly innocent delivery to North Hagia; although suspicious of him from the first, she hooks up with Nifft, who has come to conduct a secret investigation of the possibility of making a withdrawal from the island's supposedly impregnable banks. Borne by rumors of imminent disaster, thousands of other thieves gather in his wake, ready and willing to take advantage of any sudden depopulation.

There is a sense in which *The A'rak* is less adventurous than *The Mines of Behemoth*, being merely one more addition to the great tradition of menacing monster stories, unembellished by any account of the phantasmagoric underworld; its plot has more in common with *The Color out of Time* than "The Fishing of the Demon Sea." It is, however, a remarkably fine example of the "giant bug" subgenre, perhaps the best of all. The painstakingly slow revelation of the monster is handled with great dexterity, and the climactic confrontation is vividly horrific as well as providing a golden opportunity for bold and uncompromising heroics.

Michael Shea has always been the kind of writer more likely to win the fervent loyalty of a limited number of connoisseurs than the approval of a mass audience, because he cannot resist the urge to go to the limit—and then beyond—of any theme he adopts. The subgenres in which he prefers to work—farfuturistic fantasy and existentialistically sophisticated horror—are unfashionably extreme in themselves, and he has done sterling work in further extending their extremes, with hectic flamboyance and the relish of a gourmet. He is, for this reason, a uniquely precious resource within the field of imaginative fiction: an authentic pioneer.

The fact that Shea has occasionally found it convenient to appropriate materials to which others have staked a prior claim—he describes his current project as "a very delicately Lovecrafted pastiche called Mr. Cannyharme, set in the pimp-whore-drug addict heartland of the Mission" (personal correspondence, March 2, 2002)—has served to obscure the fact that he is actually a highly original writer, with an eye for the bizarre that no one else can presently match. Unlike Nifft the Lean, he is by no means a thief; he has more in common with Oscar Wilde, who could not see a thing of beauty produced by someone else without wanting to produce something akin to it that would be even more glorious—and Oscar Wilde, who bitterly lamented "The Decay of Lying," would surely have approved of a man who could envisage such a rich variety of maleficent and monstrous demons with such awesome clarity.

Selected Bibliography

WORKS OF MICHAEL SHEA

NOVELS AND SHORT STORIES

A Quest for Simbilis. New York: DAW, 1974. London: Grafton, 1985.

Nifft the Lean. New York: DAW, 1982. London: Granada, 1985.

The Color Out of Time. New York: DAW, 1984. London: Grafton, 1986.

In Yana, the Touch of Undying. New York: DAW, 1985. London: Grafton, 1987.

Polyphemus. Sauk City, WI: Arkham House, 1987. London: Grafton, 1990.

I, Said the Fly. Seattle, WA: Silver Salamander Press, 1993.

The Mines of Behemoth. New York: Baen, 1997.

The A'rak. New York: Baen, 2000.

Lucius Shepard
1947–

GRAHAM SLEIGHT

SINCE HIS DEBUT in the early 1980s—explosive both in terms of the number of stories he published and their quality—Lucius Shepard has become one of the most admired writers in the genres of the fantastic. Apart from a few stories published under his name in *Collins Magazine* between 1952 and 1955, he came relatively late to prose fiction, only beginning to publish in his late thirties. Before that, he traveled widely outside the United States, and many of these biographical experiences are represented or transformed in his fiction.

BACKGROUND

Lucius Taylor Shepard's birthdate is a matter of some small speculation. He currently claims to have been born in Lynchburg, Virginia, on August 21, 1947, but the biographical note in the Fall 1965 *Carolina Quarterly* states that he was born in Daytona Beach, Florida, in 1943, and birth years of 1942, 1945, and 1946 have also been sighted. The queston of dates aside, Shepard has been consistent in stating that his father, William, was "a member of the Virginia gentry," and his mother, Lucy, was a teacher. William evidently intended his son to be a writer and, according to Shepard, made him read and learn lengthy passages from Shakespeare, the Romantic poets, and classical literature from the age of three. Lucy taught Spanish, and thanks to this Shepard had a number of trips to Latin America during his childhood, developing a facility for the language. He graduated from high school in Daytona Beach, Florida, and subsequently attended the University of North Carolina. However, he dropped out and began traveling in Latin America, the Caribbean, Europe, and the Middle East. According to the jacket biography for his first story collection, *The Jaguar Hunter* (1987), "During this peripatetic period of his life, the author smuggled marijuana, taught Spanish at a diplomatic school, owned a T-shirt company, worked as a janitor in a nuclear facility and bouncer at a whorehouse in Málaga, and, most recently, 'beat his brains out' as a rock musician." Shepard returned to the United States in the 1970s, where he married and had a son; the marriage subsequently ended in divorce. It was during this period that he was most involved in music, principally as a singer/songwriter and keyboard player.

EARLY WORK AND *THE JAGUAR HUNTER*

Shepard attended the Clarion science fiction writing workshop at Michigan State University in 1980, where his teachers included Algis Budrys, Avram Davidson, Damon Knight, and Kate Wilhelm. His first sale was "The Taylorsville Reconstruction" to Terry Carr's *Universe 13* in 1983, and he subsequently became extremely prolific. He published at least six stories a year—mostly novelettes and novellas—from 1984 to 1989. Almost all of these stories use the tropes of the fantastic not as ends but as means to the moral examination of the characters and the societies in which they find themselves.

"The Jaguar Hunter," originally published in the *Magazine of Fantasy & Science Fiction* in May 1985 and set in contemporary Honduras, is a fine example. Esteban Caax, the hunter of the title, undertakes to kill a jaguar that has been terrorizing a local barrio. In return for this, the debt his wife incurred to a local appliance dealer, Onofrio Esteves, in buying a television, will be written off. Esteban's marriage, though, is loveless—his wife is more interested in watching *Murder Squad of New York* than in him; and Esteves wants the jaguar dead so that he can have a vast property development built on the untouched barrio. So when Esteban reaches the barrio and meets Miranda, a girl who shares his Patuca Indian heritage, and who seems to have magical powers, he begins to have second thoughts about his task. Miranda is also, it transpires, an avatar of the jaguar. Eventually Esteves, tiring of Esteban's lack of success in completing his assignment, comes to the barrio with armed reinforcements. Esteban is wounded as they try to kill the jaguar and sees the creature dive into a river. Looking into the water, he sees Miranda swimming downwards, perhaps to some transcendent opening into another world. As the story ends, he dives in and swims down after her.

Such a summary may convey what happens in the story, but cannot convey the grace and power of Shepard's writing, as when describing the jaguar's first appearance: "It seemed at first that a scrap of night sky had fallen on to the sand and was being blown by a fitful breeze" (p. 14). Both from sentence to sentence and cumulatively, Shepard's prose has an intensity and an evocative precision rare in any genre.

In addition to his shorter work, Shepard's first novel, *Green Eyes,* appeared in 1984 as part of Terry Carr's revived Ace Specials series—which also included the first novels of William Gibson, Kim Stanley Robinson, and Michael Swanwick. *Green Eyes* has a science-fictional premise, but its tone and setting are closer to horror. A private scientific project in Louisiana's bayou country has found a way of reviving the dead. Recently dead bodies are injected with dust from an old slave graveyard, creating "zombies" with charismatic, archetypal personas. The revival only works for a limited time, though, and the end of a zombie's life is marked by the bacteria fluorescing in its irises: green eyes.

The plot of the novel revolves around the escape of the poet-zombie Donnell Harrison, together with his therapist from the project, Jocundra Verrett. As their odyssey through the rotting landscape of the Deep South unfolds, Donnell becomes a kind of faith healer, and it becomes clear how apt the novel's title is, for *Green Eyes* is centrally concerned with his transformed perception. In the end, voodoo lore—which provided the original rationale for the project's experiments—gives Donnell a gateway to death or transcendence. However, although the set pieces of the novel are as vivid as those in his shorter works, the structure of the book is somewhat ramshackle, with a plot that begs more questions than it answers and jumps somewhat uneasily from place to place.

Shepard's talents were displayed to their best advantage in the short fiction assembled in *The Jaguar Hunter,* which won the World Fantasy Award for best collection. Apart from the title story, there were such tales as "Mengele," depicting the Nazi doctor continuing to live in the Paraguayan jungle thanks to his own surgical and genetic advances. Again, the premise is science fictional, but the tone is that of horror—specifically, morally informed horror, as becomes apparent when the protagonist, a pilot whose plane crashed near Mengele's hidden estate, returns to the United States at the end of the story. He begins to seek out people on the streets with the same deformities as he saw in Mengele's experiments, but he comes to realize that whether he finds them or not, Mengele's dull evil has pervaded the world anyway, palpable in the everyday cheapening and deadening of experience around him.

"The Night of White Bhairab" is an account of a generational haunting, in some ways conventionally structured, but made memorable by Shepard's imagery and the setting, tourist-infested Katmandu. Stories such as "Black Coral," "A Traveler's Tale," and "The End of Life as We Know It" use their settings in Latin America or the Caribbean not as decoration but as integral parts of the story. The latter, for instance, follows Richard and Lisa, an affluent American couple with a disintegrating marriage, on their holiday around Lake Atitlán in Guatemala. Lisa begins to become aware of a magical transformation coming over the world through her conversations with Murciélago, a local *brujo*, or wizard. Richard scorns her new outlook, and the story closes with Lisa setting out for the volcano where Murciélago lives, as the world shimmers and changes around her.

"A Spanish Lesson" draws explicitly on Shepard's own experiences as a traveler. Couched as autobiography, it depicts Shepard as part of a community of not particularly lovable bohemians in the Spanish village of Pedragalejo in 1964. The autobiographical thread sits side by side with a fantastic one, of the narrator becoming involved in sheltering time-travelers from an alternate universe where the Third Reich reigns supreme thanks to occult powers. Although opinions differ on how successfully the story integrates these two aspects, it concludes memorably, with an explicit and forcefully delivered moral about the need for each of us not to abdicate responsibility for the world's troubles, no matter how much they may seem out of our hands.

Most of the stories in *The Jaguar Hunter* are difficult to categorize as purely fantasy or science fiction. Reviewers have often made comparisons between Shepard's work and the magical realism of Gabriel García Márquez, but Shepard himself has said (for instance, in his 1990 interview with Wendy Counsil) that he feels such comparisons are inaccurate. One might suggest the work of Joseph Conrad, Paul Bowles, or Graham Greene as carrying the same charge of what John Clute has described as "the born exile's passionate fixation on place" (In Encyclopedia of Science Fiction, 1993). Within the genres of the fantastic, Shepard is clearly uninterested, though, in the generic games of rationalization and explanation. The supernatural powers in his stories are frequently amoral rather than purely evil or good, and act for reasons which humans cannot fathom. Perhaps for similar reasons Shepard has often eschewed the comfort of conventional resolutions for his stories.

In this context, "The Man Who Painted the Dragon Griaule" is an unusual story in *The Jaguar Hunter*, a wholehearted venture into pure fantasy. It is set in the Carbonales Valley, a region dominated by the body of a six-thousand-foot-long dragon, Griaule, alive but frozen into immobility by a spell cast millennia before. Meric Cattanay, a young artist, arrives in the valley and proposes that the dragon's vast hide be painted with pigments that will ultimately poison it and free the surrounding communities from its malign influence. Although the tale is told, unusually for Shepard, in a consistently "high" tone, its ambivalent ending and allegorical richness make it a piece with the rest of his work.

The stories from *The Jaguar Hunter* that attracted the most immediate attention, however, were "Salvador" and "R & R," depicting the United States fighting a near-future war in Central America. "Salvador," with its coruscating vision of American soldiers going into firefights while high on combat drugs and returning home as psychic walking wounded, makes explicit what had been implicit in the rest of Shepard's work: his visceral political engagement, in particular against the cruelties the developed world inflicts on poorer countries. As a polemic against the Ronald Reagan administration's global outlook, "Salvador" has few equals.

Although "R & R" is less graphic in its depictions of the horrors of war, largely taking place during a soldier's rest and recreation weekend, it is at least as harrowing. It is partly organized around the idea held by some soldiers that the war they are waging for Free Occupied Guatemala is in some sense magical, that "fate" or "chance" in such a context is just the enactment of a larger design that can be understood and manipulated. David Mingolla, the central character, spends his R & R in a quiet Guatemalan town and finds himself participating in a street lottery game run by a woman called Debora. He wins repeatedly, prompting suspicion from the locals, and subsequently talks inconclusively with Debora, who tells him about Psicorps, the elite army unit using psychic powers to affect the course of the war. Through that, and subsequent encounters with street children, two fellow soldiers, and the permanently helmeted pilots who ferry them back and forth to the front line, Mingolla's terrible dislocation from "normal" life is potently conveyed.

"R & R" took a Nebula Award in 1987 and became the first section of Shepard's second novel, *Life During Wartime* (1987). The novel follows Mingolla's progress deeper into the heart of this fictional war. He is recruited into Psicorps and encounters Debora again, discovering that she has been working for the other side in the war. Moreover, it becomes clear that the war is a manifestation of a larger, centuries-old conflict between two families in which Mingolla is to play a central role. Not for the first or last time in Shepard's work, the devices of science fiction act as openings into the structures of fantasy. Nonetheless, and despite the consistently compelling level of Shepard's writing, there was something of a loss in seeing the potent ambiguities and mysteries of "R & R" being given genre explanations.

THE ENDS OF THE EARTH

Shepard's second collection, *The Ends of the Earth* (1991), is if anything more varied than *The Jaguar Hunter*. Like its predecessor, it gained the World Fantasy Award. The title story revisits archetypal Shepard territory in its narrative of the reappearance of ancient gods in an out-of-the-way Guatemalan coastal town. However, its central section, recounting the protagonist's apparent possession, has a surreal force unmatched in Shepard's earlier work. Similarly, "Aymara" uses its fantastic tropes and Central American setting to provide a stunning vision of a world unmade and reborn.

Elsewhere in the collection, "Shades" and "Delta Sly Honey" provide scathing retrospectives on the Vietnam War. "The Exercise of Faith" is a supernatural story of a priest who, like Donnell Harrison at a revivalist meeting in *Green Eyes,* decides to tell his flock the opposite of what they have heard before. "Nomans Land" is a contemporary horror story set on an isolated island off the coast of Massachusetts, while "Bound for Glory" presents a nightmarish train journey through the heart of America as a psychic odyssey for its protagonists. "Fire Zone Emerald" returns to the territory of war in Central America; in a 1987 interview with Rafael Sa'adah, Shepard characterized it as an outtake from *Life During Wartime*. And "On the Border" makes concrete Shepard's implicit arguments about the relations of the United States with its southern neighbors, with its image of the Mexican border in the near future: "A curtain of shimmering blood-red energy that appeared to rise half-way to the stars before merging with the night sky" (p. 363). The border is, of course, lethal.

The Ends of the Earth contains a second Griaule story, "The Scalehunter's Beautiful Daughter" (also published as a separate volume); a third, *The Father of Stones,* was published as a novella chapbook in 1989 but remains uncollected. Although the Griaule stories have little in common but their setting and tone, Shepard has spoken in interviews of a fourth Griaule work, tentatively entitled "The Grand Tour," which will complete the sequence.

"The Scalehunter's Beautiful Daughter" is a rich moral allegory that follows the eponymous Catherine, who has been born and brought up in Hangtown, a settlement built on Griaule's vast back. Following an attack by local thugs, Catherine is forced to enter Griaule's mouth, and she dwells for many years in the strange ecosystem that lives within him. At the climax of the story, the dragon's heart beats once, freeing Catherine to return to Hangtown, which she now sees with new eyes. The superb close of the story encompasses many years of her life in a few pages, beautifully conveying what she has renounced and what she has accepted.

"Surrender," the final story in *The Ends of the Earth*, marks as clearly as possible the end of a period in Shepard's work. On its first publication in *Isaac Asimov's Science Fiction Magazine* (August 1989), the accompanying note stated that the author intended to set no more stories in Central America—in other words, that he seemed to be abandoning his best-known setting. The content of the story made amply clear his reasons. The narrator, a cynical and self-loathing journalist called Carl, stumbles across an experimental farm in Guatemala whose produce has transformed the natives into brain-damaged, nocturnal mutants. A gun battle erupts outside the room where Carl is interrogating one of the heads of the project. Shepard uses the strangeness of Carl's situation to make a point about the realities of Latin American life:

> This was, you see, a particularly poignant moment for me. I realized the horror that was transpiring outside was in character with all the other horrors I'd witnessed. I'm sure that reading this as fiction, which is the only way I can present it, some will say that by injecting a science-fictional element, I'm trivializing the true Central American condition. But that's not the case. What was going on was no different from a thousand other events that had happened over the previous hundred and fifty years or so. This was the *rule*.
>
> (p. 474)

Carl's, and Shepard's, rage at the Central American condition, and what the United States has done to create it, are uniquely forceful in "Surrender"; the story is narrated at a pitch of anger and horror that even Shepard's other work cannot equal. After reading its closing pages of fury at the self-satisfied contentment of the United States and its dependency on the agonies of the poor, it is difficult to imagine anything more being said on the subject.

KALIMANTAN, THE GOLDEN, AND SHORT FICTION

Shepard has spoken eloquently about these political issues, as well as about his approach to writing, in various interviews. These are an indispensable source for anyone interested in his work: in many ways, he is his own best critic. In his 1990 interview with Wendy Counsil, he stated that he planned to travel to Borneo in the near future to research a major new vampire novel that he planned to set there. This project seems to have split in two, as there followed the Borneo-set science fiction-tinged novella *Kalimantan* (1990) and the vampire novel *The Golden* (1993). *Kalimantan* makes more explicit than ever Shepard's debt to Joseph Conrad and, in particular, to *Heart of Darkness*. The main story is narrated by a down-at-the-heels British jewel dealer, Barnett, to an unnamed listener, and concerns the Kurtz-figure Curtis MacKinnon and his discoveries in the jungle upcountry. These discoveries have an explicitly science-fictional rationale—a vast alien spaceship—which does not perhaps mesh well with Shepard's otherwise striking evocation of Borneo and its culture. Again, it is a culture that the influence of the developed world is causing to mutate into strange new shapes.

The Golden, by contrast, is a full-length horror novel, a vampire story of striking intensity.

Its principal setting, Castle Banat, is in the extensive tradition of edifices in fantasy or horror that are almost characters in themselves—from the House of Usher and Gormenghast through Gene Wolfe's House Absolute to the libraries of Borges. The story itself concerns a nineteenth-century gathering of vampires at the castle to sample the Golden, a mortal whose bloodlines have been planned over many centuries to have the finest possible bouquet. However, the Golden is killed and drained of blood before this planned ceremony, and Michael Beheim, a former Paris detective, is assigned by his vampire mentor, Roland Agenor, to investigate the crime. It's difficult to imagine a more amoral premise for a novel to have, and yet the reader begins to identify with Beheim. As ever, the generic elements in the story—in this case, police procedural as well as erotic horror—exist in a moral context, that of the examination of evil. In its formalized tone, *The Golden* belongs with Shepard's Griaule stories. It is arguably his most wholly successful novel to date.

Meanwhile, Shepard continued to produce shorter fiction, though not at the same rate as before. Some was contained in two chapbook collections, *Nantucket Slayrides* (1989) and *Sports & Music* (1994). Perhaps the most striking work in either is "The All-Consuming" in *Nantucket Slayrides,* written with the poet Robert Frazier. It concerns Yuoki Akashini, a man who has an entry in the *Guinness Book of Records* for eating, among other things, a Rolls-Royce Corniche, a small bronze by Rodin, and Lee Harvey Oswald's rifle. He comes to a town on the edge of the Malsueno, a polluted jungle region, with the intention of eating it too. The collaboration with Frazier produced a story both more surreal and more rooted in the mundane than Shepard's other work.

"BARNACLE BILL THE SPACER" AND LATER WORKS

In Shepard's third full collection, *Barnacle Bill the Spacer and Other Stories* (1997), the title story, first published in 1993, is a full-blooded space opera that won the Hugo Award. Its setting is pure science fiction: "Solitaire Station, out beyond the orbit of Mars, where the lightships are assembled and launched, vanishing in thousand-mile-long shatterings" (p. 2). But the tale of partial redemption Shepard set there could take place in many other venues, and for some readers the story is marred by his decision to render the dialogue of a major character in phonetic Cockney. "All the Perfumes of Araby" shares with "Barnacle Bill" a world-weariness even greater than in Shepard's earlier work, though its tale of supernatural happenings around the Khan al Khalili bazaar in Cairo is familiar territory. "Beast of the Heartland," the story of a boxer down on his luck, has only marginal supernatural content but is as gripping a character study as Shepard had yet published.

Shepard has said (in an interview with Nick Gevers) that he is dissatisfied with this collection, and in reviewing the book, Brian Stableford isolated a weakness in his work: "Shepard must have become painfully aware that his one crippling limitation as a writer is his inability to construct a decent plot, and the stories in [this collection] illustrate the extent to which he has been prepared to go to overcome this problem" (p. 18). Stableford's argument—that "Barnacle Bill" is Conrad's *The Nigger of the "Narcissus"* in space, just as "Beast of the Heartland" is a rewrite of *Rocky*—may be somewhat overstated, but it's true that readers do not go to Shepard for the originality of his ideas but rather for their execution.

By the mid-1990s, Shepard's published output had slowed drastically, and William G. Contento's comprehensive bibliography shows no new stories published by him between 1996 and 1999. However, Shepard returned to fiction with the publication of "Crocodile Rock" in the fiftieth anniversary issue of the *Magazine of Fantasy & Science Fiction*. His subsequent genre work to date is listed in the bibliography.

Although none of the stories from this period has yet been collected, a significant proportion of it is available online. To take a few examples from this output, Nick Gevers (one of Shepard's most thoughtful advocates) has described "Eternity and Afterward" as "a blistering existential salvo such as hasn't been seen from him since the 80s." Its setting, a Russian nightclub called Eternity, is a strikingly bizarre venue, where reality shifts to reflect back not only the protagonist's fears but also Russia's.

Other stories from this period, such as "AZTECHS," returned to the Central American settings of the 1980s with renewed vigor and clarity. The two short novels Shepard published in early 2002, *Valentine* and *Colonel Rutherford's Colt*, were presented as mainstream stories, but are substantially enriched by readings informed by the possibilities of the fantastic. *Valentine*, for instance, is couched as a love letter written by Russell, a journalist, to his lover, Kay. But Russell's account of their relationship may be unreliable, with his skill as a writer overtaking the truth, and the dark hints at science-fictional plots may need to be taken seriously. In its close, confessional tone, it is as darkly fascinating as Gene Wolfe's works in this vein.

This newest phase of Shepard's work shows his talents at full stretch, including his ear for dialogue, his powers of evocation, the sustained intensity of his writing, and his moral engagement with his characters. He also clearly wants to use a wider range of settings and tones than before. It is, of course, impossible to know how much he will continue to write within the genres of the fantastic, but his rich and complex sensibility has already added to them greatly over the last two decades.

Selected Bibliography

I'm very grateful to Richard Bleiler and Janice Bogstad for help with bibliographic information at short notice.

WORKS OF LUCIUS SHEPARD

NOVELS AND SHORT STORIES

Green Eyes. New York: Ace Books, 1984; London: Chatto and Windus, 1986.

The Jaguar Hunter. Sauk City, Wis.: Arkham House, 1987; London: Paladin, 1988. (The Arkham House edition contains a strikingly evocative jacket and internal photomontage illustrations by J. K. Potter. These were omitted in the U.K. edition, which also omitted "R&R" and substituted "Solitario's Eyes" and "The Exercise of Faith.")

Life During Wartime. New York: Bantam Books, 1987; London: Grafton, 1988.

The Scalehunter's Beautiful Daughter. Shingletown, Calif.: Mark V. Ziesing, 1988. (This novella was subsequently reprinted in *Isaac Asimov's Science Fiction Magazine*, September 1988.)

The Father of Stones. Baltimore: Washington Science Fiction Association, 1989. (This novella was subsequently reprinted in *Isaac Asimov's Science Fiction Magazine*, September 1989.)

Nantucket Slayrides: Three Short Novels. With Robert Frazier. Nantucket, Mass.: Eel Grass Press, 1989.

Kalimantan. London: Legend, 1990; New York: St. Martin's Press, 1991. (Illustrated by Jamel Akib.)

The Ends of the Earth. Sauk City, Wis.: Arkham House, 1991; London: Millennium, 1993. (The Arkham House edition again had beautiful illustrations by J. K. Potter, omitted in the U.K. edition.)

The Golden. Shingletown, Calif.: Mark V. Ziesing and London: Millennium, 1993.

Sports and Music. Shingletown, Calif.: Mark V. Ziesing, 1994. (The two stories in this collection, "A Little Night Music" and "Sports in America," were also included in *Barnacle Bill the Spacer and Other Stories*.)

Barnacle Bill the Spacer and Other Stories. London: Orion, 1997.

As *Beast of the Heartland and Other Stories*, New York: Four Walls Eight Windows, 1999.

"Crocodile Rock." *Magazine of Fantasy & Science Fiction*, October-November 1999.

"Radiant Green Star." *Asimov's Science Fiction Magazine*, August 2000.

"Eternity and Afterward." *Magazine of Fantasy & Science Fiction*, March 2001. (The March 2001 edition of *Magazine of Fantasy & Science Fiction* was a special Lucius Shepard issue, also containing the profile by Katherine Dunn and the bibliography by William G. Contento cited below, as well as Shepard's regular, acerbic film column.)

"AZTECHS." www.scifi.com/scifiction. First posted September 5, 2001.

Colonel Rutherford's Colt. Published as an e-book by www.electricstory.com, 2002.

Valentine. New York: Four Walls Eight Windows, 2002.

"Over Yonder." www.scifi.som/scifiction. (First posted January 2, 2002).

"Emerald Street Expansions." www.scifi.com/scifiction. (First posted March 27, 2002.)

BIBLIOGRAPHY

Contento, W. G. "Lucius Taylor Shepard: Bibliography." *Magazine of Fantasy & Science Fiction* (March 2001), pp. 85–88. (Contento provides a comprehensive list of Shepard's shorter fiction, as well as listing first publication of all his novels and collections.)

CRITICAL STUDIES

Clute, John. "Lucius Shepard." In *The Encyclopedia of Science Fiction*. Edited by John Clute and Peter Nicholls. London: Orbit and New York: St. Martin's Press, 1993. P. 1100.

Clute, John. "Lucius Shepard." In *The Encyclopedia of Fantasy*. Edited by John Clute and John Grant. London: Orbit and New York: St. Martin's Press, 1997. Pp. 862–863.

Counsil, Wendy. "Lucius Shepard." *Interzone*, 34:34–38 (March-April 1990). (An interview, particularly strong on Shepard's writing methods.)

Dunn, Katherine. "An Introduction to Lucius Shepard." *Magazine of Fantasy and Science Fiction* (March 2001), pp. 4–10.

Gevers, Nick. Review of "Eternity and Afterward." Online at http://www.sfsite.com/04a/fsf03101.htm. Posted 2001.

———. "Lowlife Baroque: Lucius Shepard Interviewed." *Interzone*, 168:29–34 (June 2001).

———. Review of *Valentine* and *Colonel Rutherford's Colt*. *Locus* (February 2002), pp. 29–30.

Sa'dah, Rafael. "Eye to Eye with Lucius Shepard." *SF EYE* 2:5–33. (August 1987) (Extremely interesting and lengthy interview, particularly strong on Shepard's life before writing.)

Stableford, Brian. Review of *Beast of the Heartland and Other Stories*. *New York Review of Science Fiction* (November 1999), pp. 18–19.

Swanwick, Michael. "A User's Guide to the Postmoderns." In *Moon Dogs*. Framingham, Mass.: NESFA Press, 2001. Pp. 257–274. (Swanwick's well-known essay, originally published in 1986, examined the work of the young "cyberpunk" and "humanist" authors of the time, yet found Shepard too complex a case to be placed in either camp.)

John Shirley
1953–

JEFF PRICKMAN

JOHN SHIRLEY IS a prolific author, screenwriter, and songwriter whose contributions to science fiction and, in recent years, almost exclusively horror, are significant. Often misinterpreted by critics as merely trying to shock, Shirley always adds a layer of social conscience to his fiction, no matter how twisted or bizarre the plot. Born John Patrick Shirley in 1953 in Houston, Texas, he never lived in one place for long, but grew up mainly in California and Oregon. His father died when he was ten.

Shirley began writing as a teenager, finding a niche in Portland. In "A Writer Meets Himself," he describes his early efforts: "I often sent out a story without even re-reading it....I'd tear it out of the typewriter, slap it, hands shaking, into the envelope and RUN with it to the post office. Cackling all the way" (p. 11). Eventually his short stories could not be ignored, and a turning point was attending the 1972 Clarion writing workshop in Seattle, with no less than Ursula K. LeGuin, Robert Silverberg, Terry Carr, and Harlan Ellison as instructors. Far from being intimidated, Shirley states in *The Exploded Heart*, "I entered the class by climbing up to the outside of the building and leaping in through the window" (p. 65). However, entering through a window was the least of the young Shirley's antics.

He is very candid about his wild youth, including living on the streets of San Francisco as a hustler and drug addict. Expelled from high school in Salem, Oregon, Shirley's only permanent job has been his writing. In *The Exploded Heart* he acknowledges, "I had but one or two actual jobs in my life. They only lasted about six months apiece. I tended to write at work" (p. 155). The result of his writing work ethic is a daunting array of short stories and novels, plus numerous screenplays for film (including co-writing *The Crow*) and television.

Shirley has always worn his heart on his sleeve, dedicating his books to his wife at the time of publication. He has been married at least five times, currently to Michelina Perry (since the early 1990s). Another love is rock music. References to The Velvet Underground, Iggy Pop, and Blue Oyster Cult (for whom he writes lyrics) are plentiful in his works. He has sung and released albums in bands such as Terror Wrist, The Monitors, Sado-Nation, Obsession, and, recently, The Panther Moderns.

In contrast to the chaotic nature of his life throughout his career, Shirley is remarkably consistent in the themes of his works. The evil in Shirley is always corporate malfeasance, or supernatural beings using psychic powers. The multifaceted nature of Shirley's talent and career is demonstrated in his first three novels for Zebra Books. These novels establish the tropes that Shirley uses to this day.

Transmaniacon, published in 1979 but written five years earlier, features a balkanized twenty-second century post-nuclear war America, where power is concentrated in city-states. Dolphins have become intelligent and pursue their own agenda. Ben Rackey has the ability to transfer his feelings telepathically, a talent heightened when the Exciter, a device that magnifies people's rage, is implanted below his heart. Shirley's early interest in body augmentation became a major aspect of the science fiction subgenre cyberpunk.

Dracula In Love (1979) features key Shirley horror concepts, including psychic manipulation for evil ends. Vladimir Horescu, CEO of the San Francisco-based IBEX Corporation, receives a letter from a man claiming to be his father, none other than Dracula. Dracula raped Horescu's mother, who now resides in a mental asylum. When Dracula arrives he quickly turns to an army of living dead "revenants" to do his bidding, and uses mind control to create rapists to terrorize the city. Horescu also wrestles with his feelings for his ex-wife, Lollie, a morphine addict. Their conflicting desire for each other sets the pattern most Shirley romantic relationships follow.

Three Ring Psychus (1980) features psychic energies as the basis for the plot. People begin to float upward, and suddenly have a greater awareness of the feelings of others. Richard Dreyer and Emmy Durant, the most harmonious of all Shirley couples, are conscripted by the military, which seeks to harness the newfound mental powers against the invading Russian army. Eventually The All Source arises, a Colony of hermaphrodites linked as one mental entity. The Colony sends a message of peace to everybody, ending the war. Shirley posits increased empathy and loss of ego as ultimately beneficial, but only after a painful process of adjustment and a revocation of the entire set of assumptions society is based upon.

City Come A-Walkin' (1980) is acknowledged by many, including William Gibson, as the first cyberpunk novel. Stuart Cole owns Club Anesthesia, a sleazy San Francisco bar featuring angst rock bands like The Catz Report, led by Cole's sometime lover Catz Wailen. The protection money Cole has been paying to the Mob is no longer enough. He is charged extortionist back-taxes when the Bureau of Electronic Disbursement (BED) moves all commerce to Interfund, an electronic system replacing cash. Cole faces the loss of his livelihood and attacks on the bar by moral vigilantes working for BED. The plot matches early cyberpunk's tendency to tell simple stories heavily influenced by noir elements—a small businessman fighting a criminal organization with the law on its side.

The psychic element of the novel is the city of San Francisco itself. The character City is formed from the unconscious frustrations of all of the city's residents. City leads the fight against BED, but takes over Cole's body and mind in the process (a concept appearing repeatedly in Shirley). Each city generates an overmind, which becomes part of a psychic connection. City by city, The Sweep wipes out the Mafia and its business cronies nationwide. This resolution establishes the cyberpunk formula of individuals on the fringe of society harnessing the resources to defeat much stronger foes.

At this point, Shirley's novels go back and forth between science fiction and horror. In "A Writer Meets Himself," Shirley acknowledges the split and his fear at the time of "a sort of maze-trap of ghettoized genre writing stretching ahead of me. I thought: Break into the mainstream, or at least out of SF, before it's too late" (p. 10). *The Brigade* (1981) was his attempt to do just that.

The foe in the novel is the brutal police force formed to protect the community of Salton, Oregon, from the serial murderer dubbed the Saturday Night Killer. The real horror is the abuses a group of armed men inflict on a town cut off from the rest of the world. Tony Holister, a precocious eighteen-year-old, works to expose the increasingly deadly Brigade with his high school Principal, Sonja Kramer, who is twenty-five. The sexual tension between Tony and Sonja is a highlight of the novel. The identity of the killer is perhaps predictable, but the plot is realistic in depicting how citizens participate in or fight the oppression of their neighbors.

For his next effort, Shirley returned to all-out horror in one of his most terrifying novels to date, *Cellars* (1982). He creates a Dantesque depiction of New York City in the hot summer with abandoned buildings, trash-filled streets, sub-basements, and subway tunnels evoking urban squalor. Psychic powers and the supernatural figure heavily in the plot. The main character, Carl Lanyard, reluctantly realizes he has The Gift, an ability to see black, squirming shapes from another dimension. These energies serve the Persian demon Ahriman, an entity that provides the murderers material gain in exchange for the energy fields emitted when the victims die. Lanyard obtains the crucial jade urn necessary to control Ahriman, only to be fatally betrayed at the novel's end.

Cellars is full of nasty, visceral images. Children become killers, and dog literally eats dog in one scene. Shirley describes in "A Writer Meets Himself" how the novel is "about people exploiting people, making them into cattle. It's no accident that the hideous human sacrifices performed...were rewarded with financial benefit" (p. 10). He certainly set the stage for the horror subgenre splatterpunk with this unpleasant yet compelling novel.

No novels appeared in 1983 and 1984, but, far from taking a break, Shirley was creating and writing two action-adventure series. He wrote nineteen novels published from 1984 to 1986 under two pseudonyms, eleven as John Cutter for Signet's *The Specialist* and eight as D. B. Drumm for Dell's *The Traveler*. However, in the mid 1980s, simultaneous with the publication of the pseudonymous works, he received the most acclaim and notoriety of his career, but for his science fiction rather than his horror.

Shirley had always felt like a misfit in science fiction, due to his outsider, anti-hero characters and the lack of aliens or other planets in his works. Cyberpunk's portrayals of misfits using technology to survive matched what Shirley had been doing years before in *Transmaniacon* and *City Come A-Walkin'*. He was also a friend and outspoken supporter of the key authors of what he called The Movement, fellow writers such as Gibson, Bruce Sterling, Rudy Rucker, and Lewis Shiner.

The epic *A Song Called Youth* trilogy is cyberpunk at its best, and it has rarely been surpassed since. Possessing a social conscience and plot sophistication far beyond any of the clichés that plagued the subgenre, the politics behind the series was heavily influenced by Shirley's observations while living in France in the early 1980s. He states in "A Writer Meets Himself," "I saw that the Front National, the new French fascist party, was growing more and more powerful....I see similar movements elsewhere in Europe and the potential for them here" (p. 11). In *Eclipse* (1985), America is vulnerable to fascism due to an irreversible economic decline. The daily lives of people worldwide revolve around the influential Grid, the electronic network for all entertainment and information. The effects of holograms, televised execution contests, and memory extraction are chillingly depicted, while the combat scenes are unflinchingly detailed.

The story takes place mainly in Europe, under siege from the New Soviet invasion, and on the FirStep orbital colony. The Second Alliance (SA), a corporation specializing in security and anti-terrorist services, sends in its own troops to bolster a hapless NATO. However, the real agenda behind the SA and its influential Christian Fundamentalist Worldtalk program is an ideology centered on the genetic purity of the white race. The SA is willing to use any means for genocide, including a virus designed to kill only certain races.

Steinfeld, a former member of the Israeli Mossad, leads the New Resistance against the SA and takes personal responsibility for the inevitably tragic compromises he must make to win. Dan "Hard-Eyes" Torrence becomes a major resistance leader, and his tumultuous relationship with Claire Rimpler connects various plotlines over the course of the books. Claire is the strongest woman character Shirley has created to date, deftly resuming the leadership of FirStep after a rebellion orchestrated by the SA removes her father from power. He is not quite killed, for his brain lives on using electromagnetic energy.

Bettina is another strong female character whose computer hacking skills resolve crucial plot points of *Eclipse Corona* (1990). She and her lover, Jerome-X, possess brain chips allowing access to the Plateau, a form of higher consciousness within cyberspace. Bettina is also voluptuous and black, defying the cyberpunk tendency to feature only scrawny white males (like Jerome-X) as techno savvy. The cast throughout the trilogy is racially and ethnically diverse. Shirley's thoughtful presentation of the effects of racism on personal and global levels is honest and rare in any type of fiction.

Two anthologies do an excellent job of capturing the variety of Shirley's science fiction short stories to this point. *Heatseeker* (1989) appeared during the height of cyberpunk, but contained short science fiction published between 1975 and 1988. Written in 1976 but published years later, "Sleepwalkers" (*New Pathways*, Spring 1988) presents a variation on the Shirley motif of loss of body control. Ex-junkie Jules, desperate for money to support his apathetic lover Zimm's drug habit, rents his body to the Sleepwalkers Agency. Discovering bruises after, he uses an antidote to stay awake during the next session. Shocked to discover he is part of an elaborate sexual role-playing fantasy for the wealthy renters, he accepts his fate, but vows to keep the payment for his friends, not Zimm, thus determining by whom he will be used—a standard Shirley outcome.

The previously unpublished "I Live In Elizabeth" (1988) adds a new angle on the loss of body theme. Blue and Elizabeth discover during sex that they can transfer and share consciousness. Imprisoned after being caught with cocaine for Elizabeth, in exchange for parole Blue participates in an experiment using D-17, a medication for planting subliminal suggestions during sleep. Driven to suicide by the resulting nightmares, Blue's consciousness flees into Elizabeth, and both live inside her body.

The Exploded Heart (1996) collects a different set of Shirley science fiction short stories, all but one written between 1975 and 1991. Besides the excellent author comments preceding each tale, the anthology contains Shirley's non-*Eclipse* cyberpunk short fiction (except for "Shaman"). Together these stories present a harsh vision of the future: small alliances of people try to survive riots and starvation in wrecked urban landscapes, where only fundamentalist religions and corporations still hold power.

Both collections show an approach to science fiction eschewing spaceships, robots, and alien planets (indeed, Shirley's only alien planet setting in a novel to date is in *A Splendid Chaos*). Perhaps having felt he had done all he could in the *Eclipse* trilogy, around 1990 Shirley announced his decision to leave science fiction for horror, a genre he had continued to write in, even at the peak of his cyberpunk prominence, with *In Darkness Waiting* (1988). Shirley has stayed true to his intent, with *Silicon Embrace* (1996), a lighthearted (by Shirley standards) tale about the truth behind aliens, his only recent science fiction novel.

In retrospect, 1991 is the year when, even as the last of the cyberpunk stories appeared in various anthologies, Shirley's real future direction was mapped with *Wetbones*, which makes *Cellars* seem mild in comparison. Ephram uses mental telepathy to search for and feed on victims psychically until they are literally drained. The plot strands intersect with drug counselor (and ex-addict) Reverend Garner's desperate search for his daughter Constance, who becomes Ephram's minion and endures innumerable violations. Besides the psychic evil of the Ether World Akishra beings Ephram serves, arguably the most terrifying section of the book occurs in chapters eight and nine when Garner, mistakenly believing Constance is dead, relapses and is at the mercy of crack cocaine dealers and users.

The appearance of the short story collection *New Noir* (1993) laid down the gauntlet that the nastiness of *Wetbones* was no fluke. In "Jody and Annie on TV" (*Cold Blood*, edited by Richard T. Chizmar, 1991) the title characters drive through the sun-baked, exhaust-fumed streets of California shooting people randomly. At the end of the story, having finally killed enough to get noticed, the two nobodies become somebody live on TV as the police close in. *Black Butterflies* (1998) is a more extensive collection of the rest of Shirley's 1990s horror stories.

While the stories are still quite violent, there is individual responsibility, and there are consequences for behavior. In "War and Peace" (*Fear Itself*, edited by Jeff Gelb, 1995), Oakland police officer Butch murders his wife, Della, but makes her death appear to be from gang violence. Due to a shared secret involving stolen drug money, Butch figures his partner, Hank, will never reveal any suspicions he may have about Della's death. However, Hank administers his own form of justice. "Barbara" (*Dark Love*, edited by Nancy A. Collins et al., 1995) is about a woman who turns being carjacked by teens VJ and Reebok to her advantage, getting revenge on her ex-lover and giving the young hoodlums far more than they ever bargained for. In "How Deep the Taste of Love" (*Hottest Blood*, edited by Gelb and Michael Garrett, 1993), Sid Drexel, relieved that his wife died in a car accident, successfully hits on his fantasy woman in a bar, but when they go to her place he learns, too late, that her desire, not his, is coming true.

Shirley's three most recent novels are fairly short, and use a previous story or novella as their foundation. The strongest of the three is *The View From Hell* (2001), which uses the earlier short story "V, H, and You" (*Zyzzyva*, 1991) for a Prologue. In *The Exploded Heart*, Shirley states, "In this story real life is the horror—and the supernatural world is the refuge" (p. 225). H is an inter-dimensional being fascinated by human tragedy. Unable to remain an observer, he begins to manipulate the dreams of those he watches, reveling in the chaos he causes.

Three plotlines converge by the novel's end. Jack Younger pitches a TV show to the powerful Underhill. Underhill demands one night with Younger's fiancée Linda in exchange for approving the series. After H intervenes, Younger walks into the follow-up meeting and fatally shoots Underhill and everybody else present, including himself. Jane is a real estate agent, who, thanks to H, becomes convinced the couple she is showing a home to want to kill her. She calls 911 in hysterics, assuring a deadly response from the officers who respond.

The third chapter, "Pills," is a Shirley tour de force. The author is at his absolute best here as he weaves a complicated scheme by two Topgrade Pharmaceutical executives to cover up the side effects of their drug Xanton. They knew Xanton turns women on birth control homicidal but chose to dismiss the evidence. Their deceit fails utterly when two female police officers drink coffee spiked with Xanton.

H brings many of the novel's characters together for the finale, trapping them in a series of rooms with no way out. What follows is a haunting depiction of isolation, frustration, boredom, and choosing to die, because there is nothing else to do—until even death becomes dull. Throughout the novel, Shirley shows how the indifference and selfishness people demonstrate daily provide all the ingredients H needs to make recipes for disaster.

... And The Angel with Television Eyes (2001) is based on the short story of the same name (*Asimov's*, May 1983). The Hidden Race

of plasmagnomes has periodically reduced the human population (the Biblical Flood, Atlantis). The increased microwave and electromagnetic emissions of humanity now threaten their existence. One faction wants a peaceful resolution, but another decides to attack.

Demons (2002) combines the 2000 novella of the same name as Book One and "Undercurrent," a sequel set nine years later. Extended descriptions of the demons and the havoc they wreak weaken Book One, but the first-person narrative of the main character, Ira, is appealing. Ira is in love with Melissa, the daughter of Professor Paymenz, a member of an ancient secret organization of higher consciousness called The Circle. Melissa turns out to be the Gold of the Urn, the only power capable of ending the demonic invasion.

"Undercurrent" features Steven Isquerat, a recent young hire at West Wind corporation, who wrestles with his conscience over the effects of the company's new pesticide, Dirvane 17. The strongest scenes in the novel depict the fatal devastation D-17 causes in Ash Valley, California, where it is tested without the town's consent. Ira and Melissa are now married and have a son, Marcus. After a harrowing trip to Turkmenistan, which includes the imprisonment and torture of Ira, they learn that Marcus will be a prominent figure in The Circle, but at the price of losing his consciousness to the powerful Mendel.

Shirley cleverly brings together his two standard evils, corporations and demons, through psychonomics, the psychic ability to influence economics. In exchange for this ability, corporate leaders work on behalf of the demons, including creating industrial accidents to prepare for their materialization from the astral realm to earth.

Just as *Demons* links elements of science fiction and horror, two anthologies put Shirley's career to this point in perspective. *Really, Really, Really, Really Weird Stories* (1999) is a comprehensive compilation of over two decades of short fiction, spanning 1973 to 1999, organized in order of "weirdness" by Shirley without any distinction for genre. In contrast, *Darkness Divided* (2001), another hefty collection, addresses the dual nature of his career directly, with the first section horror stories published between 1991 and 2000, and the second science fiction from 1976 to 1999. Despite the wide range of material present, there is no overlap between the two collections.

John Shirley has proved that no matter how his work may be categorized, he follows and fulfills his unique vision. The result is a copious volume of tales that, while wildly diverse, nonetheless focus on a consistent set of themes: what happens to the individual matters, and there are always hidden truths—and forces—beyond our perception.

Selected Bibliography

WORKS OF JOHN SHIRLEY

NOVELS AND SHORT STORIES

Transmaniacon. New York: Zebra, 1979.

Dracula in Love. New York: Zebra, 1979.

Three-Ring Psychus. New York: Zebra, 1980.

City Come A-Walkin'. New York: Dell, 1980. Revised edition, Asheville, N.C.: Eyeball, 1996.

JOHN SHIRLEY

The Brigade. New York: Avon, 1981.

Cellars. New York: Avon, 1982.

A Song Called Youth. Vol. 1: *Eclipse*. New York: Bluejay, 1985. London: Methuen, 1986. Revised edition, Northridge, Calif.: Babbage Press, 1999.

A Splendid Chaos. New York: Franklin Watts, 1988.

In Darkness Waiting. New York: Onyx, 1988. London: Grafton, 1991.

A Song Called Youth. Vol. 2: *Eclipse Penumbra*. New York: Questar, 1988. Revised edition, Northridge, Calif.: Babbage Press, 2000.

Kamus of Kadizhar: The Black Hole of Carcosa. New York: St. Martin's, 1988. (Based on Michael Reaves's *Darkworld Detective*.)

"Shaman." *Isaac Asimov's Science Fiction*, November 1988, pp. 76-105. (Uncollected but also in *The 1989 Annual World's Best SF*. Edited by Donald A. Wollheim with Arthur W. Saha. New York: DAW, 1989, pp. 49-81.)

Heatseeker. Los Angeles: Scream Press, 1989. London: Grafton, 1990. (Short stories, three previously unpublished.)

A Song Called Youth. Vol. 3: *Eclipse Corona*. New York: Questar, 1990. Revised edition, Northridge, Calif.: Babbage Press, 2000.

Wetbones. Shingletown, Calif.: Ziesing, 1991. London: Blake, 1993.

New Noir. Boulder, Colo.: Black Ice, 1993. (Six short stories, "Skeeter Junkie" previously unpublished.)

The Exploded Heart: The Trajectory of a Science Fiction Punk. Asheville, N.C.: Eyeball, 1996. (Short stories, plus two previously unpublished novel excerpts.)

Silicon Embrace. Shingletown, Calif.: Ziesing, 1996.

Black Butterflies. Shingletown, Calif.: Ziesing, 1998. (Short stories, two previously unpublished.)

Really, Really, Really, Really Weird Stories. Mountain View, Calif.: Night Shade, 1999. (Short stories, ten [very short] previously unpublished.)

Demons. Abingdon, Md.: Cemetery Dance, 2000. New York: Del Rey, 2002. (Includes sequel "Undercurrent." Harlan Ellison narrates audio version, Fantastic Audio, 2002.)

Darkness Divided. Lancaster, Pa.: Stealth Press, 2001. (Short stories, four previously unpublished.)

The View from Hell. Burton, Mich.: Subterranean Press, 2001.

"Her Hunger." In *Night Visions 10*. Edited by Richard Chizmar. Burton, Mich.: Subterranean Press, 2001, ppp. 93-193.

"The Claw Spurs." *Horror Garage*, 3:6-11 (2001).

...And the Angel with Television Eyes. San Francisco: Night Shade, 2001. (Slipcased edition includes chapbook *Box in My Head*.)

"One Stick, Both Ends Sharpened." *Horror Garage*, 4:32-36 (2001).

AUTOBIOGRAPHICAL MATERIAL

"A Writer Meets Himself." *Thrust*, 32:9-12 (Winter 1989).

"Violence." *SF Eye*, 13:47-53 (Spring 1994).

"Five Reasons I Wear Black (Are the Five Reasons I Write Noir)." *Horror Garage*, 2:54-57 (2000).

SCREENPLAYS

The Crow. With David J. Schow. Directed by Alex Proyas. Miramax, 1994.

"Visionary." *Star Trek: Deep Space Nine*. Story by Ethan H. Calk. Directed by Reza Badiyi. Paramount Pictures, 1995.

Night of the Headless Horseman. Directed by Shane Williams. Fox, 1999.

Robert Silverberg
1935–

ARTHUR HLAVATY

ROBERT SILVERBERG WAS born in Brooklyn, New York, on January 15, 1935, the only child of Michael Silverberg (an accountant) and Helen Baim Silverberg. A bright, bookish child, he discovered science fiction at an early age and began submitting stories to the science fiction magazines at age thirteen. For years he achieved no success with these, but in 1955 Thomas Y. Crowell published his first science fiction book, a children's novel called *Revolt on Alpha C*. He attended Columbia University, studying the modernist literature whose traces can be found throughout his own writing, such as Joseph Conrad, T.S. Eliot, and William Butler Yeats. He graduated in 1956 with an B.A. in English Literature and married Barbara H. Brown the same year, when he also won a Hugo Award as "best new writer."

In the late 1950s there were many science fiction magazines, offering an almost insatiable market for stories that satisfied the minimal standards of pulp genre writing. Silverberg made heroic efforts to fill this continuing need. Often writing as fast as he could touch-type, he turned out thousands of words, winning a reputation as someone who could provide writing on specified themes, to specified lengths, even under tight time constraints.

In 1959 the market for science fiction magazines collapsed, so Silverberg turned his prodigious writing energies to other areas, from well-researched studies of history and archeology to pseudonymous soft-core pornography. He purchased a Bronx mansion that had once belonged to Mayor Fiorello La Guardia, and the mortgage required him to produce even more wordage.

By the mid-sixties Silverberg found himself missing science fiction. Frederik Pohl, then editor of *Galaxy*, promised to buy anything he offered. With this encouragement Silverberg was soon writing at a pace not too much slower than that of his early work, but at a far higher level of aspiration and achievement. In the letter columns of the magazines his stories appeared in and elsewhere, some complained that his new work was depressing and difficult, but others praised the skill of the prose, the depth of characterization, and the strength of his vision. His peers and readers recognized the quality of his work: In 1969 his "Nightwings" was awarded the Hugo as best novella. He won a Nebula award in 1970, for the short story "Passengers," and two the following year—for his novel *A Time of Changes* and the short story "Good News from the Vatican"—then yet another, in 1975, for his novella "Born with the

Dead." In 1970 he was Guest of Honor at the World Science Fiction Convention.

He also found the time to compile a large number of science fiction anthologies, including the popular original anthology series New Dimensions, and to serve as president of Science Fiction Writers of America for 1967-1968, when it was still in its formative years.

All that work was taking its toll, however. In 1966 he suffered a thyroid malfunction that seemed serious at the time, but was eventually brought under control. He felt a continuing loss of energy from the disease, though, and in 1967 his yearly published word production fell below the million mark for the first time in many years, never to return. The La Guardia mansion was seriously damaged by fire in 1968. He was unhurt and the house was fully reconstructed, but it was another blow. In 1972 he moved from New York, his lifelong home, to northern California. He was growing weary from all the writing, and he was disappointed that many preferred his early hack work to his more serious efforts. In 1975 he announced his retirement from science fiction writing.

In 1976, however, he and his wife separated, and to buy her a house of her own, he offered to write one more book for the then-unprecedented sum of $127,500. That book, *Lord Valentine's Castle*, had a sweep and grandeur new to his writing while retaining the virtues of his sixties work. The book was widely praised, and it won the Locus award as the year's best fantasy novel. Silverberg felt encouraged to continue. He wrote more books and stories set on Majipoor, the scene of *Lord Valentine's Castle*, as well as unrelated science fiction. The awards began pouring in again: the 1986 Nebula for his novella *Sailing to Byzantium*, the 1987 Hugo for his novella "Gilgamesh in the Outback," the 1988 Locus award for his novella *The Secret Sharer*, the 1990 Hugo for his short story "Enter a Soldier. Later, Enter Another," and the 1993 Locus award for his collection *Secret Sharers*.

In 1986 he and his first wife divorced, and the following year he married fellow science fiction writer Karen Haber, with whom he has collaborated on several anthologies. As the nineties rolled on, he continued to write both fantasy and science fiction, with no desire to draw a bright line between them. At the end of the millennium, he returned to Majipoor with a trilogy—*Sorcerers of Majipoor*, *Lord Prestimion*, and *King of Dreams*—set in a time long before Lord Valentine.

***

Silverberg had grown up enthralled by fantastic literature, from the mythologies of the Middle East and classical Greece to the science-fictional writings of H. G. Wells and Robert A. Heinlein. In the 1950s, when he set out to make a living by his writing, science fiction represented not only a genre he enjoyed reading but the one form of fantastic literature for which there was a large and continuing market. He deviated little from the images of rocket ships and future societies that the editors demanded.

On his return in the mid-1960s, however, Silverberg set out to create novels and stories that stretched the boundaries of the science fiction genre, in the directions pointed by the writers he had both studied and read for pleasure. One of his best science fiction novels, *Downward to the Earth*, was enriched by references to Joseph Conrad's *Heart of Darkness*, including a character named Kurtz, but he also found fantastic imagery from creators not bound to twentieth-century Anglo-American assumptions of the necessity for realism. His very first story after his return, "To See the Invisible Man," was based on a throwaway line in Jorge Luis Borges's "The Lottery in Babylon" ("During one lunar year, I have been declared invisible—I shrieked and was not heard, I stole my bread and was not decapitated"). William Butler Yeats's Byzantium, the mythologies undergirding the work of James Joyce and Ezra

Pound, the horrific images of Franz Kafka's earthly Hells—all began to appear in Silverberg's writing.

Much of Silverberg's fiction at this time was set among the futuristic cities and gleaming rocket ships expected for science fiction, but there was one particularly notable exception. *Nightwings*, originally published as three novellas, had a richly detailed setting of the sort that has come to define "science fantasy": a baroque and decaying future like the one Jack Vance had created for his *Dying World* books and the one Gene Wolfe later devised for his masterly *Book of the New Sun*.

Early in his career, Silverberg had learned the pulp virtue of grabbing the reader's attention at the very beginning of the story. His mature writing has featured opening sentences that combine the shock of the new with imagery that will echo throughout the tale. (Thus "Born with the Dead" begins, "Supposedly his late wife Sybille was on her way to Zanzibar.") *Nightwings* is an excellent example of this approach, with the opening words, "Roum is a city built on seven hills. They say it was a capital of man in one of the earlier cycles. I did not know that, for my guild was Watching, not Remembering." Thus the reader is grounded in a world that was ours, but in some ways is no longer: Rome endures, but in a far future where words have become distorted, where there is a guild system as in the Middle Ages, but one based on wholly new categories.

The narrator, Tomis the Watcher, is apparently an ordinary human, one who has been trained in techniques to look for the desired yet feared invasion by aliens. His two companions are more unusual: Gormon is apparently a Changeling, a monster whose genes have been destroyed by the same sort of forces humanity has damaged the world with, and Avluela is a Flier, with functional pink butterfly wings sprouting from beneath her shoulder blades. The Prince of Roum seizes Avluela and forces her to become his lover, whereupon the long-awaited invasion takes place. Gormon reveals himself to be an advance spy for the aliens; he blinds the prince, then flies away with Avluela.

In the second part Tomis and the blinded prince embark on a penitential journey to Perris (Paris), where Tomis is exposed to the horrors humanity has perpetrated on the Earth and other species. The book closes with a journey to Jorslem (Jerusalem), where Tomis is reunited with Avluela, to join a new guild that will answer to the new needs of humanity: the Redeemers. *Nightwings* represents a theme Silverberg has returned to frequently: the search for religious transformation, rebirth, and transcendence. Here it appears in a richly delineated fantastic landscape.

Two other novels of that time were published as science fiction, though they reflected traditional horror themes and were presented by Silverberg without a single effort at scientific or pseudoscientific explanation. *The Book of Skulls* sends four young seekers to a mysterious monastery whose inhabitants may possess the secret of immortality: Eli, a Jewish intellectual; Ned, a gay poet; Oliver, a seemingly ordinary midwesterner; and Timothy, a rich dilettante, When it is too late to flee, they learn that the ritual of eternal life requires that two of them die, one by his own hand, and one by another's. In a stylistic tour de force, the four aspirants tell their stories in clearly distinguishable alternating chapters, as their slowly and skillfully revealed internal characteristics determine the resolution with the terrible inevitability of tragedy.

Perhaps the greatest work of this period is *Dying Inside*, a book in which the old theme of the mind reader is explored from within. In a world essentially that of the time the book appeared, David Selig is able to peek into other minds, but as he enters middle age, his power is waning. The ability has always been at least as much a curse as a blessing; Selig has never been able to establish true intimacy with any of those he has probed, and even when he meets a woman whose mind he can't read, and a male friend who shares his powers, the relationships end badly. The novel focuses on Selig's reaction to the loss of his powers, which he at first sees as a senile failing similar to the loss of sexual or creative ability, but comes to accept as a release from what was almost an illness. John Clute sees the book as being "about escaping the trap of a great gift" and suggests that it symbolizes the terrible facility of Silverberg's early writing years, which enabled him to turn out reams of competent fiction but not to create works with the power and depth of his later work, particularly *Dying Inside* itself. This theory is supported by the similarity of Selig's biographical details and intellectual interests to those of his creator.

In this creative explosion, Silverberg also produced a number of shorter works on mythic and fantasy themes; these, at their best, offered the brilliant inventions of the novels in a more focused form. The Nebula-winning "Passengers" adapts the old theme of demonic possession to aliens who use their powers for cruel ends. It is a chilling first-person tale of the horrors of this kind of possession, though its shock ending looks a bit different now than it did when the story was first published. "Sundance" is the complex, brilliantly structured tale of a Native American re-experiencing ancestral horrors as he helps colonize another world, while "The Dybbuk of Mazel Tov IV" applies Jewish folklore to a science-fictional setting. In "This Is the Road," which Silverberg placed at the end of his retrospective collection *Beyond the Safe Zone*, he looks back to the kind of science fantasy world he had created in *Nightwings* and forward to his next phase with a new tale of a quest by far-future quasi-humans.

***

In the seventies, while Silverberg was retired, some new trends in the fantastic became obvious. Popular discovery of J. R. R. Tolkien's *Lord of the Rings* led to a renewed interest in fantasy, while science fiction writers, such as Philip José Farmer and Michael Moorcock, began telling their tales in trilogies and longer series rather than in single books.

These trends grew together in two particularly popular series, Marion Zimmer Bradley's Darkover and Anne McCaffrey's Pern, which started out as science fiction stories of alien planets reached by rocket ship but began to include books based on traditional fantasy themes: the young protagonist seeking a magical item, the ruler unjustly deprived of his throne, the bewitchments of sorcery.

Silverberg returned to writing in 1976, with a tale set in such a background. Majipoor is a large world, reminiscent of Vance's *Big Planet*, but Silverberg develops and peoples it in his own way, with a lushness of description reminiscent of *Nightwings* and "This Is the Road." Patrick Parrinder describes Majipoor as "a near-encyclopedia of unnatural wonders and weird ecosystems." New animal and plant species appear throughout the book, including sentient creatures, such as the doglike Hjorts and the towering four-armed Skandars.

The story Silverberg placed in this remarkable invention is worthy of it. *Lord Valentine's Castle* begins as if in mid-sentence, with the word "and," its titular character wondering where he has been and where he is going. Valentine, who does not yet know that he is Lord Valentine, the rightful ruler of the planet, joins a juggling troupe. He begins by learning the skill of juggling, for which he has natural physical skills, and discovers that he can enter into an altered state where his feats seem to occur at a manageable pace. He finds companionship within the troupe, then deeply romantic and erotic love with a young woman named Carabella.

The politics, sociology, and psychology of Majipoor are abundantly invented and described as well. The Coronal (the title usurped from Valentine) is the political ruler, but he will eventually be expected to move on and become the temporally powerless Pontifex, living in a cave. The inner life of the people is based on dreams sent by the Queen of the Isle of Sleep, and sometimes nightmares from the darker King of Dreams. Valentine comprehends these complexities as he adventures on land and sea, visiting an enchanted island and mastering a labyrinth that is political as well as spatial. Finally he reaches Castle Mount, the capital of Majipoor, having reconstituted himself into one worthy to reclaim the throne.

The book thus combines reasoned science-fictional inventiveness with the traditional fantasy plot of the exiled prince taking back what is rightfully his. Thomas Clareson states that the book "demands that its readers re-examine the relationship between science fiction and fantasy, for in this novel, Silverberg has fused the two together." Edgar L. Chapman considers the book the culmination of Silverberg's career; indeed, he calls his book-length study of Silverberg *The Road to Castle Mount*.

Having created this wondrous world, Silverberg was understandably loath to leave it. He wrote several more stories set in this background. "Thesme and the Ghayrog" and "The Soul-Painter and the Shape Shifter" are ironic tales of love between humans and aliens. "The Desert of Stolen Dreams" is a complex adventure that provides the backstory of the King of Dreams. "Among the Dream Speakers" and "Voriax and Valentine" are light amusements. Silverberg combined ten of these stories with a frame tale in which Hissune, a young man who helped Valentine in the first book, studies these stories in the "Register of Souls." As Michael Bishop pointed out in a *Washington Post Book World* review, the resulting book, published as *Majipoor Chronicles*, thus becomes not merely a collection of tales but a *Bildungsroman* in which Hissune grows in understanding of his world by reading what we read.

Fantasy trilogies had already become a cliché at that point, but Silverberg yielded to popular demand and a substantial monetary offer from his publishers. In *Valentine Pontifex* he considers the implication of Majipoor's political system. Hissune is growing readier to take on the responsibilities of Coronal, and the old Pontifex can't last much longer, but Valentine is happy where he is. The book also looks at some of the questions that are often skimped in such works, such as the economic problems of monarchy and the oppression of the planet's native race, on which much of the humans' success has been built. Eventually, Valentine makes peace with the indigenous creatures and recognizes that there is a time to move past worldly power. Thus Silverberg concludes a successful, if originally unintended, trilogy.

After this success, Silverberg went on to imagine other new worlds. Most of his new novels, like the Majipoor books, offered quest tales and other fantasy themes set on alien planets, rather than the urban settings and technological solutions common in his earlier work. Thus *The Face of the Waters* tells of an extraterrestrial sea voyage, while *The Kingdoms of the Wall* presents an alien tribe climbing a mountain to discover the mystery of their world.

Since childhood, Silverberg had been fascinated by the figure of Gilgamesh, the Sumerian whose exploits had been recorded around 2000 B.C., as not only an epic hero but one whose conquests of warriors and demons do not help him answer the final question of mortality. In 1984 he published *Gilgamesh the King*, a strictly mimetic historical novel in which Gilgamesh retains the heroism and grandeur of the near-mythical figure in the epic, but the gods are explained away as psychological influences and Gilgamesh attains a stoic acceptance of the finality of death. Two years later, he was invited to contribute to a shared-worlds series, Heroes in Hell, edited by Janet Morris and C. J. Cherryh, in which the shades of the famous dead reappear, and he chose to bring back Gilgamesh. In the Hugo-winning novella "Gilgamesh in the Outback," the king encounters other historical figures, such as Prester John and Henry VIII.

Robert E. Howard, the writer for *Weird Tales*, finds unwanted desires stirred by this avatar of the heroic image he had limned. Pablo Picasso and Helen of Troy are stirred into the mix in the later "The Fascination of the Abomination." After the series had concluded, Silverberg brought Gilgamesh and his friends out of Hell and into New York, and Gilgamesh finds an ending more in keeping with Silverberg's usual themes of redemption and transcendence; the whole story was published as *To the Land of the Living*.

Silverberg also invoked the alternate middle ages theme that has become popular in fantasy. Back in the 1960s he had written *Gate of Time*, a young adult novel set in a world where the Black Death all but wiped out European culture. He returned to this scene in 1990 with the novella *Lion Time in Timbuctoo*, a rich, complexly plotted tale of dynastic intrigue in the dominant Africa of this world. (References are made to parallel occurrences in the tragedies set among Turkish and African courts by the minor colonial writer William Shakespeare.)

***

Silverberg's greatest strength may lie in combining fantastic vision with traditional literary virtues. He excels in setting himself narrative problems that require stylistic inventiveness. The clipped, present-tense narration of "Passengers" is perfect for a protagonist whose consciousness may be seized from him at any moment; "Sundance" expresses its protagonist's doubts in a mixture of tenses and persons; the apparent disorder of the narration of "In Entropy's Jaws" reflects the temporal flux its telepathic main character has been thrust into by a failure of his powers, while not falling into mere chaos.

His work is rich in reference to his precursors, both mimetic and fantastic. Clute says of *Dying Inside*, a particularly strong example because its narrator's erudition is an important part of the characterization, "I was conscious of constantly encountering echoes of the voices who wrote the Western World as we know it." Sometimes this is done playfully: The dolphin narrator of "Ishmael in Love" begins his story, "Call me Ishmael. All human beings who know me do."

His favorite themes are immortality, the nature of time, the quest for transcendence, and the attempt to bypass the isolation of individuality. They recur throughout his oeuvre, with each new work reflecting and reinforcing its predecessors. These are, of course, questions that much of mimetic literature has considered, but Silverberg creates imaginative experiments in which the circumstances and possibilities surrounding these questions are not as they are in present-day consensus reality, then discusses them with the skill, grace, and allusiveness we expect of serious writing.

In half a century, Robert Silverberg has gone from a prolific producer of science fiction yard goods to a major, respected figure in fantastic literature.

Selected Bibliography

WORKS OF ROBERT SILVERBERG

SUPERNATURAL AND FANTASTIC FICTION

The Thirteenth Immortal. New York: Ace, 1957.

Master of Life and Death. New York: Ace, 1957; London: Sidgwick & Jackson, 1977.
  (With Randall Garrett, under joint pseudonym Robert Randall.)

The Shrouded Planet. New York: Gnome Press, 1957; London: Mayflower, 1964.

Published under names Robert Silverberg and Randall Garrett. Newport News, Va.: Donning, 1980.

(Under pseudonym Calvin M. Knox.) *Lest We Forget Thee, Earth*. New York: Ace, 1958.

(Under pseudonym David Osborne.) *Aliens from Space*. New York: Avalon, 1958.

Invaders from Earth. New York: Ace, 1958; London: Sidgwick & Jackson, 1977.

Stepsons of Terra. New York: Ace, 1958.

(Under pseudonym Ivar Jorgenson.) *Starhaven*. New York: Avalon, 1958.

(Under pseudonym David Osborne.) *Invincible Barriers*. New York: Avalon, 1958.

(With Garrett, under joint pseudonym Robert Randall.) *The Dawning Light*. City: Gnome Press, 1959. London: Mayflower, 1964. Published under names Robert Silverberg and Randall Garrett. Newport News, Va.: Donning, 1981.

(Under pseudonym Calvin M. Knox.) *The Plot against Earth*. New York: Ace, 1959.

The Planet Killers. New York: Ace, 1959.

Collision Course. New York: Avalon, 1961.

Next Stop the Stars. New York: Ace, 1962. (Story collection.)

The Seed of Earth. New York: Ace, 1962. London: Hamlyn, 1978.

Recalled to Life. New York: Lancer Books; 1962. Revised edition. New York: Doubleday, 1972. London: Gollancz, 1974.

The Silent Invaders. New York: Ace, 1963.

Godling, Go Home! New York: Belmont, 1964. (Story collection.)

(Under pseudonym Calvin M. Knox.) *One of Our Asteroids Is Missing*. New York: Ace, 1964.

To Worlds Beyond: Stories of Science Fiction. Philadelphia: Chilton, 1965.

Needle in a Timestack. New York: Ballantine, 1966. Revised edition. New York: Ace, 1985. (Story collection.)

Planet of Death. New York: Holt, 1967.

To Open the Sky. New York: Ballantine, 1967; London: Sphere, 1970.

Thorns. New York: Ballantine, 1967; London: Rapp and Whiting, 1969.

Those Who Watch. New York: New American Library, 1967; London: New English Library, 1977.

The Time-Hoppers. New York: Doubleday, 1967; London: Sidgwick & Jackson, 1968.

Hawksbill Station. New York: Doubleday, 1968. Published as *The Anvil of Time*. London: Sidgwick & Jackson, 1969.

The Masks of Time. New York: Ballantine, 1968. Published as *Vornan-19*. London: Sidgwick & Jackson, 1970.

Dimension Thirteen. New York: Ballantine, 1969. (Story collection.)

The Man in the Maze. New York: Avon, 1969; London: Sidgwick & Jackson, 1969.

Nightwings. New York: Avon, 1969. London: Sidgwick & Jackson, 1972.

To Live Again. New York: Doubleday, 1969; London: Sidgwick & Jackson, 1975.

Up the Line. New York: Ballantine, 1969; London: Gollancz, 1977.

The Cube Root of Uncertainty. New York: Macmillan, 1970. (Story collection.)

Downward to the Earth. New York: Doubleday, 1970; London: Gollancz, 1977.

Parsecs and Parables: Ten Science Fiction Stories. New York: Doubleday, 1970. London: Hale, 1973.

A Robert Silverberg Omnibus. London: Sidgwick & Jackson, 1970. (Contains *Master of Life and Death*, *Invaders from Earth*, and *The Time-Hoppers.*)

Tower of Glass. New York: Scribners, 1970; London: Panther, 1976.

Moonferns and Starsongs. New York: Ballantine, 1971. (Story collection.)

Son of Man. New York: Ballantine, 1971; London: Panther, 1979.

A Time of Changes. New York: New American Library, 1971. London: Gollancz, 1976.

The World Inside. New York: Doubleday, 1971; London: Millington, 1976.

The Book of Skulls. New York: Scribners, 1972; London: Gollancz, 1978.

Dying Inside. New York: Scribners, 1972; London: Sidgwick & Jackson, 1974.

The Reality Trip and Other Implausibilities. New York: Ballantine, 1972. (Story collection.)

The Second Trip. New York: Doubleday, 1972; London: Gollancz, 1979.

Earth's Other Shadow: Nine Science Fiction Stories. New York: New American Library, 1973. London: Millington, 1979.

Valley beyond Time. New York: Dell, 1973. (Story collection.)

Unfamiliar Territory. New York: Scribners, 1973; London: Gollancz, 1975. (Story collection.)

Born with the Dead: Three Novellas about the Spirit of Man. New York: Random House, 1974. London: Gollancz, 1975.

Sundance and Other Science Fiction Stories. Nashville, Tenn.: Thomas Nelson, 1974. London: Abelard-Schumann, 1975.

The Feast of St. Dionysus: Five Science Fiction Stories. New York: Scribners, 1975. London: Gollancz, 1976.

The Stochastic Man. New York: Harper, 1975. London: Gollancz, 1976.

The Best of Robert Silverberg. Volume 1. New York: Pocket Books, 1976. Volume 2. Boston: Gregg, 1978.

Capricorn Games. New York: Random House, 1976. London: Gollancz, 1978. (Story collection.)

Shadrach in the Furnace. Indianapolis: Bobbs-Merrill, 1976. London: Gollancz, 1977.

The Shores of Tomorrow. New York: Thomas Nelson, 1976. (Story collection.)

The Songs of Summer and Other Stories. London: Gollancz, 1979.

Lord Valentine's Castle. New York: Harper, 1980; London: Gollancz, 1980.

The Desert of Stolen Dreams. Columbia, Pa.: Underwood-Miller, 1981.

A Robert Silverberg Omnibus. New York: Harper, 1981. (Contains *Downward to the Earth*, *The Man in the Maze*, and *Nightwings.*)

Majipoor Chronicles. New York: Arbor House, 1982; London: Gollancz, 1982.

World of a Thousand Colors. New York: Arbor House, 1982. (Story collection.)

Valentine Pontifex. New York: Arbor House, 1983.

The Conglomeroid Cocktail Party. New York: Arbor House, 1984. London: Gollancz, 1985. (Story collection.)

ROBERT SILVERBERG

Sailing to Byzantium. Columbia, Pa.: Underwood-Miller, 1985.

Tom O'Bedlam. New York: Donald I. Fine, 1985.

Beyond the Safe Zone: Collected Short Fiction of Robert Silverberg. New York: Donald I. Fine, 1986.

Star of Gypsies. New York: Donald I. Fine, 1986. London: Gollancz, 1987.

At Winter's End. New York: Warner, 1988; London: Gollancz, 1988.

To the Land of the Living. New York: Warner, 1989; London: Gollancz, 1989.

(With Karen Haber.) *The Mutant Season*. New York: Doubleday, 1989.

The Queen of Springtime. London: Gollancz, 1989. Published as *The New Springtime*. New York: Warner, 1990.

In Another Country. New York: Tor Books, 1990.

(With Isaac Asimov.) *Nightfall*. New York: Doubleday, 1990; London: Gollancz, 1990.

The Face of the Waters. New York: Bantam, 1991; London: Grafton, 1991.

(With Asimov.) *Child of Time*. London: Gollancz, 1991. As *The Ugly Little Boy*. New York: Doubleday, 1992.

Thebes of the Hundred Gates. Eugene, Ore.: Pulphouse, 1992.

The Collected Stories of Robert Silverberg. Volume 1. *Secret Sharers*. New York: Bantam, 1992; in two volumes, London: Grafton, 1992.

(With Asimov.) *The Positronic Man*. London: Gollancz, 1992. New York: Doubleday, 1993.

Kingdoms of the Wall. London: HarperCollins, 1992. New York: Bantam, 1993.

Hot Sky at Midnight. New York: HarperCollins, 1994.

The Mountains of Majipoor. New York: Bantam, 1995; London: Macmillan, 1995.

Sorcerers of Majipoor. New York: HarperCollins, 1996.

Starborne. New York: Bantam, 1996.

The Alien Years. New York: HarperCollins, 1998.

Lord Prestimion. New York: HarperCollins, 1999.

King of Dreams. New York: HarperCollins, 2001.

HISTORICAL FICTION

Lord of Darkness. New York: Arbor House, 1983.

Gilgamesh the King. New York: Arbor House, 1984.

JUVENILE FICTION

Revolt on Alpha C. New York: Crowell, 1955.

Starman's Quest. New York: Gnome Press, 1959.

Lost Race of Mars. Philadelphia: Winston, 1960.

Regan's Planet. New York: Pyramid Books, 1964.

Time of the Great Freeze. New York: Holt, 1964.

Conquerors from the Darkness. New York: Holt, 1965.

The Gate of Worlds. New York: Holt, 1967.

The Calibrated Alligator and Other Science Fiction Stories. New York: Holt, 1969.

Across a Billion Years. New York: Dial, 1969.

Three Survived. New York: Holt, 1969.

World's Fair, 1992. New York: Follett, 1970.

Sunrise on Mercury and Other Science Fiction Stories. New York: Thomas Nelson, 1975.

Project Pendulum. New York: Walker, 1987.

Letters from Atlantis. New York: Macmillan, 1990.

AUTOBIOGRAPHICAL WRITINGS

"Introduction to 'Sundance.'" In *Those Who Can: A Science Fiction Reader.* Edited by Robin Scott Wilson. New York: New American Library, 1973. Pp. 169–175.

"Sounding Brass, Tinkling Cymbal." In *Hell's Cartographers.* Edited by Brian W. Aldiss and Harry Harrison. London: Weidenfeld and Nicholson, 1975. New York: Harper and Row, 1975. Pp. 7–45.

"Introduction: The Making of a Science Fiction Writer." In *Robert Silverberg's Worlds of Wonder.* New York: Warner, 1987.

Reflections and Refractions: Thoughts on Science-Fiction, Science, and Other Matters. Grass Valley, Calif.: Underwood Books, 1997.

BIBLIOGRAPHIES

Clareson, Thomas D. *Robert Silverberg: A Primary and Secondary Bibliography.* Boston: G. K. Hall, 1983.

CRITICAL AND BIOGRAPHICAL STUDIES

Abrash, Merritt. "Robert Silverberg's The World Inside." In *No Place Else: Explorations in Utopian and Dystopian Fiction.* Edited by Eric S. Rabkin, Martin H. Greenberg, and Joseph D. Olander. Carbondale, Ill.: Southern Illinois University Press, 1983. Pp. 225–43.

Alterman, Peter S. "Four Voices in Robert Silverberg's Dying Inside." In *Critical Encounters II: Writers and Themes in Science Fiction.* Edited by Tom Staicar. New York: New York: Frederick Ungar, 1982. Pp. 90–103.

Bishop, Michael. "Majipoor Chronicles." *Washington Post Book World,* Feburary 28, 1982.

Chapman, Edgar L. *The Road to Castle Mount: The Science Fiction of Robert Silverberg.* Westport, Conn.: Greenwood, 1999.

Clareson, Thomas D. "The Fictions of Robert Silverberg." In *Voices for the Future: Essays on Major Science Fiction Writers*, vol. 2. Edited by Thomas D. Clareson. Bowling Green, Ohio: Bowling Green University Popular Press, 1979. Pp. 1–33.

Clareson, Thomas D. "Whose Castle?: Speculations as to the Parameters of Science Fiction." *Essays in Arts and Sciences*, IX: 139–43 (August 1980).

Clareson, Thomas D. *Robert Silverberg.* Mercer Island, Wash.: Starmont, 1983.

Clute, John. Introduction to *Dying Inside.* New York: ibooks, 2002. Pp. vii–xii.

Dean, John, "The Sick Hero Reborn: Two Versions of the Philoctetes Myth." *Comparative Literature Studies*, 17:334–40 (September 1980).

Dudley, Joseph M. "Transformational SF Religions: Philip José Farmer's *Night of Light* and Robert Silverberg's *Downward to the Earth.*" *Extrapolation*, 35:343-50 (Winter 1994).

Dunn, Thomas P., and Richard D. Erlich. "The Mechanical Hive: Urbmon 116 as the Villain-Hero of Silverberg's The World Inside." *Extrapolation*, 21:338–47 (Winter 1980).

Edwards, Malcolm. "Robert Silverberg." In *Science Fiction Writers: Critical Studies of the Major Authors from the Early Nineteenth Century to the Present Day*. Edited by E. F. Bleiler. New York: Charles Scribner's Sons, 1982. Pp. 505-11.

Elkins, Charles, and Martin H. Greenberg (eds.). *Robert Silverberg's Many Trapdoors*. Westport, Conn.: Greenwood, 1992. (Contains essays by Thomas Clareson, Russell Letson, Edgar L. Chapman, Joseph Francavilla, John Flodstrom, Frank Dietz, Robert Reilly, and C. N. Manlove.)

Emery, Michael J. The Invasion Motif in the Science Fiction of Robert Silverberg. *W. Ohio Jour.*, 10:138–143 (Spring 1989).

Gordon, Andrew. "Silverberg's Time Machine." *Extrapolation*, 23:345-61 (Winter 1982).

Kam, Rose Sallberg. "Silverberg and Conrad: Explorers of Inner Darkness." *Extrapolation*, 17:18–28 (December 1975).

Kilheffer, Robert. "Striking a Balance: Robert Silverberg's *Lord of Darkness, Dying Inside*, and Others." *New York Review of Science Fiction*, August 12, 1989, pp. 1, 12–14.

Letson, Russell. "'Falling through Many Trapdoors': Robert Silverberg." *Extrapolation*, 20:109–17 (1979).

Malzberg, Barry M. "Robert Silverberg." *The Magazine of Fantasy and Science Fiction*, 46:67–72 (April 1974).

McGiveron, Rafeeq O. "A Relationship More than Six Inches Deep: Love and Lust in Silverberg's Science Fiction." *Extrapolation*, 39:40–51 (Spring 1998).

Nedelkovich, Alexander. "The Stellar Parallels: Robert Silverberg, Larry Niven, and Arthur C. Clarke." *Extrapolation*, 21:348-60 (Winter 1980).

Parrinder, Patrick. "Lord Valentine's Castle." *Times Literary Supplement*, November 11, 1980.

Sanders, Joe. "Silverberg: Transformation and Death." *Science Fiction: A Review of Speculative Literature* (WA, Australia), 5:90–95 (September 1983).

Stableford, Brian M. "The Metamorphosis of Robert Silverberg." *Science Fiction Monthly*, 3:9–11 (1976).

Stewart, Ian. "Back to the Future, Part 2." *New Scientist*, 127:55–6 (July 7, 1990).

Tuma, George. "Biblical Myth and Legend in Towers of Glass: Man's Search for Authenticity." *Extrapolation* 15:174-191 (May 1974).

INTERVIEWS

Elliot, Jeffrey M. "Robert Silverberg, Next Stop, Lord Valentine's Castle." In *Science Fiction Voices #2*. San Bernardino, Calif.: Borgo Press, 1979. Pp. 51–62.

Platt, Charles. *Dream Makers*. New York: Berkley, 1980. Pp. 261–268.

Walker, Paul. *Speaking of Science Fiction: The Paul Walker Interviews*. Oradell, N.J.: Luna Press, 1978.

OTHER MEDIA

Robert Silverberg Reads "To See the Invisible Man" and "Passengers." Pelican Records, 1979. (Recording.)

Dying Inside. Caedmon, 1979. (Recorded by the author.)

Dan Simmons

1948–

GREG BEATTY

DAN SIMMONS ENTERED the fields of horror and science fiction in a much-deserved blaze of glory. In 1982 his first published short story, "The River Styx Flows Upstream," tied for first place in a *Twilight Zone* magazine competition which had close to ten thousand submissions; in 1985 his novel *Song of Kali* won the World Fantasy Award, the first time a first novel had ever done so. Since then, Simmons has published a score of books in genres ranging from horror and science fiction to historical thriller (*The Crook Factory*) and detective fiction (*Hardcase*).

Dan Simmons was born in Peoria Illinois on April 4, 1948. Growing up, Simmons lived in various small towns in the Midwest, including Brimfield, Illinois, the basis for the fictional Elm Haven in his novel *Summer of Night*. In that book, and in detailed descriptive passages throughout the novel *Phases of Gravity*, Simmons paints a bittersweet portrait of growing up in these small towns. He lingers over the feeling of community and the sensory texture of the town and surrounding farmland. He also exposes the isolation and alienation that children, especially intelligent children, can suffer in this environment.

Simmons is visible in many of the boys of Elm Haven, but one characters shows him most clearly. The passages would-be writer Duane McBride records in his notebook sound like Simmons, and align with his account of knowing he wanted to be a writer from age eight or nine on. Likewise, Duane's atheistic rationalism echoes Simmons' own self-definition; he was raised Catholic, but found his faith gradually eroded as his reason matured.

Simmons attended Wabash College, a small liberal arts school for men in Crawfordsville, Indiana. Simmons has repeatedly praised Wabash for grounding him in a literary tradition and sharpening his mind. Simmons spent a semester of his junior year in Philadelphia, where he helped teach filmmaking to inner-city kids, an experience he mined for descriptions of urban conflict in Philadelphia in *Carrion Comfort*. Simmons graduated Phi Beta Kappa in 1970, and in 1995 Wabash awarded him an honorary doctorate.

After finishing college, Simmons went on to earn a Masters in Education in 1971 from Washington University in Saint Louis—a pursuit that also helped him avoid service in the Vietnam War. At Washington, Simmons wrote his thesis on the educational television programs then emerging, such as *Sesame Street*, arguing that they had far less of an effect than their proponents claimed.

Simmons taught for eighteen years, in New York, Missouri, and Colorado. He developed, administered, and taught in a program for gifted and talented children, teaching advanced courses, some on the college level, to sixth graders. At its peak this program served nineteen elementary schools. Simmons was a successful teacher, winning awards from the Colorado Education Association. Teaching and writing are integrally related for Simmons. He developed the story of the Shrike so central to *Hyperion* by telling it to his sixth grade students, and one former student, now a professional artist, has created a sculpture of the Shrike. Simmons has taught at Clarion and at Odyssey, two science fiction writing workshops. He has also given keynote addresses at fan conventions and academic conferences; these speeches often have a pedagogical tone, as Simmons urges genre writers to higher standards, and refers to a wide range of classic models.

Simmons lives in Colorado with his wife Karen. They have one daughter, Jane, who attended Hamilton College. Simmons is close to his younger brother Wayne, a private investigator and the model for Lawrence Stewart in *Darwin's Blade*; Wayne also provided the accident investigation experience that *Darwin's Blade* is based on, and Simmons calls on his brother's familiarity with planes and weapons in several novels. Simmons is also known for doing extensive research; he visited Transylvania for *Children of the Night*, Key West for *The Crook Factory*, and so on.

***

Several themes weave through Dan Simmons' work: mortality, love, transcendence, and competence. In addition, two closely related elements unify Simmons' writing: an acute awareness of the historical traditions in which he works, and uneasiness about genre constraints. Often, these formal elements intertwine, producing a far greater attention to how the story is told than is common in genre fiction. In Simmons' best works, these formal and thematic factors come together to produce masterpieces. In his weakest, they work against one another, producing works that never cohere.

Death and pain are common enough in horror fiction. Indeed, it is hard to imagine a work of horror without them. But in *Song of Kali* (1985), Simmons foregrounds real world horrors. The novel opens with the pronouncement, "Some places are too evil to be allowed to exist. Some cities are too wicked to be suffered." These lines transform the entire city of Calcutta into a kind of haunted house. Publisher Robert Luszek goes to Calcutta to retrieve a manuscript from Das, a poet who vanished years before and is presumed dead. Luszek provides an outsider's perspective on the suffering and degradation that fill Calcutta—the detailed descriptions of which are based on Simmons' ten-week tour of India in 1977.

However, Calcutta also offers a dark passageway to the divine. While he is there, Luszek gets involved with a cult that is attempting to revive the Indian goddess Kali. As they work to unleash her upon the earth, Kali visits Luszek in dreams that blend extreme violence with moving eroticism. A rationalist in a land of divine mysteries, Luszek is a classic stranger in a strange land. Simmons captures this in crystalline prose that brought him immediate critical acclaim from such genre notables as science fiction writer Harlan Ellison and horror writer Stephen King.

After *Song of Kali* there was a brief hiatus in Simmons' career as novelist, but this was followed, in 1989, by an impressive burst of publications: three distinct works that established Simmons as a writer of note—and as unclassifiable. The first, *Phases of Gravity*, is about the mid-life crisis of former astronaut Richard Baedecker. The novel opens years after Baedecker walked on the moon. Baedecker visits India, where he attempts to reestablish relations with his son Scott, who has joined a cult reminiscent of the followers of Bagwan Rajneesh. The novel recounts the dissolution of his marriage, his discontent with his career, and the alienation he feels from both his personal life and from public attempts to honor him for his achievements.

Rather than being depressing, as this outline would suggest, Simmons' story shows us a man on a genuine spiritual quest. Without minimizing the conflicts involved, or falling prey to clichés, Simmons uses Baedecker to show readers the possibility of a positive relationship between technological competence and spiritual aspirations. Though the novel is essentially a mainstream book, Simmons' near reverence for technical competency and the subject matter of space travel links it to science fiction, while the spiritual elements suggest the supernatural, and the existence of an alternate reality beyond the details of daily life. Baedecker is the first of several Simmons heroes who are highly competent in various disciplines and able to perform complex tasks, such as flying a helicopter, while also being able to think or feel on other more spiritual levels. This duality is also seen in minor characters in *Fires of Eden* and *Carrion Comfort*, and is the defining characteristic of later lead characters Darwin Minor and Joe Kurtz.

Baedecker's name itself is also an example of the profound irony that pervades Simmons' work. Karl Baedeker was a nineteenth-century publisher whose travel books became so successful that "Baedeker" has become a synonym for travel guidebook. Travel writing is one of the roots of science fiction, and, for all that Baedecker is on a spiritual quest, one of the unifying threads of *Phases of Gravity* is its descriptions of various places: Illinois, Oregon, South Dakota, India, and of course, the moon.

The two other novels Simmons published in 1989 are longer. One, *Carrion Comfort*, a contemporary rendition of the vampire myth, won the Bram Stoker Award for best novel (given by the Horror Writers of America). The book concerns vampires who, rather than sucking blood, possess the minds of others and feed off this control—especially when it is combined with violence or degradation. Simmons interweaves narratives from several perspectives, telling part of the story through the eyes of the monsters themselves (who seem chillingly ordinary), and other sections through a handful of characters who hunt them. Chief among these hunters is Saul Laski, who was first possessed by one of these mind vampires in a Nazi concentration camp during his youth. They used him in a bizarre game of living chess, one vampire against another, in which the human pieces are killed as they are removed from the board.

The game metaphor runs throughout the book, as the core trio of monsters have played similar games throughout their lives. By the end of the book, more extensive games are played with entire islands, even with nations using nuclear weapons. Since the control these monsters exercise makes it impossible to know who to trust, an atmosphere of paranoia and threat pervades the novel. Two qualities lift *Carrion Comfort* above the level of most horror: Simmons' willingness to once again confront real-world evil, and his exposé of the banality of evil. In the novel's climax, where these facets come together, Saul confronts his ancient enemy armed only with mental images of those who suffered in the Holocaust. This interplay of cultural otherness, suffering, and identity is truly moving. It is a striking example of another of Simmons' strengths: finding ways to externalize internal realities.

In *Hyperion*, Simmons' third book published in 1989, examples of this externalization of internal reality abound, investing the book with great complexity and richness. *Hyperion* takes its title and inspiration from Keats's long poem of the same name, which examines the nature of poetry while telling an allegorical story about ancient gods. The novel's structure is borrowed from Chaucer's *Canterbury Tales*: a number of pilgrims on their way to the Time Tombs on the planet Hyperion tell their stories as they travel.

As they do so, they also describe Hyperion itself, telling of a distant planet devoted to the arts, of a complex interstellar society connected via a web of "farcasters" (teleportation devices), and of the Shrike, the greatest of the many mysteries found on Hyperion. In *Hyperion*, Simmons shows what science fiction is capable of, but also what is possible when one works within a poetic tradition, rather than largely outside of it, as is true of most genre fiction.

The alternating narratives resonate wonderfully. Each pilgrim's tale works as an independent story, pays homage to a different strand of literary history, and employs a different method of storytelling. Each is also necessary to understand the philosophical and emotional import of the planet Hyperion. The Shrike is pivotal in this understanding. Worshipped as the Lord of Pain, the Shrike can control time—but does so, apparently, only to kill, moving among humanity to slice them into pieces. The Shrike's silvery skin reflects light the way its enigmatic nature reflects back the aspects of the divine most relevant to the pilgrims, and most painful. In these accounts, Simmons shows us, almost casually, the horrific possibilities possible in every dream of transcendence, every technological breakthrough. The first pilgrim, Father Hoyt, is Catholic; he encounters a crucifixion and rebirth that turns the West's greatest miracle into grim horror. The second, warrior Fedmahn Kassad, tells of "la belle dame sans merci," a mysterious killer/lover first encountered in a virtual reality war game. For Martin Silenus, the greatest poet of the age (based on Ezra Pound, who briefly taught at Wabash, Simmons' alma mater), the Shrike is a dark muse, the evil necessary for him to write his epic poem that, like Keats's, examines the natures of humanity and poetry via a story of contesting gods.

Fall of Hyperion (1990) weaves the myriad story lines begun in *Hyperion* into a unified conclusion. The Shrike becomes the unifying thread not just for the stories, but also for the contesting worlds of humans and intelligent machines—and the literal contest between the respective gods that humans and machines have created. Despite the sweeping scope of the book, which comments on many religions and most varieties of science fiction, Simmons always takes time to humanize the characters with small details, and to find the virtue in common things, such as food, companionship, or storytelling. This blend of humane sensibility and grand ambition marked Simmons as a visionary, and his peers recognized this. *Hyperion* won science fiction's Hugo Award for best novel; *Fall of Hyperion* was a finalist for both the Hugo and the Nebula Award (given by the Science Fiction Writers Association).

Since that time, however, Simmons' novels have been less original, and varied in quality. *Summer of Night* (1991) and *Children of the Night* (1992) both won Stoker Awards for best novels. However, each book received mixed critical reactions. *Summer of Night* seemed too close to Stephen King's *It*, with its group of children banding together to fight an extradimensional menace. The Lovecraftian supernatural forces seemed to attack arbitrarily, rather than with the cosmic significance of the Shrike. Critics acknowledged the genuine chill of the political commentary in *Children of the Night*, in which AIDS and governmentally sponsored terror ravage Romania, but found the biological basis for vampirism derivative of earlier works, rather than evocative of them.

Simmons' reputation continued to grow during this period, however, due to his shorter fiction. *Prayers to Broken Stones*, a collection of thirteen short stories ranging across several genres, was also published in 1990. *Lovedeath* followed in 1993. As the title suggest, all five novellas in this latter collection deal with the interplay of love and death. One of them, "Dying in Bangkok," won the 1994 Stoker Award for best novella. Like *Children of the Night*, "Dying in Bangkok" deals poignantly with the real world horror of AIDS. Another, "The Great Lover," deals with the pain and attraction of war through the war poetry of World War I. Simmons using many period poems in the story, allowing them to speak for and through his characters as he did with the poet Martin Silenus and the cybrid (artificial intelligence/human hybrid) John Keats in *Hyperion*.

However, Simmons' next two novels stumble tremendously. *The Hollow Man* (1992) laboriously recounts of the love between two telepaths. The wife Gail dies, and becomes a Beatrice figure for her husband Jeremy, leading him through encounters based on Dante's *Divine Comedy*. Jeremy passes through a hell on earth of street violence, homelessness, and, finally, the sexualized violence of a female serial killer. Eventually, Jeremy finds God in the mind of a severely abused deaf mute child, and discovers an alternative universe where he gets his wife back and lives happily ever. As in many of his works, Simmons' love for his wife comes through clearly as a model for Jeremy's love for Gail, and the descriptive passages are striking. However, the thematic and formal elements simply don't fit, and the work ends as a tangled mess. Because the descriptions of violence and pain are so much more intensely rendered than the happy moments, the ability of the human mind to create divinity, so wonderfully evoked in *Hyperion*, is unconvincing here.

Fires of Eden (1994) is much more clearly structured, but is mostly a potboiler. Native activists opposed to capitalist exploitation of their land summon ancient demons to drive their oppressors from Hawaii. These demons get out of hand, killing people just as they did over a hundred years ago, when Mark Twain visited the islands. Twain's involvement is recounted in a journal carried by Eleanor Perry, whose aunt fought beside Twain in the 1860s. However, rather than amplifying one another's effect, the alternating narratives undercut one another, often retelling the same information. The demons lack visceral otherness of Kali or the genuine originality of the Shrike. In *Fires of Eden*, the supernatural elements are mundane, almost dull, even to the characters. One character, when surrounded by ghosts and with his life in danger, thinks, "If this is the afterlife, I'll pass. It looks like Friday night in Philadelphia" (p. 377). Individual characters, such as investment mogul Byron Trumbo and his various lovers, seem like caricatures taken from the worst of popular literature.

There are several writers in Simmons' work who might serve as mouthpieces for him, but the one that sums up Simmons' greatest achievements is *Hyperion*'s Martin Silenus. After a stroke, Silenus wrote beautifully structured poetry using a seven-word vocabulary. All of Simmons' early work is transformative, almost alchemical, as he takes images from pulp fiction and lifts them to the level of high art. However, two other figures define the later Simmons. After his initial success as a pure poet commenting on the death of Earth, Silenus must capitalize on his reputation by writing trash for money. One hesitates to say that this prediction has come true, but Simmons' work has seemed less ambitious and original as monetary rewards have increased.

The second figure suggestive of the later Simmons is telepath Jeremy Bremen in *The Hollow Man*. After his wife dies, Bremen is lost. He often escapes a harsh present by remembering happier times. Since the late 1990s, Simmons has returned to the worlds created in his earlier works. *Endymion* (1996) and *Rise of Endymion* (1997) are set in the world of *Hyperion*; *A Winter Haunting* (2002) reuses characters and settings from *Summer of Night*.

Bremen also "felt as if someone had tuned his mind to darker and darker wavelengths. Wavelengths of fear and flight. Wavelengths of power and self-induced potency" (p. 109). In 1997 Simmons suffered a bout of clinical depression intense enough to require antidepressants. Simmons uses this experience in *A Winter Haunting*, where the main character suffers from depression. Recently, he has also written several novels in which his view of mankind is much darker than it was in his earlier works, and in which the lead characters are super-competent, almost superhuman, and surrounded by incompetents. Unlike the ex-astronauts of *Phases of Gravity*, who did wonderful things but were limited, investigators Darwin Minor in *Darwin's Blade* (2000) and Joe Kurtz in *Hardcase* (2001) go years without sex, then perform amazingly, defeat crime lords on their own ground, and suffer incredible physical torment without flinching. These last two books are tightly written and suspenseful, but the moral vision that animated Simmons' early work is absent, as is any element of the supernatural.

***

One wonders where he will go from here. Readers of supernatural fiction must hope that Simmons will find his way fully home to the genre. As fun as his recent detective novels have been, Simmons must work in supernatural and speculative fiction for his talents to be shown to best effect. There he has done the miraculous, in so many ways that it is hard to catalog them even decades after his emergence in the field. Not only has he integrated a deep understanding of the canonical writers of mainstream literature, such as Chaucer, Keats, and Dante, he has adapted their techniques and tropes to address contemporary themes. What's more, he has done so in works deeply informed by science and technology. The result has been a string of works that do what speculative fiction has long wanted to do: show the spiritual impact and implications of the technological changes humans have introduced in the world. In his strictly supernatural works, Simmons has repeatedly wrestled with the most profound issues facing humanity: mortality, divinity, and ethics. Such accomplishments are rare indeed, and for them Dan Simmons deserves our respect, and our gratitude.

Selected Bibliography

WORKS OF DAN SIMMONS

NOVELS AND SHORT STORY COLLECTIONS

Song of Kali. New York: Blue Jay/Tor, 1985.

Carrion Comfort. New York: Warner, 1989.

Phases of Gravity. New York: Bantam, 1989.

Hyperion. New York: Foundation, 1989.

Fall of Hyperion. New York: Foundation, 1990.

Prayers to Broken Stones: A Collection. Arlington Heights, Ill.: Dark Harvest/Bantam, 1990.

Summer of Night. New York: Warner, 1991.

Children of the Night. New York: Warner, 1992.

The Hollow Man. New York: Bantam, 1992.

Fires of Eden. New York: Putnam, 1994.

Endymion. New York: Bantam, 1996.

Rise of Endymion. New York: Bantam, 1997.

The Crook Factory. New York: AvoNova, 1997.

Darwin's Blade. New York: William Morrow, 2000.

Hardcase. St. Martin's/Minotaur, 2001.

DAN SIMMONS

OTHER WORKS

Going After the Rubber Chicken: Three Guest of Honor Speeches. Arvada, Colo.: Roadkill, 1991.

CRITICAL AND BIOGRAPHICAL STUDIES

Bryant, Edward. "Song of Kali." In *Horror: 100 Best Books.* Edited by Stephen Jones and Kim Newman. New York: Carroll & Graf, 1988.

"Dan Simmons." *Contemporary Authors Online.* Detroit: Gale, 2001.

"Dan Simmons." In *Contemporary Literary Criticism.* Volume 44. Edited by Sharon K. Hall. Detroit: Gale, 1986. Pp. 273–275.

Gillis, Michael. "Bummer Vacation." *Necrofile: The Review of Horror Fiction,* no. 1: 12–13 (Summer 1991).

Glover, David. "Travels in Romania: Myths of Origin, Myths of Blood." *Discourse: Journal for Theoretical Studies in Media and Culture,* 16, no. 1: 126–144 (Fall 1993).

Latham, Rob. "A Paradise Botched." *Necrofile: The Review of Horror Fiction,* no. 17: 10–13 (Summer 1995).

Nicholls, Peter. "Will the Real Dan Simmons Please Stand Up?" *Necrofile: The Review of Horror Fiction,* no. 6: 1–3 (Fall 1992).

Palmer, Christopher. "Galactic Empires and the Contemporary Extravaganza: Dan Simmons and Iain M. Banks." *Science Fiction Studies,* 26: 73–90 (March 1999).

"Simmons, Dan." In *St. James Guide to Horror, Ghost and Gothic Writers.* Edited by David Pringle. Detroit: St. James, 1998. Pp. 535–537.

Trapp, Joona Smitherman. "The Image of the Vampire in the Struggle for Societal Power: Dan Simmons' *Children of the Night.*" *Journal of the Fantastic in the Arts,* 10, no. 2: 155–162 (1999).

INTERVIEWS

"OmniVisions Transcript: Dan Simmons." In *Omni,* August 14, 1997. On-line magazine; interview available at http://www.omnimag.com/archives/chats/bios/simmons.html.

Rose, Michael Alec. "World-Class Maker of Worlds: A Talk with Dan Simmons." *Bookpage,* August 1997. On-line magazine; interview available at http://www.bookpage.com/9708bp/firstperson3.html.

"Transcript of Chat with Dan Simmons on February 25, 1999." *Event Horizon,* February 25, 1999. On-line magazine; interview available at http://www.eventhorizon.com/sfzine/chats/transcripts/022599.html.

White, Claire E. "A Conversation with Dan Simmons." *Writers Write: The International Writing Journal,* 5, no. 8 (September 2001). Online magazine; available at http://www.writerswrite.com/journal/sep01/.

S. P. Somtow
1952–

GARY WESTFAHL

S. P. SOMTOW has never believed in boundaries. After living in several countries while growing up, he now maintains residences in the disparate cities of Bangkok and Los Angeles. He sometimes writes fiction and sometimes composes music, enjoying an international reputation in both fields. He crafts narratives for adults and for younger readers, and his stories simultaneously project learned maturity and youthful exuberance. His fantastic works are variously classified as fantasy, horror, and science fiction, yet individual novels may smoothly blend aspects of all three genres. While offering homages to classic authors like Homer, William Shakespeare, and James Joyce, he also infuses his writings with affectionate references to rock music, films, and television. Tellingly, the narrator of the semi-autobiographical *Jasmine Nights* (1994) introduces himself as "a creature of two worlds" (p. 1), but living in different worlds has never been challenging for this singular author.

Somtow Sucharitkul (his birth name, and the name used for his published fiction before 1985) was born on December 30, 1952, in Bangkok, Thailand, the son of Sompong Sucharitkul, a diplomat, and Thaithow Sucharitkul. Spending most of his childhood with his parents in Europe, he attended college in Great Britain, earning a B.A. from Eton College and an M.A. from Cambridge University. He originally planned to make composing his career but by the late 1970s was publishing science fiction stories in magazines, many later incorporated into *Mallworld* (1982), the Inquestor series, and the Aquiliad trilogy, and he broke into book publication in the 1980s. Despite success as a writer, he remained active as a composer, premiering in 2002 a piece commemorating the destruction of the World Trade Center, and he wrote, scored, and directed two films, *The Laughing Dead* (1989) and the unreleased *Ill Met by Moonlight*. Somtow has never married but has an adoptive son, William John Raitt, presumably the model for the young hero of *The Vampire's Beautiful Daughter* (1997), Johnny Raitt.

SCIENCE FICTION NOVELS

Somtow first attracted attention with two vastly different science fiction novels. The evocative *Starship & Haiku* (1981) depicts twenty-first-century humanity on the verge of extinction following a millennial war that generated deadly plagues, mutations, and widespread despair.

Some hope to survive by embarking on a starship voyage, but Japan's "Death Lord" wants the world to commit suicide. Meanwhile, intelligent, telepathic whales contact humans to announce that they long ago created the Japanese people through genetic engineering and are now developing another new race to join the mission to the stars. In sharp contrast to *Starship & Haiku* was the playful *Mallworld*, where advanced aliens surround the solar system with an impenetrable force field so the immature human race can develop in isolation. Frustrated by their imprisonment, people amuse themselves in Mallworld, an immense space station housing over 20,000 "shops, hotels, department stores, holopalaces, brothels, psychiatric concessions, suicide parlours, and churches" (p. 24), as well as exotic creations like bioengineered dinosaurs, unicorns, and winged horses. Lighthearted stories relate the adventures of the wealthy family that owns Mallworld as well as ordinary citizens and refugees inhabiting its hidden sectors. From the beginning, then, Somtow demonstrated that he could both move readers and make them laugh.

Despite their dissimilarities, *Starship & Haiku* and *Mallworld* share a focus on one well-realized, atmospheric setting; when Somtow's science fiction shifted to a vaster canvas in the Inquestor series (*Light on the Sound* (1982) *The Throne of Madness* 1983), *Utopia Hunters* (1984), *The Darkling Wind* (1985)), the results were not as striking. In the distant future, a powerful space empire controls a million worlds, determined to suppress any planetary government that seems utopian; a young man becomes involved in efforts to overthrow this oppressive regime. Again, whales of a sort come forward to serve as humanity's allies—the delphinoids, or star whales, who dwell in the vacuum of space. Though the novels are filled with imaginative touches, like the art form known as "lightweaving" mastered by the heroine of *Utopia Hunters*, the Inquestor series was not greatly popular and, except for two novels based on the television series *V*, Somtow has steered clear of pure science fiction since its completion.

FANTASY NOVELS

Somtow's Aquiliad trilogy—*The Aquiliad* (1983), *Aquila and the Iron Horse* (1988), *Aquila and the Sphinx* (1988)—has a science-fictional framework: amid a multiplicity of parallel universes overseen by the time-traveling Dimensional Patrol (whose members resemble little green men and ride in flying saucers), a Time Criminal introduces advanced technology into one universe's Roman Empire, enabling ancient Romans to conquer North America, or Terra Nova. Still, the overall atmosphere of the series is unmistakably more suggestive of fantasy. The protagonist is a Native American warrior named Aquila who learns Latin, becomes a Roman citizen, and embarks upon quests to locate China before joining the Dimensional Patrol. Later, an aging Aquila returns to Roman civilization, though he and his son, Equus Insanus, remain officially available to serve the Dimensional Patrol.

The Aquiliad novels are filled with humorous references and incidents, as Somtow devises new ways for the familiar names and features of America to emerge in its Roman counterpart. There are amusingly anachronistic accounts of Romans developing and employing automobiles, balloons, and X-rays; Latin names replace English equivalents (Crazy Horse becomes Equus Insanus, the New World becomes Terra Nova); in the Pacific Northwest, Aquila encounters Bigfoot, revealed as a descendant of the Lost Tribe of Israel whose members were seized and genetically engineered by the Time Criminal. When the narrator is puzzled because the Dimensional Patrol leader keeps calling the Native Americans "Indians," readers believe they understand why; but Somtow then reveals that this world emerged in a universe where North America was originally discovered by explorers from the Indian subcontinent. Parodying Mark Twain's *A Connecticut Yankee in King Arthur's Court,* Somtow describes an Egyptian captured by technologically advanced Olmecs who tries to impress the natives by announcing that he will send a dragon to eat the Sun; the Olmecs calmly reply that they have known about the imminent solar eclipse for decades.

Despite their persistent cleverness, these novels ultimately seem more like games than narratives; readers wonder not what will happen to the characters next, but what ingeniously Romanized re-creation of American history will Somtow concoct next. A more serious expression of interest in the classical world was *The Shattered Horse* (1986), a substantive effort to create a new *Iliad* and *Odyssey* as a sequel to Homer's epics. Somtow deviates from mythology to show Hector's son Astyanax surviving the end of the Trojan War, growing to adulthood, and becoming Troy's new king. He then embarks upon his own odyssey, abducts Helen again, and ignites another conflict between Greece and Troy before finding final peace in the Elysian Fields.

Even more ambitious was Somtow's Riverrun trilogy—*Riverrun* (1991), *Forest of the Night* (1992), *Yestern* (1996)—which borrowed its title from the first word of Joyce's *Finnegans Wake* and derived its plot from Shakespeare's *King Lear.* To put it mildly, the novels resist straightforward summary. Strang, ruler of the universe, has like Lear foolishly divided his kingdom between two children, the vampire Thorn and were-dragon Katastrofa, while disinheriting a third child, Ash, who declined to publicly praise him. Strang is now insanely attempting to sever the connections between worlds in the cosmos, connections that human observers envision as branches of an immense River, while battles between Thorn and Katastrofa threaten innumerable planets and billions of lives. On Earth, the Etchison family—Phil, Mary, and sons Joshua and Theo— is driving to Mexico to take Mary, dying of cancer, to a Laetrile clinic when the sons are abducted by Thorn's agents because Theo is unknowingly a "Truthsayer" whose power to see and speak the truth about everything could invaluably aid combatants in the cosmic wars. As Joshua apparently dies and Theo, Phil, and Joshua's girlfriend, Serena, keep entering strange realities and returning to Earth, Earth's history continually shifts: the Etchisons go from having two sons to having one son to having no sons to having one son again, and Serena goes from being Congressman Karpovsky's aide in America to being President Karpovsky's mistress in an alternate America called Armorica. Eventually, the efforts of Theo and a new Etchison child, Chris, cause Strang to reconcile with Ash, restore the universe to harmony, and reunite the original Etchisons, with Mary now cured of cancer.

Although Somtow threw his heart and soul into this trilogy, striving to articulate a sort of primal human narrative, the fruits of his considerable labors were decidedly uninvolving, and the publisher of the first two volumes rejected the final volume, which appeared only in an omnibus edition from a small press. The problem rests in the nature of its story: nothing is as it appears, anything can at any time become anything else, and the human characters never have any clear sense of what is going on or what they should be doing. Despite its eloquence, the trilogy is as hazy, illogical, and unsatisfying as an unending dream; protagonists haplessly stare at sequences of bizarre sights, they are abruptly told they must undertake some seemingly inconsequential action to save the entire universe, and they dutifully comply. In *Yestern,* characters convey that they themselves are starting to feel like manipulated pawns by repeatedly likening their activities to events in a trilogy, with remarks like "I had spent a trilogy's worth of adventuring" (p. 531) and "You were killed, way back, a long time ago, in a different volume of the trilogy" (p. 542). Thus the Riverrun trilogy, like the Aquiliad series but for different reasons, has the aura of a self-conscious literary exercise, lacking the sense of conviction needed to sustain a reader's interest.

HORROR NOVELS

Somtow's first horror novel, *Vampire Junction* (1985), suggested that the author had found the ideal genre for his talents, allowing him to integrate a childlike perspective with adult content in a manner that was both viscerally compelling and rhetorically sophisticated. A twelve-year-old boy in ancient Pompeii becomes a vampire during the eruption of Mount Vesuvius, inaugurating a lengthy career as a perpetual child feasting on human blood. While others plot to end his existence, he settles in contemporary Los Angeles and becomes an internationally famous rock star, Timmy Valentine. He and his circle live in an intoxicating world of sex and violence, more fascinating than repellent to contemporary readers, and Valentine recognizes that his newfound popularity—and implicitly the newfound popularity of vampire novels—are a reflection of changing values: "I am a distillation of men's most secret terrors, a summary of their million shapes of alienation. That is why I am more real than I ever was, why I am hungrier than ever before ... why for the first time I am being seen by millions, worshipped by children, lusted after by adults" (p. 14). Seeking to find peace through discussions with his analyst, Valentine is inevitably destroyed in a fire, ending his saga in a traditional manner, but he ultimately emerges, perhaps, as literature's most sympathetic vampire to date.

The thoughtful and richly textured *Vampire Junction* left Somtow with little more to say about vampires or Valentine, but its popularity inexorably engendered two sequels, *Valentine* (1992) and *Vanitas: Escape from Vampire Junction* (1995). The sex may have been kinkier, and the violence more extreme, but neither novel proved particularly noteworthy. *Valentine* involves the making of a film about the missing star, filmed in the very location where he disappeared, starring the handsome young Angel Todd. But Valentine's soul, trapped in limbo by a sinister medium, is struggling to return to life by means of Angel, who in the end absorbs Valentine's vampiric essence, making Valentine a normal human boy. In *Vanitas*, Valentine is left with nothing to do but to travel around the world on an ineffectual comeback tour while recalling additional events from his two thousand years as a vampire, including encounters with Jack the Ripper, Bram Stoker, and Dracula himself.

Having fashioned a modern American version of the vampire in *Vampire Junction*, Somtow set out to reinvent the werewolf in *Moon Dance: A Novel* (1990). Within a frame story involving a journalist in the 1960s interviewing an aging serial killer who suffers from a multiple personality disorder, Somtow tells the story of a band of European werewolves who emigrate to Dakota Territory in the 1880s, only to encounter a competing tribe of Native American werewolves; in a variety of adventures, figures from American history like Buffalo Bill mingle with well-developed fictional characters. While Native Americans are often prominent in Somtow's works, *Moon Dance* constitutes the most persuasive expression of his fascination with Native American culture, and Somtow also worked hard to craft a detailed portrait of werewolf behavior and society. Still, despite critical praise, the novel's juxtaposition of tropes from horror, western, and historical fiction was possibly too jarring for many readers.

In *Darker Angels* (1997), it was zombies animated by ancient African magic that incongruously appeared in America during the 1860s. The widow of an abolitionist meets poet Walt Whitman at the funeral of Abraham Lincoln, launching a convoluted series of flashbacks within flashbacks, eventually stretching back to Lord Byron in early nineteenth-century Britain, all involving African slaves who carry their voodoo lore into Western society, bringing the dead back to life with unsavory outcomes. Finally, to fulfill an old commitment, an African-American woman briefly revives Lincoln himself for a moment of necessary reconciliation with his son. Here, the genuine horrors of the American Civil War blend well with gruesome scenes of zombies eating human flesh, yielding a narrative that is consistently fascinating despite its sometimes frustrating structure; whenever they get to know a character well, it seems, readers find themselves jerked away into another new character's flashback.

Somtow notes that *Vampire Junction,* and its sequels, *Moon Dance,* and *Darker Angels* all occur in the same parallel world, similar but not identical to our own, laying the groundwork for additional horror novels that would combine legendary creatures, famous people from the past, and characters from previous Somtow works. He has also produced large numbers of horror stories, including "Anna and the Ripper of Siam" (1988), recasting Anna as a sexually repressed virgin meeting a homicidal English visitor in Bangkok; "Dragon Fin's Soup" (1995), about a Chinese family that hides within its restaurant an immense dragon whose regenerating flesh provides their signature dish; the award-winning "Brimstone and Salt" (1996), portraying Lot's daughter as a sexually abused woman who embraces vampirism to escape from her father; and "The Ugliest Duckling" (1997), about a handsome young AIDS victim in Los Angeles who encounters a vampire.

YOUNG ADULT NOVELS

Though regularly overlooked, Somtow's young adult novels include some of his finest work, displaying a keen sensitivity to adolescent problems and attitudes. *The Fallen Country* (1986) depicts an abused teenager who is periodically transported to a bitterly cold fantasy world where he mechanically rescues princesses and fights monsters amid emotionless people. By finding allies and triumphing over the sinister Ringmaster of the frozen land, he symbolically overcomes his cruel stepfather. Similarly blending fantastic elements with grim realities, *Forgetting Places* (1987) describes a Kansas teenager, traumatized by the suicide of his older brother, who runs away to live with an aunt in Los Angeles. While receiving mysterious messages apparently from his dead brother, he meets and bonds with a girl named Zombie McPherson, helps her as she combats her own suicidal impulses, and comes to realize that he must forget about his brother and recommit to his own life, a resolve strengthened by the discovery that the seemingly occult messages were actually prepared and timed for delivery by his brother before he died. Though *Forgetting Places* therefore is arguably not a fantasy, it remains, like *The Fallen Country,* a remarkable examination of the roles fantasy can play in both hindering and helping in the process of a young person's personal growth.

After these emotionally involving stories, *The Wizard's Apprentice* (1993) was a disappointingly glib diversion about a teenager in the Los Angeles suburb of Encino recruited by a worldly-wise wizard who sets out to fully develop the boy's latent magical powers. The only interesting twist comes when we learn that the boy's father, a Hollywood special-effects expert, turned to make-believe magic only after meeting the same wizard and proving insufficiently gifted to garner the apprenticeship his son was offered. Though *The Vampire's Beautiful Daughter* also takes place in Encino and refers to characters from *The Wizard's Apprentice,* it is stunningly superior, a haunting vignette about a maladroit teenager, Johnny Raitt, attracted to a beautiful classmate who is the daughter of Dracula and a human mother, theoretically enjoying the option of either becoming a vampire or remaining human. However, her sixteenth birthday is approaching, when she will be ritually murdered and turned into a vampire at a "devivification ceremony" (p. 58). Although Johnny halfheartedly attempts to persuade her to resist this initiation, he has observed her interacting amicably with other young vampires and understands that the eternal life of the vampire represents a heritage too powerful to renounce; so he stoically witnesses her death and transformation, accepts that he has lost her forever, and ignores her occasional nocturnal appearances in his window. In its refusal to surrender to sentimentality, its recognition that some people may be destined to remain apart, *The Vampire's Beautiful Daughter* stands out in a field of literature frequently willing to settle for facile celebrations of the power of love to overcome all obstacles. Since the novel mentions Timmy Valentine, it can also be viewed as Somtow's wistful coda to the Valentine series, reflecting a personal decision to abandon the theme of vampirism and move on to other subjects in his fiction.

Somtow has never been reluctant to travel into unfamiliar territory, although—as with his characters—this has not always been purely a matter of choice; in the late 1990s, by his own reports, Somtow was increasingly unable to find publishers for his works. Still, with characteristic energy and creativity, he forged a multifaceted strategy to endure during his adversities—reimmersing himself in composing; continuing to move in new directions, including a realistic novel, *Jasmine Nights,* and planned collections of essays and poetry; publishing new fiction from small presses; and staying in the public eye by contributing stories to thematic anthologies and writing novels for popular mass-market franchises, such as *The Crow: Temple of Night* (1999) and a projected *Star Trek* novel. To those whose horizons are limited to the shelves of major bookstores, it may appear that Somtow's career is ending; however, like many of his memorable creations, he retains the ability to spring back to conspicuous life at any time. Having transcended so many barriers during his lifetime, Somtow can hardly regard a few skeptical publishers as an insurmountable challenge.

Selected Bibliography

WORKS OF S. P. SOMTOW

FANTASY AND HORROR NOVELS

The Aquiliad. Norfolk, Va.: Donning, 1983. (Published under the name Somtow Sucharitkul). Revised edition. *The Aquiliad I: Aquila in the New World.* New York: Ballantine, 1987. (Published under the name S. P. Somtow.)

Vampire Junction. Norfolk, Va.: Donning, 1984. Revised edition. New York: Berkley, 1985.

The Fallen Country. New York: Bantam, 1986. (Published under the name Somtow Sucharitkul. For young adults.)

The Shattered Horse. New York: Tor, 1986.

Forgetting Places. New York: Tor Books, 1987. (For young adults.)

Aquila and the Iron Horse. New York: Ballantine, 1988.

Aquila and the Sphinx. New York: Ballantine, 1988.

Moon Dance: A Novel. New York: Tor, 1990.

Riverrun. New York: Avon, 1991.

Forest of the Night. New York: Avon, 1992. As *Armorica.* London: Orbit, 1994.

Valentine. New York: Tor, 1992.

The Wizard's Apprentice New York: Atheneum, 1993. (For young adults.)

Vanitas: Escape from Vampire Junction. New York: Tor, 1995.

Yestern. In *The Riverrun Trilogy.* San Francisco: White Wolf, 1996.

The Vampire's Beautiful Daughter. New York: Atheneum, 1997. (For young adults.)

Darker Angels. New York: Tor, 1997.

The Crow: Temple of Night. New York: Harper, 1999.

SCIENCE FICTION NOVELS

Starship & Haiku. New York: Pocket Books, 1981. (Published under the name Somtow Sucharitkul.) New York: Ballantine, 1988. (Published under the name S. P. Somtow.)

Light on the Sound New York: Timescape, 1982. (Published under the name Somtow Sucharitkul.) Revised edition. *The Dawning Shadow: Light on the Sound.* New York: Bantam, 1986.

Mallworld Norfolk, VA: Donning, 1982. (Published under the name Somtow Sucharitkul.) Expanded with two additional stories. *The Ultimate Mallworld,* Atlanta, GA: Meisha Merlin, 2000. (Published under the name S. P. Somtow.)

The Throne of Madness New York: Timescape, 1983. (Published under the name Somtow Sucharitkul.) Revised edition. *The Dawning Shadow: The Throne of Madness,* New York: Bantam, 1986.

Utopia Hunters. New York: Bantam, 1984. (Published under the name Somtow Sucharitkul.)

The Darkling Wind. New York: Bantam, 1985. (Published under the name Somtow Sucharitkul.)

V: The Alien Swordmaster. London: Pinnacle, 1985. (Published under the name Somtow Sucharitkul.) New York: Pinnacle, 1986.

V: Symphony of Terror. New York: Tor, 1988.

NOVELS

Bluebeard's Castle. Bangkok, Thailand: *The Nation* (serialized), 1994–1995.

Jasmine Nights. London: Hamish Hamilton, 1994. New York: St. Martin's Press, 1995.

SHORT STORIES

Fire from the Wine-Dark Sea. Norfolk, Va.: Donning, 1983. (Published under the name Somtow Sucharitkul.)

Fiddling for Waterbuffaloes. Eugene, Ore.: Pulphouse, 1992.

I Wake from a Dream of a Drowned Star City. Eugene, Ore.: Axolotl, 1992.

Nova: Short Fiction by S. P. Somtow. Translated by Thaithow Sucharitkul. Bangkok, Thailand: Vanlaya Press, 1994.

Chui Chai: Short Fiction by S. P. Somtow. Translated by Thaithow Sucharitkul. Bangkok, Thailand: Vanlaya Press, 1995.

The Pavilion of Frozen Women. London: Gollancz, 1995.

A Lap Dance with the Lobster Lady. Centreville, Va.: Bereshith Press, 1998.

Dragon Fin's Soup. North Hollywood, Calif.: Babbage Press, 1999.

Tagging the Moon. Newberg, Ore.: Nightshade Books, 2000.

FILM

The Laughing Dead. Written, directed, and scored by S. P. Somtow. 1989.

Brian Stableford
1948–

DAVID LANGFORD

BRIAN STABLEFORD IS a prolific author of science fiction based on themes of biology and sociology, disciplines in which he is academically qualified. He brings an unsparing critical intelligence to his treatment of the supernatural, in particular the vampire myth and (in his Werewolves trilogy) the possibility of "angels" with the power to alter physical laws and disrupt causality at whim.

Brian Michael Stableford was born on July 25, 1948 in Saltaire, Shipley, in the English county of Yorkshire. His parents were William Ernest Stableford, an aircraft engineer, and Joyce Stableford née Wilkinson, who had several occupations and last worked as a hypnotherapist. He attended Manchester Grammar School from 1959 to 1966 and went on to the University of York, graduating in 1969 with first-class honors in biology. After three years of postgraduate research studying the population dynamics of flour beetles, he switched to the sociology of literature in 1972, leading to his 1978 thesis "The Sociology of Science Fiction"; he was awarded the D. Phil. in 1979.

Stableford has held various full-time and part-time academic positions since 1976—chiefly at the University of Reading, Berkshire, the town in which he has lived since 1980—while pursuing a parallel career in writing. Besides publishing much imaginative literature he is acknowledged as a critical authority on imaginative literature, notably for his 1985 text *Scientific Romance in Britain, 1890–1950*. In 1999 he received the Pilgrim Award for scholarship in science fiction.

He began to publish science fiction as a teenager with the novella "Beyond Time's Aegis" (*Science Fantasy* magazine, 1965), written with his friend Craig A. Mackintosh under the joint pseudonym Brian Craig—a name later revived by Stableford for game-related fantasies written for Games Workshop. His first science fiction novels, *Cradle of the Sun* (1969) and *The Blind Worm* (1970), were colorful, exotic, and slapdash. Stableford cheerfully acknowledges the potboiler nature of his 1971 trio, Dies Irae, which essentially reworked Homer's *Odyssey* and *Iliad* as a fast-paced mixture of space opera and sword-and-sorcery.

As the 1970s progressed, his work blended entertainment with greater thoughtfulness, psychological depth, and an exhilarating sense of scale, with entire planets reengineered and viewpoints extending over gulfs of evolutionary time, as in *The Walking Shadow* (1979). *The Encyclopedia of Science Fiction* (1993) compares his better novels with the scientific romances of the visionary English writer Olaf Stapledon (1886–1950).

Stableford's first venture into book-length supernatural fantasy was the children's novel *The Last Days of the Edge of the World* (1978). The story is witty, charming, inventive, and critical of all magical wish-fulfilment. As in John Brunner's *Traveller in Black* (1971), the ultimate quest goal is to remove the taint of chaotic, irrational magic from the world so that reason can prevail.

The title's magic-poisoned edge is the last of the seven edges of a world that elsewhere has subsided into roundness. Close by is the bankrupt kingdom Caramorn, which hopes to ally itself with magic and presumed power by marrying its unlovable prince to the daughter of the last, near-senile wizard of the world's edge. Naturally the girl objects, decides to test her suitor with extremely difficult questions, and unwittingly stumbles on a spell comprising the six hardest questions of all.

Once begun, this spell must be completed. It is the last will and testament of the long-dead mage Jeahawn, who put an end to the old wars of wizardry that have left the edgelands still haunted and polluted with "curses and counter-curses stacked six or seven deep" (p. 8). Now it is time for the final decontamination, each question posing a tougher challenge—such as learning the color of a gem buried within an ancient monster's head—whose answering has more spectacular side effects. The finale is apocalyptic, with the enchanted realms collapsing in chaos and flood to give Caramorn not magical wealth but a seacoast and a fishing industry. Rationality triumphs, and the young heroine and hero (who, subversively, is not the prince) are free to go to university. *The Last Days of the Edge of the World* is an enjoyable story that seems unfortunately neglected, probably because Stableford has written very little children's fantasy and has not built a reputation in this subgenre.

In 1988 Stableford published his first major assault on the vampire mythos, *The Empire of Fear*, which opens in an alternate seventeenth-century world in which vampirism has been loose for centuries. Class divisions of Grand Normandy (England under the Gaulish empire) are made sharper and crueler by the presence of an immortal vampire aristocracy whose local prince has ruled since the twelfth century: Richard I, the Lion-Hearted (Coeur de Lion).

Here the nightmarish trappings of supernatural horror, of blood, fangs, and perverse lust, are shadows to be dispelled by the light of scientific reasoning. The story opens with Edmund Cordery, mechanician to the Court of Prince Richard, busying himself with the newly invented microscope. This, rather than garlic and crosses, is his talisman—the thin end of the wedge of understanding that will topple an empire of fear that is also an empire of ignorance. A tiny elite of undying vampires has long lorded it over millions of commoners, but now, as Cordery affirms, "Our arts mechanical have outstripped their arts magical, and they know it" (p. 9).

In fact Cordery's key insight is that vampirism in this world is not magical in origin; immortality is not a gift of God, as official doctrine claims, nor of the devil, as is whispered in folklore, but something essentially natural, biological. Therefore, knowing himself already doomed for having learned too much, Cordery conducts the final experiment of infecting himself with plague and allowing his vampire protector and sometime lover (the Lady Carmilla, a nod to J. Sheridan Le Fanu's classic vampire story "Carmilla") to take his blood. The battle between science and superstition is fought out in her veins, with fatal results.

The lamp of reason is passed on to Cordery's son, Noell, who makes a grueling heart-of-darkness journey to the African wellsprings of the vampire plague. The crater of Adamawara, center of the mystery, is guarded by jungles poisoned with a fungus-like infection called the silver death, seemingly a precursor of vampirism. Legends of a sky-god smiting the earth at

Adamawara suggest a meteor impact that brought something alien into the world, recalling the contamination described in H. P. Lovecraft's "The Colour Out of Space" (1927).

For Noell, true heroism does not lie in moral worth or brute courage but in proper use of the intellect. He sees past the trappings of the African vampire initiation ceremony—intended to terrify and overawe—to the essential facts. The tormented vampires-to-be are inoculated with something, and cruelly unmanned to ensure they can never pass that something to others.

> But [Noell], who had sat upon the knee of Francis Bacon, and carried in his flesh and spirit alike the heritage of Edmund Cordery, had seen neither gods nor devils, nor any superhuman magic, nor anything at all to humble the soul of a common man with fear and dread. He had seen only opportunity—the birth of a confident understanding which made him feel that he was no longer a bondsman in the empire of fear, but a free citizen of the republic of enlightenment.
>
> (p. 239)

Far from cowering in the face of things with which mankind was not meant to meddle, Noell knows the importance of understanding the rationale behind seeming abominations. Turning on this pivot, *The Empire of Fear* moves from supernatural horror and the dread of the unknowable to a more science-fictional prospect in which knowledge can break the vampire hegemony and bring the benefits of quasi-immortality (conveniently accompanied by reduced fertility) to the entire human race. Exceptions remain, a few who are tragically immune to immortality, and Noell himself ironically proves to be one of these.

In the final section of *The Empire of Fear*, Stableford breaks entirely with the static, petrified tradition of horror and extrapolates the benefits of vampirism into what might be called his default utopian future. This, outlined in the nonfiction work *The Third Millennium: A History of the World A.D. 2000–3000* (with David Langford, 1985) is a world transformed by "emortality," an improved human condition whereby death—still inevitable in the long entropic run—may be indefinitely postponed.

The late 1980s also brought the Orfeo trilogy of action-adventure fantasies, written under the pseudonym Brian Craig. Stableford and other British authors were commissioned to produce spin-off fiction set in the world of Games Workshop's Warhammer role-playing system. However successful as a game, Warhammer offered little originality as a fantasy setting—as suggested by the world map of such heavily copyright-protected lands as Albion, Nippon, Araby, and Cathay, peopled with innovative creatures like orcs, trolls, dwarves, elves, vampires, and the Norse. The Orfeo trilogy comprises *Zaragoz* (1989), *Plague Daemon* (1990), and *Storm Warriors* (1991); further game-related titles followed.

In the major Werewolves trilogy of 1990–1994, Stableford introduces a range of supernatural entities—werewolves, immortals, and "fallen angels" of incalculable powers—and, even more so than in *The Empire of Fear*, subjects them to severe philosophical testing by the standards of what a reasonable man might find worthy of belief. The analysis is prolonged and scathing.

The eponymous shape-shifters of *The Werewolves of London* (1990) have a literal existence in Victorian London, cheekily buttressed by an invented passage from Sabine Baring-Gould's *Book of Were-Wolves* (1865), referring in turn to nonexistent portions of Henry Mayhew's *London Labour and the London Poor* (1851–1862), which would not have been recognized by their supposed authors. Another nonhuman character is the manufactured immortal Adam Clay, or the Clay Man, who as Lucian de Terre once wrote *The True History of the World*.

But the Earth of this trilogy is "a world with many histories, none of which are true"—thanks to the possibility of supernatural "Acts of Creation" which by remaking the present also rewrite the past, rooting their changed reality in false but unfalsifiable history (p. 131).

Adam Clay, made rather than born, nevertheless has a navel implying a past that never was. In which case, as was argued by the experimental zoologist Philip Henry Gosse in his much-ridiculed *Omphalos* (1857; the title is Greek for "navel"), the Earth might be only thousands of years old, as suggested by the book of Genesis, despite the many millions implied by the geological record. Gosse's argument was that an omnipotent God could have created Earth recently but with a false geology implying its great antiquity, just as a navel implies a mother and a natural birth.

Acts of Creation are possible to the elusive beings tentatively designated as angels, who have been generally quiescent since what human myth recollects as a golden age of gods, miracles, and chimeras. Now, in 1872, there are new stirrings. In Egypt, the sequence's central character David Lydyard is bitten by a seeming snake, which infects him with apocalyptic, heretical visions of God and Satan. An angel (later taking the name Bast) has made him its creature, its eyes on a world that it cannot directly perceive.

Meanwhile the aspiring mage Harkender, who seems to prefigure the notorious twentieth-century occultist Aleister Crowley, has attempted to exploit such angelic linkage via a ritual intended to make the foundling Gabriel Gill a focus of angelic power. Lydyard's mentor and future father-in-law, the hard-line sceptic Tallentyre, must deal with inexplicable events that challenge the framework of his beliefs. The werewolves, once real wolves, still resent the angelic intervention that condemned them to spend most of their time in the less joyous human form, and take a dangerous interest in magical doings.

The book's ramified storylines climax in a tawdry, clichéd version of hell, improvised by the nameless angel (known to some as the Spider) with which Harkender communicates through ugly rituals of pain and sexual humiliation. The Spider's intimidation is limited by what it can pluck from human superstition and fear. It is Tallentyre who retorts with a more compelling vision of the cosmos as it seemed to Victorian eyes, a starry infinity whose impact on the Spider's comprehension brings the book to a pyrotechnic end.

Lydyard's visionary journey has only just begun, and continues with increasing, harrowing intensity through *The Angel of Pain* (1991), set in 1893. In this curiously static but densely argued text, external events—grave robbery, wolf attack, shocking magical killings—seem hardly more than distractions from Lydyard's and others' inward agonies and ecstasies. The Angel of Pain herself, with terrible talons and burning eyes, is no more than a symbol of Lydyard's constant torment by arthritis; yet she is a rewarding mistress whose attentions fuel his clairvoyant visions, his ability to see (his inability not to see) through certain others' eyes.

Plato's allegorical cave is a recurring image. Men chained in the cave see only shadows on the wall before them, being unable to turn and look at the real objects casting the shadows. Even Lydyard has been allowed only glimpses over his shoulder; even the angels see only metaphorical shadows, though different ones, since human and angelic viewpoints come close to mutual incomprehensibility.

The Angel of Pain culminates with a sixfold "oracle" of human characters mentally linked, through a common gateway of excruciation, for a visionary journey beyond Plato's cave. The oddly assorted six include the newly introduced Hecate, a malformed woman who like Gabriel is a conduit for angelic power, and Sterling, an ambitious biologist whose anachronistic success in inducing artificial mutations suggests covert help from an interested angel. In the final, transcendent vision that they share, there is insight at last—if only by allegory—into the angels' inhuman sensoriums. These beings might easily destroy humanity, but nevertheless need it as a mirror to help understand themselves. In a closing dream-encounter with Bast, which wins

Lydard a few concessions and some relief from pain, he addresses the angel: "You're not human, I know, but you are a thinking person. Aren't you lonely for the sight of eyes which may look into your own and have some inkling of what you are?" (p. 380). There is no reply, but for the first time it is recorded that an angel seems forlorn.

A further quarter-century passes before the closing volume, *The Carnival of Destruction* (1994), whose title quotes George Griffith's future-war novel *The Angel of the Revolution* (1893) and whose action begins in 1918 amid the carnage of a World War I that is taking a different course from our history. When Joan of Arc seems to appear to young French soldier, Anatole, as he lies dying in a shell-hole, we know that the angels have begun to meddle anew. A further example of how their powers are defined by human expectation is the transformation of a former henchman of Harkender who simplistically worshiped the Spider as Satan, and as his reward has become the immortal, invulnerable, and vestigially horned Asmodeus.

Whatever the angels may be, it emerged in book two that just seven of these transnatural entities are associated with Earth. It is time for another kind of oracle to determine the best (in whatever unimaginable scale of values) long-term relationship between angels and mankind. In scenes of considerable destructive power, various angels gather "focus groups" of human and other characters to survey the sheaf of possible futures.

Thus Mandorla, pack leader of the werewolves of London, joins the Clay Man to examine the most obvious carnival of destruction: a grim Stapledonian timeline where peace never returns after 1914, with London under gas attack in 1930, consumed by nuclear fire in 1963, uninhabitable except by deep-tunnel dwellers in the twenty-first century, and so on through increasing desolation.

Pelorus, the werewolf most sympathetic to mankind, accompanies Harkender and Sterling on a critical survey of possible utopias—from science fiction dreams (including emortality) to abstract heavens of light and ecstasy or perpetual unspoiled childhood. All are found wanting.

Anatole, meanwhile, has boldly asked "Jeanne d'Arc" for a vision of the entire universe and its workings, and together with Lydyard and Hecate experiences vast cosmological perspectives. The oracular zoom-lens ranges from immensity to submicroscopic realms. At last the nature of the angels is suggested: beings rooted in the universe's underlying quantum reality and perplexed by the strange sluggishness of matter. Yet they remain, for all practical purposes, supernatural creatures.

There is no going back after exploring the deep future, and when this coldly exhilarating carnival of destruction is over, the surviving characters are stranded, far from Victorian gaslit romance and the low-tech horrors of 1918. However, the final epilogue suggests that by removing themselves retrospectively from history in an ultimate Act of Uncreation, the angels have allowed another of the world's many histories to assert itself. In 1872, Lydyard is spared that snakebite; in 1918, World War I is ending as we expect.

This extraordinary trilogy synthesizes a vast range of myth, philosophy (that of Plato and Lucretius in patricular), invention, and literary allusion into a bleak but bracing overview of human history, from past to distant future and the ultimate limiting factor of the human imagination.

Before his Werewolves trio was concluded, Stableford returned to the vampire theme in a contemporary setting, with *Young Blood* (1992). Its heroine, Anne Charet, is a philosophy student at a very ordinary British university, low on self-esteem and carrying on a tepid affair with a postgraduate psychology researcher named Gil Molari. Then she discovers curious ecstasy ("much sexier than sex") with the shadowy being Maldureve, who identifies himself as a vampire (p. 4).

Charet willingly lets Maldureve take her blood. Fangs are not involved; as her tutor remarks in a lighthearted discussion of vampire mythology, "We can all see that Christopher Lee's canines are at least two inches apart, and the two holes in the girl's neck are never more than half an inch from one another" (p. 57). In reality, or seeming reality, the victim's flesh cooperates—voluptuously reshaping itself to allow free passage of blood.

Becoming dangerously anemic, Charet quixotically decides to go the whole way and become a vampire herself. The stage seems set for a sardonic comedy of embarrassments, but the feeding trick works equally well for her and she duly inducts or infects Molari. To him, euphoria, weakness, and hunger suggest a more literal infection. His research work involves psychotropic viruses that can alter mental states. He is certain that there has been a leakage.

Molari's rationalization proves disastrous when he is taken unawares by the craving for blood. Charet may be equally rash in assuming that Maldureve has an independent, supernatural existence. His name, after all, suggests the French for an evil thing in a dream, *mal du rêve*. Was he conjured up by a psychotropic virus, by Anne's complex emotional dissatisfaction, or by both in concert? Indeed, are these two causes necessarily distinct? "Maybe all the wars of religion were just contents between diseases of the brain. Maybe the world really was full of monsters once," Anne says (p. 296).

To deal with the dangerous, vampiric hunger, Charet journeys into her own mind for symbolic battle. She survives, and so after a fashion does Molari, but *Young Blood* ends on a note that simultaneously evokes the traditional shudder of "The End . . . or is it?" and transcends supernatural horror. Perhaps, whispers the persistent voice of Maldureve, all this has been no nightmare but the opening of a new threshold in the evolution of human consciousness. Thus is produced a science-fictional rather than a supernatural unease.

The British publishers of *Young Blood* had suggested that the author pick a different title, but retreated when Stableford gleefully offered the more—in his word—perfervid alternative, *The Hunger and Ecstasy of Vampires*. Instead this became the title of a 1995–1996 homage to H. G. Wells's *The Time Machine* (1895), which flirts playfully with Victorian gaslight-era romance, fin de siècle decadence, and the "club story," in which adventures are related to an amazed audience in a cozy club-like atmosphere.

The story opens in 1895. Professor Edward Copplestone tells the tale of how carefully compounded precognition drugs took him—or rather, his projected "timeshadow"—on dream journeys to a curiously familiar future Earth of cattle-like humanity and vampiric "overmen," recalling the Eloi and Morlocks of *The Time Machine*. Meanwhile, part of the fun for the reader is the gradual revelation of the audience members' identities.

These include the authors Dr. Watson (accompanied by an unnamed, keen-faced person on whom Watson allegedly based his best-selling detective yarns), M. P. Shiel, and young H. G. Wells himself—spluttering about plagiarism. Science is represented by the physicist Sir William Crookes, also a stalwart of the Psychic Research Society, and by the maverick inventor Nikola Tesla. Decadence is supplied by Oscar Wilde and, perhaps the mysterious "I" of the frame story, an eastern European count eventually named as Lugard. Spelled backward, of course, this gives Dragul, a variant of Dragulya or Dracula.

In the Wellsian future of Copplestone's report, humanity has all but destroyed itself. Its former evolutionary niche was opened up to the blood-drinking shape-shifters who had long lived on the fringes of civilization, and who farm the barely sapient remnants of mankind until—yet farther in the future—the ugly necessities are superseded by manufactured, synthetic blood. Listening to this account of what to him is utopia, Lugard plans to escape persecution and entirely justified rumors of vampirism by traveling forward in time.

Sequel novellas develop the situation into a struggle ranging from the beginning to the end of existence, to determine the proper structure of the universe itself. "The Black Blood of the Dead" (*Interzone* magazine, 1997) filters this through the consciousness of the Holmes-like detective who travels yet further forward in time and reports to a sceptical gathering in Paris in 1900, with the dying Oscar Wilde as a characteristically mannered frame-story narrator. "The Gateway of Eternity" (*Interzone*, 1999; also title of a 2002 omnibus collection) features a regenerated far-future Wilde but is told by the author William Hope Hodgson. Taken from the trenches of 1918, Hodgson is projected forward into a still broader arena of cosmic conflict and meets a powerful entity that he identifies with the Hog, the astral menace in the most threateningly numinous episode of his occult-detective story sequence *Carnacki, the Ghost-Finder* (1947 edition, expansion of the 1913 collection). It is confirmed that the future, with Hodgson as its instrument, can dramatically alter the past.

Throughout, Stableford's quasi-scientific extrapolation is complemented by—to quote his jacket copy for *The Hunger and Ecstasy of Vampires*—"fascination with . . . the style and sensibility of the so-called Decadent Movements." There has already been a whiff of this rich decay in the perverse rituals of pain and humiliation in the Werewolves trio, which also features two Black Masses; and like the ultra-decadent Des Esseintes in J. K. Huysmans's *À Rebours* (1884), the heroine of *Young Blood* comes to value the joys of refined sensuality above humanity and life itself.

Oscar Wilde—or at least a future look-alike who has consciously patterned himself on Wilde—features again in Stableford's *Architects of Emortality* (1999), second of the science fiction "emortality" sextet and heavy with a sense of fin de siècle uncertainty at a time of global change. This includes a sequence of decadent murders via Baudelairean "Flowers of Evil," genetically engineered to consume their victims' flesh and leave each corpse as its own floral tribute, a skeleton wreathed in black blossoms with one bloom rising stylishly from each emptied eye socket.

Stableford has edited such anthologies as *The Dedalus Book of Decadence (Moral Ruins)* (1990). He has published several translations into English of relevant French texts by various authors, including the notable decadent Rémy de Gourmont and the astronomer Camille Flammarion, both featuring in *The Black Blood of the Dead. Vampire City,* his 1999 translation of Paul Féval's text, won a Children of the Night award from the Dracula Society.

Stableford's Genesys trilogy is pure science fiction but wittily takes the shape of a fantasy quest epic set on a colonized world in which human and alien genes have been intermingled to aid survival in a lush biosystem where all manufactured objects are subject to rapid decay. The titles are *Serpent's Blood* (1995), *Salamander's Fire* (1996), and *Chimera's Cradle* (1997).

Stableford celebrated the millennium with *Year Zero* (2000), chronicling the adventures of the downtrodden heroine Molly—a woman struggling to survive on meager British welfare benefits while separated from daughters in foster care, but feisty, streetwise, and irrepressible. Her bizarre exploits begin with "When Molly Met Elvis" (*Interzone* magazine, 1997, revised and incorporated into the novel), in which a surprise meeting with Elvis Presley in a London supermarket does not lead to a dream love affair, since they have so little in common and since—due to a flawed immortality treatment—Elvis smells increasingly unwholesome. After further close encounters with a stranded angel, abduction-happy Alien Grays, and bullying Men in Black, Molly moves into a seedy thirteenth-floor apartment surrounded by literal neighbors from hell, major demons who have deserted their infernal duties. A meeting with His Satanic Majesty is inevitable.

Weirdness continues to dog Molly's footsteps. Dull employment as a pharmaceutical research subject leads to missing-time episodes and contact with a prehistoric, tentacled "mother race." Stableford winks here at H. P. Lovecraft's portrayal of a like situation as shudderingly horrific in "The Shadow Out of Time" (1936): Molly is made of sterner stuff than Lovecraft's narrator. After a trip to Faerie to ransom a stolen daughter, Molly meets the more modern nightmares of global corporate conspiracy and gruesome biological engineering, and confronts the fear that all her experiences may be the result of paranoid delusion. Next comes a plague of zombification that the government downplays as no worse than the flu.

In *Year Zero,* millennial anxiety is justified: the world really is ending. When the Rapture occurs, only thirty-seven people are saved; according to Molly, for those remaining on Earth, "Hell's finished. The Devil is moving to London. Don't ask me why—in his place I'd have picked Paris or Vienna" (p. 182). Satan and his cohorts are both reality and reification, a distilled essence of human fear and weakness. Armed only with a *"deus ex* machine" gun supplied by Heaven, Molly has the task of outwitting ultimate evil, complicated by the fact that the Father of Lies has become her elder daughter's boyfriend. *Year Zero* is an enjoyable though intermittently disquieting romp that mingles comedy, urban myths, and chiliastic terrors, and features a satisfyingly unsentimental closing twist.

A second children's novel, *The Eleventh Hour* (2001), partly echoes *The Last Days of the Edge of the World* in that the goal is to sweep away the festering remnants of magic and open an era of rationality. In theory, the land of Iridia has enjoyed a perpetual Age of Gold in the thousand years since magicians halted its inevitable "decay" into a more practical Age of Iron—by literally stopping the clock. Thinning and stagnancy followed, with a dwindling of magic, purpose, and even population.

Restarting the Great Clock of Iridia, a project rashly undertaken by a group of youngsters, will restore the full-strength magic of yore for one last hour as the Age of Gold ticks away. Unfortunately this laudable plan was initiated by long-dead practitioners of black magic who during that hour intend to return, seize power, and stop time again with Iridia frozen in eternal tyranny. There are grim struggles, triple-cross betrayals, and a high body count before the new age can begin. The survivors' only reward is the possibility and inevitability of change.

Stableford consistently rejects both the wish-fulfilment of magical solutions in fantasy and the paradoxical comfort of supernatural horror fiction that plays with terrors we know very well are unreal. Even when paying sardonic homage to the decadent tradition, he uses careful realism and close-knit arguments to imagine what follows from such counterfactual premises as the reality of vampirism, and builds to an often transcendent conclusion. Again and again he deftly negotiates the bridge from Bram Stoker to Olaf Stapledon, from horror to scientific romance. Brian Stableford is an important and much underrated genre author.

Selected Bibliography

WORKS OF BRIAN STABLEFORD

NOVELS AND SHORT STORIES

Cradle of the Sun. New York: Ace, 1969; London: Sidgwick and Jackson, 1969.
The Blind Worm. New York: Ace, 1970; London: Sidgwick and Jackson, 1970.

BRIAN STABLEFORD

Dies Irae Trilogy

The Days of Glory. New York: Ace, 1971; Manchester: Five-Star, 1974.

In the Kingdom of the Beasts. New York: Ace, 1971; London: Quartet, 1974.

Day of Wrath. New York: Ace, 1971; London: Quartet, 1974.

To Challenge Chaos. New York: DAW, 1972.

Hooded Swan Series

Halcyon Drift. New York: DAW, 1972; London: Dent, 1974.

Rhapsody in Black. New York: DAW, 1973; London: Dent, 1975.

Promised Land. New York: DAW, 1974; London: Dent, 1975.

The Paradise Game. New York: DAW, 1974; London: Dent, 1976.

The Fenris Device. New York: DAW, 1974; London: Pan 1978.

Swan Song. New York: DAW, 1975; London: Pan 1978.

The Face of Heaven. London: Quartet, 1976. (First section of *The Realms of Tartarus*, 1977.)

Daedalus Series

The Florians. New York: DAW, 1976; Feltham, Middlesex: Hamlyn, 1978.

Critical Threshold. New York: DAW, 1977; Feltham, Middlesex: Hamlyn, 1979.

Wildeblood's Empire. New York: DAW, 1977; Feltham, Middlesex: Hamlyn, 1979.

The City of the Sun. New York: DAW, 1978; Feltham, Middlesex: Hamlyn, 1979.

Balance of Power. New York: DAW, 1979; Feltham, Middlesex: Hamlyn, 1984.

The Paradox of the Sets. New York: DAW, 1979.

Man in a Cage. New York: John Day, 1976.

The Mind-Riders. New York: DAW, 1976; London: Fontana, 1977.

The Realms of Tartarus. New York: DAW, 1977. (Incorporates *The Face of Heaven*, 1976.)

The Last Days of the Edge of the World. London: Hutchinson, 1978; New York: Ace, 1985.

The Walking Shadow. London: Fontana, 1979; New York: Carroll & Graf, 1989.

Optiman. New York: DAW, 1980. Reprinted as *War Games*, London: Pan 1981.

The Castaways of Tanagar. New York: DAW, 1981.

Asgard Trilogy

Journey to the Center. Garden City, N.Y.: Doubleday, 1982. Revised as *Journey to the Centre.* London: New English Library, 1989.

Invaders from the Centre. London: New English Library, 1990.

The Centre Cannot Hold. London: New English Library, 1990.

The Gates of Eden. New York: DAW, 1983; London: NEL, 1990.

The Cosmic Perspective, Custer's Last Stand. Polk City, Iowa: Drumm, 1985. (Chapbook.)

The Empire of Fear. London: Simon & Schuster, 1988; New York: Carroll & Graf, 1991.

Orfeo Trilogy (under pseudonym Brian Craig)

Zaragoz. Brighton, East Sussex: Games Workshop, 1989.

Plague Daemon. Brighton, East Sussex: Games Workshop, 1990.

Storm Warriors. Brighton, East Sussex: Games Workshop, 1991.

Werewolves Trilogy

The Werewolves of London. London: Simon & Schuster, 1990; New York: Carroll & Graf, 1992.

The Angel of Pain. London: Simon & Schuster, 1991; New York: Carroll & Graf, 1993.

The Carnival of Destruction. London: Pocket, 1994; New York: Carroll & Graf, 1994.

Ghost Dancers. Under pseudonym Brian Craig. Brighton, East Sussex: GW Books, 1991.

Sexual Chemistry: Sardonic Tales of the Genetic Revolution. London: Simon & Schuster, 1991. (Short stories.)

Slumming in Voodooland. Eugene, Ore.: Pulphouse, 1991. (Chapbook.)

The Innsmouth Heritage. West Warwick, R.I.: Necronomicon, 1992.

Young Blood. London: Simon & Schuster, 1992; New York: Pocket, 1993.

Firefly: A Novel of the Far Future. San Bernardino, Calif.: Borgo, 1994.

Genesys Trilogy

Serpent's Blood. London: Legend, 1995.

Salamander's Fire. London: Legend, 1996.

Chimera's Cradle. London: Legend, 1997.

Fables and Fantasies. West Warwick, R.I.: Necronomicon, 1996. (Chapbook of short stories.)

The Hunger and Ecstasy of Vampires. Shingletown, Calif.: Mark Ziesing, 1996. (Shorter version serialized in *Interzone* magazine, 1995.)

Emortality Series

Inherit the Earth. New York: Tor, 1998.

Architects of Emortality. New York: Tor, 1999.

The Fountains of Youth. New York: Tor, 2000.

The Cassandra Complex. New York: Tor, 2001.

Dark Ararat. New York: Tor, 2002.

The Omega Expedition. New York: Tor, 2002.

Year Zero. Mountain Ash, Wales: Sarob, 2000.

The Wine of Dreams. Under pseudonym Brian Craig. Nottingham, England: Games Workshop, 2000.

The Eleventh Hour. Gillette, N.J.: Cosmos, 2001.

Pawns of Chaos. Under pseudonym Brian Craig. Nottingham, England: Games Workshop, 2001.

Swan Songs: The Complete Hooded Swan Collection. Abingdon, England: Big Engine, 2002. (Omnibus of all six Hooded Swan novels.)

The Gateway of Eternity. Gillette, N.J.: Cosmos, 2002 (Omnibus of *The Hunger and Ecstasy of Vampires* and its sequels *The Black Blood of the Dead* and *The Gateway of Eternity.*)

NONFICTION

The Mysteries of Modern Science. London: Routledge and Kegan Paul, 1977; Totowa, N.J.: Littlefield Adams, 1980.

A Clash of Symbols: The Triumph of James Blish. San Bernardino, Calif.: Borgo, 1979.

Masters of Science Fiction. San Bernardino, Calif.: Borgo, 1981. Rev. and expanded as *Outside the Human Aquarium: Masters of Science Fiction.* San Bernardino, Calif.: Borgo, 1995.

The Science in Science Fiction. With Peter Nicholls (co-author and editor) and David Langford (co-author). London: Michael Joseph, 1982; New York: Knopf, 1982.

Future Man: Brave New World or Genetic Nightmare? London: Granada, 1984; New York: Crown, 1984.

Scientific Romance in Britain, 1890–1950. London: Fourth Estate, 1985; New York: St. Martin's, 1985.

The Third Millennium: A History of the World A.D. 2000–3000. With David Langford. London: Sidgwick and Jackson, 1985; New York: Knopf, 1986.

The Sociology of Science Fiction. San Bernardino, Calif.: Borgo, 1987.

The Way To Write Science Fiction. London: Elm Tree, 1989.

Opening Minds: Essays on Fantastic Literature. San Bernardino, Calif.: Borgo, 1995.

Algebraic Fantasies and Realistic Romances: More Masters of Science Fiction. San Bernardino, Calif.: Borgo, 1995.

Writing Fantasy and Science Fiction, and Getting Published. London: Hodder and Stoughton, 1997; Loncolnwood, Ill.: NTC, 1998.

Yesterday's Bestsellers: A Journey Through Literary History. San Bernardino, Calif.: Borgo, 1998.

Glorious Perversity: The Decline and Fall of Literary Decadence. San Bernardino, Calif.: Borgo, 1998.

The Dictionary of Science Fiction Places. Illustrations by Jeff White. London: Simon & Schuster, 1998; New York: Wonderland, 1999.

EDITED ANTHOLOGIES

The Dedalus Book of Decadence (Moral Ruins). Sawtry, England: Dedalus, 1990. Rev. ed. 1993.

The Dedalus Book of British Fantasy: The Nineteenth Century. Sawtry, England: Dedalus, 1991.

Tales of the Wandering Jew: A Collection of Contemporary and Classic Stories. Sawtry, England: Dedalus, 1991.

The Dedalus Book of Femmes Fatales: A Collection of Contemporary and Classic Stories. Sawtry, England: Dedalus, 1992.

The Second Dedalus Book of Decadence: The Black Feast. Sawtry, England: Dedalus, 1992.

CRITICAL AND BIOGRAPHICAL STUDIES

Ashley, Mike. "Brian Stableford." In *The Encyclopedia of Fantasy.* Edited by John Clute and John Grant. London: Orbit, 1997; New York: St. Martin's, 1997. Pp. 892–893.

Bailey, K.V. "The Empire of Fear." *Foundation* 47:75–77 (Winter 1989/1990).

———. "Year Zero." *Foundation* 81:105–108 (spring 2001).

Clute, John. "The Empire of Fear," "The Werewolves of London," and "The Angel of Pain." In *Look at the Evidence.* Seattle: Serconia, 1995. Liverpool: Liverpool University Press, 1995. Pp. 81–82, 310–311, 312–314.

Clute, John, and David Pringle. "Brian Stableford." In *The Encyclopedia of Science Fiction.* Edited by John Clute and Peter Nicholls. 2d ed. London: Orbit, 1993; New York: St. Martin's, 1993. Pp. 1148–1149.

Hill, Chris. "The Loneliness of the Long Distance Biologist: The Early Work of Brian Stableford." *Vector* 211:4–6 (May/June 2000).

Jeffery, Steve. "Brian Stableford: Architect of Emortality." In *Helicon 2 Souvenir Book.* Newbury, Berkshire: Helicon 2 Publications, 2002. Pp. 10–13.

Langford, David. "Architects of Emortality." *Foundation* 77:114–115 (Autumn 1999).

———. "The Empire of Fear." In *The Complete Critical Assembly.* Gillette, N.J.: Cosmos, 2001. Pp. 233–234.

Morgan, Pauline. "Brian (Michael) Stableford." In *St. James Guide to Horror, Ghost and Gothic Writers.* Edited by David Pringle. Detroit: St. James, 1998. Pp. 560–563.

Stephensen-Payne, Phil, and Chris Drumm. *Brian Stableford, Genetic Revolutionary: A Working Bibliography.* Leeds, West Yorkshire: Galactic Central, 1997.

Peter Straub
1943–

JOHN CLUTE

EVERY BOOK BY Peter Straub is an open book. Even his latest and most difficult solo novel, *Mr. X,* is positively littered with clues to its inner meaning, Ariadne's threads leading inward to the darker chambers of the tale and the teller. It is only necessary to read the book, and it will open for you: or so it seems. Certainly the big genial voice in which Straub's novels are told, a narrative voice that is instantly recognizable under its various disguises, seems to tell readers that they are right to feel secure, even in the valley of the shadow to come: because that voice has the horrors well in hand. As none of his earlier tales are as problematical in the telling as *Mr. X,* it should therefore be relatively easy to read Peter Straub, most of whose books are, after all, best-sellers; to walk through these houses without doors, these fourteen novels, these dozen or so stories, and to gain the pleasures they promise.

This ease is, however, an illusion. The bonhomie is a trap; Straub does not write stories to be told around a fire; he is not postprandial. Littered with clues his texts may be, but those clues are elusive, embedded in texts argumentatively dark in their rendering of the nature of the world, self-conscious, gnarly, thrusting, insistent.

We are left with a paradox, or at any rate with something of a phenomenon. Out of a difficult and bleak understanding of the world, out of literary tastes (from John Ashbery to William Faulkner) that most of his readers would find rarefied, and out of an ardor to tell the truth about hard things, Peter Straub has engineered an astonishingly successful public career. His books have sold millions of copies. They are among the best sellers of our time. In the end, the explanation may boil down to the simple fact that Straub is a storyteller of great ingenuity, a writer who obeys story with all his heart and mind, who delivers what he promises. But the fact remains that his underlying instincts about the world, which suffuse every paragraph he writes, are complex and bleak: for the world he gives us is a world fallen from a sky that is godless, and can never be made whole again. This is not best-seller country.

We return to story. From the first paragraph of his first novel, we feel ourselves to be in the hands of a writer who pays intense attention to the telling of the tale, an attention which in many storytellers seems almost instinctual, something that cannot really be taught; but the long, growing success of Straub's career has almost certainly depended as well, from its inception, on brutal hard work. But although storytelling instincts are clearly important, the long, growing success of Straub's career has almost certainly depended, from its inception, on brutal hard work. Like his friend and collaborator Stephen King, though far more single-mindedly—indeed, with an intensity of application not seen, perhaps, since Charles Dickens carved his great late novels out of the raw exuberant turf of his early work—Straub has taken each book he has published as a stepping stone to the next, an example to learn from and to go beyond. Though it may be argued that everything he writes is a variation on a single underlying theme (the hunger of the fractured to be whole), no one book much resembles any other, and his later work, which builds so consequentially upon the earlier, has grown steadily in richness and resource. His oeuvre is a series of climbs toward a goal (he is not yet sixty) that may not be reached for many years.

BACKGROUND

Peter Francis Straub was born March 2, 1943, in Milwaukee, Wisconsin, a city he transforms into an almost sentient, deeply ominous, entrapping organism in "A Short Guide to the City" (in *Houses Without Doors,* 1990), where clearly intended echoes of many writers—Jorge Luis Borges, Italo Calvino, and Franz Kafka come immediately to mind—irradiate the seeming openness of the prose. From his early years he was an avid reader. At the age of seven he was struck by an automobile and almost killed; the consequences of the accident—many broken bones, operations, a near-death experience, a year away from school while confined to a wheelchair, emotional traumas whose most evident signal was a severe stutter, from which he does not now normally suffer—can perhaps be too glibly read into his fiction. But it may be safe to suggest that, at some level it is not necessary or seemly to analyze, the continual interplay in Straub's work between brokenness and the ravening desire to be whole reflects the life. He then went on scholarship to Milwaukee Country Day School, which appears thinly disguised in *Shadowland* (1980); took a degree in English at the University of Wisconsin in 1965 and an M.A. at Columbia University the next year. Also in 1966 he married Susan Bitker (they remain married) and began teaching at Country Day. In 1969 they moved to Ireland, where they lived until 1972. He failed to complete his Ph.D. dissertation on D. H. Lawrence—a work that closely resembles the thesis that the bulky, balked Miles Teagarden fails to complete in *If You Could See Me Now* (1977)—and wrote simultaneously his first novel, the unfairly deprecated *Marriages,* which was published in England in 1973. From that point he has done nothing in his professional life but write. They returned to the United States in 1979 and live in Manhattan. They have two children, Emma and Ben.

We will not linger at the absolute beginning. Straub's first incarnation as a published writer was as the author of two volumes of poetry, which assemble competent work—some of it respectably first published in magazines like *Poetry*—but, compared to his prose, work that seems shruggingly unavowed: it does not seem hugely to care to exist. Straub's poetry, and his never-completed thesis on Lawrence, are markers of first attempts at a career he signaled his unease with from the start, a career he abruptly terminated well before it took off.

MARRIAGES, UNDER VENUS, *AND* JULIA

Except for one bravura sequence, *Marriages* (1973) is not a tale of the supernatural, though the book as a whole does adumbrate much of Straub's future work, both in the concerns it articulates and in the peculiar intensity of its depiction of personalities undergoing fracture. The shadow of Henry James, whose own fracture as a man and writer is persuasively described in Joan Aiken's *The Haunting of Lamb House* (1991), can be felt throughout the text in the repeated image of a golden bowl riven by cracks (from *The Golden Bowl*, 1904), an image that surfaces time and again through the novels to come. Even more pertinent to this first tale is Straub's modeling of Owen, the protagonist of *Marriages,* on Lambert Strether, the protagonist of *The Ambassadors* (1903). Both men are Americans the nature of whose work is left disdainfully vague; both come as deadly innocents (after the fashion of Americans) to Europe. The souls of both are burned by a vertiginous confluence of culture and passion, though Owen's experiences of raw being and deep sex are direct while Strether's are anything but; and both fail—as they must—to gain for themselves the primal state of Being-in-the-World Owen craves so brutally. So hungry for wholeness is Owen that his famine seems almost to burn through his skin, which is "a hard carapace like a walnut" (p. 14). All the same, he fails to make his life cohere—the novel is told in sections whose fragmentation is a kind of body English of its protagonist's—any more than he can truly understand "the woman" he falls desperately in love with. At the climax of the tale, she blindsides Owen by sleeping casually with someone else, though she returns immediately; but Owen reacts with destructive rage at this cracking of the golden bowl, a rage he directs outward to the world and inward through his roiled guts. Again and again in Straub's work, protagonists respond similarly to the bondage of their lives, through literal spasms of vomit, as though to purge themselves of the terrible physical immanence of a world that will not let go, will not allow them any triumph of mere being.

At this point in *Marriages,* Owen attempts to follow a man of his acquaintance who eludes him in the back streets of a small French city, in scenes strongly reminiscent of Nicolas Roeg's film *Don't Look Now* (1973). The man, who has in fact died in an American prison, leads him deeper and deeper into the surreal, folded-over topology of the underside of the city, a region of night and revel we meet frequently in later novels, Hampstead in *Floating Dragon* (1982) and Hatchtown in *Mr. X* being perhaps the most vivid examples. But the coils of the city, like the coils of his gut, are coils of bondage. By the end of the novel, Owen is locked back inside the carapace of his marriage and his life. *Marriages* differs from its successors not only in its lack of a past, which haunts the present like a bad twin; it also, in the end, leaves its protagonist where he began, neither dead or in recovery.

Under Venus, written next but not published until its inclusion in the omnibus *Wild Animals* (1984), reverses the move of *Marriages:* its protagonist returns to the States after long exile in Europe, becomes deeply embroiled in a complex family and civic dispute whose roots lie deep in the past, and tries fumblingly to sort things out. Superficially more competent than its predecessor, it retreats from the blunt obsessive focus in *Marriages* on one man's cracking of the golden bowl of his daylight life. It lacks the unremittingness that marks every other Straub fiction.

Julia (1975), which does not lack unremittingness, is Straub's first tale to integrate supernatural motifs and events into a vision of the world at large, a structure of telling designed to wring the uttermost storyable meaning out of lives so torn that they cannot be understood—or told—mimetically. Julia has just left her older, domineering husband after a family tragedy. For the first half of the novel we see through her eyes almost exclusively, and our instinctive identification with her gradually darkens into a sense (not entirely accurate) that she is in fact almost totally unreliable as a point of view. Her perceptions of herself, of her friends and intimates and her granite-hard husband, Magnus, and of the hauntings that begin to torment her, have been generated out of some profound hysterical displacement.

It is only in the second part of the novel, when the single viewpoint begins to fracture into disconcerting shards of objective story, that we learn the truth: that her abhorrence of Magnus, because he had cut their young daughter's throat in an attempt to save her from choking, is misplaced, as it had been Julia herself who had cut her daughter's throat. But once her central traumatic delusion is unpacked, we find ourselves forced to begin to believe what Julia is in fact experiencing: the ravenous ghost of an earlier, murdered child of Magnus's is haunting Julia in the guise of her own daughter, longing somehow to re-embody herself. *Julia* ends in the death of its protagonist and in gestures of cruelty and self-aggrandizement all around. It is perhaps Straub's grimmest tale. Unlike later protagonists, Julia finds herself, in the end, with no story to ride. She is swallowed.

IF YOU COULD SEE ME NOW, GHOST STORY, SHADOWLAND, *AND* FLOATING DRAGON

Marriages, Under Venus, and *Julia,* which contain some unmistakable (though parodic) self-portraits, are his most naked texts. They are not yet garbed in the intricacies of telling, in the dance of allusions between raw surface story and the literary models that serve as incipits and old haunts for the novels to come. They are not yet exemplars—organons—compendiums that illustrate the many ways one may use the nature and manifested artifice of story itself to itself tell story. Nor are they able to conceal Straub's deep obsessive interest (as a writer) in what might be called the "thingness" of the absence of good; in his four "professional" novels, this sense or intuition of the procreative entangledness of the absence of good is (as it were) obscured through simplification: the knottedness of the hunger for being is opaqued into "simple" evil, profoundly unfathomable perhaps, but also somewhat lacking in novelistic interest. In their essence, the supernatural entities who threaten the surface of the world in *If You Could See Me Now, Ghost Story* (1979), *Shadowland,* and *Floating Dragon* are, as a result, quite astonishingly similar. Their absence of good evacuates them; their ravenousness defines them utterly, blanking out intricacies of story. No yin tinctures the yang.

The advances that these four novels represent are, on the other hand, various and commanding. Each of them is a work of virtuoso applied craft, and as a whole they can stand as a working encyclopedia of the contemporary novel of supernatural horror in America. It is in these novels, which remain his central achievement as an author attempting to shape the mainstream of his chosen genre, that Straub begins to show more than occasional interest in the mode of telling a story that overridingly shapes his work from this point on: the use of irony as a structuring device to maintain control over the gap between the telling of a tale (which may be conducted by a narrator hidden or manifest, or a story within a story, or a frame or a book within a book) and the events themselves. Straub's already familiar narrative voice now becomes instantly identifiable as a voice-in-control, one whose ironical edge, or slope of superiority, over the told generates both a sense of security in the reader and an almost palpable momentum. This genial, ominous, lapel-grabbing irony marks Straub off from almost all his American colleagues, except perhaps Gore Vidal, whose use of this tool in his fiction is uneasy.

The first of the professional novels, *If You Could See Me Now,* is perhaps the simplest of the lot. The story is told in the first person by its protagonist, Miles Teagarden, yet another burly, bewildered, fractured big man hungry for sense and fullness and prone to swift ecstasies of anger. The book takes the form of an actual narrative that he writes as a journal, from which he takes time off during the events recounted in order to continue composing. Everything that happens in the novel, therefore, has already happened; the irony here is temporal, not a matter of incline from teller to told. We learn that Miles's life has gone off the rails, that his marriage has ended bitterly, that his thesis on D. H. Lawrence will either be written very soon or he will lose his teaching job, that he is entering midlife on empty. He remains obsessed by the death, apparently by drowning, of his teenage love, Alison, twenty years earlier. Just before her death, they had sworn an oath to reunite twenty years later, even if they were dead. Half madly, it is to fulfill this oath that Miles has returned home to semirural Wisconsin.

Unfortunately his arrival coincides with a rash of savage killings, and the compulsive oddness of his behavior (caged admissions of which stain the edgy stuffiness of his prose) makes him an obvious, though fairly clearly innocent, suspect. A portrait of the roiled and venomous life of the small town of Arden begins to unfold, as the lives there begin to fracture, and the long summer gradually darkens and corrodes under the purely malign influence of Alison's ghost, a revenant that bears vestiges of the human girl like weeds. "Most of the odors I catch hook the nerves," Miles notes early (p. 28); later sightings of Alison are trompe l'oeil: she is simultaneously an image of the dead human and a thing made of exudations of nature: dead leaves, stones, thorns, bark, and leaves. The title is perhaps obscure, but it seems to evoke the deep horror—most succinctly presented in W. W. Jacobs's "The Monkey's Paw" (1902)—at the thought of what in truth a returning ghost might actually look like. A marriage of hungers—Miles for the whole life taken from him by Alison's death; the revenant's savage scrabble upward toward beingness—is perhaps hinted at, but ultimately declined. Miles escapes, husks the bondage of his vomitous choked psyche, and lights westward out of the territory.

Escape is less easy for the congested souls who populate *Ghost Story*, which is Straub's most professional novel, the one (along with its companion, *Floating Dragon*) whose effect on the reader is most impersonal. It is also his most commercially successful solo work. The telling of the story, which is intricate, is deployed through various voices and devices into a haunting, extremely compelling artifact of suspense. The literary incipit in this case is Arthur Machen's famous early story "The Great God Pan" (1894), which details the consequences to a group of idle gentlemen of a scientist's ruthless attempt, by operating on the brain of a young girl he has slept with and feels he owns, to open her perceptions to the true world beyond the rind of the customary, the world whose ancient liminal annunciator is the Great God Pan. The girl goes mad, nine months later gives birth to a girl child, and dies. A quarter of a century later, the gentlemanly interlocutors reconstruct the savage career of the child of Pan, who lures men through sexual excess into fatal confrontations with reality when the rind of world is peeled. Two members of the league of gentlemen then force her to commit suicide. They go scot-free.

In *Ghost Story*, Straub deliberately does nothing to complexify the convention that a woman too nakedly primordial—a woman who manifests the sexual abandon of Pan Within—may be thought of as irredeemably Other. Long before the story proper begins, the envious shape-shifter entity who incorporates this principle has taken temporary human shape, and has sexually enthralled a group of young men destined to be dominant figures over the next decades in the small city of Milburn in New York State, somewhere east of Binghamton, a backwater region adjacent to (but detached from) more vital parts of America. Almost accidentally, one of the young men, driven to a Straubian excess of anger, kills her. Realizing their careers will be destroyed unless they conceal the deed, the five youths put the corpse in a car, which they sink in the nearby lake. But she shape-changes gloatingly, and escapes the trap. Decades later, her/its vengeance begins. The slow unfolding of the pattern of deaths is superbly apportioned through a narrative texture whose almost reportorial calm tellingly contrasts with the savage dismantling of the lives of Milburn it records. For within the rind of the world of *Ghost Story*—once it peels free and becomes a threshold to the reality within—is chaos and old night: revel. The five men, now reduced to four, continue to hold regular meetings of what they call the Chowder Society, during which they tell stories as Milburn turns into an arena for Walpurgisnacht. The most effective of these stories, told fittingly enough by a character named Sears James, is a parody with love of Henry James's seminal club story, "The Turn of the Screw" (1898), though it varies the implications of that famous tale significantly. What Sears James describes is an unmistakable invasion of the supernatural, which he has experienced; he is not (as was Henry James's original heroine) arguably the source of an evil that can only wreak havoc if it is imagined into being. By extension, the members of the Chowder Society are understood to be relatively innocent victims of a similarly malign incursion.

So the remaining cast—and the readers—of *Ghost Story* are "free" to engage in the succeeding pyrotechnics without conscience. In a final scene of remarkable power, the Pan/lamia shape-changer is reduced to a wasp and destroyed, and the novel closes with a glossy click. The skillfulness of *Ghost Story* helped it gain best-seller status and inspired the filmmakers into creating the simplistic *Ghost Story* (1981). But this skill should not disguise the polished pertinence of the tale to Straub's ongoing concerns and modalities: the sense that the present rides the past like a rind upon the real; that our fallen world, which is all we inherit, is by that very token ravened after by incomplete beings, creatures (human or not) who are best understood in stories that encompass the supernatural; that, in short, to be is to be hungered after.

In contrast—almost certainly deliberate—Straub's next novel, the ungainly but vibrant *Shadowland,* is anything but polished. It is a Godgame novel (see the entry on Godgame in *The Encyclopedia of Fantasy,* 1997, edited by John Clute and John Grant), the most complex and demanding Godgame yet published in the field of the fantastic. The term comes from John Fowles's *The Magus* (1966), whose working title was "The Godgame," a text Straub discusses at length in his introduction to the 1995 reprint of *Shadowland.* The term describes a tale of initiation whose rituals are created and managed by a magus figure. With or without consent, he forces his young "victim" to undergo complex ordeals designed to test his or her readiness to enter a fuller world. Godgame tales tend to be set on islands, like Shakespeare's *The Tempest* (1611), or, like *Shadowland,* whose main action takes place in rural Vermont, in forests. Their protagonists tend to find themselves transacting labyrinths embedded in edifices—neither labyrinth nor edifice need literally exist, though usually they do—and must expect to be tempted (and tortured) sexually. The novel begins with a frame set years after the events it describes, as an unnamed narrator, who is hard to distinguish from Straub himself, encounters an old school friend, Tom Flanagan, now a stage magician of great skill. Slowly he draws from the not unwilling Flanagan the nest of stories within stories that makes up the story of Flanagan's experiences twenty years before in a great house called Shadowland, owned by a great retired magician named Coleman Collins, who is the uncle of Del Nightingale, a school friend of both Flanagan and the narrator. The tale unfolds through almost literal folds of narrative, stories and dreams overlaid with dreams and stories, some of them fairy tales, so that *Shadowland* (itself shaped as a story that frames stories) seems set in a world literally made up of story. In this intricate fashion, Flanagan reconstructs the events of one fatal story-crafted summer. After a tortured year at the appalling private school they all attend, and after a series of events that makes it clear in retrospect that the physical school is a kind of scrim (or cover story) hiding a deeper, even more corrupting pocket world, Tom and Del go to Shadowland to spend the summer with Collins, the retired magician. Both boys hope he will teach them his trade. But Collins is also a magus—protean, mocking, unstable, ultimately vicious, the "King of the Cats"—and Shadowland is both the "real" school and a labyrinth the boys must master before one of them is chosen to be his successor. But it soon becomes clear that Collins is in fact unwilling to play the game, that the Godgame of Shadowland is a cheat, that he wishes to trap the boys into eternal bondage, and that he wishes to be himself immortal. At this point the story has become so complex and multilayered—the young woman who tempts the boys sexually is, for instance, Hans Christian Andersen's Little Mermaid, and she walks on knives—that there seems no "professional" exit for Straub, no way to keep the tale on the rails. So the simplification of Collins into a figure of unalloyed malice can be understood as a necessary clarification of the narrative. In the end this purely malevolent Collins is defeated, and Flanagan graduates into the story of his own real life, the story of the years between the events at Shadowland and his telling of the tale to the Straub-like narrator: but this story he does not tell, because (we guess) it is a success.

Indeed, the destabilizing shakiness of the edifice of stories that comprises *Shadowland* seems quite possibly to be a central point the novel is intended to convey. It is a tale intoxicated by story, but also subversive of story. The faltering staccato of tales that start off the book—like the uncompletable stories that make up Gene Wolfe's even more disquieting *Peace* (1975)—constitutes a warning to the reader not, it seems clear, to trust any of them. And the story under all the stories, the story-shaped world that Coleman unfolds like Satan tempting Jesus, imposes itself upon the boys through illusion and lie, through stagecraft gone sour. *Shadowland* is ultimately not about initiation, but about betrayal—Collins's betrayal of other human beings, his betrayal of magic, of art, of story itself.

The next novel, which is the last of the "professional" tales of the supernatural, can stand as a direct contradiction of the subversive questionings of *Shadowland*. *Floating Dragon* is a kind of upscaling of *Ghost Story*, a comprehensive unpacking, through a congeries of neatly dovetailing stories, of the range of effects available in the contemporary novel of horror. Like both *If You Could See Me Now* and *Shadowland*, the novel presents itself as a text written by one of its cast (its controlling irony is again temporal); in this case, the narrator is neither the incriminated protagonist of his own tale, or a ghost Straub, but the elderly Graham Williams, once blacklisted by the House Committee on Un-American Activities and now a successful novelist, who lives in Hampstead, a Connecticut exurb of New York. (His similarity to Ricky Hawthorne, the lovable elderly protagonist of *Ghost Story,* is clearly intended.) Hampstead lies under a double curse: a principle of unslakable evil has for centuries periodically inhabited a Hampstead resident, who then becomes a serial killer and causes other havoc, including earthquakes; and a chemical experiment has gone wrong, letting loose into the air a toxic, transformative poison. These two curses interact calamitously over the course of a very bad summer.

In his afterword to the 1995 reprinting of *Shadowland*, Thomas Tessier describes *Floating Dragon* as "the largest sustained jeu d'esprit ever written," which—though he perhaps unfairly skips over Thomas Mann's *Joseph and His Brothers* (1933–1943)—points directly to the kinds of pleasure this exuberant text offers. Synopsis is impossible in any brief compass. Over the course of the summer, Williams assembles through observation and interviews a third-person narrative too full to synopsize: murders, rapes, landslides, a floating dragon, a brand-new disease of unparalleled loathsomeness, telepathy, the reconstitution of a young man as a childe with burning sword, joyous plays with other texts, most movingly L Frank Baum's *The Wonderful Wizard of Oz* (1900), with many of these events repeating themselves under various guises. Moreover, it becomes necessary for Williams to search through Hampstead's history over 300 years, and to recount—in ample detail—the evidence he gathers to confirm that the spirit of unslakable evil has been repeating itself unslakably. Despite the horrors that fill it, *Floating Dragon* is not, in the end, a very serious book, though some of the individual strands of story that weave together could, if extracted from the merry-go-round, continue to show a growing mastery in the depiction of character. Patsy McCloud, an unwilling psychic in an appalling marriage, strikes a more plangent note throughout—and indeed a detachable part of her backstory was calved off by Straub, well before publication, and transformed into *The General's Wife* (1982), a novella set in London, where she becomes profoundly entangled in a deeply compelling troilism involving her, an ancient general, and a kind of ghost/golem replicant of the general as a young man. But this story is, in the end, inexplicable; it does seem to have been properly removed from *Floating Dragon*, whose comic structure requires ultimate explanations—or at least a setting to rest—of the events Williams has been shaping into story.

THE TALISMAN, *BLACK HOUSE*, AND SHORTER FICTION

There are two collaborations with Stephen King, *The Talisman* (1984) and its sequel, *Black House* (2001). The first can be seen as a diversion for Straub, as its quest structure, its clear-cut storyline, its habit of residing far too long in individual episodes, and its secondary-world setting all signal King's dominant role in the product. *Black House*—except for a final descent into an otherworld linked clearly to King's long Gunslinger/Childe sequence—seems, on the other hand, marked throughout by Straub's methods and concerns. The third-person plural narrative voice is, to begin with, Straubian: big, genial, sweeping, ironical, and engaging in play with some earlier model, in this case the superb, very similar voice Charles Dickens developed to narrate *Bleak House* (1853), a text variously evoked throughout *Black House*. The story itself can also be understood in terms of Straub's abiding concerns: a few decades after its close, the valiant Tom Sawyer–like protagonist of *The Talisman* has turned himself—by developing amnesia over anything involving the central moments of his life—into another Straubian study in fracture. He only re-immerses himself in his real story when it becomes inescapably clear that the serial murders afflicting the small mid-western town he has retreated to are connected to that real story. He uncovers the sword that is his inner self, translates himself and his motorcycle-gang samurai crew back into the otherworld territories of *The Talisman*, destroys the foe, and is killed as far as the mundane world is concerned. The energy of telling is huge. In its way, *Black House* is as joyous as *Floating Dragon*.

After *The Talisman*, Straub turned away from supernatural fiction, and although a reading of *Koko* (1988), *Mystery* (1990), *The Throat* (1993), and *The Hellfire Club* (1996) are necessary for any complete understanding of his long self-exploratory career, that reading does not belong here. During this decade or so, Straub restricted his non-mimetic work to occasional short stories and a short novel, *Mrs. God* (1990), which he wrote as an homage to Robert Aickman after an intensive reading of his stories. A mediocre academic named Standish gains permission to spend the summer at Esswood House, a stately home in England where valuable twentieth-century manuscript archives are stored, including the papers of Standish's grandfather's first wife, Isobel. He has left his own wife behind, the anguish of the abortion he once forced upon her by no means resolved by her current pregnancy. The setting, therefore, is pure Aickman: a protagonist who is incapable of behaving chivalrously to the life he has led, and who finds himself caught in a tangle of fragmented, unreadable scenes and narratives that fleetingly seem to replicate his own fragmentation as a man. Nothing in the end makes sense, though everything is tellingly horrific. So Standish literally burns his life to ash, scalding himself into a state so close to genuine infancy that he and the aborted child he has fabricated out of the stench of his own bad faith seem pretty well identical.

Houses Without Doors (1990) assembles stories of the 1980s, some of them supernatural, including "A Short Guide to the City" and a short version of *Mrs. God*. "The Buffalo Hunter," also published here for the first time, can be read as analogous to *Mrs. God*, for its protagonist, significantly named Bunting, has also failed to make sense of his fracturing self as the middle years approach. Standish lights out for a territory that is a pathless shatter of mirrors; Bunting turns inward, hunkering infantlike in his New York apartment, where he finds himself actually entering the worlds of the Westerns he reads for escape. Fatally, however, he comes across Leo Tolstoy's *Anna Karenina* (1875–1877) and, while inside Anna's tortured story, is run over by the train that kills her.

Magic Terror (2000) assembles more recent work (see bibliography for original publication details). Each story, even the non-supernatural tales, powerfully explicates the central concerns that have possessed Straub throughout his career. Two stories are of particular interest. "Hunger: an Introduction" (1995), is the story of a failed con man and cheat, told posthumously in the first person, in an Edgar Allan Poe voice. His tale constitutes Straub's most intensely comprehensive vision of the ravenousness of the absence of good or being; the last scene, where the ghost sucks minutiae of live substance through watching a child watch television, is both excruciating and surreally hilarious. "Mr. Clubb and Mr. Cuff" (1998) is a take on Herman Melville's "Bartleby the Scrivener" (1853), though Mr. Cuff himself presumably is an homage to Sergeant Cuff in Wilkie Collins's *The Moonstone* (1868). The narrator, chief partner of a firm of accountants that specializes in criminal clients, finds that his young wife has been unfaithful, and asks his assistant to help him hire some thugs to punish her. Right on schedule (though we learn later they had never been approached) the seemingly comic Mr. Clubb and Mr. Cuff arrive, and, extract from the narrator the information they require; at the same time, they begin to transform his offices into a scene of uncontrollable revel. They perform their duties with the wife and her lover—torturing both of them to death—and then balance the books with the narrator, torturing him as well, all the while addressing each other with a camp formality that makes them seem—theatrically and inescapably—twin Lords of Misrule. His torture complete, his business ruined, his wife a corpse in the ground, the narrator returns to the fundamentalist constraints of his upstate home town, where he can be said to flourish as a clockwork man reconstrued from fractures might flourish: "Ceremonious vestments," he tells us, "assure that my patchwork scars remain unseen" (p. 325).

MR. X

The central narrative secret of *Mr. X* (1999) seems no secret if the reader knows before opening the book that its narrator is black, for there are dozens of clues throughout that make it clear that he is not white; and at least two extended sequences only make sense if this is understand, for example when a small boy with perfect pitch imitates a southern black accent with a striking accuracy that Straub renders phonetically. At the same time, these hints and sequences are laid down inconspicuously, as part of the flow of a tale of quite remarkable complexity, so that early reviewers' failure to notice Ned Dunstan's color was probably inevitable. Straub himself has said (personal communication) that

> The main thing [readers] missed was some of the humor and the suggestion that black Americans are like the doppelgängers of white Americans—feared, avoided, and necessary to the picture as a whole. If you did get it midway through the book, then you would enjoy the salutary shock of recognizing that you had all along been taking these black people as simply people, without reference to their race.

The cultural implications of this game of invisibility are in themselves sufficiently telling to justify Straub's strategy here; but as *Mr. X* is itself a novel about invisible doppelgängers who are denied but who are "necessary to the picture as a whole," then the strategy seems doubly clever.

Ned Dunstan has been shadowed all his life by his invisible quasi-ghost twin brother, Robert, while at the same time he has been tracked and haunted by his father, the eponymous Mr. X, who in turn is the demented, illegitimate offspring of the demented, philoprogenitive Howard Dunstan, a black man who lives in the large family house out of town, and Ellie Hatch, who is white. If miscegenation were itself not difficult enough to field, Ned's parents are also unduly consanguineous, as his mother, Star Dunstan, is Mr. X's niece. Since the nineteenth century, the Dunstans and the Hatches have shared an uneasy, shifting hegemony over the southern Illinois city of Edgerton (probably Cairo in real life), which only intensifies the sense that, under Straub's rendering of the family/civic arabesques riddling Edgerton, there lies an auctorial play with William Faulkner, whose greatest novels revolve around incestuous, miscegenating families. That Howard Dunstan's house finally burns down with him in it, which is what happens to the demented philoprogenitive Thomas Sutpen and his house in *Absalom, Absalom* (1936), proves, however, to be coincidental, as Straub was not familiar with that Faulkner novel.

Ned returns to Edgerton when he senses that his mother has also returned there to die. He arrives in time to say farewell to her, and to gain some clue as to his father's identity; and his subsequent search through the present and past of Edgerton, which arouses his hiding father into murderous activity, supplies the central spine around which the numerous threads of *Mr. X* are woven. Mr. X believes himself to be a scion of the Elder Gods out of the Cthulhu Mythos of H. P. Lovecraft, whom he reads literally. This belief, along with certain supernatural powers shared by all the Dunstans, makes him a dangerous dad to touch base with, and the surface action of the plot deals more than competently with various expectable scenes and encounters.

At its heart, though, *Mr. X* burns through the virtuoso devices which make reading the text an experience that can stand for the joy that, in general, reading is able to give. *Mr. X* is that joy to read. And it is funny. But in the end, it goes further: it uncovers itself as a meditation on perception, genre, race, the past, Americanness, family, sex, friendship, loyalty, betrayal. It is perhaps Peter Straub's best novel to date. We are fortunate to be able to hope for more.

Selected Bibliography

WORKS OF PETER STRAUB

POETRY AND FICTION

Ishmael. London: Turret Books, 1972. (Poems.)

Open Air. Shannon, Ireland: Irish University Press, 1972. (Poems.)

Marriages. London: Andre Deutsch and New York: Coward, McCann & Geoghegan, 1973.

Julia. New York: Coward, McCann & Geoghegan, 1975; London: Jonathan Cape, 1976.

If You Could See Me Now. London: Jonathan Cape and New York: Coward, McCann & Geoghegan, 1977.

Ghost Story. New York: Coward, McCann & Geoghegan and London: Jonathan Cape, 1979.

Shadowland. New York: Coward, McCann & Geoghegan, 1980; London: Collins, 1981.

The General's Wife. West Kingston, R.I.: Donald M. Grant, 1982. (Story.)

Floating Dragon. San Francisco: Underwood-Miller, 1982; London: Collins, 1983.

Leeson Park and Belsize Square: Poems 1970–1975. San Francisco: Underwood-Miller, 1983.

Wild Animals: Three Novels: Julia, If You Could See Me Now, Under Venus. New York: Viking, 1984. (*Under Venus* is printed here for the first time.)

The Talisman. With Stephen King. New York and London: Viking, 1984.

Blue Rose. San Francisco: Underwood-Miller, 1985. (Story.)

Koko. New York: E. P. Dutton and London: Viking Penguin, 1988.

Houses Without Doors. London: Grafton Books and New York: E. P. Dutton, 1990. (Includes "Blue Rose"; "The Juniper Tree," from *Prime Evil*, edited by Douglas E Winter, New York: NAL, 1988; "A Short Guide to the City,"; "The Buffalo Hunter"; "Something About a Death, Something About a Fire"; and "Mrs. God"—see below for longer version of this story.)

Mrs. God. West Kingston, R.I.: Donald M. Grant, 1990.

Mystery. New York: E. P. Dutton and London: Grafton Books, 1990.

The Throat. Baltimore: Borderlands Press, 1993. (Straub prefers the Borderlands Press first-edition text over the first trade edition texts from Dutton in the United States and HarperCollins in the UK.)

The Hellfire Club. New York: Random House and London: HarperCollins, 1996.

Pork Pie Hat. London: Orion, 1999. (Long story first published as "Porkpie Hat" in *Murder for Halloween*, edited by Michele Slung and Roland Hartman, New York: Mysterious Press, 1984. Also in *Magic Terror*.)

Mr. X. New York: Random House and London: HarperCollins, 1999.

Magic Terror: Seven Tales. New York: Random House and London: HarperCollins, 2000. (Includes "Ashputtle" from *Black Thorn, White Rose*, edited by Ellen Datlow and Terri Windling, New York: Morrow, 1994; "Isn't It Romantic?" from *Murder on the Run*, New York: Berkley, 1998; "The Ghost Village" from *The Mists from Beyond*, edited by Robert Weinberg, Stefan R. Dziemianowicz, and Martin H. Greenberg, New York: ROC, 1993; "Bunny Is Good Bread," as "Fee" from *Borderlands 4*, edited by Elizabeth E. Monteleone and Thomas P. Monteleone, Baltimore, Md.: Borderlands Press, 1994; *Pork Pie Hat* first published as "Porkpie Hat" in *Murder for Halloween*, edited by Michele Slung and Roland Hartman, New York: Mysterious Press, 1984; "Hunger: an Introduction" from *Peter Straub's Ghosts*, Pocket Books, 1995; "Mr. Clubb and Mr. Cuff" from *Murder for Revenge*, edited by Otto Penzler, New York: Delacorte Press, 1998.

Black House. With Stephen King. New York: Random House and London: HarperCollins, 2001.

OTHER WORKS

Peter Straub's Ghosts. New York: Pocket Books, 1995. (HWA anthology edited by Straub.)

Peter and PTR: Two Deleted Prefaces and an Introduction. Burton, Mich.: Subterranean Press, 1999. (Self-criticisms written as by PTR.)

CRITICAL STUDIES

Sheehan, Bill. *At the Foot of the Story Tree: An Inquiry into the Fiction of Peter Straub.* Burton, Mich.: Subterranean Press, 2000.

Thomas Burnett Swann
1928-1976

JOHN CLUTE

IN THE TIME since his early death, Thomas Burnett Swann has become a remote figure for the reader of fantasy. He seems as deeply embedded in the past as any of his numerous novels and stories, none of which is set later than 1875 and most of which take place in lands bordering the Mediterranean before the triumph of Christianity. To a point, the exigencies of genre publication can explain his obscurity. Of the eighteen books of fiction published under his name, seventeen appeared as paperback originals and have never been granted hardcover publication in English; as a consequence, most are difficult to obtain, and some almost impossible. The eighteenth title, *Queens Walk in the Dusk* (1977), the last of five to be issued posthumously, was released as a limited-edition hardcover by a firm whose output was restricted to this one book; it, too, is not readily available.

Swann was unfortunate in publishing most of his work ephemerally; he was also unfortunate in that the excessive productivity of his last years caused a bunching effect in the release of these titles, with eight novels being published during 1975–1977. As the market for his slender, elegiac fables was never large, the likely effect of a spate of releases was to flood that small market.

There are still further reasons for Swann's sudden disappearance from the marketplace. Of those eight final novels, two are mild, unsuccessful farces utilizing sentimentalized historical figures only dimly familiar to the readership for which he wrote, and three are "prequels" considerably inferior to the texts that they are intended to adumbrate. (*Prequel* is a term that has come into use to describe the very large number of recent science fiction and fantasy stories whose internal chronology precedes that of a previously published story set in the same venue; Swann wrote several prequels.) Only three of Swann's last novels are independent creations that fairly reflect his peculiar talents as a fantasist of nostalgia, *How Are the Mighty Fallen* (1974), *The Minikins of Yam* (1976), and *The Gods Abide* (1976). They were lost in the crowd.

Misfortunes—some of them perhaps self-imposed—dogged Swann's brief publishing career and provide a leitmotiv for any discussion of his work. Although the form in which his novels were published provides some explanation for their swift disappearance, there are further reasons for their neglect. It is clear, for instance, that Swann was more comfortable with the short story and novelette than he was with full-length fiction, yet the latter part of his career was devoted to novels and to ill-considered expansions of earlier stories. It is also clear, as any sustained reading of his fiction should confirm, that the wide variety of settings and characters in his novels is in a sense misleading, because he is a writer whose range is startlingly limited to certain obsessively reiterated themes: the rite of passage from childhood into maturity; the nature of friendship; the loss of innocence, both on the personal level, with the onset of adulthood, and on the cultural level, with the rise of the classic Mediterranean civilizations. All culminate in a constant interlinking of nostalgia and carpe them tropes.

At the heart of Swann's work lies a remarkably poignant dream of an unattainable ideal childhood. This ideal colors, and in a sense vitiates, the ostensible themes that permeate the eighteen books. This is particularly evident on any examination of Swann's treatment of the rite of passage into sexual maturity, which provides the motive force of so many of his tales.

Again, a glance at the actual presentation of his books to the market may give some hint as to the pervading cone of his treatment of this material. It is always dangerous for a book to be published with illustrations, because any artist's rendering of a world depicted through language is a kind of straitjacket; and many authors, from Gustave Flaubert on, have strenuously objected to the impoverishment of their fictions through the addition of visual material, It seems that Swann had no such qualms. He seems indeed actively to have approved of the rendering of his imaginative universe by the artist most frequently associated with his work, George Barr, whose covers and other illustrations decorate no fewer than seven of his novels; Swann even purchased three examples of Barr's work and hung them in his bedroom.

Barr specializes in cartoonlike drawings that he overlays with a watercolor wash; the effect is that of a lush, somewhat sickly innocence. Although the figures depicted exhibit the exaggerated sexual characteristics typical of popular fantasy art, they have anything but a knowing air in Barr's work, where the effect is rather that of a prepubescent pretense to adulthood and sexual maturity. In this, Barr realizes with remarkable accuracy an abiding aspect of Swann's own vision.

Thomas Burnett Swann was born on October 12, 1928 in Tampa, Florida. His parents were wealthy, and his mother, who survived him, was a significant support for him throughout his life, especially during the difficult final years. After graduating from Duke University in 1950, Swann served in the navy for four years; in 1955 he took a master of arts degree from the University of Tennessee. He had privately published his first book of poetry, *Driftwood*, in 1952; in all, he was to publish four small volumes of slender, delicate, sentimental poems. Some appear in his fiction. While earning a doctorate (1960) from the University of Florida, in July 1958 he published his first fiction, "Winged Victory," in *Fantastic Universe*, a commercial magazine of fantasy. This story, with six others, remains uncollected.

From 1960 to 1970, Swann taught intermittently at various southern colleges, publishing in the first year his M.A. thesis on Christina Rossetti. He eventually published four further books of criticism or biography, on the poet H.D., of whose classical focus (for example, *Helen in Egypt*, 1961) he strongly approved; Ernest Dowson; Charles Sorley; and A. A. Milne. He also became engaged to a fellow academic, Ann Peyton. Toward the end of the 1960s he became ill, broke the engagement, resigned from his last post at Florida Atlantic University in Boca Raton, and retired to a family house in Knoxville, Tennessee, where he concentrated on the writing of fiction. In 1972 he contracted cancer. He died on May 5, 1976, in Winter Haven, Florida, at the home of his parents.

It was a productive life and, despite his involvement with both teaching and the world of fantasy fandom, a secluded one. Although it would be impertinent to erect a psychological analysis on these bare data, the external facts of his life certainly present him as turning away from the daylight glare of the modern world and remaining as close as possible to his family roots. This unworldliness may explain some of the vagaries of his publishing career—for instance, the oddness of his relationship with the British editor and agent E. J. Carnell, who did much to Promote Swann's early career by publishing him in *Science Fantasy* but who subsequently acted as his literary agent with very little success. Whether or not Carnell agented him efficiently, it was, all the same, peculiarly unworldly of Swann, as an American writer, to have his books marketed from England. After leaving Carnell, he submitted material to Donald A. Wollheim, editor of Ace Books and from 1972 of DAW Books, which was ultimately to publish fourteen of his titles as paperback originals; but by remaining faithful to Wollheim, Swann may have forfeited some opportunities to market his fiction in a more permanent form. It is perhaps the case that he did not much care.

He wrote avidly and with scant concern for the fantasy market in general, where high fantasy adventures set in secondary universes were becoming more and more popular and more and more clamorously violent, perhaps in tune with the times. His fiction is invariably set in the past of this world, and his protagonists are generally children or women, sometimes human, sometimes creatures of myth, but all of them oppressed by patriarchy. When, as with Saul and David in *How Are the Mighty Fallen*, Swann does deal with personages on the world stage, he does so in an effort to rewrite their stories in his own terms. For Swann, male adults are redeemable only when they cast off their patriarchal trappings, put down their swords, abandon life-denying heroism, and become capable of making friends with boys, warmly sexual motherly women, and prehuman figures-dryads, paniscs, centaurs, and so forth-whose enforced departure from the world stage Swann clearly sees as analogous to the loss of innocence of children when they grow up to become the wrong kind of men. As children lose their innocence in becoming patriarchs, so the world itself loses its innocence as the gentle creatures of myth are driven underground.

Robert A. Collins' *Thomas Burnett Swann: A Brief Critical Biography* (1979) contains a "Chronology of Swann's World" put together by Bob Roehm. It is a cycle of loss, containing all of the novels and most of the shorter work. Although there are minor inconsistencies throughout from book to book, the oeuvre amounts to one large series, with a prologue, a central grouping of closely linked novels, and a series of epilogues that read as elegiac parodies of the central material.

The Minikins of Yam, set in the dynastic Egypt of 2269 B.C., serves as a prologue to the whole. Pepy, a child pharaoh, gains wisdom, sexual initiation, and true adulthood in his quest up the Nile to discover the true nature of the blight that has afflicted Egypt. His father has, in world-historical terms, rather prematurely attempted to impose a magic-denying patriarchy on the land, and it is not until young Pepy confronts and accedes to the Isis principle embodied in the ghost of his mother that the warm green fecundity of the female principle can return to rescue Egypi from drought. For a while, the world will remain in balance.

A thousand years later, in Crete, the balance has begun to tip, and from this point any reference to the haven of a golden age will be to something that, like childhood, has passed; no Swann protagonist will fail to be afflicted, at least occasionally, by moments of acute nostalgia. Swann's novels constitute that version of pastoral which deals with the rape of Arcadia. Trapped in their mountain fastness, the nonhumans of Crete who populate *Cry Silver Bells* (1977), *The Forest of Forever* (1971), and *Day of the Minotaur* (1966) are particularly vulnerable to the sexual aggressions and land-hunger of Cretan humanity. Written in reverse order—a movement into the past entirely typical of Swann's character—this Cretan trilogy compresses the theme of the loss of Arcadia into a somewhat confused narrative of the loss of innocence and freedom of the last minotaurs. Some of the confusion undoubtedly arises from the inverse order of composition and from the fact that *Day of the Minotaur*, serialized as "The Blue Monkeys" in *Science Fantasy* (1964–1965), was Swann's first novel, written before he could have more than glimpsed the full scope of the cycle to which he devoted the rest of his life.

Unsurprisingly, then, *Cry Silver Bells* shows Swann at his weakest in the construction of novel-length stories. Into the nonhuman cultures of Crete—interlinked but separate groups of centaurs, minotaurs, dryads, and the like—he introduces two young Egyptian exiles, who are duly frightened and then entranced by the beauty and gentleness of the folk they meet. (This process of introduction Swann had already gone through once, in *Day of the Minotaur*, with greater freshness and with firmer structural point.) The Egyptians are soon exiled from Arcadia by Chiron, the centaur, the vain ruler of the nonhumans; the threat of their deaths in a Cretan bullring provides a somewhat lame pretext for most of the action of this first book.

In *The Forest of Forever* the main themes of the trilogy are developed through the passage into manhood of young Eunostos, the last minotaur; his doomed affair with a dryad; and the incursion of a harsh male human into his idyllic world. Aecus the Cretan steals the dryad from Eunostos and, after she has borne his children, abducts them and returns with them to the world of men. The dryad kills herself. Eunostos lives on, with the hope of the children's return.

Achaeans invade Crete in *Day of the Minotaur*, and the children are forced to flee into the interior, where they were born. They slowly assimilate the values of Eunostos and his compatriots, though it is now too late for any sustained residence in the gentle world of the nonhumans. With the Achaeans come patriarchy triumphant, technology, life-denying religion, and modern man's relentless lust to dominate.

The children are betrayed and captured. Eunostos leads a successful counterattack but knows that the war has been lost. With the children—who turn their back on the terrible new world that is being born—he and those who have survived set sail for the Islands of the Blest. We do not witness their arrival.

In his second trilogy— *Queens walk in the Dusk*, *Green Phoenix* (1972), and *Lady of the Bees* (1976)—the scene is Carthage and Rome, though the first volume, which retells the legend of Dido and Aeneas, cleverly avoids material dealt with in later volumes. *Green Phoenix* injects a cast of dryads, fauns, and other such creatures into the later story of Aeneas. Mellonia, a young dryad, tied as are all dryads into a symbiotic relationship With her tree, has an affair with the doomed expatriate Trojan and, after his death, manages to negotiate some kind of balance between the nonhumans she has come to rule and the men who will eventually be responsible for the Roman Empire. Like the children to whom Eunostos loses his heart in the Cretan trilogy, her child is a halfling, a creature with one foot in the female and one in the male camp. For Swann, the notion of the halfling is deeply congruous with a vision of the saucy but clement innocence of retained childhood.

In *Lady of the Bees,* Mellonia, now almost five hundred years old, takes as her second lover young Remus, doomed to be murdered by his male adult brother, Romulus. Remus, who is constantly likened to a woodpecker, has the sylvan grace and love of mothering nature of a true halfling. His death and Mellonia's mark the end of any real truce in the hearts of Romans between the warring patriarchal and matriarchal principles; Romulus' guilt-ridden pledge to found a Rome whose rule of law will "resurrect" Remus seems particularly feeble.

The original story on which this novel is based, "Where Is the Bird of Fire," (*Science Fantasy*, April 1962), is told from the viewpoint of a short-lived faun whose understanding of the world is limited but who all the same conveys a sense of melancholy in his telling that becomes muffled in the flustered mélange of viewpoints through which the expanded version is recounted. Both versions end with the faun's prose poem of longing and relinquishing, but only in the story does his determination to follow the bird of fire (that is, Remus) effectively set a terminal mood: "Where is the bird of fire? Look up, he burns in the sky, with Saturn and the Golden Age. I will go to find him."

Both *Wolfwinter* (1972) and *The Weirwoods* (*Science Fantasy*, November 1965; book form, 1967) are set in an Italy subsequent to the failure of balance represented by the deaths of Mellonia and Remus, and both forsake the world stage for tales of intimate self-realization. *Wolfwinter* is much the finer work, combining the quiet balanced craft of Swann's earlier work with something of the hectic urgency of his last books, though without their incoherences of narrative and tone and their forced, saccharine rhetoric.

The frame of *Wolfwinter* depicts the protagonist, Erinna, grown old; being a sibyl, she confers some advice upon a young man whose young male friend has been murdered. She tells him to remember the Cretans, who "lived in the grace of the Mother and never feared lamplighting time because she had promised them a final, unquenchable morning" (prologue). She then recounts to him her own life, which forms the body of the novel.

Young and virginal, Erinna is seduced by a faun on the island of Lesbos and, as a consequence, is married off to a man from Sybaris, losing her love, it seems, for fauns survive only a few years, and having to leave her older friend, the poet Sappho. In Sybaris, when her husband has the halfling child exposed to wolves, she escapes civilization; rescues her son, Lysis; sleeps with an Etruscan; and is captured by nonhumans in the forest. There she sets up house with the faun Skimmer, with whom she eventually sleeps, after many adventures with humans and nonhumans; reunion with her first faun lover, who dies of age in her arms; a short visit from Sappho; and a descent into hell, from which she returns intact and blessed by Aphrodite. For the reader the heart of *Wolfwinter* lies in the brief autumnal union between Erinna and Skimmer, about which Swann is, as usual, inexplicit:

> He fell to his knees and placed the flowers in my hair, and I thought, "They are little sunbeams, they glow with their own warmth," though of course the warmth came from Skimmer's hands. I felt his breath in my face, sweet with blackberries. I felt the heat of his body, a mantle against the cold. The body of a Faun is a little forest, a place of terror and splendor and tenderness. The body of Skimmer was a forest without wolves.
> (chapter 8)

In its slightly lachrymose intensity and seeming ingenuousness, this passage is entirely typical of Swann's writing at its best: it conveys an elegiac sweetness that almost allows one to dismiss from one's response the sense that the creative energies on view have consistently been displaced from their proper locus. *Wolfwinter*, for instance, using the frail, brief lives allotted to fauns and mortals, claims to deal with the need to somehow seize the day, to live so as to merit the blessings of each day as it passes, and to accept the nature of the world, which too soon closes into death or adulthood, without mourning that necessary outcome. It might be thought, therefore, that the natural bearer of a carpe them consciousness would be the faun, Skimmer, not the human woman, who, however vividly, is rendered by Swann as viewing Skimmer's life in retrospect. The central drama of the book is thus not the locus of Swann's energies.

This turning away from the heart of the reality that he would embrace seems yet another manifestation of the central feature of Swann's life and art—a movement backward and inward that has as its goal the unsullied quietude of the unawakened child. As the child undertakes the rite of passage into sexual adulthood in so many of Swann's tales, one begins to sense a disruptive imbalance, an unresolved discord, because the rite of passage, which is meant to be read as necessary and positive, is almost always counterpointed with a depiction of the loss of balance in the world as patriarchy triumphs. This discord becomes all the more serious when the reader senses that as Swann's protagonists become sexually mature, they escape his creative control; he loses interest in them, and the text drowns in a sentimental bath of deranged pathos—sweet, distressing, perhaps rather attractive to young readers.

Indeed, all of Swann's novels are in fact juveniles. His true protagonists are male children, and the older women who sometimes substitute as protagonists serve as a complex displacement from the prepubertal male child at the heart of almost all the texts. Although the male child may —in terms inexplicit, chaste, and make-believe, though ostensibly saucy—have sexual congress with a mother figure, the undisplaced focus of his attentions seems generally to be a "friend." Bearlike or elfin, simple or preternaturally wise, this friend will be distinguished from "normal" male adults by the sweetness of his scent, the gentle givingness of his nature, and his ultimate vulnerability. Like Remus, he will very frequently be killed, and the true protagonist of the story-like the faun in "Where Is the Bird of Fire?"—will express the only undisplaced forms of mourning that Swann allows in his doomed universe.

Although it is the thematic climax of Swann's long parade of losses, *The Gods Abide* suffers from the hasty foreshortenings and excesses of his late style. At points genuinely difficult to follow, the novel represents an ingathering of oppressed nonhumans into a final haven made ready for them by the mother goddess, Ashtoreth. The book is notable for its expression of a spirited hostility to Christianity, which Swann clearly sees as life-denying, humorless, patriarchal, and disastrously Manichaean.

After *The Gods Abide*, which is set in the fourth century A.D., the world stage has been swept clear of Swann's folk, and in *The Tournament of Thorns* (1976), *Will-O-The-Wisp* (*Fantastic Stories*, 1974; book form, *1976)*, *The Not-World* (1975), and *The Goat Without Horns* (*Magazine of Fantasy and Science Fiction*, 1970; book form, 1971), the flow of elegy narrows into defiant self-parody. *The Tournament of Thorns* embodies, and vitiates the plangent clarity of, Swann's finest single tale, "The Manor of Roses" (*Magazine of Fantasy and Science Fiction*, November 1966). Set in Britain at the time of the Crusades, the tale tells of the discovery by a middle-aged widow that she is a mandrake, a creature of the woods who has taken on the semblance of a human being. As the story closes, she returns to her roots. *Will-O-The Wisp* and *The Not-World* rather unamusingly re-create historical figures—Robert Herrick in the first, Robert and Elizabeth Barrett Browning as well as Thomas Chatterton in the second–and put them through their paces as they encounter vestiges of the old Swann universe, cope, succumb, grow wiser, survive.

Oddest of these parodic texts is *The Goat Without Horns*, in which the essential Swann protagonist is divided into two aspects: the boy-man undergoing his rite of passage, in a character based on the minor poet Charles Sorley; and the undifferentiated unsullied genuine boy, impersonated in this case by a dolphin named Gloomer, who narrates the tale. The setting is a Caribbean island. Watching from the waves, Gloomer falls in love with Charlie, a glowing young orphan in early manhood who arrives to tutor Mrs. Menell's daughter. As usual in Swann's work, Charlie becomes enamored of the mother rather than of his coeval and sleeps with her. The girl's father is a were-shark, however, and the plot thickens. Gloomer is instrumental in saving the day, and at the novel's close Charlie returns to him, jumping gayly into the amniotic sea: "A big wave almost inundated him. I dove under him and he clasped my dorsal fin and we swam for the island and the passage and our own green lagoon" (chapter 12). They have become "friends." The world is well lost.

Because of the flood of displaced emotion that distorts most of his work, Swann's novels are far less attractive to read than to remember. What is read is a dissembling artifice; what is remembered can be the pure affect of elegy, the longing for a prelapsarian frolic in the mothering sea, the seizing of the day. Swann is a weak writer who evokes strong memories. His name may survive.

Selected Bibliography

WORKS OF THOMAS BURNETT SWANN

BOOKS

Day of the Minotaur New York: Ace, 1966; London, Mayflower Books, 1975.

The Weirwoods. New York; Ace, 1967.

The Dolphin and the Deep. New York: Ace, 1968. (Collection containing "The Dolphin and the Deep," "The Murex," and "The Manor of Roses.")

Moondust. New York: Ace, 1968.

Where Is the Bird of Fire? New York; Ace, 1970. (Collection containing "Where Is the Bird of Fire?" "Vashti," and "Bear.")

The Goat Without Horns. New York: Ballantine, 1971.

The Forest of Forever. New York: Ace, 1971. London: Mayflower Books, 1975.

Green Phoenix. New York: DAW, 1972.

Wolfwinter. New York: Ballantine, 1972.

How Are the Mighty Fallen. New York: DAW, 1974.

The Not-World. New York: DAW, 1975.

The Minikins of Yam. New York: DAW, 1976.

Lady of the Bees. New York: Ace, 1976. (Expansion of "Where Is the Bird of Fire?")

The Tournament of Thorns. New York: Ace, 1976. (Incorporating "The Stalking Trees" and "The Manor of Roses.")

The Gods Abide. New York: DAW, 1976. Godalming, Surrey: L.S.P.T., 1979.

Will-O-The-Wisp. London: Corgi, 1977.

Cry Silver Bells. New York; DAW, 1977; Godalming, Surrey: L.S.P., 1979.

Queens Walk in the Dusk. Forest Park, Ga.; Heritage Press, 1977.

Uncollected stories

"Winged Victory," *Fantastic Universe* (July 1958).

"Viewpoint," *Nebula* (May 1959).

"The Dryad Tree," *Science Fantasy* (August 1960).

"The Painter," *Science Fantasy* (December 1960).

"The Sudden Wings," *Science Fantasy* (October 1962).

CRITICAL, BIOGRAPHICAL, AND BIBLIOGRAPHICAL STUDIES

Collins, Robert A. *Thomas Burnett Swann: A Brief Critical Biography and Annotated Bibliography.* Boca Raton, Fla.: The Thomas Burnett Swann Fund, 1979.

"Thomas Burnett Swann: A Retrospective." *Fantasy Newsletter*, 63 (March 1983).

"Swann on Swann: The Uses of Fantasy." *Fantasy Newsletter*, 6 4 (April 1983).

Page, Gerald W. "Remembering Tom Swann." (An afterword to *Queens Walk in the Dusk* by Swann.)

Lisa Tuttle

1952–

JANICE M. BOGSTAD

LISA TUTTLE HAS been part of the emerging generation of feminist science fiction writers who participated in the women's movement of the 1960s and 1970s. Her fictional endeavors have been paralleled by work with women writers, the Women's Press in London, and the creation of collections of women's fiction and related nonfictional works.

Born in Houston, Texas, on September 16, 1952, she was a science fiction fan in high school. She was graduated from Syracuse University, in New York, with a B.A. in English in 1973. But she was also working her way into publishing through the fan community, and began a fan career in her teens, attending conventions and editing a well-known science fiction fan magazine, *Mathom* (taken from J. R. R. Tolkien's term for an unwanted gift), from 1968 to 1970. Not only did she participate at a young age, but she also was one of a small number of young women contributing to science fiction fandom at that time.

Since her early years as a fan and emerging writer, she has emigrated to England and worked as an editor for the influential Women's Press in London in the 1980s and 1990s, as a freelance journalist in the 1980s, and as an instructor of science fiction and fantasy courses for the outreach program at the University of London from 1984 to 1988. She currently resides at Harrow, Middlesex, England, and her most recent contributions have been short story-collections, the editorship of other collections, and fiction included in thematic anthologies.

The majority of Tuttle's stories are pure horror fiction and usually end with a nasty twist designed to create either a momentary frisson of fear, or, for weaker souls, *A Nest of Nightmares* (1986), as indicated by the title of one of her anthologies (a collection of stories for children). The protagonists of her fiction are rarely male, and the female characters are often hedged about with internalized or external expectations by the males in their lives and by their family members. Indeed, while reading her fiction, it is difficult to find a satisfying relationship between a man and a woman. Most of the happy women are single and almost all of the married couples and current or ex-partnerships exist in states of tense truce or outright conflict. This is also the case between other adult protagonists as well as the family members of younger characters.

Not surprisingly, for Tuttle's characters home is never a safe place to be and, whether it is the family home of "The Family Monkey" (1977), a rented home on the edge of the city for a female graduate student in *Familiar Spirit* (1983), or the home of an aunt in the wilds of California in

"Bug House" (1986), one is sure to not sleep soundly after inhabiting it with Tuttle's women.

Tuttle got her start in publishing in the 1970s with the story "Stranger in the House," but she first came to critical attention because of the publication of a novel, *Windhaven* (1981), cowritten with her then collaborator, George R. R. Martin.

She has also written a charming, illustrated book for children, *Catwitch* (1983), which combines her interests in witchcraft and animals. She regularly edits and contributes stories to anthologies, as well as to primary and secondary science fiction magazines such as *Amazing, Analog, Fantastic, Galaxy, Interzone, Twilight Zone, Isaac Asimov's Science Fiction Magazine,* and the *Magazine of Fantasy and Science Fiction*. She has written a number of nonfictional works including an encyclopedia of feminism, a book on writing science fiction and fantasy, a book on women heroes, and a "tour book" on the homes of British children's writers.

A LOOK AT SOME OF THE NOVELS

An extremely popular item that is more strictly science fiction than anything else she has produced, her collaborative work *Windhaven* focuses like most of her fiction on a female protagonist, Maris, who seeks to participate more centrally in her culture's public life. Set on another planet, Windhaven, this plot incorporates many interesting speculations on the adaptation of humans to a non-Earth planetary existence. Maris must first struggle to become an all-important flier and then to forge a life around her duties ferrying objects and messages between the many small islands that make up the only landmass available on an alien planet. Humans from Earth inhabit this planet because they crash-landed on it many centuries before.

This work has been called "atypical" of both Martin and Tuttle, as the most horrific elements are the monsters in Windhaven's waters and the stark, subsistence lifestyle forced on the unwilling settlers. And Maris's own battle is no simple one. The isolated landmasses and lack of raw materials for industrialization have resulted in a strange method of contact between islands. A very few pairs of metal wings were originally forged from the fallen spacecraft, and they are passed along as an inheritance to one worthy child of the previous owner. Unfortunately, Maris is not a legitimate heir, and the wings would normally go to her half-brother Coll, who wants to be a singer, not a flier. She is able to "gain her wings" only by challenging all the traditions of her society and becoming, in the process, a role model for others.

Where Tuttle's characters usually escape such restrictions in dreams, fantasy, and even demonic possession, in this novel Maris escapes in the ecstasy of flight. She wins her pair of mental wings that humans have learned to operate like the winged-gliders of Leonardo da Vinci's famous notebooks. Yet, like others of Tuttle's own fictions, this protagonist is a woman. Also, remarkably, we follow her from early childhood to near death rather than seeing her only in the bloom of later adolescence, as is often the case in science fiction novels up through the 1980s.

Martin's interest in ballad and music is served with the minstrels and bards that populate the novel, including Maris's own brother, Coll, and the young boy that Maris, on her deathbed, endows with the ballad of one of the most famous fliers of her lifetime. In a scene somewhat reminiscent of the encounter between King Arthur and a young boy at the end of the film *Camelot*, she gives him the fliers' view of her fallen colleague's heroic deeds. The culture of Windhaven has many analogies to late medieval Europe, with dwellings that remind one of castles, a pretechnological lifestyle, and a caste system. In this regard, the novel is also part of a trend that began in the 1970s to intermesh the literary conventions of fantasy and science fiction and lyricize the experience of life on other planets. As such it shows up in sharp contrast to the "hard science" novels so popular just a decade earlier.

Familiar Spirit (1983) and *Gabriel* (1988) are perhaps Tuttle's most famous works of long fiction, and characteristic of the greater body of her writing to date. Both deal with some kind of possession. In the case of *Gabriel*, it is reincarnation. *Familiar Spirit* employs both the structural conventions and the imagery of horror, the latter, of course, being the most obvious. Conjured demons; helpless women; pentangles; cat- and rat-familiars; and rickety, smelly old houses inhabit the pages of *Familiar Spirit* (Tuttle loves to employ the last of these, as is seen in the earlier "Bug House"). More notable are the markers of plot progression, which are in no way muted by the reader's knowledge that the young woman character, Sarah, is coming to live in a possessed house and will soon be possessed herself. The book begins with a prologue explaining how Valerie originally conjured the demon through her willful desire for power and riches. She then makes a deal with it and lures the innocent Sarah to her former house with cheap rent and promises of solitude, a commodity that Sarah wants very badly because she has lost her lover. Sarah is never comfortable in her rented house and cannot even sleep soundly from the first night as she is pursued first by bad dreams, then by rats and cats with huge yellow eyes. Rather than the stock helplessness or indecision of the gothic heroine, however, Sarah suffers from an excess of pride that becomes her undoing, and physical passion that becomes an ambivalent commodity. For some reason that is left opaque to the reader, she decides to stay in what she knows to be a haunted house, beset by bad dreams and worse wakings, as a sign of her own self-determination. It is never clear whether acknowledgment of demons as a force of evil is to be interpreted as a sign of timidity or of perspicacity. And this novel blurs the boundary between science fiction and fantasy by suggesting that possession could be an alien encounter. By contrast, most people would have fled the ambiguous situation created in the house of the *Familiar Spirit* long before Sarah does, and therefore have not shared her fate.

SHORT FICTION AND ANOTHER NOVEL

Tuttle has written very few novels and seems to be at her best writing short fiction and novellas, so it was refreshing to see the publication of a number of anthologies of her work in the 1980s and 1990s. Her first published work was the short story "Stranger in the House." It shows many signs of a fledgling writer, focusing on a young woman who thinks she is reluctantly coming back home. Her description of the old family home, miraculously restored to its condition when she was a girl, is interspersed with harangues from an obviously abusive husband. In consort with usual horror conventions, her travel back in time to become the monster under her own childhood bed is never overtly explained. The horror of the familiar, the *unheimlich* of Sigmund Freud's essay "The Uncanny" (1919) and Tzvetan Todorov's *The Fantastic* (1973), are evident here and also characteristic of much of Tuttle's other fiction.

"The Family Monkey," which got a great deal more attention than "Stranger in the House" when first published, has been anthologized widely as a result. Halfway between science fiction and more standard horror fiction, "The Family Monkey" is set on Earth in the recent past in backwoods Texas. This novelette is stylistically interesting in that there are four voices telling the story in the first person and the first voice is that of a man, William (or Billy), as he relates his unlikely courtship of Florie and their rescue of an alien they come to call Pete. One late evening, on an isolated Texas farm, they are watching meteorites and predictably, one of the falling objects is a crashing alien ship. Billy, who has not yet even put his arm around Florie, finds himself following her orders, visiting the crashed ship, carrying the alien home to a small house on the farmstead, marrying Florie, and settling down to raise a family. The second voice is the alien himself, who also ends the narrative. The alien's body, grayish and covered with bumps, also provides the author with excuses to bring out the racism of small-town Texas in the person of Florie's father. When the alien attempts to become closer physically to Florie's sister Emily, who is visiting from New York, the father senses the alien's intent but presents his objections in such a fashion that he is generally ignored and eventually dies for his insolence. The alien also befriends a grandchild, Jody, through telepathy. Of all the family, she is the only one who really understands their "shared dreams" as communication, or at least that is her reading. Jody may be special, but alien Peter's interests in her are ended abruptly when he is rescued and the reader shares his view of the kind, but boring, creatures. "Jody, still, was Jody, and he was sorry to leave her. But it was not possible to take her along, even as a pet" (in *A Spaceship Built of Stone*, p. 74).

The Pillow Friend (1996), a much later work with a younger protagonist, reiterates the perils of relaxing one's guard, even in the home. Set in another small Texas town that mirrors Tuttle's youthful experiences, the novel explores more fully the limitations of small-town life and dysfunctional family relationships, thematic strands found in much of Tuttle's short fiction— "Flying to Byzantium," "Mr. Eliphinstone's Hands," "The Horse Lord," and "Dollburger," to list only a few. It also reiterates the desperation that talented young people feel as they try to escape from these situations, and in this case, into a dream world. At the same time that we see seeds of this later effort in the many uncanny stories that make up Tuttle's major oeuvre, this novel displays characteristics of a writer who has found a unique style of horror in the everyday workings of normal life. When Agnes Grey gets a doll as a present from her flamboyant aunt, she embraces it into her small world in Houston. Agnes's mother is just as gray as her surname but Aunt Marjorie, her twin, provides excitement, adventure, and self-determination by example, and hope for the dreamy, unhappy young girl. And so does Agnes's porcelain doll, a funny-looking male figure who seems to enter her dreams and whisper to her of great things to come. This direction from her pillow friend, as Agnes matures, takes on all the markers of a possession. The author skillfully blends Agnes's observations with a narrative voice that takes the reader outside of her frame of reference just enough to feel the uncanny correspondence between Agnes's dreams and her evolving reality. Tuttle's equation of demonic and patriarchal possession are worked out within this novel more forcefully than in most of her other fiction.

OTHER ACCOMPLISHMENTS

Tuttle's nonfiction has been received with varying degrees of success. The work on writing science fiction is competent and useful to a fledgling writer. The *Encyclopedia of Feminism* (1986) is broad in scope but has been superseded by a number of other such works. The cowritten work *Children's Literary Houses* (1984), was not initially well-received but is a work(wo)manlike effort and should be honored for its intent to link real places to the fiction appreciated by children.

It is certain, however, that her horror fiction, especially in its short-story incarnations, will continue to be Tuttle's primary accomplishment. Perhaps sensing this, Tuttle has done a better job than many science fiction writers of keeping her short fiction accessible. The anthologies *A Spaceship Built of Stone* and *A Nest of Nightmares* resurrected stories that were scattered among a range of magazines in the 1970s and 1980s. Her more current *Memories of the Body* (1992) is an excellent anthology and should be in any library, even though it does not contain either her first ("Stranger in the House") or her most famous ("The Family Monkey") stories. Her many collaborations, as an editor with other writers or in thematic volumes, have somewhat compensated for the very few novels to her credit. She, like many other science fiction and fantasy writers, also publishes some of her newer work as e-books, though this medium is probably more successful as advertisement than as a commercial entity. Fortunately, science fiction and fantasy markets for shorter fiction still abound, so a writer such as Tuttle, whose mettle is best displayed in this literary form, will be available for some time to come and will offer a vehicle for the perpetuation of the pithy, compact story with a bite all its own. Just do not read a Tuttle story before getting ready to sleep, or one's dreams may be filled with the horrors from Sarah or Jody or one of the other hapless heroines upon whom Tuttle has focused her attentions.

Selected Bibliography

WORKS OF LISA TUTTLE

NOVELS

Windhaven, with George R. R. Martin. New York: Timescape, 1981.

Angela's Rainbow. Limpsfield, Eng.: Dragon's World, 1983.

Catwitch, with Una Woodruff (illustrator). Garden City, N.Y.: Doubleday, 1983. (For children.)

Familiar Spirit. New York: Berkley, 1983.

Gabriel: A Novel of Reincarnation. New York: Tom Doherty Associates, 1988.

Dreamlands, with Mark Harrison. New York: Penguin Putnam, 1991.

Lost Futures. New York: Dell, 1992.

Memories of the Body. London: Severn House, 1992.

The Pillow Friend. Clarkson, Ga.: White Wolf, 1996.

NOVELLAS AND SHORT STORIES

A Nest of Nightmares. London: Sphere, 1986. (Children's stories.)

A Spaceship Built of Stone and Other Stories. London: Women's Press, 1987. (Contains "The Family Monkey.")

Memories of the Body: Tales of Desire and Transformation. London: Severn House, 1992. (Short-story collection.)

Ghosts and Other Lovers. North Bend, Wash.: ElectricStory.com, 2001. (Short story collection; e-book; limited book edition published in 2002 by Sarob Press.)

BOOKS EDITED BY TUTTLE

Skin of the Soul: New Horror Stories by Women, with Sally Peters. London: Women's Press, 1990.

Crossing the Border: Tales of Erotic Ambiguity. London: Indigo, 1998.

NONFICTION

Children's Literary Houses: Famous Dwellings in Children's Fiction, with Rosalind Ashe. New York: Facts on File, 1984.

Encyclopedia of Feminism. New York: Facts on File, 1986; Harlow, Eng.: Longman, 1986.

Heroines: Women Inspired by Women. London: Harap, 1988.

Writing Fantasy and Science Fiction. London: A & C Black, 2001.

CRITICAL AND BIOGRAPHICAL STUDIES

Contemporary Authors. Farmington Hills, Mich.: Gale. 2001.

"Lisa Tuttle Bibliography." (http://www.fantasticfiction.co.uk/authors/Lisa_Tuttle.htm), accessed May 12, 2002.

Page, Gerald W. "Lisa Tuttle." *St. James Guide to Science Fiction Writers*, 4th edition. Detroit, Mich.: St. James Press, 1996. Pp. 940–942.

Times Literary Supplement, June 3, 1988.

Sydney J. Van Scyoc
1939–

JANICE M. BOGSTAD

SYDNEY J. VAN Scyoc has pursued a number of careers since leaving her studies at the University of Hawaii in 1964–1965 to pursue a private life. She also studied at Florida State University; Chabot College in Hayward, California; and California State University, also in Hayward, where she now resides. Her many successful endeavors have included science fiction and fantasy writer and jewelry maker and vendor.

Sydney Joyce Brown was born on July 27, 1939, in Mount Vernon, Indiana, to John W. and Geneva Brown. After a fairly normal childhood, she went to the University of Hawaii hoping for a degree in engineering, even though she had already found out that women were not considered for most programs, much less for any kind of scholarships or grants. It became rapidly clear that she would not be allowed to succeed in engineering, and she turned to marriage and writing, the latter of which she had been practicing since 1959. She married an engineer, Jim R. Van Scyoc, on June 23, 1957, and lives with him on a small farm. They have two children, a daughter, Sandra, and a son, John Scott.

Her politics (liberal), ethics (ecological or pantheistic), religion (Unitarian Universalist), and orientation toward women's emerging roles all appear prominently in her fiction, which began with a short story, "Shatter the Wall," published in *Galaxy* magazine in February 1962. Her first novel, *Saltflower*, was not published until 1971 and her entire publishing career spans 1962 to 1991, when her last novel, *Deepwater Dreams*, appeared. Her last short story, "Meadows of Light," appeared in the December 1985 issue of *Isaac Asimov's Science Fiction Magazine*.

With the first stories, Van Scyoc set a trend toward exploring changes in the human physique and psychology as they might be affected by life on other planets, with a focus on women as central authority figures and explorations of Gaia/Goddess theses through many matriarchal and some transitional societies. It is difficult to explain the absence of critical attention for her work, except that the ecological and feminist messages are very subtly embedded in engaging, readable narrative adventures. The messages are all the more powerful for the work they do in the background of these pieces, and it would be interesting to see how Van Scyoc's writerly voice would have matured with the women's movement in the twenty-first century, were she to turn her attention back to fiction. Nevertheless, her work was popular enough to be translated into German, French, Italian, and Spanish and reprinted in numerous hardback, paperback, and trade paperback editions, reaching a wide audience.

While her earlier novels, *Saltflower, Assignment, Nor'Dyren* (1973), *Starmother* (1976), *Cloudcry* (1977), and *Sunwaifs* (1981), drew some attention for their central female characters, it was a young adult series, the *Darkchild* or Brakrath trilogy (1982–1984), that drew the attention of critics and led to her inclusion in the Pamela Sargent anthology, *Women of Wonder: The Contemporary Years* (1995), which gathered the interest of the developing feminist community within science fiction fandom. Van Scyoc, whatever her personal politics, was evaluated within an emerging body of 1970s' female authors who revolutionized the literary possibilities for women writers, women characters, and women science fiction readers. Women had, up to that time, been too much in the background of this generic fictional form.

Picking up on changing women's roles, and frustrated by the limitations that traditional roles had placed on her, Van Scyoc filled her novels with female leaders, young female heroes who solved scientific and social problems, mature relationships of equality between men and women, and concern for the environment. Reacting to the emerging ecology movement, Van Scyoc also focused her novels on otherworldly dilemmas and intergalactic adventures, but each of these is explored through the eyes of young people trying to find their place under bewildering circumstances. Most often in her novels, children from twelve to eighteen years of age find themselves having to ignore what their families and societies tell them is proper behavior, a common theme in science fiction novels and novels for young adults. In these cases, however, they are faced with alien beings, sentient landscapes, and cultural and social adaptations to alien environments that add a layer of problem solving to the usual adolescent angst.

In her first novel, *Saltflower*, set on Earth in 2024, Van Scyoc depicts the planned creation of a new species of humans who can survive on the planet as it has become more polluted and inimical to traditional humans. Salt Lake City is the center for most of the story, and several themes of her later works—the interrelations of humans and the rest of the natural world, ecology, and women leaders—are prefigured in this work.

These themes, while not the focus of *Saltflower*, become very evident in the Brakrath or *Darkchild* trilogy of the early 1980s. This set of novels, also published later as a single book, *Daughters of the Sunstone* (1985), begins and ends with mysterious interactions between children who have no past and children whose past and future are totally prescribed by ritual, which they must defy. These novels, *Darkchild*, *Bluesong* (1983), and *Starsilk* (1984), trace three generations of young noblewomen and the men who assist them in stabilizing a humanoid population on a hostile world. The stories of their maturation are woven among fascinating revelations about how the humans adapted to a world in which the climate is too frigid to adequately sustain human life and how the people of the planet, now that they have adapted, must look outward and prepare to protect themselves from hostile aliens.

Enjoyable adventures are related through the meetings of young men and young women, each pair of which must change some basic element in the planetary culture. But the overriding accomplishment of these novels is the creation of broad and deep traditions out of which their dilemmas spring, dilemmas that require them, and the reader, to cast off convention and find new ways of thinking.

Darkchild begins with a young man who is dragged away from a primitive and perilous planet into an alien spacecraft. The action then quickly moves to the planet of Brakrath where a young noblewoman, Khira, prepares to see her last (of six) older sister go off into the mountains and face death as she attempts to prove her worthiness to find and wield mysterious sunstones. The sunstones are necessary to the survival of humans on this planet as they focus the energy of Brakrath's weak suns on small parts of the planet at the beginning of the growing season. This action creates an early spring and allows the population that has been hibernating over the winter to sow their crops early enough to ensure a decent harvest. Women of the noble family stay awake over the winter and, when Khira's sister does not return from her testing year, Khira must spend a second winter alone, awaiting her own trials. In this winter, she meets the Darkchild and they spend winter and summer learning about each other's problems. Khira is the last daughter, and if she is not able to pass her ultimate test the next year and take over for her mother whose powers are waning, the valley where her people live will freeze over and the people will disperse. She needs a lot of help in befriending and working with the Darkchild, who appears in a locked-off tower in the middle of the winter and is revealed to be a "ruathmage" by friendly, resident aliens studying the Brakrath culture. He has been cloned by more hostile aliens and used as a human data recorder, but Khira and the Darkchild gradually figure out how to release him from the alien's control and to keep these aliens from using the data he has gathered to take over this planet and siphon off its natural resources. In keeping Darkchild from his alien controllers, and killing off those who try to imprison him, Khira completes her "test" and becomes a sunstone queen, with Darkchild as her consort, and sets up the concerns for her own daughters and sons.

The story continues in *Bluesong*, with Keva, the daughter of Darkchild's brother and Danior, Khira's son, who, being the only boy ever born to a starstone queen, has no ritual social position, and, so he thinks, no respectable future. Keva and Danior each travel far and away to find an identity and purpose, and to link more of the people on Brakrath, uncovering yet another mystery, that of the "cloth" that sings the Bluesong, among other things. Keva and Danior in turn give birth to four daughters, three of whom die on the standard queen's quest. The fourth of these, Reyna, plans without much hope to set out on her testing year in the wilds, only to be lured by her mother on another kind of journey. For reasons Reyna cannot understand, her father leaves abruptly and her mother takes a new lover, Dariim, a young "hunter." In sorting out her resentments at the loss of her father, her sisters' deaths and her mother's defection, she finds herself on another kind of quest, along with Dariim, to the planet of the "starsilks" and back to Brakrath to help educate her people about the alien threat. The three generations of young female heroes, all central to an essentially matriarchal, nonmonogamous culture, and their equally headstrong and often ambivalent male partners, reveal Van Scyoc's ability to transform the conventional science fiction adventure plot when only a few authors had begun to do so. Her conceptualization of the ability of human genetic makeup to adapt to totally different physical conditions is implicit in these novels but much more explicit in her other works.

While *Starmother*, *Cloudcry*, and the later *Feather Stroke* (1989) touch on adaptation's human side, this theme is central to *Sunwaifs*, *Drowntide* (1987), and Van Scyoc's final novel, *Deepwater Dreams*. Of the latter three, the premise of *Sunwaifs* focuses, like the Brakrath trilogy, on harnessing the energy of the sun with a human conduit, but adds to this phantasm a human/Earth connection. *Deepwater Dreams* and *Drowntide* show humans many centuries after they have made adaptations to life on a planet with small percentages of landmass and otherwise disastrous tides and inimical human life. Van Scyoc was obviously trying out various scenarios of the Gaia thesis, that humanity has become artificially divorced from Earth, the Sun, and animals, and that these fragile and artificial barriers humans attempt to maintain will collapse as people are confronted with alien ecosystems. This is also asserted by such feminist writers as Susan Griffin and, in terms of border or barrier crossings, in writings of the 1990s of Nina Lykke, Donna Haraway, and Gloria Anzaldua. As Van Scyoc stated in the *St. James Guide to Science Fiction Writers*, "My personal orientation is increasingly pantheistic and in my longer fiction I am attempting to deal with the spiritual relationship of human to environment" (p. 954).

That Van Scyoc would use the analogical thought experiment of science fiction narrative to tease out these concepts is not unusual today, but had not been even articulated until Ursula Le Guin's famous essay "From Efland to Pokepsie" (1973), and her groundbreaking work *The Left Hand of Darkness* (1969), published less than three years before Van Scyoc's first novel, *Saltflower*.

With her novels, such as *Feather Stroke* and *Starmother*, Van Scyoc tries out some of the ideas that are forged together in the more successful Brakrath trilogy and in *Sunwaifs*. In *Feather Stroke*, a young woman finds that she is really descended from a forest people who control and fly within the bodies of birds, and is with this talent able to save her people from enslavement. In order to make the transition from selfish pursuits of personal happiness to responsible action for the benefit of at least three different forms of human culture on her planet, she must accept training and privation and learn a higher level of self-control as her lapses can kill others. The bird-mage, a mage or shaman who communicates so well with birds that she or he can cast her mind into the birds, emerged in the 1970s with Carlos Castenada's books. This emblem of the human-nature interface is reflected in both *Feather Stroke* and the later *Sunwaifs*. The bird-mage appears with one of six "odd" children, Corrie, who is so in tune with the birds of the planet Destiny that she becomes one of them. In *Starmother*, Jahna Swiss, a "star corps" worker, is brought to the primitive backwater planet of Nelding, settled by a fundamentalist religious community in the twenty-first century. Not fully trained, she has been brought to help raise "monster" children who are born to the colonists. She helps the wild humans by getting these children ready to survive within their emerging humanoid proto civilization, but not without finding herself and her charges in mortal peril from the religious fathers, the indigenous race of apelike simple sentients, and even the humanoids she has been set up to help.

That the ecosystem itself would begin to change human genotypes also appears more centrally in *Sunwaifs* and in the two water-planet novels, *Drowntide* and *Deepwater Dreams*. *Sunwaifs* brings together many analogs of the Gaia thesis through the agency of six children, Nadd, Corrie, Ronna, Trebb, Herrol, and Feliss. Nadd, the only one of these who maintains a human form as an adult, tells the story of their first fifteen years. They are the only children who survive from several hundred born in a year of excessive sunspot activity. As they grow to maturity, they each connect with a different part of the ecosystem on Destiny, with Corrie being in contact with the weather; Feliss becoming a bird woman; Ronna a transitional healer adapting humans to the alien viruses; Herroll as an intermediary to the animal sand; and Trebb as an intermediary to the plants and the earth out of which they grew. Nadd alone sees alternative futures for all their actions and tries to resist the destiny of destructive force, which the planet itself, part of each of their genetic makeup, has assigned to him. He continually mediates the efforts of his siblings to save the humans and to save the planet, which is trying to reject them like an unwelcome growth. The outline of his fragile balancing act becomes the story of *Sunwaifs* but carries the message that humanity as we know it will not persist on other planets that have their own mix of animals, plants, and weather, and that, by reflection, our own balance is equally fragile.

Drowntide is thematically connected to the Brakrath trilogy as well. Its protagonist is a "secondary" young man, Keiris, son of the ruling female monarch, who possesses the rare ability to talk with the sea creatures of this new planet. As a supernumerary son, he must go off on a quest to find his twin sister, who was stolen away by her father at their birth, and who can be their mother's successor. His quest is very reminiscent of the plot of *Bluesong* and *Starsilk*. Again, the civilizations of Keiris's planet exist because many centuries ago humans crash-landed and were forced to adapt to the waters, tides, and sea creatures found there. Keiris's mother, Amelyor, is also forced, on the death of her daughter Nandyris, to reveal a number of unhappy truths about him and his father. Keiris then goes off on a quest from the protected palace of his seashore-dwelling people to the islands in the north of the planet, where he finds a very different kind of civilization, that of his father. These humanoids not only talk to the sea creatures but also ride on and swim with them; the humanoids also participate in an odd and dangerous ritual to placate sea monsters that are anchored to the bottom of the ocean but are still capable of killing passing humans. During his journeys Keiris is transformed as he comes to understand the cost and glory of this ecosystem into which his father's people have integrated themselves and to which his sister's unique physical, social, and psychological forms are essential.

In many ways the much later *Deepwater Dreams* reprises *Drowntide*, with humans on an alien planet and two civilizations adapting very differently to life near and in the sea. Its female protagonist goes out, as did Keiris, to find her sister and discovers a totally new life, and also sentient cetacean aliens trapped for centuries in a buried spaceship. In following her and their "dreams" she rescues and frees them, finds her sister, and finds her true love. It also includes the clearest statement of Van Scyoc's pantheistic or Gaia/Goddess theme, "Concern for our resources is the living bond that joins us, the whispering voice said again. For each of us, for all of us, the concern is the same. None can be excused from the imperative that bids us never to waste and never to lay waste. For all the sea is sacred, as is the land that rises from its ancient beds. We will enjoy its riches only as long as we respect and conserve those same riches" (p. 47).

Van Scyoc's novels take young people from a personal tragedy to a sense of their mission and responsibility to their cultures, a familiar journey of maturation. This is the mundane universal story that beguiles her readers. Yet her stories also manifest a subtext of human immersion in our own ecosystem by comparison with these many genetic and subsequent social transformations. But these themes would not be successfully transmitted to her readers without a set of assumptions about the intersection of humans and the environment that are at serious odds with the positivism still strong in the contemporary scientific community, and rampant in the 1970s and early 1980s when the majority of her stories were conceived.

In Van Scyoc's stories, individuals are presented in contexts that are totally unfamiliar to us here on planet Earth, and without a historical understanding or broad view of their circumstances. In this state of forgetfulness, shored up by tradition, ritual, religion, and prescribed duty, they resemble the majority of us, a telling portrait of the inertia we suffer under as we largely ignore ecological crises all around us. In each case, young people are striving to stay within the parameters of their traditional duties and roles and must gradually relearn the history of their adaptation to this particular ecosystem in order to act in ways that will responsibly alter it. So, in addition to a series of far-reaching adventures, fascinating alien landscapes, a plethora of young people with deep commitments to their families and societies (a refreshing difference from the post-Vietnam social malaise), and creative intelligence, Van Scyoc creates a mirror in which we can rethink the future of our own civilization on planet Earth.

Selected Bibliography

WORKS OF SYDNEY J. VAN SCYOC

NOVELS

Saltflower. New York: Avon, 1971.

Assignment, Nor'Dyren. New York: Avon, 1973.

Starmother. New York: Berkley, 1976.

Cloudcry. New York: Berkley, 1977. (An expansion of the story "Deathsong.")

Sunwaifs. New York: Berkley, 1980.

Darkchild. New York: Berkley, 1982. (Brakrath or Darkchild trilogy, Book 1.)

Bluesong. New York: Berkley, 1983. (Brakrath or Darkchild trilogy, Book 2.)

Starsilk. New York: Berkley, 1984. (Brakrath or Darkchild trilogy, Book 3.)

Daughters of the Sunstone. Garden City, N.Y.: Doubleday, 1985. (Includes *Darkchild*, *Bluesong*, and *Starsilk*.)

Drowntide. New York: Berkley, 1987.

Feather Stroke. New York: Morrow/Avon, 1989.

Deepwater Dreams. New York: Morrow/Avon, 1991.

SHORT STORIES

"A Visit to Cleveland General." *Galaxy*, October 1968. (Anthologized in *World's Best Science Fiction*. Edited by Donald Wollheim and Terry Carr. New York: Ace Books, 1969.)

"When Petals Fall." In *Two Views of Wonder*. Edited by Thomas N. Scortia and Chelsea Quinn Yarbro. New York: Ballantine, 1973.

"Bluewater Dreams." *Isaac Asimov's Science Fiction Magazine*, March 1981. (Anthologized in *Women of Wonder: The Contemporary Years*. Edited by Pamela Sargent. San Diego, Calif.: Harcourt Brace Jovanovich, 1995.)

"Meadows of Light." *Isaac Asimov's Science Fiction Magazine* December 1985.

CRITICAL AND BIOGRAPHICAL STUDIES

Contemporary Authors. Farmington Hills, Mich.: Gale. 2001.

"Sydney Van Syoc." *St. James Guide to Science Fiction Writers*, 4th edition. Edited by Jay P. Pederson. Detroit, Mich.: St. James Press, 1996. Pp. 953–954.

"Sydney J. Van Scyoc." (http://www.tdl.com/~sjvan/sjvans.htm), accessed May 12, 2002. (Author's homepage.)

Jack Vance
1916–

THOMAS MARCINKO

JACK VANCE IS one of modern science fiction and fantasy's most respected and influential writers. Vance has written sixty science fiction and fantasy novels and won most of the genre's major awards: the Hugo for best novelette in 1963 for "The Dragon Masters"; the 1966 Hugo and the 1967 Nebula for "The Last Castle"; the 1975 Jupiter Award for best novelette for "The Seventeen Virgins" (incor- porated into the novel *Cugel's Saga*, itself part of the *Tales of the Dying Earth* omnibus); the 1990 World Fantasy Award for best novel for *Lyonesse: Madouc;* and SFWA's Grand Master award in 1997.

Vance is among the most series-prone of science fiction authors. In fantasy, there's the Dying Earth series and also the quasi-Arthurian Lyonesse trilogy. In science fiction, the far-flung Gaean Reach is a common background to many of his spacefaring novels. Finding the connections between books within his various series is fun but not necessary for understanding.

Under the byline John Holbrook Vance, he also pursued for a time a parallel career as a mystery writer, being one of the many authors to publish under the "Ellery Queen" name. His 1961 novel *The Man in the Cage* won the Mystery Writers of America Edgar Award. Additionally, Vance has created several science fiction detective stories, including *The Many Worlds of Magnus Ridolph* (collected in 1966) and another Gaean Reach book, *Galactic Effectuator* (1980). *The Demon Princes* also makes use of mystery/suspense devices, and the protagonist of "The Moon Moth" is trying to solve a murder. Vance has said at least once that he is not *really* a science fiction or fantasy writer. This notion is difficult to take seriously, though it is understandable that a writer might want to avoid the critical and commercial straitjacketing that often comes with the label.

Vance acknowledges the influences of Lord Dunsany, Edgar Rice Burroughs, and Clark Ashton Smith, but also of P. G. Wodehouse ("Wodehouse is my god," Vance said in a 1989 interview by Marty Halpern). Another influence little commented on is Alexandre Dumas *père*; not only did Vance title a story and collection "Chateau d'If," after Edmond Dantes' prison, but Vance's characters often speak with the urbane cynicism of the Count of Monte Cristo, and their behavior is often similarly driven.

Regardless of how he is categorized, Vance has a unique and consistent worldview that takes into account both the comic and the tragic. He is an observer of human endeavor and folly in the tradition of classic writers like Jane Austen and

Tolstoy, or Swift and Voltaire. In that way, Vance's position parallels that of many other noteworthy genre writers—his vision is large enough to interest the serious reader, if only said reader could be induced to look beyond genre labels and tacky paperback packages.

For better or worse, though, Vance has mostly been known as a writer's writer; among the science fiction and fantasy authors who acknowledge his influence can be included Gene Wolfe in his massive *New Sun* series, and Robert Silverberg in *Nightwings* and the Majipoor books. Fortunately, in recent years Vance has begun to get some much-deserved public attention. He's been championed in the *Washington Post*'s book section by critic Michael Dirda. Underwood Press, a small imprint in Lancaster, Pennsylvania, has published fifty volumes of Vance; more recently, Tor Books has been collecting his series in omnibus trade paperbacks under its Orb imprint. Still, much of Vance is out of print at this writing. An ambitious, volunteer-staffed publishing project, the Vance Integral Edition, plans to bring all his work into print for libraries and individual subscribers. The first volume in this series, *Coup de Grace and Other Stories*, appeared in 2002.

A LIFE IN PRINT

A rancher's son, Jack Vance was born in San Francisco on August 28, 1916. He served with the merchant marines in the Pacific during World War II, and his ship twice came under torpedo attack. His first story, "The World-Thinker" was published in the Summer 1945 issue of *Thrilling Wonder Stories*. A brief autobiographical note paints a portrait of the artist and also gives a sense of life during wartime:

> I am a somewhat taciturn merchant seaman.... I admit only to birth in San Francisco, attendance at the University of California, interest in hot jazz, Oriental languages, abstract physical science, feminine psychology. My chief trouble in writing at sea during this war is the FBI man who is stationed aboard my ship as some similar investigator is on every vessel of the Merchant Marine. For some reason, he seems to be especially suspicious of me....
>
> (http://jackvanceillustrated.tripod.com/pulps/)

Vance worked briefly for Twentieth Century-Fox, writing scripts for *Captain Video*, a television show aimed at children. He was reportedly fired for turning the scripts into send-ups of the show itself.

Vance's earliest work was, for the most part, unremarkable, though with touches of unusual verbal inventiveness and a sense of humor that many writers would come to describe as mordant.

While at sea with the merchant marines, Vance made a breakthrough. He wrote a series of connected stories published in 1950 as a novel, *The Dying Earth*. Set billions of years in the future, the stories describe a milieu in which our own age is little more than myth, a world that also recalls Arthur C. Clarke's famous maxim: "Any sufficiently advanced technology is indistinguishable from magic." *The Dying Earth* was published by a small publisher called Hillman Periodical, and it quickly disappeared from sight—but not from the memory of the few readers who discovered it. (Robert Silverberg describes how he turned New York City newsstands upside down in search of a copy.) Though it has echoes of Lord Dunsany, E. R. Eddison, James Branch Cabell, and Fritz Leiber, its vision was unique and its prose rich and inventive:

> [Mazirian] climbed the stairs. Midnight found him in his study, poring through leather-bound tomes and untidy portfolios.... At one time a thousand or more runes, spells, incantations, curses, and sorceries had been known. The reach of Grand Motholam—Ascolias, the Ide of Kauchique, Almery to the South, the Land of the Falling Wall to the East—swarmed with sorcerers of every description, of whom the chief was the Arch-Necromancer Phandaal. A hundred spells Phandaal personally had formulated—though rumor said that demons whispered at his ear when he

wrought magic. Pontecilla the Pious, then Ruler of Grand Motholam, put Phandaal to torment, and after a terrible night, he killed Phandaal and outlawed sorcery throughout the land. The Wizards of Grand Motholam fled like beetles under a strong light; the lore was dispersed and forgotten, until now, at this dim time, with the sun dark, wilderness obscuring Ascolias, and the white city Kaiin half in ruins, only a few more than a hundred spells remained to the knowledge of man. Of these, Mazirian had access to seventy-three, and gradually, by stratagem and negotiation, was securing the others.

Mazirian made a selection from his books and with great effort forced five spells upon his brain: Phandaal's Gyrator, Felojun's Second Hypnotic Spell, The Excellent Prismatic Spray, The Charm of Untiring Nourishment, and the Spell of the Omnipotent Sphere. This accomplished, Mazirian drank wine and retired to his couch.
(*Tales of the Dying Earth*, Tor/Orb omnibus, 2000, p. 22–23)

The Dying Earth appeared in print long before there was much demand for fantasy as a genre. It would be some time before Vance was recognized as the original he is, but he was nonetheless well on his way toward building a career and an audience.

In the occasional interview Vance has revealed interests in carpentry and pottery, and critics have seen reflections of those craftsmanlike activities in his work. Joe Bergeron, an astronomical artist and science fiction fan, wrote in his on-line account of a 1992 visit to Vance's home: "Far from being a driving force, or a release for stories and fantasies that would otherwise haunt him, he claimed that to him, writing is just a job, a source of income, a craft for which he found he has a knack." (homepage.mac.com/joebergeron)

Bergeron's essay also gives a sense of the person:

As we sat around that table, Jack began to test us. With verbal jabs and loaded questions he went about determining whether we measured up to his standards of taste and good sense.... Jack Vance is nothing if not opinionated. He had savage criticism for several artists, including some who have illustrated expensive editions of his books.... He also expressed withering views on the skills of writers whose reputation is comparable to his own. And he made the unqualified statement that jazz is the finest form of music ever devised by Man. I fell far in his estimation when I failed to agree with that.

Now legally blind and largely confined to a wheelchair, Vance lives with his wife Norma in Oakland. They have a son, John. Vance is reportedly experimenting with voice-recognition software to help him write. A new novel is expected in 2002.

A UNIQUE VOICE

Vance's work is unique and instantly recognizable, but in some ways it is easier to describe by saying what it is *not*. Vance ignores literary trends; he wrote no stream-of-consciousness/fragmented-narrative stories in the "new wave" mode of the late 1960s and early 1970s; there are no "cyberpunk" Vance stories.

Most of Vance's work can be classified as science fiction, though he often uses a fantasist's style and atmosphere to construct his distant planets. He is generally thought of as a writer whose interest in society and background overshadows plots and character. That may be oversimplifying, but his worlds are unusually rich and well drawn. The tools Vance brings to the job serve him equally well in fantasy or science fiction.

Most of Vance's work is set on other planets in the distant future, but he cannot be properly classified as a writer of space adventure in the mold of E. E. ("Doc") Smith (the Lensman series), *Star Trek*, or *Star Wars*. For one thing, he has generally avoided aliens. Upon taking the Grand Master award in 1997, Vance told a Sci-Fi Channel interview show:

The background of [my] stories are the alterations or the evolution of the ways people act when they're out on strange worlds and have to adapt to strange circumstances. I don't use in these stories what is called "aliens," which I think is cheating and silly. You could make anything happen by just putting down some funny-looking thing with eyes on stalks and sucks blood or . . . So that's comic-book, to use aliens in here. I never use 'em, except just kind of sometimes as part of the background of different worlds. But I mainly write about human beings.

(Halpern interview, www.massmedia.com/~mikeb/jvm/reviews/halpern1.html)

Human beings are strange enough, capable of enough. The fantastic creatures in Vance's work are men and women, recognizable as such despite the odd cultures they inhabit. They may be larger-than-life but they are driven by forces and emotions that most adults can identify with.

Vance has also located important work on a fantasy-Earth, either in the unimaginably distant future or in mythic times. But Vance is not a purveyor of bold sword-and-sorcery heroes à la Robert E. Howard (creator of Conan the Barbarian), nor does he cast his stories in terms of good versus evil as in J. R. R. Tolkien's *Lord of the Rings*. Most of his characters are sympathetic, but usually they come in shades of gray.

Vance paints on a huge canvas. The sweep and scope of his timeframes make most galactic milieus seem small. Take the opening lines of "The Last Castle":

> Toward the end of a stormy summer afternoon, with the sun finally breaking out under ragged black rain clouds, Castle Janeil was overwhelmed and its population destroyed.
>
> Until almost the last moment the factions among the castle clans were squabbling as to how Destiny properly should be met. The gentlemen of most prestige and account elected to ignore the entire undignified circumstance and went about their normal pursuits, with neither more nor less punctilio than usual. A few cadets, desperate to the point of hysteria, took up weapons and prepared to resist the final assault. Others still, perhaps a quarter of the population, waited passively, ready—almost happy—to expiate the sins of the human race.
>
> In the end death came uniformly to all; and all extracted as much satisfaction in their dying as this essentially graceless process could afford.

While Vance's work has cosmic scope, it is also characterized by a finely detailed sense of place, culture, language, and custom—and is laced with ironic humor. Vance gives specific and intimate detail about life on his worlds, lavishing attention on strange societies and customs. A good early example of this is the well-anthologized 1961 novella "The Moon Moth," a murder mystery set on a planet on which social interactions are governed by a complex mixture of masks and musical instruments. In this story, agent Edwer Thissell seeks advice from a fellow Terran about the complex social interactions on the human-settled planet Sirene:

> "Notice my mask. Today I'm wearing a Tarn Bird. Persons of minimal prestige—such as you or I, any other out-worlder—wear this sort of thing."
>
> "Odd," said Thissell . . . "I assumed a person wore whatever he liked."
>
> "Certainly," said Rolver. "Wear any mask you like—if you can make it stick. This Tarn Bird for instance. I wear it to indicate that I presume nothing. I make no claims to wisdom, ferocity, versatility, musicianship, truculence, or any of a dozen other Sirinese virtues."
>
> "For the sake of argument," said Thissell, "what would happen if I walked through the streets of Zundar in this mask [called the Sea Dragon Conqueror]?"
>
> Rolver laughed, a muffled sound beneath his mask. "If you walked along the docks of Zundar—there are no streets—in any mask, you'd be killed within the hour. That's what happened to Benko, your predecessor.
>
> "He didn't know how to act. None of us out-worlders know how to act. In Fan we're tolerated—so long as we keep our place. But you couldn't even walk around Fan in that regalia you're sporting now. Somebody wearing a Fire Snake or a Thunder Goblin—masks, you understand—would step up to you. He'd play his *kro-*

datch, and if you failed to challenge his audacity with a passage on the *skaranyi*, a devilish instrument, he'd play his *hymerkin*—the instrument we use with the slaves. That's the ultimate expression of contempt. Or he might ring his dueling-gong and attack you then and there."

"I had no idea that people here were so irascible," said Thissell.

(Dozois, pp. 127–128)

If societies sometimes overshadow individuals, Vance finds no shortage of conflict in struggle between caste, class, and species. "The Moon Moth"'s bizarre code of behavior enforces an extreme individualism and rigid status system. In "The Last Castle," decadent and overprivileged humans are destroyed by their servants. In "The Dragon Masters," nonhumans engineered by humans fight an Armageddon-like battle against humans engineered in turn by nonhumans. In *To Live Forever* (1956) those who come of age compete for immortality in an overpopulated world. In *The Languages of Pao* (1957) the rulers of a distant world try to manipulate their subjects by training them to speak different artificial languages. *The Blue World* (1966) revolves around a struggle for survival among competing factions on a colony planet. Tschai, setting of the *Planet of Adventure* tetralogy (1968–1970), is divided into many different zones, ruled by competing alien factions; humans (who are here because their ancestors were abducted from Earth centuries before) are second-class citizens at best. *Emphyrio* (1969) and the *Durdane* trilogy (1971–1973) concern themselves with political consciousness and revolution. Vance himself claims no political affiliation, though he sometimes shows hints of political conservatism, and more than a hint of political incorrectness.

A common motif in Vance's fiction is the quest, earnest and otherwise. In *Planet of Adventure*, omnicompetent galactic scout Adam Reith needs to get offworld and back to Earth to warn mankind of the threatening aliens who overrun Tschai; the series reads somewhat like Edgar Rice Burroughs' Mars novels, but with a dry sense of humor. In *The Demon Princes* (1997), grim and patient Kirth Gersen goes to elaborate and extreme lengths to take revenge on the five Star Kings who killed his family.

On the other end of the spectrum are Vance's comic protagonists. Cugel swindles and lies his way through two volumes of *Dying Earth* stories. Also in this mode are the con-men protagonists of *Showboat World* (1975), who reviewers aptly compared to the Duke and the Dauphin from Mark Twain. Other comedic characters are less focused. The galactic-touring cast of *Space Opera* (1965) seems to have wandered from a British drawing-room mystery into a science fiction novel. In *Ports of Call* (1998), hapless Myron Tany inherits a spaceship from his rich aunt and tries to see the galaxy, even though he can barely cope with the dull, safe planet he was born on. Myron is supposed to be looking for an immortality elixir for his aunt, which seems to have been misplaced somewhere in the galaxy; by the middle of the novel, Myron has become so dull that the author switches focus to a more interesting character.

Linguistic inventiveness is a hallmark of Vance's fiction. New words, as with the musical instruments named in the passage quoted above, abound. One industrious fan even assembled a book-length dictionary of the Vancian language. In his afterword to a reprint of the 1951 Vance story "The New Prime," Robert Silverberg pauses to admire the evocative names of mere buildings: the Legalic, the Sumptuar, the Nunciator's Confirmatory. Even a mere footnote to "The Last Castle"—Vance uses footnotes fairly often—contains a wealth of new words:

"Skirkling," as in "to send skirkling," denotes a frantic pell-mell flight in all directions accompanied by a vibration or twinkling or jerking motion. To "volith" is to toy idly with a matter, the implication being that the person involved is of such Jovian potency that all difficulties dwindle to contemptible triviality. "Raudlebogs" are the semi-intelligent beings of Etamin Four, who were brought to Earth, trained first as gardeners, then as construction laborers, then finally sent home in disgrace because of certain repulsive habits they refused to forego.

Elegantly comic dialogue is one of Vance's best skills. Even under the most mundane of circumstances, dialogue becomes a stylistic battle of wits, as in this passage from *Cugel's Saga*:

> "Your wards made off with my pouch! They threw my terces down to the teamsters, and my other adjuncts as well, including a valuable pot of boot dressing, and finally the pouch itself!"
>
> "Indeed? The rascals! I wondered what could hold their attention so long."
>
> "Please take this matter seriously! I hold you personally responsible! You must redress my losses!"
>
> "I regret your misfortune, Cugel, but I cannot repair all the wrongs of the world."
>
> "Are they not your wards?"
>
> "In a casual sense only. They are listed on the caravan manifest in their own names, which puts the onus for their acts upon Varmous. You may discuss the matter with him, or even the mimes themselves. If they took the pouch, let them repay the terces."
>
> "These are not practical ideas!"
>
> (*Tales of the Dying Earth*, pp. 481–482)

Even public signage provides an opportunity for rhetorical exercise; in *Ports of Call* we read: "Professor Gill, Curator, is a savant of trans-galactic reputation. He is currently showing a collection of objects odd, arcane, and often imbued with mystery. Serious collectors are welcome. Faddists, dabblers, and casual tourists, please pass on. We have no time to waste" (p. 269).

It's important to note, though, that however baroque the writing becomes, Vance never lets it slow down the story or render the action unclear.

VANCE'S PLACE, IN AND OUT OF THE GENRE

Though his work is both literate and accessible, usually depending on concepts that would not seem unfamiliar to consumers of science fiction bestsellers or mass media, Vance is anything but a popularizer of science fiction and fantasy. His view of humanity is not flattering, and his sense of humor and irony may have led some to distrust him as a narrator. His characters are often competent and occasionally even noble, but in his view humanity seems greedy, stupid, shortsighted, and inclined to edit the truth. This view doesn't provoke disgust, however, but laughter.

In his observant introduction to "The Moon Moth" in the anthology *Modern Classics of Science Fiction*, Gardner Dozois touches on some of Vance's unusual strengths:

> Vance is reminiscent of R. A. Lafferty in that both men break all the supposed rules of writing, and get away with it. Both eschew naturalism, each using a mannered and highly idiosyncratic prose style (baroque and stiffly elegant in Vance's case), and both have their characters spout theatrical, deliberately nonnaturalistic hieratic dialogue of a sort that never actually came out of anyone's mouth—if you were to film their work, no mumbling Method actors would need to apply; only someone with the flamboyant grandiloquence of a John Barrymore would do. Vance also ... reminds me of Philip K. Dick; each author relies heavily on a personal formula of his own, using the same basic frameworks, plots, types of characters and situations again and again (what is important in each is not creating new motifs, but refining and developing variations on their obsessive themes); each man's style is limited in technical range, but, within that range, they are the best in the business at what they do well; both emphasize how manners and *mores* change from society to society.
>
> (pp. 117–118)

To readers on his wavelength, Vance provides a reading experience not quite like any other. When we come across words like "Orwellian" or "Pythonesque" we know exactly what they mean—"Vancian" deserves comparable currency.

JACK VANCE
Selected Bibliography

THE WORKS OF JACK VANCE

SERIES

The Dying Earth

The Dying Earth. New York: Hillman, 1950. *The Eyes of the Overworld*. New York: Ace, 1966.

Cugel's Saga. Columbia, Pa.: Underwood-Miller, 1983.

Rhialto the Marvelous. Columbia, Pa.: Underwood-Miller, 1984.

Tales of the Dying Earth. New York, Tor/Orb, 2000. (Omnibus edition containing *The Dying Earth*, *The Eyes of the Overworld*, *Cugel's Saga*, and *Rhialto the Marvelous*.)

The Demon Princes

The Star King. New York: Berkley, 1964.

The Killing Machine. New York: Berkley, 1964.

The Palace of Love. New York: Berkley, 1967.

The Face. New York: DAW, 1979.

The Book of Dreams. New York: DAW, 1981.

The Demon Princes. New York: Tor/Orb, 1997. (Omnibus edition. Volume I: *The Star King*, *The Killing Machine*, *The Palace of Love*; Volume II: *The Face*, *The Book of Dreams*.)

Tschai

City of the Chasch. New York: Ace, 1968.

Servants of the Wankh. New York: Ace, 1969.

The Dirdir. New York: Ace, 1969.

The Pnume. New York: Ace, 1970.

Planet of Adventure. New York: Tor/Orb, 1993. (Omnibus edition containing *City of the Chasch*, *Servants of the Wankh*, *The Dirdir*, and *The Pnume*.)

Durdane

The Anome. New York: Dell, 1973.

The Faceless Man. New York: Dell, 1973.

The Brave Free Men. New York: Dell, 1973.

Alastor

Trullion: Alastor 2262. New York: Ballantine, 1973.

Marune: Alastor 933. New York: Ballantine, 1975.

Wyst: Alastor 1716. New York: DAW, 1978.

Alastor. New York: Tor/Orb, 1995. (Omnibus edition containing *Trullion: Alastor 2262*, *Marune: Alastor 933*, *Wyst: Alastor 1716*.)

Lyonesse

Lyonesse: Suldrun's Garden. New York: Berkley, 1983.

Lyonesse: The Green Pearl. Columbia, Pa.: Underwood-Miller, 1985.

Lyonesse: Madouc. Columbia, Pa.: Underwood-Miller, 1989.

The Cadwal Chronicles

Araminta Station. Columbia, Pa.: Underwood-Miller, 1987.

Ecce and Old Earth. Columbia, Pa.: Underwood-Miller, 1991.

Throy, Columbia, Pa.: Underwood-Miller, 1992.

Big Planet

Big Planet. New York: Ace, 1957.

Showboat World. New York: Pyramid, 1975.

NON-SERIES NOVELS AND SHORT STORY COLLECTIONS

To Live Forever. New York: Ballantine, 1956.

Space Opera. New York: Pyramid, 1965.

The Languages of Pao. New York: Ace, 1966.

The Blue World. New York, Ballantine, 1966.

The Brains of Earth/The Many Worlds of Magnus Ridolph. New York: Ace, 1966.

Eight Fantasms and Magics. New York: Macmillan, 1969. (Short stories.)

Emphyrio. New York: Doubleday, 1969.

The Worlds of Jack Vance. New York: Ace, 1973. (Short stories.)

The Best of Jack Vance. New York: Pocket Books, 1976. (Short stories.)

Green Magic: The Fantasy Realms of Jack Vance. Columbia, Pa.: Underwood-Miller, 1979. (Short stories.)

Galactic Effectuator. New York: Ace, 1980.

The Gray Prince. New York: Bobbs-Merril, 1974.

Chateau d'If and Other Stories. Lancaster, Pa.: 1990.

Night Lamp. New York: Tor, 1996.

Ports of Call. New York: Tor, 1998.

Coup de Grace and Other Stories. Oakland, Calif.: Vance Integral Edition, 2002.

CRITICAL AND BIOGRAPHICAL STUDIES

Bergeron, Joe. "A Visit to Jack Vance." Available at homepage.mac.com/joebergeron.

Cunningham, A. E., ed. *Jack Vance: Critical Appreciations and a Bibliography*. London: British Library, 1999.

Dirda, Michael. "Jack Vance's Courtly Elegance." *Washington Post*, March 17, 1988.

Dozois, Gardner. Introduction to "The Moon Moth." *Modern Classics of Science Fiction*. Edited by Gardner Dozois. New York: St. Martin's, 1991.

Eagen, Tim. "Portrait of the Artist as a Mad Poet." August 1998. Available at www.stmoroky.com/reviews/authors/vance.htm.

Hewett, Jerry, and Daryl F. Mallett. *The Work of Jack Vance: An Annotated Bibliography and Guide*. San Bernardino, Calif.: Borgo, 1994.

Mead, David G. *An Encyclopedia of Jack Vance: Twentieth Century American Science Fiction Writer*. Vol. 1. Lewiston, N.Y.: Mellen, 2002.

Rhoads Paul. "Jack Vance: Lord of Language, Emperor of Dreams." Available at www.infinityplus.co.uk/nonfiction/jvprofile.htm.

Schwab, Joe. *Vance, Magic, and Wonder: A study of Jack Vance's Fantasy Works*. M.A. thesis, Graduate School of Stephen F. Austin State University, 1992. Available at www.massmedia.com/~mikeb/jvm/reviews/thesis.html.

Sipper, Ralph B. "Jack Vance: The Prodigious Invisible Man of Science Fiction." *Los Angeles Times*, August 5, 1979, p. x08. Available at www.massmedia.com/~mikeb/jvm/reviews/sippert.html.

Silverberg, Robert. " 'The New Prime': Six Plots for the Price of One." *Robert Silverberg's Worlds of Wonder*. New York: Warner, 1987.

"Volunteers Publishing Complete Works of Jack Vance." *SciFiWS News*, October 13, 2001. On-line magazine; available from www.scifiws.com.

INTERVIEW

Halpern, Marty. "A Meeting with Jack Vance." April 15, 1989. Available at www.massmedia.com/~mikeb/jvm/reviews/halpern1.html.

INTERNET RESOURCES

The Dying Earth Roleplaying Game. Home page at www.dyingearth.com.

The Jack Vance Information Page. Available at www.massmedia.com/~mikeb/jvm.

The Illustrated Vance. Home page at jackvanceillustrated.tripod.com/pulps. Vance Integral Edition. Home page at www.vanceintegral.com.

Jeff VanderMeer
1968–

IAN NICHOLS

THE VERY BEST of fantasy is interrogative, rather than reassuring. It interrogates by showing us our own world, our human passions and fascinations, in a carnival mirror, until we question which is real, the image in the mirror or the object it reflects. It exists in that indefinable space between that which most definitely is and that which most definitely is not. Within that space, it is possible to build visions that are unique, yet consistent with the boundaries and voices of the human soul. These are not simply alien worlds, decked out with creatures of romance, and, far too often, just vehicles of escape. They are questions as narrative, as mythopoeic as the most epic of high fantasy, but as close to us as the most joyous bitterness and bitterest joy of our human experience. It is within these bounds of heart and mind that Jeff VanderMeer has made his distinctive mark.

"Fantasy is not to do with inventing another non-human world: it is not transcendental," Rosemary Jackson writes, in what could be a direct description of VanderMeer's work. "It has to do with inverting elements of this world, recombining its constitutive features in new relationships to produce something strange, unfamiliar and *apparently* 'new,' absolutely 'other,' and different (*Fantasy: The Literature of Subversion*; Methuen, London, 1981, p. 8). VanderMeer's major creation is the city of Ambergris, in and around which many of his stories are set, but he has also set stories in locations that are, apparently, a part of this world, such as New Orleans. But these stories take no comfort from their familiar settings, and, instead, reshape the settings into a richer, sometimes more sinister, background for the narrative.

***

Jeff VanderMeer was born in Belfont, Pennsylvania, on July 7, 1968. His parents worked for the Peace Corps, however, and he spent much of his childhood in the Fiji Islands. When the family returned to the United States, they came the long way home, via Asia, Africa, and Europe. Such a journey could not fail to affect a young boy, and it had a deep influence on VanderMeer. In his stories set in exotic locations, he seems to understand the landscape and the people intimately. As VanderMeer says:

> That sense of strange beauty came from growing up in the Fiji Islands, surrounded by beauty, but also allergic to most of the flowers and asthmatic and thus in constant distress. The world as a result

was very hyper-real or surreal to me. My travels as a child—seeing things very alien, foreign—helped reinforce this.

(Fantasy lecture, Tallahassee Writers' Association, March 2002)

Like Michael Moorcock, who wrote the foreword to VanderMeer's most recent novel, *City of Saints and Madmen* (2002), VanderMeer began his writing and editing career early. In 1984 he began editing *Chimera Connections*, a literary magazine that published poetry by and interviews with such writers as Enid Shomer, Carol Muske, Jane Stuart, and the Pulitzer Prize-winning Richard Eberhart, among others. This lasted until 1988, and from 1988 to 1992 he edited *Jabberwocky*, notable for publishing the early work of Kathe Koja.

In 1991 he became a member of the advisory board of the Council on the Literature of the Fantastic, an organization associated with the University of Rhode Island, and chaired by Dr. Daniel Pearlman. Its aim is to bring to the attention of the public "slipstream" and "magic realism" texts that are published in North America. Since 2001, VanderMeer has been a member of the Editorial Board for Fantastic Metropolis Website, which publishes work by and interviews with such writers as Moorcock, Michael Chabon, Harlan Ellison, Thomas Disch, and James Sallis.

In 1994 VanderMeer founded and became senior editor of the Ministry of Whimsy Press. While this was an extension of his earlier publishing house, Chimera Press, it distinguished itself with the publication of *Leviathan,* an anthology of short fiction by notable fantasy writers. This small independent press has, in a relatively short time, become a highly respected publisher, producing finalists for the World Fantasy Award and the British Fantasy Award. The works published by the Ministry are oriented toward horror, fantasy, and science fiction and, while often challenging, are always entertaining. *The Troika*, by Stepan Chapman, published by the Ministry, won the prestigious Philip K. Dick Award in 1997. It was the first time such an honor had been bestowed on an independent press. Among the writers published by the Ministry are Moorcock, Sallis L. Timmel Duchamp, Richard Calder, Rikki Ducornet, Carol Emshwiller, Rhys Hughes, and Brian Stableford.

While his achievements as an editor and publisher are admirable, VanderMeer is, first and foremost, a writer. Since 1986, he has published 60 poems and over 170 stories in more than 300 publications, in 16 different languages. These have appeared in a diverse range of volumes, from avant-garde small press magazines to mainstream anthologies, on-line in e-zines and in traditional hardcover format, and in locations ranging from Australia to the Czech Republic, from the United Kingdom to Brazil, from New York to India. His nonfiction has, in contrast, been published almost exclusively in North America, by such respected journals as *The New York Review of Science Fiction* (Pleasantville, NY).

Since winning the Michael J. Hauptmann Award for Undergraduate Fiction while at the University of Florida in 1986 at eighteen, VanderMeer has received six other awards, including the International Rhysling Award for short poetry in 1994 and the World Fantasy Award for the best novella of 2000. He has published two novels, *Dradin, in Love* (1996) and *The Hoegbotton Guide to the Early History of Ambergris by Duncan Lyric of the Highway Mariner* (1991), and a third novel, *Veniss Underground*, is in press.

VanderMeer has also had seven collections published, of poetry, prose fiction, and nonfiction. The most noteworthy of these is *The City of Saints and Madmen: The Book of Ambergris* (2002), which contains four novellas concerning the fabulous city of Ambergris, plus appendices that exemplifies his eclectic and original approach to writing. The volume is a reprint of an earlier trade paperback version, which did not contain the appendices. He has collaborated with Eric Schaller to produce *The Exchange* (2002), a "found object" that portrays yet more of the culture of Ambergris.

In 2000 VanderMeer sent the following e-mail message to writers around the world:

> Dear Writer (or Meerkat Farm Proprietor): Greetings! You may be wondering, having opened this package, why I have sent you a plastic alien baby and a disposable camera. It may not help to know that I too am wondering why, but let me assure you that it all seemed like a good idea at the time.
>
> To explain: my new author web site has a section for author photos. Upon reflection and much deep thought, I decided it might be nice to have photos of and by other writers. So I made a list of some of my favorite writers (mostly living, although I have also sent this package to the grave sites of Nabokov and Poe) and you were on it.
>
> If, by this point, you don't think I am completely nuts, I'd be honored if you would use up the roll of enclosed film on pictures of yourself, your writing space, your neighborhood, your friends, etc., and send it back to me in the enclosed self-addressed stamped envelope. One final request: although the plastic alien baby was primarily included to get your attention, could you please include it (for purposes of scale) in at least one photo?
>
> (Vanderworld Website, www.vanderworld.redsine.com)

Many replied with photographs. It is this good-humored, somewhat irreverent, approach to the entire field of writing that most characterizes VanderMeer's approach to his own work. His brand of whimsy is not capriciousness but "a fanciful or fantastic creation" (*Shorter Oxford English Dictionary*, 3rd edition). It is a deliberate attempt to change the way in which things are seen.

***

Mikhail Bakhtin pointed out that fantasy is essentially opposed to stasis, and that it juxtaposes dissimilar, often incompatible elements. It transgresses the discrete boundaries of existence, through all its elements of style, subject, and discourse. If, as the Russian formalists believed, literature is language made strange, then fantasy is literature made strange. But what is this process of "making strange?" How does the familiar become unfamiliar, our secure knowledge of what constitutes reality become shaken? It is by changing the paradigm, the framework by which we understand what it is to which words refer that the fantasist forces readers to engage their imagination, and become complicit in the text, rather than subject to it. As VanderMeer says:

> Imagination is one aspect of literature that has universal implications. It seems to me that reading—reading well, with an appreciation for more than just the basics of narrative, plot, or story—is a heroic act these days, especially considering the distractions of other media. Comic books, movies, and television shows can all be quite profound, but even the best examples provide us with ready-made immutable images. Reading a book that not only entertains but is also deeply felt—deeply realized, created from a highly personal vision—strikes me as a kind of rebellion.
>
> Reading fully engages and strengthens that long dormant muscle called the imagination, which is the most visible manifestation of the soul.
> (Fantasy Lecture, *op. cit.*)

This concern with engaging the reader's imagination is nowhere more evident than in the Ambergris stories, collected in *The City of Saints and Madmen*.

City of Saints and Madmen is not just an anthology, it is a tourist's guide to a setting as fully realized as any in literature. The four novelettes that compose the first half and the ten texts that form the appendices are experimental and challenging, yet vastly entertaining and readable. They possess a sensuality that engages the reader, and stories that provoke both laughter and tears. They also show the intellect of a writer who is prepared to push the boundaries of narrative form, and equally willing to interrogate the nature of narrative itself. It is rare to encounter a writer who can challenge while seducing, but, with *City of Saints and Madmen*, VanderMeer does exactly that.

Ambergris is a city that is as surreal as a Dali painting, and founded on the same microcosmic attention to realistic detail. It is a city where what seems unreal is based on real experience: "In my case, the setting of Ambergris quite literally incorporates quite a bit of my childhood—it is a combination of all the places I visited when my parents were in the Peace Corps. ... Things from Ambergris that seem alien have actually been taken from real life" (Fantasy Lecture, *op. cit.*). It is also based on detailed research: "I have done an extensive study of Byzantine, Venetian, and London history and tried to plug in various elements from that research to enhance the reality of the city" (Fantasy Lecture, op. cit). This verisimilitude creates a setting that is believable, however strange, and where the carnival aspects of language itself, as explored by Bakhtin in *Problems of Dostoevsky's Poetics* (Ardis, 1973), are foregrounded.

A carnival, during which the protagonist's beliefs are challenged and shattered, is a central event in the first of the Ambergris novellas, *Dradin, in Love*. Dradin is a failed, unemployed missionary recently returned from the jungles beyond Ambergris, far down the Moth River. Walking down the street, he sees a woman in a window and falls in love with her image. Just recovered, perhaps, from a real fever, Dradin falls into a metaphoric fever of passion for her, a passion that is constrained by what he sees as her purity and chasteness: "Dradin wondered if he was dreaming her, . . . so that he might once more be cocooned within his fever, in the jungle, in the darkness" (p. 5). With the help of Dvorak, a dwarf, he sends presents to her, a book and an emerald necklace, and arranges to meet her at a tavern, to watch the Festival of the Freshwater Squid. This is the major event of the Ambergris calendar, where the world turns upside down for the night, and the restraints are removed. Dradin's passage to The Drunken Boat, the tavern where he is to have his tryst, is through a host of symbols of the danger that await him: women in hunters' costumes, riding wooden horses "painted in grotesque shades of green, red and white: eyes wept blood, teeth snarled into black fangs" (p. 65). Mushroom dwellers, the sinister original inhabitants of the city, wake for the evening and leave to go to "their secret and arcane rites" (p. 66). He walks through "an archway strung with nooses," where the band sings of the "city of lies" that is Ambergris (p. 67).

Dradin waits all night, but his love does not come. Instead, the dwarf appears, and leads him into a trap. Dradin escapes and goes to his love, only to find that he has once more been betrayed, by his own perceptions. This epiphany forces a choice upon him, wherein he must decide what the nature of love might be, there and then, faced with a new and dizzying knowledge. Must he continue his precious delusion, and pursue his love, or must he accept the defeat of the spirit by the vicious rules of the world? Dradin chooses his madness, his delusion, knowing, at least, that it is *his* madness, and that it brings with it his love.

The other three novellas in the book expand upon and explain the city of Ambergris and its inhabitants. None follow the same form as *Dradin, in Love*; VanderMeer deliberately plays with form and style, and by so doing embeds the reader further in the mysteries of Amergris, creating the city by creating its documents. *The Transformation of Martin Lake* is a biography of Ambergris' most famous painter, with the author of the biography as a player in the story. *The Hoegbotton Guide to the Early History of Ambergris, by Duncan Shriek*, is an idiosyncratic account of the founding and development of Ambergris, as narrated by a laconic and sardonic historian. *The Strange Case of X* is an interview with the author of the Ambergris stories, in an attempt to determine his sanity. The nub of this sanity is whether he believes Ambergris to be real or not.

VanderMeer experiments with narrative technique not merely for the sake of variety but to refine the way in which the reader is addressed and to challenge accepted paradigms of storytelling. In *The Book of Lost Places*, which anthologizes nine of VanderMeer's short stories, the stories range from the lyrical *The Bone Carver's Tale* to the harder-edged *London Burning*, but all have an element of the magical and the surreal. In *Greensleeves*, a librarian, a keeper of books and thoughts, helps to free a bevy of mystical creatures, and is freed in her turn from the pettiness and doubt that once beset her. Some of these creatures dance to saxophone music on the floor above the library, and one of them is the eagle trapped in the stained-glass dome that covers the entire building. The librarian is aided by Cedric, a jester, and his giant frog, both from the place where the dancers belong, and to which she can never go. It is a sad, brave, happy story of love in a strange place.

※※※

For most literature, our perceived reality provides the paradigm for interpretation. We observe where the story touches against our world, and those are the points of our entrance into the story. But what if our real world can be shown to be not as we accept it to be, and if the story touches it at those points that exist, and are real, but which are most often ignored? It is then that the story, though fantastic, leads to a new appreciation of this world in which we live; the world itself is made strange, rather than discourse about the world being made strange, and so we come to see ourselves as living within a kind of narrative, and the boundaries between the real and the unreal become questionable. As VanderMeer has said:

> The world has steadily, through use of technology, become more and more surreal. I'm sure many of you have had the experience of seeing someone on the street corner who appeared to be crazy because they were talking to themselves—only to discover they had one of those wireless telephone headsets on. We walk up to machines, insert a piece of plastic, and receive cash. We "fly" places. We watch advertisements where containers of cleaning fluid talk to us and tell us stories. We are living in a fantasy world, in a sense, and therefore the idioms and ideas of fantasy can speak to us as readily as in the past, just transformed.
>
> Fantasy fiction can be truer to a psychological reality than "realistic" fiction because it is not bound to replicate a consensus reality that does not, in fact, exist.
>
> (Fantasy Lecture, *op. cit.*)

This challenge to our view of the world is present in all of VanderMeer's work. His stories act as a prism to scatter the white light of the world into its component colours, showing us things which were always there, but which could not be seen. Sometimes he achieves this through the use of dense symbolism, sometimes by using varying and inconsistent narrative positions, forms and styles. Sometimes he questions the very nature of fiction, and disguises them as non-fiction. Whatever the challenge, it is one which is worthwhile. In a field where truly intelligent, truly felt, fiction becomes scarcer by the day, VanderMeer opens doors into worlds which should have been and makes them seem as if they could have been.

Selected Bibliography

WORKS OF JEFF VANDERMEER

The Book of Frog. Gainesville, Fla.: Ministry of Whimsy Press, 1989.
The Hoegbotton Guide to the Early History of Ambergris by Duncan.
Lyric of the Highway Mariner. Troy, N.Y.: Mocturnal Publications, 1991. (Poetry.)

Dradin, in Love. Tallahassee, Fla.: Buzzcity Press, 1996.

The Book of Lost Places. San Francisco, Calif.: Dark Regions Press, 1996.

Shriek. Westborough, Mass.: Necropolitan Press, 1999.

Why Should I Cut Your Throat & Other Nonfiction. Tallahassee, Fla.: Cosmos Books, 2002.

City of Saints and Madmen: The Book of Ambergris: Prime Books, Ohio, 2002. (The earlier trade paperback, published in 2001 by Cosmos Press, did not contain the appendices.)

Howard Waldrop

1946–

JOHN CLUTE

IT IS ALMOST certainly the case that John W. Campbell Jr. had no intention of discovering Howard Waldrop, and it is also not unlikely that, had he sensed how subversive of the goals of orthodox science fiction his new find would prove, he might have sent the aspiring young author somewhere else. There remains the fact, however, that Campbell did buy Waldrop's first story—the never-reprinted "Lunchbox" (*Analog,* May 1972)—several months before Campbell's death in 1971; and that Waldrop is the last figure of importance to be brought into the science fiction field by its greatest editor.

From the first, Waldrop was—to use a phrase Harold Bloom appropriated from William Butler Yeats—one of "the ringers in the tower," one of the writers of the last decades of the twentieth century for whom the great writers of science fiction—and the institutionalized advocacy structure of science fiction itself—constituted an uneasy heritage. That heritage he has interpreted—Bloom's term is "saving misprision"—through parody, inversion, mockery; through writing fantasy garbed in the sheepskin of science fiction; and ultimately through despair. He is therefore one of the first writers of importance to signal the end of the official genre that Campbell espoused and shaped from the beginning of his career as editor of *Astounding Science Fiction* (later *Analog*) in September 1938. The Campbell/*Astounding* vision was normally darker, and almost always more sophisticated in its prognoses, than the semi-official futures envisaged through events like the New York World's Fair of 1939, where General Motors' Futurama exhibit entranced huge crowds with its vision of a sanitized technocracy. But Futurama and *Astounding* (and American science fiction in general) shared a repertory of iconic images of a future cleansed through *improvement,* a future (as it turned out in the retrospects of 2002) dangerously more storyable than the world it presumed to teach how to work.

Howard Waldrop grew up and began to write mature stories during the period—approximately 1955–1975—when the real world had begun to show the deep, hollow narrowness of the science fiction dream. The world turned out still to be dirty, unbelievably complex, compromised, anxiety-ridden, apocalyptic; it did not, in short, work right. And the icons that manifested the old story of clean progress—from spaceships to vacuum cleaners, from robot housemaids to Interstates—suffered a value change. They became tokens of loss. They became retro. Much of Waldrop's work can be plausibly read as retro homage.

But it is more complicated than simple nostalgia. At the heart of modern science fiction and fantasy American writers' sense of loss—manifest in most of those who grew up after World War II—is the knowledge that the world whose loss is mourned never in fact existed at all. Neither Futurama nor Campbellian science fiction derived from a world that could continue to become, because (the deep fear runs) it never in truth really did start to become. Insofar as science fiction attempted to base its advocacies on a testable understanding of continuous history, it had become foundling.

So "nostalgia" for 1950s icons is not nostalgia at all. A better word to describe this complex emotion, and one that deeply characterizes Waldrop's work from the early 1970s to the end of the century, is desiderium, which may be defined as an intense longing for something that is missing from the world and is now lost, something which indeed may never have actually existed in the first place, but which *should* have existed. Desiderium, so defined, points directly toward late-twentieth-century fantasy, most of whose central texts manifest, again and again, an intuition that the world not only does not work, but that the world is *wrong*.

Alternate histories are normally understood as science fiction; but under the reading of desiderium, it may be possible to suggest that alternate histories—ostensible science fiction stories set in versions of the past that differ in some fundamental way from the real past—pretty exactly fulfill a root definition of modern fantasy as being comprised of stories "set in a world which is impossible *but which the story believes*" (John Clute, in *Unearthly Visions*, p. 89). Fantasy, under this argument, differs from science fiction in that it is the story, rather than the argument, that constitutes a belief in the created world, though both fantasy and science fiction must, of course, be *told*: an science fiction story, in this context, can be understood as a text which makes cognitive estrangement storyable.

It is even possible to generate equivalences in the languages that describe the devices of science fiction and fantasy. Alternate histories, which turn, in science fiction terms, on a jonbar point—a moment in history when an alternate outcome (John Wilkes Booth's failure to kill Lincoln) generates a whole new world—can easily be understood as fantasy stories that turn on their protagonists' finding a portal into a whole new world. The isomorphy of jonbar point and portal seems evident enough. And those stories set in worlds whose otherness from ours is a unexplained given—a condition that obtains very frequently in Waldrop's work—can be described, with a similar isomorphic result, as stories set either in science fiction alternate worlds or in fantasy secondary worlds.

Waldrop's stories are stories that believe the impossible we long for.

BACKGROUND

Howard Waldrop was born in Houston, Mississippi, on September 15, 1946, but was brought up in Texas. In the early 1960s, he did artwork for science fiction fanzines which he published with Jake Saunders (and later published his first novel in collaboration with him). He attended the University of Texas from 1965 to 1970, was drafted and served in the American military, and returned to the University of Texas in 1972, but he did not graduate. He lived in Austin, Texas, for the next twenty-one years—for five years with fellow writer Leigh Kennedy—until he moved to Oso, Washington, in early 1993.

As he makes clear in various introductions and notes (those interspersed throughout *Going Home Again* [1997] are of particular interest), Waldrop has been dogged by changing circumstances and poverty for as long as he has been a professional writer. He ascribes his poverty to the fact that he is essentially a short-story writer, and that short stories do not pay well. The true story is, of course, more complicated than that. Some short-story writers

(Harlan Ellison is an example) survive at least in part by being prolific, and by writing to fit various markets (Ellison's output stands at well over a thousand stories). In the twenty-five years of his career, Waldrop, on the other hand, has published only about sixty stories; nor does much of this modest total seem to have been crafted to fit commercial markets. Poverty as a way of life may not have been a choice Waldrop consciously made, but it is an almost inevitable consequence of the kind of writing career he has engaged in.

The first novel to affect Waldrop deeply, which he read at the age of seven, was *Mists of Dawn* (1952) by Chad Oliver, a juvenile tale of time travel whose young protagonist is accidentally sent 50,000 years into the past, where he comes to terms with his fellow human beings and with nature. Unlike the dominant Campbellian juvenile science fiction novels then being published by Robert A. Heinlein, this novel does not turn upon its protagonist's competent encounter with his environment, whether personal or galactic; it is far more concerned with offering its readers a dramatic meditation on right living.

It may be that Waldrop's abiding interest in the cultural interactions between artifacts and the humans who make them had its first roots at this point. Oliver and Waldrop eventually became close personal friends and perpetual fishing companions; and the former's death in 1993 was instrumental in persuading Waldrop—according to his own testimony—to leave Texas. Whether or not any of the anthropologists who feature in *Them Bones* (1984, Waldrop's only full-length solo novel) directly resembles Oliver, much of the warmth of that deeply pessimistic book comes from its rendering of archaeologists (anthropology and archaeology are sister disciplines) in the field.

No other single writer has visibly influenced Waldrop to the same degree, except perhaps for Philip José Farmer, some of whose stories and novels in the vast Wold Newton series—which gives roles to, and tells the life history of, almost every character of any note who figures in the history of twentieth-century pulp fiction—had appeared before 1970. But as Waldrop's career began to take shape, it soon became apparent that very few specific influences would ever be easily detectable in a writer so devoted to research that his less successful stories read as little more than sawhorses over which to drape historical references. A Waldrop story can read not as the achieved final thing itself but as a kind of final exhalation of a process whose primary interest for its author lies prior to the actual writing: in the ecstasy of research. Waldrop is indeed very widely known for his habit of gestating a story for months or years before actually writing it down, a process which almost never takes more than a day or so. He reads new stories often at conventions, and it may be that an actual majority of these stories were written down (or, as it were, transcribed) at the literal last minute before the performance was due to begin.

This is no way to become prosperous. Within the science fiction and fantasy community, on the other hand, the melodrama attending a Howard Waldrop reading has done much to focus genre readers upon one of the most remarkable oeuvres to be produced in the last quarter of the twentieth century.

NOVELS

Because they are simpler than the stories, because they lack the extensive referentiality of the shorter work, and because they do not attempt very hard to fulfill genre expectations, Waldrop's novels have not been accorded a great deal of attention. At least one of them, all the same, is a work of considerable substance.

Them Bones (1984) is a seemingly simple— but in the end quite possibly unresolvably complex—time-travel story set in Louisiana. It is told in three strands, two of them fully fleshed out as narrative, one laid down mainly in the form of diaries and filled-out military forms.

The first strand is set in 1929, at an archaeological dig; a fifteenth-century burial mound turns out to contain the body of a horse (not introduced into America for another half century) shot through the head by a twentieth-century bullet. The second strand is told in the first person by Madison Yazoo Leake, on a mission to travel back in time from the year 2002 to some point early in the twentieth century, when it is hoped he (and the 140 soldiers who are due to follow him almost immediately) will be able to stop World War II and save the world from desolation. The world of 2002 is dying; soon everyone will be dead from radiation or other poisons. The only hope for the human race is to change history. What Leake and the troops backing him up are supposed to do to accomplish this goal is never made clear; nor does it much matter. Leake has not landed in 1930s Louisiana; he has plummeted back to the fifteenth century.

Meanwhile, in the third strand of the story, we see the 140 soldiers also plummet back to about the same time. They will never find Leake, however, because he has entered an alternate universe, one in which the Roman Empire never existed and the library at Alexandria was never burned by religious zealots; a world whose western bournes are now being explored by Arabs. The soldiers remain in our own world, where they infect surrounding tribes of Indians with fatal diseases and are in turn slowly slaughtered. They are completely unable to effect any change in history that might save the world of 2002.

It is their remains, and the remains of their horses, that the 1929 team discovers. The endeavors of that team to save what they can of their distressingly anomalous finds are abetted by Huey Long, governor of Louisiana; but in the end, floodwaters wash away their work.

Leake's own story—which inhabits a fantasy-like time stream—occupies the largest portion of the book. It is a gently, movingly told tale of assimilation: he is adopted by a tribe, one of whose members speaks Greek through earlier experiences with Arabs, and lives with them in peace until an Aztec-like nation kidnaps his mentor. Leake manages to rescue his mentor, who is killed all the same by the pursuing "Huastecas." Back home, disease and changing climate begin to evict everyone from Eden. But Leake remains with the remnants of his people. There is a woman he loves. There is nothing else to do, for *Them Bones*, though told with a deceptive calm, is a tale of terminus.

A Dozen Tough Jobs (1989) is a tall tale set in the Mississippi of 1925–1930, a setting also evoked in the Coen Brothers' *O Brother, Where Art Thou?* (2000), a film which, like Waldrop's novel, loosely retells Greek myth and legend, in this case the *Odyssey*, and which features a character named Vernon T. Waldrip, almost certainly a reference to Vernon Waldrip, a character in William Faulkner's short story, "If I Forgot Thee Jerusalem." There was, however, no deliberate homage to Waldrop's novel. In *A Dozen Tough Jobs*, a comic retelling of the tale of the Twelve Labors of Hercules underpins—much more cogently than the allusions scattered through the film—a veiled and melancholy patter of anecdotes about the coming of age of a black adolescent in the Deep South, who tells the story of Houlka Lee, working off a prison sentence under the supervision of Boss Eustis; the labors he is asked to perform repeat those of Hercules. The underlying world depicted by the young black, Invictus Ovidius Lace (I. O. Lace, or Iolus, for short), however relaxed his tone of voice, is profoundly bleak, as though the mythic resonances of the tale were a dream, counterfactuals to set up against a world to come.

SHORT FICTION

Almost all of Waldrop's short work of merit has been assembled in four collections—*Howard Who?* (1986), *All About Strange Monsters of the Recent Past* (1987), *Night of the Cooters* (1990), and *Going Home Again* (1997)—which have themselves been variously reassembled (see bibliography). There is relatively little development from one volume to the next, though some of the later stories are somewhat less freighted with references and feature somewhat smaller casts of protagonists and walk-ons who turn out to be historical figures, or characters from other stories in other media, or myths. But the streamlining of texture is only relative, and the intensity of rendered feeling is, if anything, greater.

The long *You Could Go Home Again* (1993), a chapbook publication that also appears in *Going Home Again*, may, for instance, boasts only five recognizable real characters—Thomas Wolfe, Fats Waller, Nevile Shute, T. E. Lawrence, and a very young J. D. Salinger—and there may in fact be almost no conventional story to tell. But the portal through which we enter this alternate history is an achingly acute manifestation of desiderium: the 1932 presidential election America has been won by Howard Scott, the historical promulgator of the Technocracy movement, which espoused the establishment of a primitive but nationwide database to keep track of supply and demand, and to institute further high-tech means to make the U.S. economic and cultural infrastructure really work. As a consequence, there is no World War II in 1940; great zeppelins fly the world; and Thomas Wolfe, though not fully recovered from his 1938 brain surgery (which killed him in the real world), is flying from the 1940 Japanese Olympics, homeward bound. Fats Waller makes an unscheduled appearance and plays inspiredly all night (Waldrop's intense love of American music from the turn of the century on is here, as elsewhere, amply unpacked); and Wolfe begins to sense, as dawn comes, what somehow he must recover in his own psyche in order to write once again at full pitch. There is nothing more to the story but detailwork; what remains is an almost unendurably potent longing for a world in which Thomas Wolfe could recover his wits, Fats Waller play forever, World War II never happen, and glorious zeppelins might sparkle the dawn winds.

An even later story, "The Heart of Whitenesse" (1997)—most conveniently reprinted in *The Year's Best Science Fiction: Fifteenth Annual Collection* (New York: St. Martin's Press, 1998, edited by Gardner Dozois)—also packs an intense emotional overload into a tale featuring Christopher Marlowe in the days approaching his murder (the murder itself is not described). The phrase "hum of pleroma," which serves as epigraph to this story, comes from an analysis by John Clute (in *Look at the Evidence*, New York: Serconia Press, 1996, p. 343)—of some of the ways in which intensity of longing may be conveyed in a venue that is not simply nostalgic. In Waldrop's tale, which replays Joseph Conrad's "Heart of Darkness" (1899), Marlowe (Marlow) embarks upon a sailing craft fitted with runners and sails up the iced-over Thames (the Congo) from London to Oxford, where he has been instructed to warn Johann Faustus (Kurtz) that he must not engage in treasonable activities.

But instead of darkness, all is epiphanic whiteness. There is a snowstorm on the Thames, but the ice ship continues—Waldrop's description of the journey is exultantly intense—through to Oxford. Marlowe's confrontation with Faust (and a prophecying demon) seems to go well. He returns to London full of plans. He does not know what the reader knows: that in hours he will be a dead man.

Like many of his later stories, "The Heart of Whitenesse" straddles, with great ease, more than one genre simultaneously. The ice ship itself is an science fiction notion; Faustus's summoning of a demon is fantasy. Their coexistence—like the collisions generated when cubist exorcisms of perception impose themselves upon collage elements in an early-mid-period painting by Pablo Picasso—becomes the point; what might seem to be an assault upon our expectations becomes the way to look. It is when he rides the interstices between genres—however artificial genres may seem to some readers—that Waldrop flourishes most eloquently. A good example is his most famous story, "The Ugly

Chickens" (1980; in *Howard Who?*), which won the 1980 Nebula Award for novelette and the 1981 World Fantasy Award for short fiction. The eponymous "chickens" are in fact dodos, a breeding population of which has survived, through a series of plausible circumstances, into the twentieth century, only to be cooked, en masse, in a barbecue.

This story has often been described as a work of science fiction set in an alternate universe—after all, in this world dodos have been extinct for centuries—but it is also a Secret History of the World, a mode of telling into which, very frequently, fantasy elements crosshatch the real. In the end, this particular tale defaults to yet another genre: the mimetic. Waldrop explains in "mundane" terms how his dodos survived so long, making it clear that their survival is something we did not know about our world, not something that requires an alternate universe to justify or a Secret History of the World to surround. But this deflation into the mimetic bears the traces of the possible worlds of discourse it has evoked in our minds, and in this sense it is an exemplary postmodern *jeu d'espirit*.

Most of Waldrop's stories feature real persons in anomalous roles, or fictional characters who have been promoted to full "reality" in worlds that are impossible (that is, are not arguable in science fiction terms as deriving from a prior jonbar point). Examples include "Save A Place in the Lifeboat for Me" (1976), "Ike at the Mike" (1982), both from *Howard Who?*; "All About Strange Monsters of the Recent Past" (1981) and "What Makes Hieronymous Run?" (1985), both from *All About Strange Monsters of the Recent Past*; "Hoover's Men" (1988) and "Fin de Cyclé," both from *Night of the Cooters*, the second being original to that volume; "The Effects of Alienation" (1992), which is a "Hitler wins" tale; and "Scientifiction," which is original to *Going Home Again*.

A full cast list of recognizable names would be difficult if not impossible to construct (walk-ons are sometimes only identified allusively). But a representative sampling of the cast may give some sense of the cultural fields Waldrop tills and blends. Almost every personage Waldrop evokes (real or fictional, human or toon) is evoked with a warmth of desiderium, an intensely conveyed feeling that the world should be thus, that the world should have been so constructed that these real folk might live aright, that these fictional folk might escape the bondage of being created daimons. When he must deal with an irrevocable fact—with a world he cannot magic into another semblance—the effect is often tragic, as in "Save a Place in the Lifeboat for Me" (1976; in *Howard Who?*), where nothing can prevent Buddy Holly from taking his fatal flight (on 3 February 1959), not even the Marx Brothers, not even Laurel and Hardy.

Figures Waldrop incorporates into his cast (some already mentioned) include Bud Abbott, Louis Armstrong, Bertolt Brecht, Bucky Bug (who featured in 1940s issues of *Walt Disney's Comics and Stories*), Natty Bumppo, John Bunyan, Holden Caulfield, Lou Costello, Charles Dickens, Donald Duck, Dwight D. Eisenhower, Lillian Gish, Goofy, D. W. Griffith, Oliver Hardy, William S. Hart, Adolf Hitler, Ernest Hemingway, Buddy Holly, Sherlock Holmes, Herbert Hoover as head of the FBI, Boris Karloff, Alfred Jarry, Waylon Jennings, John F. Kennedy, Stan Laurel, T. E. Lawrence, Huey Long, Peter Lorre, Groucho Marx (and the other Marx Brothers), Georges Méliès, Mantan Moreland, Zero Mostel, Mickey Mouse, various movie monsters of the 1950s cinema, the musicians of Bremen, Nosferatu, General George Patton, Pablo Picasso, Elvis Presley, Marcel Proust, Henri Rousseau, Erik Satie, Shemp (from the Three Stooges), Fats Waller, Isaak Walton, and Thomas Wolfe. There are many more.

Most of these figures appear in tales which variously occupy science fiction or fantasy genres, or straddle them, a spectrum ranging from the full alternate history scenario examined in *You Could Go Home Again* to the arguably this-worldly "The Ugly Chickens." Those tales that Waldrop sets in the future tend to place the reader in worlds so diffusely connected to the ongoing history of the world as almost to make them understandable as alternate histories—or otherworld representations—of futures we might have had in some other world.

The near future, post-disaster world depicted in "Mary Margaret Road-Grader" (1976; in *Howard Who?*) does not, for instance, supply more than a shapely sketch of that world. The tragicomedy at its heart—the conflict between the eponymous woman and the men who are mysogynistically loath to compete with her in a tournament of ancient road graders—unfolds with an eerie, distanced, contemplative serenity. Its closing passages much resemble the closing sections of *Them Bones;* an elegiac sense pervades both texts. It is a sense that any world in which we must live is an entrapment; that in truth the world should not be thus. This sense—that the world is wrong—lies, as we have already noted, at the heart of twentieth-century fantasy at its most penetrative.

In *Night of the Cooters,* introducing "Wild, Wild Horses" (1988), the only fantasy story he admits to having written, Waldrop presents an exceedingly narrow definition of the genre, conceived as a cast list of any Fantasyland epic: "I'm talkin' 'bout elves and demons and orcs and sea-sprites and griffons and lost swords and rings and kelpies and harpies and all that shit" (p. 169). In this light, "Wild, Wild Horses" can be seen as mildly subversive (though far less subversive than almost any other story he has ever written, most of which enact the deep grammar of fantasy without quoting any of the Fantasyland trappings common to the followers of Terry Brooks). It is a few centuries after the birth of Jesus, when Julian is emperor. Chiron, the last centaur, after long centuries among humans, longs to return home, which is an island in the furthermost West. He persuades a human, R. Renatus Vegetius, to help him get across the Roman Empire without being caught for a zoo. Vegetius, with the help of a clever slave, does so.

There is a slapstick feel to the tale (the slave reminds one of a young Zero Mostel), but this traversal of Thomas Burnett Swann territory does convey some due melancholy.

In the afterword to "Why Did?" (1994; story and afterword are in *Going Home Again*), Waldrop asks a rhetorical question of his readers:

Don't you wish sometimes you lived in a Fleischer cartoon world, with Betty Boop, Bimbo, Koko and Pudge? That when things were going great, and you were dancing, all the buildings and people and the moon and stars were dancing along with you? And when things were bad, even the trees would chase you?

Anyway, sometime in the Eighties I started referring to the "Little Moron Story" I was going to write.

(p. 130)

A world whose shape enacts the unfolding of a soul is precisely the world of any sustained fantasy story (in distinction to the diorama of tableaux vivants featured in "Wild, Wild Horses"); in science fiction terms, it is the world of Virtual Reality, in which a fantasy telling is subverted by an invisible science fiction frame. "Why Did?" itself is clearly told on a literal level: a man who thinks he is the Little Moron, from the 1950s Little Moron jokes, maintains a house and gives living space to a number of mentally deficient or disturbed characters from American literature. The big house burns down; life, although diminished, continues. This is straight enough on the page; but the implications of the tale are, on the other hand, impenetrable. Why does Benjamin—from William Faulkner's *The Sound and the Fury* (1929)—gain his senses while dying? Why does a cartoon character—Otto Soglow's Little King, who originated in the *New Yorker*—seem to take over after the deaths of the other characters? Why can they not continue in the world of their story?

Perhaps the answer, as F. Scott Fitzgerald once famously said of American life, is that there is no second act. Waldrop might add: all the

Americas of all our dreams are stages, false fronts leading into impossible worlds we can only inhabit in dream. Stories are no more real than dreams. All the alternate Americas—the real world and the imagined, the dream and the awakening—crumble and fade once a real world begins to tell on them. The bravery of life, in the stories and the example of Howard Waldrop, is to live without expecting a full story, a fixative of art, a second act.

Howard Waldrop's stories do not end. They stop when they are broken.

Selected Bibliography

WORKS OF HOWARD WALDROP

NOVELS AND SHORT STORIES

The Texas-Israeli War: 1999. With Jake Saunders. New York: Ballantine Books, 1974.

Them Bones. New York: Ace Books, 1984.

Howard Who?: Twelve Outstanding Stories of Speculative Fiction. Garden City, N.Y.: Doubleday, 1986.

All About Strange Monsters of the Recent Past: Neat Stories. Kansas City, Mo.: Ursus Imprints, 1987.

A Dozen Tough Jobs. Willimantic, Conn.: Mark V. Ziesing, 1989.

Night of the Cooters: More Neat Stories. Kansas City, Mo.: Ursus Imprints and Shingletown, Calif.: Mark V. Ziesing, 1990.

You Could Go Home Again. New Castle, Virginia: Cheap Street, 1993. (Chapbook.)

Going Home Again. North Perth, Australia: Eidolon Publications, 1997; New York: St. Martin's Press, 1998.

COMPILATIONS

Strange Things in Close-Up: The Nearly Complete Howard Waldrop. London: Legend, 1989. (Incorporates *Howard Who?* and *All About Strange Monsters of the Recent Past*.)

Strange Monsters of the Recent Past. New York: Ace Books, 1991. (Incorporates *All About Strange Monsters of the Recent Past* and *A Dozen Tough Jobs*.)

Night of the Cooters: More Neat Stuff. London: Legend, 1991. (Incorporates *Night of the Cooters: More Neat Stories* and *A Dozen Tough Jobs*.)

Dream Factories and Radio Pictures. electricstory.com, 2002. (An e-book release in MS Reader format. A compilation, except for "Major Spacer in the 21st Century," which is first released here.)

REFERENCES

Clute, John. "Notes on the Geography of Bad—and Good—Fantasy Art." In *Unearthly Visions: Approaches to Science Fiction and Fantasy Art.* Edited by Gary Westfahl, George Slusser, and Kathleen Church Plummer. Westport, Conn.: Greenwood Press, 2002.

Nancy Willard

1936–

BRIAN STABLEFORD

NANCY MARGARET WILLARD was born in Ann Arbor, Michigan, on June 26, 1936. She remained in Ann Arbor throughout her childhood, although the family was decamped to Albuquerque, New Mexico, for months at a time when her father taught summer school there. She attended the University of Michigan in Ann Arbor and was awarded a B.A. in 1958; she returned to Michigan to complete her Ph.D. in English (in 1963) after obtaining her M.A. from Stanford University in California with the aid of a Woodrow Wilson fellowship. She was already writing profusely and won five Hopwood Awards (the University of Michigan's principal literary prize, created in honor of Avery Hopwood) in three different categories: poetry, fiction, and essay. Her literary work continued to span this range, with considerable success in every category.

Willard married Eric Lindbloom in 1964; they had one son, James. In 1965 she became a lecturer in English at Vassar College, and she has remained on the faculty ever since. From 1975 she also worked as an instructor for the Bread Loaf Writer's Conference, held annually on Bread Loaf Mountain, in Vermont. She began publishing collections of poetry in 1966, beginning with *In His Country, Skin of Grace* (1967) and *A New Herball* (1968); she won a Devins Memorial Award for poetry in 1967. Her first collection of short stories, *The Lively Anatomy of God*, appeared in 1968—she won an O. Henry Award for short fiction in 1970—and her first collection of short stories for children, *Sailing to Cythera and Other Anatole Stories*, appeared in 1974. Since then the great majority of her publications have been illustrated books for younger children, but she has also written stories for older children, including more tales of Anatole, the naturalistic novella *The Highest Hit* (1978), and the fantasy novella *Firebrat* (1988). Her work for adults includes two full-length novels and several insightful essays on creative writing, some of which adopt a quasi-fabular hybrid format that qualifies them as unique works of art. Her most famous and successful book, *A Visit to William Blake's Inn: Poems for Innocent and Experienced Travelers* (1981), was the first book of poetry to win the Newbery Medal.

Although Willard's early fiction is naturalistic and often quasi-autobiographical, it is infused with a strong sense of wonder by virtue of the scrupulous religious observance featured therein. Death is a commonplace event in these stories but is always mercifully confined by faith, and monumental masonry—especially figures of angels—has a raw power that is echoed and refracted through much of Willard's subsequent work. *Childhood of the Magician* (1973) includes "The Hucklebone of a Saint," in which the superstition-stricken child-narrator benefits from an amateur exorcism, while *Angel in the Parlor* (1982) features "The Doctrine of the Leather-Stocking Jesus," in which a similar narrator experiences a brief but revealing Easter vision.

Sailing to Cythera includes two other stories in addition to the title piece. "Gospel Train" is a dreamlike account of a train journey taken by Anatole and his cat, Plumpet. In "The Wise Soldier of Sellebak" Anatole lends some assistance to an amnesiac soldier and undertakes a modest magical quest in order to help him return home. The laconically poetic surrealism of that quest set the pattern for Anatole's subsequent adventures, which carried him further and further afield. "Sailing to Cythera" finds him staying with his grandmother, in a house where things have an awkward habit of getting lost, decorated throughout with remarkable wallpaper featuring pastoral scenes. Grandma identifies one of the figures depicted in the wallpaper as Madame d'Aulnoy (who was collecting and adapting folkloristic tales for children before Charles Perrault), and she is the presiding spirit of the odyssey into the wallpaper world that Anatole eventually undertakes, meeting up with the monstrous but conspicuously mild Blimlin.

The Island of the Grass King (1979) is a novella that begins with Anatole and Plumpet staying with his grandmother again. When she regrets the loss of the particular fennel plant from which she made tea to treat her asthma, Anatole wishes on an invisible rainbow that he might recover it for her, and a rainbow horse duly carries him away on a quest to the island of Sycorax to do exactly that. It involves following a road donated by the Roadkeeper to recover a key secreted by Mother Weather-sky, which will release the Grass King, whose crown is made of the fennel. As well as Plumpet his companions on the quest are Quicksilver, his grandmother's old teapot, a glass girl named Susannah, and the pirate-turned-rabbit Captain Lark. The adventure is not without its darker moments—when Anatole and his friends first fall in with Captain Lark they are condemned to die with him for his crimes, and when they all fall into Mother Weather-sky's power extraordinary measures are required to turn the tables on her—but it includes a finer catalogue of wonders than the Sears Roebuck catalogue that Grandma uses to formulate her everyday wishes.

The Anatole "trilogy" is completed by *Uncle Terrible* (1982), an even more phantasmagorical novella in which Anatole goes to New York to stay with the eponymous relative (who is so named because he is so terribly nice). Uncle Terrible has come into possession of a wonderful dolls' house, whose library contains a book that includes a spell for reducing people to its own scale. Unfortunately, like many magical objects to be found in New York, the house is full of traps set by Arcimboldo the Marvelous, into one of which Uncle Terrible inevitably falls. Arcimboldo has also contrived to steal the thread of life from the Mother who lives in the great graveyard, and has given it to the tailor Cicero Yin to be made into a cloak. In order to undo Arcimboldo's mischief Anatole must beat the magician at checkers—a difficult feat, given that Arcimboldo's magic spectacles allow him to foresee Anatole's moves—and recruit various animal allies to the task of delaying the completion of the cloak long enough for the thread of life to be recovered. As in the earlier tales, the story's many wonders are set out with a highly effective laconism, described in beautiful and remarkable delicate prose.

Between *Sailing to Cythera* and *Uncle Terrible* Willard published numerous picture books for younger children, including *A Visit to William Blake's Inn: Poems for Innocent and Experienced Travelers*. These songs of innocence, carefully leavened by experience, take the form of a narrative series whose protagonist is conveyed by a flying gondola to an inn run by the great poet, with the aid of angels who make the beds and dragons who operate the kitchens. His fellow guests include the King of Cats and the Man in the Marmalade Hat; the Wise Cow and the Tiger are also on the scene. Willard was to pay further homage to her own sources of inspiration in several future texts, including *The Voyage of the Ludgate Hill*: Travels with Robert Louis Stevenson (1987) and the single poem embellished with remarkable pictures by Leo and Diane Dillon *in Pish, Posh, Said Hieronymus Bosch* (1991).

In her essay "The Well-Tempered Falsehood: The Art of Storytelling," first collected in *The Angel in the Parlor*, Willard observes that of the various problems facing storytellers "the most unsettling and, at the same time, most exhilarating" is that "without knowing how or why, you cross over easily from the natural to the supernatural as if you felt absolutely no difference between them" (*A Nancy Willard Reader*, p. 163). Although the crossings featured in her stories for adults had previously been far more tentative, she had made such transitions with perfect ease in her Anatole stories, and she made full use of that experience in her first full-length novel, *Things Invisible to See* (1984). The novel tells the story of a romance that develops between Ben Harkissian, a student at Ann Arbor High in the class of 1941, and Clare Bishop, who is struck and paralyzed by a baseball that he carelessly hits into the night. The ripples of causality associated with this accident spread out to affect both their families profoundly, and the resilience of family ties and family loyalties—extended and symbolized by Clare's phantom Ancestress, who proves a very valuable guide—provides a safety net that prevents disaster becoming total.

When Ben is cast adrift in a life raft while on active service in the Pacific he is fortunate enough to make a bargain with Death, which ties his fate to a baseball game. He must reunite the Ann Arbor High team, for which he was once the pitcher, in order to play a team of all-time greats assembled by Death. The odds seem stacked in favor of Death even before disaster strikes Ben's team, but the opening paragraphs of the story have established that the Lord of the Universe likes nothing better than to play ball with His archangels on the banks of the River of Time, and that Death has not as much authority within the world of men as sometimes seems to be the case. Although the Lord will not intervene directly in Ben's fateful game, because humans have free will in order to shape their own destinies, He is by no means alone in rooting for the right side. The key chapter of *Things Invisible to See* that informs Clare's little brother of the existence of the amazing "rude doctor" Cold Friday—who eventually cures her—is titled "Salvage for Victory," and in spite of the presence within it of the Lord of the Universe it is more a tale of salvage than salvation. It offers such a scrupulous account of the inhospitable conditions under which free will must operate that even though it is unrepentantly and majestically sentimental, it is not in the least sickly.

Willard's other novel for adults, *Sister Water* (1993), is also a tale of salvage, which deploys its small and subtle miracles in a similar but less flamboyant manner. Like *Things Invisible to See*, it deals with the careful repair of the shattered lives of its two chief protagonists: Ellen Hanson, who loses her husband, Mike, in a car accident; and Sam Theopolis, a young man hired to look after Ellen's aged mother, Jessie. Sam is a metaphorical ministering angel—although he does have a real pair of wings tattooed on his shoulderblades—but he requires deliverance himself when circumstantial evidence leads to his being charged with murder. The murder has actually been committed, more in folly than malice, by an aspirant rival for Ellen's affections who also has an eye on Jessie's property. The supernatural element of the story is muted, confined as well as extrapolated by the pattern of symbolism enshrined in the novel's title, but the lyricism of the prose bestows a fabular quality upon the entire work and suffuses it with a subtly magical quality. The multilayered metaphor that—among other things—likens the life-giving but sometimes misfortunate permeation of the natural environment by rivers, rivulets, and pools to the permeation of the human community by life-enhancing relationships and moral obligations is all the more effective for its discretion.

Between her two novels for adults Willard wrote another novella for children, *Firebrat*. Like *Uncle Terrible* it is set in New York and features a heroic quest into a parallel world. Molly goes to stay with her Grandma, who lives above a shop called the Silver Shuttle. She makes friends with Sean, the son of a neighbor, with whom she goes "treasure hunting" in the shop. They acquire a subway map from Eugene, an eccentric collector of exotic trivia, which leads them through a portal in an abandoned station into the disaster-stricken Crystal Empire, whose inhabitants hail them as magicians whose advent has been prophesied. Their appointed task is to overcome the Firebrat, the insectile monster that holds the empire in its terrible thrall by virtue of its seizure of the timesticks. With the aid of the guidebook *How to Fix Everything!* and Molly's talent for telling stories the two children recover the timesticks from the salamanders of the Lake of Fire and restore the Crystal Empire to its rightful lord. Although it is a more conventional fantasy than the magnificent *Uncle Terrible*, *Firebrat* reproduces the candid sense of wonder and delicate intricacy of the Anatole stories.

Although "How Poetry Came into the World and Why God Doesn't Write It" (1987) has been reprinted more than once as an essay, it originally appeared in *The Bread Loaf Anthology of Contemporary American Short Stories*, edited by Robert Pack and Jay Parini. The author, having lost the opportunity to purchase *The Lost Books of Eden*, attempts to imagine what might have been in them by casting herself as an insurance salesman visited by Adam and Eve, who are seeking compensation for what they have lost in their expulsion from Eden. Eternal life is, of course, the leading item in the claim—but there are compensating gains to be set against it in the final tally, which are far from worthless. Another item of the same hybrid kind is "Danny Weinstein's Magic Book" (1993), which offers belated compensation for the fact that a book her young self once saw the eponymous Danny carrying turned out, disappointingly, to be called *The Autistic Personality* rather *than The Artistic Personality*. Willard's other short fantasies for adult readers include "Dogstar Man," in the Doubleday showcase anthology *Full Spectrum 3* (1990), and "The Trouble with Unicorns," in Peter S. Beagle's *Immortal Unicorn* (1995). The former is a flight of fancy presumably based on the Dog Star Man snowing globe mentioned in the first chapter of *Sister Water*, while the latter tells the story of a boy in search of a replacement for his recently deceased and cremated white cat, who responds to an advertisement offering an erocinul—a fabulous creature whose presence has a remarkable effect on mirrors.

Of the many fine essays collected along with "How Poetry Came into the World and Why God Doesn't Write It" and "Danny Weinstein's Magic Book" in *Telling Time: Angels, Ancestors and Stories* (1993), the most relevant to her work as a fantasist are "High Talk in the Starlit Wood," which is about ghost stories, and "When Now by Tree and Leaf: Time and Timelessness in the Reading and Making of Children's Books." The essays, most of which originated as "craft lectures" delivered at the Bread Loaf conference, place a heavy emphasis on writing from experience, and make no bones about the fact that the supernatural plays a vital and perfectly normal role in that part of our real experience that consists of dreams, daydreams, and the stories we routinely tell one another. The element of fantasy in Willard's work is thoroughly domesticated; it is manifest not as a threatening and disturbing disruption of everyday routine but something that can fit seamlessly into it and that almost always has a constructive or healing effect. Supernatural evil hardly figures at all in her work—misfortune usually arises by unhappy accident, and such figures of menace as Arcimboldo the Marvelous and the Firebrat have more mischief than malice in their works—but supernatural good is often present, in the shape of ghostly ancestors and full-fledged angels.

It is perhaps not surprising that Nancy Willard's work should acknowledge no robust boundary between the natural and the supernatural, given that she is conscientiously disrespectful of many other kinds of boundaries. She writes for children and for adults with the same imaginative delicacy, linguistic suppleness, and thematic seriousness, with both audiences simultaneously in mind even when she is not writing texts designed to be read aloud by parents to their children. A marked preference for angels over demons is rare in modern fiction; writers are often unwilling or unable to deploy the apparatus of Heaven, not only because it is intrinsically far less melodramatic than the apparatus of Hell but also because miracles are generally the cheapest and most debased method of resolving plots. It is a tribute to Willard's great but quiet artistry that she is entirely at ease with such materials and is conscientious in their use; there is nothing false or excessively convenient about the manner in which she plies her miraculous instruments. Whenever she employs a deus ex machina she does so with all appropriate reverence. In her use of angels and other benignly magical devices she may appear to be rushing in where other writers exercise extreme trepidation, but she is never in the least foolish; her narratives are always animated by an expressive grace, a polite dexterity, and a highly refined intelligence.

Selected Bibliography

WORKS OF NANCY WILLARD

NOVELS

Things Invisible to See. New York: Knopf, 1984.
Sister Water. New York: Knopf, 1993.

SHORT FICTION

The Lively Anatomy of God. New York: Eakins Press, 1968.
Childhood of the Magician. New York: Liveright, 1973.

CHILDREN'S STORIES

The Merry History of a Christmas Pie, with a Delicious Description of a Christmas Soup. Putnam, 1974.
Sailing to Cythera and Other Anatole Stories. New York: Harcourt Brace, 1974.
All on a May Morning. Putnam, 1975.
The Snow Rabbit. New York: Putnam, 1975.
Shoes Without Leather. New York: Putnam, 1976.
The Well-Mannered Balloon. New York: Harcourt Brace, 1976.
Simple Pictures Are Best. New York: Harcourt Brace, 1977.
Stranger's Bread. New York: Harcourt Brace, 1977.
The Highest Hit. New York: Harcourt Brace, 1978.

The Island of the Grass King: The Further Adventures of Anatole. New York: Harcourt Brace, 1979.

Papa's Panda. New York: Harcourt Brace, 1979.

The Marzipan Moon. New York: Harcourt Brace, 1981.

Uncle Terrible: More Adventures of Anatole. New York: Harcourt Brace, 1982.

Nightgown of the Sullen Moon. New York: Harcourt Brace, 1983.

Night Story. New York: Harcourt Brace, 1986.

The Mountains of Quilt. New York: Harcourt Brace, 1987.

Firebrat. New York: Knopf, 1988.

East of the Sun and West of the Moon. A Play. New York: Harcourt Brace, 1989.

The High Rise Glorious Skittle Skat Roarious Sky Pie Angel Food Cake. New York: Harcourt Brace, 1990.

Beauty and the Beast. New York: Harcourt Brace, 1992.

The Sorceror's Apprentice. New York: Scholastic, 1993.

A Starlit Somersault Downhill. New York: Little Brown, 1993.

Among Angels. New York: 1994 (with Jane Yolen).

An Alphabet of Angels. New York: Scholastic, 1994.

The Good-Night Blessing Book. New York: Scholastic, 1996.

Cracked Corn and Snow Ice Cream; A Family Almanac. New York: Harcourt Brace, 1997.

The Magic Cornfield. New York: Harcourt Brace, 1997.

The Tortilla Cat. New York: Harcourt Brace, 1998.

Shadow Story. New York: Harcourt Brace, 1999.

The Tale I Told Sasha. New York: Little Brown, 1999.

The Moon and Riddles Diner and the Sunnyside Cafe. New York: Harcourt Brace, 2001.

Grandmother's Hat. New York: Little Brown, 2002.

POETRY

In His Country. Ann Arbor, MI: Generation, 1966.

Skin of Grace. Columbia: University of Missouri Press, 1967.

A New Herball. Baltimore: Ferdinand Roten Galleries, 1968.

19 Masks for the Naked Poet. Santa Cruz, Ca.: Kayak, 1971.

Carpenter of the Sun. New York: Norton, 1974.

A Visit to William Blake's Inn: Poems for Innocent and Experienced Travelers. New York: Harcourt Brace, 1981; London: Methuen, 1982.

Household Tales of Moon and Water. New York: Harcourt Brace, 1982.

The Voyage of the Ludgate Hill. Travels with Robert Louis Stevenson. New York: Harcourt Brace, 1987.

The Ballad of Biddy Early. New York: Random House, 1989.

Water Walker. New York: Knopf, 1989.

Pish, Posh, Said Hieronymus Bosch. New York: Harcourt Brace, 1991.

Step Lightly: Poems for the Journey. New York: Harcourt Brace, 1998.

NANCY WILLARD

OTHER WORKS

Testimony of the Invisible Man; William Carlos Williams, Francis Ponge, Rainer Maria Rilke, Pablo Neruda. Columbia: University of Missouri Press, 1970.

Angel in the Parlor, Five Stories and Eight Essays. New York: Harcourt Brace, 1982.

A Nancy Willard Reader: Selected Poetry and Prose. Hanover, NH: Middlebury University Press, 1991.

Telling Time: Angels, Ancestors and Stories. New York: Harcourt Brace, 1993.

Chet Williamson

1948–

T. LIAM MCDONALD

CHET WILLIAMSON ROSE to prominence in the 1980s as part of the second wave of horror fiction that followed the successes of Stephen King and Peter Straub. In a diverse career that has included musical comedy, humorous stories for the *New Yorker,* and crime fiction, he is most noted for his highly literate, character-driven horror novels and short stories.

Chester Carlton Williamson was born in Lancaster, Pennsylvania, in the heart of Pennsylvania Dutch country, on June 19, 1948, the only son of Chester G. Williamson and Helen Hershey. He has never veered far from these roots. With the exception of five years studying English at Indiana University of Pennsylvania and a year teaching in Cleveland, Ohio, he has lived in or near the small Lancaster County town of Elizabethtown his entire life. An old-world landscape of farms punctuated by small towns, where Amish wagons are still a common sight, the Lancaster County region provides the setting for most of his novels.

Acting, not writing, was Williamson's first love. Though his writing first circulated during the 1970s, when he became a member of the famous Lovecraftian writing circle known as the Esoteric Order of Dagon, he had no professional pretensions. He spent much of the 1970s employed by Armstrong World Industries, acting in—and eventually writing—their trade show productions. These lavish, professional-quality musical comedies about flooring tile eventually inspired Williamson to focus seriously on writing fiction in 1979. His first sale was the short story "Offices" (*Twilight Zone Magazine,* October 1981), about a corporate employee who sees the ghostly images of his coworkers around the office after hours. It is an image that would recur most forcefully in *Ash Wednesday* (1987), his most famous novel.

For the next five years, Williamson's career gained steam with repeated appearances in *Twilight Zone,* as well as *Alfred Hitchcock's Mystery Magazine,* the *Magazine of Fantasy & Science Fiction,* and other genre venues. He also experienced considerable success as a humorist, with the oft-reprinted "Gandhi at the Bat" appearing in the *New Yorker* (June 20, 1983) and several other humor stories being published in *Playboy.*

THE TOR NOVELS

His first attempt at a novel was *Soulstorm,* written in 1981 and published by Tor Books in 1986 to critical acclaim. In *Soulstorm,* millionaire David NeVille and his wife bring three men (a mercenary, an ex-cop, and a ruthless former corporate executive) together for a month at the NeVille family's long-abandoned "haunted house" in order to prove that there is some form of life after death. The house, however, is not merely haunted: it is hell itself, and the forces that inhabit it soon drive the five people to madness and murder.

The author deliberately chose a confined environment and a limited cast of five characters to keep things simple for his freshman effort, and the approach paid off with a claustrophobic book that mixes blood-and-thunder horror with finely wrought, unconventional characters: two things that would become a Williamson trademark. *Soulstorm* explores its central theme—man coming to terms with his own mortality and belief in an afterlife—through the confines of a haunted house novel full of violence and pyrotechnics reminiscent of Richard Matheson's *Hell House*. *Ash Wednesday*, Williamson's next and most highly regarded book, would deal with the same theme in a very different way.

In *Ash Wednesday*, the residents of the small town of Merridale wake one morning to find their town populated with the motionless, glowing blue figures of all the townspeople who ever died, frozen at the moment of their deaths. These "ghosts" do not move or speak. They are, to the reader as well as to the residents of the town, a symbol of mortality. Frightening to some, invigorating to others, the ghosts remind us that one day we all shall die. Some people are fascinated and reassured, while others are disgusted and terrified. In an audacious feat of craftsmanship, Williamson has the ghosts function as passive catalysts for the action, not as an active menace. The horror lies in how people respond to them, because the ghosts do nothing. No explanation of the ghosts' presence is ever offered. In an interview with the author, Williamson himself merely called it "a manifestation of the deity. Some Act of God." In a central passage in the book, he captures the appeal of horror and supernatural fiction:

> I want to see. Show me. Take me to the funhouse, into the dark where the boogeymen jump out and go boo and scare me. And then you can hold me tight. Hold me very tight.
>
> Show me the dead men so I can feel alive.
>
> (p. 347)

In the author's preferred version of the novel, *Ash Wednesday* featured an ending depicting this phenomenon spreading from the confines of Merridale to the rest of the world. This ending was dropped in favor of a single, overly ambiguous scene showing one of the blue shapes appearing outside of the town, thus leaving a number of plot elements left unresolved. "*Ash Wednesday:* The Final Chapter" was eventually published in the fanzine *Footsteps* (1990).

As a break from supernatural fiction, Williamson pursued his other love, detective fiction, in the novel *McKain's Dilemma* (1988). As with his previous novels, *McKain's Dilemma* uses a main character dealing with his own mortality—in this case, private eye Robert McKain, who is dying from leukemia. His physical and emotional decay are interwoven with the action of the story, with a suggestion of the supernatural emerging in McKain's belief that the people who die in the course of his investigation are actually dying in his place.

This idea of a universe balancing itself is developed more fully in *Lowland Rider* (1988). In this novel, a man named Jesse Gordon disappears into the subway system of New York after his family is murdered, vowing never to surface again. He is not sure what has drawn him there, but as he rides the trains and witnesses strange events, he becomes more certain that he was brought there for a reason. A mysterious man named Enoch seems to be the locus of an evil permeating the underground world, but things are not as they seem. Enoch is actually part of "the axis," a balancing force that keeps all of the violence and evil in the world on an even level.

After this, his fourth novel, Williamson left the stable of Tor Books as his novels grew less

STRETCHING THE BOUNDS OF GENRE

The first post-Tor novel was *Dreamthorp* (1989), Williamson's most graphically violent book to date. After Laura Stark survives an attack by psychopath Gilbert Rodman, she moves to the pleasant town of Dreamthorp, Pennsylvania, to make a new life for herself. The town, unfortunately, is built on cursed Indian land. The force of the curse, channeled through Rodman's vindictive psychic power, tears the idyllic town apart. Or does it? The Indian curse became a cliché of horror fiction in the 1980s, a fact Williamson uses to maintain ambiguity. Is the curse responsible, or Rodman, or some combination of both? In some of his most arresting passages, the buildings of Dreamthorp—the very wood itself—literally come to life to destroy its inhabitants.

Reign (1990) followed shortly after *Dreamthorp* and moved Williamson even further away from conventional horror structures. *Reign* is the story of Dennis Hamilton, a character modeled after Yul Brynner. Hamilton has grown rich and famous playing the same character—the Emperor in the imaginary musical *A Private Empire*—for years. He has played this character for so long that it eventually splits from him, taking on an existence of its own. When Hamilton retires from acting to open his own theater for new American musicals, the Emperor starts appearing, and people begin dying.

In an interesting stylistic flourish, the Emperor is depicted only in scenes written in play format, complete with stage directions and dialogue cues, emphasizing the unreal, theatrical origins of his existence. Though *Reign* is shot through with occasional violence and based on a supernatural premise, the focus of the novel is more on the characters and the theatrical milieu, inspired by Williamson's years as an actor. Like *Lowland Rider,* it also uses the doppelgänger motif to explore the complexity of human personality and the oppositional—yet complementary—forces at work in the universe. It is a trope that works well for Williamson, who never offers simple characters or easy answers. His flawed characters try to balance (and, in the case of *Reign,* unify) their good and evil natures and make the most moral choices they can.

The drift away from genre conventions continued with *Second Chance* (1995), Williamson's last stand-alone novel to date. *Second Chance* pulls off the rare feat of being nostalgic and remarkably unsentimental at the same time, viewing the 1960s in all its complex facets, both good and bad. The plot springs from a reunion organized by Woody, a successful jazz musician, to recapture the sights, sounds, and smells of his youth. Woody is haunted by the loss of his love Jen, who died helping another campus radical blow up an ROTC building. In his desperation to recapture those days, the atmosphere he creates becomes so realistic that everyone at the reunion wakes up in the past, before the bombing.

Woody is given a second chance to save his girlfriend. When the friends return to the present, Jen is with them, but something has changed. The world now contains an ecoterrorist named Pan who had not existed before, and Woody and his friends fear that by changing the past they are responsible for Pan's existence. The time travel is handled subtly and effectively, providing a springboard for the plot without being its focus. Woven throughout their story is the quest to learn who Pan is and stop him before he destroys the world, ostensibly making it a suspense novel. The result is a brilliant novel of the lost dreams, changed lives, and complex moral quandaries facing a group of mature-friends.

THE LATER NOVELS

The unconventional structure used in such books as *Reign* and *Second Chance* is both a blessing and curse, highlighting one of the central problems of genre. When does a book veer far enough away from genre conventions to become something else? Williamson's work has increasingly tread a largely uncharted zone between mainstream and genre fiction, and while it has made for some superb writing, it has also left his books out in the cold. In the time since *Second Chance,* he has written three novels that have failed to find publishers because their blend of genre elements and mainstream conventions leave them in a no-man's-land in the heavily programmed world of category fiction publishing. This approach to fiction, however, is central to his style. In an interview with the author, Williamson states:

> I never write a book about "scary stuff." I always try to write a book that's about something. That's not to say that it has a moral, or that it can't be described as horror. All horror has to deal with is the emotion of fear, and you can do that in lots of ways. I guess I deal with horror because it's such a strong emotion. I don't set out to scare the reader. I think there are some writers who do, but I don't really care. If the reader finds something and says, "Oh, that book really kept me awake at night," that's fine, but that's not the purpose of my writing. My goal is to create characters who can, through their actions or inactions, make people think more deeply about their own lives. I want some little seed to be planted. Not necessarily what I want them to think, but something I'd like them to think more about.

Since *Second Chance,* Williamson has continued to write novels, short stories, and comic books. Some of these have been novelizations, such as *Hell: A Cyberpunk Thriller* (1995; based on a computer game) and *The Crow: City of Angels* (1996; the novelization of a movie). He has also contributed to several book lines. *Mordenheim* (1994) and *Murder in Cormyr* (1996) were, respectively, a horror and a mystery novel published by TSR to tie in to role-playing games, while *The Crow: Clash by Night* (1998) was based on *The Crow* movies and comic books.

In 1998 and 1999, Williamson published a series called *The Searchers,* creating a paranormal investigation team akin to the *X-Files.* The series lasted for three books and included the titles *City of Iron, Empire of Dust,* and *Siege of Stone.* They are all finely written supernatural novels, but the focus is more on investigation and plot elements than is the case with Williamson's more character-driven work. The "Searchers" in question are covert CIA operatives Tony Luciano, Joseph Stein, and Laika Harris, who work for a shadowy figure investigating supernatural happenings. An overarching plot concerns the discovery, release, identity, and ultimate fate of "The Prisoner," a mysterious figure who may or may not be divine. These are remarkably brisk, carefully plotted, exceptionally well written, and entertaining genre fiction, but they do not have the resonance and depth of Williamson's non-series work.

Though Williamson's writing fell off in the 1990s with the decline of horror publishing, he remains one of the bright lights of his generation of supernatural fiction writers. He is kept in the public eye largely by his distinct short stories, such as the notorious "'Yore Skin's Jes's Soft 'n Purty,' He Said. (Page 243)" (in *Razored Saddles,* 1989), a gruesomely hilarious story about delusional, unrequited love in the old West; and the elegant cannibalism tale "Extracts from the Records of the New Zodiac and the Diaries of Henry Watson Fairfax" (in *999,* 1999).

Williamson's work is marked by an emotional maturity that is rare in modern genre fiction. *Soulstorm* could easily have been merely another haunted house novel and *Lowland Rider* another subway horror novel but for their use of finely shaded characters dealing in a mature way with weighty questions of life, death, God, the afterlife, self-sacrifice, and the balancing forces of the universe. A thematic consistency runs through his novels as he explores the many ways in which people contemplate and cope with death. Few works of modern horror are as stylistically daring and intellectually and emotionally jolting on the subject of death as *Ash Wednesday*, a moody meditation on mortality. An unusual aspect of Williamson's work is the primacy placed on people over plot. His plot elements are more important in the way they create unique situations for his characters to evolve and confront difficult questions than as an engine for narrative. While Williamson is certainly capable of creating rollicking, plot-driven entertainment (such as *The Searchers*), his work is most powerful when it uses supernatural situations to examine the hidden depths and nuances of characters.

Selected Bibliography

WORKS OF CHET WILLIAMSON

Soulstorm. New York: Tor, 1986.

Ash Wednesday. New York: Tor, 1987. (Horror Writers of America Bram Stoker Award Nominee, 1988.)

Lowland Rider. New York: Tor, 1988.

McKain's Dilemma. New York: Tor, 1988.

Dreamthorp. Arlington Heights, Ill.: Dark Harvest, 1989.

The House of Fear: A Study in Comparative Religions. Roundtop, N.Y.: Footsteps Press, 1989. (Chapbook of a novella.)

"'Yore Skin's Jes's Soft 'n Purty,' He Said. (Page 243)." In *Razored Saddles.* Edited by Joe R. Lansdale and Pat LoBrutto. Arlington Heights, Ill.: Dark Harvest, 1989.

Reign. Arlington Heights, Ill.: Dark Harvest, 1990. (Horror Writers of America Bram Stoker Award Nominee, 1990.)

Aliens: Music of the Spears. Milwaukee, Wisc.: Dark Horse Comics, 1994. (A four-issue graphic novel miniseries.)

Mordenheim. Lake Geneva, Wisc.: TSR, 1994.

Hell: A Cyberpunk Thriller. Roseville, Calif.: Prima, 1995.

Second Chance. Baltimore: CD Publications, 1995.

Cross. Milwaukee, Wisc.: Dark Horse Comics, 1995–1996. (Six-part graphic novel miniseries adaptation of a novel by Andrew Vachss and Jim Colbert.)

Murder in Cormyr. Lake Geneva, Wisc.: TSR, 1996.

The Crow: City of Angels. New York: Berkley Books, 1996.

The Crow: Clash by Night. New York: HarperPrism, 1998.

The Searchers # 1: City of Iron. New York: Avon, 1998.

The Searchers # 2: Empire of Dust. New York: Avon, 1998.

"Extracts from the Records of the New Zodiac and the Diaries of Henry Watson Fairfax." In *999.* Edited by Al Sarrantonio. New York: Avon, 1999.

The Searchers # 3: Siege of Stone. New York: Avon, 1999.

Pennsylvania Dutch Night before Christmas. Gretna, La.: Pelican Publishing, 2000. (Children's book.)

Uniting Work and Spirit: A Centennial History of Elizabethtown College. Elizabethtown, Pa.: Elizabethtown College Press, 2001.

The Searchers # 3: Siege of Stone. New York: Avon, 1999.

F. Paul Wilson

1946–

JUSTIN GUSTAINIS

F. PAUL WILSON earned a medical degree years before he began publishing novel-length fiction. But, unlike other physicians-turned-authors (such as Robin Cook and Michael Crichton), Wilson has not restricted his writing to medical thrillers or books with "hard science" backgrounds. He has produced such novels, to be sure, but has also penned memorable tales of fantasy, suspense, and pure horror.

Wilson, the son of Francis and Mary (Sullivan) Wilson, was born on May 17, 1946, in Jersey City, New Jersey, where he also grew up. He graduated from Georgetown University in 1968 and then went on to study at medical school, during which time he also wrote and published his first short stories. In 1969 he married educator Mary Murphy, with whom he had two daughters, Jennifer and Meggan. Wilson returned to New Jersey in 1974 and has been practicing medicine there since, although he has cut back his medical practice in recent years to devote more time to writing.

Wilson's first three novels, *Healer* (1976), *Wheels within Wheels* (1978), and *An Enemy of the State* (1980), comprise the "LaNague Foundation" trilogy, although Wilson claims he had no intent of composing a story cycle when he wrote the original books. It was only later that he discerned the connection between the three stories. These science fiction classics have been republished, along with several related short stories, in a single volume, *The LaNague Chronicles* (1992). The series, which is set in the distant future, chronicles the movement begun by the charismatic, mystical Peter LaNague in a planetary system far from earth. The Foundation organizes the nonviolent overthrow of an oppressive interplanetary government, and then must withstand a series of challenges to its own benevolent rule, both from within the home solar system and from outside it. Peter LaNague fits squarely within the tradition of the classic existential hero, and critics believe that the writings of French existentialist Albert Camus influenced Wilson's development of the character.

After the last book in the LaNague Foundation sequence, Wilson shifted his perspective from science fiction to dark fantasy and horror—a decision he admits was influenced by the tremendous success that Stephen King was beginning to enjoy in those genres. The "Adversary Cycle," a series of five books that retains a strong cult following even today, chronicles an age-old struggle between ancient forces of good and evil, with Earth as their battleground. The first volume is *The Keep*

(1981), set during World War II. A contingent of German soldiers is sent to occupy an old castle in the Carpathian Mountains—then, one by one, they start dying. What looks at first like a vampire-versus-Nazis tale (which had already been done decades earlier, in Manly Wade Wellman's well-known story "The Devil Is Not Mocked") is revealed to involve a far more powerful danger to humankind.

In *The Tomb* (1984), the old evil manifests itself in the form of the Rakoshi, a breed of savage monsters that can sometimes be controlled and directed by knowledgeable humans (just as demons, according to Christian legend, can be summoned and exploited by wizards adept in the lore of the occult). To combat this menace, Wilson introduces the character Repairman Jack, a kind of urban mercenary. Jack later reappeared as the central figure in another Wilson series, and as such will be discussed in detail below.

The Touch (1986) concerns a doctor who mysteriously develops the ability to heal seriously ill people simply by laying his hands on them. In a development reminiscent of the 1960s television series *The Immortal*, the young physician becomes the quarry of a rich and powerful villain who wants the healing power available to him alone. *Reborn* (1990) brings back the creature that represented the forces of evil in *The Keep*. Its protagonist, Jim Hanley, was raised as an orphan only to learn in adulthood that his parents are still alive. His search for them reveals (in a prefiguring of the television series *The X-Files*) that he is the product of a sinister Nazi cloning program conducted during World War II. In short, he is not quite human. In *Reprisal* (1991), Jim Hanley is dead but his son manifests a remarkable mental capacity, even from a very young age. He is also a tool of the forces of evil. The "Adversary Cycle" comes to an end with *Nightworld* (1992), which also features the reappearance of Repairman Jack. The battle between good and evil has gone beyond the individual level to assume apocalyptic proportions. The forces of darkness are ultimately defeated, but the victors pay a high price indeed.

Wilson featured his hero Repairman Jack in several short stories published during the 1990s, but it was not until *Legacies* (1998) that the character returned as the central figure in a novel. He has been the focus of much of Wilson's writing since then. Reflecting his creator's admitted libertarian sympathies, Jack is the ultimate outsider, spurning all official connection to society and the state. He has no driver's license, Social Security number, credit cards, or bank account—at least, not in his real name. He has thus acquired the freedom to move and act as he wishes, without interference or restraint from any of the powers that be.

But Jack is not a criminal; indeed, he has a highly developed moral code that allows him to do harm only to those who prey upon the weak and innocent. He calls himself the Repairman because he is willing to fix people's problems, for a price. He claims (in *The Tomb*) to have been doing so since he was eleven years old. Wilson acknowledges that Jack bears some resemblance to John D. MacDonald's character Travis McGee, the Florida-based "salvage expert" who would retrieve stolen goods in return for half their value. Some critics have also suggested that Jack has similarities to Andrew Vachss's protagonist, the streetwise vigilante known only as Burke. But the author says that the Repairman Jack stories were most closely inspired by the Fu Manchu novels of Sax Rohmer, written during the first half of the twentieth century. Repairman Jack, according to Wilson, is a literary cousin to Nayland Smith, the intrepid British adventurer who, time and again, frustrates Fu Manchu's various evil schemes for world domination.

Because of the nature of the cases he finds himself involved in, Jack also fits the mold of the occult detective—an expert who regularly investigates or contends with the supernatural. This archetype extends back to J. Sheridan LeFanu's Dr. Hesselius, continues through such characters as Algernon Blackwood's John Silence and Seabury Quinn's Jules de Grandin, and finds modern expression in literary creations like Laurell K. Hamilton's Anita Blake, Charles Grant's Black Oak investigators, and Jim Butcher's Harry Dresden, among others. However, Repairman Jack is not purely an occult detective, because some of his escapades involve creatures from other planets or dimensions, rather than ghosts or demons. Like agents Mulder and Scully of *The X-Files,* Jack deals with the paranormal, whether its source is the spirit world or another planet.

In *Legacies* (1998), Jack comes to the aid of a woman under immense pressure from her brother to sell him her half-interest in their late father's house. The father, it turns out, had invented a revolutionary new energy source and left its secret hidden in the house. The brother represents sinister foreign interests who will do anything to obtain this potentially world-changing technology.

Conspiracies (2000) allows Wilson to make sport of those obsessed individuals who see sinister plots under every rock and behind every bush. However, while seeking a missing woman in the midst of a convention full of such loonies, Jack discovers that one of the conspiracy theories is true, after all. This knowledge leads him into a near-fatal battle with supernatural evil.

The next Repairman Jack novel, *All the Rage* (2000), seems at first to be pure science fiction. A new drug, with the street name Berzerk, offers its users euphoria, confidence, and heightened mental awareness. But for some, the good times turn bad as the drug also induces intense anger, often resulting in violence—even murder. Drawn into the investigation of the drug, Jack discovers that Berzerk is distilled from the blood of a captive Rakoshi, a monster of the kind he had battled in *The Tomb.* Jack finally locates the facility where the creature is being held—only to learn that it has just escaped.

In *Hosts* (2001), Wilson introduces a member of the family that Jack has shunned his whole adult life. A woman named Kate shows up in New York, seeking the services of the man known to her only as Repairman Jack. She eventually finds him, and learns that he is her long-estranged sister. Jack agrees to help Kate find her lesbian lover, who has fallen into the clutches of a cult. He learns that all the cult members, including Kate's lover, are infected with a virus unlike any found in this world. The virus turns out to have its origin in the Adversary, the evil cosmic force that Wilson had introduced in earlier books. And it is the cult's goal to infect all of humankind.

The Haunted Air (2002) finds Jack in a spooky old mansion, with a couple of fraudulent psychics for company. His companions may be fakes, but the ghosts, it turns out, are all too real. An earthquake releases an enraged spirit from beneath the house, but the danger it poses soon seems minor once Jack understands the real nature of the menace with which he is faced.

Wilson has indicated that he plans to continue the adventures of Repairman Jack, but has speculated that the increased domestic security measures in the U.S. following the terrorist attacks of September 11, 2001, will make it even harder for a man like Jack to retain his treasured anonymity.

Wilson also has two other series in progress. The novellas that make up the "Sims" series constitute straight science fiction, focusing on projected developments in genetic manipulation. In the near future, mega-conglomerate SimGen is able to alter the genes of chimpanzees to make them bigger, somewhat smarter, and able to speak. This "product" is sold to companies all over the world, and everyone involved is very careful never to use the phrase "slave labor." *Sims, Book One: La Causa* (2001) introduces lawyer Patrick Sullivan, who is approached by a group of Sims and asked to help them end their exploitation by forming a union. In *Sims Book 2: The Portero Method* (2001), the SimGen Corporation fights back against Patrick Sullivan, using both legal and extralegal methods.

But then Sullivan meets Romy Cadman, a mysterious woman who soon becomes a powerful ally in his struggle to establish legal rights for Sims. Wilson has said that the saga will run for at least five more novella-length installments.

Wilson's other current series has not been given a title, so it will be referred to here as the "Vampire Sequence." It consists so far of three novellas: *Midnight Mass,* published as a chapbook in 1990; "The Lord's Work," written for the 1992 anthology *Dracula: Prince of Darkness* (edited by Martin H. Greenberg); and "Good Friday," which appeared in Al Sarrantonio's 1999 collection *999.* The series is based on the premise that vampires have taken over the world, leaving the few surviving humans to hide and scavenge and fight back as best they can. For this notion Wilson acknowledges his debt to Richard Matheson's classic novel *I Am Legend* (1954). The Vampire Sequence is also more or less contemporaneous with several other works by authors exploring a similar theme: the "shared-world" anthology *Under the Fang* (1991), conceived and edited by Robert R. McCammon, and Kim Newman's "Anno Dracula" series, which began with the novel of that name in 1992.

The three installments of the Vampire Sequence were written out of chronological order, but follow a logical progression when read in reverse order of publication. In "Good Friday," the vampires arrive in America, having already established dominion over Europe. Sister Carole and Sister Bernadette, in their New Jersey convent, worry over the stories and rumors they have heard. Then night comes, and the stories prove true. Sister Bernadette falls victim to the vampires, but sister Carole escapes, vowing to destroy the creatures that have killed her friend. "The Lord's Work" shows Sister Carole a few weeks later. Although mentally unhinged, she has made herself a surprisingly effective guerrilla fighter—against both vampires and the humans who collaborate with them. In *Midnight Mass,* the humans win their first important victory against the fanged oppressors.

Led by a priest and his Jewish friend, a group of them slay an important vampire commander and take back possession of a parish church—for one night, at least.

Wilson's work also includes a number of "stand-alone" books. Some are medical suspense stories, like *The Select* (1994), *Implant* (1995), *Deep as the Marrow* (1997), and *Mirage* (1998, written with Michael Costello); others, such as *The Tery* (1979) and *Dydeetown World* (1989), may be considered science fiction, while a few, like *Black Wind* (1988) and *Sibs* (1991), are unclassifiable, except as thrillers.

Wilson's short fiction runs the same gamut as his longer works: from science fiction and fantasy to medical thrillers, horror, and a few adventures of Repairman Jack (a character who transcends the genres). He won the 2000 Stoker Award from the Horror Writers Association for his 1999 story, "Aftershock."

Several of Wilson's short stories connect with his longer works in interesting ways. Three pieces in *Soft* (1989)—"Ratman," "Lipidleggin," and "To Fill the Sea and Air"—take place within the world of the LaNague Chronicles. Further, one story from *Soft* ("Dat-Tay-Vao"), as well as three stories ("Feelings," "Tenants," and "Faces") published in Wilson's collection *The Barrens and Others* (1998), are set in the fictional village of Monroe, which is also where most of the novel *Reborn* takes place. Using a fictional locale as a recurring backdrop for stories and novels is a venerable motif in supernatural fiction, as can be seen with H. P. Lovecraft's Akham, Massachusetts, Charles Grant's Oxrun Station, and Stephen King's Castle Rock, Maine.

The central theme of Wilson's work is the immense value of personal freedom. One of his early books, *Wheels within Wheels,* won the Prometheus Award, given annually by the Libertarian Futurist Society for the best science fiction addressing freedom as an issue. Repairman Jack is perhaps the ultimate libertarian, spurning any connection with the institutions that are designed to regulate, or at least monitor, human behavior. This intense concern for personal liberty comes through in Wilson's other works, as well. His medical thrillers usually feature one or two individual doctors confronting injustices perpetuated by a medical institution, usually upon powerless or unsuspecting patients. This scenario reflects Wilson's real-life view of the medical bureaucracy. In interviews, he has criticized several aspects of modern medicine, including health maintenance organizations (HMOs) and managed care, a cost-saving philosophy espoused by health insurance companies. He argues that all institutions, including those in the medical field, eventually become focused on their own perpetuation and power, to the detriment of those individuals whom the institutions are supposed to serve.

Wilson's books and stories are not didactic, and are never preachy. Nonetheless, he manages to communicate his core values clearly—while at the same time providing immense entertainment for his readers. He alternates between genres, with the goal of keeping his writing fresh and his characters compelling. Wilson's many fans offer clear testament that this goal has been achieved.

Selected Bibliography

THE WORKS OF F. PAUL WILSON

NOVELS AND SHORT STORIES

Healer. Garden City, N.Y.: Doubleday, 1976.

Wheels within Wheels: A Novel of the LaNague Federation. Garden City, N.Y.: Doubleday, 1978.

An Enemy of the State. Garden City, N.Y.: Doubleday, 1980.

The Keep. Garden City, N.Y.: Doubleday, 1981.

The Tomb. Binghamton, N.Y.: Whispers, 1984.

The Touch. New York: Putnam, 1986.

Black Wind. New York: Tor, 1988.

Soft and Others: Sixteen Stories of Wonder and Dread. New York: Tor, 1989. (Contains an "Author's Note," plus "The Cleaning machine," "Ratman," "Lipidleggin'," "To Fill the Sea and Air," "Green Winter," "Be Fruitful and Multiply," "Soft," "The Last 'One Mo' Once Golden Oldies Revival," "The Years the Music Died," "Dat-Tay-Vao," "Doc Johnson," "Buckets," "Traps," "Muscles," "Mánage a Trois," and "Cuts").

Dydeetown World. New York: Baen, 1989.

The Tery. New York: Baen, 1989.

Midnight Mass. Eugene, Oreg.: Pulphouse/Axolotl, 1990.

Pelts, Footsteps. New York: Round Top, 1990.

Reborn. Arlington Heights, Ill.: Dark Harvest, 1990.

Buckets. Eugene, Oreg.: Pulphouse, 1991.

Sibs. Arlington Heights, Ill.: Dark Harvest, 1991.

Reprisal. Arlington Heights, Ill.: Dark Harvest, 1991.

Nightworld. Arlington Heights, Ill.: Dark Harvest, 1992.

The Barrens. Newark, N.J.: Wildside Press, 1992.

The LaNague Chronicles. New York: Baen, 1992. (Includes *Healer, Wheels within Wheels,* and *An Enemy of the State.*)

The Select. New York: Morrow, 1994.

Implant. New York: Forge, 1995.

Mirage. New York: Warner, 1996. (With Matthew J. Costello.)

Deep As the Marrow. New York: Forge, 1997.

Nightkill. New York: Forge, 1997. (With Steve Lyon.)

Legacies. New York: Forge, 1998.

Masque. New York: Warner, 1998. (With Matthew J. Costello.)

The Barrens and Others. New York: Forge, 1998. (Contains "Feelings," "Tenants," "Faces," "A Day in the Life," "The Tenth Toe," "Slasher," "The Barrens," "Definitive Therapy," "Topsy," "Rockabilly," "Bob Dylan, Troy Johnson, and the Speed Queen," "Pelts," a stage adaptation of "Pelts," and the teleplay "Glim-Glim." The author provides an introduction for each story and also includes mini-essays on his writing career in several places throughout the book.)

All the Rage: A Repairman Jack Novel. New York: Forge, 2000.

Conspiracies: A Repairman Jack Novel. New York: Forge, 2000.

Hosts: A Repairman Jack Novel. New York: Forge, 2001.

The Haunted Air: A Repairman Jack Novel. New York: Forge, 2002.

OTHER WORKS

"Glim-Glim." Teleplay for the syndicated program *Monsters.* Laurel-TV, 1989.

(Editor and contributor.) *Freak Show.* New York: Pocket Books, 1992.

(Editor.) *Diagnosis: Terminal: An Anthology of Medical Terror.* New York: Forge, 1996.

BIBLIOGRAPHIES

Munster, Bill, "The Complete Bibliography of F. Paul Wilson," *Footsteps,* November 1987, pp. 15–18.

"F. Paul Wilson: Bibliography," *Weird Tales,* Winter 1992–1993, pp. 57–60.

CRITICAL AND BIOGRAPHICAL STUDIES

Gilbert, John. "Fiction File: 17: F. Paul Wilson." *Fear!,* October 1990, p. 52.

McDonald, T. Liam. "Profiles in Terror: F. Paul Wilson: The Metaphysics of Horror." *Cemetery Dance,* Fall 1990, pp. 14–20.

INTERVIEWS

Kilpatrick, Nancy. "A Graveside Chat with F. Paul Wilson." *Deathrealm,* Summer 1996, pp. 26–30.

Munster, Bill. "An Interview with F. Paul Wilson." *Footsteps,* November 1987, pp. 6–14.

Schweitzer, Darrell. "*Weird Tales* Talks with F. Paul Wilson." *Weird Tales,* Winter 1992–1993, pp. 49–55.

Wagner, Henry W. "A Conversation with F. Paul Wilson." *Cemetery Dance,* no. 32, 1999, pp. 55–60.

F. PAUL WILSON

FILMS BASED ON THE WORKS OF F. PAUL WILSON

The Keep. Screenplay by Michael Mann. Directed by Michael Mann. Paramount, 1983. (Wilson does not regard this film as a faithful adaptation of his novel.)

Midnight Mass. Screenplay by Tony Mandile. Directed by Tony Mandile. Banshee Films, 2002. (A low-budget, independent production based on Wilson's novella of the same name.)

Gene Wolfe
1931–

ROBERT BORSKI

GENE RODMAN WOLFE was born in Brooklyn, New York, on May 7, 1931, the only child of Emerson Leroy Wolfe and Mary Olivia Ayers Wolfe. Roy Wolfe was employed in various enterprises, and the Wolfes moved often during the 1930s, living alternately in New Jersey; Peoria, Illinois; Massachusetts; Ohio; Des Moines, Iowa; and Dallas and finally Houston, Texas. Wolfe, as a child, contracted polio, although there were no lasting deleterious effects. As perhaps befits a writer of the fantastic, he attended an elementary school named after Edgar Allan Poe. In high school, Wolfe received an appointment to West Point, but the appointment was not honored by the newly elected U.S. senator from Texas, Lyndon Johnson.

In 1949 Wolfe entered Texas A & M University, but dropped out in his junior year, losing his student deferment. Drafted, Wolfe was sent to Korea, where he served in the Seventh Infantry Division and earned the Combat Infantry Award. The G.I. Bill allowed Wolfe to return to school and he completed his degree requirements for a B.S. in mechanical engineering at the University of Houston in 1956. That same year, he converted to Catholicism (he was raised Presbyterian) and married Rosemary Dietsch, who had been a childhood playmate of Wolfe's in Illinois; they had four children, two boys and two girls.

From 1956 to 1972 Wolfe worked as a project engineer for Proctor and Gamble in Cincinnati, where he helped design the machine that makes Pringles potato chips. In 1972 Wolfe joined the staff of *Plant Engineering* magazine, based in Barrington, Illinois, remaining there as a senior editor until 1984, when he left the magazine in order to write full-time. Wolfe had previously contributed to his college humor magazine, and first attempted to write professionally in 1956. Nine years later, he sold his first short story, "The Dead Man," to *Sir*. By 2002 he had written twenty-one novels and over 250 short stories, and his work had received three World Fantasy Awards, two Nebula Awards, the Rhysling Award, the British Science Fiction Association Award, the Chicago Foundation for Literature Award, the John W. Campbell Memorial Award, and the French Prix Apollo.

Although he has written works that are primarily science fiction, fantasy, and horror, much of Wolfe's work is infused with elements of all three and can therefore be difficult to categorize. The Book of the New Sun, for example—a quartet of novels that chronicles the rise of the ambiguous hero Severian—is, despite being replete with giants, witches, undines, sea monsters, sorcerers, and talismanic weapons, nominally science fiction and hence outside the purview of this discussion, as are Wolfe's other two solar series, the four-volume Book of the Long Sun and the three-volume Book of the Short Sun.

Regardless of genre, however, the typical Wolfe work is deftly executed, being highly readable, employing familiar tropes and conventions (although quite often with a twist), and yet within this genre-ized framework is intellectually rigorous, drawing upon a wide literary tradition that includes such forebears as Marcel Proust, Rudyard Kipling, G. K. Chesterton, Jorge Luis Borges, Charles Dickens, Lewis Carroll, and Robert Graves. It is only when the reader attempts to comprehend Wolfe on a non-superficial level that difficulty ensues, Wolfe being notoriously complex and intricate, and the master of a labyrinthine style requiring the reader to attend to every word. Moreover, the overall narrative is often unreliable or incomplete, filled with lacunae, anachronistic sequencing, applied misdirection, and formidable symbolism. The diligent reader, therefore, does not so much tread his or her way through Wolfe, but retraces, paying strict attention to every detail along the way, salient as well as inconsequential (perhaps even more so the latter), and hopes that he or she will not be led astray or inveigled by Wolfe's literary pyrotechnics. In many respects his tendency toward inexplicitness makes Wolfe a mystery writer (indeed, Wolfe's 1990 juvenile novel, *Pandora by Holly Hollander*, although not fantastic, is explicitly a mystery), and his work often features embedded puzzles that must be solved—especially since the author steadfastly refuses to endorse outside solutions by his readers. Thus Wolfe's artistic conceit seems to be this: All life is ambiguous, and nothing is ever as neat and tidy as we would like it to be.

And yet far from being a mere monger of despair or fringe nihilist, Wolfe is an ardent Catholic, and his faith informs much of his work, though it is often to a degree so subtle that the nonsensitive reader will miss it. However, while there is a moral dimension to his writing, Wolfe clearly understands that evil triumphs over good at least as often as the other way around. No stodgy moralist, Wolfe also has a prankish sense of humor, perhaps best evidenced in his frequent tendency to insert into his work either himself—in the way that the film director Alfred Hitchcock made cameo appearances in his films—or a lupine proxy—either an actual wolf or its lycanthropic cousin. For example, the name of the narrator of Wolfe's second novel, *The Fifth Head of Cerberus*, can be worked out to be "Gene Wolfe" through a variety of clues, while the major character of one of his series is a werewolf.

Because of the complexity of Wolfe's fiction, it is important to discuss how best to approach him as readers, since a number of stratagems may be employed to wrest the most meaning from his work. The first of these is onomastics. Names, in Wolfe's stories and novels, mean something, either etymologically or through broader association with any number of religious or mythic belief systems, the arts, sciences, history, popular culture, and so on. Wolfe is also adept at picking names that are multivalent, having a number of contexts, all of which must be teased out and followed up on to understand a particular work. A potent example here is the character Robert Peacock from Wolfe's 1975 novel *Peace*. Peacock is one of the suitors of Olivia Weer, the maiden aunt of the book's protagonist, Den Weer. But peacocks are not only birds, they also have a color named after them (peacock blue), as well as an intermediate stage in the alchemical transformation of base material to gold; and in medieval folklore were believed to be slayers of snakes. Each of these aspects plays an important role in the novel's overall scheme, contributing not only to our understanding of several characters' motivation and actions, but also helping to solve one of *Peace*'s smaller mysteries.

Another technique used by Wolfe is conflation; he will take a number of story elements from well-known works by other authors and combine them within his own fiction. These elements then not only resonate within Wolfe's piece as homages to the original writers, but shade and inform plot points and subtext therein. Perhaps the best example of this can be found in Wolfe's "Houston, 1943" (collected in the 1988 anthology *Tropical Chills*, edited by Tim Sullivan), one of his finer, more horrific, and most autobiographical novellas. In it the life force of a sleeping boy named Roddie is summoned by two Haitian voodoo practitioners, who are seeking the location of sunken treasure. (Onomastically, "Roddie" is a combination of Rodman, Gene Wolfe's middle name, and Roderick Usher, the protagonist of Edgar Allan Poe's "The Fall of the House of Usher.") Roddie, however, sees everything through the sensibility of a young boy; having no understanding about what is going on (to say nothing of the practice of voodoo), he thinks he is having a nightmare. Thus the first two apparitions initially sent to retrieve him—formerly a pair of seamen who have been hung in chains and tarred—he identifies as Jim Hawkins from Robert Louis Stevenson's *Treasure Island* and *Peter Pan's* Captain Hook. (Earlier, it is the planting of a mummified glory hand—which is supposed to keep the inhabitants in a deep sleep while a household is plundered—under Roddie's house that allows his *ti bon ange*, or soul, to be captured.) They, in turn, will reveal to Doc and Sheba, the voodoo practitioners, where the sunken treasure is if Roddie will agree to give them both a proper Christian burial.

In the tropical heat wave that frames the story, various bizarre events take place, and soon everyone winds up at a wilderness shack where Roddie encounters a one-eyed cat he identifies as Pluto, from Poe's "The Black Cat." Then later, during the fiery climax, the voodoo serpent god Damballah himself appears. Roddie, however, sees him in the only relevant context he has—as the crocodile from *Peter Pan*, complete with ticking clock, who has come to finish off his repast of Captain Hook. The final image is one of consummate terror: Roddy, reunited with his *corps cadavre* (his zombie twin, in the same way that the cataleptic Madeline Usher is Roderick's), is being silently rowed by the latter in a boat (think Charon, who in Greek mythology ferries the souls of the dead over the Styx), accompanied by Pluto, "through an endless dark to which there came no day"—otherwise known as hell. Thus, by incorporating characters and situations from other writers, Wolfe is able to tell a powerful tale from a child's unique point of view, leaving the background details to be worked out by his readers. (The word "voodoo" itself is never mentioned, and we must infer the narrative context from, among other things, further onomastics, an observed ritual, complete with sacrificed black chicken, and such terms as "peto man.")

This limited, filtered perspective is common in Wolfe's fiction, especially where children are the viewpoint characters. (And perhaps because Wolfe himself was an only child, such stories form a substantial part of his oeuvre.) We also expect and accept narrative restrictions in such cases. Less so, however, may be the case when adults are involved, and it is here that Wolfe often plays our expectations against us. Quite simply put: when an adult in any given work by Wolfe makes a statement of either certitude or supposition, it is almost certainly false, either by design, ellipsis, or miscalculation. Wolfe, we note again, is a master of subterfuge, and he delights in intentionally misleading his readers.

Peace, Wolfe's third, but first supernatural, novel, has the distinction of being not only perhaps his best work, but the finest supernatural novel of the latter half of the twentieth century. In it, the ghost of Alden Dennis ("Den") Weer (liberated some years after his death by the falling of an elm tree planted on his grave) recalls his life and times in the small town of Cassionsville, in the midwestern United States. Wolfe, in part, uses the structure of a memory palace, a mnemonic device where one associates items to be remembered within a familiar building, to revisit important events in

Weer's earthly transit, and thus freed of the constraints of time and sequence is able to jump about chronologically; but mostly the novel follows Weer's life from childhood to old age.

As a young boy, Den Weer is responsible for the accidental death of a playmate, Bobby Black; we are not told this directly, of course—hence Weer's guilt is problematical—but rather characteristically must piece together the details from sparse clues (Den pushing Black down a stairs during horseplay, Bobby later dying from his injuries). Apparently scandalized by their son's role in the tragedy, Weer's parents take off for a European vacation that lasts years, and Den goes to live with his father's sister, Olivia. Olivia—a feminist free spirit whose interests include not only the sciences, but pottery, especially if it has anything to do with China—has a number of male suitors, but eventually marries a pharmacist named Julius Smart. Smart soon devises an instant orange-flavored drink that can be made from potatoes, and the production of it becomes a major industry for Cassionsville. Den will work in Smart's factory his entire adult life, first as an ordinary laborer (during which he may be responsible for another death—that of a coworker, during a prank), then later when his uncle dies, as president. Before, during, and along the way, we meet various of his inamorata; his high school sweetheart, Maggie Lorn; a treasure-seeking librarian, Lois Arbuthnot; and a promiscuous teenager, Sherry Gold, who may become pregnant by him; as well as Sherry's father, Louis, who, while claiming to be a finder of rare books—among them the *Necronomicon* from H. P. Lovecraft's Cthulhu mythos—actually forges them.

Finally, in his sixties, Weer reaches his terminus after a second cardiovascular event. (The first, a stroke, has left him limping—a common attribute of Wolfean characters, stemming from the author's childhood bout with polio.) Throughout the course of the book, we are also treated to a number of interpolated tales; pastiches really. Among these, there is an Irish folktale about a banshee, something that might have come from the *Thousand and One Nights,* and a Damon Runyonish version of Cinderella—although oddly enough, few of these tales are ever concluded. Each, in turn, must be further evaluated for typological relevance and how events in them relate to the larger mainframe of *Peace.* Take, for example, the bedtime fairy tale read by Den, "The Princess and Her Four Suitors." It is about how a princess on an isolated island is wooed by four men representing air, water, earth, and fire. We are told beforehand by a wizard's prophecy, however, that "fire will win her." And so as we watch real-life equivalent Olivia Weer entertain her bevy of admirers, we are not surprised that she passes on Professor Robert Peacock (air), merchant Stewart Blaine (water), and banker James Macafee (earth), and marries modern-day alchemist Julius Smart (fire). Given also that Smart, despite being minimally present, is called the central character of the novel and that his chapter, "The Alchemist," is the book's longest, it seems almost certain that Wolfe wants us to explore the broader significance of alchemy as a thematic element (and it is substantial, if beyond the scope of this essay to discuss). But perhaps more important still is the central question raised by Den Weer's review of his life; that is, will he now find the repose suggested by the title and thus be able to end his ghostly exile?

Any number of interpretations are possible; but if one accepts a purgatorial model for *Peace,* the fact that Weer refuses to acknowledge his responsibility for Bobby Black's death, or his roles in either the factory prank that results in another death or Sherry Gold's pregnancy, leads one to believe that the answer is no. We can also heed the unfinished nature of the inserted supernatural tales; as Den himself is a ghost, his story too is not meant to conclude. And lastly there is both an onomastics clue—*weer* in Dutch means "to begin again"—and the novel's final line, which suggests that, like the soldier in the Chinese pillow tale, Den will be forced to undergo another cycle of "existence"—at least until he somehow redeems himself. But regardless of whichever interpretation the reader favors, what makes *Peace* extraordinary is Wolfe's loving and lyrical evocation of an America gone by—from its houses and cars to the ambience of small-town ways and picnic countrysides to the artifacts of childhood, especially a beloved scout knife. *Peace* may be filled with ghosts, but what haunts Alden Dennis Weer (and ultimately the reader) is not so much his remembrance of things lost, but their bittersweet retrievability.

Memory and how it affects us is perhaps Wolfe's grandest and most frequent concern. Owing to a head wound he received in battle, Latro, the narrator of a story told in two volumes, *Soldier of the Mist* (1986) and *Soldier of Arete* (1989), has little memory at all, losing his retention of the day's events each night as he sleeps. Hence Latro must constantly strive to recall not only where he is or his companions' names, but even simple matters of identity, such as who he is. "Latro" itself is actually a *nom de convenience,* meaning, as Wolfe tells us in the foreword to *Mist,* "brigand, guerilla, hired man, bodyguard or pawn," and Latro, a mercenary in the Persian army of King Xerxes, has in all likelihood heard his fellow soldiers describe him by the term.

Wolfe allows us to share in his protagonist's amnesiac confusion by detailing his struggles in the form of a diary, which Latro must update and review on a regular basis. This presents interesting reading in several respects; whenever Latro "freshly" describes someone we know well, such as Io, the pubescent slave girl accompanying him through much of the series, we experience what the French might call *déjà lu;* but when Latro fails to fill in the blanks between entries, since he has no remembrance of what needs further amplification or closure, we must somehow attempt to forge our own continuity. (The reader paying close attention will find that a relevant aside or detail is often dropped by a Wolfe character later in the narrative). Latro also literally translates the place names of the various towns and cities he visits, creating another layer of estrangement; hence, Athens is "Thought," Corinth is "Tower Hill," and Sparta is "Rope," although the latter is a mistranslation on his part.

Yet despite Latro's various faults as both scribe and practitioner of mnemonics, he does have one gift none of his fellows have, in that he can see and converse with the gods and goddesses of his time. Indeed, because he transgressed on Demeter's temple during the Battle of Marathon, Latro has been cursed with "the wolf's tooth"—almost certainly lycanthropy, or the ability to assume the form of a wolf (*latro* also means "I bark" in Latin, something Wolfe scrupulously avoids telling us)—and thus the stage is set for the series, as Latro attempts to recover his memories (we eventually learn that his real name is Lucius and that he hails from Latium), but must contend with not only the Great Mother and the forces allied against her, but a sex-changing sorcerer, a fellow werewolf, centaurs, various paramours of either human or mythic origin, and even a few historical personages, most notably Pindar the poet. Unfortunately, after two books, Wolfe abandoned the series, although there are some indications that he may return to finish Latro's story. Still, for the ancient world that it accurately portrays, and the challenge Wolfe has given himself by featuring a first-person amnesiac narrator, the Soldier books are well worth reading.

As Greek mythology is integral to the Latro books, Celtic mythology, with a special emphasis on Arthurian legend, drives the plot of Wolfe's *Castleview* (1990), perhaps the least well understood of the author's novels. The story, however, is relatively straightforward. Most of the book's events take place on a single day, Samhain (our November 1), the Celtic equivalent of New Year's; signally, Samhain marks not only the beginning of winter, but according to tradition is also the one day on which the borders between this world and the Otherworld are most permeable, allowing for denizens of each to cross over into the other (again, Wolfe assumes a certain amount of background knowledge on the part of the reader).

Into the upstate Illinois town of Castleview—named for an atmospheric mirage that allows the inhabitants to glimpse what looks likes a castle; perhaps the refracted skyscape of downtown Chicago—comes a plethora of beasts led by one Viviane Morgan. She, in the guise of a phantom hitchhiker, is searching for the modern-day descendent of King Arthur—the death of whom may allow for the permanent opening up of the Otherworld. But while Viviane Morgan conflates the figures from legend—the fairy Morgan Le Fay and the sword-wielding Vivienne, the Lady of the Lake—a much more diverse roster of candidates contends for the role of Arthur: Tom Howard (who is murdered before the first page of the novel is turned), his son Seth, the newly relocated car dealer Will E. Shields, his senior salesman, L. Bob Roberts, and the ranch hand Wrangler Dunstan, who works at a local riding school for girls.

Viviane and her fey companions, including Dr. von Madadh—*madadh* means "wolf" in Gaelic and the doctor seems a likely avatar of Mordred—are also looking for Excalibur's scabbard, clues to the location of which may be found in a museum diary. Various shenanigans involving the Shields's and Roberts's families, as well as the employees and patrons of the riding school, take place, and Wolfe ratchets up the suspense by intercutting between events at crucial moments. The reader also has to contend with the changing identities of several characters (if ever any creature had a special place in the heart of Gene Wolfe, it is the shape-shifter, which frequents much of his fiction): Viviane, whose major alternate form can be seen weeping at Tom Howard's casket visitation, as well as Lucie d'Carabas, who may be a certain gun-toting feline special operative. Observational biases account for other seeming discrepancies: people see and hear what they expect to see and hear; while parochial versions of certain archetypes further contuse the novel's often frenetic plot. The giant horseman who appears from time to time and who must die at the novel's end because winter yearly kills summer is variously Odin, the Celtic god of nature Cernunnos, and Gawain's Green Knight. And finally there is a face-off between human and fairy antagonists, with one of the Arthurian candidates (although not necessarily the noblest) stepping forward to face von Madadh.

All in all, *Castleview* is an interesting mix of action, social commentary (the Shields's marriage is less than ideal), and mythic fun, and besides paying tribute to Wolfe's Celtic heritage, the novel may be a homage to Charles Williams—with C. S. Lewis and J. R. R. Tolkien another of Oxford's Christian writing dons—whose supernatural thrillers, especially *War in Heaven,* and Arthurian poems, seem a likely influence. Wolfe also argues convincingly in the book that such creatures as the Sasquatch may exist, and there is something ennobling (and perhaps some scientific truth) in Wolfe's notion that any of us, no matter how flawed our lives, could be Arthur, the once and future king.

Though it partakes as much of science fantasy as anything else, Wolfe's other contemporary urban novel, *There Are Doors* (1988), may almost be read as an early working model for *Castleview*—or, to change slightly a term coined by the editor Terry Carr to describe several of Wolfe's stories with inverted themes and titles, a fugue prequel. A woman from another world—her name is sometimes Lara Morgan—is looking for the latest incarnation of her eternal lover, and there is a castle of sorts, though it is more a literary artifice than an actual edifice. But while Lara Morgan is described as a long-lived goddess—in our continuum she may be the inspiration for the Greek goddess Cybele—other than the breach between worlds (the titular aperture), there are few other supernatural elements.

Lara's world is also different from ours in the following biological distinction: men die after mating a single time, like male bees. Wanting a lover for more than a single occasion, Lara has come into our world, where she takes up with

Wolfe's viewpoint character (the Greek exemplar would be Attis), a mental patient whose real name is never stated, but is probably William Green. Green's struggle to find Lara—she abandons him in the first chapter—leads him in and out of several psychiatric institutions both here and in Lara's world, and involves him with a violent Nixon-loving revolutionary, William North. Thus, because of these various mental and physical displacements, much of Green's sojourn has an absurdist, often oneiric, quality to it, recalling Franz Kafka. In fact, Wolfe directly mentions Kafka's book *Das Schloss* (1926) at one point, Lara's world features the same snowscapes and Eastern European retro-tech found in that book, and not only does Wolfe import Kafka's character Klamm (here making him a Henry Kissinger type advisor to the female president), but on several occasions Green is addressed by and as the synonymous equivalent of Kafka's Herr K. *There Are Doors*, therefore, may be Wolfe's version of Kafka's *Castle,* but one in which the mysterious unobtainable object is no building, but a woman, and where the absurdities and inanities of life can be navigated by following the heart's compass out of personal darkness. Wolfe on several occasions has said that *There Are Doors* is his favorite of his novels and this may well be because the novel seems a response to its own first sentence, "Do you believe in love?"

Also among Wolfe's non-science fiction novels is the juvenile historical novel, *The Devil in a Forest* (1976), perhaps the least reflective of any of Wolfe's titles, since the alleged devil, wayfarer Wat, is no more demonstrably evil than several of the book's other characters. *The Devil in a Forest,* however, does accurately portray the superstitious mindset of a medieval peasantry caught between Christianity and the older pagan religion, and while the Barrow Man (a tumulus-haunting entity) appears in a dream to young Mark, who will grow to manhood in the course of the book's events, the only other fantastic element to be found in the novel is in Wolfe's vivid portrait of Mother Cloot—no true weird sister with actual powers, just the ability and mien to appear so, and perhaps she is Wolfe's most aptly (and realistically) described witch in all of his work.

Much more likely to appeal to lovers of epic fantasy, if also intended for a younger readership, will be Wolfe's first new series of the millennium, the Wizard Knight, wherein a high school boy wakes up in a medieval world in which the Norse religion is prominent. The series is said to feature a roster of characters that includes (among others) the Queen of the Green Aelf, numerous giants, a dead witch, her talking cat, a talking dog, and a human woman who marries the King of Jotunland, and it will be interesting to see how Wolfe stakes out his territory in the post-Harry Potter literary landscape.

Much of Wolfe's shorter work remains uncollected. As might be expected for a writer of Wolfe's playful nature, werewolves predominate in several tales. The one encountered by Nadan Jaffarzadeh in "Seven American Nights" (in *The Island of Doctor Death and Other Stories,* 1980) may actually be the shape-changed Ardis Dahl (her off-putting bedroom deformity perhaps being the laser burn he inflicted the previous evening on an attacking lycanthrope). But it is in "The Hero as Werwolf" (also in *The Island of Doctor Death*) that Wolfe has written one of his better short stories (the "werwolf" of the title is the intended spelling, Wolfe being more than a casual lover of recondite words), as young Paul Garou must survive in a radically changed future in which those with an unusual burden of bad genes may be more human than anyone. The story has a fair amount of Christian subtext, but the ending is pure Wolfe, with Paul seeking to save both himself and his new wife, Janey, in a manner that is both animalistic and redemptive.

Similarly, Wolfe tackles other familiar supernatural themes, but always in his own inimitable style. "In the House of Gingerbread" (in *Endangered Species,* 1989), for example, updates and inverts the story of Hansel and Gretel, but this time, rather than be the victims of a "witch"—in this case, their widowed stepmother, whose money they covet—the teenage duo seek to victimize her. Neither Tina Heim, the children's stepmother, nor the old house in which she and her family live, however, are as innocent as they initially seem.

Yet another malevolent building can be found in "The Haunted Boardinghouse" (in *Strange Travelers*, 2000), a strongly allegorical tale that posits a future as imagined not so much by Wolfe as by Nathaniel Hawthorne or Poe. The milieu is steam-driven, neo-Victorian, and years after a war with Mexico has been fought and won, with upstate Illinois the venue. (Another autobiographical element; Illinois has been Wolfe's home since the early 1970s.) An impoverished student, Enan Bambrick, is forced to abandon his studies as a classics major (his love of Latin aphorisms is revealed in the way that they stud the text), but is eventually able to secure a position as a librarian and tutor at the Seely New Lake School in Granville. The building that houses the school consists of four sides, each done in a different architectural style and corresponding to a different age. Forced to walk the final ten miles to Granville, Enan falls through the ice as he attempts to cross the frozen water that surrounds the fortified town. When he awakens, he is being cared for at the school, but is now desperately ill. Mysterious events begin accreting—he encounters flying shadows, sees a boy (who had previously seemingly fallen to his death) climbing from a high window, and meets a young woman described as "a maiden in black." But are these occurrences really happening or merely the images out of feverish dreams? (There seems to be an echo of Henry James's 1898 story *The Turn of the Screw* here.) Enan eventually works his way into the good graces of the headmaster, but is not above sleeping with the headmaster's wife, Kore. And then just when he begins to be recognized for his scholarship and teaching skills, another invasion by Mexico takes place, although this one is much more phantasmagoric, and we, more than Enan, perhaps better understand his final disposition, especially if we realize that Kore (aka Persephone) is Greek for "maiden." And yet despite the implications of this, unlike Wolfe's previous travelers in the hereafter, Roddie and Den Weer, Enan comes to know a genuine, everlasting peace.

Whether the protagonist of Wolfe's "Game in the Pope's Head" (in *Ripper*, 1988) is experiencing a similar metaphysical transit or we are indeed inside the pope's head must be decided by the individual reader (although the fact that the game player in the story believes his name to be Randolph Carter may be a clue). However, this short tale, which unfolds like a hallucinatory exercise in free association, combining Jack the Ripper lore, the natural history of flies, the evolution of psychoactive plants, and various board games, including (and perhaps most significantly) role-playing ones, is genuinely creepy and disturbing.

Indentureship to supernatural beings is another theme mined by Wolfe in various pieces of short fiction. In "Cabin on the Coast" (in *Endangered Species*, 1989), a young man of Irish ancestry, named after his politician father, is tricked by one of the Fair Folk, or fairies, into providing two decades of servitude. When he finally returns from the Otherworld to the cabin where he last saw his girlfriend twenty years earlier, he finds that no time has elapsed at all in the real world, although he himself now resembles his once older father enough to pass as his twin. "Cabin on the Coast" reprises the Wolfean notion that the global prevalence of folk beliefs in "little people" is too substantial to be based on pure imagination. In "Queen of the Night," (in *Strange Travelers*), despite being mistaken for a fairy, the main character is an orphaned human boy taken up by a loving family of ghouls in medieval England. At puberty he is reluctantly given up to the White Lady, who uses him for her erotic divertissement, but when she is done with him, and he is returned to a human family he had previously victimized, time has passed in the normal manner (which probably means she is not one of the Fair Folk either, but Death personified), and it is his aging stepfather who rues on the passage of time and how childhood innocence, once lost, can never be retrieved—Wolfe suggesting that the onset of sexuality dooms the child in us all.

More mythic, if hybrid, recasting takes place in Wolfe's ironically titled "The Friendship Light" (in the 1994 collection *The Best from Fantasy and Science Fiction: A Forty-fifth Anniversary Anthology*) wherein a man, deciding to take revenge on his crass brother-in-law, plays a number of tricks (he is clearly Norse god Loki, bedeviler of thunder god Thor), eventually culminating in the rigging of the light so that it draws down certain special agents of the Erinyes—Greek Fates sanctioned to avenge grievous family wrongs—who exact a horrible due. Once again, however, while Wolfe has never shirked from working in allusions to various mythologies, he has always done so less for effect than because it seems to reflect his belief that both folklore and storytelling draw on ancient tropes and themes that are universally shared. This at least is the attitude epitomized by Dr. Samuel Cooper, a professor of folklore who is featured in a number of Wolfe's tales.

In the first of these, "The Nebraskan and the Nereid" (in *Endangered Species*), Cooper, outward bound in Greece, is attempting to find out why the belief in a certain class of nymphs has never died. He does, of course, eventually encounter a Nereid, who both is and is not the mermaid we first think of. Then, in "Lord of the Land," originally published in the 1990 tribute anthology *Lovecraft's Legacy,* Professor Cooper traces the Midwestern tale of soul-catcher back to ancient Egypt and an extraterrestrial parasite of Cthulhoid ilk, only to see it reborn in a frightening final paragraph. Time and again, obviously, we glimpse this in Wolfe—the notion that the creatures of folklore, although viewed through the prism of various belief systems, were once real, and only the onset of modernity (science as well as widespread urbanization) prevents us from glimpsing them today or viewing them as anything other than regressive, the product of either less sophisticated mindsets or simple superstition.

Doubtless this knowledge informs what is probably to Wolfe, as a Catholic, his most personally horrific tale, "The Detective of Dreams" (in *Endangered Species*). In it a private investigator (modeled almost certainly after Poe's character C. Auguste Dupin) is hired to find the so-called Dream-Master, believed to be an actual man, who is haunting several persons' dreams to dire effect. In one, a celibate woman is turned out from a gala banquet by the kingly figure of the Dream-Master, who, although he seems familiar, she cannot identify. In another, an accountant is forgiven an enormous debt by the Dream-Master, only to turn around and demand of a fellow servitor the money owed to him; sinisterly, each night, the accountant begins to see more and more of a reptilian arm that is engaged in opening a numinous separating door. With its early-twentieth-century pseudo-Austrian setting, sense of foreboding, and unexplained, if deducible, burden of guilt shared by the dreamers, the tale again owes more than a little to Kafka, but even more so to the New Testament parables of Saint Matthew, which the dreams recapitulate, making the Dream-Master none other than Jesus Christ—forgotten, it seems, despite his ready visibility at a nearby church, as easily as we ourselves have already forgotten the fairies, werewolves, demons, and haunts that once dominated mainstream thoughts and folkways.

Lest Wolfe be seen as a lone wolf, it is notable that he has contributed to the shared-world Liavek series edited by Will Shetterly and Emma Bull, as well as collaborated twice with the British-born writer Neil Gaiman, himself now an American Midwesterner, and perhaps the one writer whose work, though uniquely his own, most recalls Wolfe—primarily in *Sandman: Book of Dreams* (which can be compared with Wolfe's "Ain't You 'Most Done?"). In *A Walking Tour of the Shambles,* the duo take us on a somewhat tongue-in-cheek tour of the Shambles, an area that escaped the Great Fire of 1871, and home to much else that is sinister.

Selected Bibliography

WORKS OF GENE WOLFE

NOVELS AND SHORT STORIES

Note: Most of Wolfe's novels and collections remain in print as Orb paperback editions from Tor.

Peace. New York: Harper and Row, 1975; London: Chatto and Windus, 1985.

The Devil in a Forest. Chicago: Follett, 1976; London: Panther, 1985.

The Island of Doctor Death and Other Stories. New York: Simon & Schuster, 1980; London: Gollancz, 1986. (Contains "The Hero as Werwolf" and "Seven American Nights.")

Soldier of the Mist. New York: Tor, 1986; London: Gollancz, 1986.

Storeys from the Old Hotel. Worcester Park, Surrey, U.K.: Kerosina; New York: Tor, 1992. (Contains Wolfe's two Liavek stories, "The Green Rabbit from S'Rian" and "Choice of the Black Goddess.")

There Are Doors. Tor, New York, 1988; London: Gollancz, 1989.

"Game in the Pope's Head." In *Ripper.* Edited by G. Dozois and S. Casper. New York: Tor, 1988.

"Houston, 1943." In *Tropical Chills.* Edited by Tim Sullivan. New York: Avon, 1988.

Endangered Species. New York: Tor, 1989; London, Orbit, 1990. (Contains "Cabin on the Coast," "The Nebraskan and the Nereid," "In the House of Gingerbread," and "The Detective of Dreams.")

Soldier of Arete. New York: Tor, 1989; London: New English Library, 1990.

Castleview. New York: Tor, 1990; London: New English Library, 1991.

"Lord of the Land." In *Lovecraft's Legacy.* Edited by R. Weinberg and M. Greenberg. New York: Tor, 1990.

Young Wolfe: A Collection of Early Stories. Weston, Ontario, Canada: U.M. Press, 1992. (Includes Wolfe's two stories published while a sophomore at Texas A & M, the second of which, "The Grave Secret," is a ghost story.)

"The Friendship Light." In *The Best From Fantasy and Science Fiction: A Forty-fifth Anniversary Anthology.* Edited by E. Ferman and K. Rusch. New York: St. Martin's, 1994.

Strange Travelers. New York: Tor, 2000. (Contains "The Haunted Boardinghouse" and "Ain't You 'Most Done.")

A Walking Tour of the Shambles: Little Walks for Sightseers, Number 16. With Neil Gaiman. Woodstock, Ill.: American Fantasy, 2002.

BIBLIOGRAPHY

Stephensen-Payne, Phil, and Gordon Benson, Jr. *Gene Wolfe: Urth-Man Extraordinary: A Working Bibliography.* Leeds, West Yorkshire, U.K.: Galactic Central, 1991.

CRITICAL STUDIES

Borski, Robert. "Wolves in the Fold: Lupine Shadows in the Works of Gene Wolfe." *New York Review of Science Fiction* 155:14–15 (July 2001).

GENE WOLFE

Broderick, Damien. "Thoughts on Gene Wolfe's *Peace.*" *New York Review of Science Fiction* 91:16–17 (March 1996).

Christopher, Joe R. "A Second View of Castleview." *Quondam et Futurus: A Journal of Arthurian Interpretations* 3, no. 3:66–76 (1993).

Gordon, Joan. *Gene Wolfe.* Mercer Island, Wash.: Starmont, 1986.

Locey, Kathryn. "Three Dreams, Seven Nights, and Gene Wolfe's Catholicism." *New York Review of Science Fiction* 95:1, 8–12 (July 1996).

Chelsea Quinn Yarbro
1942–

JANICE M. BOGSTAD

YARBRO'S FICTIONS TAKE us on journeys around the world, back through time and into the realms of both fantasy and the fantastic. She has settled in San Francisco, which offers a wealth of research opportunities for a versatile and scholarly author such as she. Born in Berkeley, California, on September 15, 1942, to Clarence Erickson, a cartographer, and Lillian (Chatfield) Erickson, an artist, she attended San Francisco State College from 1960 to 1963 but left to join the family cartography business, where she worked from 1963 to 1970. On November 3, 1969, she married Donald Paul Simpson, but they divorced in January 1982, well after she had established herself in a writing career. She has no children and continues to live in California with her music, her animals, and her writing. "I am a working writer," she often states, and has proven this by producing more than seventy books, more than three per year since her debut novel, *Time of the Fourth Horseman* (1976). She continues to pursue her early interests in music, horseback riding, mystery, science fiction and fantasy, magic, and the occult, both in fiction and in reality. While she does not list history as an avocation, her affinity for historical research is clear in all of her writing. The historical accuracy of settings for her vampire series and her young-adult novels have received particular praise and, were the characters themselves not so fascinating, one might almost see the fiction as a vehicle for historical writing and especially for the history of everyday life that transformed historical studies in the academy during the 1960s.

Ms. Yarbro is something of an industry all her own. In addition to writing successful science fiction and fantasy novels, including the Saint-Germain vampire series for which she has acquired a sort of cult following, she is also praised for her occult series "Messages from Michael," which she identifies as nonfiction. She has been honored with awards and critical attention for her several mystery series. She has often discussed her use of music as a soothing background for the writing process and calls it an "avocation" ; she also has written several musical pieces, some of which have been performed, and she has earned a living by teaching music to young students. The task of doing justice to her range of fictions alone is therefore daunting.

Like many women writers of science fiction and fantasy entering the field in the 1970s, she did not gain much critical attention for her first novel, *Time of the Fourth Horseman*, a grim apocalyptic tale about a mysterious plague, which looks " a little like polio" under a microscope but is eventually revealed as a government plan for population control. Her notoriety really began with the happy conjunction of two forces, the inclusion of an excerpt from her second novel, *False Dawn*, in the celebrated anthology *Women of Wonder* (1974, edited by Pamela Sargent) and the infusion of a growing body of women into science fiction readership and fan organizations. Additionally, her early participation in such conferences kept her in the public eye, and she continues to appear at science fiction and fantasy conventions including WisCon, the feminist-oriented science fiction fan convention that began in 1977 in Madison, Wisconsin. When her first vampire novel, *Hotel Transylvania*, was published in 1978, her readers were already waiting for it. Twenty-four years and fourteen books later (or twenty-two if you count the three spin-off series), they are still waiting for each one.

SAINT-GERMAIN AND OTHER VAMPIRES

The resurgence in interest in vampire fiction that gripped the 1970s and 1980s has been commented on widely in relation to Yarbro's fiction. Sarah LeFanu offers a useful explanation in *Feminism and Science Fiction* (1988). Linking it to the Gothic sensibility, she mentions a number of influential writers—Suzy McKee Charnas, Yarbro, Anne Rice, Jody Scott—and discusses both the social and sexual symbolism:

> The image of the vampire represents transgression, the breaking of the social codes, a denial of death. It is interesting that so many women writers are attracted by this image for the vampire is traditionally a male figure, active over his female victims' passivity; a barely concealed symbol of phallic penetration. It is perhaps that this identification with the vampire figure allows a claim to be made for a liberation sexuality for women, a transgression—no longer the prerogative of men—from the constraints of social order.
>
> (p. 83)

Even at this late date, however, she could not have predicted the long-term interest in Yarbro's unusual, sympathetic vampire, Saint-Germain.

Hotel Transylvania, named for the mid-eighteenth-century Parisian home of Count Saint-Germain, is an unpretentious little novel about a 4,000-year-old vampire. Its eponymous hero is sympathetic to women's plight and generally tries to improve the lives of people around him, regardless of their social class. Books in the series are more often classed as romance than horror or fantasy fiction, but in them Yarbro mixes generic conventions. She explores romantic love without conventional sexuality, writes female-focused narratives, and includes much of the visual description common in romance fiction. There are abundant vampire and occult references from supernatural fiction and graphic violence from horror fiction. *Hotel Transylvania* is by far the shortest novel in Yarbro's series, only 252 pages where the rest are between 400 and 600. It is lovingly embellished with descriptions of food and dress (especially that of Saint-Germain, and of the women around him), along with a number of less savory but nonetheless vivid portraits of everyday life. Soon after its publication, Saint-Germain had already gathered a sizable following among feminists and science fiction and fantasy fans as well as a larger readership. In fact, by 1983, Yarbro had published four others and related stories. The short explanatory essay "My Favorite Enigma: the Historical Comte de Saint-Germain," found in *The Saint-Germain Chronicles* (1983), addresses the available background information on the historical figure, reported first in Paris in 1743 and with two reported deaths, France in 1786 and Cairo in 1817. Yarbro determines that he must have been Czech, probably a wealthy merchant's son, who used makeup to conceal his true age and who had also traveled extensively by his early twenties. Thus her first novel is set in 1743 and she uses that period as a jumping-off point to establish the character and allude to his dark and long history.

Her extensive use of the vampire conventions to delve into historical accounts is also less evident in *Hotel Transylvania*, but the history of the occult is specifically addressed in Saint-Germain's contact with would-be sorcerers who are eager to do his bidding. She also establishes some of Saint-Germain's fictionalized personal history early in the novel. Hailed as Prinz Rogoczy of Transylvania, he is patterned after the French accounts of the actual historical figure who wore almost exclusively black, white, and red clothing, with fabulous waistcoats, and surrounded himself with fantastic biographical mysteries. Yarbro extrapolates from this confusion when, on page 12, she tells her readers in the third-person narrative: "He reflected that the name was as much his as Saint-Germain was. Or Balletti had been. He had used Ragoczy for many years, in Italy, Hungary, Bohemia, Austria, and the German City of Dresden." Thus the reader is quickly alerted that he is in some way unusual. Additionally, as in the subsequent vampire novels, letters from various individuals provide additional details and the mundane flavor of the time and place in which the story is set. In this case, the letters introduce a sweet young virgin from Provence who has been sent to Paris to find a husband, and they set the stage for her destruction.

Stylistically the letters enrich the narrative on several planes, adding perspective, detail, a contrasting writing style, and some suspense. By their presence in this first novel, they also acknowledge the epistolary forms, which were one of the few literary outlets for European women from the medieval period well into the nineteenth century. And, in fact, female characters pen a significant number of the letters that appear throughout her vampire series. Since many also comment on the details of daily life, home, family, marriage, private fears and hopes, the details of dress and, equally importantly, the effects of major public events on individuals, they are brilliant shorthand for enriching the text.

While it is difficult to cover these many novels or even to pick a few favorites and do them justice, it is possible to describe a few characteristics. (Other descriptive notes, such as the historical place and time of the main action in each novel, are indicated in the bibliography below.) Like many historical romance writers, she picks recognizable periods so that the reader has some idea of the background. Unlike other writers, however, she specifically dates the period and peoples it with believable characters, some of whom are also recognizable to a reasonably educated reader. She also uses the horror-novel convention of picking periods of acute disaster such as the Spanish Inquisition, the invasion of the Mongols into China and India, or the Crusades and the plague years in Europe, to name a few. Purist fans of historical romance, mystery, or horror fiction might find some of their expectations frustrated by the mixing of conventions from these genres, but most readers will delight in Yarbro's versatility and obvious knowledge of these genres.

In the reviews of her work, it is clear that critics and readers have chosen their least and most favorite Saint-Germain novels. Until *Communion Blood* (1999), one might have criticized *Blood Games* (1979) for its voluminous amount of graphic violence. However, historical breadth and expertise is noteworthy in the early *Path of the Eclipse* (1981), set in China before the fall of the Northern Sung dynasty (960–1279) and the establishment of the Mongol-ruled Yuan (1260–1368). Saint-Germain is a teacher and adviser, first in the old Tang (618–907) capital of Lo-yang and then in a remote Northern stronghold. His love interest is an unlikely female warlord, Chih-yu, who needs his military expertise in the absence of adequate troops and funds. Yarbro's charming use of the old Wade-Giles transliteration system for Chinese lends this work the tone of a nineteenth-century narrative. Saint-Germain ranges widely in this novel, and his travels also take him to India and to another woman in distress. While demonstrating knowledge of Far East and Middle East history, history, Yarbro uses her knowledgeable vampire to link it to that of Europe and the last of the Cathars fleeing the rage of the Church triumphant. In fact, checking her historical details is half the fun of reading the novels.

A second favorite, *A Feast in Exile: Saint-Germain in India* (2001), falls much later in the publishing chronology (fourteenth) and has received somewhat less praise, perhaps because the usual reviewers of generic fiction are not ready for its length and complexity. The novel inserts our favorite vampire into India's fourteenth-century battle to protect itself from the invading Mongol, Tamerlane. Known as Sanat Ji Mani in this novel, the vampire manages to escape Tamerlane's imprisonment of him, retain his own "humanity" and sensitivity, and preserve the lives of some around him. While Yarbro seems to prefer continental Europe to other parts of the world, with the majority of the novels set in France, Spain, or Italy, and most in the twelfth to seventeenth centuries, it is clear she isn't limited by either her own publishing history or the expectations of readers and critics.

Yarbro has interspersed novels about her most popular character with two trilogies about female vampires from his history. The first, The Olivia Clemens series, follows an atypical chronological path, beginning with sixth-century Byzantium in *A Flame in Byzantium* (1987). This is followed by a twelfth-century tale of one of the great Christian crusades (*Crusader's Torch*, 1989) and the series ends in the seventeenth century when this female vampire falls in love with D'Artagnan from Alexandre Dumas's classic, to which it makes a number of literary gestures (*A Candle for D'Artagnan*, 1989). In the course of her adventures here, Olivia really, and gratefully, dies. The Brides of Dracula trilogy, published in the late 1990s, is another such exploitation of Saint-Germain characters.

Then there is Yarbro's newest Saint-Germain spin-off, two books currently available only in electronic form. These two long, complicated and excessively cross-genre novels, *Magnificat* (2000) and *In the Face of Death* (2001) may be too unusual for the increasingly restrictive publishing market, despite Yarbro's popularity. Both flesh out another female character, Madelaine de Montalia, who was transformed into a vampire during her rescue in *Hotel Transylvania*. *Magnificat* is 635 pages in length and has been described as a "metaphysical thriller," while *In the Face of Death* shows Madelaine's earlier career as she attempts to live with Native Americans before the American Civil War. A copy of William Tecumseh Sherman's memoirs (he is Madelaine's love interest in the novel) is bundled with the electronic novel as a free bonus.

THE MICHAEL SERIES

While engaged in the production of mysteries, historical vampire fiction, children's literature, science fiction, and movie novelizations, many of which incorporate the world of the occult, the alchemist, the magician, or shaman, Yarbro has apparently also developed a real-life interest in these areas of human endeavor. Some of her experiences are concentrated in a series of polemical volumes under the title of "Michael." A mixture of Rosicrucian, Taoist, Hindu, and selected Western philosophies, the pronouncements of the group entity Michael are not her own words. In the preface to *Messages from Michael* (1979), the author says: "The following material has been compiled from the transcripts of literally thousands of hours of mediumistic dictation beginning almost a decade ago." It is not clear whether she intended at the time to produce more than this first work. It places the "teachings" of Michael in the context of "fictionalized" gatherings of friends that begin their metaphysical quest as a party entertainment around a Ouija board. The narrative style is reminiscent of the theosophical books published around the turn of the last century, with a liberal dose of pantheism and biblical reference. Within a very few years, Yarbro had gained a following for the Michael teachings, which provide the opportunity for followers to be in touch with their and others' illustrious ancestors. She has also identified and lends her assistance to an official "Michael" group and discourages the impromptu creation of others. Yarbro's last of these books, so far, is *Michael for the Millenium* (1995).

OTHER GENRE FICTION

Yarbro has also produced a bewildering number of other types of fiction. *Crown of Empire* (1994) narrates the culmination of the plot David Drake began in *Crisis of Empire* and is one of very few of her fictions not set on Earth in a pre-twentieth-century period. This work follows Drake's classic space adventure, potboiler style, and reminds the reader of her many borrowings from other novelists such as Dumas and Ariosto. *To the High Redoubt* (1985) is done in the style of sword-and-sorcery fantasy and is set in a sixteenth-century Islamic/Arabic empire. While exploring magic and shamanism, this narrative takes the reader from Warsaw to North Africa and details the differences between white (good) and black (evil) magic that takes some of its thematic content from the Michael series. *Firecode* (1987), set in 1980s America, is an occult work introducing biblical numerology into the world of technology we all take for granted. Its shaman/wizard is aware that special sequences of numbers will cause fires to erupt and manages to induce his victims to set them on the microwaves, computers, and other such devices they use every day. Another genre crossover, this is also a supernatural detective novel, in which a young, female insurance adjuster must unravel the mystery. Young women placed in the way of harm appear in many standard horror plots. The novel could thus be a science fiction, mystery, or occult thriller. In fact, even by the end of the novel, readers don't know if they were dealing with technological or occult forces.

Less interesting to the literary reader are her novelizations of horror movies. *Dead and Buried* (1980) and *Nomads* (1984) are classic dark-horror fiction, much in the tradition of the film "Night of the Living Dead." For true fans of graphic violence, these works present sadistic scenes of torture and dismemberment that are true to the original movies and offer interesting secondary characters. In fact, the author dedicates the first: "For Donald: Craft for Art and a Toyota." While neither of these will appeal to a more sensitive taste in fiction, it is notable that *Dead and Buried*, film and book, were very popular, and that Yarbro was novelizing the work of script masters such as Dan O'Bannon.

Among Yarbro's various mystery series, the five titles in the Mycroft Holmes series use the brother of Doyle's Sherlock Holmes to explore supernatural mysteries in England and Scotland. Written with Bill Fawcett under the pseudonym of Quinn Fawcett, the books are as fraught with nostalgia as with mystery. Her popular Charlie Spotted Moon mysteries follow a Native American detective who uses extrasensory abilities to solve crimes, not unexpected in a Yarbro series, and two of them focus on another passion of hers, music. *Music When Sweet Voices Die* (1976) and *False Notes* (1991) mix science fiction and mystery conventions with a liberal seasoning of classical opera references.

Most writers of genre fiction stick to one genre or another. It must already be clear that, while skillfully mixing genre conventions, Yarbro has also been successful in many genres, with multiple audiences. Much of her fiction is very long, and she has been plagued with criticisms for the length of texts and volume of detail, especially in the otherwise beloved vampire series. Yet she is also a successful short-story writer, a respectable market in science fiction with its many fiction magazines. She has published a number of notable short-story collections, some connected to the Saint-Germain series and others full of "cautionary tales," as she named the first of these collections. Wordy or pithy, her works have made a mark.

Nor does she limit herself to adult fiction. Yarbro has to date completed four novels for young adults, two of them linked to her Saint-Germain novel *Blood Games* by being set in Nero's first-century Rome. All four make remote historical periods accessible to younger readers and focus on youthful protagonists, both male and female. Like her Saint-Germain fiction, they demonstrate Yarbro's love for historical accuracy and details of everyday life. The best of these, according to her many enthusiastic reviewers, are the first, *Locadio's Apprentice* (1984) and the second, *Four Horses for Tishtry* (1985). Locadio's apprentice, Eneus Cano, is a fourteen-year-old boy learning medicine in Pompeii, in the turbulent years after Nero's death. He survives the eruption of Vesuvius and helps some of its victims. As he matures and learns his trade from the infinitely wise Locadio, Eneus travels around the port city of Pompeii, serving as the reader's eyes into a long-lost era. To add intellectual spice, his conversation includes many Latin names for objects of everyday life, medicines, and treatments, all of which are explained in a seven-page glossary.

The later novel, set in Nero's (37–68 A.D.) Rome at the height of the public games, is told through the perspective of Tishtry, a thirteen-year-old female slave and a talented performer on horseback. Cast much more in the adventure mode, this novel follows her to major cities of the Roman empire and allows for glimpses of a broad range of everyday life, especially for slaves, merchants, and the lower classes. Tishtry herself seems very remarkable for a thirteen-year old. While this was close to the age of majority in ancient Rome, and it is also a respectable age for a gymnastic performer, the ease with which she manages travels, her sale to several masters, and the rigors of her circus act, verge on the incredible. It nevertheless makes an engaging and entertaining story. The novel, like its predecessor, is followed by a glossary of Latin and historical terms relevant to the time period.

Accorded somewhat less notoriety, Yarbro's other two young-adult novels are not historically or thematically linked but demonstrate her wide-ranging interests. They both contain more conventions of the supernatural. *Monet's Ghost* (1997) is an illustrated account of a contemporary, artistic young girl who can literally walk into paintings until she finds herself lost in one in Monet's gardens. *Floating Illusions* (1986) is Yarbro's young-adult mystery novel and is set on an ocean liner at the turn of the century. Its plucky young heroine, Millicent, is fascinated by the onboard magician and by a murder investigation. Both these novels have received relatively lukewarm reviews. Yet Yarbro implicitly encourages young people to trust their abilities and carries through in these novels with intelligent, talented, active young women in the midst of high adventure. They compare well to Lloyd Alexander's Vesper Holly series (such as *Illyrian Adventure*, 1987, and *Jedera Adventure*, 1990.)

Yarbro also enjoys frustrating the established genre conventions with alien characters in her mystery novels and what amounts to magic in her science fiction, and this can result in undeserved criticism. She has written two novels about the experienced Sheriff Jason Russell set in a small town in Colorado. *The Law in Charity* (1989) and *Charity, Colorado* (1993) have received little attention in the sheer mass of Yarbro's work and have been described in *Library Journal* (February 14, 1994) as "trying for a mixture of the Western, horror, and mystery genres, doing justice to none."

A convincing argument could be made that historical romance, horror, and fantasy conventions have been combined to produce the success of the Saint-Germain novels. Even her fantasy novels, *Baroque Fable* (1986) and *Ariosto* (1988), carry an underlying spoof on the conventions of this popular contemporary genre, the first as an amusing tongue-in-cheek tale of witches, wizards, maidens, princes, and dragons, although the same character may change shape and function as you read. The novel *Ariosto* transforms Ludovico Ariosto, the actual sixteenth-century writer of *Orlando Furioso,* into a high-fantasy character in a story he writes to avoid the reality around him.

Despite her common assertion that she writes to be read and that "the reader should not be aware of the mechanics of language as they read" (*Contemporary Authors*), Yarbro obviously takes pride not only in historical accuracy but also in experimentation in style, form, publication venue, and genre convention. As with all experiments, some of hers are not successful. Her works mirror the literary fads of the 1970s, 1980s, and 1990s but also spoof, improve on, and violate some of their basic tenets, becoming commentaries as much as paradigmatic examples.

Although one could wish that all of her works were as carefully crafted as some of them, we can just enjoy what she has given us, in all its profusion.

Selected Bibiliography

WORKS OF CHELSEA QUINN YARBRO

VAMPIRE SERIES

The Saint-Germain Chronicles (annotated for time period and place)

Hotel Transylvania. New York: St. Martin's Press, 1978. (Paris and Provence, c. 1645.)

The Palace. New York: St. Martin's, 1978 (Italy, late fourteenth century).

Blood Games. New York: St. Martin's, 1979. (rome of Nero, c. 65 A. D.)

Path of the Eclipse. New York: St. Martin's, 1981. (China, India, c. 1216.)

Tempting Fate. New York: St. Martins, 1982. (European travels, c. 1914.)

The Saint-Germain Chronicles. New York: Pocket Books, 1983. (Stories.)

Signs & Portents. Santa Cruz, Calif.: Dream Press. 1984. (Stories.)

Out of the House of Life. New York: Tor, 1990. (Egypt, alternates between Pharaonic Egypt and c. 1825–1828.)

The Spider Glass. Eugene, Ore.: Pulphouse, 1991. (Stories.)

Better in the Dark. New York: Orb, 1993. (Germany, Saxony, c. 940.)

Darker Jewels. New York: Tom Doherty Associates, 1993. (Russia, sixteenth century.)

Mansions of Darkness. New York: Tom Doherty, 1996. (Spanish North and South America, Peru, c. 1640.)

Writ in Blood. New York: St. Martin's, 1997. (Russia, Germany, 1910–1912.)

Blood Roses. New York: Tom Doherty, 1998. (Provence, France, c. 1345.)

Communion Blood. New York: Tom Doherty, 1999. (Rome, seventeenth century.)

Come Twilight. New York: Tom Doherty, 2000. (Spain, Catalonia, seventh–twelfth centuries.)

A Feast in Exile: Saint-Germain in India. New York: Tom Doherty, 2001. (fourteenth century India.)

Night Blooming. New York: Warner Books, 2002 (eighth century France).

Atta Olivia Clemens Trilogy (female vampire) *A Flame in Byzantium.* New York: Tom Doherty Associates, 1987. (Constantinople, sixth century.)

Crusader's Torch. New York: Tom Doherty Associates, 1989. (France, Holy Land, twelfth century.)

A Candle for D'Artagnan. New York: St. Martin's, 1989. (France, seventeenth century.)

MADELAINE DE MONTALIA SERIES (E-BOOKS)

Magnificat. San Jose, Calif: Hidden Knowledge, May 2000. www.hidden-knowledge.com. (Alternative Rome, late twentieth century.)

In the Face of Death. San Jose, Calif.: Hidden Knowledge, 2001. www.hidden-knowledge.com. (Loosely based on W. T. Sherman's memoirs. Life with American Indians in 1840s and 1850s.)

BRIDES OF DRACULA TRILOGY

Kelene: The Angry Angels. New York: Avon, 1998.

Fenice: Soul of an Angel. New York: Avon, 1999.

Zhameni: The Angel of Death. New York: Avon, 2000.

MYSTERY SERIES

Mme. Victoire Vernet Series (as Quinn Fawcett, with Bill Fawcett)

Death Wears a Crown. New York: Avon, 1993.

Napoleon Must Die. New York: Avon, 1993.

MYCROFT HOLMES SERIES (AS QUINN FAWCETT, WITH BILL FAWCETT)

The Adventures of Mycroft Holmes: Against the Brotherhood. New York: Tor Books, 1997.

The Further Adventures of Mycroft Holmes: Embassy Row. New York: Tor Books, 1998.

The Further Adventures of Mycroft Holmes: The Flying Scotsman. New York: Tor Books, 1999.

The Further Adventures of Mycroft Holmes: The Scottish Ploy. New York: Forge, 2000.

The Further Adventures of Mycroft Holmes: Glastonbury Haunts. New York: Tor Books, 2001.

CHARLIE SPOTTED MOON SERIES (AS C. Q. YARBRO)

Music When Sweet Voices Die. New York: Putnam, 1976.

Ogilvie, Tallant and Moon. New York: Putnam, 1976. As

Bad Medicine, New York: Jove, 1990.

False Notes. New York: Jove, 1991.

Poison Fruit. New York: Jove, 1991.

Cat's Claw. New York: Jove, 1992.

HORROR FICTION (NON-VAMPIRE)

Dead and Buried. New York: Warner Books, 1980. (Novelized screenplay.)

Sins of Omission. New York: NAL, 1980.

The Godforsaken. New York: Warner, 1983.

LYCANTHROPY, INQUISITION
Nomads. New York: Bantam, 1984. (Novelized screenplay.)
Writting in Blood. New York: St. Martin's, 1998.

FANTASY
Ariosto. New York: Tom Doherty Associates, 1980.
Baroque Fable. New York: Berkley, 1986.

OTHER NOVELS
Time of the Fourth Horseman. Garden City, N.Y.: Doubleday, 1976. London: Sidgwich and Jackson, 1980. (First published novel.)
False Dawn. Garden City, N.Y.: Doubleday, 1978.
A Taste of Wine. As Vanessa Pryor. New York: Pocket Books, 1982.
Hyacinths. Garden City, N.Y.: Doubleday, 1983.
A Mortal Glamour. New York: Bantam, 1985.
To the High Redoubt. New York: Warner Books, 1985.
Firecode. New York: Warner Books, 1987.
Taji's Syndrome. New York: Warner Books, 1988.
Beastnights. New York: Warner Books, 1989.
The Law in Charity. Garden City, N.Y.: Doubleday, 1989.
Blood and War. With David Drake and Christopher Stasheff, created by Gordon Rupert Dickson. New York: Baen Books, 1993.
Charity, Colorado. M. Evans and Company, 1993.
Crown of Empire. New York: Baen Books, 1994.
Dance to the Piper. With Anne Stuart et al. New York: Harlequin, 1995.
Dark Light. New York: Pocket Books, 1999.

YOUNG ADULT BOOKS
Locadio's Apprentice. New York: Harper and Row, 1984.
Four Horses for Tishtry. New York: Harper and Row, 1985.
Floating Illusions. New York: Harper and Row, 1986.
Monet's Ghost. Illustrated by Pat Morrissey. New York: Atheneum Books for Young Readers. 1997.

COLLECTIONS
Cautionary Tales. Garden City, N.Y.: Doubleday, 1978. Expanded, New York: Warner and London: Sidgwich and Jackson, 1980.
On Saint Hubert's Thing. New Cast, Va.: Cheap Street, 1982.

OCCULT WORKS
The Michael Series

Messages from Michael: On the Nature of the Evolution of the Human Soul. Chicago: Playboy Press, 1979.

More Messages from Michael. New York: Berkley, 1986.

Michael's People. New York: Berkley, 1988.

Michael for the Millenium: The Fourth Book in the Michael Teaching. New York: Berkley, 1995.

CRITICAL AND BIOGRAPHICAL STUDIES

Altner, Patricia. "Yarbro, Chelsea Quinn," In: Vinson, James, ed. *Twentieth Century Romance and Gothic Writers.* Detroit: Gale, 1982.

Bogstad, Jan. "Chelsea Quinn Yarbro interviewed," *Janus* vol.5, no. 2 (Autumn 1979): 6–9.

Contemporary Authors. Vols. 65, 68. Detroit: Gale, 1981.

Contemporary Authors New Revision Series. Vols. 9, 25, 77, 103. Detroit: Gale, 1981.

Fitzgerald, Gil. "History as Horror: Chelsea Quinn Yarbro," In: Schweitzer, Darrell, ed. *Discovering Modern Horror Fiction II.* Mercer Island, WA: Starmont, 1988. Pp. 128–134.

Kies, Cosette. "Chelsea Quinn Yarbro: Can Monsters Be Humanized?" In: *Presenting Young Adult Horror Fiction.* New York: Twayne, 1991. Pp. 96–105.

Lawler, Amy and Donald Lawler. "The Saint-Germain Series." In Magill, Frank N., ed. *Survey of Modern Fantasy Literature*, vol. 3. Englewood Cliffs, N.J.: Salem Press, 1983. Pp. 1343–1346.

Pederson, Jay P., ed. *St. James Guide to Science Fiction Writers.* Detroit: St. James Press, 1996. Pp. 1041–1042.

Pringle, David, ed. *St. James Guide to Horror, Ghost, & Gothic Writers.* Detroit: St. James Press, 1998.

Russell, Sharon A. "Introducing Count Saint-Germain: Chelsea Quinn Yarbro's Heroic Vampire." In Heldreth-Leonard-G. and Pharr-Mary (eds.). *The Blood Is the Life: Vampires in Literature.* Bowling Green, OH: Popular, 1999. Pp. 141–153.

INTERNET RESOURCES

"Chelsea Quinn Yarbro Bibliography." Online at Fantastic Fiction. http://www.fantasticfiction.co.uk/authors/Chelsea_Quinn_Yarbro.htm.

Yarbro's Web site. http://www.chelseaquinnyarbro.

Jane Yolen
1939–

GARY K. WOLFE

ALTHOUGH HER PRIMARY reputation remains that of a prolific and varied author of children's books—in fact, one of the most important children's book writers of the twentieth century—Jane Hyatt Yolen is also a fantasist, poet, editor, and storyteller of considerably broader scope. Along with the impressive string of honors her children's and young adult literature has brought her, she has won Nebula Awards from the Science Fiction and Fantasy Writers of America (where she also served two years as president), three Mythopoeic Society Awards, and a World Fantasy Award. Her reputation as both editor and author is such that from 1990 to 1996 she was given her own editorial imprint, Jane Yolen Books, at Harcourt Brace. She edited a series of original fantasy anthologies, the *Xanadu* series, for Tor Books from 1993 to 1995, and also has edited a number of often-thematic anthologies covering fantasy, science fiction, horror, and folktales, such as *Werewolves* (with Martin Greenberg, 1988), *Vampires* (also with Greenberg, 1991), and *Favorite Tales from around the World* (1986). Her broad scholarship and insightful understanding are reflected in a number of nonfiction works, of which the most notable are *Touch Magic: Fantasy, Faerie, and Folklore in the Literature of Childhood* (1981), expanded from work done for an unfinished doctoral program in education, and *Guide to Writing for Children* (1989).

Yolen, the daughter of Will and Isabelle (Berlin) Yolen, was born in New York City on February 11, 1939. She attended high school in Westport, Connecticut, and Smith College, where she received a B.A. in 1960, followed by a master's degree in education from the University of Massachusetts in 1976. She married David Stemple, a computer scientist, in 1962, and has two sons (Adam and Jason) and a daughter (Heidi)—all of whom have occasionally collaborated with her. In the 1960s she worked as an editor for various magazines in New York, as well as for such book publishers as Gold Medal (1961-1962), Routlege (1962-1963), and Alfred A. Knopf (1963-1965). Yolen became a full-time writer in 1965. In addition, she has been active since then as a professional storyteller on stage and in classrooms, and as a folksinger and songwriter.

Yolen's first children's book, a nonfiction account of women pirates titled *Pirates in Petticoats* (1963), already anticipated the detailed historical research and feminist sensibility which would inform much of her later work. Although her subsequent work included picture books for very young children as well as chapter novels for older readers, it soon became apparent that some of her more compelling and original fantasies might attract the attention of adults as well. For example, *The Magic Three of Solatia* (1974), set in the mythical land of the title, is a sequence of connected tales in which the heroine, together with her father and son, learn to use the magical powers of three buttons given to them by a sea witch. The question of how such supernatural powers ought properly to be used—essentially the ethics of magic—was a theme that would recur often in later works. Similarly, the Pit Dragons trilogy (*Dragon's Blood*, 1982; *Heart's Blood*, 1984; *A Sending of Dragons*, 1987), although it is a science fiction series set on a former penal-colony planet, conveys much of the feel of a fantasy narrative in its tale of a boy slave who seeks to win his freedom by raising an enormous red fighting dragon. By the early 1980s, Yolen was regularly contributing short stories to such genre publications as *The Magazine of Fantasy and Science Fiction* (many of these were collected in *Tales of Wonder*, 1983), and her first adult novel, *Cards of Grief* (1984), was another science fiction tale. Written in the form of anthropological reports concerning a culture in which grieving is a form of artistic expression, *Cards of Grief*—like the Pit Dragons series—develops a strong fantasy component through its astute insights into the role of storytelling in a culture's structure and development.

Despite her wide popularity and the growing crossover appeal of her young adult work, it was not until 1988 that Yolen emerged as a major novelist in the adult fantasy genre, with *Sister Light, Sister Dark*, the first of her "Great Alta" novels. In that same year she also published a groundbreaking young adult novel that is now regarded as one of her most enduring classics. This was *The Devil's Arithmetic*, a "timeslip" fantasy in which a petulant young girl named Hannah, uninterested in her Jewish heritage and bored by the survivors' stories of her aging relatives, finds herself inexplicably transported back in time to a *shtetl* in occupied Poland during 1942. She is cast in the role of unheeded Cassandra among the locals, who are incredulous when Hannah—drawing on half-remembered classroom studies—tries to warn them about the Holocaust. Although time travel is a trope conventionally associated with science fiction narratives, it is hardly uncommon in fantasies as well, from Mark Twain's *Connecticut Yankee in King Arthur's Court* (1889) to Octavia Butler's *Kindred* (1979), in which a contemporary African American woman is transported back to the slavery era. Like those writers, Yolen makes no attempt to rationalize the time travel experience as anything other than a fantasy device: Hannah, asked to perform the ritual opening of the door for Elijah during a family Passover Seder, steps out and finds herself in 1942, where she is known as Chaya. Unlike the more conventional movement of a fantasy narrative in which the protagonist must learn the rules of the new world, Hannah finds herself at a disadvantage because she knows *too much* about what will happen to her and her new friends. Even her own considerable storytelling skills, established earlier in the narrative when she regals her younger brother with the plot of a horror movie, seem to work against her: her marvelous stories of life in a modern America prove no more believable than her warnings of the coming Holocaust.

But soon even these stories seem to abandon her: after the family is finally rounded up and transported to the concentration camp, Hannah finds that her memories of contemporary life all but disappear when her head is shaved. She thus becomes a courageous leader among the young people based entirely on her own natural resources. She learns the "devil's arithmetic" of surviving by adding one day to the next, and when she chooses to enter the gas chamber called "Lilith's Cave" in place of her newfound friend Rivka, she makes the choice heroically, and not as a time traveler who realizes she is ultimately safe. After the darkness of the chamber resolves itself into the hallway of her grandparents' apartment in the Bronx—when, in effect, Hannah returns from the dead—she learns that her Aunt Eva, whose tales of survival had so annoyed Hannah earlier, had been known in her village as Rivka. (Lest there be any mistaking the tale for a dream fantasy, Hannah brings back information that only Aunt Eva would have known.) Hannah's closing line in the novel, "'I remember. Oh, I remember,'" is an ironic echo of her opening complaint, "'I'm tired of remembering.'"

The Devil's Arithmetic was immediately recognized as one of Yolen's most important and courageous novels, receiving numerous awards and citations including the National Jewish Book Award for Children's Literature and even placing as a finalist for the Science Fiction Writers of America's Nebula Award. But the book did not arrive without controversy, and the editor of an influential children's book journal criticized it—in an editorial, not a review—both for its unusually graphic portrayal of suffering and death in a novel for young people, and for the use of the time travel device as a convenient escape hatch for the protagonist. In fact, Yolen's quiet integration of this genre device into a story that is firmly rooted in historical reality may be viewed as one of the novel's most successful aspects. Time travel is used both to draw the reader into this historical reality and to underline the critical survival value of storytelling and memory.

Yolen's next Holocaust novel, another strong brief for the cultural value of storytelling, also came under attack—for a fairly bizarre reason. *Briar Rose* (1992), written as an adult novel for a series of modern fairy tale redactions edited by Terri Windling at Tor Books, was conceived by Yolen after seeing Claude Lanzman's documentary film *Shoah* (1985). The film includes a description of Chelmno, a brutal concentration camp located in a castle, from which few escaped alive—a real-life horror story which suggested to Yolen a terrifying perversion of the "Sleeping Beauty" or "Briar Rose" tale. *Briar Rose* frames its account of a young woman named Becca seeking to learn of her grandmother's mysterious past with excerpts from a distorted version of the tale that the grandmother told her and her sisters as children. On her deathbed, the grandmother Gemma insists to Becca that the tale is true, and that she herself was the princess Briar Rose. Aided by a journalist friend and clues found in a box after Gemma's death, Becca undertakes a quest which leads her first to Fort Oswego, New York—site of the only wartime camp for Holocaust refugees sponsored by the U.S. government—and eventually to Chelmno itself. In Chelmno, she and her young Polish guide meet Josef Potocki, an aging homosexual who rescued Gemma from a pit of corpses and later worked in the resistance with her. Potocki's tale, taking up more than a quarter of the novel, neatly unpacks the mysteries of Gemma's past and constitutes a moving Holocaust narrative in its own right. One aspect of this narrative, Josef's account of his earlier secret gay life and eventual betrayal, led to a public burning of the book in Kansas City—by a parents' group who rather perversely felt that having a character like Josef as a hero glorified homosexuality.

Briar Rose is not strictly an adult novel, since its indomitable young girl heroine—whose problematic relationship with her family suggests another fairy tale, "Cinderella"—generates a strong appeal for young adult readers. It is also not truly a fantasy novel (although it was nominated for a World Fantasy Award), but is rather an historical narrative embedded in a mystery. But like *The Devil's Arithmetic*, the novel has the form of a fairy tale and is so thoroughly concerned with the survival value of storytelling that it never quite violates the fantastical terms of its source text.

Briar Rose wasn't Yolen's last experiment in adapting the fairytale form to grim subject matter. In the short story "Granny Rumple" (1994), the tale of Rumpelstiltskin provides the frame for an all-too-believable account of circumstances leading to an anti-Semitic pogrom in a Ukrainian village early in the twentieth century—and at the same time the suggestion emerges that the original tale itself may contain subtle anti-Semitic references. "Sister Death" (1995) is a version of the myth of Lilith, in which Lilith is portrayed as an immortal vampire and grim reaper who is nearly undone when a young condemned girl at a Nazi death camp welcomes her as a mother. "Allerleirauh" (1995), drawn from the Grimm Brothers' Cinderella variant of the same title, forgoes the happy ending to posit a grim view of father-daughter incest as an almost inevitable outgrowth of the tale's initial premises.

Just as Yolen explored harsh realities in her fairy tale and young adult fiction, so too she was unsparing in her view of women's lives in her first major adult fantasy work, the two-part novel made up of *Sister Light, Sister Dark* (1988) and *White Jenna* (1989). Although released originally as separate novels (and separately nominated for Nebula Awards), these two volumes actually constitute one continuous narrative, and were eventually published together as *The Books of Great Alta* (1990). Based on the 1983 short story "Sister Light, Sister Dark" (later incorporated into *White Jenna*), the novel features a fair number of familiar fantasy conventions. These include a setting called the Dales which is clearly a kind of mythical alternative England; a child of humble birth with an unusual characteristic (white hair), who a prophecy claims will be the savior of her people and who grows up to become a formidable woman warrior; a sacred text called the Book of Light, which is the source of the society's moral authority; and the magical ability of the women who live in segregated enclaves called the Hames to summon up dark "sisters" who represent their own darker selves. The child of prophecy is Joan-enna, or Jenna, whose life is traced from infancy to the eventual assumption of her destined role, to her humbling of opponents called the Cat and the Bear, and finally to confrontation with a usurper named Kalas. Jenna's own "dark sister," Skada, provides her with blunt and unsentimental advice along the way.

While there is a strong feminist subtext to the tale of White Jenna, the novel's most striking element is the manner in which it explores the dynamics of storytelling itself. Throughout the novel, the narrative is presented in varying and sometimes conflicting forms: the story, myth, legend, history, songs and ballads (complete with sheet music), even a series of aphorisms. The sections headed "The Story" present the tale through straightforward narration, while in "The Legend" the same material has been transformed into folklore, and in "The Myth" it takes on the authority of religious parable. The songs and ballads are intermediary forms of expression, still based in the culture of the Hames, but the segments labeled "The History," written in a parody of academic prose, show how later generations can drain stories of all their mystery and conspire to suppress or rationalize any evidence of the miraculous (a significant subtext of these chapters involves the cultural marginalization of anything resembling fantasy). As a kind of postmodern questioning of the sources of authority (we are tempted to view "the story" as reliable and "the history" as fatuous, but why?), this technique of using shifting narrative forms is nothing short of brilliant—but Yolen never permits it to interfere with the forward movement of the action.

Sister Light, Sister Dark and *White Jenna* were followed nearly a decade later by a sequel, *The One-Armed Queen* (1998), creating the impression among some readers that the story is a trilogy, rather than a two-part novel and its sequel. In fact, the sequel was never part of Yolen's original plan, emerging instead from a story, "The One Armed Queen," which Yolen had written in 1995 for an anthology edited by Lois McMaster Bujold and Roland Green. Although part of the newer novel focuses on the aging Jenna's struggle with parenting and with the problem of being a warrior queen in a peaceful, post-heroic age, this book is mainly concerned with Jenna's adopted daughter Scillia, who will grow up to become the one-armed queen of the title. Using the same multiple-narrative technique (and this time with original music by Yolen's son Adam Stemple), the novel introduces Scillia as a stubborn thirteen-year-old, born with only one arm, who resents her mother's tales of heroism much as Hannah in *The Devil's Arithmetic* resented her own family's preoccupation with the past. She is also resentful of her brother Jemson's taunting about her being adopted, taunting that proves ironic when Jemson, who is sent to the rival nation of Garun-over-the-sea as part of an exchange meant to guarantee peace, becomes a willing pawn in a deceitful Garunian plot to recapture the Dales. Prematurely cast into the role of leader of the resistance to the Garunian invasion, Scillia, aided by her other brother Corinne, finds herself becoming a Warrior Queen similar to her mother, whose legend she had always felt so oppressed by. In the end, though, she refuses the crown and turns the Dales over to a governing council. While continuing and extending the strengths of *Sister Light, Sister Dark* and *White Jenna*—the various legends and histories take on a richer and more ironic resonance, for example—*The One-Armed Queen* also allows Yolen to rethink some of the issues raised by the earlier, more traditionally heroic epic. New perspectives are created through the mother-daughter relationship of Jenna and Scillia, then through Scillia's problematic relationship with her brothers and her own growing sense of responsibility for three orphaned girls who come to view her as a mother.

Throughout the 1990s, Yolen's children's books continued to focus on myths and legends in a manner that often resonated with adult readers as well. One of them also eerily anticipated a worldwide craze. *Wizard's Hall* (1991) concerns an unheralded young wizard named Henry, who is the 113th recruit at a school for wizards, where he turns out to be the most powerful of all; eventually he saves the entire school from an evil wizard who formerly taught there, and who is aided by a kind of patchwork dragon assembled from the worst traits of the personalities of its victims. Predating the Harry Potter series by some eight years, the novel ironically went out of print at Scholastic Books the year before that same publisher began releasing J. K. Rowling's famous novels. Other children's books of particular interest during this period include *The Wild Hunt* (1995), a sometimes enigmatic and elliptical tale based on a common European legend. Set initially in a house that straddles two worlds, the novel's central characters are two boys who, each unknown to the other, live in the house with a mysterious white cat. Eventually they learn that they are champions of the Goddess in her fight against the Wild Hunt. Unusually for an illustrated children's book, the story also experiments with alternate versions of the same chapter, fragmentation of narrative, and minimal characterization. A number of interesting stories and poems also appear in Yolen's series of collections about imaginary beasts, *Here There Be Dragons* (1993), *Here There Be Unicorns* (1994), *Here There Be Witches* (1995), *Here There Be Angels* (1996), and *Here There Be Ghosts* (1998).

Yolen revisited the Arthurian legends in *The Dragon's Boy* (1991)—in which the young Arthur, called Artos, is mentored by a giant dragon who turns out to be the aging alchemist Merlinnus—and also in her "Young Merlin" trilogy (*Passager*, 1996; *Hobby*, 1996; *Merlin*, 1997), which focuses on the boyhood of Merlin in a manner often more suggestive of realistic historical fiction than of fantasy. In *Passager* the seven-year-old Merlin is presented as near feral: he has lost his ability to speak and even forgotten his own name, and survives alone in the woods until rescued by a falconer. *Hobby* describes Merlin as a twelve-year-old living in the falconer's home until a catastrophic fire sends him back into the world, where he becomes involved with an itinerant magician and a vengeful king. In the third volume, Merlin, still at the age of twelve, is captured by a wild tribe called wodewoses and imprisoned in a camp where he meets the child Arthur. Rich in sensory detail and characterized by spare, restrained prose, the series received the Mythopoeic Fantasy Award for Children's Literature in 1998.

In 1998 and 1999 Yolen won back-to-back Nebula Awards for short fiction, an unusual feat that helped bring attention to her adult work. In 2000 she published her most substantial collection of adult fiction to date, *Sister Emily's Lightship and Other Stories*, which contained twenty-eight stories from the preceding two decades, including three original to the volume. All but a few relate in some way to fairy tales, myths, or earlier authors from Shakespeare to O. Henry, but collectively they reveal a good deal about Yolen's short story techniques. One such technique, common in her poetry as well as in her stories, is to approach a tale from an unexpected point of view. The narrator of "The Thirteenth Fey" (1985), for example, is the "bad" fairy who places the curse on Sleeping Beauty; she is revealed to be a somewhat klutzy but well-meaning younger fairy who, intending to grant long life to the princess by means of a magic thread, pulls the thread from the spindle too abruptly, breaking it and thus accidentally cursing the child with premature death. "Lost Girls" (1997), one of the collection's Nebula winners, reexamines the Peter Pan story from the point of view of Wendy, who turns out to be a kind of feminist labor organizer unwilling to accept the role assigned girls in a classic boys' wish-fulfillment fantasy. "Granny Rumple" (discussed earlier) uses Rumplestiltskin as its model for a tale of a Jewish moneylender, but the viewpoint is that of the moneylender's wife.

Another technique Yolen uses to transform her source material involves shifting the setting of the original. "Snow in Summer" (2000) is a haunting version of "Snow White" set in Appalachia, where the wicked stepmother belongs to a fundamentalist snake-handling sect, while "Belle Bloody Merciless Dame" (1997) presents the title character of Keats's famous poem "La Belle Dame sans Mercie" as an anorexic elfin seductress in a contemporary Scottish village. A third technique involves grafting together disparate sources, as with "The Gift of the Magicians, with Apologies to You Know Who" (1992), in which "Beauty and the Beast" and O. Henry's "The Gift of the Magi" are combined, or "Under the Hill"(2000), in which elves are pitted against Damon Runyon-style gangsters. The autobiographical "Speaking to the Wind" (2000) combines classic fairy tale elements (especially George MacDonald's *At the Back of the North Wind*) with an account of a real hurricane experienced during childhood. A fairy family becomes involved with Romeo and Juliet in "Dusty Loves" (1988) and with Christianity in one of the book's funniest pieces, "The Uncorking of Uncle Finn" (1986), which concerns an elf who becomes completely insufferable on finding religion. "Dick W. and His Pussy; or, Tess and Her Adequate Dick" (1997) is a ribald variation on "Dick Whittington's Cat" that seems designed purposely to proclaim that Yolen is not as innocent as her children's-book reputation might suggest.

The broad awareness of worldwide storytelling traditions reflected in Yolen's collections of international folk tales is also evident in her short fantasy fiction. "Journey into the Dark" (1995) draws on Mayan mythology, while "Memoirs of a Bottle Djinn" (1988) is based on Arabian Nights lore, "The Sleep of Trees" (1980) and "Sun/Flight" (1982) borrow from Greek myths, and "Words of Power" (1987) is inspired by Native American folklore. The latter story, a tale of a girl's coming of age after she learns her own magical words, is a particularly good example of the kind of expanded narrative perspective that makes some of Yolen's best folktales read like compressed novels. A similar narrative sweep is achieved in "Become a Warrior" (1998), about the making of a female warrior who eventually gains revenge on those who murdered her family. Even when Yolen tries her hand at a fairly traditional romantic ghost story, such as with "A Ghost of an Affair" (2000), set largely in a small Scottish village not far from Yolen's part-time St. Andrews home, the sense of a place and a culture—and the narrative voice itself—is pronounced and individual.

Yolen's science fiction also often turns on themes of storytelling and language. The alien who gives Emily Dickinson a brief tour of outer space in "Sister Emily's Lightship"(1996; Nebula winner) is barely more than a mechanism for dramatizing Dickinson's intensity of vision, and the mission of the time traveler in "The Traveler and the Tale"(1995) is to plant a folktale which is designed to change the future of the Auvergne region, because, as she muses, "Only through stories, it seems, can we really influence the history that is to come."

Yolen seems truly to believe that only stories can influence "the history that is to come," and her body of work explores, often brilliantly, nearly all the transformations of which storytelling is possible. More than almost any other contemporary fantasy writer, she has learned how to modulate the classic storyteller's voice, and she knows that for this voice to remain authentic, it must be neither slavish nor condescending toward its sources, neither fashionably ironic nor willfully ingenuous. While her output may be too prodigious for all of it to be truly memorable, it seems almost certain that the best of her work will endure.

Selected Bibliography

WORKS OF JANE YOLEN

CHILDREN'S AND YOUNG ADULT NOVELS

The Magic Three of Solatia. New York: Crowell, 1974.

The Transfigured Hart. New York: Crowell, 1975.

Dragon's Blood. New York: Delacorte, 1982. (First novel in the Pit Dragon series. Reprinted in *The Pit Dragon Trilogy.* Garden City, N.Y.: Science Fiction Book Club, 1998.)

Heart's Blood. New York: Delacorte, 1984. (Second novel in the Pit Dragon series. Reprinted in *The Pit Dragon Trilogy.* Garden City, N.Y.: Science Fiction Book Club, 1998.)

The Stone Silenus. New York: Putnam, 1984.

A Sending of Dragons. New York: Delacorte, 1987. (Third novel in the Pit Dragon series. Reprinted in *The Pit Dragon Trilogy.* Garden City, N.Y.: Science Fiction Book Club, 1998.)

The Devil's Arithmetic. New York: Viking Kestrel, 1988.

Dove Isabeau. New York: Harcourt, 1989.

The Dragon's Boy. New York: Harper, 1990.

Wizard's Hall. New York: Harcourt, 1991.

The Wild Hunt. New York: Harcourt, 1995.

Passager. New York: Harcourt, 1996. (First novel in the Young Merlin series.)

Hobby. New York: Harcourt, 1996. (Second novel in the Young Merlin series.)

Merlin. New York: Harcourt, 1997. (Third novel in the Young Merlin series.)

ADULT NOVELS

Cards of Grief. New York: Ace, 1984.

Sister Light, Sister Dark. New York: Tor, 1988 (First novel in the Great Alta series. Reprinted in *The Books of Great Alta.* Garden City, N.Y.: Science Fiction Book Club, 1990.)

White Jenna. New York: Tor, 1989. (Second novel in the Great Alta series. Reprinted in *The Books of Great Alta.* Garden City, N.Y.: Science Fiction Book Club, 1990.)

Briar Rose. New York: Tor, 1992.

The One-Armed Queen. New York: Tor, 1998. (Third novel in the Great Alta series.)

SHORT STORY AND POETRY COLLECTIONS

Tales of Wonder. New York: Schocken, 1983.

Dragonfield and Other Stories. New York: Ace 1985.

Merlin's Booke. New York: Ace, 1986. (Short stories.)

Storyteller. Framingham, Mass.: NESFA Press, 1992.

Here There Be Dragons. New York: Harcourt, 1993. (Short stories and poetry.)

Here There Be Unicorns. New York: Harcourt, 1994. (Short stories and poetry.)

Here There Be Witches. New York: Harcourt, 1995. (Short stories and poetry.)

Here There Be Angels. New York: Harcourt, 1996. (Short stories and poetry.)

Here There Be Ghosts. New York: Harcourt, 1998. (Short stories and poetry.)

Sister Emily's Lightship and Other Stories. New York: Tor, 2000.

OTHER WORKS

Touch Magic: Fantasy, Faerie, and Folklore in the Literature of Childhood. New York: Philomel, 1981. Rev. ed., Little Rock, Ark.: August House, 2000. (Nonfiction.)

(Editor.) *Favorite Folktales from Around the World.* New York: Pantheon, 1986.

(Editor.) *Dragons and Dreams.* New York: Harper, 1986. (With Martin H. Greenberg and Charles G. Waugh.)

"The Profession of Science Fiction, 37: The Author as Hero." *Foundation*, 43 (1988): 47–49.

(Editor and contributor.) *Xanadu.* New York: Tor, 1993. (With Martin H. Greenberg.)

(Editor and contributor.) *Xanadu 2.* New York: Tor, 1994. (With Martin H. Greenberg.)

(Editor and contributor.) *Xanadu 3.* New York: Tor, 1995.

CRITICAL AND BIOGRAPHICAL STUDIES

Brown, Charles N. "Jane Yolen" (interview), *Locus* 360 (January 1991).

———"Jane Yolen" (interview), *Locus* 439 (August 1997).

Krueger, William E. "Jane (Hyatt) Yolen," In *Dictionary of Literary Biography.* vol. 52 of *American Writers For Children Since 1960: Fiction.* Farmington Hills, Mich.: Gale, 1986.

Weil, Ellers R. "The Door to Lilith's Cave: Memory and Imagination in Jane Yolen's Holocaust Novels," *Journal of the Fantastic in the Arts* 5,2 (1993): 90–104.

Roger Zelazny
1937–1995

JANE LINDSKOLD

IN MOST CASES, categorizing a Roger Zelazny piece as either science fiction or fantasy is not a simple matter. There are a few stories that neatly fall into one area or the other, but these are the exceptions. As Zelazny said in his essay "Fantasy and Science Fiction: A Writer's View," collected in *Frost and Fire* (1989): "I have often wondered whether I am a science fiction writer dreaming I am a fantasy writer, or the other way around. Most of my science fiction contains some element of fantasy, and vice versa"
(p. 281).

In the same essay, Zelazny credits his peculiar tendency to write "science fantasy" to the manner in which he encountered some of the varied ways humanity has tried to explain the universe. First came mythology, then folklore and fairy tales, and finally, when he was eleven, science fiction. Not long after, Zelazny became interested in science itself and started reading widely in various areas, for pleasure as well as for personal edification. It was a practice that he continued until his death.

When Zelazny began to write fiction, all of these means of explaining the universe coexisted within his imagination, each valid in its own way. His early stories blended these approaches, creating tales that were unique, even among the increasingly experimental and sophisticated "New Wave" science fiction and fantasy of the early 1960s.

BACKGROUND

Roger Joseph Zelazny was born May 13, 1937, in Cleveland, Ohio, the only child of Joseph and Josephine (Sweet) Zelazny. His mother was American Irish. His father was born in Ripon, Poland—at that time under the control of Tsarist Russia.

From age eleven, Zelazny knew he wanted to be a writer. His father supported his interest, making him a gift of his first typewriter. This parental support and approval meant a great deal—so much so that Roger kept the typewriter for the rest of his life.

In 1954 Zelazny sold his first story, "Mr. Fuller's Revolt," to *The Literary Cavalcade,* but otherwise collected rejection slips. Gradually, he shifted his primary focus to poetry, mastering a discipline that would have a tremendous impact on his later prose. However, Zelazny was realistic enough to know that few poets could make a living from their art. "A Rose for Ecclesiastes," written in 1961, was not only his homage to the old Mars of the pulps, but was also his farewell to dreams of making his living as a poet.

A similar practicality shaped Zelazny's education. He attended Western Reserve University (now Case Western Reserve) in Ohio, where, initially, his undergraduate major was psychology. However, as interested as he was in the material—an interest reflected in his Nebula Award–winning novella "He Who Shapes" (later expanded into the 1966 novel *The Dream Master*)—Zelazny didn't think he'd enjoy working in psychology . In his junior year, he switched his major to English, reasoning that he could always teach if his writing career didn't work out. After graduating from Western Reserve with a B.A. in 1959, Zelaney entered Columbia University, finishing his course work for a Master's degree within a year.

While waiting for his thesis to be passed, and to take his comprehensive exams, Zelazny enrolled in the Ohio National Guard, in which he would serve in various divisions for the next six years. Since this was not full-time work, in 1962 Zelazny took a job as a claims representative with the Social Security Administration. He continued working for them until 1969, when he resigned to write full-time.

In 1964 Zelazny married Sharon Steberl, from whom he was separated in less than a year. The couple divorced in 1966, the same year in which Zelazny married Judith Alene Callahan. Zelazny remained married to his second wife for the rest of his life, although they were separated during the last year before his death. They had three children: Devin (b. 1971), Jonathan Trent (b. 1976), and Shannon (b. 1979). After leaving Ohio in 1965, Zelazny lived in Baltimore, Maryland. In 1975 he moved to Santa Fe, New Mexico, a location that would appear frequently in his fiction thereafter.

In early 1994, while contemplating separating from Judy and moving in with fellow writer Jane Lindskold, Zelazny discovered he had cancer. He went into treatment almost immediately, and his condition temporarily improved. In mid-1994 he and Lindskold set up housekeeping in Santa Fe, in order to remain close to his mother and children.

Despite his illness, during the last year and half of his life Zelazny's enthusiasm for writing was, if anything, more intense than it had been for the previous decade. He completed several short stories, edited two anthologies (*Forever After* and *The Williamson Effect*), contributed to a computer game (Chronomaster), and worked on two novels: *Donnerjack,* and *Lord Demon.* At his request, the latter two were completed by Lindskold after his death.

He died on June 14, 1995, in Santa Fe, New Mexico.

AWARD-WINNING WORKS

The majority of Zelazny's awards were for works of "science fantasy" rather than for what might be termed pure fantasy. Looking in detail at some of these works provides a means of examining the themes to which Zelazny persistently returned, and also gives an idea of the range of material he incorporated into his writing.

1966 was a remarkable year for Zelazny in that he won three of the field's major awards. "He Who Shapes" won the Nebula Award for novella, while "The Doors of His Face, the Lamps of His Mouth" won the same award in the novelette category. ". . . And Call Me Conrad," later published as the novel *This Immortal,* won the Hugo Award.

Both "He Who Shapes" and "The Doors of His Face, the Lamps of His Mouth" are science fantasy within which the science dominates the fantasy. In each case, however, mythic undertones add to the depth of the story, freeing it from the limits of mere intellect.

For "He Who Shapes" Zelazny created the profession of neuroparticipant therapy, a type of psychotherapy in which the therapist uses a blend of technology and trained telepathy to enter a patient's dreams and reshape them for therapeutic purposes. The protagonist is Charles Render, an expert in neuroparticipation therapy.

Render's client, Eileen Shallot, is a resident in psychiatry who hopes to specialize in neuroparticipation. There is one difficulty; blind from birth, Shallot would not be prepared for the visual elements in her clients' dreams. Initially, she claims that all she wishes is for Render to use his abilities to acclimatize her to sight. However, it rapidly becomes apparent that what Shallot really desires is to experience sight, even if secondhand.

The tale is too complex to summarize here, for Zelazny takes what could have been a simple account of the clashing of two strong wills and infuses it with added depth through the use of a wide variety of images drawn from myth and legend. However, touching on at least one thread of imagery gives some idea of the artistry that made Zelazny virtually unique for his time.

As her name suggests, Eileen Shallot is linked by Zelazny to the Lady of Shallot, who died from grief over Lancelot. She is simultaneously Elaine, who bore Lancelot his son, Galahad, but could never win his love. As Eileen exploits Render's unresolved guilt over the death of his wife and daughter—as well as his strong sexual attraction to her—she also becomes a powerful and destructive witch in the mold of Morgan Le Fay. Repeatedly, Eileen Shallot forces Render to assume the role of a knight in shining armor, her imagined rescuer. In the end, the suicidal impulse towards which Render's unresolved guilt has been driving him makes Render a prisoner within the dream Eileen had created, long after she herself has been withdrawn. Render's entrapped incarnation blends the knight in Keats's "La Belle Dame Sans Merci," the wounded Fisher King, and Tristam forever waiting for Isolde.

"The Doors of His Face, the Lamps of His Mouth" is one of two stories Zelazny wrote as an homage to the pulps that had shaped his own early reading. Set on a steamy, living Venus— rather than the dead planet whose reality science would confirm soon thereafter—"The Doors of His Face, the Lamps of His Mouth" takes its most obvious inspiration from Melville's tale of Captain Ahab and his vengeful quest after Moby Dick. However, Zelazny does not simply retell the tale, he remolds it. Carlton Davitts, while simultaneously longing for another chance, does not pursue his Moby Dick. He actively avoids the beast, until forced after it by another. Moreover, unlike Ahab, Carl succeeds in his final confrontation, and he succeeds precisely for one of the reasons Ahab fails— an ability to feel with and for another person.

This Immortal introduces what would become a recurring character type in Zelazny's work, the immortal or nearly immortal hero. Zelazny says that the trilogy by George Sylvester Viereck and Paul Elderidge sparked his interest in this sort of figure: "When I was growing up I read the 200-year Trilogy (each volume from a different viewpoint) many times, and was doubtless influenced thereby in my own writing" (letter to Jane Lindskold, August 29, 1990). The novel also brings to the fore another type of character who would recur in various forms throughout Zelazny's career: the extremely competent, multifaceted man (Zelazny's main characters are almost always male), who confronts his problems from outside the established power structure. When these qualities are combined with immortality, they make for frequently captivating protagonists.

Conrad, to give the main character of *This Immortal* the preferred of his many names, is several hundred years old. The product of an Earth that has been devastated by some unnamed, but presumably nuclear disaster, Conrad was born near a Hot Spot. His unusual physical characteristics—one leg shorter than the other, a hairline that reaches to near his brow, extraordinary strength, mismatched eyes, a hirsute body, and the aforementioned resistance to aging—are apparently the result of radiation-induced mutation. Or are they? At one point Conrad relates how, after his ill-omened birth on Christmas Day, his parents left their deformed child to die, as was the custom of the place. They were forced by the local priest to reclaim their child, and always maintained that the baby they brought back was not their own.

Conrad's birth on Christmas Day not only ties him into the Christ myth—an identity he never claims, though there are others who would like him to be their savior—but also with the Greek legend of the *kallikanzaroi,* destructive trickster figures related to fauns and satyrs. Conrad never quite denies being one of these creatures. Indeed, at times he hints that he is one, but given his liking for keeping his associates off balance, this could be just another facet of his sense of humor.

In *This Immortal* Zelazny does not only draw from Christianity and Greek mythology. He also incorporates elements of voudoun, Islamic demonology, and smatterings of other mythological traditions, so that a multicultural, multifaceted future Earth is evoked, quite unlike the Western Christian or agnostic futures found in so much other science fiction of the period.

This Immortal is also interesting in that it marks Zelazny's transition from being primarily a writer of short stories to being a writer of novels. As with his transition from poetry to fiction, part of this move was purely practical. He explains in the introduction to his collection *The Last Defender of Camelot* (1980):

> I had started out as a short story writer, and I still enjoy writing short stories though I no longer do nearly as many as I used to in a year's time. The reason is mainly economic. I went full-time in the late '60s, and it is a fact of writing life that, word for word, novels work harder for their creators when it comes to providing the necessities and joys of existence. Which would sound cold and cynical, except that I enjoy writing novels, too.
>
> (p. 1)

However, despite this strong awareness that he had to make his living and support his growing family through his writing, Zelazny never ignored the lure of a story that clamored to be told. Later in Zelazny's career, he would call these impulse projects "hobby books"—books he wrote not to fulfill a contractual obligation, but because he felt driven to write them.

Following *This Immortal,* Zelazny published *Lord of Light* (1967), winner of the 1968 Hugo Award for Best Novel and perhaps the archetypal work of science fantasy. In it, Zelazny unfolds the tale of Sam, also known as Mahasamatman and Lord of Light, who sets himself up as the sole opposition to the Deicrats, those who would combine technology and mutant abilities to reign as gods while keeping the rest of humanity in a permanent technological twilight. After the initial introduction of Sam and his core group of allies, the story is unfolded in a series of flashbacks, these concluding with the final battle between Sam's Accelerationist forces, the zombies of the last Christian (Nirritti the Black), and the Deicrats.

As with all of Zelazny's stories, in *Lord of Light* nothing is simple. Even the question of whether or not the gods are indeed gods is open to debate. The reigning Deicrats have fine and facile arguments to support their claims. These would seem to be so much politics, but for the fact that the energy beings who are the aboriginal inhabitants of the world, and who can see the "flames" of a person's soul, state that some of the gods' souls do seem to bear the mark of the forces they claim to embody. Even Sam himself admits that certain of his allies—Yama and Sugata in particular—have achieved a more than human status. This theological debate adds a level of complexity to what could be a stereotypical tale of rebellion against autocracy.

"Home is the Hangman," winner of both the Hugo and Nebula Awards for Best Novella in 1976, is the Frankenstein tale framed as a murder mystery. As a dual award winner, it deserves mention here, but being more purely science fiction than is usual for Zelazny it cannot really be termed "supernatural" fiction.

"The Last Defender of Camelot"—for which Zelazny won the Balrog award in 1980, and after which he titled his 1980 short fiction collection—is wholly fantasy. After an apparently chance meeting in San Francisco, Lancelot is convinced by Morgan Le Fay to join forces with her to defeat Merlin, who she reveals as the true enemy of Camelot. In some ways, "The Last Defender of Camelot" is akin to Mark Twain's *A Connecticut Yankee in King Arthur's Court,* in that it views Merlin and his manipulation of events and ideals in a less than favorable light. However, Zelazny combines Lancelot's own poignant emotional dilemma with action and intrigue in a fashion that makes the tale unique.

"Unicorn Variation," which won the Hugo Award for Best Novelette in 1982, is fantasy with strong science fiction undertones. The story examines humanity's responsibility for its own actions and future, a theme prevalent in numerous of Zelazny's other works. In it, Zelazny presents the interesting notion that when humanity dies out, its myths will survive—or perhaps it is that they have had their own existence all along, independent of those who thought they created them. The collection the story appears in, also called *Unicorn Variations* (1983), won two awards, the Daicon for its Japanese translation, and the Balrog. In the introduction included in the collection, Zelazny presents an unusually detailed look at the forces that went into the genesis of the title piece, demonstrating that market forces do not preclude the creation of powerful fiction.

"Twenty-Four Views of Mount Fuji by Hokusai," which won the Hugo for Best Novella in 1986, and "Permafrost," which won the Hugo for Best Novelette in 1987, are both science fantasy—but with the science dominating the fantasy elements. However, both stories feature literal gods in the machine, once again blurring the question of where science ends and the fantastic takes over. "Permafrost" adds a goddess to the mix in the form of a woman who has become the intelligence of a living planet. "Twenty-Four Views of Mount Fuji by Hokusai" is perhaps the more successful of these two pieces because within it Zelazny examines the responsibilities of godhood as he did in *Lord of Light,* rather than merely settling for the flash and dazzle available to those who use divinely powerful beings as characters.

AMBER NOVELS

Although only one of the ten Amber novels ever won an award (*Trumps of Doom,* winner of the Locus Award for Best Fantasy Novel of 1986), much of Zelazny's general popularity rests on these books. For many years, the Science Fiction Book Club offered the first five novels, collected into the two-volume *Chronicles of Amber,* as a bonus to new subscribers. This doubtless exposed Zelazny's work to a host of readers who might not otherwise have encountered it. In 1999 a massive omnibus volume containing all ten novels was published as *The Great Book of Amber.* Despite the fact that it contained no new material, this collection briefly reached number one in sales rank on Amazon.com.

Over the years the Amber novels have spawned a computer game, the "Choose Your Own Adventure" books, a visual guide, a comic book series, a role-playing game, and numerous pieces of art, including entire decks of the elaborate Trumps the Amberites use for communication. The movie options for Amber have been repeatedly purchased over the years, although as of this writing no movie has been completed. Zelazny himself felt a particular fondness for the series. When he incorporated it was as "The Amber Corporation."

Yet, despite the series' wide readership, it is regularly dismissed by critics as light adventure, unworthy of being assessed in the same breath with works such as "A Rose for Ecclesiastes" or *Lord of Light.* This dismissal is hardly a just assessment of the Amber novels. Although swashbuckling and filled with magic and mayhem, they have a distinguished lineage, complex overall story arc, and prose poetry as fine or finer than is found elsewhere in Zelazny's works.

When one attempts to fit the early Amber novels into the context of Zelazny's writing overall, publication dates are deceptive. Zelazny began writing the series in 1967, several years before *Nine Princes in Amber* (1969) was published. An unfinished version of *The Guns of Avalon* (1972) was shelved in 1969. Thus, these novels are contemporaries of *Lord of Light* and *Isle of the Dead*. *Creatures of Light and Darkness* (1969), Zelazny's earliest "hobby book," was also written around this time, a fact that provides some insight into Zelazny's incredible creative energy at this early stage of his career.

The first five Amber novels (*Nine Princes in Amber*, *The Guns of Avalon*, *Sign of the Unicorn*, *The Hand of Oberon*, and *The Courts of Chaos*) are told from the first-person point of view of Corwin of Amber. The books begin with Corwin suffering from amnesia and imprisoned in a sanitarium. Almost immediately, both the reader and Corwin himself realize that he is something out of the ordinary. Despite two recently broken legs, he overwhelms a burly orderly and escapes his captors.

Although by the end of *Nine Prince in Amber* Corwin believes he has regained his memory, the next several novels make amply clear that remembering who he is is the least of his problems. Repeatedly lied to and manipulated by those who would use him in the power games surrounding the throne vacated by Oberon (King of Amber and father of the eponymous nine princes), Corwin rapidly learns that truth and identity are a great deal more complicated than one would think.

Zelazny intended the Amber novels to be "a comment on the nature of reality and people's perceptions of it. I was thinking of Lawrence Durrell's 'Alexandria Quartet' when I began the first book" ("Roger Zelazny: Forever Amber," interview in *Locus* 1991, p. 5). Although the Durrell influence was undoubtedly present, Zelazny was also influenced by *The Dark World*, a novel by Henry Kuttner that was one of Zelazny's childhood favorites. As in the Amber novels, *The Dark World* features parallel worlds, a liberal helping of figures based on myth and legend, and even as in the Amber novels, a central character named Ganelon.

Among his many talents, Corwin of Amber is a poet. Therefore, many of the passages in his first-person narrative voice become prose poetry. This is most obvious in the segments describing "hellrides"—the means by which the denizens of Amber travel between the alternate realities known as Shadows. To travel between Shadows, an Amberite changes what is present into what could be. The more drastic the change, the faster the journey and the greater the risk involved. Zelazny's use of prose poetry for these sections allows readers to step within the dizzying experience of reshaping the universe, rather than leaving them standing on the outside, watching the narrator undertake the process.

After the publication of *The Courts of Chaos* in 1978, Zelazny didn't write any new Amber novels for several years. The publication of *The Trumps of Doom* in 1985 reopened the universe, but, true to his plan to make the Amber novels an examination of reality and perception, with this book Zelazny switched to a new narrator. Merlin "Merle" Corey had been introduced briefly in the previous sequence. The child of Corwin and Princess Dara (whose mixed lineage links her to both Amber and its rival, the Courts of Chaos), Merlin seems to belong firmly within his mother's chaos heritage. However, as *The Trumps of Doom* makes clear, Merlin belongs to both worlds and is something of an outsider in each.

As with the Corwin cycle, Merlin's story takes five volumes to unfold, beginning with *The Trumps of Doom,* and continuing through *Blood of Amber* (1986), *Sign of Chaos* (1987), *Knight of Shadows* (1989), and *Prince of Chaos* (1991).

The Trumps of Doom begins approximately eight years after the previous novel. Merlin has been living on our Earth, a "Shadow" in which his father had dwelt during the long years of his amnesia-induced exile. Far from being the exotic mage princeling he had seemed in the earlier work, Merle Corey is a computer programmer, bookish, and even a bit nerdy. Of course, like his father, Merle is more than he seems, and a series of attempts on his life force him to develop his abilities and resources.

Unlike the Corwin novels, which concentrated largely on the vicinity of castle Amber and the politics therein, Merlin's adventures take him through numerous Shadow realms and deep into the complex politics of not only the courts of Amber and Chaos, but of those various allied realms which are only vaguely alluded to in the earlier novels.

The Amber novels, though ostensibly fantasy, employ a liberal dose of the kind of technology usually foreign to such sword and sorcery tales. In *The Guns of Avalon* Corwin and his allies find a way to bring functioning firearms into Amber, thus drastically altering the balance of power. The mingling of technology with magic is even more prevalent in the Merlin novels. Merlin's Ghostwheel, a computer that magically scans Shadows, has roots in both traditions. However, computers, firearms, and electricity are balanced by the increased importance of the Pattern and the Logrus, primordial deific figures who predate creation, and whose rivalries provide the driving force behind much of the action.

After concluding the Merlin novels with *Prince of Chaos,* Zelazny began writing short stories that expanded or otherwise filled in some of gaps in the larger tale. These stories also permitted Zelazny to continue his on-going experiment in examining reality from varied points of view. Zelazny's original intent was to write enough of these stories for them to be gathered in one volume, but unfortunately his death prevented this from happening.

OTHER FANTASY SERIES

The Amber novels are Zelazny's best-known fantasy works, but there are several others that deserve more than passing mention.

Another extended series features Dilvish, a hero called "the Damned" because of an extended banishment to the Hell of his world. This sequence of works began as a series of short stories, which were then combined to form the novel *Dilvish the Damned,* published in 1982. Despite its origins, the book is not merely a patchwork of unconnected tales. The stories progress in chronological order, complete with internal reference links, and Zelazny also wrote several new sections to further unify the work. The sequel to this novel is *The Changing Land* (1981), a high fantasy with elements of H. P. Lovecraft and William Hope Hodgson as undertones.

The Dilvish stories provide a particularly fascinating look at the evolution of Zelazny's stylistic preferences. The first several stories in the series (published between 1964 and 1967) are written in an affected, high fantasy style. When Zelazny resumed writing about Dilvish in 1979, the style he chose was more casual and breezy. This style continued to be used in the final novel, with the tone of the stories becoming more openly humorous.

Jack of Shadows, published in 1971, was inspired in the fantasy portions by the works of Jack Vance, an influence Zelazny acknowledges through the name of the title character. Jack, a thief and sorcerer, is one of Zelazny's less savory protagonists; he is cold and calculating, even by the standards of a society known for such traits. He draws his power from the twilight region between the dark and light sides of a world permanently fixed so that it does not rotate, and is one of the rare persons who travel between both sides. Jack is also featured in "Shadowjack," a prequel written specifically for *The Illustrated Roger Zelazny* (1978).

Zelazny's other fantasy series consists of two novels, *Changeling* (1980) and *Madwand* (1981). A third novel, *Deathmask,* was intended, but was uncompleted, unoutlined, or otherwise developed at the time of his death. *Changeling* was initially written at the request of someone interested in animating an original Zelazny piece. For that reason, Zelazny wrote the magical sequences to make them as visual as possible. This, in turn, gave a freshness and originality to the material.

Although largely fantasy in tone, *Changeling* and *Madwand* are more science fantasy than either the Dilvish or Jack of Shadows stories. In *Changeling*, Pol Detson is spirited away to our world upon the death of his father, Det, to protect him from enemies that Det—a very black sorcerer—had made. There Pol takes the place of Daniel Chain, who in order that the balance of matter between these parallel worlds not be disturbed, is taken to Pol's birth world. Each grows up a misfit. Pol's very presence causes electronic devices to malfunction. Daniel Chain, now known as Mark Marakson, is obsessed with things mechanical, a very bad trait in a world that has only evil memories of technology. Eventually, the old sorcerer who first worked the exchange returns Pol in the hope that he will defeat Mark, and a final conflict between magic and technology occurs. True to Zelazny's fascination with both, Mark is a fanatic, but he is not evil. A true exploration of evil is left to the book's sequel, *Madwand*.

FINAL WORKS

In his Introduction to Zelazny's *Four for Tomorrow* (1967), one of the earliest assessments of Zelazny's work, Theodore Sturgeon wrote: "Roger Zelazny is a writer of such merit that one judges him by higher standards than one uses on others—a cross he will bear all of his writing life" (p. 10). Sturgeon proved to be all too correct.

Yet, despite having to deal with the pressure of such high expectations, in the end Zelazny remained truest to what is any writer's own best and truest audience—himself. A quick look at the stories he wrote in the last years of his life show him continuing to stretch out, trying new things, and developing new tricks.

As has already been mentioned, during this last decade of his life he expanded the Amber universe. He also entered into several collaborative projects, mostly with peers whose work he had long admired. In addition, he launched into several "hobby book" projects.

The book that became *A Night in the Lonesome October* (1993) had been lurking in Zelazny's imagination since 1979, always as an illustrated project, never as simply a novel. Gahan Wilson, the artist Zelazny hoped to have do the illustrations, was interested, but unavailable at that time. The project lay fallow until December of 1991, when Zelazny came across his initial notes and found that this time the idea would not let him go. He wrote the entire manuscript in a surprisingly short time, contacted Wilson again, and this time the project came off.

A Night in the Lonesome October—as its dedication makes clear—is Zelazny's homage to many of authors who influenced him. The story opens with deceptively simple prose, introducing what may be one of Zelazny's strangest and most unique narrators: "I am a Watchdog. My name is Snuff. I live with my master Jack outside of London now." This simple opening expands into a humorous yet suspenseful tale, full of complex twists and turns, which recounts what happens when the stars align themselves into the proper position for magic, and thus bring the Openers and Closers into conflict over whether or not to let loose various nameless horrors.

Of the two novels Zelazny left unfinished at his death, *Donnerjack* (1997) had been conceived and conventionally contracted-for based on a proposal, while *Lord Demon* (1999) was one of Zelazny's "hobby books." In the case of both books, the chapters that introduced the majority of characters and set the action into motion had been written. When Zelazny realized he might not "make it," he asked his companion, Jane Lindskold, if she would finish the projects for him. Zelazny did not leave outlines or extensive notes. However, he and Lindskold discussed both projects, so the books are very much Zelazny's creations.

Donnerjack is classic Zelazny science fantasy. Partly written in response to cyberpunk's dystopean vision of the World Wide Web, *Donnerjack* reflects Zelazny's long-term interest in the merging of human and machine consciousness. In an undefined future, the Web crashes. When it starts up again, users discover that a sentience is present that had not been there before. Soon regular interaction between Virtù (this new presence) and Verité (as our reality comes to be known) is established. The novel has several intertwining plot lines, but the action revolves around John Darcy Donnerjack Jr. (also known as Jay), a child born of the seemingly impossible union of Virtù and Verité.

Unlike most of Zelazny's fantasy books, *Lord Demon* has an Asian rather than European source for its imagery. It is pure fantasy, despite the fact that the story—as is often the case with Zelazny—begins not in some faraway land, but in our own time and place. The protagonist is Kai Wren, a demon sorcerer and pocket-universe creator, who is drawn from self-imposed seclusion when his trusted servant is murdered. Layer upon layer of intrigue is revealed before Kai Wren learns who killed Ollie. Along the way he learns some uncomfortable truths about himself.

CONCLUSION

Much has been said here about Zelazny's unique blending of fantasy and science fiction, much about his use of myth and legend, much about his awareness of the far-reaching implications of human action. Numerous critics have praised Zelazny's elegant, poetic prose, but few have noted the appeal of his sly, sometimes earthy humor. It just doesn't do to note that a great writer might slip a pun or two into a Great Work. Zelazny did so repeatedly. Zelazny laughed at his own jokes, wept over the tragedies he created, lived and breathed each world as he wrote about it. That passion makes his novels as fresh as the day they first appeared, and will continue to make them fresh into the future.

Selected Bibliography

WORKS OF ROGER ZELAZNY

NOVELS

The Dream Master. New York: Ace, 1966.

This Immortal. New York: Ace, 1966.

Lord of Light. Garden City, N.Y.: Doubleday, 1967.

Damnation Alley. New York: Putnam, 1969.

Isle of the Dead. New York: Ace, 1969.

Creatures of Light and Darkness. Garden City, N.Y.: Doubleday, 1969.

Nine Princes in Amber. Garden City, N.Y.: Doubleday, 1970.

Jack of Shadows. New York: Walker, 1971.

The Guns of Avalon. Garden City, N.Y.: Doubleday, 1972.

To Die in Italbar. Garden City, N.Y.: Doubleday, 1973.

Today We Choose Faces. New York: Signet, 1973.

Sign of the Unicorn. Garden City, N.Y.: Doubleday, 1975.
Bridge of Ashes. New York: New American Library, 1976.
Doorways in the Sand. New York: Harper, 1976.
The Hand of Oberon. Garden City, N.Y.: Doubleday, 1976.
My Name Is Legion. New York: Ballantine, 1976.
The Courts of Chaos. Garden City, N.Y.: Doubleday, 1978.
The Chronicles of Amber. 2 vols. Garden City, N.Y.: Doubleday, 1979.
Roadmarks. New York: Ballantine, 1979.
Changeling. New York: Ace, 1980.
The Changing Land. New York: Ballantine, 1981.
Madwand. New York: Ace, 1981.
Dilvish, the Damned. New York: Ballantine, 1982.
Eye of Cat. New York: Timescape, 1982.
Trumps of Doom. New York: Arbor House, 1985.
Blood of Amber. New York: Arbor House, 1986.
A Dark Traveling. New York: Walker, 1987.
Sign of Chaos. New York: Arbor House, 1987.
Knight of Shadows. New York: Morrow, 1989.
Prince of Chaos. New York: Morrow, 1991.
Here There Be Dragons. Hampton Falls, N.H.: Donald M. Grant, 1992.
Way Up High. Hampton Falls, N.H.: Donald M. Grant, 1992.
A Night in the Lonesome October. New York: Morrow, 1993.
The Great Book of Amber. New York: Avon Eos, 1999.

COLLABORATIVE NOVELS

Deus Irae. Garden City, N.Y.: Doubleday, 1976. (With Philip K. Dick.)
Coils. New York: Tor, 1982. (With Fred Saberhagen.)
The Black Throne. New York: Baen, 1990. (With Fred Saberhagen.)
The Mask of Loki. New York: Baen, 1990. (With Thomas T. Thomas.)
Bring Me the Head of Prince Charming. New York: Bantam, 1991. (With Robert Sheckley.)
Flare. New York: Baen, 1992. (With Thomas T. Thomas.)
If At Faust You Don't Succeed. New York: Bantam, 1993. (With Robert Sheckley.)
A Farce to Be Reckoned With. New York: Bantam, 1995. (With Robert Sheckley.)
Donnerjack. New York: Avon, 1997. (With Jane Lindskold.)
Psychoshop. New York: Vintage, 1998. (With Alfred Bester.)
Lord Demon. New York: Avon, 1999. (With Jane Lindskold.)

SHORT STORY COLLECTIONS

Four for Tomorrow. New York: Ace, 1967.
The Doors of His Face, the Lamps of His Mouth. Garden City, N.Y.: Doubleday, 1971.

ROGER ZELAZNY

The Last Defender of Camelot. New York: Pocket Books, 1980.
Unicorn Variations. New York: Avon, 1983.
Frost and Fire. New York: Morrow, 1989.

UNCOLLECTED SHORT FICTION RELATED TO THE "AMBER" SERIES

"The Salesman's Tale." *Amberzine,* 6 (February 1994): 32–44.

"The Shroudling and the Guisel." *Realms of Fantasy,* 1 (October 1994)

"Blue Horse, Dancing Mountain." In *Wheel of Fortune.* Edited by Roger Zelazny. New York: Avon, 1995. Pp. 240–246.

"Coming to a Cord." *Pirate Writings,* 3, no. 2 (June 1995)

"Hall of Mirrors." In *Castle Fantastic.* Edited by John de Chancie and Martin H. Greenberg. New York: DAW Books, 1996. Pp. 11–32.

POETRY

When Pussywillows Last in the Catyard Bloomed and Other Poems. Carlton, Victoria, Australia: Norstrilia, 1980.

To Spin Is Miracle Cat. San Francisco: Underwood/Miller, 1981.

Hymn to the Sun. Radford, Va.: DNA, 1995.

OTHER WORKS

"Two Traditions and Cyril Tourner: An Examination of Morality and Humor Comedy Conventions in 'The Revenger's Tragedy.' " Unpublished Master's Thesis, Columbia University, 1962.

(Editor.) *Nebula Award Stories Three.* Garden City, N.Y.: Doubleday, 1968.

The Illustrated Roger Zelazny. Edited by Byron Preiss and illustrated by Gray Morrow. New York: Baronet, 1978. (Short stories recast as graphic novels.)

Roger Zelazny's Visual Guide to Castle Amber. New York: Avon, 1988. (With Neil Randall.)

(Editor.) *Warriors of Blood and Dream.* New York, Avon, 1995.

(Editor.) *Wheel of Fortune.* New York: Avon, 1995.

(Editor and contributor.) *Forever After.* New York: Baen, 1995. (With Robert Asprin, David Drake; Jane Lindskold, and Michael A. Stackpole.)

(Editor.) *The Williamson Effect.* New York: Tor, 1996.

BIBLIOGRAPHIES

Levack, Daniel H. C. *Amber Dreams: A Roger Zelazny Bibliography.* San Francisco: Underwood/Miller, 1983.

Sanders, Joseph. *Roger Zelazny: A Primary and Secondary Bibliography.* Boston: G. K. Hall, 1980.

Stephensen-Payne, Phil. *Roger Zelazny, Master of Amber: A Working Bibliography.* San Bernardo, Calif.: Borgo, 1991.

CRITICAL AND BIOGRAPHICAL STUDIES

Cowper, Richard. "A Rose Is a Rose Is a Rose. . . . In Search of Roger Zelazny." *Foundation: The Review of Science Fiction,* 11/12 (1977): 142–147.

Delany, Samuel R. "Faust and Archimedes." In *The Jewel-Hinged Jaw: Notes on the Language of Science Fiction.* Elizabethtown, N.Y.: Dragon, 1977. Pp. 191–210.

Francavilla, Joseph V. "These Immortals: An Alternative View of Immortality in Roger Zelazny's Science Fiction." *Extrapolation,* 25 (Spring 1984): 20–33.

———. "Promethean Bound: Heroes and Gods in Roger Zelazny's Science Fiction." *The Transcendent Adventure: Studies of Religion in Science Fiction/Fantasy.* Edited by Robert Reilly. Westport, Conn.: Greenwood, 1985. Pp. 207–222.

Fredericks, S. C. "Revivals of Ancient Mythology in Current Science Fiction and Fantasy." In *Many Futures, Many Worlds: Theme and Form in Science Fiction.* Edited by Thomas D. Clareson. Kent, Ohio: Kent State University Press, 1977. Pp. 50–65.

Friend, Beverly. "Virgin Territory: The Bonds and Boundaries of Women in Science Fiction." In *Many Futures, Many Worlds: Theme and Form in Science Fiction.* Edited by Thomas D. Clareson. Kent, Ohio: Kent State University Press, 1977.

Krulik, Theodore. *Roger Zelazny.* New York: Ungar, 1986.

Lindskold, Jane M. "All Roads Do Lead to Amber." *Extrapolation,* 31 (Winter 1990): 326–332. Reprinted in *Amberzine,* 2 (August 1992): 20–27.

———. "Zelazny's Santa Fe." *Amberzine,* 1 (March 1992): 17–23.

———. *Roger Zelazny.* New York: Twayne, 1993.

———. "Starting Backwards." *Amberzine,* 3 (April 1993): 22–26.

———. "Burn the Innocent." *Amberzine,* 4 (August 1993): 14–20.

———. "Imprinting Imagination: Kuttner's *The Dark World* As a Pattern for Amber." *Amberzine,* 5 (November 1993): 27–30.

———. "Zelazny and the Zelaforms." *Amberzine,* 6 (February 1994): 14–20.

———. "Cards on the Table." *Amberzine,* 8 (November 1995): 22–28.

———. "Zelazny and the Comics." *Amberzine,* 9 (January 1996): 9–12.

Morrisey, Thomas J. "Zelazny: Mythmaker of Nuclear War." *Science Fiction Studies,* 13 (1986): 182–192.

Rhodes, Carolyn. "Experiment As Heroic Quest in Zelazny's 'For a Breath I Tarry.'" In *The Scope of the Fantastic: Culture, Biography, Themes, Children's Literature: Selected Essays from the First International Conference on the Fantastic in Literature and Film.* Edited by Robert A. Collins and Howard D. Pearce. Westport, Conn.: Greenwood, 1985. Pp. 190–197.

Sanders, Joseph. "Zelazny: Unfinished Business." In *Voices for the Future: Essays on Major Science Fiction Writers.* Edited by Thomas Clareson. Bowling Green, Ohio: Bowling Green University Popular Press, 1979. Pp. 180–196.

———. "Dancing on the Tightrope: Immortality in Roger Zelazny." In *Death and the Serpent: Immortality in Science Fiction and Fantasy.* Edited by Carl B. Yoke and Donald M. Hassler. Westport, Conn.: Greenwood, 1985. Pp. 135–143.

Yoke, Carl B. *Roger Zelazny: Starmont Reader's Guide 2.* West Linn, Oreg.: Starmont House, 1979.

———. "Roger Zelazny's Bold New Mythologies." In *Critical Encounters II: Writers and Themes in Science Fiction.* Edited by Tom Staicar. New York: Fredrick Ungar, 1982. Pp. 73–89.

———. "What a Piece of Work Is Man: Mechanical Gods in the Fiction of Roger Zelazny." In *The Mechanical Gods: Machines in Science Fiction.* Edited by Thomas P. Dunn and Richard D. Erlich. Westport, Conn.: Greenwood, 1982. Pp. 63–74.

ROGER ZELAZNY

FILMS AND TELEVISION PROGRAMS BASED ON THE WORKS OF ROGER ZELAZNY

Damnation Alley. Film directed by Jack Smight. 20th Century-Fox, 1977.

"The Last Defender of Camelot." *Twilight Zone.* Screenplay by George R. R. Martin. CBS, April 11, 1986.

Index

Arabic numbers printed in boldface type refer to extended treatment of a subject

À Rebours (Stableford) 897
A'rak, The (Shea) 842, 843
Abarat (Barker) 67
"Abe Lincoln in McDonald's" (Morrow) 752
"About a Secret Crocodile" (Lafferty) 599
Absalom, Absalom (Straub) 912
Ackroyd, Peter **1–8**
Acorna series (McCaffrey) 699
Acorna: The Unicorn Girl (McCaffrey & Ball) 699
Act of Love (Lansdale) 605
Adept series (Kurtz & Turner) 580
Adept, The (Kurtz & Harris) 580
"Adept's Gambit" (Leiber) 644, 646, 648
"Adrift Just Off the Islets of Langerhans" (Ellison) 333
Adventures in Unhistory (Davidson) 254, 260, 261
Adventures of Doctor Eszterhazy, The (Davidson) 260
Adversary Cycle series (Wilson) 971–975
Aegrisomnia, The (Collins) 221
Aegypt (Crowley) 250
Aegypt series (Crowley) 245, 247–250
"Affair at Lahore Cantonment, The" (Davidson) 253, 256
After Silence (Carroll) 204, 206
Again, Dangerous Visions (Ellison) 333
"Agents" (Di Filippo) 288
"Agitators, The" (Ellison) 336
Agyar (Brust) 165
Aickman, Robert **9–19**
Aiken, Joan **21–31**
"Ain't You 'Most Done?" (Wolfe) 989
Aleph (Constantine) 230
"Alice, Alfie, Ted, and the Aliens" (Di Filippo) 285, 288
"Alien Graffiti" (Bishop) 85
All About Strange Monsters of the Recent Past (Waldrop) 954, 956
"All About Strange Monsters of the Recent Past" (Waldrop) 956
All Darkness Met (Cook) 234
"All on a Golden Afternoon" (Bloch) 105
"All Pieces of a River Shore" (Lafferty) 599
"All the Angels Living in Atlanta" (Carroll) 201

All the Bells on Earth (Blaylock) 93
"All the Birds Come Home to Roost" (Ellison) 335
All the King's Men (Mayne) 689
"All the Lies That Are My Life" (Ellison) 334
"All the Perfumes of Araby" (Shepard) 850
All the Rage (Wilson) 975
All the Weyrs of Pern (McCaffrey) 700
All You've Ever Wanted (Aiken) 27
"All-Consuming, The" (Shepard) 850
"Allegra's Hand" (Bishop) 85
"Allerleirauh" (Yolen) 1006
Althalus series (Eddings & Eddings) 325
Alvin Journeyman (Card) 189, 191, 192
Alvin Maker series (Card) 190–193
Alvin Master (Card) 193
Always Coming Home (Le Guin) 614, 618, 622
Amazing Maurice and His Educated Rodents, The (Pratchett) 797
Ambassadors, The (Straub) 905
"Amber out of Quath" (Norton) 772
Amber series (Zelazny) 1013–1015
Amber Spyglass, The (Pullman) 813, 814
"America" (Brite) 150
American Ghosts and Old World Wonders (Carter) 209, 211
American Gothic (Bloch) 109
American Gothic Tales (Oates) 776
American Nomad (Erickson) 344, 345
"Amerikanski Dead at the Moscow Morgue " (Newman) 763
Amnesiascope (Erickson) 341, 344, 345
"Among the Dream Speakers" (Silverberg) 867
"Among the Hairy Earthmen" (Lafferty) 595, 596
Amsterdam (McEwan) 719
Anackire (Lee) 635, 637
Anatole series (Willard) 959
Ancient Images (Campbell) 182
"And Don't Forget the One Red Rose" (Davidson) 256
And Eternity (Anthony) 47, 49
And on the Eighth Day (Davidson) 258
…And The Angel with Television Eyes (Shirley) 859
Anderson, Poul **33–43**
Andy Warhol's Dracula (Newman) 760

"Angel Down Sussex" (Newman) 764
Angel Fire East (Brooks) 156
Angel in the Parlor, The (Willard) 960, 961
"Angel of Death, The" (Shea) 841
Angel of Pain, The (Stableford) 894
Angel of the Revolution, The (Stableford) 895
Angels on Fire (Collins) 223
"Angels" (Brite) 147, 148
Angry Candy (Ellison) 334, 335, 337
Angry Lead Skies (Cook) 236
Animal Castle (Lee) 633
Animal Planet (Bradfield) 124–126
"Anna and the Ripper of Siam" (Somtow) 887
"Anne" (Di Filippo) 287
Anno Dracula (Newman) 757–764
Anno Dracula series (Newman) 757, 761, 976
Antar and the Eagles (Mayne) 689
Anthony, Piers **45–51**
Anti-Man (Koontz) 555
Antiquities (Crowley) 251
Antrax (Brooks) 157
Anubis Gates, The (Powers) 91, 786, 787
Apocalypses (Lafferty) 598, 599
"Apollo" (Disch) 295
Apprentice Adept series (Anthony) 48
Approaching Oblivion (Ellison) 334
Aquila and the Iron Horse (Somtow) 884
Aquila and the Sphinx (Somtow) 884
Aquiliad series (Somtow) 883–885
Aquiliad, The (Somtow) 884
Arabel and Mortimer series (Aiken) 25
Arc d'X (Erickson) 343, 344
Archipelago (Lafferty) 594, 597, 598
Architects of Emortality (Stableford) 897
"Are You Listening?" (Ellison) 332
Are You Loathsome Tonight? (Brite) 150
Argos Mythos series (Lafferty) 597
Ariosto (Yarbro) 998, 999
"Arise" (Brite) 150, 151
Armageddon Rag, The (Martin) 668, 669
"Arms and the Woman" (Morrow) 752
Arrive at Easterwine: The Autobiography of a Ktistec Machine (Lafferty) 594, 598

Arrow's Fall (Lackey) 586
Arrow's Flight (Lackey) 586
Arrows of the Queen (Lackey) 586
Arrows series (Lackey) 585
"Ash of Memory, the Dust of Desire, The" (Brite) 149
Ash Wednesday (Williamson) 967, 968, 971
"Asian Shore, The" (Disch) 294
"Assemblage of Kristin, The" (Morrow) 751
Assignment, Nor'Dyren (Van Scyoc) 930
Association, The (Little) 662, 663
Asylum (McGrath) 725
At the City Limits of Fate (Bishop) 85
"At the City Limits of Fate" (Bishop) 84
Athyra (Brust) 162, 164
Atlantis: Three Tales (Delany) 280
Atonement (McEwan) 720
Attempted Rescue, The (Aickman) 11, 12, 15
Atwood, Kathryn: see Ptacek, Kathryn 803
"Auggie Wren's Christmas Story" (Auster) 57
Aurelia (Lafferty) 598
Auster, Paul **53–60**
"Automatic Pistol, The" (Leiber) 645
"Autopsy, The" (Shea) 842
Avalon series (Bradley) 136–137
"Avenger of Death, The" (Ellison) 334, 335
Avenue X and Other Dark Streets (Collins) 223
"Avenue X" (Collins) 223
"Aye, and Gomorrah …" (Delany) 279
"Aymara" (Shepard) 848
"Aztechs" (Shepard) 851
Baal (McCammon) 706
Babel-17 (Delany) 278, 279
Babylon Sisters and Other Posthumans (Di Filippo) 288
Bachman, Richard: see King, Stephen 526, 534
Back in the USSA (Newman & Bryne) 759
Bad Brains (Koja) 543, 544, 546
Bad Dreams (Newman) 758
Bad Seed, The (Collins) 223
Bag of Bones (King) 533, 761
Ballad of Beta-2, The (Delany) 278
"Bar Talk" (Lansdale) 604
"Barbara" (Shirley) 859
Barbarians of Mars, The (Moorcock) 738
Barclay, Bill: see Moorcock, Michael 738
"Bard's Tale, The" (Lackey) 588

Bardic Voices series (Lackey) 587
Barker, Clive **61–70**
Barnacle Bill the Spacer and Other Stories (Shepard) 850
Baroque Fable (Yarbro) 998
Barrens and Others, The (Wilson) 976
Barrens, The (Smith) 776
"Basilisk" (Ellison) 333
Bast and Sekhmet: Eyes of Ra (Constantine & Coquio) 230
Bastard Prince, The (Kurtz) 577
Batman: Captured by the Engines (Lansdale) 609
Battlefield, The (Mayne) 687
"Bazaar of the Bizarre, The" (Leiber) 647
"Bazaar of the Horse Jewelers" (Davidson) 255
Beagle, Peter S. **71–77**
Bear Went Over the Mountain, The (Kotzwinkle) 563
Beardless Warriors, The (Matheson) 673
Bearing an Hourglass (Anthony) 47
Beast from Twenty Thousand Fathoms, The (film) 119
"Beast of the Heartland" (Shepard) 850
Beast That Shouted Love at the Heart of the World, The (Ellison) 333
Beastchild (Koontz) 552
Beasts (Crowley) 245
Beasts (Oates) 781
"Beasts of Barsac, The" (Bloch) 103
Beauty and the Beast (television series) 669
Beauty's Punishment (Roquelaure) 820
Beauty's Release (Rice) 820
"Become a Warrior" (Yolen) 1008
Bedlam's Bard series (Lackey, Guon & Edghill) 588
"Beetles" (Bloch) 101
"Before the Play" (King) 528
Beggars and Choosers (Kress) 572
Beggars in Spain (Kress) 572
Beggars Ride (Kress) 572
Beginning Place, The (Le Guin) 621–622
"Behold the Man" (Moorcock) 744
Being a Green Mother (Anthony) 47, 49
Belgarath the Sorcerer (Eddings) 323, 324, 328
Belgariad series (Eddings) 323–325
Belinda (Rice) 819
"Belle Bloody Merciless Dame" (Yolen) 1008
Bellefleur (Oates) 778, 779
"Belsen Express" (Leiber) 649
Benjamin, Paul: see Auster, Paul 53
"Bethane" (Kurtz) 577, 578

Bethany's Sin (McCammon) 706
Between, The (Due) 310–311
Bewitchments of Love and Hate, The (Constantine) 227, 229
"Beyond the Light" (Lansdale) 607
Beyond the Safe Zone (Silverberg) 866
"Beyond Time's Aegis" (Stableford) 891
Beyond World's End (Lackey & Edghill) 588
BFI Companion to Horror, The (ed. Newman) 759
Bible Stories for Adults (Morrow) 752
"Bible Stories for Adults, No. 17: The Deluge" (Morrow) 751
"Bible Stories for Adults, No. 31: The Covenant" (Morrow) 751
"Bible Stories for Adults, No. 46: The Soap Opera" (Morrow) 753
Bid Time Return (Matheson) 674, 677, 679, 680
"Big Binge, The" (Bloch) 102
Big Blow, The (Lansdale) 605
"Big Fish, The" (Newman) 759, 763
Big Time, The (Leiber) 36, 646
"Billy Fearless" (Collins) 223
"Bingo Master, The" (Oates) 775
Bio of an Ogre (Anthony) 47
Birthgrave series (Lee) 636
Birthgrave, The (Lee) 633, 636
Bishop, Michael **79–87**
Bishop's Heir, The (Kurtz) 577
Black Alice (Disch & Sladek) 293
"Black Barter" (Bloch) 102
Black Blood of the Dead, The (Stableford) 897
"Black Blood of the Dead, The" (Stableford) 897
Black Butterflies (Shirley) 859
Black Cocktail (Carroll) 204, 205
Black Company series (Cook) 235
Black Company, The (Cook) 235
"Black Coral" (Shepard) 847
Black Dogs (McEwan) 719
"Black Ferris, The" (Bradbury) 118
"Black Glass" (Leiber) 649
"Black Gondolier, The" (Leiber) 649
Black Gryphon, The (Lackey) 586
Black Hearts in Battersea (Aiken) 24
Black House (King & Straub) 535, 910
Black Jade Road, The (Grant) 805
Black Rose, The (Due) 310, 312, 313
Black Swan, The (Lackey) 588
Black Unicorn (Lee) 636
Black Unicorn, The (Brooks) 156
Black Water (Oates) 779
Black Wind (Wilson) 976
Blackouts (Auster) 54
Blades of Mars (Moorcock) 738
Blake (Ackroyd) 1

INDEX

Blameless in Abaddon (Morrow) 753, 754
Blaylock, James P. 786
Blaylock, James P. **89–97**
Bleak Seasons (Cook) 235
Blemyah Stories, The (Mayne) 689
"Blessed Event" (Schow) 836
Blind Worm, The (Stableford) 893
Bloch, Robert 779
Bloch, Robert **99–113**
Blonde (Oates) 781
Blood And Gold (Rice) 822
Blood and Water and Other Tales (McGrath) 726
Blood Autumn (Ptacek) 804, 805
Blood Dance (Lansdale) 605
Blood Games (Yarbro) 997, 998
Blood of Amber (Zelazny) 1018
Blood of Roses, The (Lee) 637
Blood Opera series (Lee) 634
"Blood Rape of the Lust Ghouls" (Schow) 836
Blooded on Arachne (Bishop) 84
Bloodsmoor Romance, A (Oates) 779
"Bloody Assizes" (Beagle) 76
Bloody Chamber, The (Carter) 210, 211
"Bloody Chamber, The" (Carter) 210, 212
Bloody Red Baron, The (Newman) 759, 762
Bloody Sun, The (Bradley) 133
Blue Adept (Anthony) 47, 48
Blue in the Face (film) 57
Blue Kansas Sky: Four Short Novels of Memory, Magic, Surmise and Estrangement (Bishop) 85
Blue Mirror, The (Koja) 546
"Blue Monkeys, The" (Swann) 918
Blue World (Mccammon) 709
Blue World, The (Vance) 939
Bluesong (Van Scyoc) 930, 935, 935
Boat of a Million Years, The (Anderson) 34, 40
"Body Politic, The" (Barker) 63
Boggart and the Monster, The (Cooper) 243
Bone Carver's Tale, The (VanderMeer) 949
Bones of the Moon (Carroll) 203–206
"Boogey man, The" (King) 535
Book of Atrix Wolf, The (Mckillip) 731
Book of Atrix Wolfe, The (Mckillip) 730, 733
Book of Hob Stories, The (Mayne) 689
Book of Lost Places, The (VanderMeer) 949
Book of Love (film) 565
Book of Skulls, The (Silverberg) 863
Book of the Beast, The (Lee) 636
Book of the Damned (Lee) 634

Book of the Long Sun series (Wolfe) 982
Book of the Mad, The (Lee) 634
Book of the Short Sun series (Wolfe) 982
Books of Blood, The (Barker) 61, 62–63, 64
Books of Great Alta, The (Yolen) 1006
Books of the Last Herald-Mage series (Lackey) 586
"Born of Man and Woman" (Matheson) 673
Born to Run (Lackey & Dixon) 588
"Born with the Dead" (Silverberg) 863
Bottoms, The (Lansdale) 605, 610
"Bound for Glory" (Shepard) 850
"Box, The" (Ketchum) 521
"Boy and His Dog, A" (Ellison) 333, 336
"Boy to Island" (Mayne) 689
Boy's Life (Mccammon) 705, 710, 711
Bradbury, Edward P.: see Moorcock, Michael 738
Bradbury, Ray **115–122**, 674, 836
Bradfield, Scott **123–127**
Bradley, Marion Zimmer **129–145**, 866
Brain Wave (Anderson) 33–35
Brakrath series: see Darkchild series (Van Scyoc) 930
Brave Little Toaster Goes to Mars, The (Disch) 295
Brave Little Toaster, The (Disch) 294
Briar Rose (Yolen) 1005
Bride of Frankenstein (Campbell) 183
Brides of Dracula series (Yarbro) 998
Bridge of Lost Desire, The (Delany) 279–281
Brigade, The (Shirley) 860
Brighten to Incandescence (Bishop) 85
Brightly Burning (Lackey) 587
"Brimstone and Salt" (Somtow) 887
Brite, Poppy Z. **147–152**
Brittle Innings (Bishop) 82, 83, 85
Brokedown Palace (Brust) 162, 165
Bromeliad series (Pratchett) 798
"Brood of Bubastis, The" (Bloch) 101
Brooks, Terry **153–160**
Brothel in Rösenstrasse, The (Moorcock) 737, 744
Brust, Steven **161–167**
"Bubba Ho-tep" (Landsdale) 609
"Buchanan's Head" (Davidson) 256
Buddha Boy (Koja) 545
Buffalo Gals and Other Animal Presences (Le Guin) 623
"Buffalo Gals, Won't You Come Out Tonight" (Le Guin) 619, 622, 623, 626
"Buffalo Hunter, The" (Straub) 910
"Bug House" (Tuttle) 924, 925

"Bully and the Beast, The" (Card) 195
Bundle of Nerves, A (Aiken) 27
Burn, Witch, Burn! (Leiber) 649, 674
Burning Water (Lackey) 587
Burying the Shadow (Constantine) 227, 228, 230
Businessman: A Tale of Terror, The (Disch) 295
"Button Molder, The" (Leiber) 649
"By His Bootstraps" (Bradley) 130
"By the Hair of the Head" (Landsdale) 604
By the North Gate (Oates) 778
By the Sword (Lackey) 586
Byzantium Endures (Moorcock) 737, 744
Cabal (Barker) 64
"Cabin on the Coast" (Wolfe) 988
Cadigan, Pat **169–176**
"Calcutta, Lord of Nerves" (Brite) 149
"Calendar Girl" (Schow) 836
Calenture (Constantine) 230
California Gothic (Etchison) 350, 351
"Call 666" (Etchison) 348
Call of Earth, The (Card) 195
Camber of Culdi (Kurtz) 576, 580
Camber the Heretic (Kurtz) 576, 581
"Camera, The" (Davidson) 255
Camp Concentration (Disch) 293
Camp Pleasant (Matheson) 680, 681
Campbell, Ramsey **177–187**
"Campbell's World" (Di Filippo) 287, 289
Candle for D'Artagnan, A (Yarbro) 998
Candlefasts (Mayne) 687
Candyman (film) 63
"Caphtor and other Places" (Davidson) 255
Captain Scatterday's Quest (Leiber) 646
Card, Orson Scott **189–199**
Cardinal Detoxes, The (play) 293
Cards of Grief (Yolen) 1004
Carnival of Destruction, The (Stableford) 893
Carpe Jugulum (Pratchett) 794
Carpet People, The (Pratchett) 793
Carrie (King) 527–529
Carrion Comfort (Simmons) 877, 877
Carroll, Jonathan **201–207**
Carter, Angela **209–219**
Cast of Corbies, A (Lackey & Sherman) 587
"Castle in the Desert: Anno Dracula 1977" (Newman) 760
Castle of Deception (Lackey & Sherman) 588
Castle of Wizardry (Eddings) 323
Castle Roogna (Anthony) 47, 48

Castleview (Wolfe) 985, 986
Cat People (Newman) 759
Catacomb Years (Bishop) 80
"Catalyst" (Kurtz) 577
"Catch that Zeppelin!" (Leiber) 649
Catch Trap, The (Bradley) 130, 132
"Cathadonian Odyssey" (Bishop) 84
Cathedral School series (Mayne) 686
"Catnip" (Bloch) 103
Catteni series (McCaffrey) 699
Catwings series (Le Guin) 614, 622
Catwitch (Tuttle) 924
"Cavalerada" (Collins) 223
Cellars (Shirley) 857, 858
Cement Garden, The (McEwan) 716
Ceremony (Cook) 233
"Chair, The" (Etchison) 349
"Chairmany" (Davidson) 256
"Chaney Legacy, The" (Bloch) 109
"Change of Season, A" (Contantine) 230
Changeling (Zelazny) 1017, 1018
Changeling Sea, The (McKillip) 730
Changeling series (Zelazny) 1017
"Changeling" (Norton) 772
Changing Land, The (Zelazny) 1017
Chapman, Lee: see Bradley, Marion Zimmer 131
Charade (Newman) 762
Charity, Colorado (Yarbro) 998
Charlie Spotted Moon series (Yarbro) 997
"Chateau d'If" (Vance) 935
Chatterton (Ackroyd) 3, 7
"Cheese Stands Alone, The" (Ellison) 335
"Chemyst, The" (Ligotti) 655
"Chihuahua Flats" (Bishop) 85
Child across the Sky, A (Carroll) 203–205
"Child and the Shadow, The" (Le Guin) 621
Child in Time, The (McEwan) 718
Childe Morgan series (Kurtz) 579
Childhood of the Magician (Willard) 960
"Children of Noah, The" (Matheson) 675
"Children of the Corn" (King) 585
Children of the Mind (Card) 195
Children of the Night (Lackey) 587
Children of the Night (Simmons) 876, 878
"Children, Women, Men, and Dragons" (Le Guin) 619, 621
Chimera's Cradle (Stableford) 897
Chinese Agent, The (Moorcock) 737, 744
"Choice of Weapons" (Aickman) 14
Christine (King) 530, 535

Christmas at Fontaine's (Kotzwinkle) 561
"Christus Apollo" (Bradbury) 118
Chrome Circle (Lackey & Dixon) 588
Chronicles of Amber (Zelazny) 1015
Chronicles of Pern: First Fall, The (McCaffrey) 700
Chronicles of the Deryni series (Kurtz) 577
Chronicles of Thomas Covenant series (Donaldson) 300–303
Churchman, The (Leiber) 644
Ciara's Song (Norton) 768
Cipher, The (Koja) 541–543, 544, 545
Ciphers (Di Filippo) 289
City Come A-Walkin' (Shirley) 856, 857
City in the Autumn Stars, The (Moorcock) 743
City of Glass (Auster) 54
City of Iron (Williamson) 970
City of Saints and Madmen (VanderMeer) 946, 947,948
City of the Beast (Moorcock) 738
City of Truth (Morrow) 752, 754
"City on the Edge of Forever" (Ellison) 336
Claiming Of Sleeping Beauty, The (Roquelaure) 820
Clara Reeve (Disch) 297
Clash of Kings, A (Martin) 670
Clash of Star-Kings (Davidson) 258
Climate of Change (Anthony) 47
Clingfire series (Bradley & Ross) 136
Clive Barker's Salome and The Forbidden (film) 64
"Cloak, The" (Bloch) 102
"Clock Watcher, The" (Aickman) 17
Clockwork (Pullman) 812, 814
Clockwork, or All Wound Up (Pullman) 811
Close Encounters with the Deity (Bishop) 84
Cloudcry (Van Scyoc) 930, 931
Cockatrice Boys, The (Aiken) 26
Codex Derynianus (Kurtz) 578
Cold Blood (Shirley) 859
Cold Copper Tears (Cook) 236
Cold Fire (Koontz) 554, 556
Cold Shoulder Road (Aiken) 25
Coldheart Canyon (Barker) 67
"Collaborating" (Bishop) 84
Collected Stories (Matheson) 675
Collector of Hearts, The (Oates) 776, 780
Collins, Nancy A. **221–225**
Colonel Pyat series (Moorcock) 737, 744
Colonel Rutherford's Colt (Shepard) 851

Color out of Time, The (Shea) 841, 843
Colour of Magic, The (Pratchett) 792, 793
Colvin, James: see Moorcock, Michael 738
"Come Lady Death" (Beagle) 73, 74
"Come Then, Mortal, We Will Seek Her Soul" (Shea) 840
Comfort of Strangers, The (McEwan) 715, 717
"Coming of the Doll, The" (Cardigan) 170
Coming of Wisdom, The (Duncan) 316
"Coming Soon to a Theatre Near You" (Schow) 835
Communion Blood (Yarbro) 995
Companions on the Road (Lee) 636
"Company of Wolves, the" (Carter) 210, 211, 215
"Compulsory Games" (Aickman) 17
Conclave of the Shadows series (Feist) 358
"Confessions of Ebenezer Scrooge, The" (Morrow) 752
Conjure Wife (Leiber) 645, 647, 649
Conrad Aiken Remembered (Aiken) 22
Conspiracies (Wilson) 975
"Conspiracy of Noise" (Di Filippo) 288
Constantine, Storm **227–232**
"Consuming Passion" (Moorcock) 744
Conte Cruel (Leiber) 647
Continent of Lies, The (Morrow) 750, 751
"Continued on Next Rock" (Lafferty) 599
Continuum (McCaffrey) 697, 698
Cook, Glen **233–238**
"Cool Theory of Literature, The" (Brust) 166
Cooper, Susan **239–244**
"Coppola's Dracula" (Newman) 757, 760
Corum series (Moorcock) 741–742
Couch, The (Bloch) 108
Count Geiger's Blues (Bishop) 82
Count Karlstein (Pullman) 810
Count of Eleven, The (Campbell) 182
Country Life (Ackroyd) 1
Coup de Grace and Other Stories (Vance) 936
Courts of Chaos, The (Zelazny) 1016
"Courtship Rituals" (Due) 312
Cover (Ketchum) 519
Cradle of the Sun (Stableford) 891
Cradlefasts (Mayne) 687
Craig, Brian: see Stableford, Brian 891
"Cream of the Damned, The" (Leiber) 646

INDEX

Creatures of Light and Darkness (Zelazny) 1016
"Creeper in the Crypt, The" (Bloch) 102
Creepy Company, A (Aiken) 27
Cretan series (Swann) 917
"Cricket" (Aiken) 27
"Crickets" (Matheson) 675
Crisis of Empire (Yarbro) 997
"Croatoan" (Ellison) 334
"Crocodile Rock" (Shepard) 850
Crook Factory, The (Simmons) 875, 876
Crooked House, The (Duncan) 320
"Crossing, The" (Oates) 780
Crosswicks Horror, The (Oates) 779
"Crouch End" (King) 536
Crow: City of Angels, The (Williamson) 970
Crow: Clash by Night, The (Williamson) 970
Crow: Temple of Night, The (Somtow) 886
Crow: The Lazarus Heart, The (Brite) 150
Crowley, John **245–252**
Crown of Empire (Yarbro) 997
Crown of Silence, The (Constantine) 231
Crusade of Fire (ed. Kurtz) 580
Crusader's Torch, (Yarbro) 996
Cry Silver Bells (Swann) 917, 918
Cry to Heaven (Rice) 820
Crystal City, The (Card) 193
Crystal Gryphon, The (Norton) 768, 771
Crystal Line (McCaffrey) 698
Crystal Singer, The (McCaffrey) 697
Cube Route (Anthony) 48
Cuckoo Tree, The (Aiken) 24
Cuddy (Mayne) 690
Cugel's Saga (Vance) 935, 940
Cujo (King) 525, 526, 529–531
Cursed, The (Duncan) 318–321
Cutter, John: see Shirley, John 857
Cutting Edge (Etchison) 347
Cutting Edge, The (Duncan) 317
Cycle of the Werewolf (King) 530
Cyrion (Lee) 638
Daemonomania (Crowley) 247, 249, 250
Dagger Magic (Kurtz & Harris) 580
"Dagon" (Davidson) 254
Damnation Game, The (Barker) 63
"Dan Cohen" (Davidson) 255
Dan Leno and the Limehouse Golem (Ackroyd) 3, 6
Dance for Emilia, A (Beagle) 76
Dancer from Atlantis, The (Anderson) 38

Dancers at the End of Time series (Moorcock) 739, 742
Dancing at the Edge of the World: Thoughts on Words, Women, Places (Le Guin) 614, 620
Dandelion Wine (Bradbury) 116
Dangerous Games (Aiken) 24
Dangerous Visions (Ellison) 333
"Danny Deever" (Davidson) 256
"Danny Weinstein's Magic Book" (Willard) 962
Danse Macabre (King) 526–528
"Dark Beauty of Unheard Horrors, The" (Ligotti) 656
Dark Country, The (Etchison) 348
"Dark Country, The" (Etchison) 349
Dark Dance (Lee) 637
Dark Entries (Aickman) 16
Dark Half, The (King) 531
Dark is Rising series (Cooper) 239–243
Dark Is Rising, The (Cooper) 239–241, 243
Dark Ladies (Leiber) 649
Dark Matter (Due) 310
Dark of the Woods (Koontz) 555
Dark Rivers of the Heart (Koontz) 551
Dark Side of the Sun, The (Pratchett) 791
Dark Tower II: The Drawing of the Three, The (King) 534
Dark Tower III: The Waste Lands, The (King) 534
Dark Tower IV: Wizard and Glass, The (King) 534
Dark Tower series (King) 528, 534
Dark Tower: The Gunslinger, The (King) 534, 536
Darkchild (Van Scyoc) 930
Darkchild series (Van Scyoc) 930–931
Darker Angels (Somtow) 886, 887
Darkest Part of the Woods, The (Campbell) 183
Darkest Road, The (Kay) 509, 510
Darkfall (Koontz) 553, 554
Darkfall's (Koontz) 554
Darkling Wind, The (Somtow) 884
Darkness at Sethanon, A (Feist) 356
Darkness Divided (Shirley) 860
Darkness in My Soul, A (Koontz) 553
Darkness, I (Lee) 637
Darkover Landfall (Bradley) 133
Darkover series (Bradley) 132–135, 772, 866
Darkside (Etchison) 349
Darwin's Blade (Simmons) 876, 880
"Dat-Tay-Vao" (Wilson) 976
Daughter of Dracula (Campbell) 183
Daughter of Regals and Other Tales (Donaldson) 304
Daughter of the Empire (Feist) 357

Daughter of Troy (Franklin) 320
Daughters of the Sunstone (Van Scyoc) 930
Davidson, Avram **253–265**
Dawn of Fear (Cooper) 239
"Day of Reckoning" (Matheson) 678
"Day of the Glacier" (Lafferty) 594
Day of the Minotaur (Swann) 917, 918
Day of Their Return, The (Anderson) 36
"Day the Martels Got the Cable, The" (Cardigan) 170
"Daybroke" (Bloch) 105
Days between Stations (Erickson) 341, 343–345
"Dazzle Redux" (Bradfield) 124
"Dazzle" (Bradfield) 124, 126
"Dazzle's Inferno" (Bradfield) 124
De Lint, Charles **267–276**
De Vermis Mysteriis (Bloch) 100
Dead and Buried (film) 997
Dead Beat, The (Bloch) 108
"Dead Cop, The" (Etchison) 351
Dead in the West (Lansdale) 605
"Dead Love You, The" (Carroll) 205
"Dead Man, The" (Wolfe) 981
"Dead Travel Fast" (Newman) 760
Dead Zone, The (King) 529–531
Deadly Streets, The (Ellison) 332
"Deadtime Story" (Etchison) 351
Dealings of Daniel Kesserich, The (Leiber) 644, 649
"Death and the Single Girl" (Disch) 294
Death Artist, The (Etchison) 351
"Death from Exposure" (Cardigan) 170
Death Instinct (Emmons) 662
Death Instinct (Little) 661, 662
Death of an Adept (Kurtz & Harris) 580
Death Qualified: A Mystery of Chaos (Oates) 781
Death series (Pratchett) 794
Death's Master (Lee) 634
Deathbird Stories (Ellison) 331, 333
"Deathbird, The" (Ellison) 331, 333, 335, 337
Deathmask (Zelazny) 1017
"Deathtracks" (Etchison) 348
Decision at Doona (McCaffrey) 698
Declare (Powers) 787, 789, 790
Dedalus Book of Decadence (Moral Ruins), The (ed. Stableford) 897
Deep as the Marrow (Wilson) 976
"Deep Breathing Exercises" (Card) 195
Deep, The (Crowley) 245
Deepwater Dreams (Van Scyoc) 929, 931–933
Delany, Samuel R. **277–283**

"Delivery" (Shea)
"Delta Sly Honey" (Shepard) 847
Demon and Other Tales (Oates) 776
Demon Knight (Hood) 319
Demon Lord of Karanda (Eddings) 324
Demon Princes, The (Vance) 935, 939
Demon Rider (Hood) 319
Demon Seed (Koontz) 555
Demon series (Brooks) 156–157
Demon Sword (Hood) 319
"Demon with a Glass Hand" (Ellison) 336
"Demoness, The" (Lee) 635
Demons (Shirley) 860
Demons by Daylight (Campbell) 179
Demons Don't Dream (Anthony) 47, 48
Dervish Is Digital (Cadigan) 170, 172, 173
Deryni Archives (Kurtz) 577
Deryni Checkmate (Kurtz) 577
Deryni Magic (Kurtz) 576, 578
Deryni Rising (Kurtz) 575–577
Deryni series (Kurtz) 575
Deryni Tales (Kurtz) 579
"Descending" (Disch) 293
"Desert of Stolen Dreams, The" (Silverberg) 867
Desperation (King) 525, 532, 533
Destiny of the Sword, The (Duncan) 316
Destiny Times Three (Leiber) 646
Destroy All Brains! (Di Filippo) 286
"Detective of Dreams, The" (Wolfe) 989
"Devil Disinvests, The" (Bradfield) 124
Devil in a Forest, The (Wolfe) 987
Devil Is Dead series (Lafferty) 597
Devil Is Dead, The (Lafferty) 597, 598
"Devil with You, The" (Bloch) 102
Devil's Arithmetic, The (Yolen) 1004, 1005, 1007
Dexter, John: see Bradley, Marion Zimmer 131
Dhalgren (Delany) 279
Di Filippo, Paul **285–291**
Diamond Throne, The (Eddings) 325
Diana Tregarde Investigations series (Lackey) 587
"Diary of a Mad Deity" (Morrow) 751
"Dick W. and His Pussy; or, Tess and Her Adequate Dick" (Yolen) 1008
Dickens (Ackroyd) 1, 2
Dido and Pa (Aiken) 25
Die Panische Hand (Carroll) 205
Different Seasons (King) 535, 536
Digging Leviathan, The (Blaylock) 90, 91
Dilvish series (Zelazny) 1017
Dilvish the Damned (Zelazny) 1017

Dinner at Deviant's Palace (Powers) 787, 789, 790
"Dirty Work" (Cardigan) 171
"Disappearing Act" (Matheson) 675
Disappearing Dwarf, The (Blaylock) 90
Disch, Thomas M. **293–298**
Discworld Companion, The (Pratchett) 797
Discworld series (Pratchett) 791–798
Dispossessed: An Ambiguous Utopia, The (Le Guin) 614
"Distances" (Koja) 541
Diversions of Purley, The (Ackroyd) 1
"Do the Dead Sing?" (King) 536
"Do You Believe in Magic?" (Di Filippo) 287
Doctor Rat (Kotzwinkle) 561, 563, 565
"Doctor Wu's Portable Decryption of Ciphers" (Di Filippo) 289
"Doctor's Case, The" (King) 536
"Doctrine of the Leather-Stocking Jesus, The" (Willard) 960
"Dog Park, The" (Etchison) 350, 351
"Dogstar Man" (Willard) 962
"Dolan's Cadillac" (King) 536
Doll Who Ate His Mother, The (Campbell) 179
"Doll, The" (Oates) 781
"Dollburger" (Tuttle) 926
Dollmaker, The (Cooper) 239
Dolores Claiborne (King) 525, 526, 532
Domains of Darkover (Bradley) 130
Domes of Fire (Eddings) 325
Dominion (Little) 662
Donaldson, Stephen R. **299–308**
Donnerjack (Zelazny) 1012, 1018, 1019
Doomstalker (Cook) 233
Doona series (McCaffrey) 700
Door through Space, The (Bradley) 133
"Doors of His Face, the Lamps of His Mouth, The" (Zelazny) 1012, 1013
Double Edge (Etchison) 351
"Double Felix, The" (Di Filippo) 285
"Down in the Hole" (Collins) 222
Downward to the Earth (Silverberg) 864
"Dowry of Angyar, The" (Le Guin) 614
Dozen Tough Jobs, A (Waldrop) 954
"Dr. Bhumbo Singh" (Davidson) 256
Dr. Haggard's Disease (McGrath) 725
Drachenfels (Newman) 758
Dracula In Love (Shirley) 856
Dradin, in Love (VanderMeer) 946, 948
Dragaeran Empire series (Brust) 162–165
Dragon (Brust) 162, 164
"Dragon Fin's Soup" (Somtow) 887
Dragon Hoard, The (Lee) 633, 636

Dragon in the Sword, The (Moorcock) 741
"Dragon Masters, The" (Vance) 935, 939
Dragon Never Sleeps, The (Cook) 234
"Dragon Scale Silver" (Norton) 772
Dragon Tears (Koontz) 556
Dragon's Blood (Yolen) 1004
Dragon's Boy, The (Yolen) 1007
Dragondrums (McCaffrey) 700
Dragonflight (McCaffrey) 694–700
Dragonfly (Koontz) 555
"Dragonfly" (Le Guin) 617, 625, 626
Dragonquest (McCaffrey) 699
"Dragonrider" (McCaffrey) 694
Dragons in the Trees (Davidson) 260
Dragonsdawn (McCaffrey) 700
Dragonseye (McCaffrey) 700
Dragonsinger (McCaffrey) 700
Dragonsong (McCaffrey) 700
Drangonriders of Pern series (McCaffrey) 694–696
Drawing Blood (Brite) 149, 150
Drawing of the Dark (Powers) 789
Drawing of the Dark, The (Powers) 786–790
Dread Empire series (Cook) 234
"Dread" (Barker) 63
Dream Master, The (Zelazny) 1012
Dream of the Wolf (Bradfield) 124
"Dream of the Wolf, The" (Bradfield) 124, 126
"Dream Smith" (Norton) 772
"Dream-Makers, The" (Bloch) 105
Dreamcatcher (King) 534
"Dreamclown, The" (Collins) 221
"Dreamers" (Newman) 758
Dreaming Place, The (De Lint) 270
Dreaming Revolution: Transgression in the Development of American Romance (Bradfield) 123
"Dreams Must Explain Themselves" (Le Guin) 620
Dreams of Steel (Cook) 235
Dreams Underfoot (De Lint) 270
Dreamthief's Daughter, The (Moorcock) 740
Dreamthorp (Williamson) 969
Dressing Up: Transvestism and Drag, the History of an Obsession (Ackroyd) 1
Driftwood (Swann) 916
Drink Down the Moon (De Lint) 269
Drive-In 2, The (Lansdale) 608
Drive-In, The (Lansdale) 607, 608
"Driven" (Ptacek) 806
Drowntide (Van Scyoc) 931–933
Druid of Shannara, The (Brooks) 156
Drumm, D. B.: see Shirley, John 857
"Duck Hunt" (Landsdale) 605

INDEX

Due, Tananarive **309–314**
"Duel" (Matheson) 674
Duncan, Dave **315–322**
Durdane (Vance) 939
Durdane series (Vance) 939
"Dusty Loves" (Yolen) 1008
"Dybbuk of Mazel Tov IV, The" (Silverberg) 866
Dydeetown World (Wilson) 976
Dying Earth series (Vance) 935
Dying Earth, The (Vance) 936, 937, 939
"Dying in Bangkok" (Simmons) 878
Dying Inside (Silverberg) 865, 866, 868
Dying of the Light, The (Martin) 667
Dying World (Silverberg) 865
E Pluribus Unicorn (Sturgeon) 130
E.T.: The Extraterrestrial (Kotzwinkle) 561, 563, 564
"Each Night, Every Year" (Ptacek) 806
"Eager Dragon, The" (Bloch) 102
Eagle and the Nightingale, The (Lackey) 587
Earl Aubec (Moorcock) 744
"Earth Dwellers, The" (Kress) 569
Earthborn (Card) 196
Earthbound (Matheson) 675, 678
Earthfall (Card) 196
Earthfasts (Mayne) 685, 686, 688
Earthfasts series (Mayne) 686–687
"Earthly Mother Sits and Sings, An" (Crowley) 251
Earthquake Weather (Powers) 787
Earthsea Revisioned (Le Guin) 614, 619, 621
Earthsea series (Le Guin) 614, 615–621
East of Midnight (Lee) 636
Eclipse (Shirley) 857, 858
Eclipse Corona (Shirley) 858
Eclipse series (Shirley) 858
Eddings, David **323–330**
"Edge, The" (Matheson) 675
"Eenie, Meenie, Ipsateenie" (Cardigan) 170
"Effects of Alienation, The" (Waldrop) 956
Egyptian Birth Signs (Constantine & Phillips) 231
"Eidolons" (Ellison) 335
Einstein Intersection, The (Delany) 278, 279
"El Vilvoy de las Islas, El" (Davidson) 257
"Elder, The" (Brite) 147
Elenium series (Eddings) 325
"Elephant's Ear" (Aiken) 27
Elephantasm (Lee) 635
Eleventh Hour, The (Stableford) 898
Elf Queen of Shannara, The (Brooks) 156
Elfin Ship, The (Blaylock) 89

Elfstones of Shannara, The (Brooks) 155
"Elle est Trois (La Mort)" (Lee) 634
Ellison Wonderland (Ellison) 332
Ellison, Harlan **331–339**
Elric series (Moorcock) 739–740
Elvenbane (Lackey & Norton) 588
Elvenblood (Lackey & Norton) 588
Elvenborn (Lackey & Norton) 588
"Emissary from Hamelin" (Ellison) 333
Emmons, Phillip: see Little, Bentley 662
Emperor and Clown (Duncan) 317
Emphatically Not SF, Almost (Bishop) 84
Emphyrio (Vance) 939
Empire of Dust (Williamson) 970
Empire of Fear, The (Stableford) 892, 893
Empire series (Feist & Wurts) 357
Empire Star (Delany) 278
"Enchanted Fruit, The" (Campbell) 179
Enchanters' End Game (Eddings) 323
Enchantment (Card) 193, 194
Enchantments of Flesh and Spirit, The (Constantine) 227, 229
"End of a Summer's Day, The" (Campbell) 179
"End of Life as We Know It, The" (Shepard) 847
"End of the Pier Show, The" (Newman) 764
Ender's Game (Card) 189, 195
Ender's Shadow (Card) 195
Ends of the Earth, The (Shepard) 848–849
Enduring Love (McEwan) 719
Endymion (Simmons) 879
Enemy of My Enemy, The (Davidson) 258
Enemy of the State, An (Wilson) 971
"Engine of Samoset Erastus Hale and One Other, Unknown" (Davidson) 257
Engine Summer (Crowley) 245
English Music (Ackroyd) 4, 5, 7
"Enoch" (Bloch) 103, 107
Enquiries of Doctor Eszterhazy, The (Davidson) 254, 260
Ensign Flandry (Anderson) 36
"Enter a Soldier. Later, Enter Another" (Silverberg) 864
"Entr'acte" (Schow) 836, 837
"Environment Problem" (Moorcock) 744
Epic Fantasy in the Modern World (Donaldson) 303
Epitaph in Rust (Powers) 786, 789

Equal Rites (Pratchett) 792, 793
Eric (Pratchett) 793, 797
Erickson, Steve **341–346**
"Escape from Evening" (Moorcock) 741
Essential Ellison: A Thirty-Five-Year Retrospective, The (Ellison) 332
Estcarp/Escore series (Norton) 768
Etchison, Dennis **347–353**
Eternal Champion, The (Moorcock) 741
Eternal Footman, The (Morrow) 753
"Eternity and Afterward" (Shepard) 851
"Eumenides in the Fourth Floor Lavatory" (Card) 195
"Eurema's Dam" (Lafferty) 599
"Events Which Took Place a Day before Other Events" (Davidson) 256
Everville (Barker) 66
"Everybody Needs a Little Love" (Bloch) 109
Everything's Eventual (King) 535, 536
Exchange, The (VanderMeer) 947
"Executioner's Beautiful Daughter, the" (Carter) 216
"Exercise of Faith, The" (Shepard) 848
Exile, The (Kotzwinkle) 562, 563
Exit at Toledo Blade Boulevard, The (Ketchum) 520
Exit To Eden (Rampling) 820
Expensive People (Oates) 779
Exploded Heart, The (Shirley) 855, 858, 859
Exquisite Corpse (Brite) 149, 150
"Extra, The" (Shea) 842
"Extracts from the Records of the New Zodiac and the Diaries of Henry Watson Fairfax" (Williamson) 970
Extremities (Koja) 545
Eye (Schow) 836
Eyes of Darkness, The (Koontz) 552
Eyes of the Dragon, The (King) 528
"Eyes of the Mummy, The" (Bloch) 101
Eyes of the Overworld, The (Vance) 744, 839
Ezra Pound and His World (Ackroyd) 1
Face of Fear, The (Koontz) 556
Face of the Waters, The (Silverberg) 867
Face That Must Die, The (Campbell) 178, 179, 183
"Faceless God, The" (Bloch) 101
"Faces" (Wilson) 976
Faded Steel Heat (Cook) 237
Faerie Queene, The (Spenser) 301
Faerie Tale (Feist) 358
Faery Lands Forlorn (Duncan) 317

"Fafhrd and Me" (Leiber) 643
Fafhrd and the Gray Mouser series (Leiber) 647–648
Fahrenheit 451 (Bradbury) 115–117, 119
Fairy Tales of London Town: See-Saw Sacradown, The (Mayne) 690
Fairy Tales of London Town: Upon Paul's Steeple, The (May 690
Faithless Lollybird, The (Aiken) 27
"Falcon Blood" (Norton) 772
Falcons of Narabedla (Bradley) 132
"Fall from Innocence: The Body" (King) 536
Fall of Atlantis (Bradley) 131
Fall of Hyperion (Simmons) 878
Fall of Rome, The (Lafferty) 598
Fall of the Dream Machine, The (Koontz) 555
Fall of the Towers, The (Delany) 278
"Fall River Axe Murders, the" (Carter) 210, 211, 214
Fallen Country, The (Somtow) 887
"Falling Expectations" (Di Filippo) 285
"Falling Man, The" (Schow) 833, 834
False Dawn (Yarbro) 994
False Memory (Koontz) 557
False Notes (Yarbro) 997
Familiar Spirit (Tuttle) 923–925
"Family Monkey, The" (Tuttle) 923, 925, 926
"Family" (Oates) 776
Famous Monsters (Newman) 759, 760, 763
"Famous Monsters" (Newman) 758, 763
"Fane of the Black Pharoah" (Bloch) 101
Fantastic, The (Tuttle) 925
Fantasy Worlds of Peter S. Beagle, The (Beagle) 74
Far Forests, The (Aiken) 27
Farm That Ran Out of Names, The (Mayne) 689
Farthest Shore, The (Le Guin) 616–618, 621
"Fascination of the Abomination, the" (Silverberg) 868
"Fat Face" (Shea) 841, 842
"Fat Man, The" (Landsdale) 604
Fata Morgana (Kotzwinkle) 565
Father of Stones, The (Shepard) 848
Favorite Tales from around the World (ed. Yolen) 1001
Fawcett, Quinn: see Yarbro, Chelsea Quinn 997
"Fear Planet, The" (Bloch) 105
Fear That Man (Koontz) 553
Feast in Exile: Saint-Germain in India, A (Yarbro) 996

"Feast in the Abbey, The" (Bloch) 100
Feast Of All Saints, The (Rice) 820
Feather Stroke (Van Scyoc) 931–932
"Feelings" (Wilson) 976
Feet of Clay (Pratchett) 795
Feist, Raymond Elias **355–359**
"Fetch, The" (Aickman) 12, 17
"Fever" (Ellison) 336
Fevre Dream (Martin) 668
"Fiddler's Fee" (Bloch) 101
"Field of Vision" (Le Guin) 625
Fifth Elephant, The (Pratchett) 795
Fifth Head of Cerberus, The (Wolfe) 982
"Fin de Cyclé" (Waldrop) 956
"Final Shtick" (Ellison) 334
"Finder, The" (Le Guin) 618, 626
Fine and Private Place, A (Beagle) 72–76
Fionavar Tapestry series (Kay) 509–510
"Fire Balloons, The" (Bradbury) 118
Fire in His Hands, The (Cook) 234
Fire Rose, The (Lackey) 588
"Fire Zone Emerald" (Shepard) 848
Firebird, The (Lackey) 588
Firebrand, The (Bradley) 136
Firebrat (Willard) 959, 962
Firebug (Bloch) 108
Firecode (Yarbro) 997
Firefly (Anthony) 47, 49
Fireman, The (Kotzwinkle) 561, 565
"Fireman, The" (Bradbury) 121
Fires of Eden (Simmons) 877, 879
Firestarter (King) 525, 529, 530
Firework-Maker's Daughter, The (Pullman) 811
"First Anniversary" (Matheson) 678
"First Book of the Art" (Barker) 65
First King of Shannara, The (Brooks) 157
First Light (Ackroyd) 3, 7
First Love Last Rites (McEwan) 716
"Fish Night" (Landsdale) 604
"Fisherman . . . A Tashlich Legend, The" (Davidson) 255
"Fishing of the Demon Sea, The" (Shea) 840, 843
Five Hundred Years After (Brust) 162, 164
Flame in Byzantium, A (Yarbro) 996
Flame Is Green, The (Lafferty) 598
Flat Earth series (Lee) 634
"Flesh and the Mirror" (Carter) 216
Flight from Nevèrÿon (Delany) 81, 279
Flight of Vengeance (Norton) 768
Floating Dragon (Straub) 905–907, 909, 910
Floating Illusions (Yarbro) 998
"Flying to Byzantium" (Tuttle) 926
"Foetus, The" (Disch) 294

Fog, The (Etchison) 348
"Foghorn, The" (Bradbury) 119
Folk of the Air, The (Beagle) 74, 75
"Folksong from the Montayna Province" (Le Guin) 614
Follow the Footprints (Mayne) 685
Fools (Cadigan) 169–171
For Love of Evil (Anthony) 46, 47, 49
Forbidden Tower, The (Bradley) 130, 134
Forbidden, The (Barker) 64
"Forbidden, The" (Barker) 63
Forest House, The (Bradley) 136
Forest of Forever, The (Swann) 917, 918
Forest of the Night (Somtow) 885
Forests of the Heart (De Lint) 271
Forever After (ed. Zelazny) 1012
Forgetting Places (Somtow) 887
Forgotten Beasts of Eld, The (Mckillip) 729–731
Forms of Heaven (Barker) 62
Fortress of Frost and Fire (Lackey & Emerson) 588
Fortress of the Pearl, The (Moorcock) 740
Four and Twenty Blackbirds (Lackey) 587
"Four Dark Fables" (Oates) 781
Four for Tomorrow (Zelazny) 1018
"Four Ghosts in Hamlet" (Leiber) 647
Four Horses for Tishtry (Yarbro) 998
Four Past Midnight (King) 535, 536
Fourth Mansions (Lafferty) 597, 599
Fox Gate and Other Stories, The (Mayne) 690
Foxfire (Cooper) 239
Foxfire: Confessions of a Girl Gang (Oates) 779
Fractal Paisleys (Di Filippo) 285–288
Frankenstein (opera libretti) (Disch) 293
Franklin, Sarah B.: see Duncan, Dave 320
"Franklyn Paragraphs, The" (Campbell) 179
Freedom and Necessity (Brust) 162, 165
Freedom Flight (Lackey & Guon) 588
Freedom in the Family (Due) 310
"Freedom of the Race" (McCaffrey) 693
Freedom's Landing (McCaffrey) 699
Freezer Burn (Lansdale) 610
"French Key, The" (Davidson) 256
"Friend's Best Man" (Carroll) 205, 206
"Friendship Light, The" (Wolfe) 989
"Frog on the Mountain" (Lafferty) 594
"From A to Z, in the Chocolate Alphabet" (Ellison) 334–336
"From Elfland to Poughkeepsie" (Le Guin) 615, 616, 620

INDEX

From the Dust Returned (Bradbury) 115–117
From the Teeth of Angels (Carroll) 205
"Frost Monstreme, The" (Leiber) 648
Fulfillments of Fate and Desire, The (Constantine) 227, 229
"Full Count, The" (Landsdale) 604
"Function of Dream Sleep, The" (Ellison) 334, 335
Funeral for the Eyes of Fire, A (Bishop) 80
"Funnel of God, The" (Bloch) 106
"Furies in Black Leather" (Collins) 223
"Further Developments in the Strange Case of Dr Jekyll and Mr Hyde" (Newman) 763
Future Imperative (Duncan) 320
Gabriel (Tuttle) 925
"Gaffer, The" (Davidson) 256
Galactic Effectuator (Vance) 935
Galilee (Barker) 67
"Game in the Pope's Head" (Wolfe) 988
Game of Dark, A (Mayne) 688
Game of Thrones, A (Martin) 670
"Game of Time and Pain, The" (Delany) 280
"Gandhi at the Bat" (Williamson) 967
Gap into Conflict, The (Donaldson) 305
Gap into Madness, The (Donaldson) 305
Gap into Power, The (Donaldson) 305
Gap into Ruin, The (Donaldson) 305
Gap into Vision The (Donaldson) 305
Gap Series (Donaldson) 305
Garan the Eternal (North) 767
Gardner, Mirian: see Bradley, Marion Zimmer 131
Garrett series (Cook) 235–237
Gate of Time (Silverberg) 868
Gates of Sleep, The (Lackey) 589
"Gateway of Eternity, The" (Stableford) 897
Gather, Darkness! (Leiber) 645, 646, 649
General's Wife, The (Straub) 910
Genesys series (Stableford) 897
Gentleman Junkie and Other Stories of the Hung-Up Generation (Ellison) 333, 334
Geodyssey series (Anthony) 47
"Georgia Story, A" (Brite) 147
Gerald's Game (King) 532
Get Off the Unicorn (McCaffrey) 698
Getting Into Death and Other Stories (Disch) 294
"Getting Into Death" (Disch) 294, 297
Ghastly Beyond Belief (ed. Newman & Gaiman) 757

Ghost Dance (Ptacek) 805, 806
"Ghost Light, The" (Leiber) 649
"Ghost of an Affair, A" (Yolen) 1008
Ghost Story (Straub) 907–908
Ghostlight (Bradley) 137
Ghosts (Auster) 54
Giant Bones (Beagle) 74
Gila Queen's Guide to Markets, The (Ptacek) 806
Gila! (Simons) 801
Gilded Chain, The (Duncan) 320
Gilden-Fire (Donaldson) 299
"Gilgamesh in the Outback" (Silverberg) 864, 867
Gilgamesh the King (Silverberg) 867
"Gills" (Schow) 834
Girl Next Door, The (Ketchum) 519
Girl Who Loved Tom Gordon, The (King) 533
"Girl with the Blackened Eye, The" (Oates) 780
"Girl with the Hungry Eyes, The" (Leiber) 649
Glass Ball, The (Mayne) 686
"Glass Floor, The" (King) 526
Gloriana (Moorcock) 739, 744
"Glowworm" (Ellison) 332
Gnosis (Crowley) 247
Go Home Again (Waldrop) 952
"Goat Song" (Anderson) 38
Goat Without Horns, The (Swann) 918
"God's Hour" (Bishop) 85
"Goddess in Glass, The" (Shea) 841, 842
Godhead series (Morrow) 752, 754
Gods Abide, The (Swann) 915, 920
Going Home Again (Waldrop) 952, 954–957
Gold Unicorn (Lee) 636
Golden Barge, The (Moorcock) 739, 741, 744
Golden Bowl, The (Straub) 905
"Golden Gate" (Lafferty) 593
Golden Grove, The (Kress) 571
Golden, The (Shepard) 849, 850
Golem in the Gears (Anthony) 47, 48
"Golem, The" (Davidson) 253, 254, 256, 259
Gone South (Mccammon) 705, 711
"Gone" (Ketchum) 521
"Gonna Roll the Bones" (Leiber) 647
"Good Friday" (Wilson) 976
"Good Knight's Work, A" (Bloch) 102
"Good News from the Vatican" (Silverberg) 864
Good Omens (Pratchett) 798
"Goodbye, Miranda" (Moorcock) 744
Gorgon and Other Beastly Tales, The (Lee) 638
"Gorgon, The" (Lee) 634

"Gospel According to Gamaliel Crucis, The" (Bishop) 84
"Gospel Train" (Willard) 960
Gotham Handbook (Auster) 53
"Grail" (Ellison) 335
"Grand Tour, The" (Shepard) 849
"Granny Rumple" (Yolen) 1005, 1008
Grant, Kathryn: see Ptacek, Kathryn 803
Grass Rope, The (Mayne) 686
Grave, Stephen: see Schow, David J. 834
Gravelight (Bradley) 137
Graves, Valerie: see Bradley, Marion Zimmer 131
Great Alta series (Yolen) 1004
Great and Secret Show, The (Barker) 65, 66
Great Book of Amber, The (Zelazny) 1015
Great Fire of London, The (Ackroyd) 2
Great Game trilogy (Duncan) 319
"Great Globe, The" (Davidson) 259
"Great Lover, The" (Simmons) 878
"Great San Diego Sleazy Bimbo Massacre, The" (Ketchum) 520
"Great Tom Fool or The Conundrum of the Calais Customhouse Coffers" (Lafferty) 594
"Greater Conqueror, The" (Moorcock) 744
Green Boy (Cooper) 243
"Green Child, The" (Crowley) 251
Green Eyes (Shepard) 846, 848
Green Flash, The (Aiken) 27
Green Mile, The (King) 532
Green Millennium, The (Leiber) 646, 647
Green Phoenix (Swann) 918
"Green Tower, The" (Kurtz) 579
Greenmantle (De Lint) 269
Greensleeves (VanderMeer) 949
Greenwitch (Cooper) 239–241
Greetings from Earth (Bradfield) 124
Grey King, The (Cooper) 239, 240, 242
Griaule series (Shepard) 848
Grigori trilogy (Constantine) 228
Grim Fairy Tales (Pratchett) 794
Grimscribe (Ligotti) 655
Grotesque, The (McGrath) 723, 724
"Grotto, The" (Ptacek) 806
"Growing Boys" (Aickman) 15
Gryphon in Glory (Norton) 768, 771
Guardians of the West (Eddings) 324
Guardians of Time (Anderson) 36
Guards! Guards! (Pratchett) 794
"Guerilla Pop" (Erickson) 341
Guide to Writing for Children (Yolen) 1003

Gummitch and Friends (Leiber) 647
Guns of Avalon, The (Zelazny) 1016, 1017
Gypsy, The (Brust & Lindholm) 165
"Hades Business, The" (Pratchett) 791
"Hair" (Ptacek) 806
Halfblood Chronicles series (Lackey & Norton) 588
Halfblood Chronicles, The (Lackey & Norton) 588
Halloween (Martin) 348
Halloween II (Martin) 348
Halloween III: Season of the Witch (Martin) 348
"Hand Me Downs" (Carroll) 201
Hand of Oberon, The (Zelazny) 1016
Hand to Mouth (Auster) 54
Handful of Men series (Duncan) 317
"Hang-Up, The" (Livingston) 518
"Hanging the Fool" (Moorcock) 744
"Happy Valley at the End of the World, The" (Di Filippo) 287
Hardcase (Simmons) 875–880
Harlan Ellison's Dream Corridor (Ellison) 336
"Harlem Nova" (Di Filippo) 288
Harp of Fishbones, A (Aiken) 27
Harp of the Grey Rose (De Lint) 268
Harper Hall series (McCaffrey) 700
Harpist in the Wind (Mckillip) 729
Harrowing of Gwynedd, The (Kurtz) 577
Harry Potter and the Chamber of Secrets (Rowling) 825, 828
Harry Potter and the Goblet of Fire (Rowling) 829–831
Harry Potter and the Philosopher's Stone (Rowling) 825
Harry Potter and the Prisoner of Azkaban (Rowling) 826, 828
Harry Potter and the Sorcerer's Stone (Rowling) 825, 826–828, 830, 831
Hart's Hope (Card) 193
"Haunt, The" (Ketchum) 521
Haunted Air, The (Wilson) 975
"Haunted Boardinghouse, The" (Wolfe) 988
Haunted Shore, The (Pullman) 809
Haunted: Tales of the Grotesque (Oates) 776
"Haunted" (Oates) 780
Haunting of Hill House (Jackson) 183
Haunting of Lamb House, The (Aiken) 26, 904
Hawksmoor (Ackroyd) 2–7
"He Who Shapes" (Zelazny) 1012
"Head Down" (King) 536
Healer (Wilson) 973
"Healer's Song" (Kurtz) 577
"Healing Touch" (Ptacek) 806

Heart of Darkness (Shepard) 849
"Heart of Whitenesse, The" (Waldrop) 955
Heart's Blood (Yolen) 1004
Heart-Beast (Lee) 637
Heartfire (Card) 192
Heartlight (Bradley) 137
Hearts in Atlantis (King) 533, 535
Heat and Other Stories (Oates) 776
Heatseeker (Shirley) 858
Heidelberg Cylinder, The (Carroll) 206
Heirs of Babylon, The (Cook) 233
Heirs of Saint Camber series (Kurtz) 577
Hell House (Matheson) 674, 675, 677
"Hell through a Windshield" (Landsdale) 607
Hell: A Cyberpunk Thriller (Williamson) 970
Hell's Gate (Koontz) 552
Hellbound Heart, The (Barker) 64
Hellfire Club, The (Straub) 910
Hellraiser (Barker) 61
Hellraiser (film) 64
"Henry Miller and the Push" (Ketchum) 518
Heralds of Valdemar series (Lackey) 586
Here There Be Angels (Yolen) 1007
Here There Be Dragons (Yolen) 1007
Here There Be Ghosts (Yolen) 1007
Here There Be Unicorns (Yolen) 1007
Here There Be Witches (Yolen) 1007
Heritage of Shannara series (Brooks) 156
Hermetech (Constantine) 230
"Hero as Werwolf, The" (Wolfe) 987
"Hero, The" (Martin) 667
Hero! (Duncan) 317
Herr Nightingale and the Satin Woman (Kotzwinkle) 565
Hidden City, The (Eddings) 325, 328
Hide and Seek (Ketchum) 519
High Crusade, The (Anderson) 37
High Deryni (Kurtz) 577
High Hallack series (Norton) 768, 770
High Hunt (Eddings) 323
"High Talk in the Starlit Wood" (Willard) 962
Highest Hit, The (Willard) 959
Hill Road, The (Mayne) 687
His Dark Materials series (Pullman) 809, 811–813
"His Mouth Will Taste of Wormwood..." (Brite) 148
Histories of King Kelson series (Kurtz) 577
History of Luminous Motion, The (Bradfield) 123–126

"History of Snivelization, The" (Di Filippo) 288
"Hitler Painted Roses" (Ellison) 334
Hob and the Goblins (Mayne) 689
Hob and the Peddler (Mayne) 689
Hobby (Yolen) 1005
Hoegbotton Guide to the Early History of Ambergris by Duncan (VanderMeer) 946, 948
Hogfather (Pratchett) 794, 796, 798
Hogg (Delany) 281
"Holiday Man" (Matheson) 676
"Holiday" (Schow) 836
Hollow Man, The (Simmons) 879
Holly from the Bongs (play) 685
"Home is the Hangman" (Zelazny) 1014
Homebody (Card) 194
Homunculus (Blaylock) 91
Honeybuzzard (Carter) 210
"Honeymoon" (McCaffrey) 698
Honoured Enemy (Feist & Forstchen) 357
Hood, Ken: see Duncan, Dave 319
Hook (Brooks) 157, 158
"Hoover's Men" (Waldrop) 956
Hope of Earth (Anthony) 47
Horn Crown (Norton) 768, 771
"Horror on the #33, The" (Shea) 842
Horror: The 100 Best Books (ed. Newman & Jones) 757
"Horse Lord, The" (Tuttle) 926
"Hospice, The" (Aickman) 15
Hosts (Wilson) 975
Hot Jazz Trio, The (Kotzwinkle) 562
Hotel Transylvania (Yarbro) 994, 995, 996
"Hottentots" (Di Filippo) 286
Hottest Blood (Shirley) 859
"Hound, The" (Leiber) 645
House of Doctor Dee, The (Ackroyd) 5–7
"House of the Hatchet" (Bloch) 103
House of Thunder, The (Koontz) 555
House on Nazareth Hill, The (Campbell) 183
House on Parchment Street, The (Mckillip) 729
House That Fear Built, The (Knye) 297
"House the Blakeneys Built, The" (Davidson) 257
House, The (Little) 662, 664
"Houses of the Russians, The" (Aickman) 17
Houses Without Doors (Straub) 910
"Houston, 1943" (Wolfe) 983
How Are the Mighty Fallen (Swann) 915, 917
"How Deep the Taste of Love" (Shirley) 859

INDEX

"How It Was with the Kraits" (Collins) 223
How Precious Was That While (Anthony) 47
Howard Who? (Waldrop) 954, 956, 957
"Hucklebone of a Saint, The" (Willard) 960
"Hungarian Rhapsody" (Bloch) 103
Hunger (Auster) 54
Hunger and Ecstasy of Vampires, The (Stableford) 896, 897
Hunger and Thirst (Matheson) 674
"Hunger: an Introduction" (Straub) 911
Hungry Moon, The (Campbell) 181, 182
Hunted, The (Ptacek) 806
Hunters of the Red Moon (Bradley) 132
Hunters' Haunt, The (Duncan) 318
Hyperion (Simmons) 876–879
"Hypocrites of Homosexuality, The" (Card) 189
I Am Legend (Matheson) 674, 675, 976
"I Do Not Love Thee, Dr. Fell" (Bloch) 105
"I Have No Mouth and I Must Scream" (Ellison) 331, 333, 336
"I Live In Elizabeth" (Shirley) 858
I Was a Rat! (Pullman) 812
I, Said the Fly (Shea) 842
Icebound (Koontz) 556
If You Could See Me Now (Straub) 904, 906, 909
Ignored, The (Little) 662, 664
"Ike at the Mike" (Waldrop) 956
"Ikon of Elijah, The" (Davidson) 256
Ill Fate Marshalling, An (Cook) 234
Ill Met by Moonlight (film) 883
"Ill Met in Lankhmar" (Leiber) 647
Illearth War, The (Donaldson) 299
Illustrated Man, The (Bradbury) 119
Illustrated Roger Zelazny, The (Zelazny) 1017
Ilse Witch (Brooks) 157
"Imaginary Friends" (Brooks) 158
Imajica (Barker) 65, 66
Immortal Unicorn (Beagle) 962
Immortal, The (Wilson) 974
Implant (Wilson) 976
In a Foreign Town, in a Foreign Land (Ligotti) 655
"In a Green Tree" (Lafferty) 600
In a Green Tree" series (Lafferty) 600
In Between the Sheets (McEwan) 716
In Darkness Waiting (Shirley) 858
In Dreams (ed. Newman & McAuley) 758
"In Entropy's Jaws" (Silverberg) 868
"In Fear of K" (Ellison) 334

In His Country, Skin of Grace (Willard) 959
In Silence Sealed (Ptacek) 805
In the Beginning (Leiber) 644
In the Blood (Collins) 224
In the Country of Last Things (Auster) 55, 57
In the Face of Death (Yarbro) 996
"In the Fourth Year of the War" (Ellison) 334, 335
"In the Hills, the Cities" (Barker) 63
"In the House of Gingerbread" (Wolfe) 987
"In the Lilliputian Asylum" (Bishop) 85
"In the Memory Room" (Bishop) 85
"In the Penal Colony" (Etchison) 349
"In the Realm of Ice" (Oates) 779
In Yana, the Touch of Undying (Shea) 841
Incarnate (Campbell) 180
Incarnations (Barker) 62
Incarnations of Immortality series (Anthony) 48–49
Incredible Shrinking Man, The (Matheson) 674
Influence, The (Campbell) 181
Inhabitant of the Lake and Less Welcome Tenants, The (Campbell) 179
"Inner Circles, The" (Leiber) 647
"Inner Room, The" (Aickman) 12, 14
Innkeeper's Song, The (Beagle) 74, 75
Innocent, The (Mcewan) 718, 719
Inquestor series (Somtow) 884
"Inside the Cackle Factory" (Etchison) 351
Insomnia (King) 532
"Instability" (Di Filippo) 288
Institute for Impure Science series (Lafferty) 594
"Insufficient Answer, The" (Aickman) 14
Intensity (Koontz) 551, 557, 558
Interesting Times (Pratchett) 793, 796
Interview with the Vampire (Rice) 817, 818, 819–820
"Interview with the Vampire" (Rice) 819
Into the Green (De Lint) 268
"Into the Wood" (Aickman) 15
"Introduction: "What Killed Science Fiction?" (Di Filippo) 287
Intrusions (Aickman) 17
Invasion (Wolfe) 556, 557, 558
Inward Revolution, The (Constantine & Benstead) 230
Is (Aiken) 25
"Is Betsy Blake Still Alive?" (Bloch) 105
Is Underground (Aiken) 25

"Ishmael in Love" (Silverberg) 868
Island of the Grass King, The (Willard) 960
Island under the Earth, The (Davidson) 260
Isle of the Dead (Zelazny) 1016
Isle of Woman (Anthony) 47
Issola (Brust) 162, 164
It (King) 525, 531
It (Mayne) 689
"It Happened Tomorrow" (Bloch) 105
"It Only Comes Out at Night" (Etchison) 348
"It Wasn't Syzygy" (Bradley) 130
"It Will Be Here Soon" (Etchison) 349
It's All in Your Mind (Bloch) 102
Ives, Morgan: see Bradley, Marion Zimmer 131
Ivory and the Horn, The (De Lint) 270
Jack in the Box (Kotzwinkle) 565
Jack of Shadows (Zelazny) 1017
Jack, the Giant-Killer (De Lint) 267, 269, 270
"Jackdaw's Last Case, The" (Di Filippo) 287
Jago (Newman) 758, 759, 761, 764
Jaguar Hunter, The (Shepard) 845–848
"Jaguar Hunter, The" (Shepard) 846
"Jane Doe no. 112" (Ellison) 332
"Jane Fonda Room, The" (Carroll) 205
"Jaqueline Ess: Her Will and Testament" (Barker) 63
Jargoon Pard, The (Norton) 768, 771
Jasmine Nights (Somtow) 883, 888
Jason Striker Martial Arts series (Anthony & Fuentes) 47
"Jeffty Is Five" (Ellison) 331, 332, 334
Jekyll Legacy, The (Bloch) 109
Jersey Shore, The (Mayne) 688
Jewel Seed, The (Aiken) 26
"Jewels in the Forest, The" (Leiber) 645
Jewels of Aptor, The (Delany) 278
Jhereg (Brust) 162–164
Jingo (Pratchett) 795, 797
Jinx High (Lackey) 587
"Jody and Annie on TV" (Shirley) 859
Joe's Liver (Di Filippo) 289
"John Ford's 'Tis Pity She's a Whore" (Carter) 211, 212, 217
Johnny Alucard (Newman) 760, 762
Johnny and the Dead (Pratchett) 798
Johnny Maxwell series (Pratchett) 798
Jonah Hex: Two-Gun Mojo (Lansdale) 609
"Josie and the Elevator" (Disch) 294
"Journey into the Dark" (Yolen) 1008
Joyleg (Davidson) 257
Judgment of Tears: Anno Dracula 1959 (Newman) 759, 762–764

Julia (Straub) 905, 906
"Julie's Unicorn" (Beagle) 75
"Junior Teeter and the Bad Shine" (Collins) 222
"Junk Yard, The" (Landsdale) 604
"Just a Song at Twilight" (Aickman) 15
Juvies, The (Ellison) 332
Juxtaposition (Anthony) 47, 48
Kachina (Ptacek) 804
Kalimantan (Shepard) 849
Kar-Chee Reign, The (Davidson) 258
"Karuna, Inc" (Di Filippo) 288, 289
"Katherine and Jean" (Rice) 818
Kay, Guy Gavriel **506–516**
Keep, The (Wilson) 972, 974
"Kerowyn's Tale" (Lackey) 586
Ketchum, Jack **517–523**
Key to Midnight, The (Koontz) 556
"Keyhole" (Bradley) 130
Kiai! (Anthony & Fuentes) 47
"Kid Charlemagne" (Di Filippo) 285
Kidnapper, The (Bloch) 106
Kill Riff, The (Schow) 835
Kill the Dead (Lee) 637
Killashandra (McCaffrey) 698
Killashandra series (McCaffrey) 697
"Killashandra-Coda and Finale" (McCaffrey) 698
Killer Savant (Little) 662
Killing Time (film) 349
King Javan's Year (Kurtz) 577
King Kelson's Bride (Kurtz) 577
King of Dreams (Silverberg) 862
King of Elfland's Daughter, The (Beagle) 73
King of Shadows (Cooper) 243
King of the Murgos (Eddings) 324, 327
King of the Swords, The (Moorcock) 742
King of Ys, The (Anderson) 34
King, Stephen **525–540**
King's Blade series (Duncan) 320
King's Buccaneer, The (Feist) 357
King's Daggers series (Duncan) 321
King's Justice, The (Kurtz) 577
Kingdoms of the Wall, The (Silverberg) 867
Kink (Koja) 543, 545
Kissing the Beehive (Carroll) 205, 206
"Kittens" (Koontz) 551
"Knife in the Darkness" (Ellison) 336
Knight and Knave of Swords, The (Leiber) 648
Knight of Ghosts and Shadows, A (Anderson) 36
Knight of Ghosts and Shadows, A (Lackey & Guon) 588
Knight of Shadows (Zelazny) 1016
Knight of the Word, A (Brooks) 156

"Knighting of Derry, The" (Kurtz) 577, 578
Knights of the Blood (Kurtz & McMillan) 580
Knights of the Blood: At Sword's Point (Kurtz & McMillan) 580
Know Your Waterways (Aickman) 9
Knuckles and Tales (Collins) 222
Knye, Cassandra: see Disch, Thomas M. 297
Koja, Kathe **541–549**
Koko (Straub) 910
Koontz, Dean **551–560**
Kotzwinkle, William **561–568**
Kress, Nancy **569–573**
Krondor: Tear of the Gods (Feist) 357
Krondor: The Assassins (Feist) 357
Krondor: The Betrayal (Feist) 357
Krondor: The Crawler (Feist) 357
Krondor: The Dark Mage (Feist) 357
Kurtz, Katherine **575–583**
L.A. Weekly 344
Lackey, Mercedes **585–592**
Ladies' Night (Ketchum) 520, 521
"Lady in the Tower" (McCaffrey) 698
Lady of Avalon (Bradley) 136
Lady of the Bees (Swann) 918
"Lady of the House of Love, The" (Carter) 210, 214, 215
Lafferty, R. A. **593–602**
Lammas Night (Kurtz & Harris) 579, 580
LaNague Chronicles, The (Wilson) 973
LaNague Foundation series (Wilson) 973
Land of Dreams (Blaylock) 92, 94
Land of Laughs, The (Carroll) 201–203
"Land of Sinim, The" (Davidson) 255
Land of Ten Thousand Willows series (Grant) 803, 805
"Land of the Great Horses" (Lafferty) 595
Language of the Night, The (Le Guin) 614, 615, 621
Languages of Pao, The (Vance) 939
Lansdale, Joe R. **603–612**
"Larger Than Oneself" (Aickman) 16
Lark and the Wren, The (Lackey) 587
Lasher (Rice) 822
Last Call (Powers) 787, 788
"Last Castle, The" (Vance) 935, 938–940
Last Coin, The (Blaylock) 92
Last Continent, The (Pratchett) 793, 796
Last Days of the Edge of the World, The (Stableford) 892, 898
Last Defender of Camelot, The (Zelazny) 1014

"Last Defender of Camelot, The" (Zelazny) 1014, 1015
"Last Feast of Harlequin, The" (Ligotti) 655, 656
Last Hero, The (Pratchett) 797
"Last Illusion, The" (Barker) 63
"Last Reel, The" (Etchison) 350, 351
"Last Rung on the Ladder, The" (King) 536
"Last Song of Sirit Byar, The" (Beagle) 75
Last Testament of Oscar Wilde, The (Ackroyd) 2, 6
Last Unicorn, The (Beagle) 72, 74, 76
Last Viking, The (Anderson) 34
Last Voice They Hear, The (Campbell) 183
"Last Wizard, The" (Davidson) 256
Late Breakfasters, The (Aickman) 11, 13, 15
"Late Shift, The" (Etchison) 348, 349
Laughing Dead, The (film) 883
Laurel and Hardy Go to Heaven (Auster) 56
Law in Charity, The (Yarbro) 998
Law of the Wolf Tower (Lee) 636
"Lawnmower Man, The" (King) 536
Lawson, Philip: see Bishop, Michael 87
Lawson, Philip: see Di Filippo, Paul 87
Le Guin, Ursula K. **613–631**
"Lean Times in Lankhmar" (Leiber) 647
Leap Year (Erickson) 343–345
Lee, Tanith **633–642**
Leese Webster (Le Guin) 623
Left Hand of Darkness, The (Le Guin) 133, 614, 932
Legacies (Wilson) 974, 975
Legacy of Lehr, The (Kurtz) 579, 581
"Legacy, A" (Oates) 778
"Legacy" (Kurtz) 577
Legend of Hell House, The (film) 674
Legends of Camber of Culdi series (Kurtz) 576
Leiber, Fritz **643–651**
"Lennon Spex" (Di Filippo) 285
Leronis of Darkover (Bradley) 129
"Letter from the South Two Moons West of Nacogdoches" (Landsdale) 606
Letters to Jenny (Anthony) 47
Leviathan (Auster) 53, 56, 57
"Liberty of the Subject, The" (Davidson) 256
Life During Wartime (Shepard) 848
"Life Hutch" (Ellison) 332
"Life of My Crime, the" (Carroll) 205
Life of Thomas More, The (Ackroyd) 1
"Life Partner" (Schow) 834
Life's Lottery (Newman) 760

INDEX

Light Fantastic, The (Pratchett) 792, 793
"Light House, The" (Bloch) 106
Light on the Sound (Somtow) 884
Ligotti, Thomas **653–658**
"Like Daughter" (Due) 312
"Likeness of Julie, The" (Matheson) 678
"Lila the Werewolf" (Beagle) 73–75
"Lilies" (Bloch) 100
Limbo Lodge (Aiken) 24
"Linda and Phil" (Di Filippo) 288
"Linda, Daniel, and Spike" (Disch) 294
"Lineaments of Gratified Desire, The" (Davidson) 257
"Lion and the Lamb, The" (Leiber) 646
Lion Time in Timbuctoo (Silverberg) 868
Lions of Al-Rassan, The (Kay) 510, 512–513
"Lipidleggin" (Wilson) 976
"Little Contrasts" (Ptacek) 806
Little Country, The (De Lint) 268, 269
Little Doors (Di Filippo) 285, 286, 288
Little Knowledge, A (Bishop) 80
"Little Sacrifice, The" (Oates) 781
Little, Bentley **659–665**
Little, Big (Crowley) 245–247, 248, 251
"Little-Known Side of Elvis, A" (Etchison) 350
Lively Anatomy of God, The (Willard) 959
Lives of the Mayfair Witches series (Rice) 822
Lives of the Mayfair Witches series series (Rice) 821
Living Blood, The (Due) 310–313
Living God, The (Duncan) 317
Livingston, Jerzy: see Ketchum, Jack 517
"Lizzie Borden Took An Axe" (Bloch) 103, 107
Locadio's Apprentice (Yarbro) 998
Locked Room, The (Auster) 54
Lodge of the Lynx, The (Kurtz & Harris) 580
London Burning (VanderMeer) 949
London Lickpenny (Ackroyd) 1
London: The Biography (Ackroyd) 2, 7
"Lonely Songs of Laren Dorr, The" (Martin) 670
Long Lost, The (Campbell) 183
Long Walk, The (Bachman) 534, 535
"Long Way Home, A" (Oates) 777
Longdirk series (Hood) 319
Lord Demon (Zelazny) 1012, 1018, 1019
Lord Foul's Bane (Donaldson) 299
Lord Kelvin's Machine (Blaylock) 91
"Lord of Central Park" (Davidson) 257

Lord of Emperors (Kay) 510, 513
Lord of Illusions, The (film) 63
Lord of Light (Zelazny) 742, 1014–1016
Lord of the Fire Lands (Duncan) 320
"Lord of the Land" (Wolfe) 989
Lord of the Spiders (Moorcock) 738
Lord Prestimion (Silverberg) 864
Lord Valentine's Castle (Silverberg) 864, 866
"Lord's Work, The" (Wilson) 976
Lords and Ladies (Pratchett) 793, 794
"Lords of Quarmall, The" (Leiber) 647
Lore of the Witch World (Norton) 768, 772
Lori (Bloch) 109
Los Sin Nombre (film) 180
Losers, The (Eddings) 323
Lost Angels (Schow) 836
Lost Boys (Card) 194
"Lost Boys" (Card) 189, 194
"Lost Girls" (Yolen) 1008
Lost Pages (Di Filippo) 285–287
Lost Souls (Brite) 147–150
Lost, The (Ketchum) 520
Love (Carter) 210
Love Ain't Nothing But Sex Misspelled (Ellison) 333
Love and Sleep (Crowley) 247, 249
Love in Vein (Brite) 148
Love in Vein II (Brite) 148
Lovedeath (Simmons) 878
Lovelock (Card) 196
"Lover When You're Near Me" (Matheson) 678
"Loves of Lady Purple, The" (Carter) 210, 213
"Low Men in Yellow Coats" (King) 533
Lowland Rider (Williamson) 968–970
"Lucy Comes to Stay" (Bloch) 104, 107
Lulu on the Bridge (Auster) 58
Luminous Motion (film) 123
"Lunchbox" (Waldrop) 951
Lycanthia (Lee) 637
Lyonesse series (Vance) 935
Lyonesse: Madouc (Vance) 935
Lythande (Bradley) 131
M.D.: A Horror Story, The (Disch) 296
"Mad House" (Matheson) 675
Mad Man, The (Delany) 281
Madelaine de Montalia series (Yarbro) 996
Madwand (Zelazny) 1017, 1018
Mage Storms series (Lackey) 586
Mage Wars series (Lackey) 586
Mage Winds series (Lackey) 586
Magic Casement (Duncan) 317

Magic Kingdom for Sale—Sold! (Brooks) 156
Magic Mirror (Card) 193
Magic Terror (Straub) 911
Magic Three of Solatia, The (Yolen) 1004
Magic Toyshop, The (Carter) 209–212, 215, 217
Magic Wagon, The (Lansdale) 605, 606
Magic's Pawn (Lackey) 586
Magic's Price (Lackey) 586, 589
Magic's Promise (Lackey) 586
Magician (Feist) 355, 356, 359
"Magician of Karakosk, The" (Beagle) 75
Magician: Apprentice (Feist) 356
Magician: Master (Feist) 356
Magician's Gambit (Eddings) 323
Magnificat (Yarbro) 996
Magravandias Chronicles series (Constantine) 231
Mailman, The (Little) 660–664
"Mairzy Doats" (Di Filippo) 287
Majipoor Chronicles (Silverberg) 867
Malloreon series (Eddings) 324
Mallworld (Somtow) 883–884
Mammoth Book of Dracula, The (Newman) 760
Man from Mundania (Anthony) 48
"Man in the Black Suit, The" (King) 536
Man in the Cage, The (Queen) 935
Man of His Word series (Duncan) 317
Man Rides Through, A (Donaldson) 303, 304
"Man Who Collected Barker, The" (Newman) 763
"Man Who Collected Poe, The" (Bloch) 105
"Man Who Cried Wolf, The" (Bloch) 104
Man Who Fought Alone, The (Donaldson) 305
Man Who Killed His Brother, The (Donaldson) 305
"Man Who Painted the Dragon Griaule, The" (Shepard) 847
Man Who Risked His Partner, The (Donaldson) 305
"Man Who Rowed Christopher Columbus Ashore, The" (Ellison) 331, 332, 336
Man Who Tried to Get Away, The (Donaldson) 305
"Man Who Walked through Mirrors, The" (Bloch) 105
"Man Who Was Heavily into Revenge, The" (Ellison) 334
"Man with Two Lives" (Landsdale) 606
"Man, The" (Bradbury) 118

"Mannikin, The" (Bloch) 100
Many Worlds of Magnus Ridolph, The (Vance) 935
"Marie" (Kotzwinkle) 561
Marion Zimmer Bradley's Darkover (Bradley) 135
Marion Zimmer Bradley's Fantasy Magazine 135
"Marmalade Wine" (Aiken) 27
Marriage of Sticks, The (Carroll) 206
Marriages (Straub) 904–906
Martha Peake: A Novel of the Revolution (McGrath) 723, 726
Martian Chronicles, The (Bradbury) 115–117, 674
Martian Chronicles, The (television script) (Matheson) 674
Martin, George R. R. **667–671**
Martin, Jack: see Etchison, Dennis 348
"Mary Margaret Road-Grader" (Waldrop) 957
Maskerade (Pratchett) 793
"Master" (Carter) 210, 211, 214
Masters of Darkness (Etchison) 347
Masters of Darkness II (Etchison) 347
Masters of Darkness III (Etchison) 347
Masters of the Maze (Davidson) 258
Masters of the Pit (Moorcock) 738
Matheson, Richard **673–684**
Matter of Britain, The (Newman & Bryne) 760
Matter of Time, A (Cook) 234
Max's Dream (Mayne) 688
Maximum Overdrive (film) 536
Maxwell, Kathleen: see Ptacek, Kathryn 803
Mayfield, Anne: see Ptacek, Kathryn 803
Mayne, William **685–692**
Mayr, Dallas William, Jr.: see Ketchum, Jack 517
McCaffrey, Anne **693–704**
McCammon, Robert R. **705–713**
"McCarthy Witch Hunt, The" (Newman) 759
McEwan, Ian **715–721**
McGrath, Patrick **723–727**
McKain's Dilemma (Williamson) 968
McKillip, Patricia A. **729–736**
Mediums Rare (Matheson) 680
"Meeting Mr. Millar" (Aickman) 17
Member for the Marsh, The (Mayne) 686
Memnoch The Devil (Rice) 753, 822
"Memoirs of a Bottle Djinn" (Yolen) 1008
Memories of the Body (Tuttle) 926
Memory and Dream (De Lint) 270
Memory of Earth, The (Card) 195

Memos from Purgatory: Two Journeys of Our Times (Ellison) 332
Men at Arms (Pratchett) 795–797
"Mengele" (Shepard) 846
Merlin (Yolen) 1007
Merrick (Rice) 822
Messages from Michael (Yarbro) 996
"Messages from Michael" (Yarbro) 993
MetaHorror (Etchison) 347
"Metropolis II" (Ellison) 336
"Mi Casa" (Ptacek) 806
Michael for the Millenium (Yarbro) 997
Michael series (Yarbro) 993, 996, 997
"Michael" (Yarbro) 996, 997
Midnight Blue: The Sonja Blue Collection (Collins) 224
"Midnight by the Morphy Watch" (Leiber) 647
Midnight Examiner, The (Kotzwinkle) 561
"Midnight in the Sunken Cathedral" (Ellison) 336
Midnight Is a Place (Aiken) 25
Midnight Mass (Wilson) 976
"Midnight Meat Train" (Barker) 62
Midnight Nightingale (Aiken) 25
Midnight Sun (Campbell) 182
Midsummer Tempest, A (Anderson) 33, 39
Midwinter Nightingale (Aiken) 23
"Mill, The" (Di Filippo) 285
Millennium Movies: End of the World Cinema (Newman) 759
Milton in America (Ackroyd) 7
Mind Fields: The Art of Jacek Yerka (Ellison) 336
Mindplayers (Cadigan) 169–173
Mine (McCammon) 710
Mines of Behemoth, The (Shea) 842, 843
Minikins of Yam, The (Swann) 915, 917
Mirage (Wilson) 976
Mirkheim (Anderson) 36
"Miroir, Le " (Aickman) 17
Mirror of Her Dreams, The (Donaldson) 303, 304
Mirrorshades (Cadigan) 173
Misery (King) 531
"Missing" (Brite) 147
"Missolonghi 1824" (Crowley) 251
Mist (Wolfe) 985
"Mist, The" (King) 527, 536
Mistress of the Empire (Feist) 357
Mists of Avalon, The (Bradley) 131, 132, 136
Moby Dick (film) 118
Model, The (Aickman) 13, 14, 16
"Mom" (Ellison) 334
Momma Durtt (Shea) 842
Monet's Ghost (Yarbro) 998

"Monkey Treatment, The" (Martin) 669
"Monkey, The" (King) 536
"Monster Movies" (Schow) 835
Monstrous Regiment, The (Constantine) 229, 230
"Montavarde Camera, The" (Davidson) 255
Moon Cake (Aiken) 27
Moon Called (Norton) 768, 772
Moon Dance: A Novel (Somtow) 886, 887
"Moon Moth, The" (Vance) 938, 940
Moon Palace (Auster) 55
"Moonbridges" (Erickson) 341
Moonheart (De Lint) 267, 268
Moonlight and Vines (De Lint) 267, 270
"Moons & Stars & Stuff" (Leiber) 649
Moonstone, The (Straub) 911
Moorcock, Michael **737–748**
Mordant's Need (Donaldson) 303, 304
Mordenheim (Williamson) 970
Moreta, Dragonlady of Pern (McCaffrey) 700
Morgawr (Brooks) 157
Morley, Brian: see Bradley, Marion Zimmer 131
Morrow, James **749–755**
Mort (Pratchett) 793, 794
Mossycoat (Pullman) 812
Mother London (Moorcock) 737, 744
Mother of Kings (Anderson) 40
"Mother of Serpents" (Bloch) 101
Motion of Light in Water, The (Delany) 277
Mouldy, The (Mayne) 686
Mouser Goes Below, The (Leiber) 648
Mouthful of Tongues, A (Di Filippo) 289, 290
"Movie People, The" (Bloch) 105
Moving Pictures (Pratchett) 794, 795
"Mr. Clubb and Mr. Cuff" (Straub) 911
"Mr. Eliphinstone's Hands" (Tuttle) 926
"Mr. Fiddlehead" (Carroll) 205
"Mr. Fuller's Revolt" (Zelazny) 1011
Mr. Murder (Koontz) 556
Mr. Vertigo (Auster) 57, 58
"Mr. Weedeater" (Landsdale) 609
Mr. X (Straub) 688, 903, 905, 911–912
Mrs. God (Straub) 910
"Mud Puppy Goes Uptown" (Di Filippo) 285
Mulengro: A Romany Tale (De Lint) 269
Mummy, or Ramses the Damned, The (Rice) 821
Murder in Cormyr (Williamson) 970

INDEX

Murder in LaMut (Feist & Rosenberg) 357
Muse of Art (Anthony) 47, 50
Music of Chance, The (Auster) 55, 58
Music When Sweet Voices Die (Yarbro) 997
Muskrat Courage (Bishop) 84
"Mussolini and the Axeman's Jazz" (Brite) 150
Mutiny in Space (Davidson) 258
"My Boy Friend's Name is Jello" (Davidson) 254
"My Boyfriend's Name is Jello" (Davidson) 253
"My Case for Retributive Action" (Ligotti) 656
"My Dead Dog Bobby" (Landsdale) 604
"My Favorite Enigma the Historical Comte de Saint-Germain" (Yarbro) 994
"My Poor Friend" (Aickman) 16
"My Pretty Pony" (King) 536
My Soul to Keep (Due) 310, 311–312
Mycroft Holmes series (Fawcett) 997
Mysteries of the Worm (Bloch) 100
Mysteries of Winterthurn (Oates) 779
Mystery of Charles Dickens, The (Ackroyd) 2
Mystery Walk (Mccammon) 707
"Mystics of Muelenburg, The" (Ligotti) 653, 654
"Naga, The" (Beagle) 75
Nameless, The (Campbell) 180
Nantucket Slayrides (Shepard) 850
"Naples" (Davidson) 253
"Narrow Valley" (Lafferty) 595
"Nebraskan and the Nereid, The" (Wolfe) 989
"Necessity of His Condition, The" (Davidson) 253, 256
Needful Things (King) 531, 532
Needing Ghosts (Campbell) 177
Nest of Nightmares, A (Tuttle) 923, 926
"Nethescurial" (Ligotti) 654–655
Nevèrÿon series (Delany) 279–281
Nevèrÿona (Delany) 279, 280
"New Atlantis, The" (Le Guin) 622
New Herball, A (Willard) 959
"New Murders in the Rue Morgue" (Barker) 63
New Noir (Shirley) 859
"New Prime, The" (Vance) 939
New Purposes 646
New Sun series (Wolfe) 936
"New York Review of Bird, The" (Ellison) 334
New York Trilogy, The (Auster) 54, 56, 57
Newford series (De Lint) 270–272

Newman, Kim **757–766**
"Next Glade, The" (Aickman) 15, 17
"Nicholas and Jean" (Rice) 818
Nifft the Lean (Shea) 840
Night and the Enemy (Ellison & Steacy) 336
"Night Bloomer" (Schow) 834
Night Boat, The (Mccammon) 706, 707
Night Chills (Koontz) 556
"Night Flier" (King) 528
Night in the Lonesome October, A (Zelazny) 1018
Night Mare (Anthony) 48
Night Mayor, The (Newman) 758, 763
"Night of Thanks But No Thanks" (Ellison) 336
Night of the Cooters (Waldrop) 954, 956, 957
Night of the Ripper, The (Bloch) 109
"Night of White Bhairab, The" (Shepard) 847
Night Relics (Blaylock) 93
Night Shift (King) 535
"Night Surf" (King) 536
"Night They Missed the Horror Show, The" (Landsdale) 608
Night Voices (Aickman) 17
Night Watch (Pratchett) 792
Night's Black Agents (Leiber) 646
Night-side: Eighteen Tales (Oates) 776
Nightbirds on Nantucket (Aiken) 24
Nightbreed (film) 65
Nightmare Factory, The (Ligotti) 655, 656
Nightmare Movies: A Critical History of the Horror Film, 1970–1988 (Newman) 757
Nightmare Movies: Wide Screen Horror since 1970 (Newman) 757
Nightmare on Elm Street 4: The Dream Master (film) 565
Nightmares and Dreamscapes (King) 535, 536
Nightrunners, The (Lansdale) 605–608
Nights at the Circus (Carter) 209, 210
Nightwings (Silverberg) 862, 865, 866
Nightworld (Wilson) 974
Nine Princes in Amber (Zelazny) 1016
"No Time is Passing" (Aickman) 15, 17
No Truce with Kings (Anderson) 34
"No Truce with Kings" (Anderson) 33, 37
Noctuary (Ligotti) 655
Nomads (film) 997
"Nomans Land" (Shepard) 848
North, Andrew: see Norton, Andre 767
Northern Lights (Pullman) 812

Norton, Alice Mary: see Norton, Andre 767
Norton, Andre **767–773**
"Not Much Disorder and Not So Early Sex" (Leiber) 643
Not to Mention Camels (Lafferty) 598
Not-World, The (Swann) 920
"Notebook of the Night, The" (Ligotti) 655
Notes for a New Culture: Essays in Modernism (Ackroyd) 1
"Notes on the Writing of Horror: A Story" (Ligotti) 655
Nova (Delany) 278, 279
Novelty (Crowley) 251
"Novelty" (Crowley) 247, 251
Now You See It... (Matheson) 680, 681
"Nursemaid to Nightmares" (Bloch) 102
"O Brave Old World!" (Davidson) 257
"O Happy Day" (Bishop) 85
O'Brien, Dee see Bradley, Marion Zimmer 131
Oates, Joyce Carol **775–782**
Oathblood (Lackey) 586
Oathbound, The (Lackey) 586
Oathbreakers (Lackey) 586
Obsession (Campbell) 180, 181
"October 4, 1948" (Rice) 816
October Country, The (Bradbury) 117
October's Baby (Cook) 234
"Odd Boy Out" (Etchison) 347
"Odd Old Bird, The" (Davidson) 260
"Of Crystalline Labyrinths and the New Creation" (Bishop) 85
Off Season (Ketchum) 518, 519, 521
Off Season: The Unexpurgated Version (Ketchum) 519
"Offices" (Williamson) 967
Offspring (Ketchum) 519
"Ogre in the Vly" (Davidson) 255
Ogre, Ogre (Anthony) 48
"Oh, Shining Star" (Lee) 635
Okla Hannali (Lafferty) 598
"Old Woman Who Thought She Could Read, The" (Davidson) 256
Olivia Clemens series (Yarbro) 996
"Olympic Runner, The" (Etchison) 349
Ombria in Shadow (Mckillip) 730, 734
On a Pale Horse (Anthony) 47
"On Call" (Etchison) 351
On Crusade: More Tales of the Knights Templar (ed. Kurtz) 580
On Stranger Tides (Powers) 788, 789
"On the Border" (Shepard) 848
"On the Far Side of the Cadillac Desert with Dead Folks" (Landsdale) 609
"On the Slab" (Ellison) 336

"On the Street of the Serpents" (Bishop) 84
On Wings of Magic (Norton) 768
On Wings of Song (Disch) 293, 295
On Writing (King) 526, 527, 531, 534
Once around the Bloch (Bloch) 105, 109
One Armed Queen, The (Yolen) 1006, 1007
"One Armed Queen, The" (Yolen) 1006
"One for the Books" (Matheson) 676
"One for the Horrors" (Schow) 834
"One for the Road" (King) 527
"One Life, Furnished in Early Poverty" (Ellison) 334, 337
"One Morning with Samuel, Dorothy, and William" (Davidson) 256
One Safe Place, The (Campbell) 183
One Tree, The (Donaldson) 299
"One Way to Mars" (Bloch) 104
One Winter in Eden (Bishop) 84
Onion Girl, The (De Lint) 272
Only Begotten Daughter (Morrow) 751–753
Opener of the Way, The (Bloch) 102, 104
"Opener of the Way, The" (Bloch) 101
"Operation Afreet" (Anderson) 37
"Operation Changeling" (Anderson) 37
Operation Chaos (Anderson) 33, 37, 39
Operation Luna (Anderson) 37
"Optional Music for Voice and Piano" (Brite) 147
"Or All the Seas with Oysters" (Davidson) 253–255
Oracle Lips, The (Constantine) 230
Orca (Brust) 162, 164
Orfeo series (Craig) 893
Orgy of the Blood Parasites (Newman) 758
Original Dr Shade & Other Stories, The (Newman) 758, 759, 763
"Original Dr Shade, The" (Newman) 757
Other Nineteenth Century, The (Davidson) 256, 260
Other Wind, The (Le Guin) 616–619, 626
Our Lady of Darkness (Leiber) 649
"Our Temporary Supervisor" (Ligotti) 656
Out of Phaze (Anthony) 47
Outer Limits: The Official Companion, The (Schow) 834
Outside the Dog Museum (Carroll) 204–206
Over Sea, under Stone (Cooper) 239–241

"Over the Cloudy Mountains" (Aiken) 27
Over the Hills and Far Away (Mayne) 687
Owlflight (Lackey) 587
Owlknight (Lackey) 587
Owls series (Lackey) 587
Owlsight (Lackey) 587
Pact of the Fathers (Campbell) 183
"Pages from a Young Girl's Journal" (Aickman) 16
Paint It Black (Collins) 224
"Paladin of the Lost Hour" (Ellison) 337
"Pamela's Get" (Schow) 834
Pandora (Rice) 822
Pandora by Holly Hollander (Wolfe) 982
Panic Hand, The (Carroll) 205
"Paper Dragons" (Blaylock) 94
Paper Grail, The (Blaylock) 92
Paradys series: see Secret Books of Paradys series (Lee) 635
Parasite, The (Campbell) 180
"Party at Brenda's House, The" (Carroll) 201
Passage at Arms (Cook) 233
Passager (Yolen) 1005
"Passengers" (Silverberg) 862, 866, 868
Passion of New Eve, The (Carter) 209, 210, 213
Passion Play (Matheson) 675, 678
Past Imperative (Duncan) 319
Past Master (Lafferty) 595, 596, 598
"Past Master, The" (Bloch) 105
Pastwatch: The Redemption of Christopher Columbus (Card) 196
Path of the Eclipse (Yarbro) 995
Path: A New Look at Reality, The (Matheson) 679, 680
"Pathosfinder, The" (Cardigan) 170
"Patient Zero" (Due) 312, 313
"Patricia's Profession" (Newman) 758
Patterns (Cadigan) 169
Pawn of Prophecy (Eddings) 323, 324
"Pear-Shaped Man, The" (Martin) 669
"Pearls of the Vampire Queen, The" (Shea) 841
"Pedestrian, The" (Bradbury) 119, 836
Pegasus in Flight (McCaffrey) 698
Pegasus in Space (McCaffrey) 698
Pegasus series (McCaffrey) 698
"Pendulum" (Bradbury) 116
"Peninsula, The" (Davidson) 257
"People of the Crater, The" (Norton) 767
Peregrine series (Davidson) 259
Peregrine: Primus (Davidson) 259

Peregrine: Secundus (Davidson) 259, 260
Peregrine: Tertius (Davidson) 260
Perilous Seas (Duncan) 317
"Permafrost" (Zelazny) 1015
Personal Darkness (Lee) 637
Pet Sematary (King) 525, 530
Peter S. Beagle's Immortal Unicorn (Beagle) 75
Petty Pewter Gods (Cook) 236
Phantoms (Koontz) 554, 557
Phases of Gravity (Simmons) 875–877, 880
Phaze Doubt (Anthony) 47
"Philistine Syndrome" (Bishop) 82
Phoenix (Brust) 162–164
Phoenix and the Mirror, The (Davidson) 254, 258
Phoenix Bells, The (Grant) 805
Phoenix Guards, The (Brust) 162, 164
Phoenix in Obsidian (Moorcock) 741
"Pig Blood Blues" (Barker) 62
Pillow Friend, The (Tuttle) 926
"Pin Money" (Brite) 150
"Piñon Fall" (Bishop) 79, 84
Pirates in Petticoats (Yolen) 1003
Pish, Posh, Said Hieronymus Bosch (Willard) 961
Pit Dragons series (Yolen) 1004
"Pit, The" (Landsdale) 605
Plague Daemon (Craig) 893
Planet of Adventure (Vance) 939
Planet of Adventure series (Vance) 939
Planet Savers, The (Bradley) 132–134, 137
Plastic Jesus (Brite) 150, 151
Plato Papers, The (Ackroyd) 7
Plunderers, The (Shea) 842
"Poacher, The" (Le Guin) 619, 625
"Points of View" (Koja) 541
Poisoned Kiss and Other Stories from the Portuguese, The (Oates) 778
Polgara the Sorceress (Eddings) 324, 325
"Polyphemus" (Shea) 841
"Pond, The" (Cardigan) 170
"Porcelain Salamander, The" (Card) 195
Pornucopia (Anthony) 49
Portraits of His Children (Martin) 670
Ports of Call (Vance) 939, 940
"Postgraduate" (Carroll) 205
"Postscript on Prester John" (Davidson) 261
"Potential" (Campbell) 179
Power That Preserves, The (Donaldson) 299, 301
Powers of Darkness (Aickman) 16
Powers, Tim 91, **785–790**
Pratchett, Terry **791–801**

INDEX

Prayers to Broken Stones (Simmons) 878
Prentice Alvin (Card) 191
"Prentice Alvin and the No-Good Plow" (Card) 190
Present Tense (Duncan) 319, 320
"Pretty Boy Crossover" (Cardigan) 172, 173
"Pretty Maggie Moneyeyes" (Ellison) 331, 333
"Prevailing Faith in 'Free Wil'" (Oates) 781
"Priest of Hands, A" (Constantine) 230
Priest: A Gothic Romance, The (Disch) 296
Priestess of Avalon (Bradley) 136
"Priesting of Arilan, The" (Kurtz) 577, 578
"Primary Education of the Camiroi" (Lafferty) 595, 599
Prince Commands, The (Norton) 767
Prince of Chaos (Zelazny) 1016, 1017
Prince of Morning Bells, The (Kress) 569–571
Prince of the Blood (Feist) 357
Prince on a White Horse (Lee) 636
"Prince's Mixture" (Davidson) 256
"Princess and the Bear, The" (Card) 195
Princess Hynchatti & Some Other Surprises (Lee) 633
"Princess, The" (Landsdale) 604
Prison of Ice (Koontz) 556
Prison of Souls (Lackey & Shepherd) 588
"Professor Gottesman and the Indian Rhinoceros" (Beagle) 75
Psycho (Bloch) 106–107
Psycho (Bloch) 99, 106–109, 779
Psycho (film) 107
Psycho House (Bloch) 108, 109
Psycho II (Bloch) 108
Ptacek, Kathryn **803–807**
Pullman, Philip **809–815**
"Pulpmeister" (Schow) 834
"Pumpkin Child, the" (Collins) 222
Puss in Boots (Pullman) 811
Pyramids (Pratchett) 796, 798
"Quarter Past You, A" (Carroll) 205
"Quebradora" (Schow) 836
Queen of the Damned, The (Rice) 821, 822
"Queen of Air and Darkness, The" (Anderson) 38
Queen of Sorcery (Eddings) 323
"Queen of the Night" (Wolfe) 988
Queen of the Wolves (Lee) 636
Queen, Ellery: see Davidson, Avram 257
Queen, Ellery: see Vance, Jack 935

Queens Walk in the Dusk (Swann) 915
Quest for Saint Camber, The (Kurtz) 577
Quest for Simbilis, A (Shea) 839, 840
Quest for Tanelorn, The (Moorcock) 741, 742
Quest for the White Witch (Lee) 636
"Quickening, The" (Bishop) 84
Quicksilver Highway (film) 63
"Quietus" (Card) 195
Quorum, The (Newman) 758, 759
"R & R" (Shepard) 847, 848
"Racism and Science Fiction" (Delany) 310
"Raft, The" (King) 536
Rage (Bachman) 534
Rage of a Demon King (Feist) 358
Rainy Season, The (Blaylock) 94
Rampling, Anne: see Rice, Anne 820
Ramses (Rice) 821
"Ratman" (Wilson) 976
"Ravissante" (Aickman) 14
Rawhead Rex (film) 63
"Rawhead Rex" (Barker) 63
Razored Saddles (Williamson) 970
"Reach, The" (King) 536
"Reading My Father's Story" (Carroll) 201
"Real Bad Friend, The" (Bloch) 107
Really, Really, Really, Really Weird Stories (Shirley) 860
Reap the East Wind (Cook) 234
Reaper Man (Pratchett) 794, 796
Reave the Just and Other Tales (Donaldson) 304
Reaver Road, The (Duncan) 318, 320, 321
Reborn (Wilson) 974, 976
Red (Ketchum) 520
Red as Blood, or Tales from the Sisters Grimmer (Lee) 638
"Red Light" (Schow) 834
Red Planet (Powers) 785
Red Prophet (Card) 191
"Red Reign" (Newman) 758
Red Star Rising (McCaffrey) 700
Red Unicorn (Lee) 636
Redemption of Althalus, The (Eddings) 323, 325–327, 329
Rediscovery (Bradley & Lackey) 136
Reefs of Earth, The (Lafferty) 595, 596
Regina's Song (Eddings) 323, 328, 329
Regulators, The (King) 532, 533, 535
Reid, Desmond: see Moorcock, Michael 738
Reign (Williamson) 969
Reigning Cats and Dogs (Lee) 637
Reluctant Swordsman, The (Duncan) 316
Renegades (McCaffrey) 700

Renegades of Pern, The (McCaffrey) 700
"'Repent, Harlequin!' Said the Ticktockman" (Ellison) 332, 333
Reprisal (Wilson) 974
"Rescuing Andy" (Di Filippo) 285
"Residents Only" (Aickman) 15
Restoree (McCaffrey) 693
Return to Harken House (Aiken) 26
Return to Nevèrÿon (Delany) 280
"Return to the Sabbath" (Bloch) 101, 105
Revelation, The (Little) 659, 660, 662
"Revelation, The" (Oates) 781
Revenge of the Rose, The (Moorcock) 740
Revolt on Alpha C (Silverberg) 861
Ribofunk (Di Filippo) 286, 287
Rice, Anne **817–824**
Riddle of Stars series 729, 732
Riddle of the Wren (De Lint) 268
Riddle-Master of Hed, The (McKillip) 729
Ride on the Red Mare's Back, A (Le Guin) 623
"Riding the Bullet" (King) 536
"Rifle, The" (Ketchum) 520
RiftWar Legacy Series (Feist) 357
Riftwar series (Feist) 355–357
Rime Isle (Leiber) 648
"Ringing the Changes" (Aickman) 9, 16
Rise of a Merchant Prince (Feist) 358
Rise of Endymion (Simmons) 879
Rivan Codex, The (Eddings) 324, 326
River Runs Uphill, The (Aickman) 11
"River Styx Flows Upstream, The" (Simmons) 875
Riverrun (Somtow) 885
Riverrun series (Somtow) 885
Rivers, Elfrida: see Bradley, Marion Zimmer 131
"Roaches, The" (Disch) 294
Road Kill (Ketchum) 519
Road to Castle Mount, The (Silverberg) 867
Roadwork (Bachman) 534, 535
Robin and the Kestrel, The (Lackey) 587
Robot Adept (Anthony) 47
"Rock On" (Cardigan) 173
Rockabilly (Ellison) 332
Rogue Dragon (Davidson) 258
"Rogue Tomato" (Bishop) 84
Rolling Season, The (Mayne) 686
"Roman Question, A" (Aickman) 16
"Romance, A" (Barker) 67
Roquelaure, A.N.: see Rice, Anne 820
Rork! (Davidson) 258

1041

"Rose for Ecclesiastes, A" (Zelazny) 1011, 1015
Rose Madder (King) 525, 532
Rose-Red City, A (Duncan) 316, 319
Rowan series (McCaffrey) 698
Rowan, The (McCaffrey) 698
Rowling, J. K. **825–832**
Rubicon Beach (Erickson) 341–343
Ruby in the Smoke, The (Pullman) 810, 811
Ruby Knight, The (Eddings) 325
Rumble (Ellison) 332
Running Man, The (Bachman) 534, 535
Running with the Demon (Brooks) 156, 157
Russian Intelligence, The (Moorcock) 737, 744
Sabella;, or, The Blood Stone (Lee) 637
Sacrament (Barker) 66
Sacred Ground (Lackey) 587
Sadeian Woman (Carter) 212
"Sadness of Detail, The" (Carroll) 205
Sailing to Byzantium (Silverberg) 864
Sailing to Cythera (Willard) 960
"Sailing to Cythera" (Willard) 960
Sailing to Cythera and Other Anatole Stories (Willard) 959, 960
Sailing to Sarantium (Kay) 510, 513
Saint Camber (Kurtz) 576
Saint Fire (Lee) 635
Saint Germain series (Yarbro) 994
Saint-Germain Chronicles, The (Yarbro) 994
Saints (Card) 190
Salamander's Fire (Stableford) 897
'Salem's Lot (King) 525, 527, 528, 659
Sally Lockhart series (Pullman) 810–811
Saltflower (Van Scyoc) 929, 930, 932
"Salvador" (Shepard) 847, 848
"Salvage for Victory" (Willard) 961
"Same Dog, The" (Aickman) 17
Sand (Mayne) 686
"Sandkings, The" (Martin) 667, 668
"Sandmagic" (Card) 195
Sapphire Rose, The (Eddings) 325
Sarantine Mosaic series (Kay) 513–514
Satan's Angel (Ptacek) 803
Satan's World (Anderson) 36
"Save A Place in the Lifeboat for Me" (Waldrop) 956
"Saved" (Landsdale) 604
"Scalehunter's Beautiful Daughter, The" (Shepard) 848, 849
Scales of Justice, The (Kay) 509
Scarf, The (Bloch) 106
Scarlet Fig, The (Davidson) 259
"Scartaris, June 28" (Ellison) 335
Scenting Hallowed Blood (Constantine) 227, 228, 230

Schow, David J. **832–838**
Science Fiction/Horror: A Sight and Sound Reader (ed. Newman) 760
Science of Discworld, The (Pratchett) 795
Scientific Romance in Britain, 1890–1950 (Stableford) 891
"Scientifiction" (Waldrop) 956
Scions of Shannara, The (Brooks) 156
Scream, The (Aiken) 26
"Screaming People, The" (Bloch) 105
"Scrimptalon's Test" (Bishop) 85
"Scylla's Daughter" (Leiber) 647
Sea and Little Fishes, The (Pratchett) 794
Sea Came in at Midnight, The (Erickson) 344, 345
Sea Dragon Heir (Constantine) 230, 231
"Sea-Scene, or Vergil and the Ox-Thrall" (Davidson) 259
Searchers series (Williamson) 970
Searchers, The (Williamson) 970, 971
"Seasons of Belief" (Bishop) 84
Seaward (Cooper) 243
Second Book of Fritz Leiber (Leiber) 643
Second Chance (Williamson) 969, 970
Secret Ascension, The (Bishop) 83
Secret Books of Paradys series (Lee) 635
Secret Books of Venus series (Lee) 635
"Secret in the Tomb, The" (Bloch) 100
Secret Life of Houses, The (Bradfield) 124
"Secret Life of Houses, The" (Bradfield) 123
"Secret of Sebek, The" (Bloch) 101
Secret Sharers, The (Silverberg) 864
"Secret Songs, The" (Leiber) 647
"Sect of the Idiot, The" (Ligotti) 654
Seed of Lost Souls, The (Brite) 148
Seeing Red (Schow) 834–836
Seeress of Kell, The (Eddings) 324, 325, 328
Select, The (Wilson) 976
Self-Made Man (Brite) 150
Sending of Dragons, A (Yolen) 1004
"Sequel on Skorpios" (Bishop) 85
Serpent's Blood (Stableford) 897
Serpent's Shadow, The (Lackey) 588
Serpentwar series (Feist) 357–358
SERRAted Edge series (Lackey, Dixon & Lisle) 588
Servant Of the Bones, The (Rice) 820
Servant of the Empire (Feist) 357
"Seven American Nights" (Wolfe) 987
"Seven Devils" (Collins) 222
Seven Stars (Newman) 760, 763, 764
"Seven Stars" (Newman) 763

Seven Steps to Midnight (Matheson) 680, 681
"Seven-Day Terror" (Lafferty) 595
"Seventeen Virgins, The" (Vance) 935
Seventh Son, The (Card) 190, 191
Seventh Sword trilogy (Duncan) 316–317
Several Perceptions (Carter) 209
"Sex Opposite, The" (Bradley) 130
"Sex, Death, and Starshine" (Barker) 63
"Shades" (Shepard) 848
Shadow (Duncan) 316
Shadow Dance (Carter) 210
"Shadow from the Steeple, The" (Bloch) 101
Shadow Games (Cook) 235
Shadow Guests, The (Aiken) 26
Shadow in the Plate, The (Pullman) 810
Shadow Matrix (Bradley) 133
Shadow of a Dark Queen (Feist) 357
Shadow of All Night Falling, A (Cook) 234
Shadow of the Hegemon (Card) 195
Shadow of the Lion, The (Lackey & Flint) 589
Shadow Puppets (Card) 195
Shadoweyes (Ptacek) 804
Shadowfires (Koontz) 556
"Shadowjack" (Zelazny) 1017
Shadowland (Straub) 904, 906, 908, 909
Shadowline (Cook) 233
Shadowman (Etchison) 349
Shadows Linger (Cook) 235
"Shadows" (Delany) 277
Shaft, The (Schow) 835
"Shaman" (Shirley) 858
"Shambler from the Stars, The" (Bloch) 101
Shame of Man (Anthony) 47, 50
Shannara series (Brooks) 154–156
Shards of a Broken Crown (Feist) 358
Sharra's Exile (Bradley) 133
Shatterday (Ellison) 331, 332, 334, 335
"Shatterday" (Ellison) 331, 332, 334
Shattered Chain, The (Bradley) 133, 134
Shattered Horse, The (Somtow) 885
"Shattered Like a Glass Goblin" (Ellison) 333
She Is the Darkness (Cook) 235
She Wakes (Ketchum) 519, 521
Shea, Michael **839–844**
"Shed of Rebellion" (Ellison) 336
Shepard, Lucius **845–853**
Shining Ones, The (Eddings) 325
Shining, The (King) 527–529
"Ship of Shadows" (Leiber) 649

INDEX

"Ship That Returned, The" (McCaffrey) 698
Ship Who Sang series (McCaffrey) 589, 696–697
Ship Who Sang, The (McCaffrey) 696, 698
"Ship Who Sang, The" (McCaffrey) 696
Ship Who Searched, The (McCaffrey & Lackey) 589
Ships of Earth, The (Card) 196
Shirley, John **855–862**
"Shobies' Story, The" (Le Guin) 625
Shock II (Matheson) 674
Shock III (Matheson) 674
Shock IV (Matheson) 674
Shock Waves (Mccammon) 706
Shock! (Matheson) 674
Shon the Taken (Lee) 636
"Short Guide to the City, A" (Straub) 904, 910
"Shortest Day, The" (Cooper) 239
Showboat World (Vance) 939
Shrinking Man, The (Matheson) 674–676
Shudder, The (Martin) 349
Sibs (Wilson) 976
Siege of Stone (Williamson) 970
Sign for the Sacred (Constantine) 230
Sign of Chaos (Zelazny) 1016
"Sign of the Asp, The" (Collins) 223
Sign of the Unicorn (Zelazny) 1016
Silent Children (Campbell) 183
Silicon Embrace (Shirley) 858
Silver Eggheads, The (Leiber) 647
Silver Gryphon, The (Lackey) 586
Silver Heart (Constantine & Moorcock) 231
Silver on the Tree (Cooper) 239, 240, 242, 243
Silver Pillow, The (Disch) 295
Silver Spike, The (Cook) 235
Silverberg, Robert **863–874**
Silvercloak (Duncan) 320
Silverheart (Vance & Constantine) 744
Silverthorn (Feist) 356
Simes series (Wilson) 975
Simmons, Dan **875–881**
Sims Book 2: The Portero Method (Wilson) 975
Sims, Book One: La Causa (Wilson) 975
Sinful Ones, The (Leiber) 645, 646
"Singing Each to Each" (Di Filippo) 285
Sir Stalwart (Duncan) 320
"Sister Death" (Yolen) 1006
Sister Emily's Lightship and Other Stories (Yolen) 1008
"Sister Emily's Lightship" (Yolen) 1009

Sister Light, Sister Dark (Yolen) 1004, 1006, 1007
"Sister Light, Sister Dark" (Yolen) 1006
Sister Water (Willard) 961, 962
"Six Fingers of Time, The" (Lafferty) 595
Six Stories (King) 535
"Sixth Sentinel, The" (Brite) 148
Skeleton Crew (King) 535, 536
Sketch, The (Aickman) 16
Skies Discrowned, The (Powers) 786, 787, 789
Skies of Pern, The (McCaffrey) 700
Skin (Koja) 543, 544, 546
"Skin Deep" (Koja) 541
Skin Spinners, The (Aiken) 22
"Skin Trade, The" (Martin) 668
"Skinned Angels" (Ptacek) 806
"Skip" (Carroll) 201
"Skull of the Marquis de Sade, The" (Bloch) 103, 108
"Sky Blue Ball, The" (Oates) 780
Sky of Swords (Duncan) 320
"Sky" (Lafferty) 599
Slater, Ray: see Lansdale, Joe R. 605
"Slaughter House" (Matheson) 678
"Slave of the Flames" (Bloch) 103
"Sleep of Trees, The" (Yolen) 1008
Sleeping in Flame (Carroll) 203, 204
"Sleepwalkers" (Shirley) 858
Slippage (Ellison) 331, 332, 335
"Slovo Stove, The" (Davidson) 256, 257
"Slow Tuesday Night" (Lafferty) 595
Small Gods (Pratchett) 795, 796
Small Pinch of Weather, A (Aiken) 27
Smith, Rosamond: see Oates, Joyce Carol 776
Smoke (Auster) 58
Smoke from Cromwell's Time (Aiken) 27
"Smoke Ghost" (Leiber) 645, 649
"Smooth Talk" (film) 779
"Snapshots from the Butterfly Plague" (Bishop) 85
"Snow in Summer" (Yolen) 1008
"Snow Sculptures of Xanadu, The" (Newman) 759, 763
"Snow" (Ptacek) 806
"Sociology of Science Fiction, The" (Stableford) 891
"Sock Finish" (Bloch) 105
Soft (Wilson) 976
"Soft Come the Dragons" (Koontz) 552
Sojan the Swordsman (Moorcock) 738
Soldier of Arete (Wolfe) 985
Soldier of the Mist (Wolfe) 985
"Soldier" (Ellison) 336

Soldiers Live (Cook) 235
Sole Survivor (Koontz) 552
Solitudes, The (Crowley) 248
Solomon Leviathan's Nine-Hundred and Thirty-First Trip Around the World (Le Guin) 623
Someplace to be Flying (De Lint) 271
"Something Rich and Strange" (Davidson) 255
Something Wicked This Way Comes (Bradbury) 115, 117, 118
Sometimes the Magic Works (Brooks) 158
Somewhere In Time (film) 674, 679
Somewhere in Time (Matheson) 674
"Somewhere to Elsewhere" (Crowley) 245
Somtow, S. P. **883–889**
Song Called Youth series (Shirley) 857
Song Called Youth, A (Shirley) 857
Song for Arbonne, A (Kay) 510–512
Song for Lya, A (Martin) 667
Song for the Basilisk (Mckillip) 730
Song of Ice and Fire series (Martin) 670
Song of Kali (Simmons) 875, 876
Song of Roland, The (Anderson) 38
Songmaster (Card) 195
Songs of a Dead Dreamer (Ligotti) 655, 656
Songs of Stars and Shadows (Martin) 668
Sonja Blue series (Collins) 221
"Sorcerer's Apprentice, The" (Bloch) 104
Sorcerers of Majipoor (Silverberg) 864
Sorceress and the Cygnet, The (Mckillip) 730–732
Sorceress of Darshiva (Eddings) 324
Sorceress of the Witch World (Norton) 768, 770
Soul Music (Pratchett) 794, 796
"Soul-Painter and the Shape Shifter, The" (Silverberg) 867
Soulstorm (Williamson) 967, 968, 970
Source of Magic, The (Anthony) 47, 48
Sourcery (Pratchett) 793
"Sources of the Nile, The" (Davidson) 254, 257
Space Chantey (Lafferty) 597
Space Opera (Vance) 939
Spaceship Built of Stone, A (Tuttle) 926
"Spanish Lesson, A" (Shepard) 847
Speaker for the Dead (Card) 189, 195
"Speaking to the Wind" (Yolen) 1008
Speaks the Nightbird (Mccammon) 705, 711, 712
Specialist, The (Cutter) 857
Spell for Chameleon, A (Anthony) 47
Spell of the Witch World (Norton) 768, 772

"Spelling God with the Wrong Blocks" (Morrow) 751
Spider (McGrath) 724, 725
Spider Kiss (Ellison) 332
"Spider Mansion" (Leiber) 645
Spiderweb (Bloch) 106
Spirits White as Lightning (Lackey & Edghill) 588
Splendid Chaos, A (Shirley) 858
Splendor and Misery of Bodies, of Cities, The (Delany) 280
Split Infinity (Anthony) 47, 48
"Spondulix" (Di Filippo) 288, 289
"Spook-Box of Theodore Delafont De Brooks, The" (Davidson) 257
Sports & Music (Shepard) 850
"Spot, The" (Etchison & Johnson
Spring-Heeled Jack (Pullman) 810
"Spy in the Domain of Arnheim, A" (Bishop) 84
Squeeze Play (Auster) 54
"Squirrel Cage, The" (Disch) 294
St. Boan series (Aiken) 25
St. Patrick's Gargoyle (Kurtz) 579, 580
Stableford, Brian **891–902**
"Stained with Crimson" (Lee) 634
"Stains, The" (Aickman) 12, 17
Stalking Tender Prey (Constantine) 227, 228
Stalking the Nightmare (Ellison) 335
Stand by Me (film) 536
Stand, The (King) 527–529, 536
Star Man's Son, 2250 A.D (Norton) 767
Star of Danger (Bradley) 133
Star Pit, The (Delany) 278
Star Quest (Koontz) 552, 553
Star Wars, Episode I: The Phantom Menace (Brooks) 158
Star's End (Cook) 233
Starfishers (Cook) 233
Starfishers series (Cook) 233
Starmother (Van Scyoc) 930–932
Stars in My Pocket Like Grains of Sand (Delany) 280
Starship & Haiku (Somtow) 883–884
Starsilk (Van Scyoc) 930–933
Starstone (Bradley) 135
Stealing Sacred Fire (Constantine) 227, 228, 230
"Steam Man of the Prairie and The Dark Rider Get Down" (Landsdale) 609
Steampunk Trilogy, The (Di Filippo) 286, 287
Steering the Craft (Le Guin) 614
Stephens, Reed: see Donaldson, Stephen R. 305
"Steppin' Out, Summer '68" (Landsdale) 609

Stinger (Mccammon) 709
Stir of Echoes, A (Matheson) 674, 676, 677
Stolen Lake, The (Aiken) 24
Stone Giant, The (Blaylock) 90
"Stone Lives" (Di Filippo) 285
"Stone Thing, The" (Moorcock) 739
Store, The (Little) 662, 663
Storm Breaking (Lackey) 586
Storm Lord, The (Lee) 635, 637
Storm of Swords, A (Martin) 670
Storm of the Century (television miniseries) 533
Storm of the Century, The (King) 525, 526, 533
Storm Rising (Lackey) 586
Storm Warning (Lackey) 586
Storm Warriors (Craig) 893
Stormbringer (Moorcock) 740
"Storming the Bijou, Mon Amour" (Bishop) 84
Storms of Victory (Norton) 768
Strange Angels (Koja) 543, 544
Strange Case of X, The (VanderMeer) 948
Strange Doings (Lafferty) 598
Strange Eons (Bloch) 109
"Strange Flight of Richard Clayton, The" (Bloch) 103
Strange Highways (Koontz) 551
Strange Trades (Di Filippo) 285, 286, 288
Strange Wine (Ellison) 333, 334
"Stranger in the House" (Tuttle) 924–926
Strangers (Koontz) 552
Stranglehold (Ketchum) 520
Strata (Pratchett) 791
Straub, Peter **903–913**
Straydog (Koja) 545
Stress of Her Regard, The (Powers) 786
Stricken Field, The (Duncan) 317
Strings (Duncan) 317
Sub, The (Disch) 296, 297
Subtle Knife, The (Pullman) 813
Sudden Fear (Koontz) 555
"Sufferings of Charlotte, The" (Rice) 818
"Summer of Corruption: Apt Pupil" (King) 536
Summer of Night (Simmons) 875, 878, 879
Summer Tree, The (Kay) 509
Summoned to Tourney (Lackey & Guon) 588
Summoning, The (Little) 662
Sun, the Moon, and the Stars, The (Brust) 161, 165
"Sun/Flight" (Yolen) 1008
"Sundance" (Silverberg) 866, 868

"Sunday-Go-to-Meeting Jaw, the" (Collins) 222
Sung in Blood (Cook) 234
Sung in Shadow (Lee) 638
Sunglasses after Dark (Collins) 221, 224
Sunwaifs (Van Scyoc) 930–932
Supernatural Minnesota series (Disch) 295
"Surrender" (Shepard) 849
Survivors, The (Bradley) 132
Svaha (De Lint) 267
Swamp Foetus (Brite) 148, 150
Swan Song (Mccammon) 708, 709
Swann, Thomas Burnett **915–922**
Swarm in May, A (Mayne) 686
Swatting at the Cosmos (Morrow) 752
Sweet Silver Blues (Cook) 236
"Sweet Sixteen" (Bloch) 103
"Sweets to the Sweet" (Bloch) 104
Swell Foop (Anthony) 47
Sword of Aldones (Bradley) 132, 133
Sword of Ice and Other Tales of Valdemar (Lackey) 587
Sword of Shannara, The (Brooks) 153, 154, 157, 158
Swordbearer, The (Cook) 234
Swords Against Death (Leiber) 647
Swords Against Wizardry (Leiber) 647
Swords and Deviltry (Leiber) 647
Swords and Ice Magic (Leiber) 648
Swords in the Mist (Leiber) 647
Swords of Lankhmar, The (Leiber) 647, 648
Synners (Cadigan) 169–173
T. S. Eliot (Ackroyd) 1
Take a Thief (Lackey) 587
"Take Wooden Indians" (Davidson) 257
"Tale of Dragons and Dreamers, The" (Delany) 279
"Tale of Fog and Granite, The" (Delany) 280
"Tale of Gorgik, The" (Delany) 279, 280
"Tale of Old Venn, The" (Delany) 279
"Tale of Plagues and Carnivals, The" (Delany) 280
"Tale of Potters and Dragons, The" (Delany) 279
"Tale of Signs and Cities, The" (Delany) 279
"Tale of Small Sarg, The" (Delany) 279, 280
Tale Of The Body Thief, The (Rice) 822
Talent series (McCaffrey) 698
Tales From Earthsea (Le Guin) 617–619
Tales of Earthsea, The (Le Guin) 616

INDEX

Tales of H. P. Lovecraft (Oates) 776
Tales of Nevèrÿon (Delany) 279
"Tales of Plagues and Carnivals, The" (Delany) 279
"Tales of Rumor and Desire, The" (Delany) 280
Tales of the Dying Earth (Vance) 935, 937, 940
Tales of the Knights Templar (Kurtz) 580
Talisman, The (King & Straub) 531, 535, 910
Talismans of Shannara, The (Brooks) 156, 157
Talking in the Dark (Etchison) 351
Talon of the Silver Hawk (Feist) 358
Taltos (Brust) 162, 163
Taltos (Rice) 822
Tamastara (Lee) 635
Tamsin (Beagle) 76
Tamuli series (Eddings) 325
Tangle Box, The (Brooks) 156
"Tapestry of Little Murders, A" (Bishop) 85
Tarzan: The Lost Adventure (Lansdale) 609
Tatham Mound (Anthony) 47
Tau Zero (Anderson) 33
"Taylorsville Reconstruction, The" (Shepard) 845
Tea from an Empty Cup (Cadigan) 170, 172, 173
Teckla (Brust) 162–164
Tehanu (Le Guin) 616, 617, 619, 621, 626
"Telephone Call" (Beagle) 72
Telling Time: Angels, Ancestors and Stories (Willard) 962
Templar Treasure, The (Kurtz & Harris) 580
Temple and the Crown, The (Kurtz & Harris) 580
Temple and the Stone, The (Kurtz & Harris) 580
Tempter (Collins) 221, 222
"Tenants" (Wilson) 976
Terror (Bloch) 108
"Terror in the Night" (Bloch) 105
"Terror over Hollywood" (Bloch) 105
Tery, The (Wilson) 976
"Testimony" (Oates) 780
Texas Night Riders (Slater) 605
"That Hell-Bound Train" (Bloch) 106
"That Only a Mother" (Bradley) 130
Them (Oates) 778
Them Bones (Waldrop) 953, 954, 957
There Are Doors (Wolfe) 986, 987
There Will Be Time (Anderson) 38
"There Will Come That Evening" (Oates) 781

"Thesme and the Ghayrog" (Silverberg) 867
They Fly at Çiron (Delany) 281
They Thirst (Mccammon) 705, 707, 709
Thief of Always, The (Barker) 66
Thief of Time (Pratchett) 794, 795
Thin Air (Constantine) 230, 231
"Thing from Lover's Lane, The" (Collins) 223
Things Invisible to See (Willard) 961
Thinner (Bachman) 535
Third Ghost Book, The (Aickman) 16
Third Millennium: A History of the World A.D. 2000–3000, The (Stableford) 893
"Thirteen Lies about Hummingbirds" (Bishop) 85
Thirteen Phantasms and Other Stories (Blaylock) 94
"Thirteenth Fey, The" (Yolen) 1008
This Immortal (Zelazny) 1012–1014
"This Is the Road" (Silverberg) 866
This Is the Way the World Ends (Morrow) 751, 753
Thorn Boy, The (Constantine) 230
"Thorns of Barevi, The" (McCaffrey) 699
Three Against the Witch World (Norton) 768, 770
"Three Armageddons of Enniscorthy Sweeny, The" (Lafferty) 599
Three Hearts and Three Lions (Anderson) 33–36, 38, 39
Three Heralds of the Storm (Constantine) 230
334 (Disch) 293
Three Ring Psychus (Shirley) 856
Three Sisters, The (Aickman) 13
"Three, Four, Shut the Door" (Ptacek) 806
Throat, The (Straub) 910
Throme of the Erril of Sherril, The (McKillip) 729
Throne of Madness, The (Somtow) 884
"Through Other Eyes" (Lafferty) 594
"Thus I Refute Beelzy" (Beagle) 73
"Thus We Frustrate Charlemagne" (Lafferty) 594
Tides of Lust, The (Delany) 281
Tigana (Kay) 510–512
Tiger (Pullman) 812–814
Tiger in the Well, The (Pullman) 811
Tiger's Railway (Mayne) 689
"Tigers of Hysteria Feed Only on Themselves, The" (Bishop) 85
"Tight Little Stitches in a Dead Man's Back" (Landsdale) 604
Timbuktu (Auster) 58
Time and Relative (Newman) 760

"Time Considered as a Helix of Semi-Precious Stones" (Delany) 279
"Time Dweller, The" (Moorcock) 741
Time of Changes, A (Silverberg) 863
Time of the Fourth Horseman (Yarbro) 993
Time Patrol, The (Anderson) 36
Time Pieces (Bishop) 85
Tin Princess, The (Pullman) 811
"To Fill the Sea and Air" (Wilson) 976
To Live Forever (Vance) 939
To Reign in Hell (Brust) 165
To Ride Pegasus (McCaffrey) 698
"To See the Invisible Man" (Silverberg) 864
To the High Redoubt (Yarbro) 997
To the Land of the Living (Silverberg) 868
To Wake the Dead (Campbell) 180
To Walk the Night (Leiber) 649
"Toads of Grimmerdale, The" (Norton) 772
Tomb, The (Wilson) 974, 975
"Tomb-Herd, The" (Campbell) 179
Tombs of Atuan, The (Le Guin) 616, 617, 621
Tommyknockers, The (King) 525, 531
"Tomorrow's Children" (Anderson) 34
Total Recall (Anthony) 47
Touch Magic: Fantasy, Faerie, and Folklore in the Literature of Childhood (Yolen) 1003
Touch of Chill, A (Aiken) 27
Touch, The (Wilson) 974
Tournament of Thorns, The (Swann) 920
Tours of the Black Clock (Erickson) 342–345
Towing Jehovah (Morrow) 752
Tower and the Hive, The (McCaffrey) 698
Tower at Stony Wood, The (Mckillip) 733
Tower of Fear, The (Cook) 234
Town, The (Little) 662
Trader (De Lint) 271
"Tragical Historie of Jiril's Players, The" (Beagle) 75
"Trains Not Taken" (Landsdale) 606
Transfigurations (Bishop) 80
Transformation of Martin Lake, The (VanderMeer) 948
Transformation of Miss Mavis Wing, The (Moorcock) 743
Translator, The (Crowley) 250–251
Transmaniacon (Shirley) 856, 857
Transmutations (film) 63
"Trash Theatre" (Landsdale & Webb) 608

"Traveler and the Tale, The" (Yolen) 1009
Traveler, The (Drumm) 857
"Traveler's Tale, A" (Shepard) 847
"Traveller from an Antique Land" (Davidson) 256
Treasure Box (Card) 194
Trey of Swords (Norton) 768, 770
Triads (Brite & Faust) 150
Triads (Brite) 150
Trial of Elizabeth Cree: A Novel of the Limehouse Murders, The (Ackroyd) 6
Trial, The (Bishop) 85
"Trial" (Kurtz) 577, 578
Triton (Delany) 279
"Triumph of the Spider Monkey, The" (Oates) 779
Trouble on Triton (Delany) 279
"Trouble with Unicorns, The" (Willard) 962
"Trucks" (King) 536
"True Faces" (Cardigan) 170
Trumps of Doom, The (Zelazny) 1015, 1016
Truth Jourdemayne series (Bradley) 137
Truth, The (Pratchett) 797, 798
Tuttle, Lisa **923–928**
"Twenty-Four Views of Mount Fuji by Hokusai" (Zelazny) 1015
Twilight Eyes (Koontz) 552, 554, 556
Twilight Zone: The Movie (film) 674
"Two Cents Worth" (Schow) 836
Two Crowns for America (Kurtz) 579
Two Sought Adventure (Leiber) 646, 647
"Two Sought Adventure" (Leiber) 645
Two to Conquer (Bradley) 134
"Two-Headed Man, The" (Collins) 222
"Übermensch!" (Newman) 759, 763, 764
"Ugliest Duckling, The" (Somtow) 887
"Ugly Chickens, The" (Waldrop) 955, 957
Uh-Oh City (Carroll) 205, 206
"Umney's Last Case" (King) 536
Uncle Terrible (Willard) 960, 962
"Uncle Tuggs" (Shea) 842
"Uncorking of Uncle Finn, The" (Yolen) 1008
Under Heaven's Bridge (Bishop) 80
Under the Fang (ed. McCammon) 976
"Under the Hand of Chance" (Lee) 635
"Under the Hill" (Yolen) 1008
Under Venus (Straub) 905, 906
"Undercurrent" (Shirley) 860
Underground Alley (Mayne) 686
Underworld (film) 63

"Une Étrange Aventure de Richard Blaine" (Newman) 764
Unearth: Poems, 1970–1972 (Auster) 54
Unexpected Visit of a Reanimated Englishwoman, The (Bishop) 85
Unforgivable Stories (Newman) 760, 763, 764
"Unholy Grail, The" (Leiber) 647
Unicorn Mountain (Bishop) 81
Unicorn Point (Anthony) 47
Unicorn Sonata, The (Beagle) 75
"Unicorn Variation" (Zelazny) 1015
Unicorn Variations (Zelazny) 1015
"Unidentified Objects" (Blaylock) 94
University (Little) 662, 663
"Unmistakably the Finest" (Bradfield) 123
"Unsettled Dust, The" (Aickman) 17
"Unsound Variations" (Martin) 670
Upland Outlaws (Duncan) 317
Ursus of Ultima Thule (Davidson) 260
Usher's Passing (Mccammon) 707, 708
Utopia Hunters (Somtow) 884
"V, H, and You" (Shirley) 859
Valentine (Shepard) 851
Valentine (Somtow) 886
Valentine Pontifex (Silverberg) 867
"Valley of the Swastika, The" (Landsdale) 605
Vampire Armand, The (Rice) 822
Vampire City (Stableford) 897
Vampire Junction (Somtow) 886, 887
Vampire Lestat, The (Rice) 820
Vampire series (Wilson) 976
Vampire's Beautiful Daughter, The (Somtow) 883, 887, 888
Vampires (ed. Yolen & Greenberg) 1003
Vampyre: A Tale, The (Newman) 763
Van Scyoc, Sydney J. **929–934**
Vance, Jack 837, **935–943**
Vance, John Holbrook: see Vance, Jack 935
VanderMeer, Jeff **945–950**
Vanitas: Escape from Vampire Junction (Somtow) 886
Vazkor, Son of Vazkor (Lee) 636
"Vengeance of Hera, The" (Disch) 295
Veniss Underground (VanderMeer) 946
"Vergil and the Dukos" (Davidson) 259
Vergil in Averno (Davidson) 259
Vergil Magus series (Davidson) 258
Vic and Blood (Ellison & Corben) 336
"Victoria" (Di Filippo) 286
Videodrome (Martin) 348
View From Hell, The (Shirley) 859
"View, The" (Aickman) 15, 16
Village, The (Mccammon) 711, 712
"Vilvoy de las Islas, El" (Davidson) 257

"Vine of the Soul" (Brite) 150
Violin (Rice) 821
Viscount of Adrilankha, The (Brust) 165
Vision, The (Koontz) 554
Visit to William Blake's Inn: Poems for Innocent and Experienced Travelers, A (Willard) 959
"Visit, The" (Ptacek) 806
"Visiting Star, The" (Aickman) 16
Vittorio (Rice) 822
Vivia (Lee) 637
Vlad Taltos series (Brust) 162
"Vocation" (Kurtz) 577
Voice of Our Shadow (Carroll) 202
Voices (Aiken) 26
Von Bek Family series (Moorcock) 743
"Voriax and Valentine" (Silverberg) 867
Vows and Honor series (Lackey) 586
Voyage of the Basset: Islands in the Sky (Lee) 636
Voyage of the Jerle Shannara series (Brooks) 157
Voyage of the Ludgate Hill, The (Willard) 961
"Waiting Room, The" (Aickman) 16
Waking Nightmares (Campbell) 178
Waldrop, Howard **951–958**
Walking, The (Little) 664
Walking Shadow, The (Stableford) 891
Walking Tour of the Shambles, A (Wolfe & Gaiman) 989
Walking, The (Little) 662, 664
"Walt and Emily" (Di Filippo) 286
Wanderer, The (Leiber) 649
Wandering Fire, The (Kay) 509, 510
"War and Peace" (Shirley) 859
War for the Oaks (De Lint) 270
War Hound and the World's Pain, The (Moorcock) 743
War of the Gods (Anderson) 33, 40
War of the Wing-Men (Anderson) 36
Warding of Witch World, The (Norton) 768
'Ware Hawk (Norton) 768, 770
Warlock (Cook) 233
Warlock (Koontz) 552
Warlock of the Witch World (Norton) 768, 770
Warrior of Mars series (Bradbury) 738
Warriors of Mars (Moorcock) 738
Wars of Vis, The (Lee) 635, 638
"Watcher of the Skies" (Schow) 836, 837
Watchers (Koontz) 556
Water Sleeps (Cook) 235
"Waterfall, The" (Bradley) 137
"Waxworks" (Bloch) 102
Way of All Flesh, The (Aickman) 12

INDEX

"Way of Cross and Dragon, The" (Martin) 668
Way of Light, The (Constantine) 231
"Waziah" (Landsdale) 604
We Are For the Dark (Aickman) 12, 15
We Were the Mulvaneys (Oates) 781
Weaveworld (Barker) 64, 65
Web of Darkness (Bradley) 131
Web of Light (Bradley) 131
Web of the City (Ellison) 332
Web of the Witch World (Norton) 768, 769
"Wedding Gig, The" (King) 536
"Weird Doom of Floyd Scrilch, The" (Bloch) 102
Weirwoods, The (Swann) 919
"Well of Baln, The" (Le Guin) 624
"Well-Tempered Falsehood: The Art of Storytelling" (Willard) 961
Wells, John Jay see Bradley, Marion Zimmer 131
Werewolves (ed. Yolen & Greenberg) 1003
Werewolves of London, The (Stableford) 893
Werewolves series (Stableford) 891, 893, 895
West of January (Duncan) 317
"Wet Straw" (Matheson) 678
Wetbones (Shirley) 858, 859
"Weyr Search" (McCaffrey) 694
What Dreams May Come (Matheson) 674, 677, 679
"What is a Flounce?" (Aickman) 12
"What It Means to Be an American" (Koontz) 552
"What Makes a Cage? Jamie Knows" (Bradfield) 123
"What Makes Hieronymous Run?" (Waldrop) 956
What's Wrong with America (Bradfield) 124–126
Wheels of Fire (Lackey & Shepherd) 588
Wheels within Wheels (Wilson) 971, 976
"When Molly Met Elvis" (Stableford) 897
"When Now by Tree and Leaf" (Willard) 962
When the Bough Breaks (Lackey & Lisle) 588
"When the Sea-King's Away" (Leiber) 647
"When They Gave Us Memory" (Etchison) 350, 351
"Where Are You Going, Where Have You Been?" (Oates) 779
"Where Do You Live, Queen Esther?" (Davidson) 256

"Where Have You Been, Sandaliotis?" (Lafferty) 598
Where I've Been, and Where I'm Going (Oates) 781
"Where Is the Bird of Fire" (Swann) 918
Where the Bodies Are Buried (Newman) 757, 761–763
"Where the Bodies Are Buried 2020" (Newman) 762
"Where the Bodies Are Buried II: Sequel Hook" (Newman) 763
"Where the Bodies are Buried" (Newman) 758, 759
"Whimper of Whipped Dogs, The" (Ellison) 331, 333
Whispers (King) 528
Whispers (Koontz) 552, 556
White as Snow (Lee) 634, 638
White Dragon, The (McCaffrey) 699, 700
White Gold Wielder (Donaldson) 299
White Gryphon, The (Lackey) 586
White Jenna (Yolen) 1006, 1007
White Mercedes, The (Pullman) 811
"White Otters of Childhood, The" (Bishop) 84
White Pipes, The (Kress) 571–572
"White Rabbit, The" (Landsdale) 604
White Rose, The (Cook) 235
White Serpent, The (Lee) 637
Who Made Stevie Crye? (Bishop) 80
"Why Are Americans Afraid of Dragons?" (Le Guin) 621
"Why Did?" (Waldrop) 957
"Why I Was Bachman" (King) 535
Wielding a Red Sword (Anthony) 47
Wild Animals (Straub) 905
Wild Blood (Collins) 222
Wild Cards (ed. Martin) 669
Wild Hunt, The (Yolen) 1007
Wild West Movies (Newman) 758
"Wild, Wild Horses" (Waldrop) 957
Will to Kill, The (Bloch) 106
Will-O-The-Wisp (Swann) 920
Willard, Nancy **959–965**
Williamson Effect, The (ed. Zelazny) 1012
Williamson, Chet **967–972**
Willow Garden, The (Grant) 805
Wilson, F. Paul **973–979**
Windhaven (Martin & Tuttle) 668, 924
Winds of Change (Lackey) 586
Winds of Darkover (Bradley) 132–134
Winds of Fate (Lackey) 586
Winds of Fury (Lackey) 586
Windscreen Weepers, The (Aiken) 27
"Windstorm Passes, The" (Landsdale) 606

Wine of Violence, The (Morrow) 750, 754
"Wine-Dark Sea, The" (Aickman) 15
"Winged Victory" (Swann) 916
"Winter Flies, The" (Leiber) 647
Winter Haunting, A (Simmons) 879
Winter Players, The (Lee) 636
Winter Rose (McKillip) 730, 733
Winter Sleepwalker, The (Aiken) 27
Winter Tides (Blaylock) 93
"Winter's King" (Le Guin) 614
"Winter's Tale: The Breathing Method, A" (King) 536
Wise Children (Carter) 209
"Wise Soldier of Sellebak, The" (Willard) 960
Wishsong of Shannara, The (Brooks) 155
"Witch War" (Matheson) 678
Witch World (Norton) 768, 769
Witch World series (Norton) 768–772
Witches Abroad (Pratchett) 793
Witches of Lancre series (Pratchett) 793
Witches' Brew (Brooks) 156
Witching Hour, The (Rice) 821, 822
Witchlight (Bradley) 137
With a Tangled Skein (Anthony) 47
With Mercy toward None (Cook) 234
"With Morning Comes Mistfall" (Martin) 670
With Shuddering Fall (Oates) 778
Wizard at Large (Brooks) 156
Wizard Knight series (Wolfe) 987
Wizard of Earthsea, A (Le Guin) 615, 616
Wizard's Apprentice, The (Somtow) 887
Wizard's Hall (Yolen) 1007
Wolf Moon (De Lint) 268
Wolf Star Rise (Lee) 636
"Wolf" (Moorcock) 744
Wolf's Hour, The (McCammon) 709
Wolfe, Aaron: see Koontz, Dean 558
Wolfe, Gene **981–991**
Wolfman, The (Campbell) 183
Wolfwinter (Swann) 919
Wolves of Willoughby Chase series (Aiken) 22–25
Wolves of Willoughby Chase, The (Aiken) 23
Women as Demons: The Male Perception (Lee) 638
Women of Darkness (ed. Ptacek) 803
Women of Darkness II (ed. Ptacek) 803
"Women Only" (Bradley) 129
Wonderful Story of Aladdin and the Enchanted Lamp, The (Pullman) 811
Wonderland (Oates) 778

"Wood" (Aickman) 17
Wooden Sea, The (Carroll) 206
"Word of Unbinding, The" (Le Guin) 614
"Words of Power" (Yolen) 1008
"Working with the Little People" (Ellison) 334
"World of Difference, A" (Matheson) 679
World of Shannara, The (Brooks) 157
"World Wars III" (Di Filippo) 288
World Wreckers, The (Bradley) 133
"World-Thinker, The" (Vance) 936
Worm in the Well, The (Mayne) 690
"Worst Thing in the World, The" (Collins) 223
Would It Kill You to Smile? (Lawson) 83
Wounded Land, The (Donaldson) 299, 301, 302
Wraeththu series (Constantine) 227, 229
Writing Popular Fiction (Koontz) 555

Wyrd Sisters (Pratchett) 793
Xanadu series (ed. Yolen) 1003
Xanth series (Anthony) 47–48
Xenocide (Card) 195
Yarbro, Chelsea Quinn **993–1002**
Yarrow: An Autumn Tale (De Lint) 269, 270
"Yattering and Jack, The" (Barker) 62
Year and a Day, A (Mayne) 688
Year in the Linear City, A (Di Filippo) 289
Year of the Unicorn (Norton) 768, 770, 771
Year Zero (Stableford) 897, 898
Years of Longdirk trilogy (Duncan) 319
"Yellow Rome, or Vergil and the Vestal Virgin" (Davidson) 259
Yendi (Brust) 162–164
Yeovil, Jack: see Newman, Kim 757
Yestern (Somtow) 885
Yolen, Jane **1003–1010**

You Could Go Home Again (Waldrop) 955
"You Don't Have to Be Mad..." (Newman) 764
You're All Alone (Leiber) 645, 646, 649
"Yougoslaves, The" (Bloch) 109
Young Blood (Stableford) 895
Young Merlin series (Yolen) 1007
"Young Vergil and the Wizard" (Davidson) 259
Young Warriors, The (film) 674
"Yours Truly, Jack the Ripper" (Bloch) 103
"Yukio Mishima Cultural Association of Kudzu Valley, Georgia, The" (Bishop) 84
Zaragoz (Craig) 893
Zarsthor's Bane (Norton) 768, 772
Zelazny, Roger **1011–1023**
"000-00-0000" (Bishop) 85
Zeppelins West (Lansdale) 609
Zombie (Oates) 775, 779, 780
"Zombie" (Oates) 775